EX LIBRES

SHERMAN
FEUER

A PRIDE
OF ROYALS

ALSO BY JUSTIN SCOTT

Normandie Triangle
The Shipkiller
The Turning
Treasure for Treasure
Many Happy Returns

WRITING AS J.S. BLAZER

Lend a Hand
Deal Me Out

A PRIDE OF
OF

ROYALS

BY
Justin Scott

ARBOR HOUSE
New York

To Gloria Hoye,
For the music that lingers . . .
my love, my beauty, my friend.

BOOK

I

Victoria's Children

1

Mauve drapes of lined velvet muffled the noise of the Paris street below the Frenchwoman's bedroom. Worn-out truck motors, clattering draft horses, even the prolonged tramp of infantry on night march, sounded remote. But a deeper, richer noise penetrated the cloth; from sixty miles east of Paris came the determined rumble of German artillery barraging the French trenches.

Kenneth Ash lay awake, propped against the pillows, watching the face of the woman who had fallen asleep with her head on his chest, and listening intently to the distant assault. Across the sumptuous boudoir, among the ornate mirrors, a loose glass rattled sympathetically in its frame. The guns had rumbled all night like the heartbeat of a stranger who had followed them here to spy on their lovemaking.

Ash had toured both sides of the battle lines. He knew what the guns meant. Between the opposing trenches cold December winds had hardened the mud in no-man's-land; the Germans would conclude the barrage with an infantry attack at dawn. It was the start of the third winter of the World War. The new year, 1917, would see Kaiser Wilhelm's armies defeat the combined forces of the English, French and Russian allies, unless the United States intervened to defeat Germany and end the slaughter.

The candles he had carried upstairs from the dining room still burned on the sconces around her bed. In the golden light her skin looked as soft as it felt, smooth as the silk-covered quilt which had spilled off their bodies and lay half on her bed and half on the carpet. She was a woman, not a girl, and faint lines had gathered beside her eyes and mouth. Her elaborately coiffed hair had come undone, like a diary scrawled in the dark of what they had done. Ash kissed her hair, savoring her perfume.

11

He had to leave, had to report back to the American Embassy. Duty called, such as it was. A despatch to Berlin, too important to trust to cable or letter, yet not so momentous that the ambassador himself had to make the journey. Call in the navy instead—Lieutenant Commander Kenneth Ash, special attaché to the American Embassy in London, discreet diplomatic courier, neutral observer of how the Allies and Central Powers were conducting their war, and, some might suggest, glorified mailman . . . But only one more month. Then at last a berth on a fighting ship.

She shivered; a chill had crept back into the room because the coal fire her maids had lighted while she and Ash had eaten late supper had burned low, flickers of blue flame among white ash. Ash pulled the coverlet over them, over her shoulders until only her face showed. She tightened her arms around him. Ash cupped her breast and she smiled, still half-asleep.

His gaze shifted to the room. It was a voluptuous concoction of silk and velvet, gilt carving, marble, crystal, and everywhere the gleaming, ornate mirrors. She had straddled him and they had shown her in a dozen, subtle variations. She was a *comtesse*—wealthy, arrogant and secure. Ash knew jewelry and the blood-red ruby on her right hand could finance a torpedo boat, or a townhouse on Washington Square. Like most he had met of the *gratin*—the rich and titled crust of French society—she was a passionate sportswoman and an anglophile in her tastes. *Le betting à le steeplechase* slipped incongruously from her tongue. They usually didn't like Americans, but for Ash she had made a rather grand and, as it turned out, thorough exception.

At a reception this evening at the embassy she recalled he had skippered an American yacht in the Brenton Reef Cup cross-Channel race a year before the war, and invited him to leave with her. Nightlife was officially banned in Paris, but there were places to dance in the Montmartre section behind closed doors, doors which opened to a password, or a bribe, or a name like hers. Inside they were doing a new dance, a slow gliding version of the fox-trot called the Nurse's Shuffle.

Ash supposed if he hadn't spent the years he had in Europe he might have been appalled by the cynical response to the millions of war casualties. The English, by contrast, worried less about appearances, allowing dances everywhere except by officers in uniform. Their new dance was the Saunter, an intricate, precision duet which borrowed from several American dances. The style was to appear nonchalant. When Ash showed her, the *comtesse* was not impressed. She had just returned from Petrograd, and the Russians, she told him, were mad for the Tango.

Her husband was a general, headquartered in Rheims, the champagne city a few miles inside the trench line, and near, judging by the sound, tonight's German artillery barrage. This house was her own, as were the servants, which was a comfort because French army officers from the country nobility were notoriously eager duelists and neither the United

States State Department nor the navy approved of special diplomatic couriers skewering French generals, no matter how incompetent the generals were.

"You're smiling," she said suddenly. "What are you thinking?"

"I was wondering what it would be like to be married to you." He spoke with a faint West Virginian plantation drawl, which had been softened, modified and nearly erased by fifteen years of kicking around Europe and England. She was taken aback until Ash grinned at her. Then she laughed. "I don't recommend it. Particularly to a naval officer."

"I'm rarely at sea."

"You would be with me, Commander."

Now Ash laughed, stung a little by the reminder of the gulf between them. *"Touché, comtesse.* But on occasion I've managed pretty well at sea . . . ." True, years past. Last summer he had wangled a temporary command in the Philippines. Now it looked as if his luck was improving as the navy finally began building ships again. He had orders next month to become executive officer on a new cruiser and he could hardly wait, because for most of his fourteen years of navy service he had assisted staff officers and diplomats—errand boy, an officer of the line might call it. Bright young polished aide to Admiral Thayer Mahon, to President Teddy Roosevelt, to Taft, recently to Teddy's young nephew, Franklin, Assistant Secretary of the Navy; still a bright aide, still well-mannered, but not quite so young. And forty had appeared on the horizon like an unexpected landfall; or, more likely, an error of navigation.

"I've made you sad." She smiled.

Ash kissed her; it was in his nature to fall in love, for the moment at least, with women he made love with, and at this moment he could have spent more time with the *comtesse* than he knew he would be invited to. The sound of the guns grew softer. Perhaps the wind had shifted.

"What is this?" She touched a round scar that pocked his shoulder like a raindrop in a pond.

"A bullet."

"From love or from war?" she smiled, tracing it with her finger.

"An anarchist," said Ash. She raised her brow, and he said, "He was aiming at someone else."

She pressed his hand where he held her breast, then raised her fingers to his face. The blood-red ruby glittered like an eye in the dark. She stroked his cheek, then held the ring aloft to direct a ray of reddened candle light into his eyes. Down his nose. To his mouth. She kissed where the red beam touched his mouth, moved it, and followed it with her lips. The quilt slid away again as she spiraled her body to follow the descending glow.

She knew how to tease. She lifted her head abruptly, flashed the ruby in his eyes and kissed his mouth. "Yes, you have managed rather well. Very well." She turned the ring toward a candle flame and gazed into it; touched the jewel to her lips.

"What a fine stone," Ash said. "Did you get it recently?"

She gave him a quizzical look. "How did you know?"

"You wear beautiful jewelry. Your necklace is lovely." It lay on the coverlet, a cascade of brilliant diamonds entwined with Ash's gold attaché's aigullettes. The *comtesse* was not the first woman to choose the golden shoulder cords as an elegant accoutrement to her lovemaking. Nor, he supposed, would she be the last as long as he had to wear them.

"But you take your jewelry for granted—except for this ruby."

"I smuggled it out of Petrograd. It belongs to my cousin."

Intrigued, Ash asked why.

"Her husband is a Russian noble, and a member of the Duma. There will be a revolution. They're sending out all they can before the Czar falls. It's mine until she leaves Russia."

"But if the Czar falls the eastern front will collapse."

"Who cares?"

"*Who cares?*" Ash sat up. "You'll care if Germany wins the war. The Kaiser will rule all of Europe, *including* Paris."

She looked at him with cold eyes. "Better Kaiser Wilhelm than the socialists."

Ash's face betrayed him. The *comtesse* laughed, sprawling back on the sheets and opening her arms to him. "Forgive me, *chéri.* I forgot you were American. You don't understand."

"I understand pretty well that French and British soldiers are fighting a war to end autocratic militarism. They're *told* it's a war for freedom—"

"I am already free, Commander. I'd prefer a French King, but I'd rather a German King than a French peasant republic, which is what all this freedom will bring us." She extended her soft hand and again directed the ruby light into Ash's eyes. "But most of all, I would prefer you. Again."

Ash stared at her, frankly put off by what amounted to treason.

"*Chéri,*" she said, lying back and tapping the sheet impatiently, "this is not the Chamber of Deputies. My bed is no place for debate."

"Does your cousin in Russia prefer a German King too?"

"There is already a German cabal in the Russian court. Everybody knows that. The Czarina is German, is she not? She and the Czar are both the Kaiser's cousins—"

"And King George of England is cousin to all of them."

"Do you think King George cares who wins the war?"

Ash actually knew George V, but the first rule of a royal friendship was discretion. One did not bandy it about, so all he said was, "Of course he cares. He's a British patriot first, a royal second."

14

"Then he's a fool. The royalty and the nobility—we are international. . . . Now be quiet, or leave my bed."

She said it with a smile, but Ash didn't doubt she meant it. He didn't exactly hate himself for staying, but he wasn't exactly proud of himself either. He might have walked out as a point of honor when he was younger, he thought, but at age thirty-six a man developed an eye for opportunities not taken that he'd sorely miss later. And there was, after all, a peculiar grain of truth in what she had said—millions *were* dying in the name of God and three royal cousins, Czar, King, and Kaiser, who knew each other by their Christian names.

The artillery ceased rumbling abruptly. It meant dawn in the trenches. Ash could visualize the event sixty miles away. Soldiers were already climbing over the top, charging across no-man's-land into the fire of any machine guns that had survived the night-long bombardment; and from what Ash's English friends had told him, one always seemed to.

Around the bed the candles began guttering out simultaneously.

"I have to go."

She nodded drowsily, sleep drifting back into her eyes, dismissing him.

A kitchen maid was lighting the stove fire; she kept her head down as Ash strode out the back door into the cold. He found a gate in the murky dawn light, opened it just wide enough for his body and slipped into a lane that connected stables to the street. There were no lights because of the war.

As he walked past the front of the *comtesse*'s house and looked up at the dark windows where she slept, a man stepped out of the shadows across the street. Ash reached inside his boat cloak.

"Commander. . . ."

Ash recognized Captain Wesley, senior naval attaché to the United States ambassador to Great Britain, and let go of his sword. How in hell had he found him here?

"I didn't know you were in Paris, sir," Ash said as he saluted and attempted to steer him away from the *comtesse*'s house, and Wesley boomed in his quarter-deck voice, "Thought you'd never come out, Ash."

"How did you happen to find me, sir?"

"Somebody at the reception saw you get into her car. Here." He hauled a thick envelope from his greatcoat. "From Ambassador Page."

Ash looked at him. What could be so important that it had to be hand delivered by his superior officer? Captain Wesley looked like he wondered the same thing. Ash handed him a gold matchbox a woman had given him in Berlin and excitedly broke the seal. Wesley lit a match. Ash shielded the flame with his cloak.

Ambassador Page ordered him to break off his trip to Berlin and return immediately to England to attend a shooting party at Sandringham, the country home of King George V. With the orders were priority travel documents—gaudily stamped and beribboned passes to get him swiftly aboard crowded trains and steamers.

Something was definitely up, Ash thought, the excitement building. Surely some kind of action. All this was very strange . . . royal invitations always allowed weeks to cancel conflicting engagements. And Ambassador Page would have wired orders and had travel documents issued by the Paris embassy, unless he had a reason to keep the invitation quiet. But it was no state secret that Kenneth Ash was considered a friend by the King of England . . . . Besides that, it was late in the year for shooting pheasant in Norfolk.

"Anything I can do to help?" asked Captain Wesley.

"Thank you, sir. Please could you ask someone to get my bags from the embassy and send them to London?"

"Anything else?" Wesley asked silkily and Ash realized the captain was not exactly happy to have been sent out to retrieve a subordinate officer. Ambassador Page had really stepped out of channels.

"Are you off to Berlin, sir?" Ash asked.

"Yes, dammit, doing your job."

They exchanged salutes again and shook hands, and Ash set out for La Gare du Nord, plotting the fastest route—train to Calais via Amiens because the Boulogne line was jammed with ambulance trains, thanks to another bloody British offensive against the Germans' vital railroad link to Bapaume, then the Channel ferry from Calais to Dover and with luck an express to London. Nine hours if he was lucky, a full day if he wasn't.

Despite his Medal of Honor, which admittedly attested to bravery, and Ash's reputation as fencing champion of the Naval Academy and a boxer with a wicked left hook in his midshipman days, Ash, in Captain Wesley's opinion, was an irresponsible bachelor with nothing to spend his pay on but uniforms and liquor. Also a bit of a conniver, with political pull as well. After all, lieutenant commander was a pretty heavy rank for a man Ash's age who had served most of his time in the diplomatic corps around Europe, yacht racing, shooting and playing polo like a millionaire sportsman at public expense. Before the World War at any rate. Damned little of that tomfoolery left now.

Maybe he was feeling sour because he hated the trip to Berlin in the

16

winter. Actually, he liked Ash. Decent enough looking man, well-built, with an easy blue-eyed gaze and tousled brown hair women seemed to like —if half those rumors were true. But his lean face was barely marked, even if he had been at sea, and his broad smile was maybe a little too quick to trust . . . And for sure that damned European officer mustache didn't help, didn't seem American, somehow.

Halfway down the street, Ash suddenly turned around and called out, "Roses."

"What?"

Ash ran back and pressed a couple of francs in Captain Wesley's hand. "Would you do me a favor, Captain? Send some roses to the *comtesse?* . . . White, if they've got 'em, sir."

2

An hour after dawn a cold, wet North Sea wind sloughed through the bare woods as thirty beaters whooped, whistled, tapped the trees with sticks. The King's gamekeeper trailed on horseback, straightening their line with sharp commands. Pheasants, partridges and woodcocks retreated uneasily; ahead, the woods came to an abrupt stop at a mowed field where four guns, Ash among them, waited.

Why was he here? Ash wondered, motionless, double-barrel shotgun draped in ready position. King George was one of the finest shots in the realm, but easily half a dozen English guns could offer His Majesty top-hole competition if sport was all he wanted. So Ash's last-minute invitation suggested a charade to keep the real reason for bringing him to Sandringham private, whatever it was. And an elaborate charade at that, right down to his regular loaders crouching silently behind him with second and third guns and bags of shells; Eddison an estate gardener, Martin a mechanic in the Royal Garage, both too old to be conscripted.

The King had placed Ash fifty yards to his right for the first stand of this blustery winter morning. To Ash's right, at an equal distance, the King's equerry, Alex Farquhar, paced in impatient little circles as the noise of the beaters modulated with the changing wind; and another fifty yards beyond him was a man Ash hadn't met before, Lord Exeter, a giant of a man whose vast, unmoving bulk seated on a shooting stick and wrapped in enough houndstooth twill to clothe a village put Ash in mind of a deeply entrenched artillery piece puffing gun smoke each time Exeter exhaled in the cold, damp air.

When Ash had arrived from Paris yesterday evening the King had been closeted with advisors. He had gratefully requested a supper tray in his room, cleaned his guns, and gone to an early bed to sleep off the grueling trip. The King had offered no hint at their hasty breakfast.

But in London, in the car from Charing Cross to the Royal Train at Paddington Station, Ambassador Page had explained that prior to the invitation the King's private secretary had approached him in his club and discreetly sounded him out about the courier duties Ash performed for the United States' European embassies. He had been particularly interested in confirming whether Ash continued to make regular runs to Berlin.

The beaters sounded closer. Ash grinned at the sight of Farquhar, pacing and talking to his loaders. No mistake the King had placed him where he had. The equerry was unintentionally acting as a flanker for Ash and the King. All that activity would drive more birds their way. A lone pheasant ran from the woods and took flight with a warning cry and drumming wings. She spotted the guns, veered and flew low and fast, paralleling the gun line from left to right. The King brought her down with a cross shot.

A mass of birds broke from the edge of the woods, rising swiftly in a tightly formed hard, dark cloud, climbing higher and faster than Ash had ever seen at Sandringham. The tight whirr of a hundred wings drowned out the beaters; then the loud flat popping of the guns began.

Ash fired and hit, fired again and hit, reached for his second gun without removing his eyes from the birds. Eddison took the empty Purdey and placed the loaded Holland and Holland in Ash's hands. Ash fired twice, missed once, took his third gun, the Westley Richards, and hit a fourth and fifth bird before the first fell to the ground.

"Good 'un, sir," Eddison murmured as he exchanged the Purdey he had reloaded for the empty Westley Richards.

They were old-fashioned hammer guns, handmade. Ash's favorite had been a gift from the gunmaker. There'd been nothing so crude as any suggestion that he tout the weapon, but the simple fact that Commander Ash used it lent the expensive fowling piece a cachet wealthy sportsmen would find hard to resist. Ash shrugged away the doubt. Fact was, it was a good weapon, and, he thought ruefully, the most valuable thing he owned.

Lord Exeter and Farquhar were firing sporadically, wasting time choosing targets and coping with the thinner flyover caused by Farquhar's earlier pacing. To Ash's left, the King banged a steady, rhythmic string of salvos into the sky, while pheasant rained at his feet. Like Ash, the King had held onto his old hammer guns, and for the same reason; the hammers made fine sights for lining up the birds. Both men were in constant motion, shifting their feet like boxers as they took the proper stance for each shot. Years before, when they had met yacht racing and the King was still the Duke of York, he had taught Ash how to shoot. It was basically an athlete's sport, although few who shot realized it and you had to keep moving.

The last birds flew over like ellipses at the end of a long sentence and

Ash and the King turned around and brought them down. A moment's silence followed the final shots, broken by the beaters emerging from the trees and the loaders inspecting the corpse-littered ground, counting the score.

It was a modest bag by prewar standards, when a dozen guns and scores of beaters had killed thousands of birds in a single day. The beaters straggled onto the field, dressed in the traditional long blue twill smocks, and they too bore the mark of war. They were mostly old men, now, and boys. Those few in their prime years were maimed, with empty sleeves flapping from their coats or, in the case of one, struggling to keep up on crutches, their expressions less bitter than dismayed.

A game wagon drawn by an old plow horse trundled out of a distant thicket, the driver, back home on the estate, where he'd been born, coughing steadily from gas-rotted lungs. The birds were hung by the neck from the game wagon racks; a slew of rabbits flushed earlier on the walk out to the field were already trussed by the hind feet.

The King waved Ash over and they started toward the next stand. He was a small, compactly built man with a short beard and mustache, younger looking than his fifty years, vigorous, his face ruddied by the cold damp. Quiet and shy, King George was the direct opposite of the outgoing showman and *bon vivant* his father King Edward had been. This eight thousand acres of lovingly tended game lands on the North Sea coast of Norfolk was his great joy, but Sandringham House itself was far less lavish than dozens of English country houses.

But in matters of manners and dress he was the image of his father—a stickler for propriety. A boy approached with cider and glasses and commenced to pour for Ash and the King. The King stopped him. "Laddie, when you're old enough to have a sweetheart you may clasp her about the waist, but be so kind as to hold a bottle by the neck."

They started over the rough ground again. The King was an inch shorter than Ash and he walked with a limp. "Slow down, Ash. Damned leg still drags on these wet days."

"Sorry, sir." The King had had a bad fall from a horse a year before while reviewing a Royal Air Force unit. Ash had played polo with him and knew what a freak accident the fall must have been. He said, "Maybe the French are right about eating horses."

The King laughed. "I say, Ash, you did rather well for a man who hasn't shot recently."

"Thank you, sir. . . . May I ask, am I getting older or are the birds flying faster and higher?"

The King scooped a bird off the ground. Its breast was speckled red where the shot had pierced it. "Feel this."

Ash took the bird. It was thin.

"She's had to fend for herself," said the King. "I doubt a man your age has ever seen a wild-fed pheasant in England before. But we can't feed them grain anymore, of course."

The Defense of the Realm Act outlawed feeding precious grain to game birds while German U-boats were sinking Britain's food ships. The birds Ash had shot at the big shoots before the war had been raised expressly for the sport, pampered animals too fat to fly fast or very far, though still hard to hit on the wing. In fact, during those luxurious times when the rich European empires were still at peace, the beaters' job had often been to persuade the birds to take to the air rather than light out on foot.

That afternoon, as the dusk was gathering and cold rain blew in from the sea, the King said, "We'll have a talk, Ash. After dinner."

All Ash had ever envied the King of England was his marriage. He had been his guest often, at Sandringham for shooting, and Osborne on the Isle of Wight for sailing at Cowes, and he had come to regard the royal union as a partnership built on mutual enjoyment. Queen Mary, May of Teck, was a beautiful and intelligent woman, as shy as her husband, and considerably better educated than most European royalty.

She did Ash the honor of inviting him to sit on her right at dinner, and reminded him of their conversation of a year ago when he had recommended the poetry of Robert Service. "He seems a little rough to me," she said, "though certainly a proper antidote to Mr. Emerson's lives of quiet desperation. Have you read Rupert Brooke?" Ash had, and admired him, but he regretted that this was not the place to bring up the more recent war poets like Sassoon with their grimmer assessments of the carnage overtaking their generation.

The dinner guests were a mixed bag of Royal household and Norfolk neighbors, landowners whose lives revolved around their shooting estates. Ash knew most of them. Other guests were conspicuous by their absence —neighbors' sons killed in France, including a boy whose death marked the end of a line that descended from the Angle kings of the eighth century.

Lord Exeter sat on Queen Mary's left, across from Ash. Indoors, he seemed ever larger, a vast mountain of a man, whose bulk seemed incongruous in the light of the nervous deference he paid the King and Queen. He was in his fifties, face red and lined as if from drink, and Ash recalled now that he was rumored to be somehow connected with the secret service.

Ash looked around the table again and realized that Exeter and his wife and he himself were the only guests outside of the King's immediate circle of neighbors and household. Windsor Castle, the official country residence of the King, saw admirals and members of Parliament, European statesmen, Hungarian counts and the like purposefully gathered for political motives, but Sandringham was home. Whatever the King had in mind for Ash was private and most probably involved Exeter too.

There was no wine. George V had taken an oath of abstinence early on in hopes that his subjects would take the pledge with him to increase war production in the factories. They hadn't. The government regulated pub hours as a compromise, but the King was left dry for the duration. Ash had had some brandy in his room from his traveling flask, but it was wearing off under the onslaught of cider and lemonade.

As usual, conversation started about the shooting but shifted quickly to the war, to the new government being formed by Prime Minister Lloyd George, to the rumors of peace. Ash listened intently and said little. This was the sort of informal conversation at the seat of power that the embassy expected him to report, not mix in. But Ambassador Page had instructed him to try to make one point clear to the King—that at least he, Page, did *not* expect the British to accept President Wilson's latest proposal of peace without victory—British sacrifices had been too great.

1916 had been a terrible year for the Allies—England, France and Russia. They were reeling. On the Western Front six months of murderous attacks had gained the French and English little, and as winter set in the Germans were as strongly entrenched along the Somme as they had been in the spring.

French troops had mutinied, and the previous Easter a full-scale rebellion had broken out in Dublin. The cost to Britain of putting it down with army troops had included great anger in America. And Lord Kitchener, the embodiment of the British Army, the old soldier pointing from a million recruiting posters, had drowned on a mission to Russia when his cruiser struck a German mine. So important had Kitchener been in the mind of the British public that rumors abounded that he was still alive, working on a secret plan to end the war.

At sea the great miracle weapons of the twentieth century—dreadnaught battleships, the cause of a treasury-draining fifteen-year arms race —had finally clashed, inconclusively. Despite great loss of life on both sides, the ferocious Battle of Jutland had not affected the balance of naval power in the slightest. England continued to blockade Germany with surface ships, and Germany blockaded England with submarines—a situation that naval officers the world over, Ash included, still had difficulty believing, not to mention the stalemate on land, where the unexpected defensive power of machine guns had mired millions of infantry in trenches to the astonishment of an entire generation of military strategists.

But the Allies' predicament was most perilous on the Eastern Front, where Russian armies continued to grind themselves to death on the opposing artillery of the Central Powers. True, the Russians had won some significant victories against the Austrians, but Germany had made up for her partners' deficiencies by meting out stunning defeats from Rumania to the Baltic. And the terrible, preeminent question was—how long could the Russians last? A collapse of the Russian government, a collapse on the battlefield, a separate peace with the Central Powers, and Germany could wheel three thousand guns and a million men against the Western Front.

Lord Exeter seemed informed about Russia. The Czar's armies were "bewildered peasants, underarmed and underfed, driven rather than led. This winter the Russian railroads are on the verge of collapse, and when I left Petrograd last month food supplies were already said to be falling short in the cities."

"Will there be a revolution?" the Queen asked.

"Ma'am, no one knows . . . least of all the Czar."

"Poor Alix," she murmured, so quietly that only Ash and Exeter heard her. "Poor Nicky." They exchanged a look. Nicholas and Alexandra, autocrats of the Imperial Russian Empire, were not remote figures to her.

"What *precisely* is the United States waiting for?" Lady Exeter asked suddenly, turning on Ash with an expression that indicated she demanded much and expected little. "Surely you're not *still* choosing sides."

"No, ma'am," replied Ash, thinking to himself, *Thank you for the opening,* and presenting Ambassador Page's message with a casual glance at the King. "In fact, I just yesterday overheard the American ambassador assure the British foreign minister that Britain deserves recompense for her struggle against—"

"We don't need recompense," she shot back. "We need, sir, an *ally.* Where the blazes are you?"

Lady Exeter was twenty years her husband's junior, a handsome woman with stern, chiseled features, extravagant red hair and a fiery glint in her eye. She had been, Ash recalled, a leader of the radical suffragette movement before the war. Had she gone to prison? He couldn't remember, but so many had. Probably not if she was welcome at his table, though you couldn't tell, the war had realigned so many things . . .

Ash started to explain that President Wilson, reelected the previous month on a promise to keep out of the World War, had to deal with a Congress that represented a peace-minded citizenry that resisted entanglement with what it considered ancient rivalries among . . . forgive him . . . corrupt and reactionary European states.

King George interrupted. "Commander Ash does not make foreign policy for the United States. Correct, Kenneth?"

"No, sir, but I *can* say—"

"But surely, sir," Lady Exeter said to the King, "an officer of the United States Navy, attached to the American Embassy, has *some* inkling of his country's intentions?"

"A democracy's intentions," Ash replied, "are not as predictable as—"

Lady Exeter interrupted with an indignant snort and the King quickly interrupted her. "Lady Exeter, Kenneth Ash is a fine sportsman who also happens to hold a commission in the United States Navy. Forgive me if I insist that he be allowed to be only a sportsman when he's a guest at my shoot, and *not* be pestered with questions best addressed to—"

"Your Majesty, I merely—"

The King laid the extended fingers of one hand firmly on the tablecloth. "My dear woman, this is a shooting estate, not your London salon."

Lord Exeter intervened before his wife could answer. "His Majesty's right, m'dear. Ash is a first-rate helmsman and a splendid shot. Don't burden the chap with concerns he can't be expected to respond to."

Lady Exeter bowed her handsome head to the King, then turned to Ash, her jewels flashing with the quick movement. "*Forgive* me, Commander, if I have cast a *pall* on your sport."

Ash returned a smile he'd last offered the captain of a destroyer who'd rammed his minesweeper at a Philippine coal dock. He did not relish being considered a fool or a fop, but a sportsman who happened to hold a commission in the navy came uncomfortably close to the way he too had been feeling about himself since this war began—a sort of relic of a time when a neatly cornered race buoy or the shooting maxim "Aim high, keep the gun moving, and never check" had actually seemed important.

The King had intervened out of kindness, but he would have preferred to answer Lady Exeter himself, which he was fully prepared and able to do. But the ambassador wouldn't have tolerated it. In his own mind Ash saw Germany as the enemy already, and to hell with neutrality. German militarism had been a frightening spectre since his midshipman days at Annapolis, the Imperial German Army and the High Seas Fleet growing stronger each year, bolder, testing the older empires, challenging, attacking. They'd own the Philippines today, he thought, if a very angry, brave Admiral Dewey hadn't put the American Fleet in their way in 1898, and they had pulled similar stunts in Europe and Africa.

German officers drank a toast—*Der Tag*. "To the day," the day Germany would cast off the restraints of peace. So the war seemed a logical, direct macabre outcome of all the German threats and boasts. But even Ambassador Page, who so badly wanted to intervene, had to contain his utterances on the war, and tonight Ash sympathized and wished he too could stop some of this diplomatic playacting, however good he might be at it, and swing back. He settled, instead, for a pinprick. "It was a small pall, Lady Exeter, in the light of His Lordship's praise."

She gave him a spirited grin and another barb. "You're rather witty . . . for an American." Lord Exeter, perhaps noting the glance of appreciation between them, intervened again. "Any American who doesn't respond to an introduction with 'Pleased to meet you' is all right in my book. Why do your countrymen do that, Ash? You don't."

24

"May I suggest, Your Lordship, that the next time one says 'Pleased to meet you,' inform him, 'You damned well ought to be.' "

Exeter laughed, as did his wife and the King, who then glanced at Queen Mary. She rose with a warm smile for Ash.

"Ladies, shall we leave the gentlemen to their cigars?"

A butler presented a mahogany humidor to each man and a circle of blue smoke formed above the table. Conversation reverted to the shooting, and the King's neighbors, who'd sat silently through the earlier discussion, finally had something to talk about. But it was a brief respite for the rustics; Ash barely had his cigar going when the King suggested that they join the ladies. He started to snuff it out, but the King stayed him with a gesture as the others pushed back their chairs.

Farquhar ushered them out, and very quickly Ash and the King were alone in the empty dining room. A long expanse of white linen interrupted by candelabra and ashtrays lay between them. "Move on up here, Kenneth. Bring your cigar."

Ash moved to the head of the table and took the chair Lady Exeter had occupied to the King's right. The King's invitation was a signal that complete ease would exist between them while they talked, like a ship's captain temporarily dropping formalities with a subordinate officer. The charade was drawing to a close.

"Awfully good to see you again, Kenneth. Envied you being back at sea."

"I was hardly there before they hauled me right back here for diplomatic work." He shrugged. "My reward, I guess, for speaking foreign languages and knowing the difference between a knight and a baronet."

"Oh, what I would give for a command again. If I could have my wife near me I would be the happiest man alive if the Royal Navy gave me back my minesweeper . . . So, you were sorry to give it up?"

"I've orders to join the cruiser *San Diego* next month. As executive officer. The navy promised me a destroyer in a few years. Thank God I'm finally getting back to sea. I'm damn tired of watching the race from the committee boat."

The King smiled. "May I give you some advice? Don't fool yourself about a naval command. You're used to a rather freer life—you're a diplomat at heart, almost a politican. You like being at the center of things. You like Europe. Right here is the sort of action you've always enjoyed."

"That may have been true before the war. But diplomacy has failed, Your Majesty. Somehow, if I may be frank, charm and good manners don't seem to make a great deal of difference anymore."

"You're a man of parts, Kenneth, including a good deal more than just charming. I've seen you in action and—"

Ash shook his head.

"You're not the retiring sort, as I am," the King insisted. "You *feast* on Europe. London . . . Paris . . . and we know how you admire the ballet," he added with a smile that suggested he might be referring to Ash's long, intermittent affair with Tamara Tishkova, *prima ballerina assoluta* of the Imperial Russian Theater. He hadn't seen Tamara in three years, but people remembered. He wondered, Did she?

"Look here, Kenneth . . . you know the Kaiser . . . ?"

"Yes, Your Majesty. I last saw Kaiser Wilhelm at his daughter's wedding to Duke Ernst August." He was puzzled; the King knew perfectly well that he had met the Kaiser on several occasions, particularly that one.

"Beat him at the Cowes once, didn't you?"

"And promptly lost the next race to you, sir." Ash replied, still puzzled. It wasn't like the King to state the obvious.

"You lost to the *Britannic,* not to me—Kenneth, I want you to do something for me."

"Of course, Your Majesty."

"Don't be too quick to answer. I want you to take a message to Berlin. To my cousin Willy."

"To the *Kaiser?*"

"You should see your face," King George said.

Ash was astonished. He had guessed that the King had a private courier mission in mind. Armed with a diplomatic *laissez-passer,* a neutral courier like himself could travel most anywhere with a private message, cross borders without search. But it never occurred to him that the King wanted to communicate privately with Britain's mortal enemy.

"I said, my *cousin,*" the King continued. "It's a family matter, an extremely sensitive one. I can't send an Englishman to the Kaiser, obviously, and I can't risk commercial cable or the mails. Nor can I communicate through a neutral embassy because I can't put my message in writing. If it were exposed I'd have to abdicate. And, just as important, it must be presented both privately and persuasively to Kaiser Wilhelm. I need a man not in the fight, but one whom I can trust like my most loyal subject."

Ash said, "I'm honored that you'd consider me, sir."

But his mind was tumbling through the aspects of the King's request—pride that he'd been chosen, excitement to get in the action, worry that such a mission put him at odds with the responsibilities of his commission and his attaché duties, tricky waters at best, if not plain illegal . . . But the King had not asked an American naval officer to help him. He had asked a friend . . . a friend who just happened to hold a commission in the United States Navy . . . Ambassador Page would approve the King's mission in a flash. Anything to help Britain. The navy, however . . . but the navy—of course—was the target of the King's charade. A week's shooting at San-dringham was time enough for Commander Ash to travel secretly to Germany and return before he was due in London. And if the Kaiser tossed him into a German prison? Page and the navy could innocently disown him. So would the King. But what a chance to play the game as if it really mattered.

"I can do that, sir."

But instead of thanking him, King George gazed into the forest of candelabra that lit the long table and said, "There's more. . . . My message to the Kaiser is only the beginning . . ."

The King's fingers trembled slightly as he raised his cigar to his lips. "My ambassador to Petrograd and my consuls throughout Russia are convinced that my cousin Czar Nicholas's government will fall. Either to revolution-aries or palace intrigues. I'm told it's a matter of when, not if . . . ." He looked closely at Ash. "I intend to rescue my cousins Nicholas and Alexan-dra and their children and give them asylum in Britain."

Ash's first and foremost excited thought was that the United States would intervene in the World War on the side of the Allies the moment the Romanov tyrant was removed from Russia. And in the process would defeat Germany and end the war . . .

"How do you intend to carry out the rescue, sir?"

"I shall send a British cruiser to Murmansk."

Ash nodded. But Murmansk was over a thousand miles north of Petro-grad—a long, hard run in the middle of a revolution. He asked, "And the Kaiser, Your Majesty? What does the Kaiser have to do with your plan?"

"Protection. Another Kitchener sinking, with the Romanovs aboard, would be terrible. I want you to ask Willy to guarantee safe passage for my cruiser."

Ash nodded slowly. To Europe's rulers, the death of the old general was a terrible reminder of the indifference, even the insolence of modern weapons that held no respect for rank. But he said, "I beg your pardon, Your Majesty, but the Kaiser can't *guarantee* safe passage through mines and U-boats. Mines drift, U-boats venture beyond wireless range. You would literally need a German escort from Russia to England to guarantee the Czar's safety."

"Exactly! An escort is precisely what you are going to ask for. You must convince Kaiser Wilhelm to protect my cruiser."

"That's a pretty tall order, Your Majesty. German U-boat—"

"Willy loves Nicky in a fatherly way, and loves our cousin Alix, as well he might—she's the most beautiful woman, except for my wife, that I have ever seen. Willy is not the monster he's made out to be, regardless of what the newspapers must print to encourage the nation."

"You believe the Kaiser will put family above nation . . ."

"Do you know, Kenneth, that our grandmother Queen Victoria died in

27

the Kaiser's arms? He cried like a baby, then tried to take over the entire funeral. That's his way . . . but he's always been kind to Nicky, if not a little too forceful in his advice on how to rule Russia. He'll see this my way. And if he does, it will help convince Nicky to accept asylum. Nicky's stubborn, though not the fool he's made out to be. With the offer of sanctuary coming from both myself and Willy, Nicky and Alix will accept . . ."

All these Willys, Nickys and Alixes made the King's remarkable scheme sound as innocuous as a house party, and Ash felt obliged to put in an objection. He couched it very carefully; King George was no fool but he was still a King and even the best of them, as this man surely was, did not easily take advice. "Of course, I don't know who you've confided in, sir, but—"

"No one. I've told you, this is a family affair. It is to be handled privately and involve only those directly concerned. We will rescue Nicky and let our governments proceed with this damnable war . . . and we'll beat Willy, in the end, but God, what a price . . ."

"Yes, but don't you run the risk of being associated with actions that might smack of undermining your own Russian ally."

"We have no intention of appearing to undermine anything," the King snapped, shifting abruptly to the royal *we*. "It is not our intention to weaken our ally, Kenneth. It is our intention to rescue our cousin—regardless of his many shortcomings, Nicky and Alix and the children will live out their lives peacefully in British sanctuary."

"Who do you intend to send to Russia, sir?"

"Well, as you've suggested, until the Czar is replaced by an orderly Russian government, appearance *is* vital. Therefore I can't send an Englishman to the Czar, whether he be military officer or diplomat. I can't blur the lines between family and nation."

"How about a Russian?" Ash said. "One who knows his way around the Czar's court?"

"Not without becoming inadvertantly involved in one of their intrigues."

"Then a private citizen, like Lord Exeter? He seems to know Russia."

The King shook his head, and Ash had an awful feeling he would never sail on the *San Diego*. "No. Even a private agent exposed as an English subject would bring the worst implications down upon the British Crown. But I could send a neutral . . . an American . . . When does your posting to the *San Diego* take effect?"

"Next month, sir. But I don't see how I could possibly get to Russia and back before January . . ."

"I know it's a good deal to ask, Kenneth. Please feel free to decline—"

"I've been playing diplomat a long time, sir. I need action before I lose my edge."

28

"Kenneth . . . I've seen you in action. Surely you haven't forgotten Berlin. I know I haven't . . ."

"I suspect if I'd had time to think I might have moved more slowly." Ash smiled. "I just happened to be standing in the way."

"It's precisely what you did before you thought that distinguished your actions and saved my life."

May, 1913; nearly four years ago, and the King was still haunted by the demented glare of the assassin's face—a look of total hatred, made even more terrifying by his expression of triumph that he had slipped past the guards. The fact that his bullets were intended for his cousin Nicky was little comfort.

All the years his father Edward had been king before him had been disrupted by periodic anarchist attacks on European royalty. They went, the King of Italy had once said, with the job. And suddenly in a Berlin palace garden, moments after a lavish wedding pageant, it was happening to him. It had been typical of anarchist attacks of the prewar era, confused —the assassin mistook him for the Czar—the man was especially danger-ous because he had no regard for his own life. Six inches to one side and the first shot would have gone through the King's head. A foot the other way and his Queen would have died.

The King had realized later that he had noticed the man for days as he, in retrospect, stalked the wedding guests at the elaborate pageant the Kaiser had staged to marry his only daughter to Ernst August of Bruns-wick-Luneburg. A happy occasion in which the marriage of a plain dowdy girl cemented an ancient rift between the houses of Hollenzollen and Brunswick. It was the last time he and Nicky and Willy had all been together and ironically the last grand royal pageant before the World War destroyed the myth that the European royals possessed the power to keep the peace.

The assassin had posed as an orthodox priest, and for all their Germanic efficiency the Kaiser's Imperial Guard never caught on. The final proces-sional over at last, and the Kaiser's plain daughter finally packed off on her honeymoon, an informal party had continued in the gardens. Czar Nicho-las had just walked away to address the Kaiser when the King had spotted Ash with his friend the Russian ballerina, apparently a guest of the Grand Duke Valery, her paramour—the Russians were tolerant of that sort of thing; the King had been surprised, but at least she hadn't been in the church.

The King had summoned Ash, who was part of a small American delega-tion from their Berlin embassy, where Ash was attached at the time. The Queen had expressed a curiosity to meet the ballerina. They were just shaking hands when the gunman rushed up in his black robes, drew his revolver, fired. People screamed and the Guard rushed up. It was over in seconds, the gunman dead, May clinging to him like a child, Ash's shoulder smashed by a bullet and the dancer kneeling beside him in tears. The King would swear to his dying day that Ash had stepped in front of the gun, and Stamfordham, his private secretary, confirmed it, even though Ash steadily claimed that all he had done was throw a left hook and try to draw his sword . . . .

"Kenneth, you're the only man for the job." The King ticked off the reasons persuasively. "You're a first-rate officer. I can trust you to do the right thing at the right time. I can trust you to operate on your own, as you will have to. Once in Petrograd, you'll receive precious little help from me. I must remain detached for all the reasons you yourself have mentioned. In addition, you know the Kaiser and the Czar. They know I know you and know I would send you for this sort of thing. No need for elaborate introductions. And you *know* the Russians. Your friendship with Mademoiselle Tishkova has, I am sure, over the years given you a deeper insight into the Russian character than most, which should be quite useful in persuading the Czar and those around him."

Ash shook his head. The hint earlier had not been idle. "Please understand, Your Majesty, that I can't turn to Mademoiselle Tishkova for anything—"

"I was referring only to your knowledge and contacts acquired in the past—"

"It's over," Ash said. "Once and for all . . ."

"Of course, forgive me for bringing it up. I am so concerned that . . . I ask you to reconsider your position . . . perhaps you could find a way to have your orders postponed. Surely I could put in helpful words, indirectly?"

"Perhaps," Ash agreed, though he knew he couldn't. Executive on a brand new cruiser was a plum a dozen officers would be waiting in line for . . . It was a lot to give up—a career even—for a friend. An awful lot. But it wasn't only a choice between friendship and career. Russia, he realized, would be a far more palatable *American* ally with Czar Nicholas out of the way. America could then intervene in Europe, help defeat Germany and end the war. And the King, never mind if for his own personal reasons, had offered him the chance to help make it happen. Ash said, "You honor me by your request. I'll give it a try."

The King reached over and gripped his arm. "Thank you. But I don't honor you, I believe you can do it."

"I have one stipulation. I must clear this with my superiors."

30

To Ash's surprise, the King didn't object. "Of course. But could you confine your report to Ambassador Page?"

Ash nodded. "I think so. It so happens that my immediate chief is in Berlin at the moment."

"Excellent," the King said. "Ambassador Page will understand the situation, I'm sure . . . I wish I could give you more help. However, you may call on Lord Exeter in Petrograd for introductions and the like. He has commercial interests in Russia."

"Exeter?" Ash asked as he stood with the sovereign. "May I ask is His Lordship with the Secret Service?"

"Lord Exeter is serving me in a private capacity," the King replied, leaving Ash's question largely unanswered. It would need some investigation. Ash had no desire to act as an unknowing point man for the British Secret Service, and he wouldn't put it past that service to climb aboard the King's personal mission and steer it to the aide of a mission of their own.

The King now was saying, "In fact, Lord Exeter is waiting to take you by motor car tonight to Yarmouth for the steamer to The Hague."

"No—"

"No? But I thought—"

"No, Your Majesty. I'll go to Yarmouth in the normal manner, by train from London."

"Speed is essential, Kenneth. Russia is, as they say, reeling. Let Exeter deliver you to the midnight boat. You'll be in The Hague tomorrow morning. Surely your meeting with Ambassador Page can wait until you return from Berlin."

"It's not that, Your Majesty. But Holland is the main neutral entry into Germany. The entire route is crawling with spies. And I would strongly prefer that German agents didn't observe me pull up to the steamer in Lord Exeter's motor car."

3

"**Y**ou're back early," said Walter Hines Page. "Shoot a beater?"

The American ambassador to Great Britain was a sick man and his illness, harsh and chronic, seemed to show in the dark pools beneath his enormous eyes and pinched his high-browed face. He extended Ash a bony hand and a shaky smile. He was sixty-one and looked ten years older.

Ash attributed his uncommonly informal manner to Page's long career as a newspaper and magazine writer. Woodrow Wilson had awarded him the ambassadorship to the Court of St. James for his early support of his presidency, and Page had taken happily to diplomacy; he enjoyed intrigue, admired the British as perhaps only a gentleman of the Old South could, and regarded German militarism as the curse of the century.

" . . . Since Captain Wesley is in Berlin, I thought it best to report directly to you, Mr. Ambassador."

"What did the King want?" Page asked, brushing aside the chain of command with an impatient wave of his skeletal hand.

"Well, sir, it regards an extremely sensitive personal matter—"

"Spit it out, man. I've got to meet a train."

Ash took a quick breath and tried it all in a sentence. "King George wants to join forces with Kaiser Wilhelm to rescue their cousin the Czar from what the King fears is an impending revolution."

"Rescue? You mean somehow get him out of Russia?"

"Yes, sir. He's offering asylum in Britain."

"With the *Kaiser?*"

"The King will send a Royal Navy cruiser to Murmansk if the Kaiser will provide a U-boat escort for it to Britain."

"And just who in hell is going to talk the Kaiser into conspiring with the Allies?" Page asked.

"I guess I am, sir, with your permission, of course."

Page's eyes closed to narrow slits. "And provided you can, who is going to present this . . . scheme . . . to the Czar?"

"With your permission, sir, it seems I'm again elected to give it a try. The King feels he must use a neutral. I'd of course need some sort of extended leave of absence from my current duties, sir, as well as from my January posting to the cruiser *San Diego.*"

"I thought you were all fired up about getting back to sea."

"I *am.* But, sir, it's true, isn't it, that Congress would look a good deal more favorably on intervention if the Czar were gone . . . ?"

"I see . . . end autocracy in Russia *and* defeat German militarism in a single blow. Quite an achievement for a young officer, wouldn't you say, Commander?"

Ash felt a little foolish. "I know I'm just a naval officer, sir. Actually a courier, a glorified mailman—no Admiral Dewey, for sure—but, sir, I guess what's going through my mind is what President Roosevelt used to say. He said he wanted to grab history and make the right thing happen. I'm not saying I'm the man to do it but couldn't we—"

"What makes the King think you're the man to grab the Czar?"

"I don't know that I am, sir, but . . . well, the King seems to have a somewhat overblown opinion of me . . . thinks I'm sort of a man of parts or something . . ." Ash no longer felt foolish, he felt like an ass.

"Sort of a Count of Monte Cristo?" Page asked drily. "You'd have damn well have to be to pull off something like this."

With that, Ash was sure Page would deliver a flat no. He was almost relieved. But after a long moment a smile lifted Page's cadaverous cheeks.

"Marvelous."

"I beg your pardon, sir?"

Page tugged his watch chain and squinted at the time. "Get your coat, Commander. We're going for a drive."

Hooting its chrome horns, the embassy's Pierce town car cut through the line of black ambulances that snaked into Charing Cross and onto the platforms under the glass-roofed train shed. Walter Hines Page felt damned proud when a policewoman waved them past with a smart salute for the American flags flying from the fenders—still another sign that United States stock was rising as the European empires battered themselves bankrupt.

"Don't get out of the car," he warned Ash. "I don't want anyone to see you with us."

Ash settled back looking puzzled, and perhaps a little sorry he had confided in Page. Wait until he heard the rest of it. Page pulled down the window. The station reeked of locomotive coal smoke. Hundreds of men in battle dress were hurrying to the trains. Women walked with them, holding their arms; some cried, but most had assumed the mask of a stiff smile.

"Admiral Innes!" Page called hoarsely. "Mr. Banks!" The effort to make himself heard above the shuffle of hundreds of boots hurt his throat, but he barely noticed in his excitement. For too long, in his judgment, he had been President Wilson's stalking horse, drawing fire each time he urged the American people to stand with the Allies. Now intervention was in his grasp, provided he could persuade Banks and Admiral Innes to support Ash, and provided Ash was up to the job.

The portly Admiral Innes caught sight of the car. Banks, a lanky white-haired civilian in a trenchcoat, hurried beside him. "They're just back from inspecting French Atlantic ports," Page told Ash. "For troop transports if we manage to wangle our way into the war." Ash attempted to salute sitting down as they scrambled into the car. Admiral Innes was in his late fifties, neat and rotund, a hero of the battle of Manila; in the navy he was known as a maverick. Banks, a Midwesterner, was a confidential advisor to the President; like Colonel House he spoke for the President. Holding no official title, he was in effect senior to the admiral and Page himself—the man Page had to convince. When they were seated opposite in the passenger compartment, Page introduced Ash.

"Mahon's aide, weren't you, Commander?"

"Yes, Admiral. At The Hague."

Banks shook Ash's hand and displayed a politician's memory.

"I had the pleasure of meeting your father at a Bull Moose convention in 1912. He told me that T.R. had sent you to the Portsmouth Peace Conference—how'd you happen to choose the navy for a career? Your father intimated he'd hoped you'd pick up his cudgels—shrewd old gentleman, your father," Banks added with frank admiration. "And proud as the deuce of you."

"We differed on how exciting smalltown life is." Ash smiled.

"Small town? He practically lives in the State House."

"We also disagreed on how exciting the action was in the State House. I was a little young to settle down to law and politics."

"Well, you certainly have gotten around, haven't you?"

"Wait until you hear where he's been this time," Page interrupted drily. "Tell them what you just told me, Commander. Go ahead."

Ash stopped smiling. "Sir . . . may I remind you of the conditions under which we spoke? I can't betray a confidence—"

"You can with us."

"I'm sorry, sir, I gave my word."

34

Admiral Innes purpled. "Commander, what the devil are you ranting about?"

Ambassador Page apologized. He had provoked Ash, already testing whether he had the "sand," as the British put it, to conduct his one-man mission into Russia.

"Gentlemen, for reasons that will become apparent, this conversation is to remain strictly confidential."

"Does that apply to the President as well?" Banks asked.

"Until Commander Ash agrees otherwise . . ." Turning to Ash, who looked equal parts mystified and angry, and decidedly not buffaloed by all the rank in the car, Page explained, "To help you trust us, Commander, let me say that Mr. Banks, Admiral Innes and myself lead an unofficial inner circle created by President Wilson to expedite American entry in the war. We've been laying groundwork, even trying to provoke some incident that would tip the Congress to take action."

"With President Wilson's knowledge?"

"I report to the President," Banks told him. "As does Ambassador Page. Admiral Innes is in close contact with Assistant Navy Secretary Franklin Roosevelt."

"We've been pretty successful preparing the way for American troops to arrive in France," Page said, "but less so in finding a way to get the Congress to get off its rear. But we're trying . . ."

"In other words," Banks said, "the pacifists will lynch us from the Capitol dome if you tell them what Ambassador Page just told you. So you see, we're very much on the same side here."

"I think I get your point, sir."

"Yes, it would seem we're presumably engaged in the same cause."

"Yes, sir," said Ash, and began to describe in detail the King's mission to rescue the Czar.

The car sat still, trapped in a sea of stretchers. As the driver had loaded Banks's and Innes's bags, a dark ambulance train, one of a dozen that shuttled daily between London and the Channel ports, had glided ominously into the station. Nurses and orderlies carried the badly wounded to the ambulances; and a hundred and fifty "walkers" shuffled by the car under their own steam in mud-splattered khaki and bloody bandages.

". . . I felt," Ash concluded, "that with Captain Wesley in Berlin, that I needed at least tacit approval from Ambassador Page."

Page looked at Banks and Innes.

"Sounds a damned sight better than anything we've come up with," the Admiral said. "No matter how you cut it, the Czar is the real sticking point with Congress. The United States doesn't want to defeat Germany only to put Bloody Nicholas in control of central Europe."

"Hold on," Banks said.

"What the devil for?" Admiral Innes demanded. "If Ash can get the son of a bitch out of Russia he'll get rid of the taint of despotism from the Allies—"

Page put in, "The American people won't spill blood in a war between some damn foreign tyrants, but they'll fight *against* a tyrant. I think we're getting somewhere."

The car started rolling. Outside the station, under a sky gray with coal smoke and cold drizzle, the walking wounded were helping each other into taxis. Some of the people in the large, silent crowd of Londoners bought bouquets from the flower girls and handed blossoms into the taxis as they trundled to the hospitals.

"Why not have Ash here just get rid of the Czar?" Banks asked. "Why go to all the trouble of getting him to England when . . . dispatching him would achieve the same purpose?"

Ash started to protest but Page cut in. "Any action that threatens the stability of Russia and the Russian Army directly threatens the United States."

"How's that?"

"Tell him, Commander."

"Well, the Czar's sudden death . . . his violent death . . . could collapse the government and with it the Russian Army and the Eastern Front. Germany could wheel her whole eastern army—a million men and three thousand guns—west . . ."

"And just as our boys were arriving in France," Page finished for him. "He's right, Mr. Banks. Order in Russia is vital. Assassination would be a disaster." He turned to Ash. "Just getting King George's royal cousin out of a pickle won't, I'm afraid, be enough. You've got to pluck Czar Nicky very damn gently out of Russia, gently as a single pickup stick."

Page turned to the window to let them chew on it. The streets were dull; he missed the chestnut men and the coronet players. London was filled with soldiers. Civilians, who seemed mostly women and old men, were shabbily dressed, shop fronts unpainted. The German U-boat success against British shipping was reflected in the number of horse-drawn carriages that the gasoline shortages had dragged from the stable for the first time in fifteen years. No question Britain was being squeezed.

"The Kaiser . . ." Banks said as they drove past a long line of people standing outside a movie theater showing the documentary "Battle of the Somme," which was drawing bigger crowds than Charlie Chaplin.

"What about the Kaiser?" Page asked. He had seen the film and had been shaken by its eloquent portrait of the hopeless, endless nature of this new kind of war; and it had shown him why the men in the trenches had dubbed the mightiest British offensive of 1916 the Great Fuck-Up. Page hoped he was not just another old man scheming to send more young men to their deaths . . . He consoled himself with the thought that America would not only send new blood—new blood alone would be sponged up as swiftly as the old—but new spirit and a sense of the possible. The tanks in the Battle of the Somme, a brilliant new invention, had been wasted by the British. Too few of the trench breakers and not enough follow-up. Weary blood and dying spirit. America could change all that. And face it, he thought, the prize was worth it. Not only would democracy win out . . . the country that won this war would win preeminence in the whole world. He very much liked to think of America in that role. About time a democracy called the tune.

"Why would Kaiser Wilhelm join a scheme that would strengthen his enemies?" Banks demanded.

"Family loyalty is a powerful thing to the royals," Ash said. "Family and bloodlines, after all, are the source of their power. And, excuse me, but I doubt the Kaiser will see the King's plan as strengthening the Allies. Being an autocrat himself, I suspect he'll reason that removing the Czar would very much *harm* Russia."

"Whereas," Innes said, "a constitutional monarch like King George would conclude just the opposite—that a good government would save his ally Russia."

"Is that the King's real motive?" Banks asked.

"I think family is the King's only motive," Ash said. "The Czar and Czarina are his first cousins—"

Banks raised a white eyebrow. "No other motive, Commander?"

Ash shrugged. "Well, I would like to know more about Lord Exeter. Is he Secret Service?"

"I've heard he is," Page said. "I'll find out more."

Banks said, "I think we can assume that the British Secret Service has its own interests in Russia. Interests that perhaps even go beyond the war . . . . The British are heavily invested in Russian industry. Don't make the mistake of thinking our idea of a democratic government for Russia will be the same as theirs. They have too much at stake to worry only about the war."

Ash said, "I'd also like to have more information about conditions in Russia. No one I've talked to really seems to know what's going on there."

"We'll have reports waiting when you get back from Germany," Page said. "Though I warn you that the American Embassy in Petrograd is, shall we say, a rudimentary affair."

Banks said, "We seem to have come around to approving this . . . this escapade—with one strict proviso. President Wilson must approve."

"You can't put this in a *cable*," Page said. "Even in code. It's too sensitive, the risk of compromise—"

"I *know* that. That's my job—speaking privately for the President . . . . Now we might as well let Commander Ash get started on his mission to the Kaiser. Good chance just to see what's going on there. And afterward he can start for Russia . . . But I'm also warning you now that if the

President doesn't agree when I get back to Washington, Commander Ash is going to find a cable waiting for him in Petrograd ordering him back to London."

"Understood," said Page. "That way you can report to President Wilson personally and we won't waste any time here."

"One more question, Commander," Banks said, "before we loose you on an unsuspecting Imperial Russian Empire . . . Why you? Why did the King choose you of all people? I mean apart from your being a man of parts."

"Well, as I said, sir, he needs a neutral officer."

"You can't be the only neutral the King knows."

"He and I have shot and sailed for years and—"

"I know the British put great stock in sport, Ash, but surely he must have more reason than that for picking you for a mission so obviously important to him."

Ash seemed reluctant to answer. "Well . . . once in Berlin I happened to be standing in the right place at the right time and the King thinks I saved his life . . ."

"A Count of Monte Cristo, I believe, Page suggested."

Ash shrugged. What the hell could he say?

Actually Banks knew a good deal more about Ash than he had let on. Teddy Roosevelt had told him about Ash the last time Banks had visited at Sagamore Hill. As usual, T.R. had greeted Banks warmly, glad of a visitor from "the front," as he put it.

Banks had long since patched up the cracks in their friendship caused by his support of Wilson against Bull Moose Roosevelt's bid for reelection in 1912. He served winners, and Roosevelt and Taft splitting the Republican vote had guaranteed Wilson a winner.

T.R. had seemed lonely. And bored, even though he was stumping the country making speeches in favor of intervening in the World War. Inviting Banks into his library, he displayed a panorama he had constructed of the Battle of San Juan Hill, his heroic charge of nearly twenty years earlier; it was complete with papier mâché hills and tin soldiers.

"McKinley was lucky getting shot," he replied with uncharacteristic gloom when Banks complimented the panorama. "I doubt death will ever be as anticlimactic as leaving the White House."

"I'm sure you know how grateful President Wilson is that you're speaking out for war preparedness, Mr. President."

"I'm not doing it for Wilson," T.R. growled. "I'm doing it for the country. We better raise an army before the Kaiser wrecks what's left of the world." He smacked a fist in his palm. "I'll be damned if I made this country a major power to inherit dust."

Banks had proceeded to give T.R. a personal report on the situation in Europe, and Roosevelt had been almost pathetically grateful. Banks realized why he preferred back rooms to front offices; a man was always welcome in his own back room.

Roosevelt, of course, knew about the Inner Circle, so they had discussed the group's slow progress toward provoking intervention. The conversation had turned to Ambassador Page's staff. Who was smart and trustworthy?

"Ash," said T.R. abruptly. "Page's second attaché. Look him up sometime. I gave Ash to Mahon and he went to Portsmouth for me in '06. Bully chap. The state department lost a fine diplomat the day he got his first whiff of cordite and salt air. First-rate officer. He came up San Juan Hill with us, you know?"

"I think I'd heard that. Was he in the navy then?"

"He was still a midshipman at the Academy—summer duty on a transport. I met him in the harbor and invited him along for the fun. And if he didn't save my bacon, he sure helped save my reputation. We got pinned down just as the flanking troops were reaching the top." He grinned. "Which was no way for a Colonel to lead his men to victory."

T.R. marched Banks back to the panorama.

"The Spaniards occupied these ridges, here, here and here. They were armed, by and large, with single-shot and bolt-action carbines. We started up. Charge! Suddenly a unit here opened up with a gatling gun. Lord knows where they got it, probably in Mexico from the Indian wars. Ancient, but still in fine working order, as we in the middle unit learned when they started hosing down this slope. Caught me and my boys by surprise. I could hear the others cheering as they scrambled up, but we stayed pinned down under terrific fire. Now, Ash was here . . ." He took a swagger stick from the table and poked at a gully. "When the boys heard he was a clay pigeon shooter at the Academy, they scared him up a pump action shotgun—sort of a joke, but he was damn glad to have it . . . Well, sir, suddenly this seventeen-year-old youngster lets out a war whoop would have turned a Commanche's hair white and goes up the gully like a brave on firewater . . ." Eyes sparkling, T.R. turned the swagger stick into a gatling gun, holding it in both hands and aiming at Banks. "The Spaniards saw him coming and swung the gatling gun his way and started firing— you know, a kind of ragged pop-pop-pop. The boys yelled at Ash to get down, but he let loose with that shotgun, pumping buckshot like the Spanish were offering to buy it by the ounce. Blew the gatling gun into the next block. *Adios* Spaniards."

"Sounds either very brave or very foolhardy," Banks said. "Which was it?"

"Neither. He saw a clear field of fire and knew the closer he got, the better his chances with the shotgun. Remember, the boy was already a crack shot."

"So would you say it was really just a calculated risk?"

Roosevelt looked at Banks over the gulf that he felt inevitably separated men who had been shot at from men who had not. "I would say that Ash deserves his Medal of Honor."

"Would you say Ash is a very independent officer?"

Roosevelt showed his teeth in another big grin. "To me that's the same as asking is he a good officer. I think he's a *damned* good officer . . . ."

How good and how independent was what Banks wanted to know before he recommended Ash to President Wilson.

"But why hasn't Ash advanced further in the navy?" Banks had asked Roosevelt. "He's got the rank, but no ship."

"That's complicated." Roosevelt shook his head. "The regular line officers, the deepwater men, don't approve of Ash's diplomatic service. And frankly, there was something about a Russian woman—got himself tangled up fair and proper—but the main damned problem is Ash doesn't seem to know his own strengths. The boy has never seen himself for what he is, and he's just not aware of what he can do."

Teddy Roosevelt was right, though Ash was no boy anymore. He *looked* like a navy recruitment poster. Fit and handsome in immaculate dress blues, sword at his side, eyes holding Bank's with a direct gaze, he was the picture of a solid officer. And yet he did not seem to understand that King George had picked him over other men because the King had no doubts that Ash could deliver. All right, if not knowing his own good points was sidetracking his career, that was Ash's problem. But was Ash also savvy enough to keep the U.S. out of hot water if he went to Russia?

"Commander, can you think of any *other* reason why King George would have chosen you for this mission?"

To Banks's relief, Ash cut to the heart of his question.

He said only, "I'm aware, sir, that whatever goes wrong, the blame will fall on me, not on the King."

"How about the United States Navy?"

"I've already asked Ambassador Page for leave."

Page said, "Rather than leave, I'm going to arrange a legitimate assignment to Petrograd. To make it look—if something should go wrong—as if Commander Ash took the opportunity to pursue his . . . private interests."

"Sure you want to do this, Commander?" Banks said with a lazy smile. "There'll be no cruisers coming to *your* rescue."

And Banks was relieved again. Ash might not know his own strengths, but he pounced on that opportunity. "I'd be more sure," he said, "if I knew my berth on my own cruiser was still waiting for me when I got back— I've got orders to join the *San Diego* in January as her exec. I've been looking forward to that for a long time. But I won't be back by January."

"If you can manage to get the Czar out and leave Russia intact," Page said, "I'll personally see to it you get your own command. We can do that, can't we, Admiral Innes."

"Would a minesweeper suit you?" Innes said.

"Make it a destroyer and you're on, sir."

4

Kaiser Wilhelm II, Emperor of Imperial Germany, had always reminded Ash of Teddy Roosevelt—boisterous and charming when he was happy, sheer hell when he wasn't. Right now, it seemed that he wasn't.

"*Wer?*" The Kaiser's voice echoed belligerently in the gigantic reception hall he was using as an office in Schloss Bellevue, his Berlin palace. Ash knew that he hated the frigid city palace, and he wished he had found him in his favorite Neueu Palais several miles out in the country. The elaborately uniformed courtiers and army officers hovering around his desk looked terrified.

"Ash," repeated the aide-de-camp, who had promised to present him because, he had confided, His Royal Majesty was unhappy and perhaps a visitor from better days would cheer him up. Unfortunately, it seemed the Kaiser had forgotten his name.

Ash had first been presented to the Kaiser at The Hague Peace Conference of 1899 when he was aide to then Captain Alfred Thayer Mahon, the American advocate of sea power. The Kaiser had shocked the newly commissioned ensign by pulling one of his famous practical jokes, squeezing Ash's hand so hard that his rings bit painfully. Ash, too young and surprised to react diplomatically, had squeezed back until the Kaiser yelped. Captain Mahon, who was the sensation of battleship-happy Europe and whom the Kaiser greatly admired, had smoothed over the fuss, and the Kaiser had invited them both aboard his yacht.

Subsequent encounters at hunts, shoots and sailing regattas hadn't changed Ash's first impression. Both Wilhelm and Teddy Roosevelt were intelligent, forceful men tuned to the restless new century and to the

42

demands of their vigorous people for strong leadership. Yet both were flawed—erratic combinations of showman, bully and buffoon. The huge difference between them was the extent of their power. Shortcomings that were only irritants in President Roosevelt were deadly in the mighty German autocrat.

"Wer?" Screwing a monocle into his eye, the Kaiser twisted around to see where his aide-de-camp had left Ash in charge of a pair of stone-faced palace guards. His movements were quick and jerky, and his withered left arm dragged clumsily, knocking a pen off the desk. An old general swiftly bent to pick it up. The Kaiser snatched up his scepter, raised the jeweled staff high in the air and brought it down with a sharp whack on the general's ample, tightly stretched rump.

His astonished shout was drowned out by the Kaiser's laughter. Ash relaxed. Practical jokes were at least a sign that the Emperor was momentarily in a good mood. The Kaiser pounded his desk with his right hand and bellowed laughter while the other officers laughed nervously with him. He then aimed his monocle again where Ash waited and repeated, *"Wer?"*

"Lieutenant Commander Kenneth Ash, United States Navy." Ash, whose German was rudimentary, caught something to the effect of "Admiral Mahon's young aide, Your Majesty. I felt sure you would want to see him." Mahon's aide? The Kaiser knew perfectly well he had last seen Ash in May of 1913, but the subject of the assassination attempt at his daughter's wedding was *verboten.* It had put the Kaiser in a typical quandary. On one hand he wanted to take credit as the target, a perverse topping of his cousins King George and Czar Nicholas. But on the other hand he was embarrassed that a Russian anarchist had hoodwinked his Guard. His solution was typical as well. By unspoken Imperial edict it had not happened, and consequently Ash had not been there.

"Ash! Mahon's aide, of course."

The Kaiser surged to his feet, tucked his withered arm to his sword haft and swaggered toward the doors. He was decked out in a cavalry officer's uniform of bright red and the sash of an order Ash couldn't identify. His boot heels clattered and his spurs jingled and he looked as if he were prepared to review horse troops today. He was a great dresser for the occasional. When Tamara had danced *Cléopâtre* for him with Diaghilev's Ballets Russes, the Kaiser had donned the uniform of a Russian colonel.

His English was as perfect as his cousin King George's. "Ash . . . well, well, well. How did *you* get here?"

Ash saluted, bowed and even made himself bring his heels together in the Prussian manner. "By train, Your Majesty. From The Hague."

"I was right to leave Holland," the Kaiser said. "I told my army, leave neutral access to the sea. Leave the route open . . . Still would be if it

43

weren't for the damn British blockade. They're making war on women and children, Ash. Women and children. I'd have won by now. Sea power *is* all. Too bad Mahon died too soon to know he was right."

Ash resisted mentioning the U-boat blockade of England and said, "Admiral Mahon certainly knew, Your Majesty."

The Kaiser stared, wondering if he'd been contradicted, then laughed. "Yes, I suppose he did. And how's President Roosevelt? By God, I like that man." He didn't acknowledge President Wilson.

"Very well, sir, when I saw him last," Ash replied, wondering if the Kaiser knew how vigorously T.R. was campaigning to declare war in Germany. Had to know. German agents were swarming over the United States, sabotaging factories and trying to provoke the American people against England.

"What does he want?"

"I beg your pardon?"

"What does Roosevelt want? What did he send you for?"

Ash took a deep breath. The Kaiser was so mercurial, so quick to jump to conclusions. One false step and he'd be out on his ear, or in a German jail. "I have not come from former President Roosevelt," he said, stressing the *former.*

The Kaiser blinked, looked puzzled, then dangerous. "Then what do you want, if Mahon's dead and Roosevelt didn't send you?"

Ash glanced around the room. The officers grouped around the Kaiser's desk were listening curiously. "Would it be possible for you to grant me a private audience, Your Majesty?"

The Kaiser's eyes lit up. "Wilson," he breathed. "Yes, yes, of course, Ash." He turned and bellowed, *"Raus,* get out, all of you."

He put his hands on his hips and watched them scurry off. Ash was puzzled that the military men looked extremely old; hardly the type reporting from general headquarters. They were functionaries at best, ceremonial window dressing at worst, which raised a question about who was running the German army?

"Tell me," said the Kaiser when the guards had closed the gilded doors and the two of them were alone. "What is it? What does President Wilson say?"

"Your cousin King George sent me, Your Majesty."

"Georgie? What the devil does he want?"

"It's a family matter, Your Majesty." Before Ash left Sandringham, King George had reminded him that Wilhelm regarded himself as the older man, the fatherly relative to both George himself, and the Czar. It looked like the King was right. Concern erased the truculent bewilderment from the Kaiser's face. He took Ash's arm in his powerful right hand.

"What is it? Not May?"

May of Teck had been an Anglo-German princess before she married

44

King George and became Queen Mary of England. It was difficult to hate the Kaiser when he turned into a worried uncle.

"No, Your Majesty. Queen Mary is well. I saw her only yesterday and she asked me to convey her warmest regards in these hard times." That was a little more generously than she might have put it if they had discussed his mission, Ash reflected, but neither was Queen Mary alone in the Kaiser's palace in the middle of Germany.

"Thank God. Then what is the matter?" His plastic features animated, flashing from concern to an unpleasant gloating. "Georgie's fallen off his horse again?"

"It's Czar Nicholas—"

"That damned fool. What's the matter with Nicky—my God, he didn't get killed at the front, did he? No, of course not, I'd have known."

"King George is afraid for the Czar's life."

"Revolution?"

"Yes."

"The mob." The Kaiser nodded, assumed a sage expression that quickly changed to scorn as he spoke. "I've told Nicky a thousand times, shoot them down. Royalty must not treat with the mob. Particularly in Russia. Let me tell you something, Ash, all the Russian peasant understands is the knout in an iron fist. The Czarina knows. But Nicky wouldn't even listen to her. He was a damn fool when they revolted in 1905—burned some villages, hanged some peasants, which was well enough, but *then* he gave them a Duma. A council right in the middle of his capital city. I was doing my best to get rid of the Reichstag, and Nicky gives his mob a Duma."

The Kaiser glared at Ash. "Why am I wasting my time talking to an American. You don't understand these things. Just remember that Nicky is a weakling. They'll geld him worse than Georgie if he's not strong . . . Good God, if the old Queen ever saw what we've all fallen to."

And Ash knew he didn't mean the World War. He thought briefly of his French *comtesse* with the ruby ring. When he was sure the Kaiser had ended his tirade he said, "King George has a plan to save the Czar." *No,* thought Ash, he didn't mean save the Czar's throne, he meant rescue him personally . . . "To rescue the Czar if he's overthrown."

"Nicky? What the hell are you talking about?"

"A plan to rescue your cousin, the Czar."

"I know he's my cousin, for God's sake. What is all this?" He shook his head, and the dangerous glint was back in his eyes. "Ash. Who sent you?"

"King George sent me to ask for your help, Your Majesty."

"Georgie wants my help?"

"He *needs* your help. Without it he feels the Czar is doomed. Only you and he can save Nicholas from the mob . . ."

The Kaiser's left hand slipped from his sword, where it rested inconspicuously. His arm had been dislocated at birth. Hurriedly, he lifted it back with his right. Even in a glove it looked like a little claw. For a long moment he said nothing. At last he asked, "Save Nicky? Is he mad? Has he forgotten we're at war? How can I help Germany's mortal enemy to save his ally?"

Ash had thought about little else on the steamer to The Hague and aboard the train across Holland and Germany. He had wondered whether a resolution of the Kaiser's conflict might lie in the past, at the turn of the century, before the naval arms race had drawn battle lines between Germany and England, when his grandmother, Queen Victoria, had died in his arms.

"King George, of course, has a similar worry, Your Majesty. He too feels a confusion of loyalties between nation and family. But what decided him to ask the help he needs so desperately from you was another question—"

"What question?"

"What would the Old Queen have done?"

The Kaiser sighed. "Yes. Yes, of course. But . . . poor Georgie. He simply doesn't possess a military mind."

It was as much an opening as Ash was going to get. He charged in. "King George proposes to Your Majesty that he dispatch a cruiser for the Czar and his family. To Murmansk. And he asks that your U-boats—"

"U-boats?"

"Yes, Your Majesty. German U-boats to escort the cruiser safely back to England."

"England?"

"King George will offer asylum."

"Asylum? The British public won't much like that."

"King George feels it's not a public matter. It's a matter for family."

The Kaiser shrugged. "The British view of me runs the gamut. They're very fickle—which comes from being listened to." The Kaiser turned on his heel and marched, spurs and boot heels ringing, across the room to the windows. He stared out at the square for several minutes. Ash stood where he was. At least, thank God, the Kaiser hadn't said no right off.

Then he came back, took Ash's arm and asked, "Georgie thought of this?"

"Yes, Your Majesty."

"*Planned* this?"

"Yes, Your Majesty."

"No one else? No one?"

"No one. That's why he sent me, and not a British officer." Ash waited a moment, then took a chance. "Czar Nicholas's rescue is impossible without your help, Your Majesty."

Still holding Ash's arm, the Kaiser spoke quietly, as if he were thinking

46

aloud. "Georgie's father, King Edward, was a treacherous man. He lied and schemed against me. This war is his fault. The question is, is Georgie as treacherous as his father was?"

"You must realize, sir, that King George has put his throne in your hands by sending me here. He trusts you not to betray him."

"Why should he trust me? I'm not so sure I trust him."

"Family Kaiser Wilhelm. The King, I believe, has decided that in spite of the war rescuing Czar Nicholas is the duty of Victoria's children."

The Kaiser looked at Ash, his large, dark eyes suddenly deep. "My soldiers have died by the millions. What has George decided about their children?"

The color rose in his cheeks and he seemed to gather his body like an animal about to charge. In an instant, the war would triumph over the past. Ash played his last card. He had been in Europe a long time before he understood how deeply monarchs believed their source of power.

"An agreement between royals, Your Majesty, is, after all, judged only by God."

The Kaiser stared at him, intrigued but reluctant to surrender the sentimentality behind the idea of his soldiers' children. In the end royal divine right won out. A slow smile spread across Kaiser Wilhelm's face. "Yes, of course. Of *course*. Georgie is right. It's our duty to stand by Nicky. By God!"

He let go Ash's arm and gave his shoulder a friendly slap. "Good fellow. Ash, you must come hunting. Damn the war for a few days. We'll shoot the red deer at Liebenberg. Did you bring your guns?"

The German custom of slaughtering driven game was Ash's least favorite form of shooting; he was relieved to have an excuse that the volatile Emperor couldn't deny. "Forgive me, Your Majesty, but King George is waiting for your answer. He can't make a move without your agreement."

"My answer is yes. I agree. I will do anything to save Nicky . . ." He paused. "Except how shall I proceed?"

"If it pleases Your Majesty, I could approach Czar Nicholas and make the offer of asylum. When the arrangements are completed in Russia I'll ask for your U-boats." The sight of a British cruiser maintaining half-speed to permit a pack of German U-boats to keep up in heavy northern seas would, Ash decided, be the strangest of the war. "Is it possible for me to send you a message from Petrograd?"

"You mean do I have spies in the Russian capital?" The Kaiser laughed. "Of course."

"Could I approach one of your men?"

A slow smile started building on the Kaiser's face. "What makes you think they are all men? Leave it that one of my agents will approach you when the time is right in Petrograd."

"But, Your Majesty, can I be sure he'll know me? May I suggest we arrange—"

"When you approach the Czar, I will know." He tapped his temple solemnly. "You tell Georgie that I will be the *first* to know."

Ash wanted more than a boast that the Kaiser had spies in the Russian court. "But if I run into difficulties, Your Majesty, how can I turn to your agent for help if I don't know who he is?"

"They will watch you closely," the Kaiser said. "And they will approach you."

"But how will I recognize agents I don't know, Your Majesty? How can I avoid an imposter?"

"Yes . . . I see your point . . . the Czar's police are treacherous—" He snapped his fingers. "I shall give you a password."

Ash felt deflated. He had lost his maneuver to get the agents' names. "Excellent," was what he said.

"Now let me think . . . how right it is that we royals band together . . . a pride of royals. *There* is your password, Commander—a pride of royals."

The Kaiser shook his hand, pumped it vigorously. "God speed, Royal Messenger."

"Thank you, Your Majesty." But to his surprise, the Kaiser, who had been ebullient an instant before, suddenly frowned; his deep, liquid eyes screwed up small and hard and his mouth tightened. What in hell had he done wrong? . . . The Kaiser's gaze fell ominously on their clasped hands. Ash kicked himself for an idiot. He had automatically tightened the hard muscle of his own hand to protect his fingers from the Kaiser's rings, but he had forgotten to pretend to wince.

He winced. The Kaiser stopped frowning, let go with a laugh and clapped him on the back.

"Your Majesty?"

"What? What is it now?" He was already propelling him toward the door, but Ash needed one more thing.

"The police delayed me at several railroad stations. May I have your *laissez-passer?*"

"Speak to my chamberlain."

"Your Highness, King George has told no one about this . . . this family matter. No one but you, and myself."

"And he is right. It's none of their business—ah, yes, I see what you mean. . . ." He went quickly to his desk, scribbled energetically, reminding Ash of Teddy Roosevelt again, and affixed his royal seal to the letter. Ash stole a glance at it. The ploy had worked. In his haste, the Kaiser had neglected to specify the route to Holland.

"Off you go. And tell Nicky I warned him something like this would happen."

Georgie, what are you scheming?

The Kaiser had reverted to form, and was now wondering if Cousin Georgie was trying to steal a march on him. He went to the window to watch Ash leave. Behind him he heard his courtiers returning, huddling by his desk, waiting anxiously for him to notice them; their presence eased his mind. Georgie was too simple a fellow to scheme against him. It was true he didn't possess a military mind. If he did, he would never undermind England's ally by removing her Czar . . .

He watched Ash come out, cloak swirling like wings in the snow. He walked fast, snapping back the salutes offered by junior officers. The Kaiser felt a brooding gloom descend on him. He had strutted like that before the war, fast and proud like the American, when he was still the sun around which the German Empire revolved. But the war had turned into a catastrophe for him. He couldn't pinpoint the moment when he'd lost control of the army. He only knew that today, thanks to the infernal combination of machine guns and trenches, which made war total, Ludendorff and Hindenburg made decisions at army headquarters while the Kaiser was elsewhere—isolated, and surrounded by young upstarts and old failures. For twenty-eight years, since he had taken the crown, he had inspired the military to spearhead German Imperialism, to make Germany the most powerful nation in Europe so she might take what was hers in the world. Inspired by his example, there wasn't a German boy worth his salt who didn't dream of glory in the army or the High Seas Fleet . . . But no one thanked him anymore . . . There was a time, not so long ago, when barbers made their fortune curling officers' mustaches in the exact manner he curled his. Officers copied his stance, practiced his facial expressions, his very manner of talking. And there was a time before the war when his simplest request was an Imperial command. "As Your Majesty commands," was the instant response by generals and ministers alike. Now General Hindenburg and General Ludendorff seemed even brusque when they made their daily military report.

Ash disappeared out the gates, but the Kaiser remained by the window staring at the snow filling the American's footsteps, alone with his gloomy thoughts. A Kaiser not fully in command was not a Kaiser, hardly better than a silly constitutional monarch like the King of England . . .

He longed to regain his power.

Not for himself, of course. For Germany. Because, of course, Germany needed her Kaiser again. This abomination of a war would go on forever if Germany weren't first starved into defeat by the British blockade. Shortages had become so bad that people were actually criticizing the Kaiser himself for extravagance for maintaining his stables and Imperial train on the luxurious scale, which they didn't seem to understand was vital for morale. Germany needed her Kaiser restored to full power to win the war —or at least to stop it—and make things good the way they used to be . . . But how? . . . Strange, the way Georgie's messenger had stirred up all his thinking . . . Well, it felt good to be doing something again, even if it was only saving poor Nicky's silly neck. It had been a long time since he had been able to do anything worthwhile. He thought of Ash and resolved, impulsively, to send his best man to help the American on his royal mission.

"Send me a guardsman!"

"Yes, Majesty."

An officer in the uniform of the Imperial Bodyguard marched into the reception room. Up close he smelled of a combination of thoroughbred horse and French cologne.

The Kaiser liked cavalry men; a fall on the head now and then only deepened their simple loyalty. He put his arm around his shoulder and spoke quietly. The army hadn't yet taken *all* his power.

"Inform Count von Basel his Kaiser needs him."

Poor Georgie, so weak he had to ask an American to rescue Nicky. Well, thanks to Kaiser Wilhelm, Ash would have the help of the finest German in his realm . . . And if George *was* scheming, using the American against him, what better man than von Basel to stop Ash in his tracks? Dead in his tracks.

An army spy at the Kaiser's court reported the mysterious visit and the long private audience to Major Konrad Ranke, German Imperial General Staff, Gruppe IIIb—secret service. Ranke called for Gruppe IIIb files on Commander Ash, found them oddly full for an American officer, and noted that Ash often acted as a high-level courier.

Ranke promptly telephoned General Headquarters at Spa, the resort town in occupied Belgium. A superb military communication system—as well as a conviction in the German Army that the ever-volatile Kaiser bore close watching—had Ranke connected in minutes to First Quartermaster General Erich Ludendorff.

Ludendorff was in a rare reflective mood. His staff had prepared casualty lists for the year about to end so he could calculate conscription requirements for 1917. In two great battles the German Army had held the line along the River Somme but failed to break the French fortress of

Verdun. It had suffered 437,000 casualties at the Somme and had lost a third of a million men at Verdun. One might as well count grains of sand.

"This is Major Ranke, Gruppe IIIb, Berlin, Herr General. His Majesty received an American naval officer in private. Whatever transpired between them, His Majesty has been extremely agitated since the American left."

"Where did the American come from?"

"England."

"What do you know of him?"

"His Majesty apparently met him before the war at sporting events. He is second naval attaché to the American ambassador to England. A confidant of King George. He was wounded in the anarchist attack of 1913."

"King George? . . ." General Ludendorff brushed a heavy hand over his closely cropped, half-bald head. He had a small black mustache, a big nose and a prissy mouth that might have gone better on a greedy shopkeeper than the second-ranking soldier in Germany. "What," he asked, "do you speculate, Major Ranke?"

"The American perhaps brought the Kaiser another negotiating plan from President Wilson," Ranke ventured.

Ludendorff glanced down at his waist. A roll of fat bulged through his tunic as if some barracks prankster had attached it the night before as a practical joke. Ranke was the only major he allowed to report directly to him. The Kaiser left unwatched was like a child with a box of matches, but Ranke suffered a serious lack of imagination.

"More likely the American brought the Kaiser a peace offer from King George."

Major Ranke, in his fashion, said: "What shall we do?"

General Ludendorff pressed the telephone receiver more tightly to his ear. Artillery at Liège the first summer of the war seemed to have an occasional effect on his hearing. Major Ranke thought the general hadn't heard at all and repeated the question, adding, ". . . since we are not sure what was the real purpose of the visit . . ."

He *had* heard Ranke's question the first time. Gazing at the casualty lists, counting his grains of sand, he answered coldly, "You say you are not sure, but you suspect that the American persuaded His Majesty to treat for peace behind the army's back?"

"Yes, General."

"And you suspect that the American is at this moment returning to whomever sent him with the Kaiser's agreement about some peace scheme?

"Agreement of *some* scheme . . ."

"And you agree that whatever they may have talked about, it is dangerous . . . because whatever else he may be the Kaiser could still convince the German people to accept peace. Behind the army's back . . ."

"Yes, General."

"And you still ask me what to do about the American?"

"I await your orders, General," Ranke replied nervously.

"Major Ranke, kill him."

5

Major Ranke wired Holland. The steamer to England offered promising circumstances in which to kill Kenneth Ash; one more body in a North Sea already brimful of bodies.

The job fell to an agent posing as a Dutch seaman who called himself Hendrik van Brunt. Van Brunt missed Ash when the train passengers from Germany transferred to the steamer. The boat was at sea by the time a fellow agent, a deck steward, provided a passenger list.

Ash's name was not on it. Van Brunt and the steward made a painstaking search of the boat, confirming the identity of the deck and cabin passengers. The only man who might vaguely fit the detailed physical description Major Ranke had wired turned out to be a legitimate French diplomat. Fortunately, van Brunt had warned Gruppe IIIb that he had not seen Ash get off the train.

Ash had already decided that if he were going to Russia alone he would need help. He had friends in Zurich, and friends in Paris. And some of them had friends in Russia. So Ash headed south.

The royal *laissez-passer* gave him *carte blanche* to travel anywhere in Kaiserin Germany, on any conveyance, to any border. Racing the nearly four hundred miles from Berlin to Munich, Ash brandished the letter at stationmasters in Leipzig and Plauen to force his way aboard faster trains.

He made Munich in twelve hours—good time even before the war allowed the German Army to commandeer the rails. Ahead was Switzerland, his destination. But an arm of Austria-Hungary separated Germany from Switzerland, and he worried that the Kaiser's letter would carry less weight in the German ally's territory than in Germany itself.

Major Ranke polled his agents along the rail line from Berlin to The Hague. No one had seen Ash. What if, Ranke speculated, Ash had gone to Vienna instead to include the Austrian in whatever scheme he and the Kaiser were hatching? He cast Gruppe IIIb's net wider. And when the telephones began ringing back, and the telegraph keys took up their busy clatter, and radio signals slithered into his Berlin headquarters, Ranke was rewarded by reports that Ash had gone south—traveling fast with the Kaiser's own *laissez-passer.*

Ranke alerted his Munich agents to cover the railroad station, and organized ambushes on the routes east to Vienna and south across the Austrian border through Innsbruck to Switzerland.

Ash weighed his options at Munich Station. West on local lines to enter Switzerland directly at Thaingen was tempting, but those lines were often jammed by troop and munitions trains bound for the German front, where the tail end of the trenches stopped at the Swiss border. Innsbruck beckoned despite the difficulty of passing through Austria.

He noticed a man in a suit watching him while he studied the time tables; he crossed the station and bought a newspaper and the man followed, pushing roughly through a group of wounded Austrian soldiers begging for money for food.

Ash went out to the taxi queue. As his taxi pulled away from the train station the man in the suit shouldered ahead of an army lieutenant; in Germany officers were yielded seats and conveyances, but the man in the suit showed the lieutenant something in his hand, and took the cab without protest.

"Bayerischer Hof," Ash told his driver, and when he got to the hotel the man in the suit was right behind him. Ash went inside, showed the Kaiser's letter to the manager and demanded a ranking *polizei* officer who spoke English. Being followed in wartime Germany was hardly an uncommon experience for a foreigner, but Ash wanted to arrive in Switzerland with a empty wake. He took a chair in the elegant lobby and let the manager order coffee, which arrived when the *polizei* did.

He pointed out the man in the suit, sitting across the lobby reading a book. The coffee was ersatz. The police officer returned in a few minutes.

"Could there be a mistake, Commander? The gentleman is an army officer recuperating from wounds."

"The mistake will be yours if that man is allowed to follow me another foot while I am on the Kaiser's mission."

The officer flushed. "Perhaps I should detain him then."

"I would think it's imperative," Ash said, got up and left. Army? Why would the army be following? The police usually did the following in Germany. It made him damn uncomfortable. Getting the man arrested bought some time, but not much if he really was army.

He was heading for the train station again when it occurred to him that December snow had slowed infantry fighting. If artillery had taken up the slack, the Germany Army Transport Corps would be moving more shells than troops. Checking his Baedecker, he ordered his driver to head in a new direction.

An hour later night had fallen when Ash arrived alone at the railroad yard furthest from the center of Munich. Heavily guarded gates told him he had guessed right, that from here the German Transport Corps sent munitions trains highballing west on cleared track. A veteran of several hunting excursions with the Kaiser's entourage before the war, and several courier trips to Berlin since, Ash felt that Wilhelmine German officials responded best to orders clearly and loudly stated, followed by arrogant silence.

"Lieutenant Commander Ash, United States Navy, on orders of Kaiser Wilhelm. Take me to the commandant."

Whether the sergeant of the guard believed, or even understood his clumsy German, the sound of it impressed him sufficiently to send Ash, escorted by four men, to the commandant's aide-de-camp. Ash showed him the Kaiser's letter, following another of his rules—never to show papers before it was necessary. The aide asked if he could be of assistance and Ash told him firmly he could not.

The commandant's office overlooked a vast rail yard surrounded by warehouses and high walls, and lighted by lanterns and electric lamps. Switch engines were disassembling the freight trains that snaked in from the surrounding darkness and sending new trains back out as if the entire yard were a single machine and the freight cars—passing from darkness into light and back to darkness—the moving parts.

The commandant, an engineering officer, read the Kaiser's letter. He spoke English, as so many of the German officers did, but with a thick accent.

"There is passenger service from Munich to Innsbruck. There you change for Zurich."

"I haven't time to deal with the Austrians."

The commandant remarked with unexpectedly open scorn for his ally, "Who does?"

"Then you see my problem, and why I require fast passage to Thaingen."

"However," the commandant countered, "the fact that our Austrian allies are dunderheads does not alter the situation here. This yard, as you have evidently surmised, is a stage for munitions trains arriving from the factories with cargoes bound for the front. It is a military post barred to foreigners."

"But the Kaiser gave me this letter of free passage to relieve just such legitimate concerns on the part of his officers. In short, the Kaiser demands that you aid me—*immediately and in any manner I ask.*"

"The Kaiser does not have responsibility for supplying our cannon with shells."

Ash had never heard such independent talk in Germany. The commandant folded the letter and returned it. Ash said, "The United States is a neutral. I offer no threat. I merely want to ride aboard a fast train west. And I suspect that your trains are the fastest."

"What makes you suspect that?"

"I've seen every rail yard in Europe. I know what the good ones look like." There was truth in that. One of the reasons Germany was winning her two-front war was that she'd built a railroad system specifically designed to shuttle her armies from front to front.

The compliment softened the commandant enough to make a joke of his refusal. "But if the United States declares war on Germany while her neutral courier is aboard my munitions train, wouldn't her neutral courier automatically become a spy?"

"Then you, sir," Ash said with a straight face, "will have the honor of capturing the first American prisoner." He glanced at the blackboard behind the commandant on which were chalked the trains leaving that night and added, "And I expect to be treated well, since you're obviously a gentleman."

It didn't work. The commandant said, "I can't help you, Commander. And tell your good friend the Kaiser that the *army* will beat the English and the French and the Russians, but we'd appreciate it if he'd keep the Americans out."

Unsure of the reception he would find in Munich, Ash paid a taxi driver triple rate to drive him to a suburban station west of the city.

Major Ranke was summoned from his wife's bed moments after entering it. A staff car took him through Berlin's pitch-black streets to Imperial General Staff Headquarters. Ash had disappeared. Worse, the American had used the Kaiser's *laissez-passer* to provoke an incident between Gruppe IIIb and the Munich police. One of his agents was still in the Munich jail at Ash's request.

Ranke polled the telegraphers and telephone operators for agent reports along Ash's various possible routes. Vienna reported no sighting. Then Ranke's chief officer in Munich switched him a telephone call from the commandant of a Munich munitions depot—Ash had tried to board a munitions train to the front. The commandant had sent him away. Now he had second thoughts. Was the American a spy? Should he have arrested him, regardless of the Kaiser's *laissez-passer?*

Ranke dressed him down. When transport officers spent too much time managing civilian train personnel they lost their edge. Ranke alerted Munich. Ash had probably left already. Search all the trains, passenger and freight.

Ash slept the night sitting up in a second class carriage on the local to Thaingen. He woke up in the morning when the conductor shooed the other passengers out of his compartment. An army captain—a heavily built officer with close cropped hair and a face slit by a dueling scar from his eye to his jaw—entered and asked, "Commander Ash?"

"Yes," Ash said, rubbing the sleep out of his eyes and noting that the conductor had already backed respectfully away.

The captain told him he was under arrest.

6

"I am a United States Naval officer and diplomatic courier traveling with the Kaiser's *laissez-passer*. On your way out tell the orderly to bring coffee."

The captain read the Kaiser's letter and tore it in half.

"Captain, if you're looking for trouble, I assure you you've found it."

The train began to slow. The captain motioned Ash to his feet. Ash sat still. The German shifted the trenchcoat he was carrying over his arm, unsnapped his holster, drew out his Luger.

"Get up."

"You're making a mistake, Captain."

The captain gestured with the long-barreled automatic pistol, and Ash rose slowly as the train pulled into a small village station and onto a siding. Passengers boarded and disembarked, but the captain marched Ash through the train to the rear car before he allowed him to step onto the platform. He held his gun close to his side, and when three country *hausfrauen* passed near them he covered it with his coat. All very professional, Ash couldn't help thinking.

"That way." He pointed at a stair at the back of the platform that led away from the station. A path paralleled the main line, which curved out of sight of the station. Two hundred yards down the line the path veered across the siding and ended at a freight depot. Ash looked back and caught a last glimpse of the back of the train, which apparently was waiting on the siding for an express to overtake it.

As they walked toward the depot the freight master came out and hung a big canvas mailbag on the mail pickup hook beside the express track. He hailed the captain, who ordered him away. The captain kept the gun under his coat and watched until the freight master had trudged out of sight around the curve. Only then did he slide open the depot door.

A lieutenant, bearing similar dueling scars, sat at the wheel of a truck whose cargo area was shrouded by canvas. Ash felt the gun prod him in the back, pushing him toward the truck.

"Hold on," Ash said. German officers, like British, never performed what they considered menial tasks. The long walk from the station, the concealed gun, and now an aristocrat at the steering wheel spoke more of a kidnapping than an arrest. "Where are you taking me?"

"Headquarters."

"What unit?"

The captain glanced at the lieutenant, which was just time enough for Ash to kick him in the stomach, draw his dress sword as the German doubled over and slash at his hand. The Solingen blade drew blood through the captain's glove. He dropped the gun. Ash kicked it across the floor and went at the lieutenant, who got tangled between the wheel and the gear shift. Seeing Ash charge, he launched himself out of the truck, gave up trying to unsnap his holster flap and fell back, drawing his own sword.

Ash kept at him. The lieutenant slashed broadly—plunging strokes in the German manner of saber fighting—and reached across his waist for the Luger strapped to his right hip.

He too had dueling scars, but as was the case with most German swordsmen, his training had been weighted more toward the courage to receive wounds than the skill to inflict them. When his wild high slash missed and his blade had traveled too low to parry, Ash thrust as if his saber were a foil, and managed to impale his wrist.

A murmur was the only sound that came from the German, but bravery couldn't keep his weapon from falling from his convulsing fingers. Ash glanced at the captain, who was getting uncertainly to his feet, tapped the lieutenant's holster with the point of his sword, then directed it at his face.

The lieutenant pawed it open with his left hand, his eyes on Ash's blade. Gingerly he removed the gun. The captain then made a rush for his own gun across the freight room. Ash flicked the gun from the lieutenant's hand, shoved him aside and covered the captain, who stopped short and slowly raised his hands. Ash motioned them to stand together. "Where is headquarters?"

They looked back at him. Silent.

Ash raised the Luger and fired. The shot passed between them, close to the captain's ear. Both flinched but said nothing. Ash fired again. The express train was now closer, its engine pounding.

"Last chance."

They looked at each other.

"You were going to kill me. Why?" And he fired again, very close. The captain grabbed at his ear. Ash aimed at the lieutenant's face. "Why?"

"Orders," the man said, raising his hand as if to stop the bullet.

"*Whose* orders?"

"The major."

"To kill me?"

"Yes."

"How?"

"We were supposed to throw you from a bridge, look as if you had fallen. Like an accident—"

"Shut up," the captain said.

Ash snapped a shot past his other ear. "Who told the major to kill me?"

The lieutenant shrugged. The captain gazed into the barrel as he said, "I don't know. I swear it."

Ash sighted down the barrel at a point between the man's eyes. The captain actually drew himself stiffly to attention. Ash figured he had to be telling the truth. The express was blowing its whistle and it sounded near and moving fast, with no stop planned at this local station.

The door behind the Germans banged open, kicked in by four soldiers carrying Mauser rifles. They moved quickly, crouching, looking for the source of the gunfire. The officers threw themselves flat and shouted to fire. Ash went for the front door. Shots exploded—heavy rifle fire. Bullets cracked past his head, splintered the wooden door. Ash hit the floor rolling, slid the door open, squeezed through and surged to his feet, dodging and weaving, knowing he had two or three seconds before they reached the door and got him in their sights again.

The express rounded the curve, blowing long, piercing wails. Ash scrambled toward the tracks and threw himself in front of the locomotive. He made it across, all but one boot, which the engine brushed. The impact threw him in the air in a full circle. The post office, the woods, the side of the speeding train raced across his vision. He landed hard, on gravel.

The mail pickup. The mail sack hung from a hook five feet off the ground beside the rails. Between the roaring wheels Ash saw the legs of the soldiers waiting for the train to pass, and the pale smears of their faces when they bent down to look. He headed for the mail pickup, shoved the Luger in his belt and threw his arms around the mail sack as the baggage car hurtled toward him. He caught a glimpse of a hinged hook, and the next instant the mail sack tried to explode out of his arm.

He saw a blur, the force broke his grip, wrenched him sideways. He slammed into a heap of mail sacks. An ancient postal clerk holding a teacup stared.

"Special delivery," said Ash, feeling absurd but relieved as he said it.

The clerk raised his hands uneasily. Ash looked at his own hand; he was surprised to see that he was still holding the Luger.

60

"What's the next stop?"

"Thaingen."

Near Schaffhausen on the Swiss border. They'd search the area around the country station for a long time before they figured what he had done. He just might make it. He sagged back on the mail sacks, breathing hard. It had been a long time since he'd been in a killing fight. The attack on King George didn't count, over too fast. A long time, and those he remembered had been fought at a distance—a skirmish with the Spanish fleet in 1898, T.R.'s charge and a rifle duel with Philippine insurgents in '02. Like most American officers his age he was schooled in the killing trades, but not practiced. Whacking polo balls and fencing steeled the eyes and limbs, but not the nerves. . . . Count of Monte Cristo? Hell, he hadn't even managed to get out of Germany yet.

He had three shots left in the Luger and the no-man's-land between Schaffhausen's German and Swiss border posts was guarded by four riflemen. It was a hundred-foot stretch of road, fenced on both sides and cleared of snow. *Polizei* watched the travelers trying to leave Germany while the customs house clerks inspected their papers and poured through official telegrams pertaining to criminals and spies. Ash knew his only hope was that the army officers who had tried to kill him were operating unofficially.

Well, at least being the chief attraction at an assassination sharpened the mind . . . he made a count of the German guns and targeted the closest three. From the smallest soldier he would take a sidearm, spray the *polizei* as fast as he could pull the trigger, shoot the remaining rifleman and take off for Switzerland if he were still on his feet. A plan, anyway.

Attempting to cross the border at an unguarded point was futile; there was none. And if he tried and was caught, whoever in the army who was trying to kill him would do it one night in his cell while the embassy was still maneuvering to spring him. Why they were trying to kill him he didn't know. The *polizei* had been accommodating in Munich, and the Kaiser's pass had worked wonders until the captain shredded it. Nor had the munitions depot commandant stopped him, and he was army . . . But if he were wrong that his attackers were unofficial, a wired order to stop him would already be waiting at this post. Which was why he was counting guns.

He submitted his diplomatic passport and reached inside his boatcloak for the Luger. Three shots. The customs house clerk rifled through a stack of telegrams, reading each one. Then he got up, bowed and returned Ash's passport with apologies for the delay. Five minutes later, on the far side, the Swiss attached a visa stencil to his papers and showed him aboard the train to Zurich, leaving Ash to conclude that in some way, somehow related to his visit to the Kaiser, he had aroused the considerable displeasure of some section of the German army. Or had maybe stumbled into a feud at the Kaiser's court? He also tried the notion that the Kaiser might have changed his mind and double-crossed him, except that didn't make any sense. If the Kaiser were against him, he'd be dead by now.

No answers, but at least he was alive . . .

7

Two thousand miles northeast in the Russian capital an informer's note arrived on the desk of Vasily Moskolenko, captain in the Czar's secret police, the Okhrana. Moskolenko spent a long time verifying the seal before he broke it.

His office in Petrograd's Litovsky Prison looked like a cave hewed from the stone walls. Moskolenko seemed both at home behind his rough wood desk and oddly out of place. His bony head, skeletal frame and emotionless gray eyes were appropriate to the notorious political prison, but there was a restless energy and swift grace to his movements which hadn't been nurtured at a desk in a gloomy room.

The note was from one of the very few police informers who had direct and private access to the Okhrana captain. Moskolenko deciphered the few words. Although he was alone, a slight movement around his hard mouth, which on another man might have been the beginning of a smile, was his only visible reaction. Then something dark flickered in his eyes and burned suddenly bright. He lifted a telephone.

"Where is Orlov?"

"In the interrogation cell, Captain."

Moskolenko rose and walked the long stone halls to Orlov's favorite cell. Two guards waiting outside snapped to attention when they saw that Captain Moskolenko himself had descended to this remote corner of the prison.

"Open it."

They hesitated. "Lieutenant Orlov—" one began before Moskolenko cut him off with a glance. They opened the door.

Orlov was in the act of mounting a female prisoner he had strapped to a table. He turned angrily toward the intrusion, his bald face flushing. He calmed down when he saw Moskolenko, who said only, "I will be away for a week or two. You are in charge."

Moskolenko boarded the train to Europe at the Warsaw Station. An officer highly placed in the Czar's secret police had many privileges and he used them freely. Six artillery subalterns returning to the front were rousted from their compartment. Moskolenko ordered tea and locked the door. He had taken care to eat before he left. Food was not to be trusted on a Russian train these days. He would not eat again until he was deep in Germany.

The express, such as it was, took fifteen hours to cover the three hundred and fifty miles to Dvinsk at the front. Or, more accurately, the outskirts of Dvinsk, since the city itself was firmly in the hands of the German army. Moskolenko detrained and slipped carefully into the night.

He found a point a few miles south of the city where a unit of Siberian Rifles was dug in on the bank of the Dvina. The Germans held the western shore. The frozen river was no-man's-land, a flat stretch broken here and there by barbed-wire entanglements. He inspected the no-man's-land inch by inch through a field periscope. A few stars cast a revealing blue glow on the snow-covered ice. Cover was scarce.

The Germans had nested a machine gun on the other side, and he spent a long time plotting routes around it. The periscope showed five separate wire tangles. At the third, he would head down the river to an upthrust ridge of ice . . . He returned the field periscope to the *unteroffizier* acting as his guide and demanded a wire cutter.

The soldier was contemptuous of noncombatants in general and police from Petrograd in particular.

"This is the single least likely place to cross the lines, Captain. Even the most basic knowledge of trench warfare would tell you—"

"I hope the Germans agree with you. Now take me to the nearest field kitchen." Mystified, the soldier led him to a kitchen and watched, outraged, as he appropriated precious flour his men were making into bread and covered himself with the white powder head to toe. He seemed to make a point of doing it in full view of the sullen troops.

"*Halt.*"

Thin snow was falling when a German sentry found him resting at dawn. By then the flour camouflage had rubbed off his front and had mixed with melting snow on his back to form a striped paste. The sentry pointed a

Mauser and bayonet. Mud oozed around the duckboards on the trench floor and clung to his boots. He looked like a conscript, and his accent was a Ruhr factory worker's when he demanded the password.

The Okhrana captain raised his hands. "Take me to an officer"—in perfect German. The sentry shouted for help. Two soldiers came running, searched him. When they were finished, surprised not to find a weapon, Moskolenko said, "It's a sword," and contemptuously tossed them his heavy cane. When the carved head was twisted and the sword withdrawn, four prongs unfolded to form a cross guard. The blade was a whippy length of light steel sharpened on both sides like a saber.

The infantrymen marched their mysterious prisoner through the zigzagged communication trench that led to the rear, passing him up the ranks to a weary and very young Junker *leutnant* in a mud dugout. The Junker, a Prussian aristocrat who in happier times would still be a cadet in training, slapped the prisoner's face.

"State your name and unit before I tell my sergeant to kick your Russian teeth down your Russian throat."

"I am Count Philip von Basel . . . And your best hope in this life is that I board a train to Berlin within the hour."

Forty-five minutes later Count Philip von Basel was luxuriating in a deep bath aboard a private car attached to the Berlin Express and the officers who had accomplished the hasty arrangements returned, with relief, to the trenches. As far as they knew the young *leutnant* was the only man who had ever slapped von Basel and stayed alive. Von Basel was aware of the oversight but decided it couldn't be helped. It was not a matter of the war—the trenches were as good a place to kill a man as any; nor did the *leutnant*'s extreme youth bother him. Duels were exercises in skilled killing, but no opponent was unworthy. It was merely a question of not enough time. After all, his Kaiser had summoned him. Priorities.

8

Ash remembered Zurich as a sleepy backwater before the war, but it had turned abruptly cosmopolitan when Switzerland emerged as a neutral island for bankers, diplomats, spies and political exiles. A dozen nationalities thronged the financial district's Bahnhofstrasse above Lake Zurich.

He went first to the American consulate, where he had lunch with the military attaché, an army captain he had served with in Berlin in 1913. He asked where various people they knew were staying and he asked about the Russian revolutionary exiles living in Zurich. His friend thought those in Zurich were mostly fragments of the prewar movement, but he promised to scare up the names of their leaders.

"Lunatic Bolsheviks," the captain warned. "The sensible ones stopped their agitating when the war began. Hunkered down to fight the Germans."

Ash wired Ambassador Page not to expect him in London for a week as he was planning short stays in Zurich and Paris. He closed with, "All's well," which was not exactly the truth, considering that *some* elements of the German army were trying to kill him, but Page would know from his message that he had persuaded the Kaiser to help King George's plan, which more importantly meant that their own scheme was underway.

Having lost his bag when he was arrested on the train, he bought a dark suit. He had dinner with the president of the Bank of Rome's Zurich branch, an old friend from a Roman fencing *salle* he'd attended the summer Tamara Tishkova left Russia for what she called "tuning" with an Italian dance master. Albioni had given up the sword, and the lack of exercise showed in his thickening waist, though it didn't seem to bother him. Albioni's position in Zurich was a plum for a man his age, which was also Ash's age, and his mistress had come along while his wife remained at home with the family.

"All and all, my friend, not an unpleasant state of affairs. And you?"

"I'm going to Petrograd." Up until five days ago he had been telling people about his transfer to sea duty.

Albioni nodded. "Tishkova?"

"Unfortunately no. But I did wonder whether you could introduce me to your counterpart in Petrograd . . . Signor de la Rocca?" It might be handy to know a banker in Petrograd, particularly one married to a Russian baroness.

He visited a brothel late that same night with an English so-called economist he had sailed with in the Fastnet Race and who had turned up at his hotel one night years before the war in Berlin with a bullet hole in his arm and a story about an irate husband that Ash hadn't believed for a minute. Rumor suggested he was in the habit of poking his sailing yacht up various restricted German estuaries to gather naval secrets. Ash had patched him up and found papers to get him across the border. The fact that he was in Zurich meant he was probably in the spy business again; and that his cover story was that he was teaching economics at the University.

Taplinger—he was part German though completely English in manner —was anxious to take a Roumanian beauty upstairs, but Ash persuaded him to have a quiet brandy first.

"I need some information. I'm going to Petrograd."

"I'd be quick off the mark, old chap. There might not be a Petrograd very soon."

"What do you hear about the revolution?"

"It's going to happen."

"What do the Bolsheviks want?"

Taplinger cast a longing eye at the Roumanian before he answered. "You know, old son, I do believe she's got her eye on you." Ash had already noticed, but tonight the only reason he'd come here was because Taplinger had insisted; as long as he had known Taplinger, the man had had an obsession with bordellos. This one, with its rococo drawing rooms, French Academy paintings, women of almost infinite European variety and a clientele drawn from the diplomatic corps and the banking elite illustrated one more irony of the war: lavishly appointed sin in western Europe was now most available in formerly staid Switzerland.

"What do the Bolsheviks want? Everything, I'd say. And it's for the taking. The old monarchies can't rule modern industrial nations. The Bolsheviks, of course, are as conspiratorial and ruthless as the Borgia, and they well sense the opportunity. Marxism and socialism aside, the Bolsheviks understand power as well as any emperor. They're going to be our new royals, Ash, whether we like it or not—and *now* may we pay our respects to that lady?"

"Two more questions—"

"Ash, the woman has to earn a living. Be fair."

"Give me a rundown on the Russian parties against the Czar."

"Briefly—dammit—Bolsheviks are sort of left-wing Social Democrats without a social or democratic bone in their bodies. Mensheviks are right-wing Social Democrats, democratic in their organization and, therefore, of course no match for the Bolsheviks. Social Revolutionaries want all power to the people and will bomb and shoot whoever stands in their way; the Social Revolutionaries are the violent lunatics. Last, and perhaps Russia's best hope, are the Kadets, the Constitutional Democratic Party. The Kadets are a powerful party in the Duma and could provide the leadership of a new government."

"*Will* the Czar be overthrown?"

Taplinger peered owlishly across the smokey room. "I believe she's going to come over here and rescue me."

Ash glanced at the Roumanian woman sprawled impatiently on a chaise longue, fluttering a Chinese fan. A portly, expensively dressed Belgian was trying to speak with her, but she ignored him and smiled at Ash, or Taplinger; the room was too wide to tell for sure.

"*Will* the Czar be overthrown?"

"I'm just an economist," Taplinger protested. "But it's significant, perhaps, that the Czar regards the Kadets, those parliamentarian liberal democrats, as revolutionaries. With that attitude . . ."

"Who is Lenin?" The military attaché at the American consulate had come through with a few names; Lenin was supposed to be a cut above the others.

"Vladimir Lenin. Agitator, theorist, Bolshevik leader and damned good speaker. Or used to be. Going down hill these days, people tell me. Why?"

"I want to know what's going on in Russia before I get there."

Taplinger looked at him curiously, but said only, as if from professional courtesy, "There's a café where the Russians hang out. Lenin won't be there, but look for a woman, a Madame Armand. I'm told that Lenin and Madame Armand conduct their dialectic in a reclining position . . . If your legendary charm hasn't deserted you—and by the adoring look on that Roumanian lady's face it hasn't—perhaps you can convince Madame Armand to introduce you to the Bolshevik."

"What does she look like?"

"Honey blonde, delicious—here comes our Roumanian lady."

She was tall and dark-haired, her skin olive where her breasts swelled above her low bodice. Swaying slightly, she fixed her eyes on Ash.

"Dammit, she wants you," Taplinger said.

"I don't think I'm up to it . . ." Tamara's name cropping up so often had

68

left him unsettled again, but the main reason he didn't want to stay was that the Germans kept informers in brothels like these; he purposely hadn't told Taplinger anything that mattered about the mission to rescue the Czar. Or at least so he thought.

As she approached, the Belgian came up to her again, insistent, waving his diamond studded hands. Again she brushed him aside and headed for Ash.

"It's you she wants," Taplinger said. "Damn it."

Ash returned her smile. She was, after all, extraordinarily pretty.

"Probably a German spy," Taplinger said *sotto voce*. "Diamonds usually do the trick in a place like."

"Usually," said Ash, standing up for her. In escaping the Belgian she had turned completely around, revealing a beautiful back and swelling hips beneath her tightly cut gown. "Good evening, *Mademoiselle.*"

"*Bon soir,* Commander. My English *très* bad. *Oui?*" She ignored Taplinger. Ash agreed to speak French. They danced to the string orchestra in the next room, and she asked his name. Ash told her. Her name was Margo. She said she was worried about her grandmother who lived in Germany. Ash said he had just come from Germany and she asked why Ash was in Zurich.

"Just passing through," Ash told her. What else? "What news from home?"

"Home?"

"The German invasion?"

The attack on Roumania had just begun and looked to be over in a few more days as the Germans threw the Roumanian army headlong into the Russian lines.

"I don't understand about war," she said. "Only about soldiers. And maybe sailors. Where do you go from here?"

Ash told her that he traveled as a diplomatic courier. Taplinger looked away angrily as Ash took her upstairs. The room was sumptuous, an original bedroom, unpartitioned for the mansion's new function. The bed was turned down with sheets of fine crisp linen. Margo came back from the bathroom in her chemise, barefoot except for stockings, and it occurred to Ash that she had very pretty feet for such a tall girl.

Smiling, apparently enjoying herself, she posed for him while he sat in an armchair beside the bed. She danced in slow circles around the carpet, pulled the chemise over her head and, passing near him, laid the perfumed silk on her shoulder.

A black whalebone corset lifted her breasts, flattened her belly and thrust her buttocks out in a full, rich curve. She noticed his reaction and posed accordingly. She left her corset in place as she finally untied the ribbons that secured her drawers at the sides and let them fall away.

She pulled an ottoman into the middle of the room in front of Ash, straddled the low, narrow piece, laid flat, and arched her back. She looked at him over her shoulder and asked if there was something special he might enjoy, something to remember wherever he traveled.

"A fantasy," Ash said, his mouth dry as sand, his heart pounding. He stood up and unbuckled his sword.

"What fantasy, *chéri?*" Margo asked, undulating softly side to side as she watched him.

He held the scabbard in one hand, his sword hilt in the other and stepped closer. The straps and buckles dangled in front of her eyes. She arched her back higher and ground her spread thighs against the cushion, playing the game. There were many possibilities—the straps, the buckles, the scabbard, the blade itself. She wasn't afraid. Ranking officers in uniform did not injure girls in a house like this one.

He drew the blade and she still wasn't afraid; a French colonel had flogged her once with his empty scabbard, the discomfort amply rewarded in gold francs.

"What fantasy?" she whispered.

"Pretend I'm the German officer you report to."

He turned his wrist and the blade flicked beside her cheek.

9

Now that he had her, Ash had to deal with her. He gave her what he hoped was a murderous look, one to convince her that he would actually cut her. Somehow he kept the blade rock steady. She stared back at him, hugging the ottoman. And then she went rigid.

"His name."

"I don't know his name. He comes here."

She started crying. Ash steeled himself, but when goose bumps of fear prickled her flesh he had to remind himself that they had already declared war on him.

"What does he want to know about me?"

"Where you are traveling . . . please don't—" Her eyes went to his, then back to the tip of the sword.

"What else?"

"Who you are visiting—"

"What else?"

". . . What the Kaiser told you—"

"*What?*"

"Please—" She sucked in her breath. Ash's hand had moved convulsively. *The Kaiser?*

Ash sheathed his sword and buckled it around his waist. She lay there crying, still straddling the ottoman, still damned provocative. Ash forced himself to the door.

"What can I tell him—"

"Tell him I told you absolutely nothing."

"He won't believe me."

"Tell him what I told you when we danced. And tell him I was so overwhelmed I gave you this. Here . . ." He went back to her and laid five gold sovereigns beside her face on the cushion. "With a tip like this he'll believe I had the time of my life."

Ash ate lunch in the Russian café Taplinger had told him about, ordering dishes he recalled from Petrograd; he was pleased he remembered the Cyrillic alphabet well enough to read the menu. It was a cheap place with dirty tables and steamed-up windows. It smelled of wet wool, soup and sweat and heavy tobacco and rang alternately with gloomy shouts and bellowed laughter—smells and sounds Ash remembered from his brief trips to Russia long before the war.

Conversations flowed endlessly in loud and passionate Russian, spiced with snatches of French and English. In Petrograd, English and French were the languages that mattered among the diplomatic corps and the so-called upper levels of society. Russian was spoken to servants, and in the countryside. Here, though, it was the primary language, and Ash was at a disadvantage because most of his Russian was love talk he'd learned from Tamara.

All of a sudden, when the place had filled to capacity and the early night was falling a group turned on a man sitting alone, surrounded his table and stared at him, silently. The man pretended not to notice but it was an impossible sham and he got up and left, pursued by scornful laughter and mocking shouts. They turned next on Ash.

One called out in Russian. There was more laughter. Ash stared him down and waited. There were more calls, then someone said a word Ash recognized. *Police.* And then, *spy.*

Ash faced the man who'd asked the mocking question and said in English, "No. No, I'm not a spy. I'm not from the Czar's police—"

"Then what are you doing here?"

Ash stood up. A very beautiful woman with a red feather in her hat approached his table. She was in her thirties or early forties, he guessed. She looked at him with an intelligent, derisive gaze. Her accent was French, her splendid cheekbones, Russian. Her clothing reflected wealth and taste, luxury unknown to the others in the café, yet instead of regarding her resentfully they gathered around her with respectful silence and waited for Ash's reply. Taplinger's "delicious" was precisely right. Madame Armand. There couldn't be two of them in the same city.

"What do you want?"

Doubting that navy credentials would gain her trust, Ash said, "I'm a correspondent, ma'am. . . . I'm on assignment to write a story about the Russians in Zurich."

"For what newspaper?"

"I doubt you've heard of it. The Atlanta *Constitution.*"

She had. "You don't speak with the accent of a man from the American South."

Ash tried the Ash smile, searching for an opening. "If you know Atlanta, Georgia, ma'am, you probably know that many northerners have settled there. I'm from West Virginia, myself, which is sort of midway between Dixie and Yankeeland but I haven't been down home in a long time."

"What is it you want?" She had, again as advertised, golden blonde hair and almost seemed to glow in the warm, steamy café; her eyes were greenish, and she managed to appear reasonably friendly, though with no hint of an invitation.

"Would you care to join me?" Ash asked, indicating his table.

"No, thank you. What do you want to know?"

"I want to write about the revolution—"

"Which revolution?"

"In Russia."

For a brief moment she allowed him just enough of herself to say that she found him attractive but had other commitments, more important plans. Her eyes went to his suit and shoes. She seemed to sense a false note in his story, and Ash realized he probably was several shades too well-dressed for the average newspaper reporter. There was nothing to do about it now but smile and remind himself that although his story was a lie he presented no danger to these exiles.

She made up her mind suddenly. "Why don't you ask Lenin?"

"Who?" He wanted to see how her story compared with Taplinger's.

"I think you could find Lenin on the library steps in the morning. Around eight forty-five."

"I'm sorry to sound so ignorant, but I'm new to all this revolution business. Could you tell me something about this Lenin?"

"He is a theorist. And a leader."

"Will he talk to me?"

"He might." She moved closer as if afraid those at the other tables would overhear. "Take him to lunch, why don't you?"

"Will you be there?"

"No," she said, turning away. "Do that for him. Please."

"I don't understand . . ."

She faced him again. "You look like you can afford to buy the man a good lunch."

"So do you," said Ash.

"It wouldn't be the same for him. For his spirit . . . it's a very difficult time . . ."

She hadn't exaggerated.

The short, powerfully built, bald-headed man standing on the library steps was shivering in a threadbare overcoat that was no match for the unusually cold wind blowing up the Limmat River from Lake Zurich. His round peaked workman's cap did not conceal much of his baldness, and his battered shoes and cracked leather briefcase looked years beyond repair.

When he saw Ash approaching he asked anxiously in French what time it was. A mustache and a stubbly brown beard circled his obstinate mouth. Small, deep-set eyes lent a dogged look to his face, and Ash was reminded of a gambler riding out a long streak of bad luck.

"Almost ten to nine," Ash said. "Do they open on time?"

He seemed less comfortable in English. It took a moment before he said, "Yes. Yes. The Swiss are good about time."

"Are you Lenin?"

"Who are you?"

"I'm an American, a foreign correspondent. My newspaper is considering sending me to Petrograd but they want some reports from Zurich first about the exiles who live here and about the state of the revolution." He grinned. "In other words, my bosses want to know if it's worth sending me to Russia, or should I just stay in France to cover the fighting."

"How do you know my name?"

"You *are* Lenin? Well, I heard your name in a café when I asked the same questions. Someone told me you might be the man to talk to. Could you spare me the time?"

"I'm very busy here." He glanced at the library doors, which still were shut.

"I've heard you're a writer too. So you know my problem. They might even yank me home if I don't come up with a beat . . . say, how about lunch? Do you ever stop for lunch?"

Lenin nodded. "I could stop for lunch."

"I'll meet you here at noon."

"What paper did you say?"

"Atlanta *Constitution*. Atlanta, Georgia."

"How is Mr. Grady's New South doing these days?"

The question threw Ash so completely that for a long second he just stared. Mr. Grady. Who the hell was Mr. Grady? It rang a bell . . . he should know . . .

Lenin looked up at him, even showing a slight smile. "I would expect that even the stupidest reporter from America would know the name of the founding editor of his own newspaper, Henry Grady."

Idiot, thought Ash. Henry Grady. The proselytizer of an industrial New South after the Civil War. "He was before my time," Ash said lamely.

The library doors on top of the stairs opened with a sharp snap of released latches, and Lenin darted up the steps with surprising—to Ash, at least—athletic grace and vigor. At the threshold he turned back and looked down at Ash, who was watching helplessly. "Perhaps I'd have lunch with you out of curiosity. You have three hours to dream up a better story."

Taplinger, who should have known better—hell, he did—and had fired agents for less, had been indiscreet. When he finally got his turn with the Roumanian girl, she had gushed how handsome was his friend the American naval officer, and Taplinger, piqued, had informed her that unfortunately Ash was leaving for Russia and she had better concentrate on the job at hand; namely himself. Other German agents had already reported Ash's arrival in Zurich, and next morning the astonishing news that he had climbed the library steps to talk to the revolutionary Nikolai Lenin. Later that same morning the American consulate booked him a seat on the train to Paris as well as a luncheon table for two at the Carleton-Elite.

Major Ranke had traveled to Spa to report personally on the bungled assassination attempt and Ash's escape. Before seeing Ludendorff he telephoned Berlin in hopes of better news.

"Russia. Lenin?" What was the Kaiser up to? Subverting Russian revolutionaries was army business.

"Paris next," his aide-de-camp reminded him. "We have a conductor on that train . . ."

"Tell him what to do—and order Gruppe IIIb agents to stay clear of the Okhrana." Even in Zurich the Czar's secret police stuck to Lenin and his sort like pilot fish to a shark; except they were pilot fish with teeth.

But when Major Ranke reported to General Ludendorff, skimming lightly over the debacle his men had made of things so far, Ludendorff promptly ordered him to *tell* the Okhrana about Ash and Lenin. "Let the Russians kill him for conspiring with a revolutionary."

"I would venture to guess that the Okhrana already knows of their meeting this morning, Herr Quartermaster General. Surely they watch him at the library." Ranke was congratulating himself on his forthrightness when he realized General Ludendorff was looking at him oddly. He felt the early twinges of panic. "Sir . . . do you think the Okhrana would risk attacking an American navy officer?"

Ludendorff spoke slowly, as if to a demented child, and it was chillingly clear that he was getting fed up with Gruppe IIIb and Major Ranke.

"Tell the Okhrana that Ash is masquerading as a naval officer and that in fact he is an American revolutionary from New York City . . . it's full of them . . . who is supplying Lenin's forces with guns and explosives." He glared at Ranke, who wished he had thought of it, and added, "At least that way I won't have to depend upon whatever idiot you've put aboard the train to Paris."

10

Lenin bounded down the library steps at twelve on the dot. Ash joined pace beside him, and they walked to the Bahnhofstrasse, past the banks to the Carleton-Elite Hotel. Winter sun streaming in tall windows lighted the pastel dining room exquisitely.

Lenin's gaze traveled over the flowers on the tables, the pâtisserie trolley, the linen and the silver, and settled on the silent waiters padding about the lush carpets. "I imagine it's a romantic failing on my part, but something innocuous about the Swiss makes their wealth less grating than it is in Russia."

"I suppose there is a difference," Ash said, "between ostentation and tasteful comfort."

Lenin's bleak smile suggested that his romantic failing had been indulged enough.

"Try your new story on me, Mr . . . ?"

"Ash."

"A pseudonymous name if I've ever heard one."

"Kenneth Ash, Lieutenant Commander, United States Navy."

A waiter had poured mineral water when they sat down. Lenin had his halfway to his lips. He lowered the glass untouched. "Lieutenant Commander, United States Navy? What the hell do you want?"

"Shall we order first?"

"I'm not hungry. What do you *want?*"

"I want to know what's going on in Russia. Are they going to throw the Czar out on his ear?"

"You're asking the wrong man. I haven't seen a Russian newspaper in a month. I haven't received a letter from Petrograd in five weeks. The last interval between letters was six weeks. The censors."

Ash had done some more checking on Lenin and the Bolshevikii since Taplinger had mentioned them. In the jigsaw puzzle of left wing and revolutionary political parties—a puzzle he had paid little attention to in the past since the slightest suggestion of revolution would send Tamara into a pro-Romanov rage—the Bolshevikii, preaching class warfare and the overthrow of factory owners by factory workmen, *seemed* to fall midway between the moderate socialists, who wanted to install a democratic parliamentary government in place of the Czar, and the anarchists, who wanted to destroy all governments. But however radical and violent they had been before the War, Lenin's Bolshevikii, if indeed they were still his, had since suffered the same loss of popular support as all the European socialists.

"You're not the wrong man," Ash said. "From what I've heard, if anyone knows what's going on, Lenin does."

"If I did, and I don't, I don't know why I should tell you."

"Why not? It's possible we want the same thing."

"I doubt it. *I* want a revolution. I want the oppressed, the proletariat installed on the oppressor's throne. I want the wealth of the few restored to the many. And I fail to see how the United States navy would want any of that."

"I'm not speaking of the navy," Ash said. "The navy doesn't know I'm here. If the navy did I'd be facing a long line of officers with an even longer list of questions."

Lenin did not smile. "I repeat—what do you want?"

"The only way to end the war is to get America to help England, France and Russia beat Germany. But the only way to get America to help Russia is to kick out the Czar."

After a moment Lenin said, "You don't look young enough to believe in just wars."

"Maybe it's because I'm American."

"Maybe it's because you think I'm stupid enough to be entrapped in some sort of provocative scheme."

Ash sipped his mineral water and motioned to the waiter for a wine list. "I only know one thing for sure about you, Mr. Lenin. You're not stupid. I'm talking on the square. Try to believe that. Besides, what could I possibly provoke *you* into doing?"

Ash was satisfied to see a note of interest in Lenin's eyes. He waited silently, until Lenin said, "Go on, Mr. Ash. I'm listening."

"I'd like to get your assessment of the revolutionary situation in Petrograd, for openers. And then some advice about the Czar. What will happen in Russia in the next, say, two months?"

Lenin brought his fingers to his lips. "My assessment, such as it is, taking into account how removed I am, is that the war has brought the socialist movement to Russia to a full stop. The moment the factory workers began producing munitions and the peasants shouldered the Czar's rifles, our case lost its appeal. The same thing happened in Germany, and France and England. *Only* when the war is ended can we even begin to speak of revolution."

"Our goals seem mutual," Ash said, flipping casually through the wine list to hide his alarm. Lenin was considerably less optimistic about revolution than the supposedly learned Professor Taplinger and intelligence gatherers in the British Embassy in Petrograd. And if revolution was not a powerful threat it would be impossible to persuade the Czar and his family to leave . . .

"How is that, Mr. Ash?"

"We both want to end the war, for our own reasons. I want to end it by removing the Czar. You want to end it *to* remove the Czar. We agree—"

Lenin banged the table and the silver jumped. *"No, we don't agree.* The worse the better, for me. The more killed on the battlefield, the angrier they'll be at home."

Ash was ready to walk out of the restaurant. Lenin returned his gaze mildly. Ash shook his head. "I thought I'd heard it all in Europe, but you are the most cynical . . ."

"Finish your sentence, Lieutenant Commander. Or do words fail you? Do you suppose that because I can sit in a fine restaurant and drink your wine that I'm a cretin who can't accept the truth of the revolution? Am I a semi-idiot who hopes that Czars and Kaisers will surrender their thrones without a fight? . . . I repeat, the worse the suffering the better the chances of the revolution. The more killed on the battlefield, the longer the war, the angrier the people."

"But how long can *you* wait? How long can you sit around Zurich? How many years before the revolution passes you by? A whole new generation of young men and woman who've never seen Lenin?"

Lenin shrugged, almost allowed himself a smile. "Perhaps that's why I'm still talking to you . . . What advice or help do you want?"

"If you could go to Petrograd—"

"The Czar's police would lock me up in Peter and Paul Fortress on arrival. If I survived the arrest I'd be exiled to Siberia. They put lead weights in your shoes and make you walk."

"But if you—if you were me, for instance—how would you convince the Czar that his time had come?"

"I would shoot the son of a bitch."

Ash started to laugh but stopped himself when he saw the pain in Lenin's eyes. So he had feelings after all; and he meant it, he would shoot the Czar, and with passion, not merely as a political expedient.

Ash said, "I would have to demonstrate it in some other way."

"Groups demonstrate, not individuals. And please remember that if you convince a group of Russians to demonstrate you will provoke a counterattack by the police. And if your group proves too strong for the police, the army will attack it. I'm afraid it really is hopeless in wartime."

"But in wartime," said Ash, "doesn't the army depend on conscripts? Aren't they less likely to attack demonstrators?"

"Who knows? It's the demonstrators themselves who will receive the definitive answers to your hypothetical question. You're talking about blood in the streets. Blood for no gain—"

"*If* the army fires."

"If! If! I can discuss theory with a hundred Russians here in Zurich anytime I can stand it. You've come from the outside. Tell me something I don't hear every day."

"The Russian nobility are smuggling out their jewels."

"Good. What else?"

"British secret intelligence fears a Russian revolt at any moment."

"Could these be the same intelligence officers who predicted a war won by Christmas 1914? Or perhaps they're the ones who planned the Gallipoli campaign."

"German intelligence agrees."

"German intelligence *hopes*. If they agreed they'd send me and my comrades home to Petrograd. No, Mr. Ash, we're in a terrible bind. No revolution until the war ends, and it seems the war will never end."

"Tell me who I can talk to in Petrograd."

"About what?"

"Demonstrating to the Czar that he should step down."

"You're convinced I have a cell there, aren't you? I don't. The revolution is here in Zurich. In the library, believe it or not."

"There must be someone I can contact in Petrograd."

"Who do you know in Petrograd?"

"I know a few Russian diplomats and naval officers. Men I met in Portsmouth, New Hampshire, in 1905 during the Russo-Japanese peace negotiations, and again at the 1906 disarmament conference at The Hague."

"You can be assured that the competent ones among them have long been relieved of their offices. The Imperial bureaucracy has been corrupted from the top down. Since the Czar resumed command of the army the Czarina Alexandra controls the ministries and appoints fools and thieves recommended by the monk Rasputin. Rasputin is the government now . . . Who else do you know?"

Ash hesitated. "I have friends in the Imperial Ballet."

"Procurers to the aristocracy," Lenin said. "Is that all?"

"I'm afraid so."

"Wonderful. You're on various terms of intimacy with representatives of perhaps one percent of the Russian people. Do you know any merchants?"

"I don't think so."

"Intellectuals?"

"Maybe through the ballet."

"Peasants?"

Ash thought of the drunken sledge drivers who had driven hunting parties to the bear caves in the countryside. "Not really."

"Workers?"

"I've toured some of your naval shipyards . . . Can you put me in contact with people who may know the state of the revolution inside Russia itself?"

"Don't be coy with me," said Lenin. "You want me to name a revolutionary."

"One who will talk to me."

Lenin looked up at the chandeliers. A waiter came running over. He waved the man away. Suddenly he smiled, as if savoring a private joke. "Kirichenko."

"Who's he?"

"Kirichenko is, or was if he's not been shot, an SR fighting squad leader."

"Where do I find him?"

"He's underground. I imagine if you persisted in asking about him in the right places that he would find you. If he does, you have my permission to try to dissuade him from shooting you by mentioning our lunch together. Tell him I congratulate him if he's still alive. Tell him that if there is ever a revolution in Russia it will owe its rebirth to Kirichenko because Kirichenko stayed while the rest of us tucked our books under our arms and ran."

Lenin rose, as if to leave, his face bitter.

"Hey, you haven't eaten."

"I'm not hungry."

"Mr. Lenin, forgive me for saying that you look like you could use a good meal. Please stay. My train doesn't leave for a couple more hours."

Lenin settled back and nodded listless agreement as Ash ordered for both of them. He sipped his wine gloomily but brightened after the soup, and it occurred to Ash that the revolutionary's swift changes of mood were similar to the Kaiser's.

"What train are you taking?" Lenin asked.

"To Paris. I guess we'll cross in to France at Boncourt. How did you happen to know about Henry Grady?"

"Madame Armand told me she'd met you at the café, so I looked it up. I have a list of newspapers I try to sell articles to."

"She's a lovely woman," Ash said.

"She is a flame," Lenin replied softly. "A flame in the night." The

81

thought seemed to cheer him further. He asked, with a sly grin, "Tell me, Lieutenant Commander, have you ever *worked* for a living?"

"From the age of fifteen until I entered the Naval Academy I worked my way around the world on sailing ships."

"Bourgeois adventuring isn't work."

Ash put down his knife and fork, reached across the table and laid his hand, palm up, beside Lenin's plate. "Turn your hands over." Lenin glanced at Ash's calloused palm and turned his own to the light. It was a strong hand, but untried. Ash said, "You work on a ship and you don't notice politics at sea."

"Nonsense. The sailors of the Imperial Navy have been the fiercest supporters of political revolution. Time and again they've defied their officers."

"Maybe if they had less mutiny on their mind the Imperial Navy might have done better against the Japanese."

Lenin flushed. "The mutiny came *after* the defeats. Besides, they'd have beaten the Japanese if they'd been better led."

"You sound like a patriot," Ash remarked.

Lenin stared back, long and hard. "If you don't understand Russian patriotism, you haven't a hope in hell of persuading anyone to leave—*including* the Czar."

Lenin walked Ash to his train. "I probably shouldn't have given you Kirichenko's name," he said. "He's not stable. He could kill you. I would avoid him."

Great, thought Ash. The one contact he'd pried out of Lenin was a nut of some kind. He supposed that other than some interesting talk, the lunch had been a waste of time. On the other hand he'd never before had the chance to sit face to face with a revolutionary . . . Lenin seemed almost ordinary, except for his cold eye on the world. It was funny, but if the Kaiser reminded him of T.R., Lenin was strangely similar to another American president—the cold and remote Woodrow Wilson.

The whistle blew. Lenin surprised Ash by giving his hand a quick shake, thanked him for lunch and disappeared along the platform in wreaths of steam and train smoke.

A conductor was drawing the corridor curtains in Ash's compartment and had already placed a "Private" notice on the door. But just as the train started moving, two men entered, ignoring the sign, and sat down opposite him.

Ash said, "This is a private compartment."

They merely looked at him. He tried French with similar results. One

spoke to the other. Russian. The hell with it, he had plenty of room anyway
. . . As the train cleared Central Station and began to pick up speed, one
of the Russians latched the door and the other drew a Luger, pointed it
at Ash and asked, "What did you talk about at lunch?"

11

"**I** am Lieutenant Commander Kenneth Ash, serving as diplomatic courier for the United States of America. Please take that goddamn gun out of my face." Well said, Ash, but who do you think you're impressing?

Well, they were obviously Russian police—Okhrana, probably, to have trailed Lenin so far from home. Ash wished he were wearing his uniform, but his passport should help. The Czar's police weren't, he hoped, about to offend an officer of his potential American ally. All he had to do was concoct a plausible reason for meeting Lenin. He reached for his passport—

"Raise your hands, *Commander Courier*," the Russian said, contemptuously, and, then, "how many guns did you promise Lenin?"

"Guns? There's some mistake—"

"No mistake. Raise your hands."

Ash smelled tobacco smoke heavy on their clothing. Ordinarily the luxurious paneled compartment sat six; now it felt distinctly crowded by three. The Luger he had appropriated from the German captain was buried deep in his satchel, under his uniform, his sword strapped to the bag in a closed traveling scabbard. He raised his hands.

"Who is to receive your *shipment* to Russia?"

"I don't know what you're talking about. Will you let me show you my passport? I'm a diplomatic courier—"

"Why does an American diplomatic courier meet with the revolutionary Nikolai Lenin?"

"Lenin applied for a visa to visit the United States. I was delegated to see whether he is dangerous—"

"He is."

84

Ash had started to reach for his passport again. "I want to show you my papers."

"We know your papers. What did you ask Lenin, Commander Courier?"

Was this a mistake or a setup, Ash wondered. Either way he was in trouble. "I . . . asked him about the revolution."

"You asked the wrong man, you should ask the Czar's police."

"Is that who you are?"

The gunman said nothing.

"All right," Ash said, "I'll ask you. What can you tell me?"

The reply was grave, deliberate. The police detective actually sounded scholarly. "I can tell you that we have more to fear from the population than we do from revolutionaries. You scum are finished but the people . . . the people are threatening . . ."

Ash glanced at his partner, who was waiting silently, his expression blank. Obviously he didn't understand English.

"Now it's your turn to answer my question. You're no more a diplomat than I am. You watch my gun like a leopard—Answer me. Whose money do you bring to the revolutionary Lenin? What messages do you take back? Who brings the weapons to Russia?"

"Let me show you my passport."

The Russian gestured Ash's hands higher with his gun and nodded to his partner, who reached into his coat and pulled out a foot-and-a-half length of stiff wire that had lead weights welded to each end. He slapped it against his palm.

The detective with the gun said, "This is a Cossacks' flail—first-rate for dispersing crowds from horseback. I think you can imagine what it would do to a man's face."

Ash could imagine. Too well to keep quiet. "You touch me with that thing and I'll—"

The flail leapt at Ash's eyes, blurring, humming through the air. Tipped by the gunman's nodded command, Ash was already levering up from the seat and lowering his hands. He blocked the Russian's swing with his left, absorbed a blow that stung the length of his forearm and punched with a right. The Russian fell backward, knees buckling.

Ash kicked at the other man's gun, missed. The Russian swung back. The gun grazed Ash's forehead. He grabbed for it, got the barrel. The sight ripped his palm. He held on, pushing it up and away. The gunman now hit him hard with his free hand. Ash pressed against him, kicking, kneeing, using the confined space to push off from the seats, the door, the big window.

They stumbled over the man who'd collapsed half on the seats, half on the floor.

The Russian jerked his gun out of Ash's hand and managed to land the butt on his head and neck. Momentarily stunned, Ash brought his knees up into the man's stomach, snapping high like a sprint runner. The Russian pushed away, raising the gun like a club. Ash threw three quick jabs under it, thrusting the Russian backward, and then brought a deep left up from his knees.

The gunman slammed into the window. The glass broke. Cold air and locomotive coal smoke blasted into the compartment as the Russian tumbled over the side of the train. His partner jumped on the gun. Ash fell on him, slapping at the gun, trying to shove it under the seat. It bounced off a strut, slid across the floor into the Russian's hand.

Ash pounded his wrist, but the big man kept his grip and began to stand up, lifting Ash on his back. Ash punched at his head but the Russian kept rising, ignoring the blows, gathering his enormous strength, and abruptly threw Ash off his back with a sudden twist.

Ash dropped low, got under the Russian, shouldered him toward the broken window. The Russian aimed the Luger. Ash got an awful glimpse down the black bore, then lashed out, driving the Russian's arm against the jagged glass. The gun fell from his fingers as he tumbled backward.

Ash hung out the broken window, gasping in the bitter cold mountain air, watching the second Russian roll down the slope onto the snowy pines that lined the railroad embankment. He felt blood on his forehead, blood was oozing from his cut palm. He had skinned the knuckles of both hands and shuddered with the sudden onset of nausea.

The compartment was a shambles. Ash threw the flail out the gaping window, tossed the Russians' bags after it. He mopped the blood off his face and hands, stuffed the Luger in his bag and left the car. He was too shaky to deal with train conductors and the inevitable police.

Just in time. He glanced back as he passed through the vestibule between his car and the next. The conductor was entering the car from the other end. He went directly to Ash's compartment, pulled something the size of a baseball from his pocket, carefully opened the door, tossed it in and ran. Ash had only a moment to wonder what the hell before a loud explosion blew smoke and glass out of his former compartment into the corridor.

"What went wrong in Paris?" General Ludendorff demanded.

Major Ranke glanced elaborately at his watch. "According to the reports from Calais, Commander Ash is no doubt arriving in London just now, General, so may I suggest—"

"*What happened in Paris?* And stand at attention when you address me!"

Major Ranke stiffened like glazed ceramic. "Commander Ash met with

86

Chevalier François Roland, dance writer for the newspaper *Le Monde* in Paris. He also met Count Leonard Fasquelle, director of Russe-Franc Viande, a company which imports Russian caviar. Both are apparently old friends of Ash. Fasquelle has many highly placed associates in Russia. Roland left Paris for Russia immediately after he met Ash, but my sources say his trip was already arranged—to report the season."

"What *season?*"

"The dance, sir. In Petrograd the ballet season starts after the Russian New Year—"

"You still haven't answered my question, Major Ranke. Why did Ash leave Paris alive? Why is Ash back in London reporting to God knows whom?"

"He . . . managed to be fortunate enough to escape the trap our agents set—"

"How?"

"We sent Ash an invitation, purportedly from a woman, a French *comtesse* with whom, our agents had learned, Ash had recently shared a *liaison.* But somehow Ash discovered it was a device. He came to the place of meeting with Chevalier Roland. Both were armed. Fortunately the only agent who knew anything about Gruppe IIIb's connection escaped."

"The *dance* reporter stopped your agents?"

"François Roland is also fencing champion of France, general."

"They routed your agents with *swords?*"

"Lugers."

"And where, I wonder, did they get Lugers?" Ludendorff muttered to himself. Ranke kept quiet. In a few more awful minutes he would be on his way home to the relative safety of Berlin. But Ludendorff wasn't through. Belatedly, Ranke realized that Ludendorff's sarcasm was rooted in a far deeper rage than he'd so far expressed. His neck turned red, flushed all the way up into his bristly hair.

"There is another matter, Major Ranke."

"Yes sir."

"Did you know that Count von Basel was back in Germany?"

Was that all? "Of course, General. Von Basel reported to Gruppe IIIb last week—after, I might mention, returning unexpectedly from Russia and without orders to do so, though of course we on Staff have learned to put up with the peccadillos of field agents—"

"Really? And where is von Basel now?"

"He departed for what he claimed was, to use his own words, a well-deserved holiday."

"Did you know that he had another reason to cross enemy lines?"

"No sir."

"Did you know that his holiday as you call it was spent with the Kaiser?"

Ranke felt a chill.

"Are you aware that von Basel has been the Kaiser's protégé for some thirteen years?"

"Of course," Ranke whispered.

"Did you know that the Kaiser ordered von Basel to return immediately to Russia and that he has already done so?"

"How . . . ?"

"Are you asking how do I know? Fortunately your so-called observer in the Kaiser's entourage is not my only source . . . Would you care to speculate who von Basel and the Kaiser discussed? I will tell you. A man who just happens to be on *his* way to Russia . . ." He leaped from his desk and stood nose to nose with Ranke. "Well, Major, *would you?*"

"Ash . . ."

Ludendorff turned to his aide-de-camp. "Inform this major that he is to report to me through regular channels from now on."

"Dismissed," the aide-de-camp said.

For Major Ranke it was like a death sentence.

Some instinct, Ludendorff reflected, had warned him from the start about Commander Ash and the Kaiser. And unfortunately he had been right. Count von Basel was a murderous psychopath with two passions in his life —to mutilate men with his saber and serve his buffoon of a Kaiser. Kaiser Wilhelm loved him like a son.

Ludendorff still did not know precisely what the Kaiser was plotting, except that it clearly pointed at Russia, but the fact von Basel was summoned meant he regarded it as vital. King George was also likely in on it. President Wilson could be. Certainly Ash could serve either or both. But if Count von Basel left his post as a German plant in the Russian secret police in Petrograd, risking crossing Russian lines twice to deliver a report to IIIb that could have been sent by simpler means, it was clear that he had actually been summoned by the Kaiser for instructions about a plot . . . a peace plan? . . . in Russia. And peace could only bring disaster to Ludendorff and the German army.

Ludendorff paced his office. Von Basel . . . the man was a relic—an old-fashioned, out-of-date servant to royalty, one of those hidebound Junkers who still believed that the nobility existed to fight for the royalty, and utterly blind to the idiot the Kaiser had turned out to be. But for his part the Kaiser had chosen well, because von Basel was both brilliant and dangerous.

Within the closed world of the Prussian Junkers he had secured his reputation at age fifteen by humiliating his father, a highly respected duelist himself, into suicide. A year later he was notorious as the Heidelberg swordsman who refused to accept a dueling scar.

The absence of "beauties" scarring his face was due neither to squeamishness on von Basel's part nor lack of trying by his fellow students. The ancient German Student Corps demanded that first-year students be "free as a lad" and earn manhood by fighting frequent courtesy *mensuren*. To display bravery and obedience, the principals stood toe to toe and slashed at each other's faces until ordered to halt.

The duels were expected to yield blood on both sides so that arms and bodies were padded to prevent incapacitating wounds and ears were taped to the head to minimize the risk of losing one. The resultant wounds on cheeks and brows and lips were sewn shut by medical students and doused with wine to enhance the scarring that set the elite Student Corps alumnus apart from ordinary men and coincidentally guaranteed social position through life.

Count von Basel had mocked the *mensur* ritual and scorned the Student Corps, because, he announced on his arrival from remote Eastern Prussia, volunteering to be hacked into bloody ribbons betrayed the highest ideals of Kaiserin Germany. Where was the skill a nobleman should cultivate to serve his Kaiser on "Der Tag?"

Muth, moral courage, to accept pain was not enough. Germany needed winners. Besides, surrender bred servility. He scorned the blunt-tipped *schlager.* The *sabel*—the heavy curved saber capable of cleaving a skull in half and running a man through the heart—was a real test not only of swordsmanship but of footwork, and the courage required to face death as well as trifling flesh wounds. As an afterthought, von Basel noted that many of low rank joined the Student Corps to advance beyond their station.

Stepping on another student's dachshund's tail was sufficient to provoke an insult duel, questioning the purity of his sister equally effective. But to characterize all the members of all the Student Corps as servile, social-climbing cowards was to insure challengers for the entire school year.

Gradually, though, it dawned on the mutilated challengers that von Basel had provoked the entire incident for the sheer pleasure of proving his own superiority in birth, courage and skill. He took great pains not to kill. A man who killed had to leave the University; he could join another, but if he killed again he was barred from all.

At last, when sufficient eyes had been put out and the use of many hands ended forever with severed tendons, there were no more challengers and the entire *mensur* ritual ground to a sullen halt. Remarkably, von Basel had suffered only one wound, when a Bavarian twice his weight had managed to slam through his guard and slice off a small chunk of his scalp, for which he paid with both ears. Then a dragoon officer, who was a

Student Corps alumnus and a fencing master, intervened on behalf of the noble tradition.

The new challenger was fifteen years von Basel's senior and when he entered the tavern where the insult *mensur* was scheduled, von Basel realized by his walk alone that his opponent far outclassed any others he had faced. While the servants were wiping the blades with disinfectant, he informed the master in a discreet whisper that because he was not yet skilled enough to let him off with flesh wounds, he would kill him if he insisted on fighting.

The cavalry officer laughed and attacked, shredding the younger man's defenses, which, as he'd suspected, were less formidable than his attacks. And when he catalogued them all, and knew for certain that all von Basel had left was his bewildering speed and the incredible strength in a seemingly tireless wrist, he loosed a series of feints to lower von Basel's guard, and when he had, he slashed. Von Basel's speed saved his skull, but the saber still laid his brow open to the bone.

Von Basel's left cheek was next, the officer announced as the student surgeons stanched the bleeding so he could see. Then the right cheek, and then his nose and lips, which this master informed him he could feed to his dachshund if he didn't offer a public apology.

The spectators were still laughing, when von Basel ran him through. The man was incredible . . .

Ash, Ludendorff told himself, had to be stopped before he reached Russia. Von Basel was beyond stopping. He was so secretive about his activities in Russia that even his superiors—if you could call them that—at IIIb didn't know his actual Russian identity or even how he got the information he got. They were reasonably sure he served in Petrograd, though it could have been Moscow. Von Basel was damn near as mysterious in Germany as in Russia.

But this Ash . . . Ash was part of the Kaiser's scheme, part of a scheme to make peace behind the army's back—indeed apparently was integral to it. The linchpin. Ash *must* be stopped before he reached Russia, somewhere along the way . . .

He called in his aide-de-camp. "Bring me a Russian."

"A Russian?"

"Yes. One of the revolutionaries. A young earnest one."

"Yes, General."

"And bring me a German officer who speaks Finnish."

"Yes, General."

Ludendorff felt better. German agents had done a fairly good job of stirring up national feelings in the Russian Grand Duchy of Finland. Of late they had established renegade army units to disrupt the telegraph and stop trains. The Finns could remove Ash from the train, if the revolutionary didn't get him first.

12

"**W**hy the devil did you go to Zurich and Paris?" Admiral Innes grumbled when Ash had finished his report. "I understood you were to deliver the King's message to the Kaiser and come home."

"I had no specific orders, sir. I went where I went because I had to—"

"You almost got yourself killed—"

"Not because he didn't come straight back to London," Ambassador Page interrupted. "Go on, Ash."

"I'll be operating alone and unofficially in Petrograd, sir. I've had to turn to friends and acquaintances to jury rig my own network to draw on in Russia. Now I believe I have connections with various people, including an Italian banker and his wife who's a Russian noblewoman. My friend Count Fasquelle has kindly written a letter of introduction to Sergei Gladishev, a Moscow millionaire who happens to be in the Kadet movement in the Duma—"

"What's the Kadet movement?" Admiral Innes put in.

Taplinger in Zurich had explained the basic political parties . . . "The Kadets are constitutional democrats. Gladishev could eventually be involved in a new government—"

"Good," Page said.

"And Chevalier François Roland—who happens to be going to Petrograd as I figured he would be—is a very handy man in a fight. The sort you'd want covering your back."

"Then how come he's not in the army?"

"He lost his left arm at Verdun."

"So you feel ready?" Page asked. Throughout their meeting, Innes had tended to challenge Ash and Page support him.

"As ready as I will be, Mr. Ambassador. I'm counting on tapping a few friends in Petrograd when I get there—if they're still around. The point is I'm not blundering into Russia all by myself. Nor will I have to depend entirely on Lord Exeter."

"That's a blessing," Innes agreed. He looked at Page and nodded. "Well, you got back and that's what counts. Any idea why the Germans tried to kill you?"

"No, sir. Mostly bad guesses."

"Well, the German army shouldn't be a problem in Russia," the admiral said, standing up to go. "I'm sailing to New York to report to Assistant Secretary Roosevelt. Mr. Banks left last week. But Ambassador Page'll get you squared away. Good luck, Ash."

When the admiral had gone Page asked, "How did you know the invitation from that woman was a German trick?"

"Well, I was flattered until Chevalier François suggested that the *comtesse* was not known to invite a gentleman back a second time. We checked up and found she was away in the country."

Page smiled. "Admiral Innes is right. The German army won't be much of a problem in Russia."

"Probably not," said Ash.

Page handed him an envelope. "King's equerry brought this for you this morning."

Ash opened it. Written was an address in Belgravia. And the time, eight-thirty.

"Exeter?" Page asked.

"Sailing orders."

Ash took the Lugers to his gunmaker in New Bond Street. The seven-shot pistols had been developed some years earlier for the German army; the Luger was a dependable gun and, at thirty ounces, considerably lighter than the British Webley or a U.S. Navy Colt.

When he gave his gunmaker the pistols they were eight and three-quarters inches long. When he returned that evening they were much smaller—only six inches long and less than twenty-five ounces; one could fit under his dress uniform tunic in a chamois holster in the small of his back; the other was a spare he would carry in his traditionally inviolate diplomatic pouch. The chamois holster was necessary, the gunmaker explained, or his perspiration would rust the weapon.

"But you won't hit much at long range," he warned, indicating the foreshortened barrel.

"At long range, I'll still have some options."

He checked the mirror as he dressed that evening. The gun did not

92

show, nor the fact that he had had his dress saber ground to razor edges. Who was trying to kill him, or why, he didn't really know. But the next son of a bitch who tried at least was going to have his hands full.

The address in Belgravia was in a row of elegant townhouses that twined the bend in a curving street with marble steps and creamy white columns lit by gas lamps. Ash knocked. The butler led him to the library. Lady Exeter put down her book.

"Good evening, Commander. I've been delegated to entertain you until my husband is done meeting with a rather dreary Royal Navy officer in the next room."

Ash bowed over her hand. "I hope it's a long meeting."

Her extravagant red hair was piled high tonight; wisps escaping across her cheeks softened her stern face, and he thought she looked prettier than he'd remembered and more in her element in the city. She wore black silk.

"Commander," she said with a quick smile, "the Irish side of my family bequeathed me red hair and a fine ear for blarney."

"I have a drop or two of French blood on my mother's side," Ash said. "It left me with a taste for claret and an eye for beauty."

Lady Exeter turned to her butler. "Graham, bring this gentleman a whiskey. And please tell His Lordship that I am growing impatient."

"Have I offended you?" Ash asked when the butler had left.

"I imagine you can't help yourself, but I find your proprietary attitude toward women not overly flattering—one feels like a candidate for a very large club with an undiscriminating membership committee."

"I'm sorry—"

"Good God, you meant it . . . forgive me, a friend was killed in France today. I'm in no mood to entertain. I was against the war in the beginning and now I find myself praying for total victory . . . Where the *hell* are the Americans?"

They sat in stiff silence until the whiskey came.

"I understand you were in Germany."

Ash said nothing, but was surprised and angered that someone had apparently told her more than he should have.

"I have no idea why you went, but I am curious about the Germans. Are they really starving?"

"The best hotel in Munich had no coffee."

"What about the ordinary people?"

"They looked tired. The soldiers looked tough as nails."

Lord Exeter came in, apologizing for being detained, enormous in evening clothes. In his own home he was much more direct than when Ash had met him at Sandringham. "Hello, Ash. My dear, could you excuse us? We'll be an hour."

"Dinner at ten," she said, and turning to Ash said, "We have a friend from Petrograd staying with us that I thought you might enjoy meeting."

Ash watched her go. She walked with an erect carriage, and the billows of her black gown seemed hard put to keep up. When he felt Exeter's eyes on him he said, "Is it possible that someone in your organization is a traitor?"

"I don't know what organization you're talking about," Exeter said, "but if you're referring to my efforts to assist the King in the rescue of the Czar then the answer is no. My organization, as you call it, consists of myself, you and a chap from the Royal Navy who happens to be distantly related to the King and has agreed to lay on the cruiser."

"I'm referring to British Secret Service. I've had you checked out." . . . Up to his eyeballs in espionage was how Ambassador Page had put it about Lord Exeter.

Exeter shrugged. "So far as I am concerned I am performing a personal service for His Majesty. Just as you are."

"The King knows I had to report to Ambassador Page. Can you—?"

"I am not similarly bound. I report to no one. Now I want you to meet this navy man, and I can assure you he is not a traitor . . . I only brought him in this afternoon." He looked puzzled. "Why did you ask?"

"Three attempts were made to kill me after I saw the Kaiser. Somebody knows we talked."

"Ah. Perhaps it is the Kaiser who has a traitor."

"Perhaps."

"Or has changed his mind?"

Ash had thought of that. "I'll find out in Petrograd if his agent doesn't contact me."

"Mercurial fellow, the Kaiser . . . Were I His Majesty I might have looked for another way to protect my cruiser . . ."

Lord Exeter moved some books, opened a wall safe, pulled a slim leather slipcase from the dark inside and handed it to Ash.

Ash opened it and spread the contents on Exeter's desk, a nouveau fantasy of polished marquetry. There were letters of credit with Barclays' and the Russian & English Bank.

"What limit?" Ash asked.

"None."

Ash looked at him. "None?"

"Merely present that code number and take what you need."

Ash opened a thick envelope. It was filled with British pound notes and Russian roubles.

"A thousand pounds," Exeter said as he started to count it.

Ash counted it anyway. A thousand pounds was more by some than his yearly pay as a lieutenant commander in the United States Navy. He counted the roubles; the Czar's face was on each, the Imperial double-headed eagle on the back. Another thousand pounds at the current exchange.

"I need a personal letter and *laissez-passer* from the Russian Embassy," Ash said. "I had trouble with the Okhrana in Zurich. They seem to have me down as an American revolutionary."

"I'll take care of it," said Exeter. "We don't want you stopped at the frontier." He didn't ask why the Okhrana had Ash down as a revolutionary and Ash was grateful not to have to explain.

Exeter said, "Cooks Travel is empowered to book you any form of transport at any time on account. And included there is my card with my Petrograd address. I'll be along soon. I've got factories up the Neva that need tending to."

"Your own?"

"I had to leave the army to take over the family business when my brother died a number of years ago. I'm often in Russia. We produce munitions. The fuel shortages are killing us, I can assure you."

Ash wondered if Lady Exeter traveled with him.

"At the risk of repeating the obvious, you are not under any circumstances to approach British Ambassador Buchanan. And please don't even go near the British Embassy, except when it's time for His Majesty's cruiser. Then you will contact Captain Cromwell, who would appreciate a week's notice if possible."

Lord Exeter went to a door and returned with a tall Royal Navy captain who looked Ash over with a disapproving stare. "Frankly I fail to see why one of our own can't conduct this mission."

"It was His Majesty's wish that Commander Ash carry out his plan, Captain."

"All the same . . ." He shook hands reluctantly and said, "The cruiser will fly a plain green ensign beneath the Union Jack when she enters Murmansk. You will please instruct your German contacts that their U-boats should do the same. Any German boat not flying the green ensign will be sunk."

"May I suggest white, sir."

"What?"

"White. So they can see it at night."

"All right. If you insist. White it is. They should be of sufficient dimension to be seen at a thousand yards. That's all." He turned and headed for the door.

"Sir?" Ash called. "Is Lieutenant Skelton still serving in the Baltic?"

"That's not the sort of information I'm likely to bandy about, Commander. Why do you ask?"

"Skelton and I played some polo at the Royal Durber in India. I recall he has a submarine based at Reval. I'll be close by. I thought maybe I'd stop in and see him if he's still there—he wasn't sunk, was he?"

Cromwell almost softened. "He's well. I'll tell him you said hello. Good evening, Exeter."

"Thank you for coming, Captain Cromwell."

Exeter walked him to the door and Ash returned the money and letters to the slipcase, thinking he was lucky he had a close friend much closer to Petrograd than Murmansk, with his own submarine.

"He'll be back in Petrograd a week or so after you arrive," Exeter said. "Shall we join the ladies? My wife has a delicious little number visiting from Petrograd. A ballerina."

Ash followed him apprehensively, hoping it wasn't one of Tamara's friends.

"Can I assume your wife knows nothing about your work?"

"Nothing," Exeter said.

Lady Exeter was sitting by the fire in a drawing room with the ballerina. Exeter made the introductions. Her name was Vera. Vera Sedovina. Ash didn't know her. Anyway she was too young, only a girl.

She was tall for a dancer, slim, and her hair was blonde. She had a little bump on her nose which would keep her from being a great beauty, but there was a feeling of vulnerability and contrasting certainty about her that made Ash think she had at least the personality to be a great dancer.

Her eyes were startling ice blue. She must have Swedish or Finnish blood, but so slim, perhaps a Dane. She said hello with a light accent. A pretty voice, yet quite serious. Ash figured she was about sixteen and wondered what she was doing in London; no ballet had performed in London since 1914.

Lady Exeter seemed to cherish the girl like a newly acquired oil painting—something exotic by the French. "Mademoiselle Sedovina," she said, "has come to London to dance in the Christmas Pantomimes at Covent Garden."

He nodded. There were small roles for balletic dancers in the children's shows that would be starting in a week. Ash asked if this was her first trip to London; she said it was.

"Commander Ash is off to Petrograd," Exeter said. "I've been recommending restaurants and gypsy bands."

She looked at Exeter gravely. "The restaurants have become very expensive since the food shortages."

Graham came in and announced dinner.

Vera seemed awed by the Exeter's lavish dining room. They clustered at one end of a long table, and Exeter turned somewhat grandfatherly around her, inquiring if she liked the wine and the savory and then, when the main dish was served, remarking, "I'll have you know that bird on your plate met his demise at the hand of Commander Ash. His Majesty insisted I take a few home . . . Have you many friends in Petrograd, Commander?"

Ash saw where he was leading and went along. "A few. I suspect most of them will be at the front . . . But I'll be meeting plenty of people. My embassy has asked me to survey popular sentiment in Petrograd concerning the war . . ."

"They are fed up," Vera said forcefully. "The war is a disaster. The people have suffered too long—"

Lady Exeter interrupted. "I doubt the people Commander Ash intends to talk to have suffered as much."

Ash agreed. "I've orders to speak to military officers and people in government. Unfortunately I always find it hard to find people who haven't been primed to answer in a specific way."

"Vera," said Exeter, "your father's a *tappeur*, isn't he?"

"Yes. He plays the piano at Society balls."

Ash noticed that she laid a disapproving stress on "Society."

"Could Commander Ash call on him—the *tappeurs* know everything, Ash. Everything going on at court and the city. Handy chap to know."

"He likes Americans," Vera said, looking Ash straight in the eye for the first time since they had been introduced.

"I'd like very much to meet him."

"I'll give you a note to him," she said. "His name is Vadim Mikhailov."

"Vadim Mikhailov."

Then she added gravely, "But you really ought to meet real people too. My father can't help you there. He's too much of a snob."

Late that night when everyone in the house was sleeping, Vera Sedovina emerged out of the kitchen door and into the streets of London. She walked to the vegetable markets around Covent Garden and met a Russian merchant seaman in a pub open to the market workers. He was shipping out to New York from Liverpool the next day. She was a courier for the Bolshevikii; being hired to dance a few weeks in London was an opportunity to send word of conditions in Petrograd to party exiles in New York and Zurich—words of hope, that their day was near . . .

Ash's final bit of business remaining in London was a charade for the benefit of Captain Wesley, representing the United States Navy, and Ambassador Page's chargé d'affaires. Unknown to them, both men were being set up as witnesses to prove that Ash had gone off on his own in the event something went wrong in Russia.

Ash reported to Page's office early the morning after he met with Lord Exeter. Page, Wesley and the chargé were waiting. Page said, "Good morning, Commander. Something very unusual has come up, but before we go into it, let me be the first to congratulate you." He pushed himself painfully up from his desk and extended his hand. "Cable arrived this morning. You've been promoted to full commander."

For a moment Ash forgot why he was there. Full commander at age thirty-six! Damn near unheard of. A glance at Captain Wesley told Ash that Wesley thought so too. Wesley had been forty-six when he'd made commander, fifty-three for captain. And by now Wesley had to know he would never wear the broad stripe of a commodore whereas Ash's promotion made him a candidate for flag rank before he was fifty.

"Commander?" Page smiled. "Are you all right?"

Suddenly, Ash had a lot to lose. "Yes, sir. Thank you. I'm very surprised, and pleased. Thank you."

Of course Page had engineered it, and probably with the help of the President or Assistant Secretary of the Navy Franklin Roosevelt to get it so fast. And a wise notion for the sake of the mission. Europeans were extremely conscious of rank, and the Russians most of all. Commander put him on the level of an army lieutenant colonel, a rank the Russians would take seriously, the rank, by their lights, of an aristocrat.

Captain Wesley willed himself to step forward and shake Ash's had. "Congratulations, Commander." Ash admired the effort. No line officer, which Wesley had been for years, liked political pull. That was the dark side of the windfall. If Ash hadn't made any new enemies in the navy, he'd certainly made no friends.

"Sit down, both of you," Page said, collapsing into his chair like a bundle of sticks and pausing to catch his breath. "Ash's good fortune couldn't come at a better time, don't you agree, Captain Wesley?"

"Yes, sir. Shall I tell him, or will you?"

"Go ahead."

Wesley turned to Ash. "The new American ambassador to Russia has asked that his family be allowed to join him in Petrograd. He's got plenty of political pull back in Ohio or some damned place so he's used to getting his own way. The family is already in London and they're leaving for Petrograd this afternoon. You'll travel with them as escort."

Ash glanced at Page. A good cover.

"Further," Wesley continued, "you'll be attached to the Petrograd embassy to—"

"Informally," Page interrupted, "you will still be attached, officially, to my embassy here in London."

"Yes," Captain Wesley said. "Informally, just in case we've got to evacuate women and children from Petrograd."

"Evacuate?" Ash asked.

"Reports from Petrograd are not good. We don't really know what's going on politically in Russia but it's our general feeling that it wouldn't hurt to have a few extra officers in Petrograd in case we have to evacuate our women and children. Now, while you're there, you can make yourself useful meeting Russian naval officers. Inspect their Baltic fleet if you can —although I'm not really sure why you'd want to—get a look before the Germans sink the rest of it, I suppose. Also, might as well look into the Russians' new torpedo boats. They've got something new and fast and we ought to know more about it . . ."

From the corner of his eye Ash noticed Page fidgeting with his papers. Apparently he had so taken in Wesley that the captain felt obliged to make sure Ash stayed very busy while away. "There's talk of an Allied military war plans conference occurring in Petrograd in January. You'll still be there, I imagine, and you might attach yourself informally to it . . ." He paused, running down, and finally asked, "Everything understood?"

"Yes, sir."

"Steamer and train tickets will be issued. You'll have access to embassy funds in major cities along the way—Christiania, Stockholm, Haparanda, although we'd hardly call that a city."

Page cleared his throat.

"Did you want to add anything to Ash's instructions, Mr. Ambassador?"

"Yes, Captain, thank you . . . Ash, keep your eyes open in Russia. I'd like some more accurate reports on these rumors—"

"But may I interrupt, sir?" Captain Wesley said. "Don't step on any toes in the Petrograd embassy, Ash. Whatever you do. They've got their own military attachés to gather intelligence, don't you agree, Mr. Ambassador?"

"Sure, Captain Wesley. I'd imagine the American ambassador has his own operatives assessing the situation, though one might wonder from their reports—all right, listen to this, Ash. Why don't *you* send *me* the occasional private note in the embassy pouch or via the King's Messenger. The Foreign Office will forward it to me. The King's Messenger comes from Petrograd every two weeks. And if you send it to me directly instead of through navy channels to Captain Wesley there can't be any suggestion of stepping on toes . . . How does that sound to you, Captain Wesley?"

"Sounds all right, sir," Wesley said slowly, his tone denying his words.

A knock at the door. When Wesley looked toward it, Page gave Ash a wink. It was fine cover, giving Ash complete freedom of movement, not to mention one that would allow Page to deny any connection with Ash if something went wrong.

His secretary came in. "They're here, Mr. Ambassador."

"Ambassador Hazzard's family," Page explained. "Yes, show them in."

Since Page had mentioned them, Ash had been expecting a midwestern American matron and four or five bashful children suffering the effects of a winter Atlantic crossing. Instead, what walked in were a beefy fellow in his late twenties wearing a loud suit and a very pretty girl, sixteen or seventeen years old. Both were fair-faced and blond and when the ambassador introduced them by name Ash thought he saw a faint resemblance in their wide mouths and big blue eyes.

Catherine Hazzard was the ambassador's daughter. She was petite, a little shy and seemed very serious. Something about her suggested strength and intelligence—a girlish version of Lord Exeter's fiery wife, though as yet perhaps unformed.

Andrew Hazzard, her second cousin, looked like a fast-talking sales-man, the sort, Ash thought, that farmers meant by a city slicker. In the course of shaking hands Andrew managed to announce that he was sell-ing railroad wheels to the Imperial Russian Railroad for an Ohio steel mill whose owner, Ash recalled, had been one of his father's friends. Russia, Andrew described loudly as a market the United States had just begun to tap, now that Krupp of Germany could not trade there any-more. He added that the English and the French had better look out because the United States would be selling Russia everything from Fords to farm tractors.

Ambassador Page blessedly interrupted. "Commander Ash will be your escort to Petrograd."

Full commander, Ash thought. Same old address but a big jump from lieutenant commander.

Catherine and Andrew looked at him again, and Andrew said, "Well, thanks a lot, Mr. Ambassador, but that's not necessary. Catherine's father asked me 'specially to take care of her. We've gotten this far just fine without the navy."

Page smiled warmly, as if to suggest that anticipating the needs of midwestern entrepreneurs was one of the delights of his job.

"I'm speaking less of protection, young man, than of the difficulties of wartime travel. Commander Ash is familiar with conditions in Europe. You'll find him a competent and interesting guide. I'm sure you'll be happy I've sent him along. Also, I'll rest easier knowing that he'll get you and my fellow ambassador's daughter safe and sound to Petrograd."

Andrew scowled unhappily. Ash sympathized. It was pretty clear he was in love with his young cousin and didn't want another man along. Cather-ine, who was just as clearly unaware of his infatuation, asked, "How long will the journey take, Commander Ash?"

"We have to go the long way because of the war, up the Swedish coast around the Gulf of Bothnia. Figure two days on the steamer from Newcastle to Christiania, Norway. And five to seven days on the train. If we're lucky."

Andrew asked, "What'll be the holdup if we're not lucky?"

"German U-boats in the North Sea. And Russian border guards at the Grand Duchy of Finland."

13

The embassy booked Ash three first class berths on the sleeper to Newcastle on the northeast coast of England. There they boarded the *Nord Kapp,* a thousand-ton Norwegian mailboat for the North Sea crossing to Christiania. Her Scots captain cast off in the snow. Beyond the sea wall, where a brutal North Sea chop was already promising a grim winter voyage, snow and fog erased the harbor tugs like lead smudges.

The weather was a mixed blessing. So long as it stayed thick it would hide them from prowling submarines; but if a German U-boat stumbled on them in the fog it might easily mistake the neutral boat for a belligerent.

Three-and-a-half thousand miles to the west, a much larger ship, the American liner *George Washington,* steamed into New York Harbor. Off on the pilot boat, hours before the liner tied up at her Chelsea pier, Harold Banks hurried to Pennsylvania Station, where he caught a train to Washington, D.C.

Eight hours later he was admitted into the White House. President Woodrow Wilson—lean as a steel rail and about as warm, in Banks's opinion—perfunctorily welcomed him home from a trip which had taken him to five European capitals in six weeks and asked how the Europeans had reacted to his latest proposal to negotiate a peace without victory.

"Britain's new government wants to keep fighting," Banks told him. "So do the French and the Germany army. The civilians in the German government aren't so sure, and the Kaiser is on the fence. Unfortunately the army isn't listening to the government anymore and Hindenburg and Ludendorff definitely want to keep fighting."

President Wilson didn't seem surprised or even especially perturbed. He asked Banks, "When will they let loose their U-boats again?"

Banks shrugged. "It's only a matter of time. The British blockade is starving them. Do you think U-boat attacks on American ships would provoke the Congress?"

"I'm not hopeful," Wilson replied gloomily. Banks knew he had backed himself into an impossible position on the war, having campaigned for reelection the month before on a promise to keep out, despite a powerful conviction that the United States had a mission to save world democracy. "People just don't want to get involved. The international situation is as remote as the moon, and what little they do know of Europe they don't like."

"Mr. President, Ambassador Page has come up with a scheme that might interest you . . ."

"If he sends me one more British propagandist I'll transfer him to Mexico."

Banks laughed appreciatively; the jocular threat was the full extent of the humor he would hear in the Oval Office these days.

"No, Mr. President, not a propagandist." Then he described the King's fortuitous plan to rescue the Czar. Banks and Page were undeniably rivals for the President's affections, but Banks freely gave Page the credit for usurping the King's plan for American purposes. One reason he did so was that Ambassador Page was too sick to live long; for another, if the very risky attempt to rescue the Czar and keep Russia in the war backfired, Harold Banks definitely wanted none of it sticking to his boots.

When Banks was done President Wilson rubbed the red marks his glasses left on his nose and asked, with characteristic astuteness, what Banks believed was the most pertinent question—the one he had prepared for. "Who is this Commander Ash? We're putting a lot of trust in a single officer. Can't I send you or Colonel House? He could carry the King's message to the Czar."

"It might involve much more than merely carrying a message, Mr. President. Russia's a nest full of rattlesnakes waiting for a prairie fire. And Ambassador Page told me he feels certain King George made a wise choice in asking Ash."

"I don't like it," Wilson said flatly. "A single officer, alone, six thousand miles from Washington, implementing a dubious scheme based on a notion dreamed up by the King of England? He could undermine years of our work preparing this nation for war. All Congress wants would be an American officer accused of being an *agent provacateur*. What if Ash makes a dangerous mistake? How can I stop him? No, it won't do."

"I anticipated your concern, Mr. President. The moment I learned about Ambassador Page's plan I made arrangements for someone to keep a close eye on Ash and, if needs be, a tight rein.

"Who?"

"Ambassador Hazzard's nephew, young Andy."

Wilson's lips wrinkled disdainfully. "The Lord should spare us from rich businessmen and their wastrel offspring."

"Andrew is capable of relaying orders."

"I suppose it's better than going the official route through the embassy."

"Much better, sir. We can always drop Andy overboard."

"You are certain, then, that I'll be able to stop Ash?" the President asked again.

"Whenever you wish," Banks told him. "But we should time any such action so that we don't leave him out on a limb, over a pack of revolutionaries."

Wilson gave him a sternly professorial look. "The needs of democracy will dictate the timing, not the fate of a single navy officer . . . and I suggest you prepare something to put into his records in the unfortunate event we may be obliged to disassociate the navy from Kenneth Ash, to, as you say, drop him overboard as well . . ."

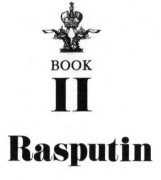

BOOK
II
Rasputin

14

The twelve-year-old Czarevich Alexis, heir to the Imperial Russian Empire, lay screaming in a room full of expensive toys. His four sisters watched him, young girls, the eldest twenty. Alexis's mother held his hand while her hollow eyes darted between his swollen knee and the door. She glimpsed her reflection in the shiny mirror the boy used to dress in his beloved uniforms. Twelve years of dreadful anticipation had made her old.

Doom hovered capriciously; without warning a bump, a mild blow, a child's fall made a bruise which bled inside, and bled and bled. The blood collected in a nearby joint—his knee this time—and filling it, squeezed his nerves. There was no pain like it in the world, no torture so refined, and when it happened the little boy, her baby, screamed until he fainted. Unable to watch his contorted face anymore, or his poor swollen knee, and wondering would this be the time he died, the Czarina Alexandra stared at the door, waiting for her friend Father Gregory Rasputin to save him.

Czarevich Alexis's sisters, the grand duchesses Olga, Tatiana, Marie and Anastasia felt grief tinged with guilt. It had started, they thought, with a pillow fight the night before. Alexis had egged them into it, pleading in his way for an unguarded moment of childish fun, and they had given in, playing carefully, fearfully; in terror of a nosebleed. Instead Alexis, growing excited, had led a chase through their dressing room and had careened through a curtain and smacked into their silver bathtub. The bruise was dark, just above his knee. The blood inside was filling the joint, increasing pressure on the nerves, and starting to bend his knee into a locked, rigid angle the grand duchesses knew well from past accidents. The tighter the angle, the louder the little boy's cries.

Anastasia started his train set and wound up his floating model warships, but he was too far gone to be distracted by the locomotive whistles, the miniature gate crossings, the tiny church bells or the whir of the ship propellers. And at last, they too, turned from his suffering face, and watched the door, waiting.

Father Gregory's shadow fell across the threshold. He was immensely tall, with long black hair and a thick beard and as he paused, sweeping the room with piercing gray eyes, he filled them with hope. The grand duchesses saw in his gaze that Rasputin knew they were at fault, knew but forgave them. The Czarina thanked God he had come.

Rasputin let them stay. Whatever helped calm the child would help stop the bleeding. He knelt by the Czarevich's cot; he was so tall that kneeling he was still taller than Anastasia. The Czarina knelt beside him to pray. He let her do that for a while, best to calm her too, to calm everything in the room. Toys were clattering on the train board. He pointed a long blunt finger at it and Grand Duchess Tatiana, the great beauty of the four sisters with dark, wide-set eyes and perfect lips, stopped the toys.

Quiet smothered the room, quiet but for the boy's whimpers. His strength was failing. He would faint soon, blessed relief from the pain. But Rasputin did not want him to faint. Not yet. Relief from the pain was not enough. It would make his mother happy for the moment, but only for the moment. The boy had to be conscious for Rasputin to work his magic. If he fainted, the bleeding inside would continue. And Rasputin had to stop the bleeding first, before it killed him. *He had to stop the bleeding.*

He spoke, his voice deep, sonorous, rumbling and steady; it was a voice he brought from inside his chest, and it calmed. It did indeed. He prayed aloud for the benefit of the Czarina, who believed that God could only hear her through Rasputin. And then he spoke to the boy after motioning to Tatiana to dim the lights. She glided about the room, regal as the Empress, beautiful as the stars, achingly unattainable. For the moment.

"*Alexis . . .*"

The boy's eyes opened at the sound of Rasputin's voice and rolled feebly, searching. The monk's eyes seemed like deep pools in which he had been taught to swim. Float. Drift. Forget.

"*Alexis . . .*"

Rasputin, the monk, was enormous, shaggy like a bear, his nose enormous. Deep lines scored his face, and a boy might be afraid of him if it were not for his voice. Rich, liquid, clear as the Siberian air, rumbling like benevolent thunder from a storm that cooled a summer's day, Rasputin's voice promised thrilling stories, and above all, peace where there was pain.

Alexis thought he smelled funny, like the kennels where the wolfhounds lived mixed up with his sisters' perfume; not quite as stinky as the wolfhounds, not quite as nice as his sisters, but somewhere in the middle like

. . . like a Rasputin. But when he hurt, the awful way he hurt now, and when he was frightened that this time he would die, then Rasputin smelled wonderful, sounded even better . . .

Alexis tried to speak. He could hardly move his tongue. Rasputin leaned close and put his big hairy ear to his mouth and said, "What?"

"Tell me a story."

The monk's voice made wondrous vibrations in the mattress. "That is what I came for."

Alexis wondered through his pain which story would it be. Maybe the secret story, the one he wasn't supposed to tell, and didn't. About how while his father was so busy commanding the army that Alexis himself should be made Czar and his mother regent until Alexis grew up. No, not while his mother was listening. He didn't like the story anyway. He'd rather be a soldier than a Czar . . .

Rasputin laid his big hand on the boy's chest and another on his chilly forehead and felt the little body strain, like tight guitar strings. The Czarina was staring at his hands. People thought his powers came from his eyes and his hands and surely they were good, but his power, God's power, was in his voice, and the boy knew it. Felt it . . .

Rasputin spoke his name again. *"Alexis,"* and then he told him how once he had walked all the way from Siberia to Greece. Two thousand miles across Russia and into the beyond—to a monastery on Mount Athos. Alexis knew the story, had heard it again and again. But two thousand miles was a long way and anything could happen on such a long walk. Tonight Rasputin told him about a camel with gold teeth, smiling occasionally at the weeping Czarina.

A camel alone was a delight—a horse with a hump—and the boy loved to hear about camels. A camel with gold teeth, and how the beast got such teeth. It held his interest, and so kept him awake to hear the soothing, mesmerizing tones of Rasputin's voice.

Inside the little body, Rasputin sensed, the vessels that carried blood grew strong when he was calm, and weak when he was afraid. He didn't know why—and he didn't particularly care why—but fear, he was certain, made bleeding. And doctors made fear. They frightened the Czarevich almost to death. It was a joke, a very funny joke, at which only Rasputin could laugh. The more worried the doctors, the more they frightened the boy and the more they frightened the boy, the more he bled.

At last the boy began to fall asleep. Rasputin watched him closely, making sure it was not a faint but real sleep which came from well-being, and happiness and trust in his savior and friend, Rasputin. He rose wearily from the bed, made the sign of the cross for the Czarina's sake and walked quietly from the room.

They brought him a chair and gave him wine. He sipped at it, resting, letting them bask in his power. He truly was tired. There were energies he transferred from his body to the boy's in ways he himself didn't understand, but which nonetheless left him drained.

Gradually he revived.

The Czarina came tiptoeing back from the boy's room. "He's still sleeping," she whispered.

"He will sleep," Rasputin intoned. "He will sleep. The bleeding is done."

"Thank God."

"God has heard our prayers."

She sank down beside his chair and took his hand and pressed it to her cheek. The grand duchesses gathered around them, the long vigil over. He felt like their uncle; welcome in their house, this magnificent palace, trusted and loved. He said, "I had a dream last night."

They looked at him expectantly, and the Czarina pressed him to tell the dream.

"When the German artillery shoot at our Russian soldiers, our soldiers should run forward *under* the flight of the shells, which will explode harmlessly behind them." With his hand he inscribed the arc of an artillery shell; he made it look like a thrown rock.

"I will tell my husband," the Czarina said.

Rasputin looked at her. "I also think that General Brusilov must be warned again not to advance another step. Innocent Russian lives are being wasted . . . Purishkevich attacked me again in the Duma . . . " He laughed. "The Duma—dogs barking."

"But their barking keeps other dogs quiet."

Rasputin beamed. It was a phrase he had taught her years ago. He pulled some scraps of paper from his pockets on which he had written names. "I met a good woman today. Her husband, a religious man, has waited years for a promotion. He works in the Admiralty. Do you suppose you could help him?"

"Of course, Father Gregory."

He pressed the papers in her hand, then returned to the subject of the Duma. "Sometimes I fear your enemies in the Duma will kill me."

"I won't permit that," she said. "God would never forgive me."

"If they do kill me," Rasputin intoned, "everything will be swept away . . . even the boy's throne . . . "

She heard him, and believed him.

15

Ash stood lookout for periscopes and drifting mines when the fog lifted. The Germans had torpedoed a Norwegian mail boat a month before in November. Andrew Hazzard said Ash was nuts to stay out on deck in the bitter cold.

Ash reminded him of the Channel steamer *Sussex* and the liner *Arabic*.

"Accidents."

"How about the *Lusitania?*"

"Where've you been, Commander? Everybody knows she was carrying munitions."

"Well, just in case 'everybody' gets the idea that Norwegian mail boats are carrying munitions, I'll stand watch."

An hour before the early northern dusk of the second day, when the steamer was in sight of the Norwegian coast, Andrew came out from the smoking lounge to show Ash a package he had bought from another passenger. Ash glanced away from the empty horizon to take in a beautifully scrimshawed whale tooth.

"Told me it's from Antarctica."

"A beauty," said Ash. "But you better find some regular wrapping paper."

"Newspaper's fine," Andrew said, rolling the tooth up again in the *Daily Mail*.

"Get rid of it, or we'll be a week at customs convincing the Russian police it's not some kind of revolutionary literature."

A sinister-looking black stalk broke the surface two cable lengths from the bow.

111

"Periscope. Port bow."

"Where?" Andrew said suspiciously. "I don't see nothing."

Ship's officers and crew came running, training their glasses. The Scots captain ordered the boats swung out. The periscope paced the steamer while her passengers braved the cold to watch and speculate.

"Catherine," Andrew shouted. "What are you doing here? Get back inside."

"Stay here, miss," the captain told her. "Let the Hun have a good look. And the rest of you pray he's still got an eye for a pretty lass."

Catherine pulled a ribbon from her hair and let it blow in the wind. The periscope lingered, trailing a thin wake. Abruptly it veered toward the distant coast and disappeared in the chop. They watched until a snow squall swept the deck. Ash was following the others into the lounge when he heard two loud cracks from a four-inch gun.

He ran back on deck, afraid the Germans had decided to shell the steamer from the cover of the snow squall. But there were no hits. The captain was leaning from the bridge wing, scanning the squalls with binoculars, apparently as puzzled as Ash.

In twenty minutes they saw a reddish glow in the middle of the squall, like a spark of sunset. A sailing bark lay on her side, her masts in the water, flame spouting from her hull. Half a dozen sailors were pulling away in a long boat; several were wounded. The steamer slowed to pick them up. As the captain jockeyed alongside, Ash saw the sinking bark's cargo spilling into the water. Soon the sea was thick with logs.

"Why would they sink a little boat like that?" Catherine asked. Andrew nodded agreement. "It wasn't hurting anybody."

The dying wooden ship reminded Ash of a bark he had sailed in the South Pacific copra trade when he was Catherine's age. He pointed to the logs bumping against the steamer's hull.

"Pit props from Norway. The British can't mine coal without pit props. *That's* why . . ."

The snow chased them up the fjord to Christiania. Inland, it looked like a blizzard and when the cab driver said there was talk of cancelling trains Ash decided to spend the night at the Grand, a modern hotel overlooking a snowy square up the hill from the harbor.

He counted himself fortunate to get a small suite, though he had to share a room with Andrew; Christiania, the capital of the new nation of Norway, was riding a crest of war profits. The small fishing and trading town had exploded into a sort of Klondike gold rush city and the hotels were packed.

The neutral Norwegians were shipping at high wartime rates for the Allies and supplying canned meats to the German army. Consequently, Ash noticed, the dining room of the Grand Hotel was crowded with rich old gents and pretty young girls.

Andrew and Catherine, so obviously American, and he in his dress blues drew a good deal of attention at dinner. A bewhiskered sea captain sent over a bottle of champagne, and several men asked Catherine to dance, bowing first to Ash for his permission, ignoring young Andrew, who seethed at each intrusion. For her part, Catherine treated Andrew like a younger brother, in spite of their ten-year age difference.

When she came back to their table Catherine reported that the Norwegians favored the Allies.

"What do you expect them to tell you when they've got their arms around you?" Andrew asked.

"No, it's because the Germans have torpedoed so many of their ships. And they asked me when the United States was going to enter the war."

"Never. That's when. This isn't our fight. Uncle Sam's too smart to get mixed up with a bunch of worn out old monarchies—"

"What did you tell them?" Ash cut in.

"I told them our position was quite similar to Norway's," she answered seriously.

Ash gave her a smile of approval . . . He had learned by now how far Page had stretched the situation. Catherine's mother had become sick in Petrograd and was on her way home to Columbus, Ohio, via the Trans-Siberian Railway and the Pacific. Catherine was supposed to take her place as her father's hostess—a considerable job in a city as formal as Petrograd; still, if tonight was any example, Ambassador Hazzard's daughter would by no means embarrass him in Russia . . . Ash caught her giving him an appraising look, part girlish curiosity, part womanly speculation. He was flattered, and intrigued; of course she was very young, but she was also already a real beauty, and her rather grave manner often tended to make her seem more mature than she perhaps was. Extracting the Czar was going to be complicated enough without the seduction of, or by—Ash couldn't predict which—the U.S. ambassador's extremely lovely and precocious sixteen-year-old daughter. Quickly he blocked out that notion by remarking how anxious he was to get to Petrograd to see his old friend Tamara Tishkova dance at the Maryinski Theater.

Catherine was, literally, wide-eyed. "A ballerina? Did you meet her in Petrograd? Or in Paris."

Ash had neglected to mention that when he'd last heard, Tamara had finally succumbed to the Romanov Grand Duke Valery and had let him install her in her own mansion on the banks of the Neva River.

"Where'd you meet her?" Catherine persisted.

"Portsmouth, New Hampshire, as a matter of fact."

"How'd you meet a Russian ballerina in New Hampshire?" Andrew demanded.

Ash stood up. "Bedtime. Early train to Stockholm."

"Come on, Commander, how'd you meet her?"

The dining room had begun to roar. The Norwegians looked as if they had settled in for a long night's drinking. Ash waved his thanks to the sea captain who'd sent the bottle. "I met Tamara in nineteen hundred and five at the Russian-Japanese peace conference. I was naval aide to President Roosevelt's negotiator. Okay?"

"Well, well . . . you must have been a real live wire back then to get a job like that," Andrew said, and waved the bottle invitingly.

Ash didn't really feel like going upstairs alone, not yet. He sat down again and accepted more champagne when Andrew poured.

"Okay, seriously, how'd you get a job like that?"

"Do you remember when Teddy Roosevelt led the Rough Riders up San Juan Hill?"

"Sure. We read about it in school. Spanish-American War, 1898."

"Well, you probably didn't read that right before the charge—on foot, incidentally, since we left Florida too fast to pack the horses—Colonel Roosevelt slipped off a gangway and fell in the drink. As luck would have it, I was standing in an open loading port and the colonel practically landed at my feet. I reached in, hauled him out and lent him a pair of dry pants. The rest, as they say, is history. The good colonel was generous in his thanks and shortly after became President, for reasons you also read in school." Ash drained his glass. "I've been sailing in his wake ever since."

"What happened when the damned Democrats took over?"

"T.R. passed me along to his nephew Franklin."

Andrew reddened. "That man has all the earmarks of becoming a traitor to his class . . . Can I ask you something?"

"Sure." Andrew looked several sheets to the wind, and Catherine was nodding. Wait 'til they hit the Russian vodka, Ash thought.

"With all the opportunities in the good old U.S. of A., why the hell would a fellow with gumption want to join the navy and live on the public payroll?"

"Not everyone has the ability to sell railroad wheels."

"Come on . . . don't be smart—"

"All right. Here it is . . . my father gave me two choices. Join his law practice or run the plantation."

"Plantation?"

"Every Southerner who can support one owns a plantation. Ours has kept the family in a kind of splendid poverty for generations. Neither of the Old Man's choices appealed to me and I'd already been to sea and liked it. So I joined the navy."

114

"You're from West Virginia?"

"Lewisburg. Just outside Greenbriar."

"I know it. Is your father Charles Ash?"

"Yes."

Andrew whistled amazement. "He practically owns the state."

"No. He practically *runs* the state. He *owns* damned little. A big difference." The difference being, Ash thought, that you couldn't inherit what your father only ran.

"What about the ballerina?" asked Catherine, blinking herself awake.

"Good morning to you . . . What about her?"

"What was she doing in Portsmouth, New Hampshire?"

"Tamara was . . . along for the ride, you might say."

"Well, are you still . . . are you going to marry her?"

"It seems she has her sights set a little higher than the navy."

"How high?" Andrew demanded.

"I really am going to bed," said Ash, suddenly very unhappy with the direction of the talk. How high? Higher, damn it, than he had ever been able to offer.

The Stockholm train pushed a rotary snowplow out of the Christiania station, and they were applauding the good fortune of having a compartment to themselves when a Russian in a shabby overcoat stumbled down the corridor with two big satchels and spotted the empty seat. He came in apologetically, hoisted his bags onto the luggage rack before the porter trailing him could help. The train conductor came in and seemed surprised when he produced a first class ticket.

He spoke good English and turned out to be as talkative as Andrew Hazzard. Before the train had climbed past the first farms above Christiania, he had introduced himself and told what he did and where he was going. Like Andrew, he represented himself as a salesman, but there was something off-key about him that made Ash uneasy.

His name was Protopopov—no relation to the Czar's incompetent Minister of the Interior, he hastened to assure them—and he was heading home to Moscow from a sales trip for a Russian match factory that had been built by a Scottish manufacturer on the upper Neva River above Petrograd. British investors, he said, were attracted to the location by the cheap labor and the waterpower and by the Russian government's wise investment incentives; the only difficulty was the natural laziness of the Russian worker.

"Same damned thing back home," Andrew put in.

"It's been suggested that the Russian working class—the so-called proletariat—are misled by incompetent factory managers," Protopopov said. "But that's not true."

Ash asked, "How can you sell matches abroad while Russia's at war?"

"Russia needs to trade for currency to buy arms. Our factories are a disgrace. I mean, we can't produce enough arms."

"How come you're not in the army?" Andrew asked.

Protopopov responded with an enormous, slow shrug that took Ash back to the Russia he remembered; the gesture seemed to marry European sophistication and Oriental fatalism. "There are ways not to be drafted . . . if you know important people. But what I do is necessary—as good to pay for rifles as shoot them. Yes? The peasants at the front have no weapons. They're told to pick up the rifle when the man carrying it is shot. It is criminal. If you can believe the truth of such a story."

"What if the Russian army just quits fighting?" Hazzard asked.

"They won't," Protopopov answered gloomily. "The Russian army is a peasant army and the Russian peasant knows how to suffer."

"What does that have to do with it?"

"Suffer? There's only one way to suffer. You wait. And our peasant soldiers can wait longer than the Germans."

Ash invited Protopopov to join them for lunch in the dining car, which seemed to please Catherine. Inside his oversized, badly cut wool suit was a well-built young man who reminded Ash of a ballet dancer. He had a handsome face, a little too thin, and dark, soulful eyes which settled increasingly on the ambassador's daughter as he answered a steady barrage of questions from Andrew. He attacked the lunch of pickled fish like a starving man.

Ash ate quietly, listening while Andrew did his work for him, asking questions about Russia which seemed provoked as much by his wary appraisal of the mutual attraction smouldering between Catherine and Protopopov as by a traveler's curiosity.

"What's Russia's big problem in the war? Why can't you folks get moving?"

Chaos at home, Protopopov told him. "Everyone is saying the Czar must go, the Czar must go. The Czar's ministers are corrupt fools. The Czarina has usurped the government while the Czar tries to command the army . . . But we Russians are great complainers."

"But if they can't run the government, maybe they ought to be kicked out."

Protopopov shrugged. "The railroads are the real problem. All trains are commandeered for troops. Nothing else moves. No food, no fuel. It is criminal that the railroads weren't ready for war."

"Isn't that the Czar's fault?"

"There are some who say so."

"But not you," Catherine said as their eyes met.

116

"Not me."

"My father agrees with you. He's the American ambassador to Russia—"

"The American ambassador?" Protopopov said it with appropriate awe.

"Yes, and he wrote me that all this talk against the Czar sounds like nothing more than a lot of talk to him. A bunch of hot air."

Protopopov blinked. "May I ask has your father been in Petrograd long?"

"Two months."

"Ah."

Swedish customs officials boarded the train at the Norwegian frontier with elaborate questionnaires and strict warnings about imports. Ash presented a diplomatic *laissez-passer* Ambassador Page had procured from the Swedish Embassy, then went back to the baggage car to prevent any accidental inspection of his bachelor chest. When he returned, the Swedes were still scrutinizing Protopopov's satchels. Matchboxes were spilled all over the seats.

Why, if he was selling Russian matches abroad, was he returning to Russia with matches, Swedish customs demanded to know. Could it be that he was importing Norwegian matches into Sweden?

Protopopov patiently showed them the Cyrillic Russian lettering on the matchboxes. "I am not permitted to sell these samples. I must return the samples. I can only take orders." He showed them his order book, pages filled in neat Cyrillic letters and Arabic numbers.

Andrew watched in a way that reminded Ash of himself when he had first come to Europe—slightly astonished by everything he had seen, often amazed, occasionally awed. Protopopov finally convinced the customs men, and the train started the two-hundred-mile leg across lower Sweden to Stockholm. The Russian became silent and gazed out the window at the snow, the fir trees on the gentle slopes and the frozen lakes.

Ash felt their chill.

"What kind of a city is Petrograd?" Catherine asked Protopopov after several earlier questions had failed to cheer him up.

"Petrograd is a pit of corruption."

Catherine looked astonished. She turned to Ash, "You've been there before, Commander. Do you agree?"

"Not as recently as Mr. Protopopov, but I think it's the most beautiful city I've ever seen."

Protopopov snorted disagreement. "A swamp."

Ash said, "Remember Mr. Protopopov told us he was born in Moscow. So asking him about Petrograd is like asking a man from Chicago what he thinks of New York. I think Petrograd's the most attractive city in Europe."

"You haven't seen it since Rasputin's taken power."

Catherine nodded. "That's the weird monk father wrote about."

"Sounded like a strange character," Andrew said.

"Rasputin is a pig." Protopopov turned red and his lips actually started quivering under his thin mustache. "Actually, he's a monster."

"What does he do that's so—?"

"Rasputin controls the Czarina. She's German already and the monk corrupts—" He paused and reconsidered and continued more calmly. "There are rumors that she . . ." He glanced at Catherine, ". . . has been corrupted by him. Terrible stories. And some people believe them and think that she is betraying Russia to Germany. They say that Rasputin forces her to appoint ministers he selects. Corrupt incompetents and fools. And she forces the Czar to do things Rasputin tells her and the Czar goes along because he's busy leading the army, which he is incapable of doing —or so I am told." He seemed uneasy.

"Sounds to me like the Czar's as dumb as the rest of the kings who got Europe into this stupid war," said Andrew.

"It would be better not to talk that way when you get to Russia," Protopopov told him. "The police are everywhere."

"What can they do to me? I'm an American citizen. So's Catherine. Plus we've got the navy along to protect us. Right, Commander Ash?"

"You can't go far wrong being a good guest, Andrew."

"Sure, Commander, but don't you find it tough being an American and having to put up with all this royalty nonsense over here? These guys couldn't get elected dog catcher back in Ohio."

Ash was watching a pair of Swedish peasants trying to pry a sledge out of a snowdrift beside the tracks. One had his shoulder to the sledge, the other was beating a shaggy pony with a stick.

"Like it or not," Ash said, "the royals are the center of social, military, political and cultural life in Europe. The Kaiser's tastes in architecture and art, his brand of patriotism are Germany's; the King of England is the pillar of the English aristocracy, who control Britain's wealth; and the Czar rules a hundred and eighty million Russian peasants who've been raised to think Nicholas II is their direct link to God."

"That's got to change."

Ash looked at him sharply. "Well, if you want to understand Europe you've got to understand that these three royals have power unlike anything we've got at home. If they're ever gone they'll leave a huge vacuum in Europe. Who knows what would fill it."

Catherine said, "The United States will. Don't you agree, Commander Ash?"

Who knew what senator's vote the ambassador's daughter might some-

118

day control with her serious smile? So Ash said, "Not without a bigger navy." But his private thoughts were much more on the Czar, his removal without chaos and the U.S. getting into the war on the side of the Allies.

Protopopov disappeared to send a cable in Stockholm and almost missed the train. They had changed to a sleeper bound north up the coast of the Gulf of Bothnia, the northern arm of the Baltic Sea. Russian Finland lay a short boat trip across the water, but here in the Baltic the naval situation between the Allies and Germany was reversed.

The Baltic was a German sea. The Czar's navy hid in port and German squadrons controlled the surface, except for a handful of brave, even lunatic, British submariners—Ash's friend Rodney Skelton among them— who attacked German shipping from the shallow depths. The railroad took the long way around.

The terrain, broken occasionally by small towns and villages, remained the same for the rest of daylight and was the same the following morning when the sun finally came up at eleven. It sloped gently to the east, down to the gulf—green fir trees, white birches, rivers and lakes flattened under snow and ice. The sun hung low on the horizon, barely clearing the treetops and lighting a spectacularly colored dawn that kept on looking like dawn even as the afternoon approached and the train neared the Finnish border. Ash had never been so far north—fifteen degrees from the Arctic Circle, higher on the planet than most of Alaska. The train tracks ended at Haparanda on the bank of the Tornea River.

Protopopov had the same difficulties as he had entering, convincing the Swedish inspectors that his Russian match samples were indeed from Russia. Outside the customs building sleighs were waiting that carried two people each, with luggage. Ash took Catherine aside.

"Please ride with Andrew."

"But I already promised Misha." During breakfast Protopopov had invited her to use the diminutive for his given name Michael. "Why shouldn't I ride with Misha?"

"Because I don't want you seen arriving with him."

"Catherine," Protopopov called from the sleigh. "Hurry up." Andrew waited truculently by another sleigh.

"Why in the world can't I arrive with whom I please?"

Ash briefly considered threatening to turn her over his knee. "You're the daughter of the American ambassador, Catherine. You shouldn't be connected with Protopopov if he has trouble entering the Russian Duchy of Finland."

Ash expected another question. Instead, she promptly said, "All right, Commander. Then I'll ride with you." She walked to an empty sleigh and extended her hand for Ash to help her in. Protopopov looked appropriately sad. Andrew glared.

The sleigh drivers cracked their whips and they started through the streets of the town—packed snow tracks between frame houses—Ash and Catherine's sleigh in the lead. The cold, the wind and pale sun were exhilarating after the hours on the train.

Suddenly the sleigh swooped down onto the frozen river. The horse broke into a fast trot, heading for a windswept island in the middle a quarter mile away. *"Cold,"* Catherine said between clenched teeth, "but isn't this beautiful?"

Ash pulled the lap robe over their legs. The sun glinted in her hair, and when the sleigh lurched she took hold of his arm. Ash glanced back. Andrew and Protopopov were sitting stiffly in the next sleigh, which was far behind them. He would have preferred that Andrew not be with the Russian either, because Protopopov really did seem destined for trouble at customs.

Catherine's eyes darted everywhere—the broad river, the low island, the forested slopes on the other side and the train of sleighs behind.

"Look!" A long line of freight sledges were crossing the river upstream and the sun etched their silhouettes darkly against the snow.

The horse broke into a canter, gathering momentum for the banks of the island. Catherine grabbed Ash's arm with both hands, laughed excitedly as it scrambled up the slope and dragged the bouncing sleigh to a sudden halt in front of a wooden turnstile.

A soldier wearing dirty sheepskin and a balisk hood watched them climb down from the sleigh. Beyond the gate was a loose cluster of rough wooden buildings—warehouse, barracks and customs house, all unpainted and reminding Ash of pictures of western frontier towns. The soldier put his shoulder to the gate and pointed at the customs house. Their driver threw down their luggage, whipped his horse back toward the river and left them standing alone in the snowy square on the edge of the Russian Empire.

16

A portrait of Czar Nicholas, looking fit and handsome and very much like King George, gazed paternally down on the customs desks. But a silver-framed life-size icon depicting Christ on the cross dominated the dirty, whitewashed room. Beneath it sat an old woman in black, selling candles.

The Russians among the train travelers—officers from the battalions lent to France, military attachés and a few civilians like Protopopov—crowded around the icon, bought her candles and lighted them in silver holders. By the time the Swedish sleighs had deposited the passengers and the shaggy, bearded Russian porters had dragged the luggage in from the square, the icon blazed in candle flame.

The Czar's police opened their registers, began running their fingers down endless columns of names, whispering to each other as the travelers presented their papers. Andrew urged Ash ahead. Ash told him to ease up. No one was leaving the island, it was clear, until the Russians had checked everyone through the border post.

Soldiers guarded the doors, the entrances to a foul-smelling restaurant, to private offices, and the stockade, where Ash had seen forlorn faces peering through the cracks. He showed their papers, including the *laissez-passer* Ambassador Page had acquired from the Russian Embassy in London. Attached were copies of the Russian Embassy's orders to correct Ash's file and officially apologize for the "inconvenience" Ash had suffered on the train from Zurich. A lamentable "blunder" in the embassy's words, for which Ash deserved "every courtesy."

Catherine and Andrew stayed close. Andrew, awed at first into rare silence by the grim-looking customs examiners, the conspiritorial muttering among the police and the anxious expressions worn by many of the train passengers, finally whispered to Catherine, "Boy, they look scared . . . say, there's Protopopov. I'd say he looks scared too."

The Russian stood on line nearby, fingering his papers and casting a worried eye on his satchels, which a porter had dropped beside the examiner's desk. He looked their way and gave Catherine a weak smile.

The commandant of the border post burst through the privet office door, welcomed by the police and soldiers with a flurry of salutes. He was a youngish-looking, cold-eyed man wearing a spotless green police uniform with captain's insignia. He greeted Ash in precise English, then bowed over Catherine's hand. "The daughter of the American ambassador honors our outpost." His manner was cool, formal. Catherine introduced Andrew. The commandant nodded, then turned back to Ash. "May I have your party's papers, Commander Ash?"

Ash handed them to the commandant, who tested the papers' weight with his fingertips as he passed them to an officer seated before an open register and said to Ash, "A necessary formality in time of war."

"Of course, Commandant. You will be particularly interested in this letter from the Russian ambassador to Great Britain."

"You will excuse me, please." He saluted, turned and disappeared with their papers.

"Friendly so and so," Andrew remarked.

"Keep it down, Andrew—"

"Don't get that way with me, *Commander*, I've had about enough of your telling us what to do—"

"Andrew, please . . ." Catherine said.

Ash said quietly, "If you say or do the slightest thing that delays us on this miserable island I will take you out to the river, chop a hole in the ice and shove you through it."

"Commander!"

"That's okay, Catherine, he's just talking big. He won't be so big in Petrograd, just another—"

Ash silenced him with a sharp look. Beside them, Protopopov's turn had come. The Russian started clasping and unclasping his hands as his satchels were opened. Nervous and it showed, thought Ash. But why? The Swedes had already let him pass.

The Czar's police noticed his fidgeting. They gathered around, ignoring the other travelers, and watched one examiner spread the matchboxes on the table while another poured over his book of names.

"What's he looking for?" Andrew muttered.

"They keep lists of undesirables," Ash said quietly. "Revolutionaries, criminals and spies. Since the war . . ."

"Is that why he took our papers?"

"Checking they weren't forgeries."

122

The customs examiner asked Protopopov a question in Russian. Protopopov answered. Another question. A second officer joined the interrogation, bringing another ledger.

The commandant came back, fired questions at Protopopov, who continued to answer coolly and had, by visible effort, managed to get his hands under control, though his fingers kept clawing at his pant leg.

The commandant dumped the contents of one of the satchels on the desk. Matchboxes spilled out, and the room grew quiet as the other travelers stopped their own whispered conversations to watch.

"Here we go again," Andrew muttered. "I'm glad as hell I don't have to carry my samples around like he does."

The commandant felt inside Protopopov's bag for a false bottom. There was none, and he threw it aside in disgust. He turned his attention to the heaped matchboxes. Protopopov spread his hands, said something in Russian. The commandant ignored him. Suddenly he scooped up a single matchbox and pulled it open and scattered the matches on the table.

"What's he doing?" Catherine whispered. "It's only matches."

Ash watched the commandant. A bird dog sniffing the wind. At random, he emptied six more match boxes, found nothing and seemed ready to give it up. Then an examiner shoved his ledger triumphantly under the commandant's nose.

"Commander *Ash* . . ."

"Captain?" Ash said coolly, reminding the Russian that beyond this outpost Ash was the ranking officer.

"Did you travel with this man?"

"We boarded the same train in Christiania."

"And did you travel with him the entire way?"

"Yes."

"Through Norway?"

"Yes."

"Through Sweden?"

"I told you yes, Commandant. We were on the same train . . . the only train, Commandant, so far as I could see."

"Did he have these satchels when he boarded your train?"

"He showed them when we crossed the Swedish frontier."

"It is not my name," Protopopov interrupted calmly. "It is a mistake in the book. I am Mikhail Vladimirovitch Protopopov. You have found Mikhail *Vadimovitch* Protopopov. A man I do not know." He spread his hands in innocence and added, "Perhaps related to the new Minister of the Interior."

Ash saw immediately that Protopopov had made a terrible error; the boy hadn't the experience to know that one needed to treat functionaries very seriously. The commandant flushed at the jibe; the Interior Minister's vast domain included the police.

He snapped his fingers and picked up a matchbox. He spilled the matches out as he had before, but this time he ripped the box itself apart.

Inside was a sheet of paper folded many times until it was as thick as a piece of cardboard. Slowly, his eyes on Protopopov, he unfolded it, spread it out on the table, then waved it triumphantly on the air. Black Cyrillic letters stood oversize on a white background, like a headline on a tabloid.

The soldiers seized Protopopov's arms and, at the commandant's orders, dragged him away, protesting loudly.

"*Misha,*" Catherine called after him.

Ash encircled her with his arm to hold her back, but she already had regained control, which seemed to settle something for Protopopov. He stopped struggling, protesting. At the door he squared his thin shoulders and said, rather melodramatically, "Good-bye, Catherine."

The commandant looked from one to the other, unsure. Ash held her tightly. Protopopov threw off the guards, and in the instant before they grabbed him again, he thrust a clenched fist into the air and shouted, "*Kill the Czar . . .*"

Ash kept hold of her after the door slammed shut. "What *is* it? What happened . . . ?"

The commandant turned to her, read the situation correctly. "Not to concern you, young miss. We have detained a revolutionary."

"What did the piece of paper say?"

The commandant picked it up disdainfully. "Inflammatory leaflets, smuggled from Germany. He's a spy and a revolutionary. This paper incites the workers to strike and the soldiers to stop fighting."

"What will happen to him?"

"Commander Ash," said the commandant. "Here are your papers. We apologize for the delay. The war . . . Your sleigh will be ready in a short while." He glanced around the room, flushed with excitement. "In the meantime will you and your charges do me the honor of sharing a toast in my office?"

"Thank you—"

"Excuse me, I will come right back."

Catherine grabbed Ash's arm when he had gone. "No. I *won't* go with him. Poor Misha . . ."

"You would be honored," Ash said quietly, forcing a gentle smile. "And so would Andrew. The commandant has captured a spy. He wants to share his triumph with an important person like you."

"I'm not drinking with him," Andrew said.

"If you don't, Andrew, he will telegraph a friend or relation who works in the Ministry of Interior who knows a man who knows a man who knows someone whose job it is to buy railroad wheels. And when you call on that man, *he* won't drink a toast with *you.*"

"The hell with him, I'll buy my own. Coming, Catherine?" When she hesitated, he stalked off.

Ash said, "I guess we can admire Andrew for doing that. Unfortunately, you and I have more than ourselves and some railroad wheels to consider."

She went with him, asking, "What will they do to Misha?"

He hurried along without answering.

Another picture of the Czar, a large oil, hung in the commandant's office; a more intimate painting, it revealed dreamy eyes and a mouth less strong than King George's. The commandant poured vodka in short glasses, offered a toast to America and tossed it back. He poured again. Ash nodded to Catherine and she spunkily offered a toast to Russian victory. She was learning. A servant in a dirty jacket appeared with a tray of smoked fish and caviar. Before the commandant could persuade Catherine to try it, a soldier came in and conferred with the commandant, who glanced several times at Ash, then dismissed the soldier. "Would you be so kind, mademoiselle, to excuse Commander Ash and myself a brief moment." He stepped out and Ash followed. In the hall the commandant said, "The prisoner has confessed something unusual. It concerns you . . . you had better hear it yourself." He took Ash through a pair of guarded doors and into a windowless cell. Protopopov was slumped in a chair, breathing harshly through his mouth. They had broken his nose and there was blood on his face and deep cuts around his eyes. He flinched as he looked up. But when he saw Ash he tried to smile, revealing blood on his teeth.

Ash was through being diplomatic. "Was this necessary?" he asked coldly.

"He is a revolutionary and a German spy," the commandant replied just as coldly.

"I am not a spy."

"Then why were you following Commander Ash?"

"What?"

Protopopov looked at Ash. "I'm sorry. They gave me passes and train tickets if I would tell them where you were going."

"Who?"

"Germans."

"*What* Germans?"

"I don't know. The Germans who help the revolution."

"The German army," the commandant answered for him. "The army sends spies. We catch them every time."

"I am *not* a spy. I only did it to return to Russia—"

"What exactly did you do?" Ash asked him.

"I telephoned the German Embassy in Stockholm and told them you were still on the train and heading to Petrograd."

"What did they say?"

"They . . . they told me to kill you."

Ash's head was reeling from the vodka. "And what were you waiting for?" This was Catherine's "poor Misha"?

Protopopov's bruised eyes opened wider. "I couldn't. I only said I would to make them send me home."

"But you would kill the Czar," the commandant said.

"That is different."

"You're at best a fool," the commandant said. "A German dupe—"

"What did they say in Stockholm when you said you hadn't killed me?"

"They were angry. They threatened to hurt my comrades in Germany. They made me promise to telegraph if you left the train in Sweden."

"What about in Finland? What about Petrograd?"

"No. Only in Sweden."

"Misha," Ash said, crouching beside the chair to meet him eye to eye. "Misha. Didn't they ask you to report from Petrograd?"

"No. They only said to telegraph if you left the train in Sweden." He looked briefly at the commandant, then at the floor. "It was a general who told me to kill you."

"Which general?"

"I don't know."

"Where?"

"Spa. In Belgium . . ." He murmured something then to Ash.

"What did you say?" the commandant broke in.

Misha looked up. "I asked him to kiss Catherine's hand for me." Russian to the last, Ash thought.

And then he also thought . . . Spa. German Army Western Front Headquarters were at Spa . . . Ludendorff? Had he, Ash wondered, gotten caught up in some conflict between General Ludendorff and Kaiser Wilhelm? Had he stepped in the middle of a powerplay between the Germany army and the German monarchy?

Ash looked back at Misha, huddled in the cell. Well, the boy had done his job. Now the Germans knew he was in the Russian Duchy of Finland . . . Except what could the German army do to him in Russia . . . ? Well, what had they done already . . . ? He thought of their agents, the girl in the Zurich brothel and the conductor who had tossed the bomb on the train. Switzerland was neutral, easy for German agents to penetrate. But France sure as hell wasn't neutral and they'd come at him again with all four feet right in the middle of Paris. . . .

Halfway to the shore of Finland, Ash heard the firing squad.

Catherine started beside him. "What was that?"

126

The ragged volley was wind-whipped and muffled by the snow. Ash pointed down river at the endless line of freight sledges moving across the snow-covered ice. The caravan stretched for miles, hundreds of horse-drawn sledges in close formation. The shots could have been the snap of whips, or even the ice cracking, he told her. She nodded as if she believed him, but when Ash looked down at her a moment later, he saw tears on her cheeks. Without saying a word he slipped his arm around her shoulders and held her close to him for several long moments.

Ahead, the Finnish forest rose on gentle slopes along the river, green northern firs sprinkled with birch, similar to the forests they had seen in Sweden. But suddenly there spouted like fire from the green trees a dazzling red—the low sun blazing on a cluster of golden onion-dome church spires.

Catherine stared at the gleaming steeples, blinking and brushing her coat sleeve at her eyes. Ash gave her his handkerchief. His own astonished first glimpse of that quintessential mark of Russian territory nine years earlier and hundreds of miles to the south had been through tears too. But they had been tears of champagne laughter in Tamara's compartment as the majestic Imperial train glided home on cleared track returning the Czar's delegates from the final Hague Peace Conference. All but the chief of the delegation, the Grand Duke Valery, had stayed behind to represent Czar Nicholas at another meeting in Paris, and Tamara had invited Ash to escort her back to Russia. It had been the best of times. Tamara . . .

"Civilization," Andrew Hazzard crowed happily when they boarded the Finnish National Railroad for Petrograd. Outside the train Russian soldiers and bearded porters tramped about in the snow and the strange Cyrillic letters adorned the Torneo station signs, but aboard were soft velvet, polished wood and glass, and English-speaking attendants in dapper European uniforms.

The third bell rang and the train moved out—a sealed capsule of Europe gliding through an alien land. Catherine's station had garnered three adjoining compartments. Ash took the center one, which they agreed to use as their sitting room.

Andrew flopped down on the plush seat and mopped his face with a handkerchief. "Say, I got a terrific bun on drinking those Russian highballs."

"You've been drinking?"

"Well, yes I have."

"I thought father wrote that they had banned the sale of vodka for the war."

"Oh they did. So they sell it in tea glasses. Big tall ones. Blew me into the next block."

Catherine took the furthest seat from him and stared out the window, her face a mask.

"Know what I heard?" Andrew asked. "A fellow told me that the Russians laid their tracks wider than Europe to keep invaders out. Didn't work, though. It never occurred to the ninnies that it's easy as pie to narrow railroad tracks. All the Germans had to do was pick up one rail and shove it over. Japs did it to 'em in the last war. On the Siberian railroad. Then the cunning little devils cut the ties off. These folks are really backward, aren't they, Commander?"

Ash was wondering what Tamara would do if he came knocking. He couldn't begin to guess what her feelings would be after these three years; his own were still chaotic, the rare times he let them surface. But one thing was certain, if he ever did drop in on her, which he swore he wouldn't, Tamara would show him what she felt. She was not a woman to hide anger, or excitement, passion, or even as he knew too well, cold regret. He tried to smile as he thought of the way she tossed her jet black hair when she was happy, and the fire in her dark, sloe eyes, but it hurt too much. If only . . . if only—

"Aren't they, Commander?"

"What . . . ?"

"Backward."

"I suppose . . . three thousand miles and two centuries from Europe."

Andrew laughed. "That makes 'em six thousand miles and *three* centuries from the U.S."

"Just remember the Russians think they're the center of the world."

"That's rich." Andrew laughed. "Center of nowhere, you ask me."

The sun had dropped beneath the horizon, and a blue darkness was gathering on the snow in the forests. Catherine pulled the curtains over her window. "When do we get to Petrograd, Commander?"

"Tomorrow midnight."

Ironically, Ash thought, it was Tamara's grand duke who probably could arrange the swiftest audience with the Czar, being a first cousin, and close in line for the throne himself. Unless, of course, he didn't choose to shoot Ash on sight, which, Ash reflected with a smile, *he* would certainly do if their situations were reversed. But the fact was he would not knock on Tamara's door, and certainly not for a favor. He had enough problems without falling in love with Tamara again; and it struck him that if Germany had half the spies in Petrograd people claimed, then, indeed, the German army *could* come gunning for him in the Russian capital . . .

128

He was relieved when his charges went straight to bed after dinner—Andrew half-drunk and Catherine sad and moody with reflections of the late Mr. Protopopov in her eyes. The attendants had made up the bed. He climbed in and read some Robert Service he had brought because the Queen had mentioned the author at dinner. The train was making good speed over the gentle terrain and the coach began a rhythmic swaying. Ash reached for the light switch just as there was a knock from Catherine's door.

"It's not locked. Come in." He sat up, braced his back in the corner and pulled the blankets over his chest.

He heard her unlock her side. She was wearing a wool nightgown. Ruffles topped the high neck and ran down the front. The gown touched the toes of her slippers and covered her arms to the wrists, where more ruffles half hid her hands. He was surprised by her breasts. Unrestrained by daytime undergarments they pushed insistently against the gown. Her face was the same mask it had been since they had heard the firing squad. No . . . not quite the same; her cheeks were flushed.

"I can't sleep," she said.

"Would you like a little brandy?"

"No. May I sit up with you a while?"

"If you want to." He nodded at the opposite seat, which was still in the upright position. She sat there, pulled her knees up to her breasts and clasped her arms around them. She was silent. He waited. Then she said, "Now I'm cold."

"Go get your blanket."

"Would you get it for me?"

"I'm not dressed."

"Oh." She went for it herself and returned wrapping it around her shoulders. A rag doll fell from it and landed in the doorway. She was already sitting down again on the seat and didn't notice. Ash did, and it made him smile, and tugged at his heart, at the same time.

"What did you do when your mother and father went to Russia?" he asked her.

"I made them let me try college."

"Where?"

"Smith. Mother was scandalized. College for a girl and in the East, no less . . . but I couldn't even finish the first term. When she got sick I had to leave immediately for London . . . I feel so frightened tonight . . ."

"Misha was fighting a war," Ash said, picking up her meaning immediately. "You have to understand that the people at the border thought he was their enemy. Perhaps, in a way, he was."

"He was so nice. That counts for me."

Ash said, "He asked me to promise to kiss your hand for him."

"Did he? Well, I'm waiting."

"It was the thought."

"You wouldn't deny a dying man's last wish . . ." She got up and extended her hand.

Ash held her small, delicate fingers in his, bowed his head and kissed her hand, wondering what Ambassador Hazzard would do to his career if Andrew just happened to barge in now.

She sat down. "Thank you, that was very nice . . ."

The blanket had fallen from his shoulder. She saw the scar. "You were shot?"

"It's a birthmark."

"It is not. It's a bullet hole."

"How would you know a bullet hole?"

"Andrew has one. In his leg, from when he was a Pinkerton."

"Andrew was a Pinkerton detective? When did he switch to selling railroad equipment?"

"Just a little while ago. He came along at the last minute. I guess he thinks my dad can help him . . . Do you know why I'm frightened, really? I don't know if I can take my mother's place. And my father's never even been an ambassador before."

"He's not the first," said Ash. "And with all due respect to your mother, I'm sure you're going to do an even better job than she could. Besides, you won't be all alone in this. Your father has a staff ready to help. And there are other embassy wives. In fact, I seem to remember that the British ambassador's daughter is there. She's not much older than you. She and her mother will be helpful. You'll do just fine."

"Will you be there?"

". . . I'll be around, occasionally."

"I'll make my father order you to come every day."

Ash had no doubt that she could make her father shell the Winter Palace if she felt like it. "I'd like that very much," he said. "Unfortunately Ambassador Page might miss me. But I will be around . . . Getting sleepy?"

"A little." She squirmed around in the blanket, exposing an ankle, covering it. "I hate going back in there alone tonight. I *am* upset about Misha. I'd just met him and he was killed . . . Can I just stay here?"

"If you want . . . I'm going to turn the light out now. Are you sure you're warm enough?"

"If I'm not I'll just snuggle up against you."

Ash calculated the remark to be about forty-five percent innocence and said firmly, "I wouldn't recommend that, young lady."

He turned out the light and lay on his side. The light spilling from Catherine's compartment fell on the rag doll.

"Commander Ash?"

"What?"

"Who shot you?"

130

"A crazy anarchist."

"Why?"

"He was aiming at someone else."

"Oh . . . Commander Ash?"

"*What?*"

"Why are Europeans so . . . violent?"

"Some of them ask the same question about us. I guess maybe it's got something to do with the centuries they've had to form rivalries, hatreds, to oppress each other, their own people. It's a pretty complicated subject for bedtime discussion . . ." He closed his eyes and murmured a sleepy good-night as the train wheels chattered him to sleep . . . .

Catherine woke him up, shaking his shoulder. He reached for her hand, dreaming he was elsewhere, but let go, surprised to feel such small fingers.

"The train stopped," she said.

"Go to sleep."

"There are soldiers outside."

17

Ash peered out the crack Catherine had opened in the shade. Car lights glared on the snow. He saw soldiers with rifles, heard them calling to each other. The train doors began banging at both ends of the carriage.

"Go to your compartment."

"I'm afraid—"

"Then face the wall or something, I've got to get dressed."

He threw off the blankets and got hurriedly into his blues. Heavy boots pounded down the corridor. The conductor knocked. "Commander Ash, Commander Ash. Please open your door."

"Go in with Andrew and don't open the outside door."

She knocked on Andrew's door. He was awake too and holding a snub-nosed revolver like he knew how to use it. "Put that damned thing away," said Ash. "Don't let anyone in. I'll deal with them."

"What's up?"

"Don't know yet." He closed Andrew's door and opened up to the conductor. "What the hell do you want?"

He saw two tall soldiers standing behind the conductor, who looked distinctly perturbed. "The train is delayed, Commander."

"I can see that."

"And you are supposed to go with this officer."

"What?" They were Finns bundled in sheepskin and balisk hoods.

"He has papers to take you to the local barracks, Commander."

"I'm traveling with *laissez-passer* from the Russian ambassador to Great Britain on a United States diplomatic mission. Tell him I'm not getting off this train."

Ash started to close the door. The soldiers drew pistols and two more

132

appeared behind them with rifles. "There is nothing we can do to help," the conductor said.

"Send a wire to Petrograd to the Ministry of Foreign Affairs and another to the American Embassy."

"The wires are cut. And the track is torn up. I'm sure the train will still be here when you get back."

Ash wasn't at all sure, but he had no choice. And with Protopopov's confession in mind, he didn't like the look of this at all. He reached for his sword to buckle it on; they gestured with their guns to leave it.

Northern Lights were flickering sporadically on the horizon as they marched Ash off the train and drove him away in a big open touring car with clanking chains to push it through the snow drifts. A machine gun was mounted on a tripod in the back seat. Soldiers stood on the running boards and from what he could see there were several more in a car behind. Apparently not a German among them, though none spoke English. Finns and a few squat Russians. And, he realized, no officers, despite the claim of the one with the pistol.

He looked back. The train lights had disappeared. The air was bitter cold, at least twenty below. Ice froze his mustache. They had gone two or three miles when the car seemed to set out across an open field. The land fell away flat in the starlight, and when the Northern Lights flickered again he realized the road was actually a causeway over a frozen marsh. It led to an enormous dark hunting lodge set in a pine and birch forest.

The lodge was taller than the trees. Not a window shone; nor did smoke arise from the vast chimneys that spouted from the rooflike castle turrets. Ash figured the trees for a place to run. The soldiers seemed to sense it and closed in on him as the car stopped.

They gestured him out and marched him to the lodge, up the main stairs, across a wooden verandah and through the front door. It was even colder inside the building than out. One of them carried an electric lantern that cast a yellow beam across the foyer. The light landed on a second pair of doors. They pulled them open, shoved Ash in and pulled them shut.

"Hey—"

It was pitch-black. He heard the bolts shoot home, heard their footsteps fade, thought he heard the front doors slam. He took out his gold box and lit a match. He was in a room so big the flame barely touched the ceiling and the far walls.

The match burned out. He walked toward what had looked like a sconce on the wall, fell over something soft, got up and lit another match. The sconce held an oil lamp. He lit the lamp, turned the wick up and looked around. He had fallen over one of the shrouded chairs. He lit another lamp. What the hell had they put him in here for? If they were going to shoot him, why didn't they just shoot him?

The room had no windows, like a ballroom, but the size of the rough stone fireplace and the rustic design confirmed that the house had been built as a hunting lodge—probably for water fowl on the marsh. None of which explained why he was here or why every door he tried was locked.

Should he build a fire before he froze to death? Birch logs were stacked on the hearth. He was breaking up kindling when the doors opened and two tall men in greatcoats walked in. One wore the artificial wool *papaha* of the Russian army; the other, a civilian brimmed hat. They stopped just inside the door, thirty feet across the room, but before they could speak Ash said, "I'm Commander Kenneth Ash, U.S. Navy. I am traveling under diplomatic passport with the *laissez-passer* of the Russian ambassador to Great Britian. I demand to be returned to my train, immediately."

The man with the brimmed hat spoke good English.

"Consider yourself a prisoner of war. I am a colonel in the German army assigned behind Russian lines to recruit the Czar's Finnish troops to fight for Germany . . . they object to Russia calling their nation the Grand Duchy of Finland."

"I don't give a damn who you are, I'm an officer of a neutral nation and—"

"This German-Finnish unit has brought you here to answer a simple question, Commander Ash . . . I have no desire to use physical means to force a brave man to talk, nor do I have any particular expertise in such unpleasantries. However, if you do not answer we will lock you in here with a canister of cholorine gas."

He held up a gas grenade. Ash took a step backward. One part in five thousand parts of air killed. The gas was especially deadly in the trenches because it rolled before the wind and, being heavier than air, literally tumbled into the dugouts. Since the German gas attack at Ypres no soldier went to war without a gas mask.

"What's your question?"

"First raise your hands." The man in the artificial wool cap, a Finn by the look of his long, handsome face, walked up to Ash, checked he had no gun on his hip under the cloak and patted him for a shoulder holster. When he stepped back, Ash lowered his hands slowly to his hips and asked again. "What's your question?" He knew he should be watching the Finn, the man closest, but it was hard to keep his eyes off the gas grenade.

"What did you tell Kaiser Wilhelm?" the German asked.

Ash slipped his fingers back under his tunic and drew the cut-down Luger. The German was out of range. Ash aimed at the Finn and shouted across the room. "Put down the grenade or I'll shoot your friend here."

The Finn's eyes widened. *"Nein* . . . he'll kill us both . . ."

134

But even as he turned and ran, ignoring Ash's gun, his German partner dropped the grenade and slammed the door. The canister exploded with a loud pop, like a champagne cork poorly wrapped. The Finn screamed. A sickly yellow-green cloud enveloped him and rolled toward Ash.

18

The Finn writhed inside the yellow-green gas cloud. He clawed at his throat, tried to run and collapsed in a twitching heap. The canister hissed, spewing more gas. Ash could not see the doors through the cloud and knew where the dying Finn was only by the man's strangled cough. Half the ballroom had filled with the green haze. One part in five thousand killed. And the cloud kept growing, rolling.

Ash had, he calculated, thirty or forty seconds. One part in five thousand, one microscopic inhalation. He looked for windows. If there hadn't been windows earlier there wouldn't be windows now. Twenty-five seconds. A tendril of cloud reached from the mass like a finger, beckoning, choosing. The Finn was silent.

Ash backed up until he hit the wall. Fifteen seconds. The canister hissed. One narrow, shrinking alley of pure air remained. Twelve feet in front of the fireplace. Twelve feet of pure air, now eleven, now ten. Ash backed into the fireplace, pressed his shoulders against the blackened fire wall and got ready to die.

The yellow-green chlorine gas hovered in front.

For one wild, joyous moment Ash thought that a draft down the chimney would hold off the gas. But when the cloud kept moving as the canister hissed in the eerie silence he realized that the cold inside the unheated lodge was so close to the temperature outside that there could be no down draft, nothing to keep the cloud from this last pure niche. Ten seconds?

Should he hold his breath? Or take the poison all at once to get it over with fast?

He filled his lungs with the last pure air, filled deep.

The chimney.

He looked up the great flue of the enormous fireplace. The gas was heavier than air. Maybe it couldn't rise . . . Ash stood on an andiron and grabbed the rough bricks and kicked and clawed his way up the narrow shaft. The bricks blocked his shoulders. He turned himself diagonally to the opening and reached up and pulled. His fingers found iron projections planted for the chimney sweep, and he pulled on them and hauled himself higher and got his boots planted so that he was standing inside the chimney. He took a new breath, and when it didn't kill him, started climbing.

When he emerged from the chimney Ash spotted the dotted line of train lights several miles across the flat marsh. A reddish glow flickered against the trees near the house, presumably the quiescent Northern Lights. He took a bearing on the train relative to the North Star while he rested on the chimney top. Then he scanned the steep roof for a way down.

His perch was on the back side, and higher than the peak, permitting him to see the entire roof and all its chimneys. He figured to head for a drainpipe, but it was very dark to traverse the sharply angled slate surface. The Northern Lights flared abruptly, streaming crimson across the sky, lighting the slates.

A bullet smacked into the chimney brick, inches from his hand, and a dozen shots rang out. Ash jumped some ten feet to the roof and slid down the slates. The soldiers kept pumping rifle fire at him.

He dug his heels in, slowed his descent and tried to scramble back up to the peak. The back side faced north, and the Aurora Borealis was bright enough to read by. A bullet whined past his head and caromed off the slate. He ducked behind another chimney, but they had seen him and concentrated fire around the chimney until the air was filled with ricochets.

Ash flicked his cloak tails out one side, drew their fire, and ran from the other, scrambled for the peak, flung himself over the top, out of sight of the riflemen. They had built a bonfire in front of the house beside the cars. The machine gun raked the roof from end to end, the heavy caliber slugs ripping up the slates; high shots cracking past his head like whips. He ducked and ran, zigzagging, trying not to lose control and slide to the edge. They couldn't see him as well on this side but they had the firepower to keep at it until they scored.

Ash slid behind another chimney. They were shouting to each other from several corners, and he realized they were climbing the drainpipes.

They'd seen him, and now trained a spotlight from the second car on the chimney. He heard the touring car's engine start as he hid from the light. They moved it several yards to give the machine gun a better field of fire, and again ricochets and broken slates were all around him.

He ran for the next chimney. They were slow with the light, and he got to the chimney first. He heard them climbing, calling back and forth. He jumped, caught the top of the chimney in his hands and hauled himself up to the top, then lowered himself into the flue.

If he had come up this way he could go down. He felt for the chimney-sweep's footholds, anchored his boots, started down, fast. They'd figure it out soon enough too. The flue descended twenty feet of total darkness, then branched. Ash took the widest, but it stopped suddenly. He tried to turn around in the cramped space, found it impossible, then realized the obstruction wasn't brick. It was clay. Clay. A smoke chamber in a Scandinavian tile stove. He battered it with his feet, it gave way on another wall, and another.

He heard shouting in the chimney. Were they on to him so soon? He kicked through a third wall and tumbled with a clatter of broken clay and tile into a room lighted by the bonfire flickering through a big French window. He looked out the window. Twenty feet below, two soldiers manned the machine gun; a third, the light on the other car. The rest were nowhere in sight, presumably climbing to the roof and covering the back. He ran from the room into a hallway, found a staircase and headed down. He smelled the chlorine gas beginning to permeate the house.

He reached the ground floor, silently opened a window and swung through onto the verandah. Thirty feet away they were training the light on the roof and firing sporadically. He ducked behind the verandah railing, edged closer, drew his Luger.

He waited until the machine gun fired again and snapped a shot at the light. It went out, amid yells from the machine gunners. Ash vaulted the railing and charged ahead.

The machine gun belt-feeder spotted him first and called out. The triggerman spun the barrel toward Ash, started spinning his crank, firing as the gun bore around. Six slugs stitched through the snow. Ash kept running at the gun. The seventh shot grazed his boot heel and threw him off his feet. He hit the snow rolling, came up beside the machine gunners, and shot them down. The soldier on the ruined searchlight pulled a pistol. Ash winged him, got himself behind the machine gun, clumped up a few folds of the belt so he could fire alone, found the crank and raked the corner of the house as the rest of the unit streamed around it.

He hit a few, saw a few shadows disappear, sprayed the opposite corner, then directed a long stream into the hood of the other car. He jumped over the front seat, jammed the touring car into gear and headed for the causeway.

Rifle fire pursued him. The windshield exploded into glass shards. The tires took several hits, but they were hard rubber and the chains kept digging through the snow. A shot whined off the windshield post. Ash ducked, stuck his head over the low door and steered by the light of the crimson sky. At last he was out of range. He crossed the marsh, following their track in the snow, and turned toward the train.

It was where he had left it, venting steam forlornly, and he wondered who he could draft to help hold off the renegade army unit if they came for him again. The machine gun tipped the odds his way, but he needed a belt feeder. He saw a repair train had arrived from the south, and with it a unit of Russian soldiers guarding the men laying new track.

Ash knew by the relieved look on the face of the lieutenant in charge that he had already read the Russian Embassy's *laissez-passer* and had been wondering how he would explain losing an important passenger from a train passing through his sector.

Freezing, Ash brushed past the lieutenant and made a beeline for the warm train. But when he climbed up into the vestibule he recoiled from his image in the mirrors. No wonder the passengers in the corridor were staring. Black with chimney soot from head to toe and his lean cheeks sunken wearily, he looked like a coal miner dragged half-dead from a cave-in.

The Russian scrambled up after him. "What happened?"

Ash's blue eyes seemed wild in their black sockets. His once-brown hair was pasted to his skull like a greasy black helmet. His small, even teeth shone white beneath a mustache ordinarily highlighted by glints of red and gold.

"What happened, Commander Ash?"

"Initiation rite for a Finnish fraternal order."

"I don't understand," the Russian officer said. "Where are the troops who took you?"

Catherine came running down the corridor in her dressing gown, dodging the other passengers. "Lord . . . are you all right?"

"Fine," Ash said, and patted her shoulder reassuringly, leaving black prints on her gown. He then turned back to the officer, who was grinning knowingly at the girl's concern. Ash pointed first at the shot-up touring car, then in the direction from which he had come. "There's a renegade Finnish unit at a lodge across that marsh. About a dozen men left, and maybe their German commander. I'm not sure if I hit him. They can't have gotten far in one car. You might just catch 'em."

The Russian didn't look enamored of the idea of night-fighting Finns on Finnish snow. He asked, "Does that machine gun work?"

"Very well."

The train steamed south and southeast, down the Gulf of Bothnia and then diagonally across Finland's lake-pocked interior, pulling in late at the infrequent stations and leaving later. The system was collapsing. Ash saw railroad yards in chaos, broken-down rolling stock everywhere. Andrew Hazzard acted pleased. "Wheels, hell, they need *everything.*"

But the Grand Duchy of Finland itself was a far cry from the Russian countryside Ash had seen. Snug farmhouses and well-kept fences, reminiscent of orderly Swiss farms, indicated that the Czar's rule had not Russified the Finnish countryside. Nowhere did Ash see the squalid misery of Russian villages. It was, he thought, like expecting the worst poverty of the West Virginia back hollows only to discover the verdant Greenbriar country instead.

At midnight, when they should already have arrived in Petrograd, the train crossed the Finnish-Russian border at Bielostroff. Ash locked his door and went to sleep with the Luger under his pillow. It would be morning before they saw the capital.

Snow beat against the dining car window at breakfast, but at dawn an hour later, at nine-thirty, the sun climbed into a blueing sky. The clouds had blown away by the time the train reached Petrograd's northern freight yards, and Ash saw, as the train crept toward the Finland Station, that the plight of Russia's railroads was far more terrible than it had seemed in the Finnish province. Even Andrew was silenced.

Whole trains stood motionless; the locomotives to move them lay abandoned on back sidings. Rail workers trudged glumly over the packed snow. Many were women, shapeless creatures in black, ragged wool. In fact Ash saw very few men at all as the train wormed through the northern Viborg slums. Children walked the railroad ties, heads down, studying the snow.

"What are they doing?" Catherine asked.

"Gleaning for coal," Ash told her. "From the tenders."

Living conditions looked far worse this winter in Petrograd than any he'd seen in Berlin and Paris and London. Far worse. But this, of course, was Russia. You expected it to be worse here. He recalled Lenin's motto —the worse the better. And Protopopov's perversely proud claim that Russians excelled at suffering. If so, their time had surely come.

"What an awful looking place," Catherine said.

"Just look to your right," Ash told her. The only inspiring approach to the beautiful low-built city was from the Gulf of Finland. But even the slums offered occasional magic glimpses. Catherine and Andrew pressed to the glass. "Somewhere along here," Ash said. "Look between the buildings."

"What—oh, lord, it's *beautiful* . . ."

A razor-thin gold spire soared in the distance and speared the pale sunlight.

"What is it?"

"St. Peter's Cathedral in the Peter and Paul Fortress."

"Misha said the prison is there."

"One of them," Ash said as the train rolled into the Finland Station.

19

"**A**sh is leaving the Finland Station, Captain Moskolenko," Orlov told him, replacing the telephone on its hook.

Count von Basel finished reading Orlov's report on Ash's arrival in Russia. Orlov's typing was superb; each letter struck with precisely the same pressure. Equally precise were Orlov's facts. If the Okhrana lieutenant wrote that Ash had arrived at the Finland Station at four minutes past eleven—only ten minutes before he finished the report—he didn't mean three or five minutes. That precision, natural Russian doggedness and Orlov's yearning to control people made him a brilliant police interrogator.

Von Basel finished the report with an approving nod. "Now listen to me. Ash is to be watched carefully. But don't overdo it at the American Embassy; our regular man is quite capable of reporting who comes and goes without blanketing Fourshtadskaya Street with half the Czar's detectives."

"Yes Captain Moskolenko." Orlov scratched his bald head, hunched his thick shoulders. "May I ask the nature of our interest in Commander Ash?"

Von Basel gave him an amused smile, thinking, Shall I tell you I am really a German spy ordered by Kaiser Wilhelm to assist an American spy who has come to Russia to remove the Czar from under your nose? Shall I tell you I am concerned for Ash's safety?

"I think not, Orlov," was von Basel's answer.

"I only asked so that I could tell our men what to watch for."

"I understand, Orlov, but I am not empowered to release any more information to my subordinates. Just keep track of Ash's movements and, of course, report"—Orlov brightened, sensing that the enigmatic Captain

142

Moskolenko had decided to include him in something important—"any approach made to Ash by suspected German agents."

Orlov ducked his shiny head. "Yes, Captain Moskolenko. Report any approaches by suspected German agents."

Russians, thought von Basel. *Gullible as children.*

Count von Basel had infiltrated Russia in 1915, after the first year of war had convinced him that he had been trained a warrior for the wrong war. Sadly, he had admitted, noblemen had no special place on the modern battlefield; there was no longer a role in war for the well-born, self-reliant fighting man.

The machine gun had seen to that. The lowliest conscript from the most noisome Ruhr factory district could master a machine gun in a week and cut down a dozen aristocratic cavalrymen before they could draw their sabers.

Seeking a nobler way to serve his country and his Kaiser than indiscriminate slaughter in the trenches—which were really nothing better than industrial slums armed for war—Count von Basel had volunteered for the secret service, Gruppe IIIb, with the Kaiser's reluctant blessing, and invaded Russia by himself. As a spy.

The war, after all, would be won in Russia.

Von Basel spoke perfect Russian, learned from his half-Russian father, and practiced on the von Basels' East Prussian estates; he traveled in several disguises—a lame teacher, a consumptive newspaper reporter, a wounded army veteran—each of which had the dual advantage of allowing him to carry his sword-cane and having an excuse for not being in the army.

He relayed reports through the Gruppe IIIb network on the railroad breakdowns which affected Russian movements at the front. His reports had enabled German commanders to shift their numerically inferior troops with devastating effect on the blundering Russians; a unit completely out of ammunition would awaken to a German rifle charge; an artillery battery, laboriously assembled from the chaotic staging areas, would find itself the sole target of twenty German cannon.

Then he got lucky—although von Basel was convinced that pouncing on the luck the way he had would have been beyond ordinary men. He spent a night aboard a sidetracked train in the private compartment of a Russian policeman named Moskolenko. In the afterglow of physical contentment the policeman had talked, talked too much—he worked for Okhrana, security branch, secret police; he was traveling from Eastern Russia to Petrograd; the Petrograd police were expanding to crack down on the agitators who were slowing war production in the factories and he had

143

been transferred; he was excited, he had never seen the fabled capital city some five thousand miles from his home.

"What about your family?" von Basel had whispered in the dark. "Will they come too?"

"I have no family. I was an orphan. My wife and children died of cholera." Then he added mawkishly, "Now I have only nights like this."

Von Basel was not surprised. The handsome Okhrana officer had all the earmarks of an unhappy loner—too fussy for a man only thirty, a little too neatly turned out, and too querulous when small things went wrong, such as the delayed train or the poor wine in the dining car. He embraced Moskolenko again, as if to comfort him. They fit like spoons, belly to back, von Basel behind. It was difficult.

He had killed before, but only with the blade. There was no chance of the blade here in the policeman's dark compartment, only his bare hands. He caressed him toward orgasm, slowly, while he built his nerve, working his other hand up Moskolenko's chest to his neck. When he thought he could do it, he brought Moskolenko to the peak, entered him and crushed his throat just as he cried out in climax.

He stripped the body, then dressed it in his own clothes; he was traveling that night as the wounded veteran. He put on Moskolenko's clothes, threw the body out when the train began moving again and spent the rest of the journey poring over the dead man's papers.

Moskolenko's letters of introduction seemed to confirm that he had never been to Petrograd, and never met his new superiors, that he had been hired, as he had claimed, directly from his post in Siberia.

Then, when the train was on the outskirts of Petrograd, disaster. Clipped to an inside pocket was a handwritten note from an Okhrana major who promised to meet his train. It wrecked von Basel's plan to assume Moskolenko's identity. He read it again, wondering if the note held an undercurrent of an affair between Moskolenko and the major. The note ended, after all, with an invitation: "Apartments are scarce and hotels expensive. You may stay with me until you find your own lodgings." Fortunately the major had added a postscript. "If I am detained go straight to my apartment, 35 Bolshoy Prospect, Vasily Island. It is quite private."

Von Basel went straight to the Bolshoy Prospect when his train arrived. And when the dejected major returned, von Basel beat his head in with a candlestick, removed his clothing and broke up the apartment to simulate a deadly lovers' quarrel.

Afterward, not knowing whether Moskolenko had another lover waiting, he reported boldly to Okhrana headquarters. It had worked. He was allowed to take up his new post, which he had maintained for almost a year now as the cold, remote and very competent Captain Moskolenko. Better at his job than the real one, he was sure. His superiors liked his work with informers—not knowing that many were already German spies—liked how intimately he had come to know the raw underbelly of the city, and they had rewarded him with a department in the Litovsky political prison and an assistant—the simple-minded but nonetheless capable Orlov.

His reports to Germany via the Gruppe IIIb network of mock companies from neutral countries took on the highest caliber because they included information gathered by the single most reliable unit of the Czar's government, his own secret police. Von Basel had discovered how strong General Brusilov's offensive would be in sufficient time to alert German reinforcements to save the Austrian army. And just the previous month, in November, when the German invasion of Roumania was poised to begin, he had learned while interrogating a high Russian army general caught plotting against the Czar that Russia would not defend Roumanian territory if Germany invaded . . . Luck? Undeniably he had been lucky to seduce Captain Moskolenko in his train compartment. But who else, he wondered, could have grasped the luck as brilliantly as Count von Basel? Killed the Russian. Assumed his identity. No one else would have dared . . .

"And Orlov?"

Orlov, halfway to the door, froze. "Yes, sir?"

"Find out more about the incident in Finland."

"Yes, sir."

Reports were sketchy. The train had been stopped in another section's territory. Too strange to be coincidence that Commander Ash, of all people, should have been kidnapped by Finnish nationals; it smelled of German *army* subversion. But how would Gruppe IIIb know about the Kaiser's mission?

He did not know. But one thing was certain. If anyone in Gruppe IIIb or in the entire German army thought von Basel would subvert his Kaiser's wishes for them, they were terribly wrong. And any German agent who tried would find himself in Orlov's interrogation room wishing he were dead.

Thus a close watch on Kenneth Ash . . . a very close watch for Gruppe IIIb agents trying to kill Ash.

Didn't they know that the nobility had no purpose but to fight for royalty? Kaiser Wilhelm—in his wisdom—had ordered Kenneth Ash to remove the Czar to England; therefore the Czar *would* be removed to England even if it took von Basel's last breath. It was a simple matter of noble obligation . . .

Only one power on earth could stop the Kaiser's mission—the Kaiser himself, if he decided, in his wisdom, to change his mind. Actually Count von Basel hoped the Kaiser would do just that. He was loyal, but he longed to stop Ash for reasons known best to Ash himself: for insults delivered long before the war. Insults too long unavenged.

20

The American Embassy owned no car, except for a little Model T Ford Catherine said her father had bought for golfing, and no one met the chronically late trains anymore, anyway, so Ash hired porters and took Catherine and Andrew outside to bargain fares for a fast sleigh and a carriage to follow with the bags—out of the Finland Station and into a riot.

A drunken amputee, a man with one leg, a crude wooden crutch and a military greatcoat fell over a peddler's table of dubious looking meat pies; soldier, peddler and *piroshki* went down in a cursing tangle, and in seconds two dozen ragged children materialized from the crowds to fight for the food smeared on the cobblestones.

Ash shoved Catherine and Andrew back inside; the police charged, scattering the children with boots and clubs. A child fleeing crashed into another peddler's newspapers and an English-language paper blew across the square and spread a photograph of Czar Nicholas across the door with a headline that claimed the Czar was still at military headquarters, hundreds of miles south of Petrograd. Ash plucked it off the glass, but it didn't say if the Czar was coming home for Christmas; he'd have a hell of a time wangling his way into Russian Military Headquarters in the restricted town of Mogilev if the Czar stayed.

Outside, the last child fled as the police restored order. Catherine was white-faced, stunned by the sudden brutality. "How could they—"

"Russia," said Ash, taking her arm, and stepped out again into the clamor of Petrograd.

"Is it always like this?"

Ash looked around. "The war's made it a lot worse."

A horde of drivers came down on them, desperate men willing to bar-

146

gain any fare in order to feed their animals. Ash hired a *droshki*, an iron-wheeled one-horse carriage for the bags, and a smart-looking *rissak* sleigh while Catherine and Andrew gaped at the jumble of old and new, east and west that was Petrograd.

The Finland Station square was swept to dry stone, except for icy paths left for the sleighs; the work was done by old women with birch brooms dodging the brightly-painted electric trams and shouting abuse at the station porters who tromped through the neat pyramids of snow they piled for oxcarts to haul away.

Peddlers operated temporary stands and kiosks of old clothes, wrinkled carrots, moldy potatoes and greasy *piroshki*. Heavy, shapeless women in black sold shoelaces and repaired boots; all the peasant women seemed to wear black, Ash noted. All widowed by the war. Or lost their sons. The young men going in and out of the station were all in uniform.

There seemed to be more foreigners too; Allies—Englishmen, Italians, French, weary Roumanians with panic in their eyes. Small boys sold the travelers city maps and daily newspapers, but the Cyrillic alphabet made a mystery of street signs, and the Russian calender set the date two weeks earlier than it was in Europe.

Ash had sailed from Newcastle on December thirteenth, traveled eight days and arrived in Petrograd December eighth—three nights before Christmas Eve in the rest of the world. He thought, with a stab of loneliness, of Christmas down home. Somehow ham smoked on the place and wild turkeys shot by his hill-country uncles seemed much, much farther from Petrograd than the six thousand miles the maps said it was. A beggar was frightening Catherine; Ash dropped a few kopecks in the dirty hand, concluded his deal for the sleigh and put her and Andrew aboard.

The driver whipped up his half-starved thoroughbred and the overloaded sleigh trundled onto the Alexander Bridge, which spanned the broad Neva. Just downstream the river split into the half-dozen branches that separated the islands of the delta city as it emptied into the Gulf of Finland. The result was a flat city veined by canals and rivers and dimpled by low bridges. From the middle of the bridge they got their first proper view of the Russian capital and its elegant left bank, or South Side.

Catherine, as usual, hit the nail on the head. "It looks impossible." And Andrew echoed her astonishment: "How the heck did they build it?"

Ash decided to show off a little. "Peter the Great hired Italian architects to replicate the Dutch city of Amsterdam on a Russian scale in what was then a Swedish swamp. He wanted a window on Europe to show the Russians the modern world and show Europe that Russia was going to be the new boss of the North. He built the fortress, forced the Russian aristocracy to build palaces and levied a rock tax. There isn't a stone in the city that wasn't carried in."

"Misha was wrong," Catherine said in a voice soft with awe. "It's beauti-

147

ful." The sun was lighting the gold spires of the Admiralty and the cathedrals and gleaming on tall windows, and Ash thought that the splendor of the South Side of the Imperial Russian capital made predictions of the Czar's downfall seem like wishful thinking.

The grand palaces of the royalty that lined the Neva's left bank were painted soft pastel blues and yellows—as beautiful as they were incongruous in the pale northern light. Unexpectedly appropriate too was the extravagant Italianate architecture despite the fact that the Mediterranean inspirations—classical form wildly embellished by rococo decoration—sprawled on the granite embankments of a cold river aflood with swiftly moving ice.

Only the Winter Palace, which was painted dark, brooding red, looked out of place beside its smaller, sunny neighbors. Ash eyed it speculatively; it was the Czar's official residence, but Nicholas did not live there, preferring his isolated country palace, the Alexander, twenty miles outside the city of Tsarskoye Selo, the Czar's Village—like King George's remote Sandringham and the Kaiser's country palaces scattered across Germany far from Berlin.

Petrograd's smart set whispered gleefully that the Winter Palace's correct color was pale turquoise, which the architect Rastrelli had chosen and Russia's rulers had enjoyed for some hundred and thirty years before the present Czar had ordered it painted red for reasons that no one could fathom—no one, the sophisticates added, with taste. Tamara, Ash recalled, had her own theory about the color change; the shattered body of the Czar's assassinated grandfather, Alexander II, had been carried back to the Palace after the bomb attack and Czar Nicholas, still a boy, had seen the blood and torn flesh, which had left him with grim feelings for the Winter Palace. To which the sophisticates replied in even quieter whispers, because such gossip could get one exiled, that she should know since the best rumor in Petrograd said Tishkova had shared Czar Nicholas's bed. After he was married . . .

Ash looked back at the Peter and Paul Fortress. Thick granite walls thrust into the Neva, commanding the river and the city with cannon and a huge garrison. He reminded himself that it wasn't the guns within the walls but the men who aimed the guns that mattered. Mutinous troops could just as easily shell the palaces as they could repel invaders or revolutionaries.

Mansions stood near the fortress, among them, Tamara's.

The American Embassy occupied an unimpressive site between two apartment buildings and shared Fourshtadskaya Street with an army barracks, some tea shops and a coal yard. Catherine eyed the shop signs—

pictures of boots, thimbles, asparagus, telling an illiterate clientele what was sold inside. "Father wrote that he's taken a lease on a much better building. We'll be moving soon," she said.

Ash offered her his arm as they climbed down from the car at the unimposing front door; it was a drab little two-story building only slightly enlivened by a dozen flags and a Marine guard detachment that snapped to attention when the sergeant spotted what had to be the alarming appearance of a full commander swinging down from a sleigh. Nonetheless, the Russian *dvornik* leaning on the door and a pair of porters slouching beside him robbed their arrival of whatever grandeur it might have possessed. Nor could Ash help smiling at the flickers of appreciation on the stern faces of the marines who looked alarmingly like a gang of homesick kids rejoicing at the sight of a pretty American girl.

By some invisible communication the embassy foyer filled quickly with more young men—secretaries, cipher clerks and junior officers. Catherine surveyed her new domain like a duchess coming home.

Ambassador Anthony Hazzard hurried in, apologizing for being late, and running a nervous hand through his thick gray hair. Catherine threw her arms around him and hugged him, then, as he tried to introduce her to the others, pulled him over to meet Ash, who thought Hazzard looked less like a Progressive cartoonist's image of a plutocrat than he had imagined. Hazzard kept running that hand through his hair and looked exhausted and quite bewildered. Petrograd, apparently, was proving more complex than Columbus.

He shook Ash's hand and thanked him for delivering Catherine, greeted Andrew, who was giving the competition a resigned glower, and cheered him with a wink and a promise that, "There's a lot of Russian businessmen waiting to meet my favorite nephew."

Abruptly, he asked Ash to join him for a moment in his office. Ash started to open his dispatch pouch, but Hazzard waved it aside.

"What the hell happened on the train?"

"Finnish Nationals, as near as I could make out," Ash replied. "Have they hit many trains?"

"First one I heard of—'course the Russians aren't big on admitting bad news—Why you, Commander? What the hell did they grab *you* for?"

Like most successful businessmen Ash knew, Hazzard thought in a straight line, and it was hard to throw him off course. He tried again. "They might have known I was carrying the Russian ambassador's *laissez-passer* and figured I was a lot more important than I am—especially traveling with your daughter."

"My God, what if they had taken Catherine?"

Ash let that thought burn holes in the ambassador's brain before he asked, "Does this sort of thing mean the Czar is losing control?"

"Damned if I know. I suppose that's the sort of question Ambassador Page sent you out to ask."

"I suppose, Mr. Ambassador."

"Well . . . I can give you an earful, if you want one; there's no point in pretending I'm a professional diplomat—not that you have to go blabbing that to everybody."

"Of course not, sir. I appreciate your candor."

"Well, I don't know about the Czar and his government . . . but a walk around town will show you they're starving out there. And freezing. See this?"

He got up and led Ash to the tall French windows behind his desk. Opening them onto a narrow balcony, he pointed down the street. "See all those shops. Those little signs say what they sell—bread, vegetables, kerosene. Now that vegetable one hasn't been open since October. The bakery opens about twice a week. At six in the morning you see the women lining up in the cold. See those women with pails? They've been waiting all morning for kerosene. So I don't know about the Czar, but I do know that if something like this ever happened in Columbus, Ohio, folks wouldn't take it lying down for very long."

"I see—"

"I doubt you do yet, Commander." He closed the door and sat down. "This is a decent neighborhood, near the best in the city. What's going on out in the factory districts? Children must be starving. Must be the reason they have so many strikes in the factories. Can you imagine that? Strikes in the middle of the war?"

"What's the attitude toward the war?" Ash asked.

"Everybody got excited when General Brusilov started beating the Austrians. He was supposedly rolling toward Berlin. But all that really happened was the Russians suckered the Roumanians into declaring war on Germany and the Germans beat the daylights out of them in two weeks. Nobody cares about the war here, anyhow—listen, this really is just between you and me and Ambassador Page. I was sent here to negotiate commercial treaties, and the State Department doesn't want to hear bad news from junior ambassadors. I'm just giving you my personal impressions, for what they're worth."

"Thank you, that is why Ambassador Page sent me. He's concerned that if some provocative act on the part of Germany forced the United States into the war the Russian front would collapse—"

"The American people aren't going to fight for the Czar of Russia, Commander. American politics is something I do know. They'll never fight for the Czar. I don't care what Germany does."

"I've heard rumors," Ash said casually. "Rumors of a coup?"

"If rumors were firewood there wouldn't be a fuel shortage. You hear

150

about coups every day. The other night a bunch of nobles and their lady friends had a big do and the next morning everybody in town knew they'd been talking about what regiments would come over to their side."

"What happened?"

"All it was was a lot of talk. A lot of talk in this town, Commander. Hard to tell what's hot air." Hazzard ran his hands through his hair. "Not *all* talk . . . one of the grand dukes is supposedly hatching something with his ballerina girl friend."

"Which one?" Ash asked, afraid to hear the answer.

"I don't know, I just heard it."

Tamara wasn't the only Russian dancer with a grand duke, but Ash had an awful feeling it was she, and it terrified him. Plotting against the Czar was a way to get executed. If they were caught, Valery would probably just be banished, but Tamara would be hanged.

"How is the Czar reacting to all this?"

"Seemed fine when I presented my credentials. Very pleasant, I thought. Spoke good English."

"Will he be coming back to Petrograd for Christmas?"

"I have no idea. He used to receive the diplomatic corps on New Year's Day—their New Year's, not ours—but they say he canceled last year and there's no word this time. You know he's down at the Stavka, the army headquarters—all my staff hears is rumors."

"What's the latest rumor on Rasputin?"

"A real lulu. They say the monk's trying to get the Czarina to get the Czar to stop all military trains for three days."

"What for?"

"So they can carry food and coal to the cities. The shortages are getting worse."

"Sounds like a pretty good idea."

"I wouldn't know. But the monk's meddling is really upsetting people. I don't know how much he actually does, but the rumors say it's a lot. But I find it hard to believe that one illiterate peasant monk could make the Czar do anything he doesn't want to do."

Ash smiled.

"What's funny, Commander?"

"Excuse me, Mr. Ambassador. I was just thinking how pleased Ambassador Page would be if I secured an audience with the Czar—you know, asked him a few questions face to face."

"Good luck . . . the only foreigners I know who talk to him are the British and French ambassadors and they've been here thirty years."

"Wouldn't hurt to ask."

"I'll put in a request through channels, but the last time anyone from this embassy got through it took six months."

Senior staff, chargé, consular, and first, second and third secretaries were waiting in the reception room along with the military and naval attachés. Ash knew a few, vaguely; the warmth of the greetings suggested most of the staff felt they were serving in a strange and distant outpost. A Christmas tree occupied the middle of the room like a friendly totem.

After lunch, Ash presented the ambassador with private letters from Walter Hines Page and a stack of memoranda for Hazzard's staff. While he was emptying the pouch, Hazzard asked, "Did Catherine behave herself on the trip?"

"Your daughter's a lovely young lady."

"She's a kid. She'd still be in high school if she wasn't so darned smart."

"Petrograd enjoys charming young women, Mr. Ambassador. She'll be a real asset."

"I don't know how much I trust these Russians when it comes to that sort of thing. There's some pretty loose morals in this city."

Ash let it pass as he went to the office of the ranking naval attaché, whom he hadn't had a chance to talk to at lunch, ostensibly to pay a courtesy call. But after the captain welcomed him aboard, and Ash had set him gently straight regarding the official arms length nature of their relationship while he was in Petrograd on Ambassador Page's behest, Ash got down to business and started asking favors.

"I'll need a pass to visit the Czar's Military Headquarters at Mogilev."

"The Stavka," said the captain. "I'll ask Major Sheppard, the military attaché, to arrange that for you. Ambassador Page wants the navy to tell him how the Russian army runs?"

"What Page asks, I do." Ash grinned back, pretending to share the military's faintly condescending attitude toward the diplomatic corps.

An ensign sought out Ash in the captain's office. "Begging your pardon, Captain Hamilton, but Mr. Hazzard is leaving for his hotel, sir, and wonders if Commander Ash would care to ride with him in a taxi."

Ash said he would, surprised that Andrew hadn't left him to fend for himself. He said good-bye to Captain Hamilton, promised to see him soon and asked his second favor.

"Could you arrange a pass for me to the British sub base at Reval?"

"I suppose so. What do you want to go there for?"

" 'Ours is not . . .' " Ash started to quote and the U.S. naval attaché shrugged and promised to get Ash a pass to Reval.

The Nevsky Prospect, a two-mile-long shopping boulevard gaily decorated for the Russian Christmas, was Petrograd's Fifth Avenue. It was just coming awake in the early winter dusk. Thousands of officers in colorful uniforms thronged the sidewalks, so many that Ash wondered who was left fighting at the front. Russians, Frenchmen, Britons, Roumanians and Poles gazed in shop windows, were trailed by servants with packages and escorted elegant women in lustrous furs. Ash thought of a Leon Bakst set for a fanciful ballet, entitled, perhaps, "City at War."

"Look there!" Andrew said. "Singer Sewing Machine Company. I told you we're moving in."

Motor traffic, as in London and Paris, had been thinned by fuel shortages, and there were horses everywhere, drawing *likhachy* taxi carriages, and an abundance of private conveyances—two-passenger sleds for merchants' wives, fast troikas and the grand enclosed carriages of the aristocracy attended by liveried footmen and driver.

Ordinary people rode on the new electric trams, few of which had been operating when Ash was last in Petrograd. The trams went everywhere now, even, according to his new Baedecker, across the ice once the Neva froze solid in another week or two.

At the west end of the Nevsky, sprawling for hundreds of feet along the river, was the yellow and white Admiralty building, the administrative center for the four-fleet Russian Navy. Across a huge square loomed the dark red Winter Palace. *Moujiks,* peasant workers, were shoveling snow off its flat roofs.

They drove past the Admiralty, which was the hub of the city, from which the Nevsky and the other main streets radiated, around the domed and columned St. Isaac's Cathedral and into a square stacked with firewood. Across from a small palace was Ash's hotel, the Astoria, a new five-story building in the art nouveau style. Nearby was the abandoned German Embassy; its imposing red stone facade was scrawled with slogans and its doors and windows had been smashed by angry Russians in the summer of 1914.

As Ash climbed out of the taxi he saw two old women surreptitiously approach a woodpile. A soldier ran at them, rifle raised, and they scurried into an alley.

A sign on the front desk said NO ROOMS in five languages.

A clerk was arguing with a French officer in French, explaining there were indeed no rooms anywhere in the hotel. Another was explaining the same to an English businessman, and a third was coping with an angry Roumanian. Andrew pushed between them and announced that the American ambassador had reserved a suite for him. An assistant manager came up, smiling.

Ash had booked a room by cable from London. The clerks had no record of it. Ash produced the hotel's confirming cable. They apologized profusely, but they had no room.

"I intend to stay one or two months," Ash replied, slipping the man a gold British sovereign—a fortune, but worth it. The clerk reluctantly refused the tip.

"Monsieur, I wish I could oblige—I have one little flat under the eaves. But it is a little chilly."

"Show me."

The Astoria had an electric elevator, a vast affair that rose silently inside an open cage. Andrew Hazzard got off at the second floor and was ushered into a suite. Ash saw cots in the halls. At the top they walked up another flight. The room, a closet, really, with a single tiny window, was cold as a tomb.

"No," Ash said. "We'll have to do better." Petrograd was too strict socially, too conscious of rank and precedent and wealth to take seriously a man who lived in a closet when he asked to meet the Czar.

Back at the desk he was surprised to see Andrew Hazzard red-faced and shouting, "That's my suite. You can't kick me out."

"A terrible mistake, Monsieur 'azzard. We are so sorry. We'll see what we can do for you tomorrow, as for now, we have a charming little room on the top floor. Only one flight up from the elevator . . ." The manager turned to Ash, smiling broadly. "Monsieur Commander Ash, there you are. I hope we haven't kept you waiting. Your suite is ready."

Andrew purpled. "You're giving him *my* suite."

"Monsieur, it is *his* suite. It always was. And it will be as long as he remains in Petrograd. This way, Commander, if you please."

"How do you rate?" Andrew demanded. "Catherine's *father* booked for me."

"Just lucky," Ash said, straight-faced, wondering how lucky? Had Lord Exeter pulled a string to make him comfortable? Or had the arrangements been worked by a German agent? The hell with them. He had advantages on his side now. He was a neutral officer of a potential ally of Russia. He could go to the police anytime he needed help. While the Germans, if there were any more Germans, had to operate undercover.

The *important* thing was the Czar.

"Any messages?"

The clerk handed him several envelopes. Ash took them across the lobby and ordered two dozen yellow roses for Tamara. The florist replied apologetically that he would have to check his stock—"Rail disruptions, you understand, sir." While he waited Ash opened the messages. Signor de la Rocca and the Baroness Balmont invited him to dinner the following night. Sergei Gladishev and Prince Paustovsky, his friend Fasquelle's Russian partners, each invited Ash to telephone on arrival. Ash assumed that some of these people could help quickly arrange an audience with the Czar.

154

A Vadim Mikhailov had enclosed his card and had written on the back, "My stepdaughter Vera Sedovina wrote me you would like to talk." The piano player. Tappeur. He would indeed. About many things. Including when his daughter was coming back.

The last card belonged to Chevalier François Roland. The address printed was the Hotel Europa, and written on the back was the address of the Petrograd Fencing *Salle,* and the time, tomorrow morning. Here a week already, the French dance correspondent would know a lot more about the state of Petrograd society than the otherwise surprisingly well-informed Ambassador Hazzard.

"Do you like these, Monsieur?" The florist thrust the yellow roses proudly at Ash. "Mademoiselle Tishkova will be pleased."

Ash stared at the flowers. For years, whenever he wangled a courier mission to the city where Tamara was performing, he had announced his arrival with yellow roses. It had been one of their love rites. His roses, her card in return and a bottle of Moët chilling beside the bed. What in the hell had he been thinking?

"Don't you remember them Commander?"

"No," he said sadly. "They won't do . . ."

21

Murder, General Ludendorff thought while he waited for the Russian assassins, was the ultimate weapon in total war; blood from the right murder *behind* the lines would flow redder than a million casualties in a pointless advance into no-man's-land. He had no patience for irony, and even less for great-man theories of history—though his own swift rise from obscure Prussian colonel to the brains behind the German army suggested to him that greatness did pace event—but he had seen the death of the right man at the right time affect events, which was why he was courting Russian assassins.

When Kenneth Ash died in Finland, for example, the Kaiser's plot to make peace behind the army's back died with him; in 1914 the murder of the Archduke Ferdinand had set off events which hastened *Der Tag.* Neither were great men, merely the right men at the moment.

Czar Nicholas was not a great man either, far from it; he was demonstrably the least competent leader in the world. But shockwaves from the Czar's murder and the murders of the Czarina and their strange monk Rasputin—the ham-handed police repression which would follow, the demoralization of already-demoralized ministers, and the ascent of the revolutionaries because Russians would see the Czar's murder as a revolutionary victory—those shockwaves would tumble the Russian government, and with it, the army.

Thus three murders in Petrograd would have greater effect than millions of deaths, his grains of sand, had had at the front; a perversely modern total-war version of medieval battle, and much like chess: kill the king and the game was yours. Check and checkmate. He had planned this a year.

Telegraph keys clattered nearby like knitting needles as his orders sped from Spa to the front and the acknowledgements returned. He had just completed regular trench inspection—this time, despite the lingering trauma of the Somme and Verdun disappointments, his positions looked stronger. The trenches were remarkably clean, the men healthy despite the weather, the field kitchens and deep, well-lit bunkers as orderly as disciplined officers could make them.

As winter deepened the army lived more comfortably on the Western Front than civilians starving in the cities. The British blockade grew ever tighter, and the food shortages were making themselves known by re-duced factory production—hungry workmen worked slowly.

The Eastern Front was a grimmer story. The Russians had such man-power—such a breeding ground was that vast empire—that German disci-pline, Krupp cannon, modern railroads and telegraphs weren't enough to dislodge their blundering army. Only a revolution would fragment their army, only a violent catastrophe to set fire to Russian cities and men against officers in the trenches.

The spark? Murder.

"They are here, Quartermaster General. Red Snow."

Ludendorff stood up eagerly, forgetting in his excitement to smooth his tunic over the roll of fat around his waist. His murderers. They called their work assassination, but murder was what it was, and Ludendorff liked to be clear.

Two Russian officers entered.

Ludendorff was surprised by their appearance. Despite the detailed reports, he had not presumed that the leadership of a Socialist-Revolution-ary terror cell called Red Snow would look like Guards officers from a noble family. But that was precisely what the brothers Vladimir and Dmi-tri Dan were.

Only in Russia, Ludendorff thought.

Their pale cheeks were clean-shaven, their dark mustaches extravagant, their black hair oiled and combed as if they had dressed for a ball. They shook hands easily, and if they were impressed by the second-ranking general of the German army—or hated him—neither Vladimir nor the younger Dmitri displayed anything but a charming smile.

Ludendorff was baffled. Where, he wondered, had such fine young men gone wrong? These were, supposedly, the flower of Russian Society. He'd seen their type fight on the Eastern Front, brave men . . . what did it to them? The answer, of course, the Russian disease—a deadly eastern com-bination of fatalism and immorality. A plague Germany must contain.

It shouldn't concern him for now, though. What mattered was that Vladimir and Dmitri had a far better chance of killing the Czar of Russia than any murderers the German army had sent before. Most hadn't made it across the border. But Red Snow was better organized, communicating with their cells inside Russia by coded telegrams sent through sham commercial firms to elude the censors, and possessing members of higher station like the Dan brothers who could infiltrate the Czar's own entourage.

"How will you enter Russia?" Ludendorff asked.

"As reported to your subordinate," Vladimir answered. "We've been stationed temporarily in France with a fusilier unit lent to the French. We will go back into France, via Switzerland, and return home in the normal manner by ship and rail. There I will take up my new commission with the Winter Palace Guard in Petrograd and Dmitri will return to his old post in the Czar's Convoy."

"You will travel with the Czar?" Ludendorff asked.

"Not precisely with him. Usually on the second train. But close."

"And getting closer," Vladimir smiled, tousling Dmitri's hair as if he and his brother were reporting home from school to a favorite uncle.

"But when the Czar is not traveling?"

"I will try to intercept him on one of his afternoon walks at the Stavka," Dmitri said earnestly.

"And if the Czar is not at the Stavka?"

"I will be housed at Tsarskoye Selo. Close to the Alexander Palace."

"Good." Ludendorff turned to Vladimir. "And how close will *you* be to the Czarina?"

"As for myself, I have made several requests to be transferred to Tsarskoye Selo, where Their Imperial Majesties live. I will use some of your gold marks to bribe the appropriate officials."

Ludendorff looked directly at Vladimir. "Are you sure you can kill the Czarina."

"Yes."

"A woman?"

"For half a million gold marks I could kill God."

"And you. Are you sure you can kill the Czar when you are actually face to face with him?"

Dmitri simply said, "Yes, I am sure," and Ludendorff believed him, noting he had made no mention of the other half million gold marks. Vladimir seemed more interested in the money then the revolution, Ludendorff thought. And feared killing a woman. But would.

"And who will kill the monk Rasputin?"

"We have left that to our comrades already in Petrograd. It is a matter of encouraging certain people without alerting them to our own purpose."

"I don't understand."

Vladimir Dan started to explain, but his brother cut him off. "The best people to kill Rasputin will themselves be killed after the Revolution. Rightists and monarchists."

Ludendorff was a highly ambitious man and appreciated intrigue, but he still did not like the way they were going about killing Rasputin. He said, "It sounds to me as if you are not trying very hard to kill the monk. Haven't we offered enough gold?"

"Rasputin will die first," Dmitri promised.

"Yes . . . he's the easiest target, but time is rushing by." He was convinced that assassinations would provoke police repression, which would in turn provoke street demonstrations in the Russian cities which would topple the government. Rasputin would start the ball rolling, and cheap at the price. Then when the Dan brothers killed the Czar and Czarina, Russia would explode. But he couldn't wait two or three months for the Czar's murder, not with the blockade squeezing his own cities. It had to start sooner with Rasputin.

Vladimir Dan smiled. "Would you care to double the price if Rasputin dies within . . . shall we say a week?"

"Of course," Ludendorff snapped. "Do it."

Vladimir grinned and Ludendorff suspected he had been taken. The monk's murder was no doubt already in progress. His aide-de-camp burst into the office. Ludendorff turned on him angrily, shifting his irritation with the Russians to his own man, who ignored his order to leave and bent over his chair and whispered, "Ash escaped." The aide-de-camp glanced at the Russians and put his lips close to the general's ear. "He's in Petrograd."

"Have the officer responsible shot," Ludendorff ordered, loud enough for the Dan brothers to hear and remember.

The aide leaned annoyingly close again, and whispered, "Apparently Ash accomplished that in his escape."

Ludendorff looked at the pair of officers lounging comfortably as if they were in their club.

"Would Red Snow be interested in earning an additional hundred thousand gold marks?"

Vladimir said it depended.

"There is an American Naval Lieutenant Commander Kenneth Ash."

"Commander," the aide-de-camp corrected, "he has been promoted."

"I suppose you also know where he's staying?"

"The Astoria Hotel in Petrograd."

"One hundred thousand gold marks," Vladimir said. "I'll do it on the way home from the train."

"*No.*" Dmitri, white-faced, stern.

"Why not?" Vladimir asked.

"It is murder."

Ludendorff looked at the young Russian incredulously. "And what do you suppose killing the Czar and Czarina and Rasputin are?"

"Revolution."

Ludendorff was silent a moment, studying the earnest Dmitri. He considered concocting a story about Ash being a counter-revolutionary, but the brothers Dan were too intelligent; and he realized he didn't understand the nuances of their lunatic hatreds. It had taken his aide-de-camp twenty minutes to explain the difference between Socialist Revolutionaries and Bolsheviks and he still wasn't sure which were which. Fortunately, Vladimir came to his rescue.

"Dmitri," he said, putting his hands on his brother's shoulders, "one hundred thousand gold marks in Red Snow's Swiss treasure box will buy guns and much food and medicine. It may take months to kill the Czar and Czarina. This Ash is a bird in the hand . . . Dmitri, we, Red Snow, need the money."

"We will pay *two* hundred thousand for Ash," Ludendorff prompted.

"Do you hear?" Vladimir said. "Two hundred thousand."

"I hear, my brother." Dmitri pulled away, gazed at the maps on the wall and finally, reluctantly, agreed.

"When?" Ludendorff demanded. "It can't wait two months. It can't even wait until you get back to Russia. It must happen now."

"We will wire the orders tomorrow from Switzerland. Ash will die before Rasputin. You may depend on it."

22

Gleaming like a predatory eye, a steel point sought Ash. He retreated; it followed. He attacked; it circled, an impenetrable fan of steel, like a spinning airplane propeller. He feinted; it waited, mockingly still. He attacked again; the hard circle resumed.

"*Relax.*"

Ash was holding his own foil too tightly; he loosened his grip, studied his stance and relaxed his right foot, which was getting rigid, and raised his guard, which, stiffening, had begun to fall.

"Good. *Attack.*"

Ash poured across the canvas strip, his body milliseconds ahead of his mind.

"*Touché.*"

François Roland gracefully slipped his foil under the stump of his left arm, removed his mask and bowed with a smile. "Excellent."

Ash pulled off his own mask. The canvas rim was drenched with perspiration, as was his entire fencing suit; Roland had really given him a workout, but Ash was smiling because he had breached his master's guard.

"Thank you."

"You've kept your speed, Kenneth—how you do it I don't know, because you obviously haven't practiced your lunges."

"I'm sorry, I haven't practiced much at all, lately. All the traveling."

"That's obvious. May I remind you that you can find a fencing *salle* in every city in Europe? Your eye is going, too. I want you to come to this *salle* every day you stay in Petrograd. You must get that eye back every day. Without your sense of distance you're a standing duck."

"*Sitting* duck." They were speaking English at Roland's request, coaching in the vernacular being the only payment the Frenchman would accept from Ash for fencing lessons that ordinarily only the very rich could afford.

"You need that sense of distance to know how far you can lunge, how close to allow your opponent. Yes?"

"Yes. Time for another bout?"

"No. Baron Zlota's a punctual fellow, for a Russian."

Baron Alexei Zlota's sister was a lady-in-waiting to the Grand Duchess Elizabeth, who was the sister of the Czarina Alexandra. An avid balletomane and an amateur dance writer—hopeless, in Roland's own words—he had agreed to meet Ash at Roland's request. Ash had already put in a request for an audience with Czar Nicholas through official channels at the American Embassy, despite Ambassador Hazzard's warning that it could take six months, and was intending to try other routes. Hazzard had promised to include him in the Embassy contingent if the Czar happened to receive the diplomatic corps on New Year's Day, but that was two weeks off, and it was doubtful it would happen in any case. An audience with the Czarina seemed more likely, and he had planned several approaches.

Roland was being very helpful; Ash hadn't told him the reason he needed royal audiences, and the Frenchman hadn't pressed, though he clearly knew it had to be more than a simple inspection tour for the American ambassador to Great Britain. The attack in Paris had made that obvious. Now, as they walked from the fencing *salle* to the Dance Society's mansion, Ash said, "The Germans took another crack at me on the train."

"And your response?"

"Escape."

"Ah." *Ah*, accompanied by a censorious droop of his expressive eyebrows, was Roland's way of closing conversations that bored him.

Ash said, "There were about twelve of them—Finnish renegades; they had a chlorine gas grenade and a machine gun."

Roland said, "I'm sure you acted according to the situation," in a voice that clearly suggested shooting it out with the German agents in Paris had been a more interesting response than escape. Ash dropped the subject.

Roland was a perfectionist; tall and lean, like a fine pen sketch. He respected beauty and talent and bravery and little else. About the left arm he had lost at the Battle of Verdun, he had admitted quietly to Ash in a moment of deep friendship, he was devastated by a fear of looking ugly with an empty sleeve. The loss had no effect on his phenomenal fencing —"Unless I run afoul of a man with a dagger in his other hand," Roland had noted with a smile. And Ash noticed as they walked along a palace-lined canal that it was still Roland's strikingly handsome face, not his sleeve, that turned the heads of women.

"Was your trip pleasant, otherwise?"

Ash said it was all right.

"And the American ambassador's daughter? I saw her at a little reception last night. Quite a beauty, from a distance at least."

"Up close she's got a pair of blue eyes that could derail a train."

"Her hands looked quite pretty."

"Small, very pretty."

"Your response? On the long train ride?"

"A regular wrong gentleman . . ."

"Surely you were tempted."

"Never even crossed my mind."

"Does she happen to have a little brother?"

"No. Just an obnoxious cousin."

"Ah."

The only duel Roland had ever fought—skill, in his mind, being more exciting than killing—he had fought with a man foolish enough to insult the foils champion of France for being a homosexual. But with a few close friends like Ash, the Frenchman was occasionally playful on the subject of his sexual preferences. Once, at the end of a long night of brandy in Paris he had asked Ash straight out if it ever bothered him to be his friend, and Ash had closed the subject with the satisfactory observation that the few people lucky enough to know real passion knew that passion made its own rules.

Baron Zlota was a round little man—a roly-poly period to Roland's stern exclamation point. He greeted Roland with a dilettante's wary respect for the professional and snapped his fingers loudly when Roland introduced him to Ash.

"I remember you. Tishkova's friend."

"Mademoiselle Tishkova did honor me with her friendship," Ash said with self-conscious formality. Tamara. My God, why did it still hurt? Baron Zlota fingered his pince-nez, perched it daintily on his nose and glanced at Roland. Ash added hastily, "I haven't seen her dance in some time."

Zlota understood, smiled sympathetically. "She is greater than ever. Please sit." Waiters, old Germans in rumpled white tunics, hurried to their side for cocktail orders.

"François tells me you wish an audience with the Czarina."

"I've been asked to report, informally, to Ambassador Page in London about conditions in Russia. An opportunity to speak with Her Royal Highness would lend a real authenticity to my report."

Zlota glanced again at François Roland, but the Frenchman's eyebrows remained noncommitally steady. "I'm sure Chevalier Roland has explained how hundreds of people every day ask for an audience with the Czarina. Her favor can advance a social position, launch a career or a charity, attract contributions to a war hospital, such as the several she herself supports, gain a ministry post—"

Roland's brow concentrated into twin peaks. "Unlikely that Commander Ash seeks a cabinet post."

"Well, yes of course," Baron Zlota said, "but I'm merely trying to explain the difficulty. It would be so much easier if he had been presented before to Her Highness."

"I was presented to His Highness the Czar at Balmoral Castle years ago and again in Berlin for the wedding of the Kaiser's daughter."

"I see. Do you intend to seek an audience with the Czar as well?"

"I would like to, but he's at military headquarters and it might be impossible to get through to him there."

"I see . . ." The drinks came and they toasted the upcoming ballet season. Roland said, "Kenneth saw Pavlova dance in New York a couple of months ago."

"She was great," Ash said.

"When's she coming back is what I want to know," Zlota grumped. "All we've got left other than Tishkova are Karsavina and Kchessinska. There's a wonderful new one, though still young. Sedovina."

"I met her in London," Ash said, and Roland beamed. This was how to get to Baron Zlota. "She was there to dance in a pantomime."

Zlota rolled his eyes. "Only the English would put a talent like hers in a kiddy show. I hope she comes back."

"She said she was."

The conversation drifted around dance gossip for a while, but when Ash and Roland left the club Baron Zlota promised, "I'll speak with my sister. Of course she and Her Highness the Grand Duchess are in Moscow at Her Highness's nunnery, but I'll telegraph immediately." . . .

It was snowing on the street. "Well?" Roland asked.

"Maybe . . . why's the Grand Duchess in a nunnery?"

"She founded her own religious order after her husband was assassinated."

"Oh."

"She's a very stylish woman. She had the habits designed by a *couturier* in Paris. Friend of mine."

"Oh?"

"Sorry. Her Highness is not on intimate terms with her dressmaker."

On his own Ash called on a Russian diplomat he had known on and off for years. Skobeleff, high up in the Foreign Ministry when last Ash had seen him, received him in an apartment heaped with packing cases. The diplomat was supervising the packing of his library. He had a bottle of champagne in an ice bucket on his desk and seemed just a little drunk. He offered Ash a glass.

"It is good to see you again. I heard they promoted you to full commander."

"You hear quickly, it just happened."

Skobeleff smiled at the compliment. But information, after all, was a diplomat's stock in trade. "What brings you to Petrograd?"

"My government has asked me to observe the Conference of Allies." It was a better lie for someone in the know like Skobeleff, and based on reality. The conference was scheduled for January.

"Unofficially, I presume?"

"Unless we declare war in the meantime."

"Which is not likely, is it?" Skobeleff asked.

"I'm afraid not," Ash conceded. "I wonder if I might ask a favor of you."

"Of course."

"Might you be able to arrange for me to meet the Foreign Minister?"

"Unofficially?"

"Of course," said Ash, thinking that he could persuade the Foreign Minister to present him at court. He could invoke his former connections with President Roosevelt. And drop hints about Ambassador Page as well. The hard part was getting to the Foreign Minister. Skobeleff shook his head. "I wish I could help you but I am afraid I am no longer in a position to request favors from the Foreign Minister."

"I don't understand."

"It's common knowledge. Several months ago I went to help a woman being molested in a box at a nightclub. I drove off the man with my walking stick, and the police arrested him. Unfortunately, for me, he turned out to be Rasputin. I was ordered to resign my position at the ministry."

"But you—"

"I had to resign. The order came from the highest levels of the court. I was about to sail for London to take a new post; instead I'm retiring to my estate in the Crimea. Maybe I'll write my memoirs."

"But you're only forty-five years old—"

"And finished . . . I'm sorry, I can't help you."

Ash was stunned. Skobeleff was one of the best. Everyone in the diplomatic corps had assumed he would one day be Russia's Foreign Minister.

That evening Ash had dinner with his friend Albioni's colleague, Signor de la Rocca, and the banker's wife, the Baroness Balmont. She was from the Baltic provinces, tall and blonde, icily beautiful and a well-known huntress. Footmen wearing the purple livery of her house served twenty-five guests a meal of duck the baroness had shot on her marshes earlier in the week.

De la Rocca, cheerful and proud of his Russian wife, held forth on the subject of the war, promising his Russian guests that the Austrian army was beginning to weaken under repeated Italian onslaughts.

Few of the Russians paid much attention, chattering instead about the upcoming social season, the dance and Rasputin's latest depredations, and when de la Rocca turned to Ash for confirmation Ash had to restrain himself from saying that *weakening* the Austrians would lead to disaster. Italy and Austria had been hacking away at each other in the mountain passes between the two countries. But if the Austrians were ever frightened into turning to their German ally for help, the Germans would, so to speak, blow Italy out of the water.

De la Rocca took Ash aside as the men rose from cigars and brandy to join the ladies. "Albioni asked that the baroness and I help you. What is it you need?"

Ash repeated his refrain about the report for Ambassador Page, who was, after all, considerably senior to the relatively inexperienced U.S. ambassador to Russia. At some point, higher up, closer to the Czarina, he would have to shift tactics and at least acknowledge that he carried a private message from King George, but the longer he waited the better chance of keeping the U.S. involvement in the Czar's removal from rumor-hungry Petrograd.

An hour later, when the other guests were leaving, de la Rocca and the baroness invited him into their library. After Ash repeated his story, she remarked on his reputation and invited him to shoot on her estates near Petrograd, which Ash declined with regret after a glance at de la Rocca told him that the Italian didn't much trust his wife alone in the country. He needed friends in court, not jealous husbands.

The baroness seemed to take his refusal with good grace and returned to the subject of an audience with the Czarina, concluding, "Not only are you a friend of my husband's friend, Signor Albioni, but the United States is a potential ally, *n'est pas?*"

Ash gave a careful nod.

"Well, we shall see what we can do."

Walking home to the Astoria that night, thinking the baroness might well not help, despite her words, because he had refused her invitation, and realizing he had mistaken de la Rocca as the power in the family, Ash noticed he was being followed. He walked straight into the Europa and watched the street from the lobby. The man looked Russian. He wore a wool overcoat, a brimmed hat and galoshes, the uniform of the plain-clothes detective in Russia, at least when following a foreign officer on the Nevsky Prospect.

Ash asked the doorman for a cab and took it home. The Czar's police followed everybody at one time or another, which was fine with him this trip. They were as good as a bodyguard.

Ash breakfasted late the next morning with Prince Igor Paustovsky, business partner of his Parisian friend Fasquelle, the caviar importer. Breakfast was a meal very rarely taken by upper crust Russians, but the prince was an gourmand of voracious proportions and seemed to relish the idea of company while pursuing his eccentric—for Petrograd—habit.

"Fasquelle cabled you were coming," he said through a mouthful of eggs and smoked salmon, forking up more with one hand and waving for the Astoria's waiters with the other. Where he had gotten his title Ash didn't know, but he seemed less the blue blood than a businessman who had married well, or somehow pleased the Czar and was ennobled for his pains. "Said you were inspecting something or other. Have some more of that."

Ash kept pace, figuring he would work it off on the fencing strip; he had another lesson scheduled with Roland and knew he damned well better spend a few days getting in shape for it. He repeated his story, made his request for help in gaining an audience.

"Good idea. Go to the top. Horse's mouth, so to speak. She's running things, you know. Making a mess of it too. Probably shouldn't tell you this, but it's all going to hell. Somebody's got to talk sense into the Czar before it's too late."

"How much longer do you think Russia can go on like this?"

"Who knows."

"Can you get me an audience with Her Highness?"

"Oh, I suspect I can. I shall work on it. Today, in fact. A matter of contacting the right people . . .

Sergei Gladishev, the Moscow millionaire and yet another partner of Ash's Parisian friend Fasquelle, received Ash in his Petrograd mansion on the Moika Canal at eleven-thirty, pointedly too early for lunch or any other socializing beyond a brief business meeting. A butler led Ash through marble reception rooms into a large, cluttered office.

Gladishev had inherited a Moscow bakery fortune and parlayed it during the last decade of explosive industrial growth into an empire of flour mills and warehouses. Several years before the war, still young, he had gone into politics. He had risen quickly through the ranks of the Kadets, the Constitutional Democratic Party, and had become a powerful voice in the Duma, the quasi-parliament that theoretically advised the Czar how to govern Russia.

He was a big man with a broad chest and belly, lavishly dressed, his velvet coat flung over the back of his desk chair, gold nugget cuff links flashing from his silk sleeves. He had thin, close-cropped hair and his high brow caused his small blue eyes to seem very bright. He was not above reminding Ash that Fasquelle and Russe-Franc-Viande were a very small part of his business.

"Fasquelle mentioned something I can't remember . . . how do you happen to know him?"

"We raced yachts."

"Yes . . . well, the only thing you'll race here for the next few months are iceboats."

"Do you?"

"Iceboats? Good God, I haven't the time . . . What is it you want?"

Ash told him.

"Impossible."

"Why?"

"The Czar and Czarina have sequestered themselves. They see few people, they listen to even fewer. There was a time I had the Czar's ear, but he hasn't talked to me since the war began. You'll find dozens like me."

"Because of Rasputin?"

"Rasputin's just a consequence. He couldn't have happened if the Czar had had any taste for governing . . . we're an autocracy without an autocrat. And when he does do something, it's just another attempt to hold off the inevitable. That's not leadership—What do you think of this house?"

"It's magnificent." Ash was surprised by the question.

"You should see my Moscow home. My estates. I'm one of the richest men in Russia, but because I'm a member of the Kadet Party, which demands liberal democracy, the Czar considers me a revolutionary. *Me.* I would be laughing, if it weren't tragic."

Gladishev's open manner seemed to invite Ash's blunt question. "How long can Russia go on like this?"

Gladishev started to answer, then seemed to change his mind. "We'll be all right, if we make it 'til spring . . ."

"Winter just started."

"Good day, Commander."

168

Two days later, after his second fencing lesson, Ash told Roland, "I've shot my bolt. Nobody who promised to help called back, and they won't answer my calls."

"Not even Zlota?"

"Nobody."

"Why do you suppose they promised in the first place?"

"They're embarrassed. I think Gladishev hit it on the head. Nobody can get through to the Czar anymore . . ."

"Maybe you're going about this in the wrong way," Roland said as they walked to the Nevsky for lunch.

"Judging by results, I'd say you were right."

"The Czarina is a woman—and a very beautiful one at that."

Ash stopped and looked at Roland. The obvious, of course, had never occurred to him.

23

"They tell me the Czarina loves pearls."

"Fabergé."

"Your mind seems to be clearing, Commander. Shall we?" They had reached the Nevsky. The jeweler's shop and workrooms were nearby, around the corner at 24 Morskaya.

"I'd better stop at the bank first."

"If you would be so kind as to sign here, sir."

The manager of the Russian & English Bank watched impassively as a senior clerk counted twenty thousand roubles onto his desk for Ash. He had not asked Ash's name; the account number Lord Exeter had given him had been sufficient for the withdrawal. Ash signed and stuffed the money into his pockets. Twenty thousand roubles was worth ten thousand dollars—three times his yearly salary.

He decided the gift would be from the King—a royal bauble for his favorite—and presumably richest—female cousin, a personal gift, delivered by a friend. After he and Roland had unanimously rejected everything on the main floor, a Fabergé manager was called. He inquired about what Ash intended to spend and on hearing the figure said, "I'm sure we have something. May I inquire about the recipient?"

"A very beautiful, mature woman," Roland said. "With expensive taste."

"She likes pearls," Ash said.

They looked some more, rejecting ropes of pearls as too ordinary, and gold hearts encrusted with pearls as too romantic. "She's a cousin," Ash told him.

The manager produced a platinum rose with the edges of the petals lined with pearls, which Ash sort of liked but Roland said to look further. The manager brought them to another room.

"*That*," said Ash.

"That is the crest of the house of Romanov, I hardly think—"

"She's sort of related," Ash said, dangling the pendant for Roland to see.

The three-inch pendant represented the top of the Russian crest—two crowned eagle heads looking to the east and west borders of the Russian Empire under a single large crown. The eagle heads' feathers were massed seed pearls, the crowns were gold, and the pennants connecting them, as well as the eagles' eyes and tongues, were cut rubies.

"What do you think?" said Ash. "A little gaudy?"

Roland shrugged. "Very Russian."

"Shall we deliver it, sir?"

"I'll deliver it personally . . ." He hoped.

"How?" Roland asked on the street.

"All I have to do is get inside her palace." That's all.

The piano player Vadim Mikhailov owned no telephone, but Ash tracked him down by messenger to a private ball he was playing that night at the Japanese Embassy. Crashing the ball just before the late supper was a simple matter of walking in in his social dress uniform and asking the first unattached attractive woman if she would care to waltz.

She was a baroness—he seemed to be running into a lot of them lately, as if they came in threes, like big waves. She invited him to join their party for supper. Sadly, her husband was at the front, unable to get leave for the ball.

The supper tables were decorated with wicker baskets of flowers brought from the Crimea on heated trains. Ash found himself with a pair of young married couples eating borscht, sturgeon and a kind of grouse. His hostess was the older sister of one of the wives.

Both men were officers. Neither had seen action. They used the English diminutives of their Russian names. Alexander was "Sandy." Ivan, "Johnny." Conversation swung from the difficulties one couple had had finishing a new summer house before the winter set in to the love poetry of Mayakovsky—" 'Cloud in Pants,' can you imagine his flies?"—to the documentary movie, "The Battle of the Somme," to bear hunting, to Tishkova's jubilee at the Maryinski and back to Sandy and Betty's summer house. The basso Chaliapin had his estate nearby. He was singing *Boris Godunov* next week at the Maryinski.

The quadrilles were lamented. Too many and too long, but the Czar had forbidden officers in uniform to dance the one-step or the tango, and as nine out of ten men in the room were wearing uniforms, what was left but a maze of old-fashioned quadrilles relieved by the occasional waltz?

Ash probed gently to see whom they knew at the Czar's court. To his surprise the baroness herself was related to a Count Dolgorouki, who was Master of the Court. It seemed he finally was getting lucky. It seemed she had already taken a shine to him. Now he looked again. She had danced well, she was quite pretty, a rather petite brunette. Cultivating her would not exactly be painful.

There was talk at the table of going to see the gypsies after the ball was over. Ash accepted their invitation and agreed to meet outside, as the baroness seemed to want to keep up appearances. He was having a cigarette by a slightly open window near the orchestra when the last dance ended and the tappeur rose like a stork from the forest of palms which concealed his piano.

He was surprisingly old to be Sedovina's father, a tall, skinny old man with a mane of white hair and a white, pencil-thin mustache. He brought out a handkerchief as Ash approached, mopped his face and gazed with satisfaction at the guests laughing and chattering on their way toward the doors.

"Monsieur Mikhailov?"

"Commander Ash? I got your message." He pronounced it *Ahsh,* as most Russians did. "Vera Sedovina's letter arrived the morning you did. You must have traveled together. How is she?"

"I met her at dinner at the Exeters. She seemed like a lovely girl."

"She is too serious."

"She did seem that," Ash agreed. "She told me you know a lot of people in society here."

The old man seemed to preen, and again Ash was reminded of a bird.

"I have played piano in Petrograd for four Czars. I have played so long that I remember when the only orchestra you ever heard at a ball was in the Winter Palace. Now they don't trust the old man to make enough noise by himself so they surround me with band instruments. Tonight was an exception. I think the Japanese are too tightfisted to hire a whole orchestra. Did you like my music?"

"Very much . . ." He had to break this off soon if he was going to catch up with the baroness. She looked like the better bet to get his gift to the Czarina.

"I saw you sitting with the Baroness Beauharnais. A lovely woman. Her father assumed her mother's name and title to keep the family name alive. He himself was only a count, of course, but the Czar used to allow dispensation of that kind of thing."

172

"I understand her uncle is Master of the Court," Ash said, hoping to pick up a little more about her.

"Well, that's her great uncle. His son was killed at the Battle of Tannenberg. Poor man hasn't much to live for anymore."

"But busy at court," Ash said.

"Hah. What court? Count Dolgorouki is Master of Court at the Winter Palace. The Czar is never there. So Count Dolgorouki is Master of Court which exists in name only. He's not part of the small entourage housed at the Alexander Palace with the Czar at Tsarskoye Selo. *That* is the court —such as it is."

Ash looked across the emptying ballroom. The tappeur had saved him days of futile maneuvering around the otherwise attractive Baroness Beauharnais. He said, "You seem to know a good many people . . . care to join me for a brandy?"

The old gossip beamed at the invitation. Again Ash thought of a stork, preening now, as he bowed his head and said, "Thank you, sir. You are most kind."

Ash said, "I'd like to wait a few minutes." Give the baroness time to leave without him.

"Of course . . . I will entertain you." He crowded back through the potted palms and sat at the piano. Ash followed. "I'd think you'd had enough."

Mikhailov hunched over the piano like a question mark. Wire thin as he was, his hands were enormous and thick-fingered. They poised over the keys and he looked up at Ash, a grin splitting his sunken cheeks.

"Scott Joplin?"

"Sure. Great."

The old man played Joplin's "New Leaf Rag," and stormed without pause into "Euphonic Sounds."

"What do you think?"

"I never heard it that good even down home."

"Where do you think Americans got it from? Your Negro musicians are educated in middle-European music." He played a complex variation of the "The Magnetic Rag." "That's his best one. Can we go now? I find I'm tired."

The baroness had gone and a bitter wind was blowing off the Neva. Ash saw beggars sleeping in the lee of the embassy steps. A few taxis were left, the drivers huddling in cold cars to save gasoline and eyeing hopefully the clumps of officers saying good-night.

They walked the short distance to Sedovaya Street to a nightclub that sold vodka in teacups and settled down at a table as far from the loud gypsy guitar band as Ash could bribe them.

Ash said, "I'm trying to gain an audience with the Czarina—to flesh out a report I'm writing for my ambassador."

"Then you're in the wrong place. Nobody in Petrograd is connected to the Court anymore. The Czar's gone to hide at Tsarskoye Selo. Petrograd society goes on without them."

The piano player echoed Gladishev, Ash thought. But he still found it hard to believe. "He can't hide. He's leading the army and the country—"

"Of course he can hide. Russians usually detach themselves from those they rule. It's typical. Imagine any provincial family of some wealth and possessing a fine old name. The best name in the province. Who do they associate with? The merchant who buys the grain from their fields? Hardly. The lawyers who handled their business affairs? Of course not. The teachers in the town? The representative of the railroad company? The actors who play in the little theater they support? Perhaps as mistresses and lovers. The clergy? Only to dispel evil spirits and conduct services. No. This family we imagine can only associate with themselves. And if they are rich enough and live near enough they have a house in Petrograd. If not, they live alone in a sea of peasants. And that's how the Czar lives in Russia today. The head of the great house of Romanov lives a simple, empty life twenty miles from this city. It might as well be three thousand, for all the time he spends here. They are recluses. And society has learned to get on without them."

"But there must be someone close to them."

"A few nobody ladies-in-waiting to the Czarina. A young man or two courting their beautiful daughters—beauties like you've never seen locked away like merchant's daughters. A grand duke or two who might have the Czar's ear. His dentist, if you can imagine such a thing. He sees his generals at Mogilev army headquarters, but this isn't a court . . ." Mikhailov dragged deep on his cigarette and glanced at Ash with ancient, cynical eyes. "All this talk of station and entourage must seem so odd to an American democrat."

Ash nodded. He had years ago stopped explaining to Europeans that the four hundred residents of his home town of Lewisburg, West Virginia, divided themselves into at least seven distinct social classes that separated plantation owners, railroad and coal barons, lawyers, doctors, farmers, coal miners, shopkeepers and day laborers, not to mention Negro servants and traveling salesmen.

The social lines blurred only when those who lit out for the cities returned home in better straits, and the groups mingled only in superficial and mutually agreed-on ways like at a Fourth of July picnic. The first time Ash had fallen in love was with the general store owner's nineteen-year-old daughter and because he was fifteen his father had taken him aside to explain about their different backgrounds and how their interests would diverge.

As their interests had been largely sexual, Ash had found it hard to believe his father, but the Old Man had prevailed by tempting him with a summer job on a cattle boat bound for London, which had turned out to be the first leg of his trip around the world.

"How does Rasputin fit into all this?"

"Rasputin is the sole beneficiary." The tappeur peered into his brandy. "The so-called holy man has become chamberlain, minister, major domo, privy councilor and master of the court all in one. I don't mean he has the titles, but the titles are empty, because he performs the functions of advising the Czar and Czarina, suggesting appointments, ordering the household and conveying their wishes to the state. Old Count Fredericks is still Chief Minister of the Imperial Court, but he's so old he forgets his own name. The Czar allows him to bumble along, so of course nothing important is accomplished except by Rasputin. The Czar autocrat rules through this single man, in effect, and will until some enraged nobleman kills Rasputin. Which many have sworn to do."

"Can Rasputin be as bad as they say?"

The tappeur shrugged. "I suppose it's a matter of perception. People say he whores. Well, there isn't an interesting man or woman in Petrograd who doesn't whore. The aristocracy, the liberals, the writers, the ministers, *everyone* whores in Petrograd, except the middle classes. *Everyone*, from simple affairs, to complex orgies, to sex clubs that would turn your hair as white as mine—unless, of course," he added with a smile, "your inclinations run similarly to the membership's . . . People say Rasputin is a drunkard. Show me a man or woman not drunk in this room and I'll show you a German spy. They say he blasphemes. I don't pretend to understand zealots, but I do know that Rasputin doesn't sell religious indulgences the way the Russian Orthodox church does. They say he lies and steals, but he has no need. A rich woman gives him a bag of money for pleasing her appetites and he hands it unopened to someone who needs it. They say he stinks to high heaven. Well, so does every other Russian peasant, for that is all Rasputin is—a Russian peasant, fresh from the stable."

"You sound almost as if you like him," Ash said.

Mikhailov the tappeur raised bleak eyes from his glass. *"I hate him."*

"But you've practically defended him."

"Unless he is murdered—and they say he has predicted his own murder —Rasputin will destroy the house of Romanov. And everything beautiful in Europe will die with it . . . Did you see those people dance tonight? The beauty of the women? The joy and elegance? There is nothing like this in all of Europe—not Paris, not Vienna, not that miserable bleak London. There never was, not even under the Louis and there never will be again. All because a Russian peasant who claims holy powers has hypnotized the Czarina Alexandra, who has hypnotized her husband Nicholas as only a strong, beautiful woman can. Rasputin is Czar."

"Maybe I should ask Rasputin to help me gain an audience."

175

"He wouldn't," Mikhailov said flatly. "He hates foreigners."

Ash signaled the waiter for more brandy and tried to think above the nightclub racket. He was getting an idea. "Who was that old man? . . . the one who can't remember his name?"

"Count Fredericks, Chief Minister of the Imperial Court. Or what's left of it . . ."

Ash took the pendant to the Tsarskoye Selo Railroad Station. A plain-clothes police detective asked his business when he tried to buy a ticket for the thirty-minute ride to the Czar's village.

"I'm summoned by Count Fredericks."

The detective, impressed, bowed and waved him aboard.

The train left the station on time, crossed the Obvodny Canal and slid swiftly through the factories of the Moscow District. Ash saw several works with cold, smokeless chimneys. In another, the yard of the iron mill was jammed with demonstrators; it looked like a thousand workers on strike, waving placards, cheering a man orating from a shed roof.

The train sped through a shabby suburb, passed the barracks of the First Railway Battalion and burst onto an empty, flat, snow-covered plain heading south on straight track. Railway Battalion detachments guarded bridges and grade crossings, and Ash was fascinated by the thought that this narrow line of track and telephone wire was the sole swift link between the Czar's palace and his one hundred and eighty million cold, hungry and war-weary subjects. His mission took on more and greater urgency. It was no longer merely a plan concocted from abroad. Now it impinged with an on-the-spot reality.

The elaborate court carriages waiting at Tsarskoye Selo's Imperial Station were easily distinguished by the red livery worn by their footmen. Ash eyed the Russian aristocrats and government ministers getting off the train and headed purposefully toward a carriage near the end of the line, choosing one behind an army brigadier and ahead of one entered by an imperious-looking woman who he guessed was a royal dressmaker from one of the fine shops on the Nevsky. A detective stopped him.

"Your business, sir?"

"I am summoned by Count Fredericks."

He had the pendant, gift-wrapped in its velvet box, inside his best despatch pouch, which was tucked under his arm. The Astoria's hall porter had spent half the night polishing the black leather; Ash had burnished his scabbard and visor himself—shades of midshipman inspection.

The detective examined Ash's diplomatic passport, entered his name in a notebook. "Thank you, sir." Then withdrew with a nod which threw the machinery of the Czar's Court into gear. A footman opened the carriage door, bowed low and motioned to Ash to enter. Another arranged a lap robe over his legs and shut the door, leaving Ash warm and comfortable in a plush little cabinet.

The lead carriage turned through rococo gold-and-iron gates that led to the vast park when the rest of the train passengers were seated according to station and their carriages followed in strict order with Commander Kenneth Ash, U.S. Navy, one carriage ahead of the royal dressmaker. Well, hell, it beat walking and guaranteed a serious reception at the palace, where Ash expected his Count Fredericks ploy would start to wear thin.

The broad drive, cleared of snow, was lined with aristocrats' mansions —small, elegant buildings, closely spaced. A mile into the park a blue-green palace suddenly appeared in the trees. It was long and low like the grim, red Winter Palace, but its gay color and position alone in the country made it seem magical. A cluster of gold onion domes glittered above the near wing, the only break Ash saw in the seemingly perfect symmetry that swept across the snowy gardens. The Catherine Palace.

The carriages passed it and a quarter mile ahead the Alexander Palace, the actual residence of the Czar, came into view. Smaller than the Catherine, and simpler in ornamentation, the two-story classical building still looked to hold about a hundred rooms. Wooden boxes protected the garden statues from the weather. Icicles hung from the eaves and wind sighed in the bare trees. Crows and seagulls wheeled overhead, crying.

At the gates the tall red-uniformed Cossack Imperial Guards shared their posts with plainclothes detectives in coats and galoshes. "I am summoned by Count Fredericks."

He got up the palace steps and past two lackeys in black frock coats who opened the doors before a court official in a red cape and black patent shoes approached him with the knowing eyes of a very good restaurant maitre d'hotel and asked, "May I help you, sir?"

"I am summoned by Count Fredericks." He sounded ridiculous to himself, with the rote answer.

"Your name, please."

"Commander Kenneth Ash, United States Navy."

"I've not been informed of your appointment."

Ash said nothing.

"Could you tell me the nature of your visit with Count Fredericks."

"Why don't you ask Count Fredericks? He summoned me."

"Ah. The difficulty, you see, sir, is that your name was not on the morning list—"

"Then why don't you take that up with the man who makes your lists? *After* you bring me to Count Fredericks."

"Sir . . . Please step this way." They walked from the marble entry hall and through several state rooms, each filled with fresh flowers. The palace was heavy with their perfume—an exotic effect with the views of the snow-covered gardens outside the tall windows.

Each doorway was attended by a pair of lavishly costumed lackeys and the rooms bustled with court officials passing quickly through them; the man questioning Ash led him to a small room off a ballroom and said, apologetically, "Count Fredericks is getting older, you see, and occasionally forgets appointments."

"He sounded perfectly fine to me on the telephone yesterday. Clear as a bell."

"Please wait here."

Fifteen minutes passed. Ash watched the guards and detectives from the windows. Finally a captain of the Imperial Guard entered. "Commander Ash?"

"Captain."

"Count Fredericks did not summon you to the Alexander Palace."

"Count Fredericks," Ash said quickly, "does not *remember* asking me to the Alexander Palace."

"What is your business?"

Ash glanced at the despatch case clasped under his left arm. "I am delivering a gift to the Czarina."

"To the Empress? May I ask from whom?"

Ash eyed him. "I suggest you summon your colonel."

The captain thought about it, ran his eyes up and down Ash's uniform, looked for a moment as if he would enjoy slicing Ash in half with his heavy *pallash*. "Excuse me, sir."

He returned in ten minutes with a gray-bearded colonel.

Ash saluted the colonel, explained that he was delivering a gift to Her Highness from King George V and asked the colonel if he would be so kind as to inspect the contents of his dispatch case before Ash entered Her Highness's presence.

The colonel obliged. When he got to the velvet jewelry box, he weighed it tentatively in his hand.

"Please open it," Ash said, adding, as the colonel gazed at the pendant, "of course it should be the Czarina's decision whether to make the contents public."

"Of course," said the colonel, closing the box and returning it to Ash.

"I did promise King George that I would deliver it personally, along with his *personal* greetings."

An hour later the colonel escorted him to the private wing of the palace which housed the Royal Family's apartments. He led Ash past two gigantic, colorfully garbed Ethiopians guarding the main door and turned him

178

over to a lady-in-waiting, a plump, ordinary-looking woman, who warned him, "You are not to tax the Empress. You will excuse yourself at the first indication that she is tired. I will be nearby."

The lady-in-waiting plunged into the apartments. Ash followed, clutching his despatch case. The light and airy rooms reminded him of an English country house. Pillows, shams, curtains and rugs were done in bright chintz and looked as exotic in Russia as the Crimean flowers in the midst of winter.

To his surprise, Ash was led directly into the Empress's boudoir. Mauve was the theme color in the outer rooms, and he realized she must have chosen it because her boudoir was entirely mauve—walls, carpets, furniture. Even the purple lilacs seemed bred for a pale mauve tint.

Czarina Alexandra reclined on a chaise longue.

"Commander Ash, Your Majesty," her lady-in-waiting said, and left Ash standing alone, at attention, three yards from certainly the most powerful woman in the world.

She was stunningly beautiful, with rich auburn hair flecked gray, and a delicate complexion. She wore a loose gown with lace at the neck and sleeves, and ropes of pearls. She regarded Ash through dark blue eyes and motioned him closer with a practiced languid hand.

Ash stepped to the foot of the chaise. The walls of the boudoir were hung with icons, but three pictures dominated—a painting of the Virgin Mary, a photograph of the Czarina's grandmother Queen Victoria and, ominously, Ash thought, a portrait of Marie Antoinette.

She startled him with a voice as English as the Henley Regatta.

"*What* has Georgie done?"

"He sent me with a gift, ma'am," Ash said, and to his relief, the Czarina looked delighted as any regular mortal getting an unexpected present.

"Show me."

Ash opened the despatch case, and she startled him again by patting the chaise by her feet, inviting him to sit on the edge. Ash did. She wore a lily-of-the-valley perfume. When she tried to sit up to make room for him she seemed in pain and had to brace herself with her hands. In the light shift he saw dark hollows under her eyes, and thought she looked like a woman who had suffered, and expected to suffer again. She looked, too, by the light in her eye and the set of her jaw, determined to survive. He handed her the jewelry box.

Before she opened it she gave Ash a smile that was almost shy. "My husband would be quite amused to see me accept a gift from a handsome young officer."

Before Ash could think of anything remotely appropriate in reply, he felt himself blush for the first time in twenty years. She laughed and opened the box.

"How lovely."

She gazed at it a moment, lifted the pendant from the box and held it to the light. "You have very nice taste, Commander."

"King George—"

"Does not shop at Fabergé."

She picked up a little bell; the cold rage in her eyes was frightening.

"King George did send me, Your Highness—"

"But not the gift."

"I confess, it was a device to gain an audience."

"A costly device."

"I used his money, I think he would have approved."

"Why didn't he just send me a letter?"

"He felt he could not risk that."

She put down the bell, but left it close at hand. "What is all this about? —wait . . . I know you . . . you're the man who saved Georgie's life in Berlin . . . ?"

"I was there," Ash said. "And that's one of the reasons he sent me. He seems to trust me."

"Would you please explain?"

Ash took a deep breath. He wished he were standing. Somehow sitting on the edge of the Czarina's chaise longue made it harder to say, "King George is worried about your safety, ma'am. In the event of difficulties he asks you to accept . . ." Ash hesitated. Asylum was an awful word that smacked of permanent exile. He looked at the icons and the picture of the Virgin and said, ". . . sanctuary."

"Difficulties?"

"Political difficulties. Revolution."

She was listening gravely now, her eyes on his face.

"King George is worried that Your Highnesses might be injured in an uprising."

"So he sent you here to tell me this?"

"Yes, he proposes sending a cruiser to Murmansk." Some wary instinct, perhaps stimulated by the wrecked Germany Embassy near his hotel, made Ash hesitate to invoke the Kaiser's name in her presence.

"Georgie is kind," she said at last. "And I know he means well. But you must tell him it is quite impossible. We must stay and overcome the difficulties, as you call them . . . It is our duty to Russia."

Ash reached for an answer to that one, found none. Hers had the ring of a royal edict, a manifesto, unquestionable. Might he have any more luck with her husband? Then, to his surprise, she asked him a question in conversational tones.

"How is Georgie? And May?"

"They seemed very happy two weeks ago, Your Majesty, but concerned, of course, about the war—"

"Is his leg better?"

"Yes. We shot at Sandringham and he stayed out all day."

"Good. I miss them all. What do you think of my little English heaven?" Another languid wave indicated the rooms he had walked through. Ash was ready to cling to anything that could extend his time with her. He said, "I thought I was in Devon."

"I was raised in Germany, of course, but I spent so much time in England and my mother, of course, was English . . . My husband will be touched by Georgie's kindness . . ."

"King George and Queen Mary are sick with worry, Your Majesty."

She replied forcefully, her English accent reminding Ash of Lady Exeter holding forth in her London drawing room.

"I have lived in Russia twenty-three years. I *know* what Russia needs—as does my husband."

She waited until Ash said, "Yes, I understand, but—"

"There are two Russias, you see. The disturbed Russia of the nobility and their sniveling politicians and conniving entrepreneurs is one. The happy Russia is the Russia of the peasants and their Czar. The first tries to come between the second. But when we strip the nobility and the politicians of their power—the Duma—the happy peasant Russia can live in harmony with the Czar. Do you understand?"

"I know very little about Russia—"

"It is quite simple. The Czar and I live in harmony with the peasants because we know what Russia wants—the whip! Russia loves to feel the whip."

Ash felt himself stare. He tried to digest her words in the context of her background, the pleasant decor of her apartments. It wasn't easy. Nor was she speaking metaphorically. She *meant* the whip, the Cossack's lance, the gun, the hang rope.

"It is the Slavic nature," she explained, all earnest now. "They need a firm hand—as well as our love."

Ash thought that in her pronouncement lay the best argument he had heard yet against autocracy—the system provided no way to correct rulers who were dull, foolish, or certifiably insane. . . . But why was she going on like this? Surely she had courtiers who would listen more appreciatively than he.

"Perhaps it's too late for the whip this time, Your Majesty."

She gazed at him through her long eyelashes, and it occurred to Ash that he had not the vaguest idea of what she was thinking, never mind he was sitting only inches from where she lay.

"Who is to say it is too late?" she said in a barely audible voice, tinged now with a note of honest unease.

She looked hard at Ash and Ash knew he had to answer. But if she didn't understand by now what was going on in the streets of Petrograd, or in the miserable countryside, or the bloody trenches, he could hardly enlighten her. Not about Russia.

"The war, ma'am. It's the war that has made it too late."

She looked listlessly about the boudoir, her interest fading. Talk, Ash thought. Talk like you never talked before. He said, "The war must consume so much of the Czar's strength . . ."

She brightened at the reference to her husband. "Simple peasants begged us not to fight. But they didn't know what German treachery was. How could they? We had to fight Germany."

"Of course," Ash agreed, thankful he hadn't mentioned the Kaiser. "And yet, the peasants were right, weren't they? The war has wounded Russia."

"Russia has suffered," the Czarina agreed.

"And her rulers have suffered too."

"I cannot deny that there has been . . . conflict," she said softly. "Faith has been strained . . ." She extended her hand. Ash stood up and bowed over it. "Leave me now," she said.

Ash backed away, at a loss. But then she said, "I will consider what Georgie says. Tell him . . . thank him for his kindness. I will . . . consider his offer."

She lay back on the chaise longue when Ash had gone, wincing with pain from her chronically inflamed sciatic nerve, pain that sometimes made it impossible to think; yet deep pain gave her a strange bond with her son, a way of understanding what he felt when the blood swelled his joints till they threatened to explode. She heard a noise from the elevator that led to the children's rooms. Rasputin pushed back the curtain.

The holy man held her son's hand. Alexis's leg was locked in an iron brace. It was vital to keep his knee from bending any tighter; otherwise he would be crippled as the result of the last attack.

"Alexis." She opened her arms and the boy hobbled to her and let her hold him, squirming just a little. He was recovering quickly this time. She looked up at her friend.

"You heard?" she asked in Russian.

"Yes, *Matushka.*"

182

Rasputin called her mother, as a peasant, reminding her that she and the Czar were respected as mother and father to every Russian peasant, beloved mother and father to one hundred and eighty million souls.

She asked, "What do you think?"

"I think he is the devil."

24

The mill owner's wife was waiting when a deeply troubled Rasputin got home to his Petrograd apartment the next day. She had the paper she wanted signed—some junk about the government paying for her husband's flour before the trains had delivered it to the city. The holy man's recommendation to the Minister of Interior was evidently worth a lot of roubles. This was her third visit and she knew by now exactly what Rasputin demanded for such a favor. As must her husband.

"I waited for you, Father Gregory."

"Take off your clothes."

Rasputin sat down and watched her undress; she had big breasts for such a highborn lady, but he was too worried to stay interested. The Czarina's laughter still rattled like stones in his head. Somehow, the American had apparently shaken his hold on her.

Ordinarily she listened to him, obeyed him. She prayed with him. Recognizing his saintly powers, she entrusted to him her precious children. She defended him when enemies ran to her with tales of his sins. She praised him when the Czar occasionally slipped the noose of his thrall and questioned his own holy wisdom.

Only once before had the Czarina ignored his advice. Rasputin had warned the Czar and Czarina not to take Russia to war. He had foreseen the disaster, but they wouldn't listen, deafened by the ungodly shouts of patriotism. She knew now that he had been right, but it was too late. The cart was in the middle of the stream and the horses were drowning.

The American made her afraid with his promise of rescue. All day Rasputin had brought all his very considerable will to bear on her, but still couldn't convince her that the American was a devil. And when he had called the King of England a devil too, she had laughed out loud and said, "My dearest friend, there are certain things even *you* can't understand."

Which was why the Czarina's laughter still rattled like stones in his head. His power over her demanded there be nothing he not understand, nothing she couldn't turn to him for. Curing the little Czarevich was simply not enough to sway the Empress of all the Russias in matters outside the nursery. He could not hypnotize her like the child; she was a strong woman, as strong a person as he.

To control her, he had to cure everything. She was deeply moved by prayer, so he helped her to pray, hours sometimes, until he thought his knees were broken. And she wanted to be soothed by his eyes and the God-given healing power which vibrated from his hands, as mysterious to him as it was to her.

Drugs helped when prayer wasn't enough. Drugs the doctors feared. And some drugs the doctors didn't even know. When God's healing wasn't enough Rasputin had other resources to cure what ailed the Czar and Czarina. And thank God he did, because they turned to him with all their ills.

Cocaine in the nostrils cured a cold. Opium soothed a headache. Such use was common; Rasputin had learned these drugs from real doctors and many people in Petrograd took them when uncomfortable. But the Tibetan herbs he had discovered in his youthful wanderings were more powerful. Some banished worry. Some made the mind wander among strange pictures. Some dissolved the will like water melted salt.

He kept them in bottles nestled behind the wine on his dining room sideboard. He thought of using some himself, right now, but he resisted. He needed a clear head to cure the Czarina of the American.

He hadn't thought clearly at the palace. He'd been so shocked by the Czarina's sudden independence, so upset by her laughter that he'd fallen to his knees, saying, "But you *can't* leave Russia." He'd even kissed the hem of her dress. The bond between them was like a spider web—more intricate than strong.

"We would return," she had answered soothingly, comforting *him,* even as she made up her mind.

"But Russia—"

She embraced him, held him to her breast, calmed him with soft words while the boy watched, eyes bright as sapphires . . . Recalling the moment, Rasputin cursed himself for his mistakes. He hadn't understood how worried she was about the children and had asked, "But your son's throne? What will happen to your son's throne if you go to England?"

"I would never surrender my son's throne," she replied with a smile at the boy that did not extinguish the hard fire in her eye. "*Never* . . . but I am concerned for the safety of all my children. I am considering that we take the children to England. Then when it is time to set things right again, the Emperor and I shall return—"

"Father Gregory." The mill owner's wife was waiting, standing in her pile of clothes. Rasputin's dark eyes seemed to bore through her, unseeing. He was still disturbed, frightened even . . .

There were things the Czarina didn't understand. Things only a Russian knew. The peasants would never believe in a Czar who fled. Revolutionaries would seize the throne. Or another Romanov—a grand duke from the huge squabbling family—would take the power while the Czar was in England. But neither revolutionaries nor a new Czar would give a hang for Rasputin. They would ignore him, or kill him. There were grand dukes who spoke openly of murdering him today . . .

"You will come with us," the Czarina had assured him. But the thought of leaving Russia turned his blood cold. He was only a poor Russian peasant, a wandering preacher welcome in millions of simple huts across the endless land. This was home. He believed in God and Russia and Heaven, and he never doubted that he would pass from Russia to Heaven when his time—which loomed near—came. The great beyond—Europe, England and the seas—was as mysterious as Hell, and as unappealing. His only hope was to make the Czarina stay in Russia. He'd said, "When the Cossacks burn a peasant's hut and the peasants move in with their relatives they are like cows and chickens in their new home—begging for every morsel." She had answered, "We will return, I promise you." And then God had smiled and helped Rasputin conjure a vision which had made her doubt her decision. She had seen his eyes fill with it and had asked him, "What do you see?"

"I see my blood on the American's hands."

She looked genuinely alarmed, and the little Czarevich took his hand.

"He is the devil," Rasputin repeated. "Sent to kill us all."

The Czarina looked at her son and at Rasputin. He knew he had at least frightened her a little this time. Enough to make her say, ". . . I must discuss this with the Czar. . . ."

Rasputin had hurried back to Petrograd. Her doubts were temporary, but they bought him, he hoped, time to deal with Ash . . .

"What do you want me to *do?*" asked the woman who wanted the paper signed.

"Do you speak good English?"

"Of course."

Her highfalutin airs were half the fun of bedding her. Of course I speak English, doesn't everybody? No, madame. Real Russians do not speak English. He said, "Get dressed."

Her mouth dropped open. Rasputin laughed and grabbed a handful of her ample rump on the way to the sideboard that held his herbs.

186

Ash had not let the maids unpack. Despite the size of his luxurious suite, he preferred to live out of his bachelor chest—a commodious four-foot-high brass-and-walnut traveling box that contained drawers and compartments for his dress and undress uniforms, business suit and dinner jacket, shooting clothes and the hats, shoes and boots appurtenant to them. Tamara had bought it for him the winter she'd danced in Boston.

He had lived out of it ever since, like aboard a boat with everything in its place, but the reason he did not spread into the hotel furniture was that if he had to leave Petrograd quickly, getting his belongings back would be a simple matter of wiring the Astoria to deliver his chest to the American Embassy. Provided, of course, that revolutionaries hadn't burned both buildings to the ground.

The chest contained a shaving kit, with a false bottom for jewelry, which Tamara had filled with studs and cuff links. Ash was carrying it into the marble bathroom to trim his mustache before dressing for dinner when the telephone rang. He jumped for it. A full day had passed since he'd presented King George's offer to Czarina Alexandra. He picked up the telephone hoping to hear the dignified summons of a palace operator. "You are called from the apartments of Her Imperial Majesty."

But it was only the hotel desk.

"There is a lady to call on you sir. Madame Natalia Fofanova."

"Who?"

The clerk repeated her name. It meant nothing to Ash, but he had done some lavish tipping with King George's money to cover moments like this. "Who is she?"

The clerk lowered his voice. "I believe she is married to Georgy Fofanova of the flour mills. A very important man, sir."

"Send her up." Maybe allied with the food millionaire Gladishev. But he strapped the cut-down Luger into the small of his back, in the event she was not a mill owner's wife but a German agent with friends nearby.

At her knock, Ash opened his door to a rather voluptuous, dissipated-looking woman in her thirties. She had dark good looks and a sensual face, and for a moment he wondered if the desk clerk had been fooled by a prostitute. But her pearls and diamonds looked real, and she breezed into his room with all the self-assurance of a wealthy Petrograd matron. Ash gave a quick look at the hall before he closed the door.

She introduced herself in French-accented English and said, "Father Gregory sent me."

"Who?"

"Rasputin. He wishes you to come to his home."

"Rasputin?"

"He wants to talk to you. He asks me to translate. His English is not so good."

"What does he want to talk about?" His luck was taking a turn up. Maybe.

"He did not say. Shall we go?"

Ash looked at her. "I hear he hates foreigners."

"I have no idea whether he hates you or not, Commander Ash. But he sent me to you. He wants to talk to you."

Ash ran the possibilities. A German agent? But faking Rasputin was a crazy ploy, not credible on the face of it, given the man's well-known hostility to foreigners. So if it was Rasputin, what did the monk want? Did the Czarina—she was taking too long to get back to him. She could have telegraphed her husband in hours—Rasputin had influence over her. What the hell . . . "Okay," Ash said.

But outside the hotel he made her sleigh driver wait until the plain-clothes detectives who had been trailing him for several days now had started their car.

"What's wrong?" she asked.

He nodded at their ordinary-looking taximeter cab, which was hard to miss in a city bereft of motor vehicles. "It seems the coppers are following me. I'd feel kind of lonely without them." He watched for her reaction but all she said was, "Yes, Father Gregory is followed too. For his protection. He's afraid someone will kill him."

Which makes two of us, thought Ash. "What does he want to talk about?"

"He just told me to bring you," she said, and sat back while her well-fed horses trotted smartly up Gorokhovaya Street to the edge of the Moscow District. Ash was surprised to see that Rasputin lived in a poor neighborhood. The streets were much darker than the Nevsky or St. Issac's Square, crowded with shop clerks and office staff walking home under the clearing sky. Bitter cold was the price of dry weather in Petrograd, and the people had the collars of their black wool coats turned up against the north wind. Yesterday, the Neva had frozen clear across.

Natalia Fofanova's sleigh stopped in front of a dimly lighted passage which led to a courtyard. At the back of the yard was an ordinary five-floor brick apartment building, as weather-worn and dirty as the others on the street. Two plainclothes detectives stopped them in the foyer.

They recognized Natalia and returned her identity papers with smirks. Ash showed his diplomatic passport. The police regarded his name and waved them to the stairs. Another detective stopped them on the third floor. The dark hall smelled of cabbage and rank cheese. Natalia knocked on a door when the detective was done with their papers.

An old woman in wool dress and felt slippers opened it. She stepped back without expression and let them enter a parlor crowded with massive oak furniture. There were carpets on the floor and icons and paintings on the walls and shaded electric lamps set about the room. Steam heat hissed, and Ash immediately felt too warm. Natalia spoke in Russian. The old woman tucked her scarf tighter over her head and disappeared down a hallway.

Ash smelled him first, perspiration and cheap perfume, as Rasputin stepped out of the shadowy hall, buttoning his trousers. He was huge, a head taller than Ash, but as he moved into the light, still concentrating on his fly, Ash thought he had rarely if ever seen a *dirtier* person. Rasputin's hair was black and greasy, hanging low over his ears. He had a long, matted beard, as thick as fleece. His clothes looked new, yet filthy—a brightly embroidered blouse, velvet trousers, and high, scuffed and water-stained boots.

Rasputin turned his weathered face toward Ash, and Ash thought that Mikhailov the piano player had been right—Rasputin was a Russian peasant, a countryman from a brutal grinding land who had somehow escaped from Russia's endless space. But then he fixed Ash with his deep, wide-set eyes.

It was like looking into the wrong end of binoculars—two gigantic shiny orbs descending into a fathomless beyond. They gave Ash a long, slow scrutiny, followed by the raising of his heavy, blunt-fingered hand in a gesture of blessing.

He motioned Ash into the dining room, which had the same heavy furniture, and sat down at a table under a bright chandelier. He muttered something in Russian. Natalia brought a bottle from the sideboard. She stood beside him as he poured two glasses of wine. The table was spread with cakes and nuts and jams. Water bubbled in a samovar. Rasputin took one glass for himself and pushed the other toward Ash. Ash draped his boat cloak over the back of the chair and sat in front of the wine.

Rasputin raised his glass.

Ash picked up his. It was a red wine, smelled sweet. A Madeira. He looked over his glass at the monk and toasted, *"Boje Tsaria Khranee!"* Long live the Czar.

Rasputin surprised him with a grin and a joke. *"Tsarinia."*

He drank noisily, poured more wine into both glasses and drank again. Stuffing a handful of cakes into his mouth, he chewed reflectively. Suddenly his eyes seemed to leap at Ash.

Ash felt a shiver as the monk's gaze connected—an electric-like jolt. Remarkable. The room seemed to disappear for a second. Then Rasputin gave a lazy smile, and the feeling subsided. Ash recalled an old bare-knuckles boxer he'd met in a Manhattan bar—half-drunk and well past his prime, but still lethal. The boxer had dropped broad hints that he could still take apart any man in the place if he felt like it, then passed the threats off with a sly grin. Rasputin was toying with him the same way, flaunting his apparently hypnotic power. Ash drank the wine. It was a damned good Madeira. Finally Rasputin spoke, his eyes holding Ash's eyes while Natalia translated.

"Rasputin says he had a dream. In the dream a navy man sailed to Russia in a big boat to—" she hesitated with the word—"kidnap the Czar. But the navy man was killed by peasants who love the Czar . . . Rasputin says you are the navy man in his dream."

"Tell Rasputin I smelled him behind the curtains in the Czarina's boudoir."

Startled, Natalia translated, and it was clear from her expression that she didn't know what was going on. Rasputin, for his part, merely refilled their wine glasses. Ash found himself thinking he was glad they weren't playing poker. Hard to tell what the monk was thinking. He took a sip of wine, then put it aside. He felt like he'd had a couple too many, probably because he hadn't eaten.

Rasputin spoke. Here it came. But all Natalia said was, "Rasputin asks would you prefer tea instead?"

"Sure." She poured boiling water from the samovar into a waiting pot, then poured Ash a glass. Ash took it. "Please tell Rasputin I'm waiting for an answer. I thought something smelled funny in the Czarina's boudoir. Now I know it was him. Go on, tell him that."

She did. Rasputin answered.

"Rasputin says the Czarina has many flowers in her boudoir." She refilled his glass. Ash tossed it back and stood up. "Tell Rasputin she needs them with him around."

Rasputin looked up at him. His eyes had changed. Two circles of gray marble polished like lenses. Deep, but opaque. Ash thought he could detect movement in the irises. They projected light. No, they couldn't. Ash realized he had frozen in a strange pose, half-standing, half-sitting. Rasputin's eyes flicked toward Ash's chair. Ash felt himself sinking back down to the table, onto the plush seat of his chair.

Rasputin spoke, and Natalia spoke and her full, sensual lips seemed to move at the same time as Rasputin's. The monk's sonorous, demanding voice seemed to rumble from her mouth. The monk spoke Russian and Ash heard English. Something was wrong with his sense of time. Their voices were simultaneous. Something was wrong.

"Navy man. Drink your tea."

Ash thought, *I'm not doing anything he tells me to.* He glared defiantly into the monk's eyes. He watched his own hand pick up the hot tea glass and lift it to his lips . . . Natalia refilled the glass, and Ash drained it again. It was warm and delicious. He pushed his glass toward her for another. Rasputin shook his head. Natalia took the glass from Ash's fingers, plucked it like a flower. She looked frightened. Ash thought something odd was happening to her face. He thought, *I should be afraid,* and Rasputin said, "No more tea, navy man. Too much might kill you."

Ash tried to stand up. He couldn't move.

"Navy man, I am stronger than they say I am. But in some ways I am weaker. I can't hypnotize a man like you without my herbs."

"Herbs?" Ash heard his own voice from a distance, clear and logical. A first-rate officer in command of the situation. *A sportsman who happens to hold a commission. . . .* The monk couldn't have drugged him. "You drank the wine too."

"I said I am stronger. I can drink many glasses of that wine and that herb. But I didn't touch your tea. Not a drop."

25

Ash saw Natalia's skin peel off her face.

It blistered up in thick pieces that fell away like an orange rind dug loose with fingernails. He tried to think, tried to explain.

"Be happy, navy man. Be happy."

Almost immediately, even as he tried to think what Rasputin wanted, Ash felt a euphoric warmth spread through his body. In a remote detached way he considered that Rasputin's drugs had made him susceptible to suggestion. Strange pictures began forming in his mind, memories as yet unformed, like a slide show out of focus, and under the pictures a thought clamored that he should not feel so happy, that Rasputin intended damage, damage to him, damage to his mission to remove the Czar of Russia . . .

The monk picked another bottle off the sideboard. Clear again, the liquid tasted like licorice when Rasputin told Ash to drink it. Time stopped. Ash's euphoria evaporated. So did the reef of clamoring thought. In their place, fear battered his mind. His brain seemed all he could see. He clung, tried to cling, to an image of the trenches. Cold mud and wet skies, a narrow gray bank of cold wet sky overhead and mud below, an image of the agony that he and Page's inner circle meant to stop . . .

The monk raised his hand. Ash actually cringed, afraid that Rasputin would do something terrible, afraid that when Rasputin did he couldn't stop him . . . Ambassador Page's face formed in his mind, old and tired, dying too soon to end the war. More pictures . . .

"Navy man. Can you hear me?"

"Yes." Ash thought of his father, wished the Old Man were here, to help him, saw his face, a big grin that faded when their eyes met. Rasputin took out a watch on a chain and swung it gently back and forth inches from Natalia's face. Ash stared. Her skin looked normal again. Her eyes followed the watch. The monk was hypnotizing her like a Viennese doctor. What the hell for? Rasputin spoke.

"You will remember nothing."

English, Russian. Ash waited.

Rasputin hit Ash with the full power of his mesmerizing eyes. He felt physical pain, as if the monk had pierced his skull. And he felt fear as Rasputin said, "You cannot take the Czar, you will leave Russia, you will *never* come back . . ."

"I can't leave," Ash said. His mind screamed. *Who said that?* but the voice, his voice, went on, echoed by Natalia's translation. "I won't leave without him."

Rasputin spoke slowly. "I will send you to a peasant village where all the sons are dead in war and I will tell the peasants that you are a German spy . . ."

Ash was overwhelmed by a sudden, vivid image of old men in black circling him with clubs. The drugs made it so clear. The women were behind the men, with knives, the old mothers and the young girls the dead were supposed to have married.

Ash couldn't stand even when he pressed both hands on the table and pushed down with all his might. The gun in the small of his back. He doubted he could lift it, much less pull the trigger.

"Stand up," said Rasputin.

Ash stood up.

"Turn around."

Ash faced the door. A minute later, or a second, or an hour, he felt his boat cloak descend over his shoulders. Rasputin stepped into view wearing a long dark coat. Beside him, Natalia, pale and eyes wide, was waiting in her sable. Rasputin's long beard, flecked with dirt and gray hair, made his face enormous, like Great-uncle Able McCoy, Ash's mother's uncle, bearded and disreputable-looking as a bear in a rainstorm. See that squirrel, boy? More pictures. The Kentucky muzzle-loader shifted in his shaggy-backed hands and the invisible squirrel dropped from the top of a seventy-foot hickory. Stick him in the sack boy . . .

The detective outside Rasputin's door watched them pass. Ash stared into his eyes, oriental eyes, tried to send a message. Help me. Oriental eyes. So common in Russia. Sloe eyes. Moody, dark purple. Tamara had them. Infinitely deep and beautiful. He nearly called out her name as Rasputin yanked him away from the detective; swallowed the sound. Rasputin would hurt her if he knew what it would do to Ash.

The pictures were getting worse, bright and weirdly colored as they trooped down the stairs. Where? Ash suddenly remembered opium. Cribs of half-naked gray men in a room as dark as this stairway. The port of

Shanghai. He'd been fifteen. Some of the other crew knew the ropes and he remembered sucking his first pipe and sinking into oblivion as the ship's carpenter promised, "The stuff won't last forever if you get scared. It won't last forever if you're scared."

But he hadn't been scared. Opium was detachment, a drifting on a benign sea. Rasputin's drug was like the tentacles of a monster rocketing out of a dark ocean.

Ash thought he heard a whimper as they passed the detectives in the courtyard and the detectives saluted with claws. They had removed their winter gloves and they had claws, brown with curved talons, ivory and razor sharp. Their faces were normal, except for long teeth.

Ash looked at Natalia. Her face was dissolving in the snow. But the sky was clear—it had been earlier—it couldn't snow. Detach yourself, Ash told himself. It can't last forever. All the buildings were white. There were many people on the street. Walking fast in straight lines. Ash felt his knees buckle. Rasputin grabbed his arms. Ash hadn't noticed earlier that the monk had a steel hand. Must have lost it in the war, like Roland. Monks didn't fight. Rasputin smiled. Steel teeth. Must have chewed it off. Powerful grip. Ash tried to imagine the number of hinges you'd need to make such a hand.

Natalia screamed. The sound echoed in Ash's head, rising in pitch. The people walking kept walking. He looked at her. She hadn't screamed, but she should have. Her face had dissolved to the bone. Rasputin told her to get in her sleigh. Where is he taking me?

Rasputin started talking, his voice deep, sonorous, a comfort. They had walked a ways. The buildings were still white, the people still walking in straight lines, but Rasputin was speaking. Russian, Ash understood only the odd word. The sleigh forged ahead of them, stopped. Rasputin helped him in. The driver cracked his whip. It echoed like Natalia's scream, and the sleigh lurched into fast motion.

The white buildings whizzed past, a white line. The running people kept pace, almost, walking straight, heads down, past the white buildings. *It won't last forever if you get scared.*

Rasputin emptied the second bottle of Madeira and threw the bottle in the street. He pulled another from his coat. Where had he gotten more? Must have a coat full of them. The monk is drunk. Ash laughed. Rasputin pressed the bottle to Ash's lips. Which was this, the drugged wine that didn't affect Rasputin, or plain Madeira? Ash swallowed.

"Listen to me," Rasputin said through Natalia. "This is your last chance. Tell me that you won't take the Czar."

It was funny, Ash thought. *He can make me do anything but that. I won't tell him I won't take the Czar. He has me now, but not in the future. It won't last forever . . .*

At the river Rasputin made Natalia's driver step down and took the reins himself. Bouncing down the snow-covered stairs of a landing, he drove onto the ice. *We'll drown,* thought Ash. But the river had been frozen for days now. How long had he been in Petrograd? Six days. The river frozen three. *We'll drown.*

"Do you swim, navy man?"

Distant, out of time, Ash heard Natalia's voice, *"No . . ."*

Rasputin made the sign of the cross, and her face turned blank as an empty page. The police, who had trailed them down the straight white streets, were gone. Natalia's coachman had disappeared. They sat alone in her sleigh, on ice, flanked by stone river walls. Above the banks, on either side of the narrow river, were dark factories. The tall smokestacks of Petrograd's electric-generating station wore rings of lights.

"Do you swim, navy man?"

Ash saw a dark hole in the ice a few feet ahead of the horses. Open water ten feet wide, wafting steam, a circle melted by the outflow from the power station's cooling pipes. The river flowed under it, moving water, black and rippled like the inside of a monster's mouth. Jagged ice on the edges were the teeth. Ash could hear the thing breathing. See its foggy breath. *It won't last forever.*

Ash looked into the mouth. He was standing on the edge of it, Rasputin behind him. He tried to remember climbing down from Natalia's sleigh. *It won't last—*

"Swim."

Ash gathered his muscles to jump into the water. How could he swim in his boots and wool boat cloak? Rasputin had had all the answers all night long. Ash turned to ask him. The monk had raised his foot as if to kick him. He seemed to kick very slowly, but before Ash could stop him, the monk's heavy boot slammed into his back. He heard Natalia scream, felt violent pain in his spine and saw the electric lights disappear as cold black water closed over his head.

26

A mile away in the Yusupov Palace, in a cellar room prepared for Rasputin's murder, a Red Snow agent presented a box of forged letters and checks to the young Prince Felix and the fiery Duma orator Purishkevich. The cellar room was well-chosen, far from the main parts of the palace and privately entered, but Narvski, the Red Snow agent, thought the killing ground looked too carefully laid out, too lovingly prepared with fine furnishings and carpets, as if Prince Felix and Purishkevich were trying to smother their fear with details. Thus the forgeries, which Red Snow hoped would goad the pair to action.

"Where did you get these?"

They knew Narvski only as an invalided soldier turned foreign currency officer for a Russian bank, a man from an ordinary family in the provinces, son of a school teacher; his mother had inherited a small textile business, and the extra money paid for a cadet education in the local military school and a commission in an artillery brigade when the war began. Fallen the first summer on the Galician Front, health forever shattered, gone to work for the bank, Viktor Narvski was as ordinary a middle-class Russian as the prince and the arch-conservative politician might meet in the capital city of Petrograd in the last week of 1916. His only secret, Red Snow.

"I discovered the checks in the course of my work at the bank." They were supposedly written by a German agent arrested the year before, and cashed by Rasputin. "I made inquiries. I was threatened. Then, these letters were given me."

"By whom?" Purishkevich asked. Young Prince Felix was dark with rage, but Purishkevich, an older, cleverer man, was not so easily led.

Narvski answered, "I can only guess that someone who was afraid to

196

show them to the authorities heard about my inquiries about the checks and sent them to me hoping I would have the courage that he lacked."

"This is disgusting," the prince said as he sifted through them the fourth time. The forged letters were written, purportedly, by Rasputin to the German agent. They contained secret information about Russian army movements that Rasputin could only have learned from the Czarina, if the letters had been written when Red Snow's forgers had dated them.

Would the forgeries be the last nails in Rasputin's coffin?

Prince Felix had been talking about killing the monk for a year. Red Snow agents, overhearing his boasts in nightclubs and bohemian salons around the city, had lent subtle encouragement, steering him toward others, like Purishkevich, who might offer to help.

All had been ready for weeks now—poison, cars to bring Rasputin to the palace and take him away, a place to dump the body, alibis, a gun if needed. Red Snow's secret revelation tonight was for courage. The final "fact" about the evil monk—ironically untrue—which would push the conspirators into action. The slender prince began pacing the vaulted room, working himself into a frenzy; Narvski had mixed feelings about Prince Felix. As heir to the richest fortune in Russia, the prince was undoubtedly the enemy of the people; yet his patriotism and love of the country he thought Rasputin was destroying was genuine, and that Narvski respected. But it was the reactionary Purishkevich, the strongest of the conspirators, that Narvski watched.

Purishkevich tugged a heavy revolver from the pocket it had been bulging and slammed it down on the table. He spoke in slow, measured cadences as if addressing the entire Duma instead of two conspirators in a cellar room. "Rasputin destroys the monarchy. Rasputin destroys the church. And now Rasputin is a traitor . . . For his crimes against Russia, Rasputin will die. *God save the Czar.*" And Prince Felix echoed, *"God save the Czar."*

Didn't they know, Narvski wondered, that Rasputin himself had predicted that if he were murdered, the autocracy would fall? Red Snow knew, and Red Snow believed him . . .

Ash clung to the ice, losing his battle against the current and the cold. The Fontanka's flow was mild but remorseless. The water temperature was brutal. Sinking once again, too weak to float, he felt the cold clamp his lungs like a spring steel. It squeezed his chest. He could scarcely breathe. His breath came in short gasps, too small to send his muscles the oxygen they needed to hold on.

The current tugged at his water-filled boots, dragging him steadily under the ice while he gripped the rim of the hole with stiffening fingers and felt the strength ooze steadily from his arms. His boots had filled when Rasputin kicked him in and he had sunk to the bottom. They were too tight to kick off. Thick mud had sucked around his legs.

Kicking frantically, seeking something to push off, he had hit some solid stone or iron from the electric power station outflow. He pushed out of the mud and kicked to the surface, only to crash into an ice ceiling. Turning instinctively against the current, he had swum and dragged himself back to the open hole.

Ash tried again to pull himself over the edge. He was too stiff and weak to lift the enormous weight of his sodden clothes. And the cold was sapping his will, even as it chiseled the drugs from his brain.

He felt a sudden surge of warmth, thought it was the delirious instinct of a freezing body simply to drift to sleep. But the cold returned, intense as before. In the black night above the stone wall of the river he saw the lights on the power station smokestacks. *The outflow.* The water pumped through the electric plant to cool the dynamos.

Gripping the ice, he worked his way around the edge of the hole, seeking warmth. Halfway around he found it. Warmer water billowed around his body. Compared to the cold, it felt like a bath. Ash hung in it as long as he dared, absorbing the warmth, building his strength for a single push.

He reached as high as he could on the ice, then kicked, rhythmically, trying to make his lower body float. It rose a little and when he was as horizontal as he knew he would ever get he kicked with all his strength and clawed the ice, inching his way up and forward. Forward. His tunic buttons caught on the edge, stopped his momentum. He started to sink back, felt his strength pour out of him like soupy clay that refused to harden. He'd never get the strength again.

Ash slammed his elbows against the ice and lifted his chest, lurched forward, clawed the rough surface and pulled until lights stormed in front of his eyes. He hauled his stomach onto the edge, his thighs, and then he was up, his chest heaving, his breath coming in shudders.

The cold air burned his face. He forced himself to stand, shambled toward the edge of the river, ran slipping, sliding along the wall to a landing and staggered up its snow-covered steps. His cloak and uniform and boots were sodden, chafing as they froze. He made for the lights of the power station. A car was pulling away from the front gate. A taxi. Ash bellowed as loud as he could and pulled a sodden wad of roubles from his pocket.

"Astoria," he gasped. Shaking uncontrollably, he huddled into a ball for warmth. He wondered if he would die. But even as the car crossed the city at a maddeningly slow pace, an idea began to form in his battered mind. Rasputin thought he was dead.

198

Ash banged on the driver's partition and gasped through chattering teeth, "Servants' entrance."

It was doubtful the driver understood English, but it would have been a dull man who would have dropped a passenger in Ash's condition any place less private at the Astoria than the servants' entrance.

Narvski left the evidence and told Prince Felix and Purishkevich good-night to let them stew alone. A troika sleigh was waiting down the bank of the Moika Canal. The man pretending to be an ordinary coachman was another Red Snow agent.

"They believed it," Narvski said as he climbed in the sleigh.

"Incredible. Why do they think Rasputin would take German bribes when he can have anything in Russia?"

"They hate him. Enough to believe anything. At least this story. Where's Ash?"

"We haven't found him yet."

Narvski took off his glove and pulled out a watch. One in the morning. "Try his hotel."

The "coachman" spoke to his horses, and when the animals were moving asked over his shoulder, "What did Ash do that we should kill him?"

Narvski knew only that orders had come through Switzerland to kill the navy officer. He knew nothing of the agreement that the brothers Vladimir and Dmitri Dan had made with the German General Ludendorff, nor, for that matter, did he even know the brothers Dan. But he believed that discipline was vital to the safety of underground cells, that too many people knowing too much could kill a revolution. There was no place for the "coachman's" question, and Narvski answered, "They will tell us when we should know."

"One wonders why an American—"

Narvski cut him off. "If one wondered less and paid closer attention to one's horses one would not have lost Commander Ash when he left his hotel earlier this evening in a woman's sleigh."

"You try driving three horses at once . . ." They rode in silence, but as they neared the Astoria, the "coachman" asked, "Why do you suppose the police follow Ash?" It was their car, a fake taximeter cab, which had spooked his horses and sent them careening across St. Issac's Square and in front of a tram on the Admiralty Prospect. Before he got them under control, Ash and the woman had vanished.

Narvski said, "I don't know. But they're making this difficult." He reached into the hiding place in the seat cushion and checked that the heavy British Webley revolver was still in place.

The back stairs were the worst. He spent five minutes slumped on the half-landing, growing colder. When he realized he could die there, he crawled. The hall porter saw Ash shambling along the corridor and unlocked his door and clucked at the muddy wet trail on the carpet.

He was vaguely aware of the telephone ringing over the roar of the water taps, but he had to get into the tub before the cold killed him. Too weak to pull off his boots, he climbed in with them on. Shivering violently, he felt like an insulated flask, his skin and flesh standing between the hot bath water and the ice in his guts.

At last the warmth penetrated. He stopped shaking. His mind drifted. Fell asleep. But wakened when the tub had cooled and realized that the telephone could have been the Czarina's answer for King George.

Gathering his strength, moving slowly, he worked off his ruined boots, started a fresh bath running, wrapped himself in towels and called the hotel desk. "This is—" His voice cracked. He cleared his throat with difficulty and concentrated hard on saying, "Commander Ash. Any messages?"

"None, sir."

"Was that you called before?"

"Yes, sir. The hall porter—is everything all right?"

Why didn't she call? Contact him? What was she waiting for? He looked at the marble clock on the mantle. Two-thirty in the morning? "I need a pot of coffee and a bottle of brandy."

He soaked in the new tub until the hall porter knocked. Then he got into bed and drank coffee and brandy half and half until he fell asleep and dreamed of Rasputin pushing him under the ice each time he tried to climb out of the hole.

He woke at noon, stiff and bleary-eyed. He was light-headed, his back hurt. It was still hard to concentrate. Two cups of coffee didn't help. Fragmented events of the night drifted past his mind. He was alive by the combination of a miracle and years of struggling to keep in fighting trim. He recalled moments in the water when a single ounce less of strength would have been fatal.

He tried a few dozen situps and pushups, which got the blood running and gave him a headache, while he catalogued his condition like a ship's engineer listening to his turbines to hear what worked and what needed servicing. He was weak, he was chilled, he still found it hard to concentrate with a strangely emptied mind, but he seemed okay, other than a light cough, which the entire population of Petrograd suffered each winter as the damp seeped out of the marshy ground.

Midafternoon dissolved in a flood of memory and speculation. Rasputin

200

had overheard his conversation with Czarina Alexandra, heard King George's offer of asylum, couldn't convince her not to leave Russia so tried to drug and hypnotize Ash into withdrawing the offer, and when that failed had thrown him in the Fontanka River. Simple enough, except Ash had managed to climb out.

But by evening the Czarina had still not sent a message. Two and a half days without a word. And Ash had to face the possibility, despite Rasputin's fears, that the Czarina or the Czar had decided against leaving Russia. He telephoned the Alexander Palace, but got no further into the court than a senior telephone operator who agreed to leave word he had called with the colonel that Ash had shown the Czarina's gift to, which meant nothing . . . He had to do more, had to get through to the Czarina, somehow persuade her . . .

He had one ace in the hole. Rasputin thought he was dead. How would the monk react to a man he thought he had murdered? Could he conceivably frighten Rasputin into interceding with the Czarina, into talking her into leaving Russia? Literally scare the wits out of him.

Mulling the idea, he had supper in his room, then put on a clean dress uniform identical to the uniform Rasputin had last seen him alive in. He was still shaky, but this seemed too good a chance to let pass . . . What if he were just sitting in Rasputin's apartment when the monk came home? Waiting among his icons . . . Not so bad. Not bad at all. Scary . . .

But to break into Rasputin's apartment Ash had to elude the monk's detectives and steer clear of the police watching the Astoria as well. He put on a navy greatcoat and a Russian fur hat Tamara had given him. They hid his face and altered the familiar boat-cloak and service-cap silhouette the Czar's police had been trailing.

Then he went out through the hotel kitchen and ducked into a channel between the woodpiles and emerged on the other side of St. Isaac's Square, where he hailed a sleigh that had just dropped passengers at the Maryinski Palace, and told the driver Rasputin's address.

The driver shrugged. No English. Ash gestured him around the corner to Gorokhovaya Street, which fanned out from the Admiralty, like the Nevsky Prospect, and angled away from the Nevsky into Rasputin's Moscow District. He indicated Rasputin's house number with his fingers. Six-four.

He had fooled the police. Checking behind him for their taxi, he saw only a troika. Carrying a single passenger the three-horse sleigh skidded off Morskaya Street and dropped far behind. He expected it to turn left on Kazanskaya, toward the Kazan Cathedral, where the troikas for hire had their stand, but it was still behind him when his sleigh crossed the Fontanka—a quarter mile upstream from where he had nearly drowned —and entered Rasputin's neighborhood.

He was wondering about the troika, and wishing he had brought a flask because the night was even colder than last night, when his driver suddenly hauled back on the reins with a surprised grunt. Half a block ahead, Rasputin careened into the street bellowing at the top of his lungs, trailed by three detectives hard put to keep up while they stuffed notebooks and pencils into their pockets and tried to button their coats.

Ash's driver jerked his horses into a courtyard, obviously wanting no part of the drama in the street. Rasputin ran past, shouting, laughing, his beard streaming to the sides while he hailed passersby with a Madeira bottle. His detectives dog-trotted after him, falling back a half block.

Fortunate timing, thought Ash. No one guarding the apartment. But what about the troika following? He caught a glimpse of it as it crossed the Fontanka, hesitated and skidded clumsily into the street beside the river. It could be *his* coppers. Why not follow Rasputin instead? Lay back until he found a good place to brace the monk?

He pressed a gold sovereign into his driver's hand and gestured he should follow the running figures back down Gorokhovaya in the direction they had just driven. The coin was worth a British pound—ten roubles before the war, for a ride which cost one or two roubles, and worth two or three times that as the rouble's value plummeted. The driver hurriedly backed his horses out of the courtyard and cracked his whip.

Rasputin ran all the way to the Ekaterinski Canal, outdistancing his detectives, who had slowed to shambling walks and seemed to be looking around for a car. At the canal he hailed a sleigh, which he rode to the Kazan Cathedral, a grand affair faced with an enormous semicircular colonnade set back from the Nevsky Prospect, where the late evening crowds turned from the glittering shop windows to stare at the not unfamiliar sight of the Czarina's holy man on a binge.

Behind the Kazan were the troikas, fast pleasure sleighs lined up for hire at great expense. The war had not changed everything, it seemed. Sporting hats adorned with peacock feathers, the drivers were proudly grooming sleek thoroughbreds while they waited for their wealthy fares. Rasputin leaped into one, pulled a fresh bottle from his enormous fur coat, and bellowed, "Krestovsky!"

Ash had his driver hang back until Rasputin pulled away. Krestovsky was a forested delta island where the gypsies had a permanent encampment on the Nevka, a branch at the mouth of the Neva. But it was miles out from the city; Ash's sleigh would never make it, nor could it keep up with the much faster troika. He jumped aboard the next troika and handed the driver two gold coins and gestured to follow Rasputin. He pulled a lap robe over his legs for the long cold ride and wished again he had brought a flask. Drunk, Rasputin apparently had a yen for gypsy music, as Russians tended to when they got drunk. No tame Sadovaya Street restaurant gypsies would do.

But before they had gone a mile down the Nevsky, Rasputin waved his arms and his troika swung onto Morskaya Street, passed Ash's hotel and parked in front of St. Issac's Cathedral. Rasputin took a drink from his bottle and ran up the cathedral steps, singing and fumbling with his clothes.

Ash motioned his driver to park in the shadows as Rasputin's detectives caught up in a smoking old flivver. The monk Rasputin began urinating in the colonnade. The detectives got out and conferred anxiously around their car. Then three orthodox priests in flapping black robes and head-dress stormed out a brass door and charged the monk, who was desecrating their cathedral. Rasputin backed away, laughing. A fourth priest emerged, swinging a long staff bearing the cross.

Ash started to jump down to help, terrified the priest would brain his possibly best last chance at the Czarina, but the detectives clattered up the steps and disarmed the man. Another priest fell down, tangled in his robe. Rasputin yanked a third off balance by grabbing his cross by the thick chain around the man's neck, dodged the fourth and went down the steps back to his troika, which surged out of the square while the detectives were still grappling with the priests.

Seeing a chance to get Rasputin away from his bodyguards, Ash passed his driver more of King George's gold and gestured urgently to follow. The troikas circled behind St. Issac's, ran between the Admiralty and the Winter Palace and swung onto the Dvortsov Bridge. They cut across the tip of Vassilyevskaya Island—which split the Neva in two—past the Stock Exchange, and across another bridge. Passing the Peter and Paul Fortress and prison and the Arsenal, they rode through the narrow streets of a sleeping factory district for a couple of miles. A final bridge brought them to the beginning of Krestovsky Island, where, at last, the troikas came into their own. Rasputin's picked up speed. Ash's driver waited until it was a hundred yards ahead, then spoke to his horses.

The lead horse in shafts broke into a fast trot. But the loosely harnessed outer horses, held only by leather traces, galloped wild and free. The effect was as swift as it was improbable. And eerily silent. The Russian troika had no bells like a European sleigh. The snow muffled the horses' hooves. The loudest sounds Ash heard were the animals' breathing and runners' hiss.

The silence deepened when they left the suburban fringe of the city behind and with it its dim street lights. Even Rasputin seemed awed by the silence. From what Ash could see he had stopped throwing his arms about. Nor did his shouts carry back over the snow which glistened pale blue in the starlight. He glanced back once. The starlight glinted on a mantle of frost covering his long beard. The cold was bitter, and Ash felt his mustache turn to ice.

Ash glanced back. The police car was nowhere to be seen, but another troika seemed to be following. Same one as on Gorokhovaya Street? The road curved and he glimpsed a single passenger in it, intently watching.

A birch forest moved close to the road, and Ash lost sight of him. Maybe the detectives protecting Rasputin had changed vehicles. Or maybe the police following *him* had spotted him in the square. He had better make his move now before they got to the gypsy encampment.

His driver drove standing, controlling his horses with the reins and a steady stream of conversation. Ash showed him another sovereign—his hands were too full of reins to hold it—and motioned to catch up. The conversation took on an urgent tone, the horses leaped ahead. They had halved the distance between them and Rasputin's troika when the monk tossed an empty bottle into the trees, where it shattered musically. Closer, and Ash heard women's laughter.

And then he spotted them, riding a slow-moving troika that Rasputin's sleigh was starting to overtake. The monk stood up, opened his trousers, and repeated his remarkable St. Issac's performance as his troika drew alongside the women's on a wide spot in the road. Shrieking laughter, they shook up a champagne bottle and sprayed him back.

"Now," Ash said, standing up and removing his coat and hat, and gesturing. *"Pass them now."*

27

Thirteen bottles of Madeira surely purged a man, but couldn't quiet Rasputin's fear that he had sinned in an awful way he had never sinned before. He was glad Ash couldn't take the Czarina away, but he wished he had not killed him. He had always preached that out of sin came salvation, but fornicating and drinking were not sins like murder, and for the first time in his life Rasputin doubted that God would laugh with him.

Cold champagne splashed his face as he laughed along with the women, laughed with his mouth while in his heart were tears. There were three of them—young, bejeweled and pretty in the starlight, trading ribald comments. "Put it back before it freezes," one called out, and they shrieked and hugged each other as the troikas careened side by side.

Suddenly, behind them, stood Ash.

Rasputin blinked. Ash in uniform. Standing in a troika on the other side of the women's sleigh. *Ash.* The starlight glittering on his medals and service ribbons. Gold cords on his shoulder. Sword at his side. *Alive?*

Rasputin felt the hairs straightening up the back of his neck, up his head, under his hat, standing up stiff as quills. He covered his eyes. Too much Madeira. He peeked out between his fingers. Ash saluted. Rasputin felt an earthly animal howl explode in his throat. He leaped away from the apparition, backward, off the troika, and fell into a snowdrift.

The look on Rasputin's face was almost worth drowning in the Fontanka. The monk's hair had stood up on end as if he had shoved wet fingers into an electric outlet, and his howl had sounded of terror equal to Ash's own

205

the previous night. Rasputin falling into the snowdrift was icing on the cake. Now to exploit the advantage.

He showed his eager driver another gold sovereign and motioned him to top speed. Behind them both Rasputin's and the women's drivers had stopped. They were standing the monk unsteadily on his feet. There was another howl, and Rasputin leaped on his troika and gesticulated for his driver to catch up. Perfect. Ash hunched down out of sight. When he looked back again he saw Rasputin standing beside his driver; behind them the troika following had passed the women.

The horses were breathing hard, but they were almost at the gypsy camp. Beyond the River Yacht Club, on the shore of the Srednyaya Nevka, the road veered away from the water and briefly into deep forest again. Moments later Ash's troika pulled up in a clearing lit by a bonfire. At the edge of the clearing, surrounded on three sides by fir trees was a long, low wooden building from which drifted guitar music and mournful singing.

Troikas and private sleighs were parked outside, and their drivers had grouped around the fire. Rasputin's sleigh came in moments later, the horses' coats steaming in the cold. Rasputin spotted Ash, leaped down while his troika was still moving, and ran after him, skidding on the beaten snow.

Ash ignored him and walked to the gypsies' door. Rasputin pounded up behind him, grabbed his arm and jerked him around to see his face. Ash smiled, turned away.

"Navy man?" Rasputin grabbed him again.

"Speak any English?"

"A little," Rasputin replied, fingering Ash's coat to prove he was real.

"I have powers too." Ash watched him. He was drunk. It was difficult to tell what the monk believed, but he certainly seemed, so to speak, spooked. He was not, however, going to concede mystical powers in his own territory. Staunchly, even as his wide eyes swept disbelievingly over Ash, he said, "God's will you didn't die, Navy man."

Ash went for broke. "I did die, Rasputin. God sent me back."

"*Da?*" the monk answered dubiously.

Ash felt like a snake oil salesman trying to con a circus barker. "God sent me to take you to England with the Czarina."

King George might not like a holy Russian peasant roaming around the palace, but that was one small sacrifice the Royal Family would have to make to help bring the U.S. into the war.

Before Rasputin could reply, the troika with the women pulled up and they descended laughing and calling, "Father Gregory." Ash wondered where the sleigh with the man who had passed them had gone, but the dubious, confused look on Rasputin's face was taking most of his attention. How to use it. He took his arm and steered him away from the women toward the door. "Drink?"

206

"Da." Of that Rasputin was certain.

They went inside the single, long low room. Half the space was a dancing stage and the other half a heap of pillows and blankets where the customers reclined. Twenty or thirty gypsies dressed in colorful silk, rough-cut jewels and beads, were cavorting on the stage, singing and thrumming guitars. Twice their number of revelers from Petrograd, wearing diamonds and gold, were singing, clapping time and drinking champagne on the cushions. Hundreds of candles burned in sconces around the walls. Tartar waiters, tall and dark, passed around the room pouring from bottles wrapped in gold foil.

Rasputin was still staring at Ash when people started shouting his name. "Father Gregory! Father Gregory!" He was known among the customers and known by the gypsies. Three young girls with dark eyes and thick lashes ran into his arms, laughing smiles lighting their olive faces. Rasputin scooped them up automatically but his eyes remained fixed on Ash, and a look very much like panic never left his face.

"You must convince the Czarina to leave," Ash said, glancing at the gypsy girls, whose expression confirmed they understood no English.

It took a moment for Rasputin to digest the language, but at last he did. Snatching a bottle from one of the Tartars he took a long pull and passed it to Ash. Champagne. Too sweet, but at least undrugged. Ash passed it back. Rasputin sank to the cushions, dragging the girls on top of him. Ash dropped beside them. "Listen to me . . ."

Red Snow's agent Narvski knew his moment to serve the Revolution had come. A true believer. Odd how little warning. Yesterday he was a mere courier sent to trick Prince Felix and Purishkevich; now his life was on the line. The gypsies guarded their camp, but the chance to shoot Ash was too good to pass up, and if he were killed by the gypsies, his life was not as important as the Revolution.

He could probably kill Rasputin too, but Red Snow had already decided who should do that for maximum effect; when Prince Felix and Purishkevich and their friend the young Grand Duke Dmitri were implicated—and Red Snow had plenty of evidence on hand for the police to guarantee that they would be—the news would shock the nation far more than a simple shooting in a gypsy camp. That fate would be sufficient for Ash.

Narvski took the Webley, crept through the woods behind the gypsy building. He spotted a shutter high on the side deepest in the woods. He watched that wall for ten minutes; no one walked past it. Nor were they likely to, he discovered, when he got closer. There were no footprints beside the building, no path beaten in the snow. Out front the troika drivers huddled close to the bonfire, leaving their circle only to get more firewood stacked nearby.

The gypsy chorus was nasal sounding, almost metallic. It sang loudly, and the voices had a barbaric eastern ring. The harmonies, though, were exquisite, impossibly complex. The Russians seemed drunk on the melodies, Rasputin drunker than all the rest. He thrashed around beside Ash, alternately fondling and kissing the girls and shouting the choruses led from the stage.

And all the while Ash hammered at him.

"The revolutionaries will kill you. God saved my life to save your life . . ."

Rasputin turned away.

"If the Czar falls you fall. What will happen to all your detectives? Are you afraid? Everybody hates you. They want to kill you."

Rasputin turned on him. "They hate Rasputin because they hate a peasant to screw his supposed betters."

"No matter. They hate you enough to kill you, Father Gregory. Come away until it's over. Then you can all come back." If he believed that . . .

"I'm not afraid of mixed-blood nobles. Real Russians, the *moujiks,* will defend Rasputin—"

"Could a peasant save you if a nobleman were waiting outside with a gun right now?"

"They can't kill *me.* If they kill Rasputin they all will be lost. All Russia lost . . . I see . . ."

"What is it?" Ash prompted. It was eerie, but he could see Rasputin seeing. The monk's eyes shone almost luminously, as if he were gazing through himself beyond even the future. Ash actually felt himself drawn into their liquid depths, fathomless, warm shafts into which one could sink to the center of the earth.

". . . I see heaps, masses of corpses . . . hundreds of counts and several grand dukes . . ." Ash wondered if he could see Tamara's Grand Duke Valery among them. Rasputin found a bottle and shoved the neck in his mouth, drank deep. ". . . And the Neva all red with blood—"

"*Save the Czarina,*" Ash intoned. "Save the Czar, the children. *Save yourself—*"

Ash slapped the bottle out of his hand. No one noticed, they were singing the gypsy chorus.

"*Listen* to me, you son of a bitch."

Rasputin stared at him, dumbfounded by Ash's effrontery. Ash raised his hand, and the monk actually cringed.

"If you won't save the Czarina, then you murder her. Come with me. All of you. You *must* make the Czarina do it . . ."

208

Unexpectedly, Rasputin grinned. "I can make her do anything."

The candles flickered. Ash looked up, feeling a cold draft on his face. But before he found the source, Rasputin said, "Father Czar will thank me. And the peasants will thank me."

"And the Czarina," Ash encouraged. "She will—what's wrong?"

Rasputin's eyes had filled with tears. "But what will I be in England?"

The candles flickered again. Again the draft. Ash saw an opening in the wall across the room, twenty feet from where they lay. A square hinged outward, a shutter plucked by the wind. But something black was holding it open. A short piece of pipe. Only he noticed it in the din of laughter and singing.

Ash sat up suddenly. It wasn't a pipe. The candles nearest it blew out. Rasputin shoved a champagne bottle into Ash's hand. The shutter opened wide, and in the black space of night hung a disembodied face, aiming a gun at him.

28

The gunman's eye was bisected by the front sight, and Ash was close enough to see it squint against the candle glare as he sought Ash's head. A thumb descended out of the dark toward the hammer. Ash threw the champagne bottle. It sailed the twenty feet in a hard, flat trajectory, smashed on the frame of the window. The largest piece kept going, hit the gunman as he fired.

Ash heard and felt a heavy slug part the air next to his head. The bullet clanged through a samovar. Men and women got to their feet, screaming, blocking the gun and the face in the black hole in the wall. A second shot; they all ducked down. The music stopped, the screaming doubled.

Rasputin staggered erect, swayed. "Murder, they kill Rasputin—"

"I told you," Ash said, shoving him out of the way and running for the door. He ran into the snow and around the side of the building, pulling his own weapon from his back. Ash knew he had been the real target, and he wanted the gunman to tell him why.

But he wasn't the only hunter now. A pair of gypsy knifemen followed, silent as panthers. Ash found the spot where the gunman had propped a chopping block under the window. The broken bottle lay beside it. The gypsies spotted tracks in the snow. Ash went after them, into the woods. There were dark splotches of blood in the starlight. The gypsies pointed with their gleaming blades. Ash plunged after them, determined to take the gunman alive.

Fire lanced out of the night, and one of the gypsies fell, kicking the snow convulsively as the shot boomed and crackled in the trees. The screams in the building started up again. Ash ran into the remaining gypsy, hiding

210

behind a thick tree. He saw Ash's gun and pointed across a ten-foot clearing. Ash glanced around the other side of the tree.

The gunman hid, half-crouched, breathing hard. He bolted for another tree. Ash fired and he went down clutching his leg. His gun skidded across the frozen snow. Ash picked it up and walked toward him. The gypsy slithered after him with the knife extended. Ash pushed him aside, pointed a gun at him. *"Nyet."*

When Narvski saw Ash stop the gypsy from killing him where he lay writhing on the snow, he understood that Ash wanted him alive for interrogation. The tall American approached, his uniform oddly immaculate in this miserable forest, snow crystals sparkling on his trousers where he'd broken through the crust. Narvski slid a knife from his sleeve. Ash jerked back out of reach and pointed his gun.

"Don't even think about it."

But Narvski had already made his decision.

Sacrifice was the Revolution's heart, discipline its tool, and he feared that when the Czar's police hurt him he would eventually talk. Red Snow was organized on a cell basis. He knew the name of one comrade above him, and three below, and precious little more, but even a single name was more than he would ever give the Czar. He looked at his blade a second, then drew it across his throat.

Ash tried to save him, tried to hold the wound closed and pack the torn vessels with snow. "Get help," he ordered the gypsy. But the man only gave him a murderous look and knelt beside his own dead friend. Ash saw the life disappear from the gunman's face. Oddly, he looked Russian, not German, and the dying light in his eyes was more defiant than fearful. But why had he killed himself if he wasn't afraid? Ash searched his pockets. He carried Russian papers, which wasn't surprising, and what looked like Russian army discharge papers as well. They had his picture, and if they were forgeries they were very good ones. He even had an icon on a chain around his neck, a nice touch for a German spy. But he surely looked Russian. Puzzled, Ash headed back through the woods to the gypsy house, hoping that Rasputin would still think he was the target, and that it would frighten him enough to help convince the Czarina to leave Russia.

The police arrived as he entered the clearing. He heard bells and saw their headlights coming up the road from Petrograd and ducked into the gypsy building moments ahead of a dozen police in long green uniforms followed by the plainclothes detectives who had been guarding Rasputin's apartment.

"They try to kill Rasputin, navy man . . ."

It evidently worried him enough to consume a half dozen more bottles of champagne, which lay empty beside him and the sleeping gypsy girls. He looked frightened and very drunk, and when the police came in he leaped to his feet, screaming drunken Russian, which Ash could only guess meant where were they when he needed them.

They came running, kicking the other revelers out of their way.

Rasputin snatched up a bottle and attacked his protectors, knocked a detective down and hit two more who tried to grab his arm. Spittle came to his mouth as he raged and snapped and snarled. A policeman raised his club. The others stopped him. Crazy-drunk or not, Father Gregory Rasputin was still, after all, the Czarina's favorite.

Five men wrestled him to the floor. Two more pinned his arms and legs, and Ash watched helplessly, unable to prevent the police from carrying their drunken charge home to bed . . . and with them very likely his best . . . his only? . . . chance of convincing the Czarina and Czar to leave Russia.

The "coachman," the Red Snow comrade who had driven Narvski's troika, hid in the Vyborg district in a machine-gun factory abandoned weeks earlier for lack of fuel, and it was not until late the following afternoon that Narvski's superior tracked him down and got the whole story. The coachman reported the little he knew, then pleaded for his life. It wasn't the police he was hiding from but a revolutionary party that demanded results, and Narvski's superior was accompanied by two comrades with "executioner" written all over them. "I couldn't help," he said, gazing forlornly around the cold factory. Ice had formed on the punch presses and stamping machines; half-finished Maxim guns lay on a silent, immobile conveyer belt. What a place to die. His father had been night watchman before it closed—how they had found him. "I stayed in the sleigh like Comrade Narvski told me."

"An investigation is in progress," came the indifferent reply. "In the meantime you will deliver a letter to Commander Ash at the Astoria Hotel. This evening."

Ash was three-quarters through the story of the night before, describing Rasputin's face when he passed the monk's troika, and François Roland's amusement had shredded his customary reserve, when the Astoria's

212

maitre d'hotel interrupted their dinner with an envelope on a silver tray —hand-delivered and urgent.

From the Czarina, thought Ash, although it bore no crest.

Roland's eyebrows zigzagged in protest.

"No business tonight, my friend. It is New Year's Eve—in Europe, at least—and we are invited to every embassy worth visiting, including yours with that delicious child. Let it wait."

They were dressed for the evening, Ash in social dress uniform, Roland in white tie, and were well through their second bottle of wine—a beaujolais for the pheasant that had just arrived, following a stern graves with the smoked and pickled meats and fishes the Russians called *zakouski.* And Roland was in doubly high spirits having confessed earlier that he was falling in love—"or something similar," as he had put it—with an officer of the Life Guard Preobrajenski Regiment. He had even pronounced Ash's lunge much improved at a lesson before dinner.

Ash, for his part, was celebrating just being alive, despite disappointing progress, which the envelope suggested might be about to improve. He tore it open with apologies but the letter inside was not from the Czarina. He looked at Roland. The Frenchman's eyebrows had assumed a flat, noncommittal line; Ash could tell him as little or much as he wanted to. His business.

"The son of a bitch wants me to meet him at midnight at the Yusupov Palace."

"Rasputin? . . . Which Yusupov Palace?"

"The one on the Moika."

"Perhaps he intends drowning you in a more fashionable canal. Shall I come with you?"

"No, thanks. I think I've scared him out of bothering me . . . He says he's visiting the Princess Irina. She's the Czar's niece, isn't she?"

"Yes. Prince Felix's wife. The Czar offered them any gift they wanted for their wedding and Felix took an imperial box at the Maryinski, which I rather admired."

She sounded to Ash like a very good connection.

"Wonder what Rasputin wants," Roland said, turning his knife and fork to a lean pheasant breast.

Ash had not told Roland about Ambassador Page's Inner Circle, nor the plan to remove the Czar from Russia, nor King George's mission to rescue his cousin, a matter of discretion which his friend accepted as Ash's right to decide upon. Roland knew about Ash's visit to the Kaiser, though not the reason, and was actively involved in helping him secure audiences with the Czar and Czarina. Ash had told him about Rasputin, minus certain details, because there was no reason not to. As to why Rasputin wanted to see him again, he could only hope that the monk had decided to intercede with the Czarina.

"I tried to get hold of the bastard all day, but his friends wouldn't let me near the baths where he was sobering up."

He pocketed Rasputin's letter and returned his attention to dinner. The Yusupov Palace was a short walk from the Astoria and he had plenty of time until midnight . . . It could be the monk wanted to leave Russia until things cooled down. Sounded promising . . .

All Rasputin wanted was a glass of tea. He had drunk enough Madeira to float the Baltic Fleet, but Felix kept pouring more wine. It tasted awful, like a cow had defecated in the vat, and it made him thirsty for more tea. Something was wrong with it; usually he drank a dozen bottles. No more.

But Felix insisted, kept pouring. And if that weren't enough, the Prince demanded that Rasputin eat great batches of sweet cakes. Rasputin obliged. Ordinarily he would have kicked the young pup out of the room —and be damned whose house it was—and done what he pleased, but Felix had promised to introduce him to his wife, the beautiful Princess Irina.

At last, tonight, he would have her. He had only seen pictures and they showed her to be as beautiful as people said she was. When he fixed her with his gaze, she would be his, provided Felix's wine didn't put him to sleep first, or, worse, weaken the holy shaft.

She was upstairs, entertaining friends. Rasputin could hear the music, the same song playing over and over on the gramophone. Felix said it was an American song. It just would not stop.

"Won't she be down soon?"

"I'll go ask her," Felix answered. "Have another sweet."

Rasputin gobbled down two. They were quite pleasant, and the wine was somehow tasting a little better now. As Felix headed out the door, he was hard to see, and Rasputin wondered if he had had too much to drink after all. He thought he'd close his eyes and gain some strength for the young princess. At this rate she'd be greatly disappointed. He reached into his pants and rearranged himself. It was growing distinctly soft. What the devil was Felix feeding him? Poison? Like he fed the navy man . . . ?

It was the navy man's fault. All that talk about running away to England . . . Had God sent him? . . . After the war Russia would settle down, the peasants would be happy again. Perhaps they'd slaughter the nobility— the mixed-blood vipers—perhaps kill the merchants—the thieves—and the governors—the corrupt. Then the peasants and the Czar would live together in harmony again. Burn some estates, bring the Cossacks home to restore order. God smiled.

Rasputin grinned, thought of the dark-eyed princess upstairs and felt himself grown comfortably hard again. The music stopped, suddenly. The guests were leaving. She would be down in a minute. Some excuse to get rid of Felix, send him for something.

Rasputin looked blearily around the stone-vaulted room. A thick white bearskin rug beckoned on the floor in front of the fire. He would have her on the rug, hold her down, push her clothing up around her waist and shove into her. In the moment he'd need to recover she would get used to the idea, and when he drove into her the second time she would be ready, wetted by his juices and, if she was the right sort, some of her own. He heard the door and opened his eyes for the first look at the princess.

What he saw was Felix. Felix handed him another glass of Madeira. Rasputin drank it wearily. So tired. It was hard to remember what was happening, almost what he was waiting for . . .

"Should we go to the gypsies?"

"It's too late," said Felix. His voice sounded far away.

Rasputin pulled himself out of the chair and wandered around the room. A little Chinese ebony chest caught his attention; it had compartments, doors, secret drawers and mirrors. It seemed like a whole perfect world he could happily live in forever if he were small enough.

He turned to Felix to tell him that. Felix had a gun.

"Say a prayer," Rasputin heard him say. A crucifix swam before his eyes, and the gun grew larger, and suddenly roared like the devil.

Rasputin screamed—his voice as distant as Felix's—and felt himself crash to the floor. He landed on the white fur rug and his head lolled to the side. The long white hairs tickled his face, and he thought that that was how it would have felt to the princess's wide spread thighs . . .

François Roland was drinking champagne with the director of the Imperial Theater, gossiping about the great Tishkova, who was holding court on the other side of the Italian Embassy's ballroom, when an exchange in the conversation of the next group along the bar jarred him.

"Pardon," he interrupted brusquely, surprising the director of the Imperial Theater and annoying the people he had intruded on. He did not waste time apologizing, yet the haughty challenges on the faces of the officers melted to ingratiating smiles when they recognized him. He was not known as a duelist, but who wanted to be the first to provoke him into changing his habits?

"Did you say the Princess Irina is not in the city?"

"Her Highness went to the Crimea to visit her parents."

"Could she be back?" Roland demanded.

"So soon, Monsieur? It is fifteen hundred miles and the trains—"

"Excusez-moi." He rushed across the dance floor, through the quadrille, pausing only to get his cloak and stick because there was a blade in it, and raced into the street, where he hired the fastest sleigh parked in front of the embassy.

"Yusupov's Moika Palace!"

He jerked out his watch as the sleigh raced toward the Nevsky. After midnight. What had Kenneth walked into? What had Rasputin wanted? . . .

But Ash hadn't told him . . . nor had he told his friend that the note signed by Rasputin had directed him to a side entrance of Prince Felix's private wing.

And it was there that Ash crouched in the shadows of a gatepost. When he had arrived he had heard a gramophone blasting "Yankee Doodle Dandy," but when he had knocked on the door nearest the window the music was coming from, no one had answered. He had waited a while on the street. No Rasputin. He had figured he would wait five more minutes. Then two shots had boomed out and the music stopped and Ash had ducked behind the gatepost, out of sight of the main entrance on the canal.

Rasputin thought he was dead, but in his mind he drove into the princess, pounded while she wept and struggled, drove hard, but losing his hardness, until she rolled on top of him and ground her belly against his and shook him violently with her delicate little hands.

He opened his eyes.

Felix was shaking him. When their eyes met, Felix's face melted in horror. *"He's alive . . ."*

Rasputin grabbed Felix by the throat. The prince screamed again, pulled away, ripping cloth, and ran like he had just seen the devil.

Rasputin struggled into a sitting position. He hurt inside and he was confused. Felix kept screaming, somewhere upstairs, "He's alive, shoot, shoot him . . ."

Steeling his body against the pain, Rasputin tried to stand. He dragged himself to a wall, pulled up it, then worked along it to the door. Stairs. Impossible. But he remembered that they had come down the stairs immediately after he and Felix had entered the side door of the palace. If he could climb the stairs he'd escape into the street. Step by step he pulled himself up toward the outside door.

He heard their footsteps, heard Felix screaming, "Shoot him, he's getting away . . ."

He made it to the door, fell against it and shoved it open. Cold air gave him strength. His mind was clearing. They were murderers behind him. Felix had tricked him to come here, had fed him poison, had shot him . . .

216

"He's getting away . . ."

If he could just make it across the courtyard to the street . . . thirty feet across the courtyard, through the gate, into the street. There was a police station nearby. He would be safe . . . He saw the navy man at the gate.

"Navy man!" His savior.

Ash saw Rasputin stagger across the dark courtyard. When he reached the fence he seemed lost. Then he spotted Ash at the gate.

"Navy man . . ."

The monk shambled along the iron fence, pulling himself on the palings. A light from the palace windows fell on his face; he was grimacing and holding his chest.

"Help me, navy man . . ."

He started to fall. Ash hurried toward him. A man ran out the door Rasputin had come from and aimed a gun at the staggering figure. Ash pulled his own gun. "Get *down.*"

Two more shots were fired before he could take aim, a heavy revolver that sounded like a cannon, and hit like one too. Rasputin pitched forward as the first slug smashed into his back. The second snapped his head around as if he were glancing over his shoulder, and he fell hard into the snow.

Ash fired in the direction of the blinding muzzle flashes, but the gunman had ducked back out of sight. Ash knelt beside Rasputin, tried to pull him away while he watched for the gunman to reappear.

"Father Gregory . . ."

Tugging his hand feebly, Rasputin whispered, "Navy man . . ." His eye flickered. Ash leaned close and put his ear to Rasputin's lips. "Save her, navy man. Save the Czarina."

He shuddered once, and lay still.

"If you love the Czar you'll say nothing."

Ash looked up at the crazed face of a man he didn't know, holding a revolver and staring down at him. He looked drunk.

Two soldiers came into the courtyard.

"I've killed Rasputin," the man said, waving his gun.

The soldiers stared at the body, crossed themselves and murmured, one after another, "Thank God. Thank God."

Ash stood up carefully and backed away, holding his gun at his side. From the gate he took one last look at the corpse of his best hope of convincing Czarina Alexandra to persuade the Czar to leave Russia.

And then he ran.

François Roland came running along the canal toward him, the empty left dinner-jacket sleeve flapping as his opera cloak streamed behind him. Ash waved him away. The Frenchman obeyed, vanished into the shadows.

Ash turned in the opposite direction and began a roundabout route home to the Astoria. Around a corner, less than ninety feet from the courtyard where Rasputin lay, in the darkest patch between two pools of street light, two policemen were waiting, their dark green coats black in the night.

They barred the way with their clubs. Neither spoke English, but a club pointed at his gun, still in his hand, was clear enough. Ash clicked the safety on as he handed it over. They seemed to have been hiding in the dark patch, waiting. For what? Maybe for an idiot who'd responded to a forged note from Rasputin?

A long, dark car pulled alongside the curb. Plainclothes. Three men got out. One frisked him and took his sword. They looked a few notches above the cops who had been tailing him around the city. Okhrana elite, he guessed. *Secret* secret police. The sort who caught assassins and revolutionaries and people dumb enough to be caught near a murder with a gun in their hand. He had a lot of talking to do.

"I am a diplomat."

"Put him in the car."

When all four of them were crammed into the passenger compartment and the car was rolling in the direction of the Neva, Ash repeated, "I am a diplomat."

The one in charge said, "You were seen in the vicinity of the Yusupov Moika Palace."

"I was walking home to my hotel."

"With a gun in your hand. Did you hear anything unusual?"

"I heard a loud party as I passed the palace. I stopped. I saw a man shot in the courtyard. It was the monk Father Gregory R—"

"I've been there. There was no body. Several witnesses place you there, including two who confirm there was a dead man, briefly, in the courtyard. Where is he now?"

"Rasputin—"

"We are investigating," the detective cut him off again. The car raced between the Admiralty and the Winter Palace and crossed the Neva on the Dvortsov Bridge. Ash considered his position. Someone had gone to a great deal of trouble to get him arrested, almost as if deciding he was too hard to kill, they'd get him locked up a while. He must not let it work . . . "I'm a diplomat, I'm immune to arrest, I demand to be taken directly to the American Embassy—"

"My English is not so fine," the officer said. "I am not familiar with your phrases . . ."

The car turned from the bridge toward the dark shape of the Peter and Paul Fortress. It stopped before a huge, studded gate. Soldiers checked the driver's papers and signaled the gate to open. Ash glimpsed the palace lights across the Neva before the car drove into a dark tunnel through the fortress wall.

BOOK

III
The Grand Ducal Quadrille

29

Tamara Tishkova woke up near-rigid with fear. The dark canopy loomed above her. A faint line of light showed a split in the drapes. Tentatively, she moved her hand. Her fingers slid into the icy territory beyond her warmth, and she realized she was safe, alone in her own bed. The dream, again. Her nightmare.

She suffered two nightmares. The first she had dreamed nearly all her life. It was a dream common to performers—entering the stage at the Maryinski Theater she would discover herself without her costume. The dream thrived on detail; she saw the stalls, the glittering first ring, the Czar's box, three great tiers rising to the dome. Two thousand balletomanes applauded, seemingly unaware that she was naked. But the cheers turned to catcalls when the orchestra started playing music she had never heard before. She danced *Swan Lake* and the audience booed. She tried *Sleeping Beauty,* the same. *Cléopâtre, Giselle, Carnaval. Eros,* naked, and they laughed. The music—she dreamed the dream several times a year, and as she grew older had come to regard it philosophically almost as an old, familiar friend. An intruder but one who left without lasting damage.

The new dream, the nightmare she had just escaped and which left her wet with perspiration, was the fire dream. It had started with the war and there was nothing familiar or friendly about it, always different, always terrifying.

Sometimes the theater burned while on stage she danced and danced and danced. The audience stampeded, screaming, to the doors, and the tiers came crashing down on them in great explosions of red embers. Other times she saw the city burn; flames soared from the palaces—she was watching from her house—and then the fire started across the river.

Tamara spread her hands and feet into the cold areas of the big bed and forced herself to stay awake until the cold pulled the last tendrils of the nightmare from her mind. It seemed she had just fallen back into a restless sleep when her maid awakened her. The Grand Duke Valery had stopped off on his way to his audience with the Czarina.

"We'll have tea in the solarium," she ordered, shaking the night from her cloudy brain. Valery needed courage this morning. She fixed her hair, perfumed, put on a dark silk robe he liked and went downstairs to give him courage.

As she was sending him out the door Tamara rose *en pointe* and cocked his black fur hat at a jaunty angle. Valery was wearing his favorite uniform for his audience with the Czarina, that of colonel of his Life Guard Cossack regiment, and the long red coat, high fur *papaha* and heavy *pallash* cavalry sword suited a man as big as he was.

A giant, six-feet six-inches, with a square head, pink cheeks and a walrus mustache turning gray, the grand duke weighed the same two hundred and eighty pounds he had weighed since his cadet days.

Tamara could have reached his hat on ordinary tiptoe, but Valery loved it that she was a dancer, so she executed a playful arabesque, pleasing him in a way that pleased her. She stepped back to admire the effect, saw it had failed and rose again to return the *papaha* to its former staid position squarely on top of his head.

He looked, she thought, like what he was—good, dependable, and intensely loyal. He bent to kiss her. She turned her face and spoke in a firm voice . . . "Tell her this is her last chance."

"I can't threaten the Czarina like a naughty child."

"You *know* what I mean. They will be overthrown if they don't get rid of Rasputin's ministers."

"Why don't I just poke a sharp stick in her eye?" Valery protested. He knew the Czarina was in no mood to listen to reason, and calling on her today was not his idea.

Rasputin's body had been dragged yesterday from the river, three days after rumors had swept the city that he had been killed. The clumsy murderers had dropped one of his boots beside the hole in the ice. Petrograd was rejoicing, but at Tsarskoye Selo the Empress mourned. And those who knew her worried.

In her grief and rage she had already placed the Grand Duke Dmitri, one of Valery's young nephews, under house arrest, along with Prince Felix. She claimed they were implicated in the rigorous police investigation of the crime, which was being conducted by Rasputin's own protégé Interior Minister Protopopov.

But she had broken the law. The grand dukes—the Russian Czar's brothers, cousins, uncles and second sons when he had them—were above the law, and only the Czar himself had legal power over them. Tamara had played on Valery's anger to talk him into one last try to convince the Czarina to appoint new ministers.

"You must say what is right. The Czar trusts you. She should too. You have served them better by far than any other grand duke."

That was not flattery. Most of the grand dukes were quick to complain about Nicholas II, whether they were his cousin, nephew, uncle or brother, but few deigned to serve Russia the way Valery did, preferring instead to live abroad in Paris and Monte Carlo, enjoying their vast fortunes and sniping from a distance while Valery traveled constantly through Russia and Europe as the Czar's personal ambassador, negotiator and knowing observer.

"But Alexandra is the Empress," he countered gently, reaching for Tamara again. Again she stopped him, brushing impatiently at his big hands.

"If the Czarina won't listen to you then she deserves to lose her throne."

"Don't talk that way."

Tamara's sloe eyes flashed an unmistakable warning. Tamara Tishkova had inherited her Italian mother's fiery temper along with jet black hair. And with her father's broad Russian cheekbones, pale skin and eastern slant to her eyes had come a peasant stubbornness that Valery could only marvel at. He told himself he trusted her cool judgment, which he did, but actually he was also just a little cowed by this woman he loved so much.

"What's wrong?" he asked. Her nose, Serov the court painter had once observed, had been fashioned by God.

"Darling," she said, kissing his cheek but eluding his reach once again. "If the Czarina won't change, then she and Nicholas must be replaced."

"And what do we do with them then, may I ask? Shoot them?"

"Of course not. But for Russia they must just step down."

"Where?"

"Darling, don't worry about that. They must be replaced. Everyone knows it. And everyone knows that *you* are the only man in Russia to do it."

"There are many who would try," Valery objected. "They're coming out of the woodwork like termites."

"But everyone knows that only you could take the throne and *hold* it. *Everyone.* Except, sometimes, you."

"I'll do what I have to," he said glumly.

"That's all everyone asks."

"But first I will talk to her. Change her mind."

"Of course you must try, darling." She hugged him fiercely and sent him on his way, knowing full well the Czarina would never change, even with

Rasputin gone. But she hoped that one more visit to Tsarskoye Selo would convince Valery what the other grand dukes and his fellow officers had been saying for months—only a real Czar could save Russia. Not weak Nicholas and his neurotic wife, but a real leader. And that leader, the royal conspirators believed, hoped, would be the Grand Duke Valery.

She stood waving good-bye from her front door as he climbed aboard his gigantic scarlet sleigh and his Cossack guard mounted their horses, admired the sight they made clattering away from her house, then returned to her solarium, which had a splendid view of the river and the Winter Palace on the other side.

Valery's sleigh headed for the bridge; the ice was still too thin to carry its monstrous weight. She watched until it vanished among the red and blue and yellow trams. On the other side the Winter Palace crouched on its embankment like a dark red lion in the snow. Tamara gazed at it, thinking about the conspirators.

Instigators was more like it. They wanted Valery to lead them and take all the risks. They reminded her of dilettante dancers—girls from rich families with fantasies of floating in the air but unwilling to embrace the punishing work such buoyancy required.

She had had mixed feelings when they first came to sound her out about Valery's reaction to a palace coup. Open mistress to an unmarried Czar would be, in many eyes, a startling achievement for the daughter of a man born a serf. The price of a failed coup, though, would be Valery's execution.

Still, she realized that the grand ducal conspirators approaching her were the best of the Romanov family and united by their fear for Russia, as well as their hatred of the revolutionaries and the German enemy. They came to her because they suspected that she could influence Valery more than they. And with that realization, Tamara Tishkova began to experience a new dimension to her already considerable position in Petrograd.

She was a woman close to fifty years old who looked thirty and danced twenty-six, who had never married and had used the celebrity her extraordinary beauty and seemingly timeless talent had brought her to unique advantage. She knew how to get the most from a man and she had exercised strict discipline—with one aching exception—in choosing the right man. No dancers, no composers, no singers—and certainly never an impresario. They wore the same chains she did; artists were, as the system of the Imperial Theaters proved with a hundred small hurts, exotic chattle.

Even as Russia's greatest star, she had suffered a cruel reminder that no artist was above royal manipulation; and after years the memory still hurt . . . Czar Nicky, who had admired her since she was a student, had asked her to perform in private at the Alexander Palace; the new *Firebird*, no less, which had just thrilled Paris and which seemed a bold choice for such a conservative man. But His Majesty was a reader, and, well, you could never tell with a reader . . .

Tishkova rarely if ever consented to do private performances, but this was a very special exception, a considerable great honor as well as a royal command. She had submerged herself in the effort of the ballet, excited by the idea of performing for the Court and being the one to present an artist as modern as Stravinsky to an audience as venerable as the Romanov dynasty. Heady stuff, indeed, until the Czarina learned of the preparations.

Her Majesty had snapped her fingers, banned the *Firebird*. No reason given, none required. The Czar capitulated and it was over the night before dress rehearsal. Royalty had commanded a dance, royalty had changed its mind. For weeks after Tamara had felt the firebird still inside her, beating its wings with nowhere to fly . . . A mean object lesson that the right man for a dancer, including Tamara, had better possess royal blood, with inherited wealth. Millionaire careerists were, it seemed, too accustomed to fighting and winning on strictly their own terms . . . while she needed and wanted a man's protection, her own life, and art, told her to stay free of consuming, uncompromising ties. Which was why she had tried to distance herself from Kennet . . . with considerable pain, since in fact she had never gotten over him . . . and which was why the Royal Duke Valery was so uniquely appropriate, if she could keep in check her true feelings for Kennet.

Ballerinas, of course, had been sleeping with grand dukes before the invention of toe shoes, but Valery wasn't married, which made all the difference. For years she had reigned supreme on the stage and since she had finally agreed to become exclusively Valery's, after years of putting him off, she was his consort, openly and publicly, and reigned over much of Petrograd Society as well. They did not all accept her warmly, but when they bowed to Valery they bowed to her as well.

And now she was tasting what it might be like to be the power behind the throne, and she had to admit it was a delicious *mélange* of respect and worship she had known before only when she danced. There was a strong temptation to cultivate that power to carry her safely into the middle age she feared. A powerful temptation, and with it a fantasy. Were Valery to become Czar, might he not marry her? Make her his Czarina? His Empress? Empress of all the Russias . . .

She had controlled her destiny more than most performers by examining her actions and her desires as strictly as she observed and criticized her body when she danced. Now, in the course of analyzing the grand ducal conspiracy drifting around Valery, taking cautious shape, she acknowledged to herself that she would like very much to become Empress of Russia. But Valery was a careful man. He was also not ambitious for power. He would not fight for the throne unless he was totally convinced that Russia would collapse without him. So Tamara gazed across the river at the Winter Palace and prayed with her eyes wide open that the Czarina would remain her imperious and foolish self when Valery arrived at the Alexander Palace this morning—

Her butler broke into her thoughts, announcing that the director of the Imperial Theater was in the foyer. She had seen his sleigh drive up and presumed her friend had come to talk about last minute plans for the *Swan Lake*, a benefit performance she was dancing Sunday at the Maryinski to raise money for the military hospital she sponsored for the wounded.

Her last *Swan Lake*, she had decided, privately. Her jumps were going. There were limits. One more time . . . then new roles.

"Canceled?"

"By order of the Empress," the director of the Imperial Theaters said sadly. "Czarina Alexandra commands mourning for Rasputin."

"Canceled!" she repeated, her voice rising. "Tishkova? Canceled? My benefit. My *Swan Lake*? She can't."

Now she realized that the director had dressed befitting a solemn occasion. He was wearing his colonel's uniform with a tunic practically covered with overlapping ribbons and medals. They had been friends twenty-five years, and it was out of friendship he had delivered the Czarina's edict personally.

"My dear, I am so sorry."

Tamara stood up. Such a thing could not happen to her. Her every appearance on the stage was a celebration in Petrograd and confirmation to her that she had been right to cast her lot with Imperial Russia rather than dance for less demanding audiences in Europe. Here she was trained, honed and feted. By a great effort of will she kept from exploding.

"I am the greatest dancer in Russia," she said flatly. And immediately to herself, Or at least I was.

"You are, mademoiselle."

"She can't do this to me."

"Unfortunately, she can. The Empress is in mourning for the death of Rasputin. She decrees that the Imperial Theaters join her mourning and close out of respect for her murdered friend—"

"Petrograd is rejoicing. Rasputin's death is the best thing that's happened since the war began."

The director made a motion so small that it could have been a shrug, or a nod or simply an effort to relieve the strain of his high tight collar. He said only, "I don't hold political views. I can't afford to."

"She's insane. Crazy as he was."

The director rose, anxious to be away from such dangerous talk. "The Czarina's announcement will be issued publicly on Sunday in the cathedrals."

"She hates me because—"

He bowed and was gone. Tamara started after him calling out, "She can't."

The front door slammed. She ran back to the solarium, reeled about the middle of the room. Her vision seemed to turn red. The Czarina hates me because of Nicky, she wanted to scream. She picked up the nearest object at hand, the telephone, and hurled it at the distant Winter Palace. The instrument tore its wire and smashed through the double windows. Cold burst in, and the leaves nearest curled up as if the plants were wincing.

Valery! She had to call Valery. The telephone lay in the snow, the wires broken. She called for her servants, at full voice, her voice echoing in her ears. The butler came running, the footman, the coachman wielding a club to protect her, the cook, the *moujik* who tended the furnace fires, the one who fixed things. She pointed at the telephone in the snow. They scrambled for it.

The one who fixed things said he would repair the glass.

"Nyet!" It was the telephone she wanted.

She paced among the plants, calling for the servants to hurry. Then she remembered that Valery was en route to Tsarskoye Selo.

"Mademoiselle?" Her butler approached her tentatively.

"What is it?"

"A gentleman is here."

"Who? I'm not expecting anyone."

The butler squinted at the caller's card. "Chevalier François Roland."

"Throw him out. No. Wait. Tell him to wait." She had to compose herself. What did Roland want? He had accused her in a review in Paris of being too short to be a truly great ballerina. All the compliments he had heaped on her since had never fully made it up to her. What in hell am I supposed to do, she had asked Kennet. Grow? Kennet had offered to shoot the critic, with a smile for which he had slept elsewhere half the night. Now she smiled, remembering how he had still been that young then and too new to her world to understand the hurt of such a review.

When she was calm enough to think straight she called for Roland.

"Forgive me, mademoiselle," he said as he stepped in the door, "but this is terribly important."

His empty sleeve took her breath away. She had heard about his arm, of course, but he had still been too ill to make the season last year and this was the first she had seen him since he was wounded. The pain she felt for him pushed aside the vestiges of her rage at the Czarina. The poor man; if any creature on earth should not have been maimed it was this graceful Frenchman with the strong, supple arms and legs a dancer dreamed of. And he was, she knew, so vain, like a cat discovering itself in a mirror.

Tamara looked him straight in the eye. "You are still the most beautiful man I have ever seen."

He looked at her for a long moment, acknowledging the bond of perfection which united them distantly, she the dancer, he the fencer. At last he bowed. *"Merci,* my friend . . . do you know that Kenneth is in Petrograd?"

"I had heard," she said coolly.

"Did you know he was arrested?"

"What?"

"The Okhrana arrested him near the Yusupov Palace the night Rasputin was murdered. They took him to the Peter-Paul."

"But why? What did he—"

"No one can tell me why. He's just been swallowed up. I made inquiries through my ambassador who informed the American Embassy."

"And?"

"Ambassador Paléologue has the impression that Kenneth's ambassador was ordered by his State Department not to interfere. It seemed he was reporting directly to the American ambassador in London."

"They can't arrest a diplomat."

"One would think not, but they have . . . I've exhausted my own means to help him. You're the only one I can turn to."

What could she do without upsetting Valery? Much more than their relationship was at stake now—the entire grand ducal conspiracy. If Valery were distracted by Kennet . . . but *Kennet* . . . she was shocked by the raw intensity of her reaction to his arrest. Shocked by what she felt. God was a trickster, all right.

"I'll call my friend General Halle. He is chief of police for the Fourth District. He'll at least know the police side. Yes?"

"Oui, mademoiselle." Roland glanced at the *moujik* crouched on the tile floor repairing the telephone, and at the hole in the glass.

General Halle was delighted to hear from her. He listened gravely and promised to call back, which he did minutes later. When Tamara hung up the second time she turned to Roland with stricken eyes.

"They've moved him to the Litovsky."

"My God. Why?"

"They say he committed a political offense. General Halle can't help . . . No one can. The Okhrana is interrogating him."

30

At first when the guards took off his chains, Ash rated the new prison an improvement over the Peter-Paul where they had put on the shackles the night he had arrived. But by the time the guards came back for him —a few hours after the police had delivered him across the city in a cold, unlighted black maria—Ash wished he was back at the Peter-Paul.

There his cell had been eerily silent, the thick walls packed with felt to prevent prisoners from tapping messages. Here screams, faint and intermittent, echoed through the corridors from some remote corner in the depths of the cold, damp prison.

Ash rose apprehensively as the guards unlocked the bars. They shackled his hands and feet again, shoved him from the cell and pushed and dragged him down flight after flight of stone steps. The walls grew wet as they descended deeper, and the screaming louder; suddenly it stopped. If it was the guards' intent to frighten him, Ash thought, they were succeeding. But fear had the side effect of honing his mind, which days of confinement had begun to soften.

The shackles had chafed his wrists raw at the Peter-Paul, and he had feared infection in his dirty cell as his mind had begun to shift from the larger concern for his mission to remove the Czar to smaller and smaller details of daily existence. The war grew more distant, the need to stop it, remote. The chains, the silence, the constant electric light and the ever-present guards watching him through a peephole took on immediate importance until Ash had begun to wonder how people like Lenin and his comrades kept their cutting edge through long periods of prison and exile. He was going mad after four days. Maybe that's why Lenin had seemed so petty and argumentative off in Zurich.

But Lenin, at least, had friends. The Okhrana had kept Ash alone from the moment he was arrested, and the sense of isolation was so complete that he had begun to wonder if no one but the Okhrana knew he was a prisoner. François Roland had run the other way from the Yusupov Palace. So who else would have seen the police take him in their car, drive him across the Neva and through the fortress gates?

As they had entered the Peter-Paul Prison, which was isolated in one of the many bastions, the guards in the foyer had turned around and faced the walls of the small dark room until Ash had been marched through into a second room. "So no one knows who is here," the Okhrana officer had explained. Then he had ordered Ash to strip. No names. Only cell numbers.

In a room bare except for a wooden table they had confiscated his sword, billfold, passport and finally his concealed, snub-nosed Luger, which they examined with professional interest. There were hooks on the wall for his uniform, which they carred away as soon as he had hung it up, and when he was naked they gave him faded cotton pants and shirt and shackled his wrists. No one had seen him but the arresting officers.

Next up a flight of stone stairs, through a heavy iron door, with a guard who had glanced incuriously at yet another prisoner in shapeless garb undistinguishable from the prisoners before him or those who would follow. Down a long corridor lined with pairs of doors on the left side. Each wooden door had a small opening a few square inches cross-hatched with iron straps, through which the guards watched. Between each pair of cells was the square iron fuel door of a heating stove embedded in the stone. Ash's cell had been warm, comfortable even, compared to the damp chill that permeated the new prison.

The guards had pushed a key in the door and thrown it open. Ash had caught a quick glimpse of a toilet in the corner, an iron bed and table, an electric light by the table, a straw pillow, a thin mattress, a sheet and a rug on the bed and a high, barred window; they had pushed him in and slammed the door, which remained closed until several hours later when they had transferred him here.

The guards brought him up short in front of a steel door and one knocked on it with a billy club. Ash braced himself, aware that the knock was executed with a certain deference, as if the jailer feared the man behind the door. A moment passed and a scholarly looking young officer with a secretary's ink-stained fingers opened the door, stepped out and spoke to the guard, who pushed Ash firmly into the room and closed the door behind him.

It was an office with walls of stone and a coal stove that dispelled the damp common to underground rooms in Petrograd. There was a single wooden desk and behind it a lean figure sitting with his back to the desk and the door. He wore a civilian suit and appeared to be staring at the

230

stone wall while he toyed with a walking stick, unaware that Ash was standing ten feet behind him.

Ash briefly considered strangling him with the chain between his wrists; but what then? Even if he had keys, how many doors in the prison would a key alone open? Besides, the man had to know Ash was there. He was toying with Ash, building his anxiety before getting down to whatever unpleasantness he had in mind.

The wait ended sooner than Ash had supposed, and in a manner he could not have imagined. The man at the desk turned around and the moment Ash saw the cadaverous face nothing made sense, because the last person he had expected in a Russian prison in the middle of Petrograd was a psychotic German duelist named Count Philip von Basel.

"I worried you'd give me away in front of the guards."

"I don't understand."

"A pride of royals. I serve Kaiser Wilhelm."

Ash felt shock dissolve into relief and puzzlement.

"The Kaiser has quite a sense of humor, putting you and me in the same city," Ash said coldly. "Much less the same mission."

"But His Majesty doesn't know about you and me," von Basel replied with a sarcastic smile. "How could he? Don't you recall how terribly concerned you were with appearances?"

"In any civilized country, von Basel, a lunatic like you would have been locked up in an asylum long ago. I told you in Monte Carlo and I'll tell you here . . . the German army might allow its officers to go around slicing up people for the hell of it, but the U.S. Navy frowns on dueling. If you're still itching for a duel you can wait until I retire."

"A day I long for and fear you will put off, Commander. Unless you dredge up some bravery in your soul, which isn't there now."

Ash raised his shackles. "Explain this."

Von Basel smiled again, savoring the moment. The whole imbroglio in Monte Carlo had verged on the silly from Ash's point of view—a night of champagne in the casino, a deliberately insulting remark by a sneering German, and when that didn't work a grab at Tamara, which had earned von Basel a left hook that sent him sprawling across the casino floor. Followed by the tap of Basel's glove on Ash's face. A setup. Von Basel was a duelist—a sanctioned murderer who had run out of men to fight in Germany and was hunting fresh game. Ash had seen him duel once in Heidelberg when von Basel was very young and unquestionably deadly. Ash had refused to fight. It was the summer of the Kaiser's incursion into Morocco—the Agadir crisis—and Germany was itching for trouble. As a U.S. naval officer Ash had no intention of provoking an international incident, but even though he knew he had acted legitimately, von Basel's charge of cowardice still rankled, and stung again as he repeated it. But this was nonsense compared to his mission to remove the Czar . . .

"How the hell did you get here?" Ash asked.

"You might sound a little grateful, Commander. It took a lot of doing to extricate you from the clutches of the Okhrana. There were officers who wanted you to suffer the worst sort of interrogation. Others thought you should simply disappear."

"What for?"

"Somehow you're right in the middle of the Rasputin murder. The Empress is calling for blood. Some thought you would make a fine sacrifice. Fortunately I was able to persuade them that an American officer was an unlikely candidate."

"How?"

"Not your concern. No questions. I have my own position to protect—but answer me, before we get down to business, how did you get in so much trouble?"

"I think I got framed by the German army."

It was von Basel's turn to look confused. "Is this a joke?"

Ash shook the chains on his wrists. "Does this look like a damned joke?"

"Explain."

"I saw the Kaiser in Berlin."

"I know."

"Right after that, German army agents tried to kill me on the train from Munich. They tried again in Switzerland. Again in Paris. Again in Finland. And the night before Rasputin was killed a Russian tried to shoot me at the gypsy camp on Krestovsky Island."

"Why do you think they were German army?" He led Ash through a recitation of each attack, and concluded, "You're lucky to be alive. But then, again, you were always good at running."

"Let me ask you something, von Basel. Is it true you got your Heidelberg dueling scar on the cheek you sit on?"

The German flushed. "Be very careful, Ash. I could have you taken out and shot."

"By Russians? Interesting. Tell me more about your situation. . . . come on, von Basel. What are you going to do about this? I'm no good to you and your Kaiser dead."

Ash had the feeling that von Basel had already known about the Finnish attack. And he found it worrisome that von Basel looked baffled and more than a little worried himself.

"I'll make inquiries. In the meantime you will avoid your hotel. I'll arrange a flat on Vassily Island—you'll be safe this evening, no one expects you to be released. Tomorrow go to the German Embassy. We'll use the wreckage as a dropping point for messages. I'll leave a key and address just inside the side doors. I will also have you watched for your protection."

Ash took a second stab at learning how von Basel operated in Petrograd. "Are those your boys following me around in that phony taxi?"

"I told you I won't discuss my situation here. It doesn't take huge intelligence to realize I've some police contacts. But I warn you, if you threaten my position in any way I will have you eliminated. And I can assure you I will be more successful than the German army . . . the important thing is you do what the Kaiser told you to do. Rescue the Czar. Where do you stand?"

"The Czarina listened to King George's offer, but since then she's refused to talk to me. I was trying to maneuver Rasputin into influencing her when he was murdered."

"She's in no condition to make any sensible decisions now, I can tell you. Rasputin's death has devastated her."

"That leaves the Czar," Ash said.

"The Czar is on his way home from Mogilev. To comfort his wife. He will obviously stay some time at Tsarskoye Selo before returning to military headquarters. It is likely, therefore, that the Czar will receive the congratulations of the diplomatic corps on New Year's Day. I presume you can get yourself invited?"

Ash nodded. This was a break.

Von Basel tapped his desk with his walking stick. "Understand, Commander, that Rasputin's murder completely undermines the Czarina's sanity. She holds enormous power over her husband. Her condition undermines him. Russia is collapsing. And her rulers are collapsing too. You have very little time."

"Weeks?"

"If you're fortunate. But I would not be surprised if that telephone rang right now to inform me that a mob was marching on this prison."

Von Basel looked at the telephone a moment, then laid his stick down, picked up the telephone, spoke rapid Russian, then said to Ash, "You will be returned to your cell until I can make the final details for freeing you."

He stood up, walked around his desk and picked up his stick.

Ash held up his chains. "Would you mind taking these off?"

"They contribute to the authenticity of our pretenses," von Basel replied with a thin smile. "As will this." He slashed Ash across the face with his stick and kicked his shackled feet out from under him. Ash hit the floor in a red explosion of pain. Von Basel stepped on the chain holding his wrists. " 'A lunatic'? 'Locked up in any civilized country'? . . . you'll need a few bruises to convince your jailers that I dealt with you severely." He hit Ash twice more.

"Don't worry, that'll heal before the Czar's reception."

Ash came to in his cell, head aching. His uniform was laid out neatly beside him on the wooden bunk. The guards had removed the chains. They took him to another sealed black maria and drove him around the city for an hour. The lieutenant escorting him returned his papers, sword and Luger.

"Who was the officer who interrogated me this afternoon?"

"Commander, you should thank God your answers satisfied him. Don't ask stupid questions."

"I just wanted to send a little thank you note."

"By law a permit is required to bring your gun into Russia."

"You want to arrest me again?"

The lieutenant pointed at the door. The police van stopped. A moment later Ash found himself standing on Sadovaya Street, half a block from the Nevsky, staring at the back of the departing vehicle, which bore no identifying marks and disappeared among the trams and carriages.

His head still ached but the cold air felt wonderful. He started walking toward the Europa. If he had the time and didn't mind wasting his meager contacts he supposed he could track down von Basel's Russian identity. But there was no time. Nor was it worth it. Crazy as it seemed, the German count was on his side. At least he seemed to be . . .

Petrograd seemed to vibrate with color and bright lights after five days confinement. At the Europa he telephoned the Alexander Palace and got as far as the colonel who had approved his visit to the Czarina. "Her Imperial Majesty will receive no one." It sounded like von Basel was right.

Ash called Roland's room. "Meet me in the bar." He was on his second scotch whiskey by the time the Frenchman got downstairs.

"What happened? How did you get out?"

"Ran into an old acquaintance. Remember von Basel?"

"That contemptible—"

"Same one. Don't ask me how he got here 'cause I don't know."

"What happened to your face?"

"I ran into a door."

"Three of them, from the look of it."

Ash finished his whiskey and ordered a third. "Who knows I was arrested?"

"Me. The French ambassador. The American ambassador."

"How'd the French ambassador find out?"

"I saw them take you. So I went to him to help."

Ash would rather he hadn't. Now that he was out. He said only, "Do you know what the American ambassador did?"

"Nothing. My ambassador was the first to tell him, and he had the strong impression that your ambassador was ordered to stand clear."

Relieved that he hadn't been compromised, Ash said, "So no one else knows."

Roland hesitated.

"Who else?" Ash demanded.

"When it seemed hopeless I went to Tamara."

234

Ash's jaw tightened, sending a jolt of pain through his bruised face. He wanted to ask how she had reacted but said instead, "I wish you hadn't done that."

"She was my last chance." Roland shrugged. "Fanning an old flame seemed preferable to your rotting in jail. She called a police chief. Even he couldn't help, but he did learn you had been moved to the Litovsky."

"The Litovsky?" All right, von Basel. A little closer.

"We gave up hope at that point. They said you were being interrogated by the Okhrana."

"Do me a favor. Please tell her I'm all right."

"I telephoned her the moment you called."

Ash wanted to ask more but couldn't. What had she looked like? Was she happy? . . . . Was it true that her grand duke was plotting a coup? "How'd she treat you?"

"She was kind," said Roland, and looked at Ash, inviting another question, but Ash stared into his drink and said nothing.

"Why is God so cruel?" the Czarina asked. Her lady-in-waiting kept silent, knowing a hopeless question. The Empress had lain weeping all day on her mauve chaise longue. Her grief had turned briefly to rage when the Grand Duke Valery visited in the morning, but now tears were all she had.

"His Majesty's train is approaching Malaya Vishera," the lady prompted gently. "A few more hours and he'll be home."

No response. She tried another approach. "Colonel Riazhin tells me that the American who brought your lovely gift from King George has telephoned again. Shall I—"

The Czarina pushed her away. Father Gregory had seen his blood on the American's hands. If only she had listened . . . she was still crying when the Czar arrived. She went into his arms and sobbed out everything that had happened. He wore an ordinary soldier's tunic, which smelled reassuringly of cigarette smoke and oiled leather. The girls came running in in their night dresses. They all went to Alexis's room and sat around his bed while Nicholas listened to what each of them had been doing and told them how he had missed them at the Stavka.

Later, after they had put the children back to bed, they made love. And in the night he kissed the tears from her cheeks and asked, "Sunny? Tell me what exactly did Commander Ash say?"

31

Addressing his shaving mirror, and feeling mildly absurd, Ash practiced whispering, "I have a message from King George," without moving his lips. Over a hundred gossip-hungry Russian courtiers and foreign diplomats would be watching every moment at the Czar's New Year's reception.

Message was the problem word. Aspirations and grunts took care of *I, have, a, from, King* and *George,* but *message* demanded lip action. He changed it to *news.* "I have news from King George." It worked even better with a half-smile. If it worked at all.

Petrograd was nervous New Year's Day. Rumor said strikers had mobbed the police in the Vyborg District—it was the Narva District in some versions, the Moscow in others; regiments called in to restore order had supposedly fired on the police instead; a Cossack charge had ultimately returned control to the government.

Guard officers drinking champagne in the hotel bars blamed the troubles on revolutionaries aided by German spies; but the landlady of the dingy flat von Basel had rented for Ash to hide in had told Ash in broken French that the mutinous army regiments had consisted entirely of green recruits conscripted from the same factory district as the strikers. Neighbors. Ambassador Hazzard had observed again, when he invited Ash to join the American delegation to the reception, that if rumors were firewood, there would be no fuel shortage in Petrograd. But they weren't, and the woodpiles were visibly lower.

236

It seemed to Ash on the carriage ride from the American Embassy to the Tsarskoye Selo train station that every bakery had a long line of shivering women straggling into the street. The Russians, he had learned, called the line for bread or kerosene or sugar the *khvost*—the tail. The *khvosts* were everywhere on Vassily Island, where von Basel had found the flat in a slummy Maly Boulevard building inhabited by tram conductors, prostitutes and music teachers. It was twenty degrees below zero as Ash stepped down from the carriage; people were predicting the worst winter in years.

The police had roped off Zagorodny Street around the Tsarskoye Selo station and patrolled the square on horseback while eighty members of the diplomatic corps dressed in their full regalia boarded the special to present congratulations to the Czar.

"I'm delighted, *of course,* to be of service to Ambassador Page . . ." Ambassador Hazzard said with clear annoyance mixed with confusion, when the American delegation had settled onto the luxurious blue and silver Imperial Train. Unlike the uniformed chiefs of the Allies' embassies, he wore civilian dress, a swallowtail suit with white vest, tie and gloves. And far from delighted, he looked as if he wished Ambassador Page had sent Ash to China. Earlier in the week he had blown up at Ash in his office. "Are you trying to turn Russia into the Wild West? Train robbery, kidnapping, now a secret arrest. How'd you get out, escape over the damned roof?"

Ash had calmed him into admitting that the affair had been kept quiet and that he had been innocent of all charges and released with an apology.

"But I don't know how to introduce you to the Czar. Too confusing to say you represent Ambassador Page." To me as well as to the Czar, he thought.

"Say I'm posted from London, Your Excellency."

"I don't know," Hazzard grumped. "London's confusing too."

"London would explain why you're accompanied by *two* naval attachés, sir." Across the compartment Captain Hamilton was eyeing Ash suspiciously, and Hazzard's military attaché, Major Sheppard, looked put out because there were two navy men and only himself from the army.

Ash wanted the word "London" in his presentation to the Czar. Their formal introduction would last seconds only, and he needed a surefire opening. London-Scotland-King George.

"I suppose, but it's very irregular . . ."

The train started smoothly—whatever troubles plagued Russia's rolling stock did not affect this line. Hazzard took a gold watch from his vest. "Two thirty-five. Right on time. Probably the only train in Russia that is. The trip back from Moscow was awful."

The Czar's reception, which had been canceled the previous year owing to his responsibilities as commander of the army, had caught everyone by surprise. Ambassadors had scurried back to Petrograd from Moscow and vacations in Finland. Which said, Ash thought, something for Count von Basel's sources.

Ash tried to watch the route through the ice-glazed window, fascinated as he had been the first time by the idea that this single line, in winter at least, was the only practical connection between the Czar and his capital. The train gathered speed in the shabby factory districts and suburbs, passed the barracks of the First Railway Battalion and raced across the flat, empty snow-covered plain—the rails a causeway on a sea of snow, the telegraph poles hugging the line as if seeking protection from the desolation.

Separate carriages awaited each ambassador at the Tsarskoye Selo Imperial Station. The horse blankets were covered with ice. When they had taken away the ambassadors, more carriages and sleighs appeared to take their staffs through the huge rococo gold-and-iron gates leading to the Imperial Park.

A mile into the park, past the aristocrats' mansions, the beautiful blue-green Catherine Palace appeared in the trees. Brilliant sunlight shone on the gold domes of the solitary chapel. The crows and seagulls wheeled overhead, crying, as they had three weeks earlier when Ash had driven past on his way to the Alexander Palace.

The British delegation climbed the palace steps first; the chief delegation, fifteen men led by the tall white-haired Buchanan. The French and Italians—the other two Allied powers—followed, then the Americans, the Spanish, the lesser European delegations and finally a Japanese chargé d'affaires.

It was warm inside. Hundreds of servants relieved the diplomats of coats and hats. Pages from the staff of the director of ceremonies led them up a staircase lined with marble vases and into the Great Hall—a gilded ballroom with an elaborate parquetry floor, tall windows on the long walls overlooking the snowy gardens, with mirrors at the ends. The windows and hundreds of electric lamps cast light on the gold-and-red furniture.

The director of ceremonies positioned the ambassadors in a row, with their staffs lined up two steps behind them. Ash was at the back of the American line, behind Major Sheppard and Captain Hamilton, exactly where he wanted to be to draw the Czar back an extra step away from those who might hear. The Court worked like an exquisitely precise machine. The instant the director of ceremony's staff had withdrawn, the doors were thrown open and thirty generals and courtiers marched in, led by the Czar.

Nicholas II wore scarlet. He strode firmly to the British Ambassador Buchanan, shook his hand and exchanged low-voiced greetings. Buchanan then proceeded to read aloud from a paper in a voice too low for the other diplomats to hear. Hazzard's counselor and first secretary exchanged glances. Apparently the Briton had not consulted the Americans, who looked worried that Buchanan might presume to speak for the United States.

Ash thought the Czar looked thinner and quite a bit older than he had in 1913. Yet he looked at ease and was certainly very much a royal presence in his long red coat with the *pallash* scabbarded at his lean waist. The man and the title, Czar of all the Russias, were not in appearance, at least, mismatched. His entourage, however, looked anxious. Every face seemed to reflect the strain of the war—the shortages, the defeats, the uncertainty.

The Czar and Buchanan conversed five or six minutes—a long time, Ash thought, for a ceremonial greeting. At last Buchanan presented his enormous staff, and the Czar, Ash noted, took time for a word with each. He moved on and spoke briefly with the Italians. Next he went to Paléologue, the French ambassador, with whom he held a quiet conversation in French.

Nicholas was presented to the nine-man French suite, and again had a word for each. Then, still trailed by his entourage, the Czar advanced on Ambassador Hazzard and cordially shook his hand. Ash, straining to hear, heard the Czar say he recalled their last meeting three months earlier when Hazzard had presented his credentials. Hazzard replied that he had learned a lot more about Russia since then and had found much to admire.

"I'm delighted to hear that," the Czar replied seriously.

"I have been working to promote closer relations between Russia and America," Hazzard said. Ash winced. Closer relations could be interpreted in diplomatic circles as a promise to enter the war, which Hazzard had not meant. The contrast between the naive, earnest American and the wily old French and British ambassadors dramatized how much more seriously Europeans took diplomacy—though the fact of the current war made one wonder what difference it made.

The Czar smiled. "Yes," he said in his accentless English, "I have heard of your actions in that line and think considerable progress has been made."

Hazzard wished him Happy New Year and asked permission to present his staff. The Czar approached and shook hands with the counselor as Hazzard introduced him by name. They moved on to the first secretary, then the second, and the third, and Ash felt his gut tightening. Up close the Czar's resemblance to King George was uncanny, except for the eyes, which didn't bulge like the King's and were instead strangely deep, a bit dreamy. His gaze flicked over Ash for a second. Did he remember Scotland? Or Berlin?

Hazzard introduced the military attaché. The Czar shook hands. Hazzard introduced the regular naval attaché. The Czar shook his hand too. Then Hazzard said, "Commander Kenneth Ash, recently posted from London."

The Czar's grip was firm, his gaze ceremoniously noncommittal. He seemed fit and athletic for a man in his fifties, but face-to-face Ash thought him pale and too thin. Worn down.

"Have you acclimated to our Russian winter, Commander Ash?"

"I find your Russian winter stimulating, Your Majesty. Like the rain in Scotland."

"What do the Scots call it? A soft day when it rains?"

"Exactly, Your Majesty. I don't suppose you recall, sir, but I had the honor of being presented to you some years ago in Scotland at Balmoral Castle."

"You were a lieutenant then," the Czar replied without hesitation. "And almost as good a shot as King George. I doubt the winged population has recovered in that section of Scotland."

"I have news from King George," Ash whispered, dead-lipped with a half smile.

Czar Nicholas turned toward the next delegation. The Spanish rippled in anticipation. Ambassador Hazzard was still hovering as closely as protocol allowed, but even he could not hear the Czar's low-voiced, "Later."

As an officer of the Czar's Convoy, the duty fell to Dmitri Dan to escort the diplomats back to the train station after lunch. He and his men saluted from horseback as the train steamed off to Petrograd. Then Dmitri took his squad to their barracks near the Catherine Palace.

Dmitri had seen Commander Ash in the American delegation—recognized him from the pictures General Ludendorff had shown them at Spa. Now he debated whether to alert his brother Vladimir. From the beginning he had had doubts about the value and the morality of Red Snow killing the American. And now, a dead comrade later and a lot of time wasted in a failed scheme to trick the Okhrana into killing Ash for them, Dmitri Dan wondered if the German gold was worth distracting any more comrades from the business of revolution. He and Vladimir had been gone too long from Russia, and back only days did not seem the time to worry about Ash. The important jobs, now that Rasputin was dead, were killing the Czar and Czarina.

Half an hour later his squad was ordered out again to greet another special train from Petrograd. They galloped across the Imperial Park and formed up at the station just as the locomotive pulled in.

Ash got off the train. Dmitri was astonished. Ash must have boarded it in Petrograd immediately after getting off the diplomat's train. Why would a man ride from Tsarskoye Selo to Petrograd only to come straight back to Tsarskoye Selo? A Life Guard lieutenant colonel escorted the

240

American—*Podpolkovnik* Ivan Roskov, an officer who Dmitri knew was often entrusted with discreet arrangements.

It seemed, Dmitri thought as he watched their carriage slip through the gates to the park, that Commander Ash had returned for a private meeting with someone at Court, so private that even his own diplomatic delegation did not know he had returned. Escorting the carriage of the grand duchess whom his squad had been summoned for, Dmitri Dan noticed Ash's carriage continue past the Catherine to the Alexander Palace. Whoever Ash was meeting was very highly placed. Curious, he followed to the gate where the Alexander Palace guard would query whether he was authorized to come on the grounds, which he was not. Not yet.

A coal-black Ethiopian guard opened a final door in the royal apartments, and Ash's escort bade him good-bye. The Czar waited inside. He had changed into a plain, unadorned tunic, trousers and boots and stood, hands clasped behind his back, in the middle of a half dozen tables covered with military maps.

Billiard tables. A green-shaded lamp hung over each. Six pools of light —East Prussia taken, lost. Galicia taken, lost. Poland lost. Brusilov's offensive stopped. Roumania lost. The Baltic abandoned.

"Thank you for coming, Commander Ash," the Czar greeted him politely in a soft voice. "Would you be so kind as to repeat precisely what you told my wife?"

"King George begs you to accept sanctuary in England, Your Majesty."

The Czar sighed. He seemed, Ash thought, shy, almost embarrassed.

"May I call you Kenneth?"

"Of course, Your Majesty."

"It seems appropriate, since Georgie thinks so highly of you . . ." The Czar's voice trailed off. Ash waited, trying to be patient, while his mind raced. What did the Czar intend? He had made careful, deliberate arrangements to have Ash brought quietly back to Tsarskoye Selo. Clearly the Czarina had told him about King George's offer, and just as clearly the Czar was interested.

"Why," Nicholas asked suddenly, "is Georgie so worried? Does he know something about Russia I don't? Or does he fear that my soldiers will let England down?"

He went on before Ash had a chance to answer, but his voice now turned dull and tired. "You must tell King George that I am still determined to continue the war until victory—decisive and complete victory. Remind him that I have promised my armies we will take Constantinople."

Ash looked away. Constantinople—the old Imperial Russian dream of a

241

Mediterranean port. But the German army, having just seized Roumania, blocked the only conceivable route to Constantinople, and the Russians, who were still retreating, hadn't a hope in hell of dislodging them. Constantinople—and not a word of the rage crackling in his own cities.

"Is that it, Kenneth?" the Czar demanded, his voice enlivened by bitterness. "George thinks I can't make war?"

"No, Your Majesty. Not at all. King George is deeply grateful for the sacrifices of the Russian army. The Western Front would never have held without your relentless pressure on the East . . . It is the safety of you and your family . . ."

The Czar gazed back at Ash, vague and silent. Ash wasn't sure if he had heard him, hadn't the slightest idea what he was thinking and at the moment wondered if the Czar knew himself.

"Unrest," the Czar asked at last. "Is it the unrest?"

"Yes, Your Majesty. Word of . . . unrest, food shortages and the troubles with your railroads has led King George to wonder whether the actions of certain ministers have perhaps undermined the Russian people's confidence in Your Majesty—"

"It is up to the people to gain *my* confidence," Czar Nicholas told him. "They must display faith in me." He walked stiffly to a billiard table with a map of Turkey and stared at it.

Ash waited. *Never say more than you have to,* his father used to say when he was grooming Ash to take over at the West Virginia statehouse. *To stop talking is the hardest thing there is.* Ash fought the temptation to answer. *Unrest?* Revolution was more like it. The talk on the delegates' train back to Petrograd had confirmed that the Cossacks *had* been called into the Narva District to disperse mutinous troops. For a few hours earlier in the week all that had stood between Petrograd and anarchy was a handful of primitive horse soldiers.

"I see," the Czar said at last. ". . . I know there is a great deal of excitement in Petrograd's smart salons . . . but I have fifteen million men under arms and surely my own police are more familiar with real conditions than the King of England."

He did not know what his mauled armies had come to. How, Ash wondered, could he imagine conscripts would fire on their own friends? As for his police, how many honest reports ever got past the Interior Minister? And how many von Basels had Germany slipped into their ranks?

"Don't you agree?" the Czar demanded.

Ash said, "Your cousin is viewing events in Russia from a great distance. Perhaps his fear for your safety makes him worry a little too much, but perhaps the distance also allows him to be more objective . . ."

To Ash's relief, the Czar did not argue, almost as if he had considered that conclusion himself. He opened and closed his hands and looked around the billiard room; glanced at and over the grim maps.

242

"What's his plan?" he blurted out, startling Ash. My God . . . he was going to cooperate . . . ?

"A cruiser will call for you at Murmansk, Your Majesty."

The Czar gave a vague smile, as if enjoying a private joke. "The navy? We each have our weakness for the sea, Georgie and I . . . one's soul feels so peaceful at sea . . ." He strolled to a table in the corner. Ash followed at a discreet distance. The Czar gazed down at the map and traced with his finger the route north from Petrograd twelve hundred miles to the coast. "The Murman railroad is almost completed," he said more to himself than Ash. Then his finger moved into the Barents Sea, around the North Cape and into the Norwegian Sea. Halfway to Scotland he lifted his finger and looked at Ash.

"Has Georgie forgotten German U-boats? Might I not step directly from, as you say, the frying pan into the fire? . . . and drown in the process?"

Ash took a deep breath. He feared this question more than any other, had hoped the Czar wouldn't raise it until the cruiser was at sea, because the Czarina had expressed such hatred of Imperial Germany. But now asked, it had to be answered, and Ash saw no way to avoid naming Wilhelm.

"King George asked your cousin the Kaiser for a U-boat escort to Scotland."

"*Willy*—Oh God, what do they think of me?" He walked back to the map of Turkey and stared at Constantinople. "Did Kaiser Wilhelm agree?"

"Immediately, Your Majesty. The Kaiser is heartsick, you know what he thinks of you, in spite of the war."

"Willy thinks I'm a dolt!" But the sudden vehemence faded quickly from his eyes, and he murmured in tones dull and lifeless as before, "Perhaps Willy's right . . ."

Was the Czar finally losing faith in himself? Perhaps he was considering the unthinkable—abdication. Could he be pushed?

"Kaiser Wilhelm told me to tell you that this is a matter of family," Ash said. "Victoria's children, was how he put it, Your Majesty. An agreement—"

"I'm the last," the Czar interrupted.

"I beg your pardon, Your Majesty?"

"I'm the last emperor. The last true autocrat. There are no others left. Willy's whole empire is an upstart. Georgie's a figurehead. Old Franz Joseph is dead. The Chinese fell years ago. The Ottoman sultans are the sick men of Europe. Who do you think will replace me, Commander?"

He's going to do it, thought Ash. *He's going to leave.*

"Who?" the Czar repeated. "Three hundred years of Romanov succession. Who will take my place?"

"You can return," Ash lied, moved by the man's genuine, deep sorrow despite his paramount goal of helping to end the war. "Your family is worried about right now . . ."

"What will the peasants think if I leave?"

Ash switched back to a firm tack. "King George said an agreement between royals is judged only by God. Kaiser Wilhelm agrees. I suppose they would say your safety is a matter for your royal families, not your peasants."

The Czar looked again at his maps; Ash guessed he wished he was back at his Stavka, where the bustle of generals and aides-de-camp gave even the worse situation the hope of sudden reversal.

"Yes, of course . . . I suppose you are right . . . poor Russia, God help her . . ."

It worked. Ash could scarcely believe it. He would have the Czar out of the country in a week. The way would be cleared for the U.S. to enter the war. And end it.

The door burst open. The Czarina stumbled in, crying, "Nicky!" Wild-eyed, dishevelled, clumsily draped in black, she clutched Rasputin's blood-stained peasant blouse to her breast. She screamed when she saw Ash.

32

Weaving frantically through the maze of billiard tables, the Czar extended his arms to her. "Sunny. Darling—"

She jerked away, screaming hysterically at Ash. "Father Gregory saw his blood on your hands."

Her hair was tangled, loose to her waist, her skin deathly white, her eyes red from crying. The Czar reached for her again. "Darling, calm—"

"I didn't listen. I didn't listen. Father Gregory warned me you are the devil. I should have listened." Another outburst of tears. Nicholas held her, rocked her in his arms, murmured softly to her. Her body heaved, and she flung her hands about as if to hit Ash. The Czar looked over her head, his eyes begging Ash to leave.

"Your family sent me," Ash said. "I'm not the devil. Your own cousins asked me to help—"

"We will not leave Russia."

"They want to help you and your children—"

The Czarina covered her ears. "Make him go away!"

"*Leave us,*" the Czar commanded.

"Your Majesty, please—"

"Get *out.*" The huge black guard opened the door. "Take him out," the Czar snapped, then turning on Ash as he backed toward the door, he said, "It is God's will we are here and God's will we stay."

The Ethiopian took his arm and guided him firmly out of the billiard room, down narrow corridors and back stairs. He threw open a final door, the state reception room. "Mind the step, suh."

Ash was halfway through the door when he realized the black man had addressed him in the soft, southern drawl of one of his father's own servants. He looked at him and the black man smiled. "The other boys are real Africans, suh, but I'm American."

"How—"

"Long story, suh," he replied, closing the subject and the door, nodding at the stairs as he did. "That's a pretty good man up there. And a real nice family."

Grand Duke Valery sat alone in the gloomy smoking room of the Yacht Club, wondering if his small band of Cossacks could hold Palace Square long enough to convince the Russian Army to accept him as the new czar. A half dozen grand dukes, cousins and uncles, eyed him anxiously from their quinze game in the next room. Interesting, he thought, now that they had persuaded him to take action few of the conspirators would risk being seen with him—even in the most private club in Russia.

Valery snorted a laugh, and an old German waiter came running. "Vodka."

He supposed he was suited to be the czar . . . if anyone was. Certainly he had more Russian blood in his veins than most of the Romanov clan— poor Nicky had barely a drop, if that, when you gave Catherine the Great's mysterious antecedents a close look, as his Tamara had been fondly reminding him of late—more Russian in blood, yet more widely traveled than most, including the Parisian cosmopolitans who never came home.

Besides, he had Tamara, who had a frightening way of thrusting the world at him. He often felt like a little boy with her, but afterward he stood more the man than his limited peers. How long could he hold the throne? Longer than Nicky. Long enough to beat Germany before the troops rebelled and simply turned around and walked home.

What next? No one knew. Feeding the peasants and the workers would quiet their anger at first, but enriching the peasants always had the effect of enriching the townspeople far more. And for some damned reason the more they got the more they demanded, the louder their children complained in the universities. And most strange, the more they left the land for the festering cities.

Never mind. Winning the war was the first and immediate task. All the Russian army needed was support at home—guns, food, ammunition. He remembered the awe and pride he felt in 1914 when Russia mobilized. Masses gathered at the railroad stations. More Russian men than anyone had ever imagined existed. Hordes of the Czar's subjects, thousands, millions, until the trains couldn't carry them all. And still they walked out of the countryside—trailed by saddened wives and wary fathers—brave men who deserved more from Father Czar than Nicholas II had the power to give them.

246

Valery knew his Cossacks would fight for Palace Square to the last man. He had provided for their families on his estates since they had been assigned to protect him during the 1905 revolt. He let them recruit their replacements in their traditional way of choosing the best young man each year from their villages—a young man who would never return except in disgrace. But even the most loyal hundred fighters, he realized sadly, couldn't be more than shock troops. Unfortunately, the bold conspiritors who had promised regiments were hesitating.

He surged abruptly to his feet and headed for the door. Six pairs of eyes trailed him from the card room, their owners sensing like a herd of sheep that the wolf was up to something. Who was he meeting tonight? The colonel of the Preobrajenski Regiment? A reactionary Black Hundred member of the Duma? A district police chief? What conspirator had agreed to make the first move?

Valery left them with a grim smile. He felt less the wolf than a bear lost in the forest. As for tonight, he was taking his Tamara to the French ambassador's ball.

The Czar had a friend, Lieutenant Colonel Ivan Roskov of the Imperial Convoy, who served him as a private royal courier—much the way Ash occasionally served the King of England—when Nicholas felt the need to operate with greater secrecy than his court could guarantee. He turned now to *Podpolkovnik* Roskov.

The two men had met as nineteen-year-olds nearly thirty years ago; Nicholas, then the Czarevitch, had been given command of young Roskov's Horse Guard squadron. The years had treated them differently, yet their friendship had remained strong. Nicholas hardly looked older, except when he was tired or grief-stricken for his son, and the placid, dreamy light in his eyes often reminded Roskov of their youth.

Roskov, however, looked like the crusty old veteran he had become fighting Russia's wars. His hair and beard had long ago turned iron gray. A Japanese saber cut inflicted during the Yalu River campaign creased his brow. A Chinese lance encountered in Manchuria, occupied during the Boxer Rebellion, had marked his leathery neck. Fragments of a revolutionary's bomb picked up in the course of a punitive expedition still caused a limp, and a German gas attack in Poland left him too short of breath to serve on the Front.

The Czarina complained he was too rough but she agreed with Nicholas that Roskov was shrewd and loyal, and she knew that he reminded her husband of the bracing, manly atmosphere the Czar loved at the Stavka and missed at home, living with so many women.

The Czar issued Roskov's orders in Russian, the language he required his officers to speak instead of the foreign French and English so many preferred. "Bring back Commander Ash."

Podpolkovnik Roskov arrived by train in Petrograd within the hour. Commander Ash was not at his hotel, but the staff informed him that the American had been invited to the French ambassador's ball.

Ash had not been surprised by a last minute invitation to the French ball. An American naval officer arrested by the Okhrana, only to show up two weeks later chatting like an old friend with the Czar at his New Year's reception, had to be of some interest to a witty gossip like the short, stout French ambassador.

His Excellency, however, was too polite, and too cagey, to launch a frontal attack. He opened instead—when Chevalier Roland introduced Ash on the reception line—with an apology that he could not recall where they had first met.

"The Hague, Your Excellency. I had the honor of serving Admiral Mahon."

"*Mon Dieu,* so long ago. And such a fruitless endeavor *that* turned out to be."

French diplomats preferred comment to small talk, but Ash had no intention of opening a discussion on his arrest by thanking the ambassador for helping Roland try to find him. He said, "Perhaps the peace conference bought time for the Allies to discover their friends."

The ambassador covered his disappointment with a smile. Now *he* had to say, "Who knew in 1907 who would fight whom." The line of guests was getting long; Ash thanked him for the invitation and all the ambassador had time left to say was, "I hope we have the opportunity to meet again while you are in Petrograd. *Intime?*"

"You should parry so well on the strip," Roland remarked on their way to the champagne bar.

"He was distracted. Something's bothering him."

"He had an audience at Tsarskoye Selo this morning. I understand he was not encouraged by the Czar's grip on reality."

No wonder. The French ambassador had only one job in Petrograd and that was to keep his Russian ally fighting their common enemy, Germany. If he had seen what Ash had seen New Year's night . . . Ash could not get out of his mind the Czar's preoccupation with Constantinople; nor forget the anguish on Nicholas's face when his wife broke down in hysterics. It seemed that with Rasputin dead and the Czarina grief-stricken, the Czar was desolate, alone.

The French ball was a high point in the social season—the French ambassador being a favorite of Petrograd Society. The cream of the nobility—the aristocracy, the army and the government as well as the diplomatic corps—had braved a blizzard howling off the Gulf of Finland. Ash eyed the glittering throng, wondering if there was a single man or woman here capable of removing the Czar before Russia collapsed and the revolutionaries took over, ending the chance for America to enter the war on the side of the Allies.

Of all the means by which Russians traditionally flaunted their wealth, Ash thought that the most impressive was the manner in which Russian women dressed for a ball. He had grown accustomed to the great pastel palaces strung along the rivers and canals, to the perfect teams of matched thoroughbreds, to the retinues of docile servants. But neither palaces nor the languid splendor of their country estates, which Ash had sampled on previous visits, nor fine horses showed off Imperial Russia's surface glitter quite as vividly as the play of precious gems on naked female skin.

Petrograd was a city of achingly beautiful women, which the Russian upper classes spawned in infinite variety from raven-haired exotics to regal blondes. Their gowns swept low, and when they let their sables fall from their milky shoulders they revealed masses of brilliant diamonds, dazzling emeralds, rubies like blood. A quick motion to extend a shapely hand, a slow half-turn to impart a smile, and jewels shimmered wildly— emeralds, sapphires, matchless pearls—reminding one that one-sixth of the earth's surface was still theirs in contiguous possession.

Suddenly, across the cream-colored ballroom ablaze in electric chandeliers, Ash saw Lord Exeter parting the sea of gowns and uniforms; and at his side, lean as a frigate, Lady Exeter. Her gown covered her shoulders and her arms, and her only jewelry was an emerald brooch, yet in a room full of half-naked beautiful women, she still managed to look interesting.

Exeter, one of the few men not in uniform, smiled benignly when Ash bowed over Lady Exeter's hand, exchanged inconsequentials about their arrival in Petrograd, until Lady Exeter fell into conversation with a bohemian-looking noblewoman on the arm of an aristocratic poet; then he drew Ash aside and glanced around to see if it was safe to talk.

A lively quadrille was pounding across the ballroom; the noise of the dancers and Mikhailov's orchestra would compete with an artillery duel.

"I heard most of what happened. I presume prison was some ghastly error."

"I'm okay."

"Still useful?"

"Apparently. My arrest was not widely known and my embassy stayed out of it. I think I can continue as if nothing happened."

"And nothing has happened, has it?"

"What do you mean?"

"I mean I haven't heard about any request for the cruiser yet."

"The Czarina listened to what I had to offer," Ash said. "But when I got out of jail I received a strong indication that she was not interested in British asylum. I managed an audience with the Czar; I'm afraid he's not interested either." Not after the Czarina's outburst, he added to himself.

"What are you going to do?"

"I don't know. The Rasputin killing has shaken them up pretty badly."

"Bloody hell," Exeter said mildly, sounding, as only the English could, neither surprised nor upset. "Well, if they can't see the truth themselves, you'll just have to persuade them in a somewhat more forceful manner . . ."

Ash looked at the floor, as if Exeter's suggestion had spilled on the shiny parquet like something unpleasant. He had resisted Exeter's part in the King's mission from the beginning, worrying about his Secret Service connection. Ambassador Page and President Wilson's special assistant Harold Banks had raised the same doubts in the car at Charing Cross Station.

British capital was a pillar of Russian industrial modernization; there wasn't a mill or a railroad in Russia without British money in it, nor a town worthy of the name not served by a British consul. King George might be concerned only for his cousin—which meshed perfectly with Ash's goal to make Russia a palatable American ally by removing the taint of despotism —but the British Secret Service's goals might well transcend the war if Secret Service and the foreign office feared that Russian revolutionaries might put a major trading partner out of business.

Ash's goal was simpler. Get a situation in which American could enter the war. End the war. Which meant no more Czar, and no revolution.

"Exeter, I came this close to disengaging myself from His Majesty's scheme. I waited outside your house after our dinner and I promised myself that if one person who looked remotely like one of your superiors at Secret Service came to the door, or if you visited one, I would quit." He would not have quit, but Exeter had to be made to understand that Kenneth Ash would not be a stalking horse for British Secret Service.

"You're a bit of a spy yourself."

"No. But I'm learning."

Ash could have added, but did not, that *someone* had left the Exeter town house—the Exeters' houseguest, the ballerina Vera Sedovina, whom Ash had followed, because three o'clock in the morning was no hour for an innocent girl to be out alone, particularly when she had slipped like a shadow from the side door of a darkened house and met some strange characters in Covent Garden.

Exeter laid a hand on his sleeve. For such a fat man he had delicate fingers, Ash thought. Ash looked at him and he removed it, saying, "You must convince the Czar to leave."

"Put a gun to his head? What are you driving at?"

"You know Tishkova, the dancer?"

Podpolkovnik Ivan Roskov, the Czar's emissary, stalked into the French ball, handed the ambassador's major domo his snow-covered cloak and went looking for Ash among the several hundred guests. But just as Roskov was about to approach him, he was surprised to see the American become involved in an intense conversation with Lord Exeter.

A lifetime of watching for the Czar's safety made Roskov cautious. Puzzled that the two men would even know each other, he decided to observe from a distance before telling Ash the Czar wished to see him. As a lieutenant colonel in the Czar's Convoy, Roskov was regularly briefed by the Okhrana. He knew that Exeter worked for the British Secret Service, knew the English lord spent long evenings at the Imperial Yacht Club, surely plotting with the increasingly treacherous grand dukes. What had such a man to discuss with Kenneth Ash? . . . Whatever the subject, it appeared that Ash did not like it. He looked like a man about to draw his sword.

"Yes, I know Tishkova. What of it?"

"I hear rumblings that the Grand Duke Valery is cooking up some sort of palace revolt."

"Exeter, what the hell are you doing in Petrograd?"

"His Majesty asked me to help you, but I'd be here anyway. I may have mentioned that my family owns munitions and cloth works up the Neva, near Lake Ladoga. Vital to the war push, but production's lagging, what with strikes and fuel shortages. I've come out to stir things up."

"Is that all you're stirring up?"

Exeter took hold of Ash's arm again and this time he did not let go. "Ash, my sources say that Grand Duke Valery has a damned good chance of pulling it off. Tishkova, of course, is allied with him."

"If *you* know about it," Ash said coldly, "what about the Okhrana?" Tamara . . . what in hell had she got herself into? "Don't you think the police know too? It didn't take long to banish Grand Duke Dmitri and Prince Felix for shooting Rasputin."

"This is different—"

"Damned right it's different. They'll execute them for treason."

"No," said Exeter. "The Grand Duke Valery can succeed. But they need help with certain logistical problems. You might get in touch—"

"*No.*"

"Why not?"

"I didn't come to Russia to overthrow the government. I came to rescue the Czar." He had come to *remove* the Czar, but that was between him and Ambassador Page's Inner Circle.

"Well, who do you suppose is going to replace him?"

"Why don't we let the Russians worry about that? If you and the British Secret Service tip them over the brink with some damned fool scheme, the whole Eastern Front will collapse."

"Is that your only reason?"

"It's my best reason. Any other isn't any of your damned business."

Ash saw the Baroness Balmont, the banker de la Rocca's wife, and hurried toward her, shedding Exeter as he made his way through the crowds.

Lord Exeter watched Ash's progress in the mirrored walls. A line from Kipling's "Recessional" ran through his mind: "The Captains and the Kings depart."

But who, he wondered, shall inherit what they leave behind? Neither the meek, nor the scrupulous, he was certain. Not even the cautious . . .

The tall Baltic blonde greeted Ash with a kiss on each cheek and repeated her invitation to come shooting on her estate. Her long white arms and high bosom were complimented by a dark blue gown; sapphires cascaded and glittered between her breasts. Ash inquired about her husband's health, and the Baroness Balmont replied that she had just had a channel dug so that one of her marshes opened directly into the Gulf of Finland to accommodate winter-bound yachtsmen who cared to try their hand at iceboating.

Ash admitted he was tempted. A day of shooting and iceboating and a night in the baronial bed might be just the antidote to the catastrophe he had reaped so far. Exeter's nibbling around the edges was irritating and very likely dangerous; and his suggestion to turn to Tamara for help was downright depressing. Was *she* why the King had chosen him in the first place? That possibility was even more depressing, but whether the King had or not, Ash knew he had to do *something,* and damned soon. The wood piles outside the Astoria were getting lower every day, and the blizzard howling past the French Embassy was only the first big storm of winter.

Vladimir Dan recognized Ash from photographs General Ludendorff had shown them. Only yesterday his brother Dmitri had seen Ash at Tsarskoye Selo. Twice, once at the Catherine Palace and later, mysteriously, at the Alexander. It scemed Ash was more than just a navy commander, which would explain partly why General Ludendorff was so anxious to buy his death.

The Red Snow leader had been disappointed when he got back to Petrograd to learn that the American was still alive; the German bounty had seemed like money in the bank. Instead, a comrade had died and Vladimir's brother Dmitri was complaining it wasn't worth the effort. Vladimir had gone hunting anyway, only to discover that Ash never slept in his hotel. Spotting Ash at the ball tonight was a piece of luck.

"Who are you looking at?" asked his fiancée, a pretty girl from a rich family who knew nothing about Red Snow but was a necessary accoutrement to his carefully maintained existence as a loyal young officer to the Czar. Her only drawback was a habit of uncommon jealousy, and while he was looking at Ash, speculating how to kill him tonight, Elena thought he was making eyes at the very handsome Baroness Balmont. Fortunately her Italian husband came along and took her away.

But when he said, "I'm sorry I have to take you home after midnight supper," Elena pouted and accused him of planning to meet the Baroness Balmont at the gypsies'.

"I don't know where you get these ideas," Vladimir Dan protested. He rarely considered the personal effect the revolution would have on his life when it was won. He had a vague idea of continuing much as he did now, with an army career and a proper wife, a house in Petrograd and a country estate and, if her dowry was as ample as suggested, a month or so a year in Paris. None of this, of course, would be at the expense of the peasants, as such luxuries now were. A competent government run by the people would eliminate the bottlenecks of production and the rapacious middlemen who were ruining the Russian economy. His brother Dmitri envisioned a rather more spartan revolutionary aftermath, but then, Dmitri had always been the stern ascetic. With such a future in mind—and it wasn't a future he dwelled upon, just occasionally thought of—it occurred to him that Elena could be a hellish wife. Particularly when it came time to take a mistress . . . "I'm as faithful as any man in Petrograd. I'm terribly sorry, but my colonel has ordered me back to barracks early—"

"Why you?"

"The officer of the day asked to be relieved early. He hasn't fully recovered from his wounds . . ." Half-truths, because he would not put it past

253

her to have one of her many brothers trail him around the city, and he did have to go to his barracks to get a gun and maybe a hand grenade.

The quadrille grew louder. Two hundred dancers followed the lead of a couple in the middle who offered intricate steps which the rest of the Russians followed as precisely as a ballet corps. The man leading, a tall cavalry officer in a light blue uniform, called out instructions for each new figure and the ballroom resounded with laughter as the steps picked up speed. Ash had led one once with Tamara. There was nothing like it; make one wrong move and you'd send two hundred people careening into the mirrors.

"Ash!"

A short sandy-haired Royal Navy lieutenant parted the outlookers and came to rest in front of Ash, springing up and down on the balls of his feet like an aggressive terrier. Rodney Skelton, whom Ash had been intending to visit at the British submarine base at Reval. An odd coincidence? Or a good omen? Ash's emergency escape route if the cruiser were a bust. At least that had been his plan before the Czar said no.

Skelton noticed his promotion and tossed a mocking salute. "Commander? The American navy seems bound to become all chiefs and no Indians." There was an edge in Skelton's voice; they had had a set-to in India and neither had fully recovered from it. They had beaten the local Rajah's polo team in a remote province and the Rajah, in a rage, had ordered his entire team's horses put to death. Knowing nothing about it, Ash and Skelton had taken their gin-and-quinines for a walk in the Rajah's gardens and had stumbled on the slaughter. The stable yards reeked of blood, and Skelton, in the finest British tradition, had ordered the Indians to desist. Ash had seen things differently—some thirty angry men with knives intent on finishing what they had started—and had forcibly marched Skelton back to the British compound. Skelton had called him a coward; Ash had called Skelton a damned fool, and though they had continued to play polo together it had rankled through the long Coronation Durber summer.

"What are you doing in Petrograd?" Ash asked as they shook hands. "I was planning to visit you down in Reval."

"I'm a Russian hero." Skelton grinned. "Making speeches for war bonds." He had received "permission to stop shaving," as the Royal Navy put it, and had grown a luxurious yellow beard, and Ash reflected that all in all Rodney Skelton looked the epitome of the British sportsman turned warrior for king and country.

"I sank three ore ships trying to carry iron from Sweden to Germany. Ought to put a crimp in Krupp. What are you doing?"

Ash could not hide his envy, though a close look at his old teammate revealed that two years action in enemy waters had had a price; behind the open boasts Skelton was strung tight as a wire stay—but a command . . . command of a man o' war . . .

"Have you seen any action in the Gulf of Finland?"

"Sure, covering the Baltic Fleet at Reval . . . until it freezes over. Beastly shallow. Actually the entire Baltic is, and the damned salt content is so low you can't control your depth. Fact is, the censors won't let the papers print our speeches because if Jerry learns the sub commanders are dancing in Petrograd, he'll raid Reval and sink the bloody Baltic Fleet . . . What are you doing, sport?"

There were acquaintances you had to brag to, and before he could stop himself Ash was spouting his fondest hopes . . . "I might get a destroyer soon."

"When?"

When? When I rescue the Czar for your king. The same Czar who just tossed me out of his palace. "Late spring, I hope—listen I really do want to come down and see your base." Somehow, dammit, he was going to get the Czar out, but the tougher it got the more he might need an emergency escape route.

"Delighted to have you," Skelton replied with the toothy grin that usually preceded a dig. "Better wire ahead in case I have to sink a battle-ship that morning—or a couple of destroyers—ah, there's one of my hostesses. Good to see you, sport. Don't lose your despatch case."

Ash traded nods with the food exporter Prince Paustovsky, who had never called back after promising an audience with the Czarina, and who now turned quickly away. Moments later he was snubbed by Sergei Gladishev, the Moscow millionaire and Kadet Party leader. He was wishing he hadn't come when he was hailed again, this time by Catherine Hazzard, whom he had not seen since they had arrived in Petrograd.

"Commander?"

She was on her father's arm and trailed by her cousin Andrew. Her golden hair fell straight to her shoulders. She looked a little awed by the splendor and glad to see a familiar face. Her impossibly blue eyes sought Ash's. It no doubt was her first Petrograd ball. Ash bowed over her hand.

"You look lovely, Catherine. Good evening, Mr. Ambassador. Hello, Andrew."

Hazzard pulled an envelope from his evening jacket and passed it to Ash. "From Ambassador Page. King's Messenger brought it in."

Ash slipped it in his own pocket. It was thick, and he was itching to read it but had to spend a decent interval with the ambassador and his family to convince Hazzard, who still looked resentful over his arrest, that he expected such communications to be routine.

He felt Catherine's gaze and turned to her. "The ball is wonderful, isn't it?"

"I can't believe I'm here. The music is so beautiful and the colors . . ."

Ash looked around the room as if seeing it for the first time, and indeed the electric bulbs blazing in the chandeliers highlighted an incredible variety of red, blue, green and white uniforms, all dripping gold braid and ribbons; and on the arm of each officer a beautiful woman in a bright gown and shimmering jewels.

Suddenly the dancers stopped and turned expectantly toward the rococo doors from where a hush spread across the ball like a silent ocean breaker.

"Some bigwig's coming in," Ambassador Hazzard whispered.

"Oh look!" Catherine's hand closed on Ash's arm. "Oh look at them."

Ash felt a dark pit open inside his heart.

33

"**W**ho is that, Ash?" Ambassador Hazzard asked. "Looks kind of familiar."

"The Grand Duke Valery, cousin to the Czar, Your Excellency . . . I imagine he'll be representing His Majesty tonight."

Valery wore a red uniform crossed by a blue silk sash. The decorations of a lifetime serving the Czar glittered on his chest. Ash thought he looked even more arrogant and self-possessed than he had twelve years ago at the Portsmouth peace talks, but he had to admit the grand duke still stood well. Half-bald, with a graying monk's fuzz around his ears, he had a high forehead . . . like Lenin's. Ironic.

"Is that his wife?" Catherine asked.

"No . . . no, he's not married. That's Tamara Tishkova, *prima ballerina assoluta* of the Imperial Russian Theater."

Ash had never seen her more beautiful.

The Black Swan. Her gown was black silk, her lustrous black hair coiffed high on her shapely head and banded with pearls. She seemed to glide as she promenaded on the grand duke's arm, jewels flashing on her deep décolletage, long drop diamond earrings caressing her white shoulders. Valery's gifts, for flaunting her as his consort. Her sensual mouth formed the elegant half-smile she always wore in the spotlight, a smile Ash had loved to watch grow broad with laughter, full and hungry in bed.

"Isn't she the woman you told us about?" Andrew asked.

"Would you excuse me, Catherine? Mr. Ambassador?" And Ash was gone, his chest hammering, before either could reply.

Tamara was aware of their entrance. No one at the ball could guess their turmoil, not even the frightened conspirators deserting Valery. The same men, she raged inwardly behind her steady smile, who had urged him to lead a palace coup but lost their courage the instant the grand duke had returned from his visit to the Czarina announcing that she was out of her mind and had to be removed to save Russia.

There was Sirotkin strutting about in the green uniform of the Preobrajenski Guard, units of which he had promised would seize the Winter Palace but which were suddenly "too loyal" to commit *before* Valery's coup was successful. And there, Kamenev, sweet-talking Princess Paley; the men of his Jaegerski regiment were just as suddenly "conscripts too fresh to trust." And splendid in the blue of his Semonovski regiment, Captain Sokolov leading the quadrille—all he would lead, it had turned out, another noble Life Guard officer who preferred to talk while Valery fought. Tamara took some small consolation in that Sokolov danced like a monkey, waving his arms about, but she would have preferred to shoot him in his tracks.

Poor Valery. Czarina Alexandra had received him draped in black mourning, weeping, railing against the dark forces that attacked her friend Rasputin. And when Valery had tried to persuade her to release Grand Duke Dmitri, because only the Czar could legally arrest a grand duke, the Czarina had lost all control and had thrown Valery out, screaming that *she* was the Czar. Hurrying back to Petrograd, determined to overthrow her and Nicky, Valery had been astonished to discover that while his brother grand dukes and officers still swore they would support Valery *after* the Czar was deposed, no one wanted to be first.

It was a classic case of belling the cat. Every duke offered to help form a new government, and every soldier among the conspirators promised his regiment would restore order. But first, Valery had said to no avail, raging until Tamara thought he would shatter the windows of her solarium with his voice, *some* regiment had to seize the Czar. Another take the Winter Palace. And a third besiege the police. And still a *fourth* escort agreeable members to the Duma from their Turide Palace to the Winter Palace to express public support.

Risks and details. What the army called logistics. The work a dancer did to free dreams from gravity. They were lazy cowards and their desertions were gnawing at Valery's resolve. He too was on the verge of losing stomach for it. He was saying, "Perhaps if we just get through the winter . . ."

Tamara knew he was also worried about the Czar. What *exactly*, he

258

wanted to know, would happen to Nicky? What shall we do with him? Troublesome czarinas were traditionally bundled off to a nunnery. But the historical record on overthrown Czars was grimmer, Fyodor Godunov and Paul I both murdered. And Valery had already said he would take part in no palace coup that threatened to end in Nicky's death. He had demanded arrangements for the Czar's safety before he made a move.

Such cool-headedness was one of the several qualities Tamara admired in her very good if somewhat dull grand duke; his fellow-conspirators had been more willing to see what happened, as if by hoping things would work out, Nicky would miraculously not be hurt in the heat of the moment. But the question of Nicky's fate was becoming moot as one by one, day by day, Valery's allies turned cowards.

Was it perhaps for the best, she wondered, as they continued promenading about the ballroom. Who knew where poor Russia was going? Who really knew what should be done?

Tamara inclined her head, granting the merest nod to Sergei Gladishev. What a shame Valery hated the Moscow millionaire on principle. As a dancer she was accustomed to moving freely among court, Life Guard, bohemian, artist and even some merchant circles. A man like Gladishev, with his powerful allies in the Duma, could add such impetus to a coup, bring many powerful men along with him in support of a new czar. But staunchly conservative grand dukes like Valery and flashy industrialists like Gladishev distrusted each other on every issue Russia faced.

They were natural enemies—the Duma and modern industry against royalty. Yet Gladishev nodded back. Shrewd man. He understood.

And how had she become mixed up in all this? Why would a woman who reigned on two stages risk them both? Ironically, Valery himself had put it best when finally he had agreed to lead the palace coup. "If not us, the revolutionaries. Or worse, the Germans . . ." Survival.

Ambassador Page's message had been short, to the point, impatient: "What the hell is going on? Please report." In the same envelope, which had been carried to Russia by the King's Messenger, was a second message, an unsigned query which by its content had to be from George V: "We are anxious to hear whether matters are in hand." Same message. Different backgrounds.

Ash deep-sixed both in the men's room. He'd report when he had something to report, dammit. Back in the ballroom he circled the floor, careful to stay out of Tamara's way, yet unable to resist watching her at Valery's side. In a room full of beautiful women, she turned heads, on or off a grand duke's arm.

Tamara Tishkova stumbled. She was indulging Valery in a waltz when suddenly she saw Kennet. He was one uniform in a sea of uniforms, but she always knew him by his walk. She had seen him the first time walking in the sun—

"My ballerina trips?" Valery teased.

"The difference between me and an oxcart is that the ox leads." She practically gaped at Kennet as Valery steered her around the floor, stunned by what the sight of him still did to her.

She had seen him walking in the sun that first time in New Hampshire near the sea. She had climbed into a little boat tied at the end of a pier in a blue bay beside the Wentworth Hotel. A breeze was blowing from the Atlantic Ocean. The Wentworth sprawled along the shore, five white clapboard stories, big as a city, all by itself on a spit of sand and trees a few miles down the New Hampshire coast from the Portsmouth Naval Station.

She lay in the boat, looking at the Wentworth's flags and turrets, trailing her fingers in the water, thinking about Nicky and the new dance she was doing in New York, and Valery, who even then was earnestly pressing her to be his alone. The summer of 1905, eleven and a half very long years ago —magnificent years, until the war ruined them.

And then Ash had walked onto the pier. Tamara had watched him through half-shut, sleepy eyes, watched his quick walk. By the time she had awakened to the probability that she was in his boat, it was too late to move and then, suddenly, she was lost.

All thoughts of Nicky and Valery and even the dance left her mind. She saw only a young man in white shirt and trousers, his skin bronzed by summer, his unruly hair sun-streaked with gold. His footsteps shook the pier, shook the boat where it touched the pier. His gaze was focused on the bay, examining the water the way she examined a new set. He did not see her until he knelt to untie the rope.

"Have I taken your boat?" Tamara smiled up at him.

His eyes filled with her. "It's not mine. I borrowed it."

Tamara lay still, moving only to lift her fingers slowly from the water. "Then I am in your way?"

She knew her effect on him, was confirmed in it as he had answered quickly, "Not if you want to come for a sail."

She watched him prepare the boat, fascinated by his young, lean body —a fencer's body, perhaps, or a dancer's, but too big in the arms and shoulders for either. His hands were big too, and calloused from sailing. But not rough, oddly. Not rough when he touched her. No . . .

Valery invaded her thoughts again, squeezed her arm. "Are you enjoying yourself, my dear?"

260

Ash was in no mood for midnight supper, and the French ambassador's announcement that "the bold, British submariners" would make speeches during the meal cinched his feeling. When the guests began their exodus to the next room where the tables were laid, Ash had a smoke with Mikhailov while the piano player took a break. The old gossip told Ash a fantastic rumor. It was claimed by the *moujik* peasant workers that the Czar's daughter, the beautiful Grand Duchess Tatiana, had disguised herself as a lieutenant of the Horse Guard to watch the murder of Rasputin.

"She ordered the dying monk castrated because he once attempted to violate her. After that Rasputin was thrown in the river still living."

"Do you believe that?" Ash asked, knowing damned well he had seen Rasputin shot dead before his eyes.

Mikhailov shrugged. "The peasants believe in vengeance. And they know that a man drowned can never be made a saint . . .

"In other words the Okhrana started the rumor to discredit the monk."

"Perhaps . . ."

"When is your daughter coming home?"

"She's on her way. She'll be dancing Effie in *La Sylphide* next Sunday. She'd better make it soon."

"She looked more the Sylphide."

"She's made too many enemies at the theater with her political ideas to get the best parts."

Ash was not surprised, considering he had watched her pass a despatch pouch to a Russian seaman in the middle of the night in Covent Garden. Did the old boy know? "You must be happy."

Mikhailov ground out his cigarette and brought his eyes to bear on Ash. "I'm worried. I didn't want her to come back. If there's a revolution she'll be right in the middle of it."

"Maybe there won't be a revolution."

"And maybe my piano will walk to Moscow."

Ash went back in when the dancing resumed, but it looked as though Tamara had left early. He was figuring to call it a night when Lord Exeter saw him at the french doors. "Ash, be a good chap. I must go up river. There's trouble at one of my factories. Could you see Lady Exeter home?"

He looked badly agitated, so Ash, who really wanted nothing more than to be alone, agreed. Exeter pressed a coat check into his hand and hurried off, his voluminous dinner jacket flapping like the wings of a condor.

Ash got Lady Exeter's coat and waited in a corner of the foyer watching the Russians retrieve their furs. Sergei Gladishev came by with a serious-looking young woman on his arm and snubbed Ash again. His friend Skobeleff, the diplomat, left with his head bowed; probably, Ash guessed, his last ball in Petrograd, off to some dull province. He noticed a Horse Guard lieutenant colonel who seemed to be watching him; he looked like the Czar's officer who had escorted him to Alexander Palace New Year's Day. Then Lady Exeter swept grandly out of the ballroom, talking with the poet and the artistic-looking woman with short black hair, and the officer turned away.

Podpolkovnik Roskov, the Czar's emissary, had lost sight of Ash when the dancing stopped for supper. He sat with a pair of ladies he had enjoyed affairs with over the years, suffered through some interminable speeches by some insufferable British submarine commanders, who seemed to have conveniently forgotten that the last time the Royal Navy had operated in the Gulf of Finland, many years ago, it had been attacking Russia and was soundly stopped by the fortress at Kronstadt. The English had ambitious dreams and short memories.

He decided, while dining, to run Ash down at his hotel. Through the long evening the American had spoken with many people, including the American ambassador and his pretty daughter, one of the British submarine commanders who appeared to be an old friend, as well as the Baroness Balmont and her Italian husband. Exeter was the only suspicious person Ash had spoken with, so Rostov decided it was safe to bring him to the palace.

As luck would have it, he spotted Ash in the foyer, waiting with a woman's coat on his arm. Roskov hurried toward him but when the woman appeared, it was Lady Exeter, Lord Exeter's wife . . . Rostov veered away, deciding that he had better inform the Czar of Ash's strange companions.

"Commander, you look like a little boy about to cry."

"It must be the smoke, Lady Exeter. May I?" He helped her into her sable. She said, "My husband apologizes, but he had to take the carriage. I thought we might walk, if you don't mind the snow, and then the carriage can take you home when it gets back from the station. I've got boots." She raised her gown to show him, and he realized she had her pumps in her hand with her bag.

"I hope your husband's trouble isn't too serious."

262

"It is. Another strike, apparently. The last one shut the factory down for three weeks."

"What do they make?"

"Artillery shells . . . precisely what the Russian army is most short of."

Tamara huddled under Valery's fur-covered arm; he had insisted on using his favorite open red sleigh, even though it was snowing so hard she could barely see the Cossack outriders. They had taken a passenger, Sirotkin of the Preobrajenski Guard, to whom Valery was patiently explaining the necessity of immobilizing the Czar *before* he announced a new government. Sirotkin still seemed determined to waltz into the Winter Palace on Valery's coattails.

She watched the bridge lights shine on the Cossacks' lances, and thought of Kennet. God was a trickster. He had given her so much—her talent, the will to use it, her beauty and the power to manage those, like Valery, who wanted to possess her. All those gifts which made her Tishkova.

Then, He laid before her a young man, far too young, poor, a sailor, and an American democrat. That was God's joke on her, to have everything she wanted, except . . . She had almost given it all up to be alone with Kennet, to be just a dancer with her beautiful young lover, but an injury had saved her from such madness, an injured metatarsus that had been an excruciating reminder that a dancer's body had a future as uncertain as a spider web in a doorway.

The snow was falling hard, driven across the Neva by a cold north wind. They walked with heads bowed from the French Embassy on the embankment to her apartment in the Admiralty district. It was less than a mile but slow going.

"At least the wind is at our back," Lady Exeter remarked halfway.

"Shall I find a cab?" Ash stopped and faced her under a street lamp. "No, I'm fine, if you are." Her coat had a hood and the rim of dark fur around her face softened her rather angular features and highlighted her pretty eyes. Snowflakes had gathered on the wisps of red hair that escaped the hood.

Their apartment building was beside the Ekaterine Canal and overlooked the Alexander Museum gardens, now deep in snow.

"Would you like to come up for a brandy?"

Ash hesitated. He had thought he wanted to be alone, but it had been pleasant walking together and he felt better than he had all night.

"Our carriage will be back from the train station later. You'll have no trouble getting back to your hotel."

To be safe he had to go out to Vassily Island, but he could always hire a sleigh at the Europa or a troika behind the Kazan.

The Exeters' building was typical of the wealthy neighborhoods—luxurious apartments on the first and second floors and rooms for servants and coachmen, drivers and grooms on the upper floors. It was furnished in the Russian manner, which was, of course, mostly imported French furniture, and there were some good paintings on the walls.

Lady Exeter sent the butler to bed and poured the brandy herself. They sat by a fire in the library. "Feeling better?" she asked.

"Much," said Ash, "but Bonaparte is going to be annoyed when he finds out where his personal keg of brandy went."

"My husband has the most unusual sources for *everything*. Once when we were in Peking we were supplied ducks by the same farmer who raised them for the Chinese emperor."

Ash wondered if she knew Exeter was in the Secret Service. Wondered if she knew that the king had asked him to "rescue" Czar Nicholas and had asked her husband to help.

The thought flashed through his mind that Exeter might have told her to work on him to agree to team up with the Grand Duke Valery. But that seemed pretty farfetched.

"May I ask what was troubling you?" she asked, refilling their glasses.

Ash pushed his feet closer to the fire. The brandy was delicious, beginning to buzz in his head; he hadn't felt this comfortable in a long time, since the night he had supper with the comtesse in Paris, the night this all started . . .

"I saw an old friend, it was . . . it sort of upset me."

"Who?" asked Lady Exeter. Ash looked at her. An inquiring smile lighted her stern face; she seemed interested rather than curious, interested in listening if he wanted to talk. "It was hardly a secret. I was involved with Tamara Tishkova for several years. Coming back to Petrograd has stirred up a lot of old feelings."

"Involved?"

He told her how they had met and spent their years in Europe; how Tamara had changed his life, really altered its course; how she had filled the years he might ordinarily have been expected to be married; how she had made him in the process a sort of hybrid American-European, comfortable most anywhere, rarely at home.

"Is she why you remained in diplomacy?"

"I suppose. Probably there were times I turned down one duty or another to be with her." He described how he would arrange getting posted city to city when she toured. At last, after Lady Exeter had twice

264

refilled their snifters and Ash had put another log on the fire, she asked, "And now it's over?"

"Since the end of 1913. I think Tamara decided she had to settle down."

"That's three years, Commander. A long time to hold on to a memory."

Ash shrugged. "Maybe memories hang on longer than people."

"Surely you have not remained . . . shall I say *faithful* . . . to Tishkova's memory all this time?"

"Well, I haven't tomcatted around like I used to before we met."

Lady Exeter smiled, "What a horrible expression. American?"

"Down home."

"Perhaps you're just older, *n'est pas?*"

"Or choosier."

Lady Exeter stood up, smoothing her gown, went to the window and parted the drapes. "There's a Russian officer standing in the snow . . . just standing there, staring at the building . . . probably waiting for his mistress's husband to go to bed. They're so insanely romantic here, don't you think?"

Ash joined her at the window. Snow was blowing through the streetlight. The officer stood just beyond the chief light spill from the three-globe lamp, his eyes fixed on the apartment building. He wore the *papaha* of one of the Life Guard regiments.

Lady Exeter said, "They say the reason the aristocracy dislikes the Czarina so much is that she was such a prude about their affairs." She laughed. "She actually cut transgressors from the palace invitation list, but before she knew it there was no one left." She closed the drapes and faced Ash with an easy smile, betrayed by a tiny vein throbbing in her temple, and an intent glitter in her eyes.

"It's still snowing. Would you care to spend the night?"

The Czar let *Podpolkovnik* Roskov out one of the secret doors in the maze of private passageways that connected the royal apartments. Roskov had reported an hour after he had seen Ash with Lady Exeter in the foyer of the French Embassy. The Czar was drowsily sipping a glass of hot milk and examining the latest maps from the *Stavka*. Such was the sovereign's devotion to duty, Roskov noted approvingly that the maps were revised daily and sped by train from Mogilev.

The Czar had been very disturbed when he had returned without Ash.

Roskov had explained his fears. The Czar listened attentively and nodded agreement. "You were right, of course, to be cautious." He became silent. Roskov waited. He had no idea what the Czar wanted to talk to Ash about, but it seemed important . . . he seemed so worried.

"You are sure about this English lord?"

"Yes, Your Majesty. Exeter owns factories up the Neva but his activities for the Secret Service go back to the Boer War. He is no innocent."

"What could Ash want with him—and his wife? What of her? Is she a British agent too?"

Roskov hesitated. "I'm not sure, Your Majesty. But I felt it too dangerous to bring Ash here without first informing Your Majesty of what I had seen."

"You're right, of course . . . but here is what you must do—alone, without consulting the Okhrana or anyone, quickly learn more about Ash. See who else he associates with. But quickly, Rostov. I must know soon. Commander Ash could be very important to me. Very . . ."

Ash was a little surprised. She did not seem the type of woman who could carry something beyond a mild flirtation. "The French have a saying, Lady Exeter: to love another man's wife is civilized. To love a friend's wife is anarchy. I am very flattered, and while I hardly think of your husband as a friend, I did meet you together at the home of a friend, and have enjoyed your hospitality—"

"Are you stalling, Commander?"

"I suppose I am. I'm a little confused tonight, as I've told you."

"I'm not confused. I haven't slept with my husband in years."

"Do you love him?" Ash felt stupid, not sure what he wanted.

"He rescued me. My dearest friend in the women's rights movement threw herself under the racehorses in the Derby. When she died a lot of the fight went out of me. My husband has tried very hard to make me whole again. I'm not there yet but I'm gaining strength and when this damned war is over I'll be back in the fight . . ." She smiled. "Do you believe in women's rights, Commander?"

"All of them, Your Ladyship."

"Including my right to suggest you make love to me . . ."

"No," Ash said. "You've flattered me too much already." He kissed her just beneath her ear, savored her with his lips. Trembling slightly, she pulled back and eyed him. "I'll forget my husband for the night. Will you forget your dancer?"

Ash kissed her again, decided to try once and for all to bury the past. "Who?" It tore at him as he said it.

"You're kind," she said, taking his hand. "Come."

The doorbell rang.

"Damn—the telephone lines are probably out again. Probably a message for my husband. I'll be right back."

Ash picked up the telephone as she left the library. The line buzzed, the operator answered. He went to the window, opened the drape. The officer under the streetlight was gone. Ash ran after her and caught up in the foyer as she started to open the door.

"The telephone's working."

"Then it's our coachman. I'll send him home."

Before he could stop her she opened the door.

"Where is the doorman?" she asked sharply.

And then she fell back, and the officer they had seen beneath the window pushed into the foyer. Ash reached for his gun. He was too late.

34

Vladimir Dan cursed his own impatience. Red Snow deserved better. Of course the English woman was still in the apartment. It was probably hers. He should have waited for Ash even if it took all night. But the blizzard was so cold, the snow had seemed to draw blood from his face. Now he had to kill two people.

With his gun he gestured their hands into the air.

An Englishwoman and an American murdered in the exclusive Admiralty district? The police would go crazy. Such a killing would provoke them into the sort of painstaking detective work they were best at—not hunting the revolutionary he was but a common criminal. People must have seen him outside, heard him in the hall. Maybe the doorman he had eluded heard him barge through her door. What an irony it would be— caught as a criminal while committing an act of revolution, caught, like Dostoevski's Raskolnikov, by "trifles."

A lucrative act of revolution, he reminded himself, worth two hundred thousand German marks in a Swiss bank in an account held by a Red Snow company, the treasurer of which happened to be Vladimir Dan. They were watching him closely, he saw the speculation in their eyes— each wondering could he be taken. He could tell them the answer was no.

"Back," he told them, his mind whirling. He had a brilliant idea. Make it look as if her husband had surprised them in bed. Make the murder look like a crime of passion. "Back. Into the bedroom."

Twenty miles away, south of the city, in the Alexander Palace at Tsarskoye Selo, Vladimir's brother Dmitri crouched in a narrow stairwell, a few yards from the billiard room where the Czar spent so many hours staring at his maps. Dmitri had waited half the night until the palace grew quiet and the corridors were sure to be deserted except for a single Ethiopian guarding the billiard room door.

Red Snow comrades had painstakingly constructed a map of the royal apartments from the merest hints and snatches of information. At last they had discovered an unguarded, secret entrance, part of the maze connecting corridors and back stairs the servants used. It had fallen to Dmitri to don full uniform and bluff his way to that chink in the Czar's armor.

He had a gun. His plan was simple. The Ethiopians were massive men, so the guard would get three shots. Then, through the door and straight at the Czar with three more. He had a knife to finish the tyrant, but it never occurred to him to plan an escape. To think of afterward would only distract. Russia's suffering masses deserved everything Dmitri could give them.

He got up on cramped legs, pulled the gun from his tunic.

A door he had not seen because it was concealed as a wall panel opened and *Podpolkovnik* Ivan Roskov, the stern disciplinarian of the Czar's Convoy, came through it like a man half his age. Dmitri guessed instantly that Roskov, confidant to the Czar, had exited the billiard room by one of the halls.

"What the devil are you doing here, Lieutenant?"

The old gray beard's arrogant bark caused the startled Dmitri automatically to salute. And then Roskov saw his gun. The older man was fast. A powerful hand clamped hold of Dmitri's wrist, nearly broke the bones. Dmitri gasped with pain, the gun fell from his fingers and clattered on the stair.

Roskov smashed Dmitri's face with his other hand. *"Scum."*

Rage galvanized Dmitri Dan. He lashed out at the scarred face, kicked and kneed Roskov in the stomach. Roskov gasped but still tightened his grip on Dmitri's wrist and forced him to his knees.

The fate of Russia's people hung, he knew Dmitri's strength, Dmitri's ability to ignore the pain. He had to kill Roskov to kill the Czar. His wrist bones ground together as the old soldier squeezed harder. Dmitri punched him again with his free hand, punched his chest, and the wind seemed to explode from Roskov. He staggered, coughing. Dmitri slowly stood, forcing him back, broke Roskov's grip on his wrist and seized his throat in both hands. Roskov clawed at Dmitri's face, kicked, gouged. Dmitri squeezed with all the strength he had and held on as if the whole revolution depended on him.

Vladimir Dan saw the American try to comfort the English woman with a glance. Their fingers strayed together a moment before Vladimir ordered them apart. So? His scenario wasn't so farfetched. He grinned nervously at the thought that it would apply to half the highborn women in Petrograd and no one would question the conclusions. Except the husband, but the police would expect him to deny it.

"Bedroom," Vladimir repeated. The hand grenade he had taken from his barracks tugged at his belt under his cloak, but this plan was better with the gun. Required the gun. After all, what husband, even the most suspicious, entered his wife's boudoir with a hand grenade?

They backed slowly into the drawing room. Rich, thought Vladimir. Repins and Serovs on the walls. And ancient icon paintings worth a fortune. And here and there some Russian avant-garde painters. Chagall, Goncharova, Kandinsky.

"Bedroom. Not here."

Lady Exeter spoke for the first time since she had demanded the whereabouts of the doorman. "Which bedroom?"

"Yours, madam."

Ash said, "Look, Lieutenant. You and I can settle this outside—"

"Your room, madam. Quickly." He cocked his revolver, a British Webley-Fosbery he had picked up in France for its incredible hitting power and which, being an English weapon, would strengthen the case against her husband, dropping it on the way out . . .

Lady Exeter lurched against Ash and murmured, "Keep away from the bed."

"Stand apart."

Ash stopped moving, to distract him. "Leave her out of this. You're after me, I know you are and there's no reason to—"

"*Move.*"

Ash moved. The Russian was too tensed up to push any further. *Stay away from the bed.* What did she have in mind? He was waiting for the man to look the other way for a moment so he could get to his back holster.

Lady Exeter stopped at the first door in the hall, asked coolly, "Will this do?"

Vladimir glanced into the little bedroom, obviously a guest room with its two single beds. "No. Your room."

She paused at the next door, pointed again. "This is mine."

Vladimir almost laughed. It was prim as a schoolgirl's, with a narrow bed and a night table covered with books. He could just imagine a grizzled Petrograd homicide detective finding their bodies here and grunting, "Absurd."

270

"Your husband's room."

He would shoot Ash first and undress the body after he killed the woman. No. There'd be bullet holes in Ash's tunic. And it would take too long after the noise of the shots to get his clothes off anyway. *Dmitri, if only you were here.* Dmitri would not have rushed it. Dmitri would have waited until Ash came out even if the snow drifted ten feet over his head.

"Here," Lady Exeter announced at the end of the long hall. Ash crowded next to her as she pointed. Vladimir ordered them in and had a look. Good. Dimly lighted by a single lamp on a table beside the enormous bed, it was a symphony of dark wood and leather. A rich man's room. It was not hard to guess their relationship, but the bed was just right. She would have taken Ash here if he hadn't interrupted.

"Inside." He gestured, pushing her and stepping out of Ash's reach. He felt much better now, with the killing ground chosen. He pretended he was Dmitri, got control of himself to make a simple plan.

"Take off your boots, Commander."

"Hold on."

Vladimir whirled toward the woman and aimed the gun at her head. She backed toward the bed. "Do as I say. *Now.*"

Ash went to the chair in the corner. Vladimir followed him with the gun. Ash was stalling. "Hurry up."

"You don't have to kill us both."

"Shut up."

"Whoever you are, for God's sake leave her alone."

Vladimir felt the blood rushing to his face. He was working himself up to pulling the trigger. But not before the clothes . . . "Take your boots off."

Ash sat down slowly and started to tug at one of his boots.

Vladimir heard a sharp click to his left. Lady Exeter was standing where he had left her beside the bed. The night-table drawer was open. In her hands was another Webley. Her husband's gun.

Vladimir turned to fire at her. It seemed to take forever, and by the time he had her in his sights two immense blows flung him backward, slammed him to the door frame and dropped him in a heap. At last, he heard the shots.

Ash was moving across the room, tugging the Luger from his back when Lady Exeter's shots struck home and it occurred to him as he stepped on the Russian's wrist and wrenched the gun out of his hand that Lady Exeter *did* know what her husband did for British Secret Service and very probably did it with him.

"Is he dead?"

"Breathing."

271

"Towels, quickly." She brushed past Ash, knelt by the Russian and started to tear open his tunic.

"Careful," Ash said.

"Hurry. He's alive."

Vladimir's face had gone white, he gritted his teeth. She had placed the slugs little more than an inch apart high in the chest. It was remarkable that he was still breathing. His hands convulsed at his waist, and Ash now realized, too late, that he was grimacing with effort as much as pain . . . the effort it took a dying man to pull the pin from a hand grenade.

It thumped out of his hands onto the carpet, the pin ring looped around his finger. It rolled. Ash managed to push the Russian's body onto the grenade just as it exploded. The muffled boom tossed him against the bed. Shrapnel shattered a mirror, peppered a chest of drawers, but the Russian's body had absorbed most of the force of the explosion. The room was shrouded in white smoke.

"Kenneth!" Her voice was small, a note of pleading. He saw her through the smoke, trying to stand but unable to as a crimson stain spread across the front of her white dress. Redder, darker than her hair. She reached for him, and Ash caught her in his arms and moved her gently onto the bed.

"I'll get a doctor."

"Don't leave me."

"Let me see." He reached for the buttons at her neck. She stopped him with her hand. "Just hold me."

"Let me help you."

"I'm all apart inside . . . I can feel it . . ."

"Oh, God, I'm so sorry—"

"Listen to me . . . I don't know all you're doing with my husband . . . but you can't be found here with all this. Get away, please . . ."

"They'll think you—"

She took a deep breath, trying to gather strength, managed a brief smile. "I suspect where I'm going there'll be ample time to reconstruct my reputation . . . if you get the opportunity sometime tell my husband what I told you about what he did for me . . ." And she said something else, which Ash couldn't hear. He had her propped in his arms and put his ear to her mouth. "What did you say?"

"I said, Commander, I wish you and I had had another hour."

When Roskov was dead, Dmitri Dan picked up his gun and went up the stairs to complete his mission. To kill the Czar. He waited only long enough to be sure he could use the weapon in spite of the pain in his wrist where the old devil had crushed it. He opened the door a crack, sank back.

The Ethiopian was gone. No light showed beneath the billiard room door. In the ten minutes *Podpolkovnik* Roskov had fought him, the Czar had gone unknowingly to bed. But the bedrooms were much more heavily guarded. In no way could one man with a revolver get close enough to kill him.

Dmitri sat on the stairs and tried to think.

Roskov's body . . . they would treble the Czar's guard if a murder were discovered in the royal apartments. He had to move the body out of the apartments, out of the Alexander Palace. Out, he realized with grim detachment and no plan, of Tsarskoye Selo itself.

A First Railway Batallion patrol found *Podpolkovnik* Roskov's corpse ground up by a railroad train halfway between Tsarskoye Selo and Petrograd; Dmitri Dan had dropped it on the tracks. He had been fortunate. The same blizzard that had covered his exit from the Alexander Palace with the body had also covered his footprints.

And the police were preoccupied, far more interested in a spectacular killing in the Admiralty district than in one old Guards' officer who had probably fallen drunk off the train. He had been seen that night by railroad employees shuttling back and forth between Petrograd and Tsarskoye Selo like a madman. In the Admiralty district they had what looked like a double suicide—another of the bizzare death pacts which had become common among the city's wealthy bohemian classes whose salons Lady Exeter was known to frequent.

Did his brother Vladimir mingle with such people, the police asked sympathetically. Dmitri succeeded in making his rage seem like grief. Ash had killed his brother. And Roskov had ruined his own best chance to kill the Czar. Now he had to go underground. The homicide police might be fooled, but others would guess something closer to the truth about Red Snow and the plot to murder the Czar. So for the sake of the Revolution he dishonored his brother's name and said, yes, Vladimir knew such people, Vladimir talked of suicide. And yes, he knew an Englishwoman. And the police went away, for a while at least, and Dmitri Dan disappeared so that he might survive to attack again.

A frightened Czar Nicholas drew a different conclusion than his police. The officer he had sent to investigate the link between Commander Ash and Lord Exeter had been murdered.

Who could he trust?

Not Ash. Nor, he realized sadly, King George. It had been his cousin's idea to send Ash with an offer of sanctuary. Georgie could have planned the whole scheme to get him off the throne and put his own choice in his place. Somebody Georgie thought would do a better job of fighting the war.

Maybe it was all a British Secret Service trick using Georgie's name. Willy always said Georgie hadn't a military mind . . . but he would never know.

And Willy? Arrogant, bullying, bad-mannered Willy didn't know a thing about the asylum scheme. Georgie or Lord Exeter or even Ash had made that up to gain his confidence. He felt ashamed that they would even think him vulnerable to such a trick.

Poor Father Gregory had seen clearer than he would ever know. There *was* blood on Ash's hands. All around him the Czar saw treachery and deceit. Members of his own family had murdered Rasputin, Romanovs who were common criminals. And betrayal extended, he now believed, even to his royal cousin Georgie.

But he was not alone. He still had a family that mattered—his beloved wife, suffering in her grief, his beautiful girls and baby Alexis. They needed him, he needed them. Together, the seven of them would stay in Russia until whatever end God, in His wisdom, might choose for them.

35

"**Y**ou must call upon Tishkova."

Lord Exeter had chosen a cemetery on Vassily Island less than a mile across a lightly wooded field from the frozen Gulf of Finland. They drove out in sleighs from an Anglican church on the Nevsky. The grave-diggers built fires to thaw the ground. The smoke had blackened the snow around the hole. Steam billowed as the *moujiks* lowered Lady Exeter's coffin.

"The Grand Duke Valery is our only chance to remove the Czar alive."

Ash angrily wished he hadn't come. It was wrong to talk in her last minutes. But if he hadn't come Exeter would be all alone. A group of Russian painters and writers watched forlornly from the side. Her friends. It was as bleak a day as Petrograd could conjure, damp and cold and gray as lead.

"We are on the edge of chaos," Exeter murmured while the *moujiks* worked. "You don't understand the Russians, Ash. Don't imagine that Russia is the most eastward bastion of western civilization, as they say. Russia is really the most westward tentacle of the East. Fatalistic, corrupt, they're like children, and like children they love destruction. They are destructive people, Ash, like Celts."

"Where did your wife fit into that analysis? She was half-Irish . . ."

"In the middle," Exeter told him sharply. "And I'll remind you, Commander, that ignoring the effect an anarchistic revolution will have on the war won't bring my wife back to life."

Ash understood and took the rebuke, then asked, "Did you ask your wife to persuade me to go to Tishkova?"

"Did she?"

Ash stared at the hole in the ground. "She didn't get the chance."

Exeter said, "The Grand Duke Valery is the best of a bad lot. By far the best. He—"

"Then why don't *you* help him?"

"He doesn't trust me."

"I wonder why."

"These people don't like us. They don't like any foreigners. They'll take our investments and hire our engineers, but they don't like us and they don't trust us."

Ash looked at Lord Exeter, and realized that the bitterness in his voice might be directed as much at his own terrible loss as at the Russians. The Englishman was stoic, his grief buried, but not so deep. Exeter sensed Ash looking at him and turned from the grave. "Good of you to come today, Ash. She would have been pleased."

"Your Lordship, do you want to know how she died?"

"I know she didn't die the way the Russian police say."

"No, she didn't." Ash described what had happened, leaving out only her invitation and his half-hearted acceptance, and finished with, "She saved my life. And then she even tried to save Vladimir Dan's."

"You did well to get away. You'd have been finished for the King if the police had found you there."

"Thank you for saying that, sir . . . She was a lovely woman."

The *moujiks* started heaping earth on the coffin. They worked quickly, glancing at a steely snow line blowing in from the Gulf. The earth resounded on the coffin lid until a thick layer muffled the impacts.

Exeter said, "Now I will tell you something you don't know."

Ash wondered if he had guessed what had happened between him and Lady Exeter.

"This so-called bohemian Russian served with a fusilier unit lent to France."

"Yes, I heard that."

"But you didn't hear that shortly before Vladimir Dan returned to Russia he crossed into Switzerland and from there to Germany."

"Are you sure?"

"I believe a friend of yours is named Taplinger? Taplinger keeps a close eye on movements through Switzerland . . . So what was Vladimir Dan up to?"

"A Russian revolutionary working with the Germans."

"My conclusions as well. Do you know the group Red Snow?"

"Never heard of them."

"Nihilistic Social Revolutionaries, according to Taplinger. We know nothing about them except that they exist and specialize in assassinations and attract a broad spectrum of Russian zealots, from factory malcontent to someone like Dmitri Dan."

"Who's Dmitri Dan?"

"Vladimir's brother. He's in the Czar's Convoy. Or was . . . he disappeared the day after his brother killed my wife. I think it's fairly obvious that he was employed by the Germans to assassinate the Czar, don't you?"

"Who did he see in Germany?"

"We've traced him and his brother as far as Spa. Who he saw at German Headquarters we don't know."

"Ludendorff is at Spa."

"Yes, he is. And he has a penchant for Russian revolutionaries."

The snow hit hard and fast. The *moujiks* put their backs to the thick, wet, windblown flakes and shoveled a mound over the grave. Exeter stared at it, blinking, and continued talking in the same insistent tone. "I think the Czar's life is in danger. You must act, act fast, Commander. And your best hope is the Grand Duke Valery."

Ash said nothing.

"He needs you as much as you need him."

Ash was thinking about Tamara. He wondered if he had known from the moment the King asked him to rescue the Czar that it would lead to her. No good could come of it; he'd get hurt as bad as last time, like walking into an airplane propeller. A small personal price perhaps to remove the Czar and end the war—but now, if he lent impetus to the Grand Duke Valery's faltering cause, wouldn't he be putting Tamara right back into danger? The Czar of Russia and the Okhrana did not deal gently with revolt. No matter how noble its instigators, nor how beautiful.

"I heard you discussing poetry with Her Majesty at Sandringham," Exeter said. "Do you by any chance recall Lowell's 'Present Crisis'?"

Ash did. For a West Virginian the crisis of the Civil War had a particular impact.

" 'Once to every man and nation comes the moment to decide,
In the strife of Truth and Falsehood for the good or evil side.' "

Tremendous gusts blew sheets of snow; in moments the mound over Lady Exeter's grave was covered white. Exeter bowed his head. When he raised it again he said, "The evil side is Germany, Ash. Grand Duke Valery is the best hope for us. But his supporters have lost their nerve. He needs help. And you certainly need help, if you are to carry out your promise to rescue the Czar. It seems to me your course is clear."

Ash left a note inside the wrecked Germany Embassy, in a hole where an electric sconce had been torn from the wall, as von Basel had instructed, and a message arrived at the Vassily Island flat the next morning. "In front of the Stock Exchange. Five o'clock."

It was a safe place with escape possible in four directions. The Stock

Exchange overlooked the eastern spit of Vassily Island, the leading edge of the wedge-shaped island that split the wide Neva. Trams crossed the spit from a bridge to the north and from the busy streets of Vassily Island to the west. South, the Dvortsov Bridge spanned the river to the palaces. East, a fleeing man could run into the dark on the frozen river.

It was snowing. The temperature had plummeted so that fresh flakes sparkled like diamonds in the street lights. Ash turned his back to the Stock Exchange and looked east up the dark river. Palace lights shone to the right, the Peter and Paul Fortress loomed to the left. Further up river, on the same side as the Peter-Paul, their lights blurred by the snow, private mansions hugged the embankment—the homes of wealthy aristocrats and successful ballerinas.

He turned around and looked at the Stock Exchange. It was shutting down for the night, and hundreds of clerks in shabby overcoats poured down the steps, collars turned up against the snow. Suddenly von Basel materialized from the midst of a group of them queued up for a tram, dressed as they were in a dark coat and a cheap wool hat.

The German tucked his walking stick under his left arm and shook Ash's hand as if they were old friends meeting by chance. An act for onlookers. There was nothing friendly about his cadaverous face and wary gray eyes. "What's wrong?"

"Everything. Do you know Red Snow?"

"Only by name. Highly secret, highly organized fanatics. That man Narvski who tried to kill you at the gypsies might have been one of them."

"That's all you know?"

"There are three million people in this city, Ash. And only six thousand police. Why do you ask?"

"General Ludendorff hired them to kill the Czar."

Von Basel leaned on the granite railing and looked at the Neva. Snow sticking to his coat and hat made him look almost ghostly. "It seems to me you better get the Czar out of Russia fast. Do you have a plan?"

"What support can you give me?"

"What did you have in mind?"

"Can you immobilize a police station?"

"Possibly."

"Arrest certain very important people?"

"Such as?"

"Guards officers. Railroad officials. Ministers."

"For a while. Anything else?"

"Do you know any revolutionaries?"

"A few."

"Can you introduce me to Kirichenko?"

Von Basel stared. "If I knew where to find Kirichenko the Czar could

278

make me head of the Okhrana and give me one of his daughters. Where did you hear about Kirichenko?"

"From a man named Lenin in Zurich."

"I'm afraid you'll have to settle for a lesser revolutionary than Kirichenko."

"Do you know one who can blow up trains?"

"Trains? More than one?"

"Several. At once. Miles apart."

"No, I don't.

"Could Kirichenko?"

"Possibly. But first you have to find him."

"I can't if you don't call off your detectives. They're following me everywhere again." They'd missed him walking in the snow the night Lady Exeter was killed.

"For your own protection."

"Would they be protection against Kirichenko?"

Von Basel considered that. "I'll call them off."

"Start now. And try to find out where Kirichenko operates. I'll meet you here tomorrow night."

Ash headed for the tram queue. Von Basel grabbed his arm. His fingers felt like wire cable. "Where are you going?"

Ash shook him off. "Where I have to."

Jostling aboard a crowded tram, he watched the lean figure of von Basel fade in the snow. He rode a mile down river and got off after the tram crossed the river on the Nicholas Bridge. There, in the lower part of the Admiralty district, he waited for the green-and-yellow lamps of the Number Eight tram to the Finland Station. He let several pass, eyeing the homeward bound crowds until he was sure he had not been followed.

The Eight went back across the Nicholas Bridge, across Vassily Island and through the Petrograd district and over another bridge. Ash got off in front of the Finland Station and began walking toward the river, checking repeatedly to be sure no one had followed.

His heart started pounding before he laid a glove on her front gate. He pushed through the geometrically patterned wrought iron into the snow-covered entrance garden. Up her front steps to the massive carved doors. Mansions like this were laid out casually, unlike the classical palaces of Petrograd, wings and turrets set whimsically.

Ash knocked, straightened his cloak and hat, waited. Last time he had seen her she lived in an apartment in the fashionable Liteinaya Quarter, not far from the British Embassy. She earned a fortune dancing, but she sure as hell hadn't bought this place on what the Imperial Theater paid her. Of course she could have socked away her earnings from her last European tour; she had, after all, danced solo to packed music halls in Paris and London. But she hadn't toured since 1912, and Ash had never known her to save a penny in her life.

He knocked again, wishing he had sent a note first. She was not a woman to forgive him for not writing just because she hadn't and they had both promised not to . . . a clean break, they'd said.

She had been his life and he was a damned fool for not . . . for not what? For not being born a Russian nobleman? If Teddy Roosevelt and Admiral Mahon had thrust Ash into the parade of Edwardian Europe, Tamara Tishkova had played the music. Music that roused him to every new moment and sweetened every day. Music that lingered. On his skin, and deeper. Much deeper.

An old butler opened the door, glowering suspiciously at a strange face. Ash squared his shoulders. "Please ask Tamara Nikolayevna if she will receive Kennet Karlovich."

The butler ushered him into the foyer. Their Christian names and patronymics, pronounced in the Russian manner, indicated that Kenneth, son of Charles, had come to call on his friend Tamara, daughter of Nikolay.

The butler returned to lead him to a solarium off the marble ballroom. Ash stopped in the ballroom to admire the Serov portrait of Tamara as Odile, the seductive Black Swan. The former court painter—he had quit after the Cossacks had massacred workers in the Palace Square in 1905— had chosen an informal setting, her dressing table. Serov had captured Tamara's pride and beauty, which was, Ash thought, a fairly straightforward matter of painting with his eyes open. But his genius showed in her laughing smile, as if he intuited how Tamara preferred to go against the grain.

Or used to . . . This was quite a house, filled with imported French furniture. The solarium housed an enormous jungle and had a breathtaking view of the palace lights across the frozen river. The floor was an elaborate tile mosaic, probably laid by Italian artisans . . .

A domestic Tamara was a little hard to imagine, though he supposed that on her it would probably wear very well, like everything else. Then he noted with relief that the house was a little untidy, as all her homes were. He walked, his heels clicking loudly, he thought, to the windows that faced the Winter Palace. Snow swirls raced down the river.

In a house like this she could have received him in a sitting room off her boudoir, but she had chosen this less intimate place. A reminder that their intimacy had ended three years ago? Ash picked up a carved ivory elephant. A gift from her father. She took it everywhere. Then this was a special room . . .

She came in with the swift exuberant rush . . . the way she always took a stage. Perfume, Coty's *Violette,* and the airy folds of her tea gown trailed her. Ash stared. He had not come within fifty feet of her at the French ball. Here, in her own home as he put down the ivory elephant and walked toward her on unsteady legs, he saw her so vibrant, still so young that it was impossible to believe that she had reigned triumphant on Russia's stages for nearly thirty years. I debuted early, she used to say.

Her dark, sloe eyes flashed when she saw him, and Ash felt his heart stop. He knew her so well, knew in the particular movement of light in her eyes that she was excited to see him. English was her third language. She spoke it with a French accent. And she called him Kennet, as she had from the first. But her greeting was stiff.

"Hello, Kennet."

"Forgive my dropping in like this, I thought at this hour it might be all right . . ." Petrograd was such a late city that at six in the evening a lady would not have begun to dress, whether she was going out or dining at home.

"I saw you at the ball the other night," she said. "You looked the same . . . But here I think I see a shadow in your eyes."

"I saw you too. You looked more beautiful than ever."

"Thank you."

Tamara extended her hand. Ash kissed it. He felt a little electric jolt. Had she shivered? Or had he?

"Kennet, why have you come here?"

"To ask your help."

"Only my help?"

"Of course not."

She looked around the solarium as if she had never seen it before. "I'm not free to . . . be with you, you know."

"I'm sorry. I guess I hoped it wasn't still true."

"It's true—oh don't look at me that way. You've known for a long time about Valery."

"Should I congratulate you?"

"A woman my age to be loved by a man like him? To be cherished? Yes, you should congratulate me."

"You've done very well. Congratulations."

"I can't dance forever, you know. And you have no right to look at me that way, or be critical of my house, as your eyes tell me you are. How dare a child like you judge."

"How long will I stay a child to you?"

"Always."

"The difference in years between us shrinks as we get older—"

"As *I* get older."

"We can't be back to that again. We've just started."

"We've *not* started anything, Kennet. It is over . . . no matter how wonderful it was." She stared at him defiantly. . . .

Two years after Portsmouth they played a French bedroom farce in The Hague. And when the grand duke had had to go to Paris, Ash had wangled a courier mission to Russia and Tamara, who was fiercely independent, then, had invited him aboard the Imperial Train, which was steaming back to Russia with the Peace Conference delegates and their wives and mistresses.

In the summers after—when the grand duke went off on army maneuvers or toured the Russian continent for the Czar—Ash and Tamara had joined in England, in the south of France, Italy and once even in Russia —long blissful months alone and free. And Ash still thought that the only thing the matter with their relationship was that it had ended. Twice he had asked her to marry him—once shortly after they met and again just before they parted—and both times Tamara had refused, saying only that she would never marry anyone . . .

Carried back to the first time, Ash heard his own voice blurting now, like a hurt kid. "It's not fair." He tried to smile. They were standing face to face, six feet apart. But all he could manage was, "I love you and I always have."

Tamara flushed and spewed a torrent of angry Russian, her nostrils flaring, her breasts straining the tea gown.

"Stop," said Ash, "stop, I can't keep up. I don't remember all those words—"

"The only words you ever learned were bed words."

"I've forgotten them too. I need practicing."

"What I *said* was, it's you who is not fair. You haven't a line. You haven't even a gray hair."

"I've grown a few on my temple just for you . . . or on account of you."

"That is not funny, Kennet," she said, her voice quiet now. "You're like a mirror. I see my face getting older in yours."

"And you are like a . . . a kaleidoscope. Every turn's more beautiful than the one before."

Tamara stepped back, a smile filling her voluptuous mouth. "Kennet Karolovich, did you mean that?"

"The Grand Duke Valery is the luckiest damned man in Russia."

"Show me that gray hair."

Ash turned his head. "It's in here, someplace."

"Bend down . . . may I?"

"Of course—*ow.*"

She held up a gray hair, kissed the spot it came from and danced lightly away. "So you've come for help?"

"I've come to take you to bed," Ash said, reaching for her.

"Well, you can't. So how else can I help you?"

Tamara pulled a bell cord and spoke to the servant in Russian.

They had tea by the fire. She rarely drank alcohol, and then only champagne. Ash felt the old electric tension still between them, undiminished. And he enjoyed, too, their easy companionship while they talked about what each had been doing since they parted.

He sometimes thought that the worst loss, the real waste, was the loss of their friendship. And he began to fancy that maybe he really was older. Mid-thirties was a much different time than the twenties. Maybe he was closer now to her feelings of age. Could it work again?

"What is the help you want?" she asked finally, reminding him why he had come, what he had to do before the palaces across the river turned to flames.

"It involves Valery . . ."

"*Kennet?* You *are* a child. Do you expect me to ask Valery to help *you?*"

"Why not? You've made it quite clear that I'm no threat to him."

"What man knows that, Kennet? Valery's as jealous of you as . . . all Valery knows is that when he first wanted me I was not available." Ash looked at her, but she would add nothing to that. She knew all his secrets —except this new one to remove the Czar. And he knew hers—except the truth behind Petrograd society's gossip that linked her with Czar Nicholas. "And when Valery finally thought I was available," she went on, "suddenly an American naval officer seemed always to be around. So you see it is too complicated. I do have my own position to consider. I would not be happy to lose Valery."

"You don't need Valery. If he left you tonight ten thousand men in this city would rejoice."

"Perhaps, Kennet. But how many would be grand dukes?"

Ash shook his head. Arguing with Tamara had always been like dueling with twelve-inch guns—direct hits and damned few ricochets.

"Do you realize," he said, "that Valery and I have never met?"

"A mystery maintained with some difficulty, I can tell you . . . No, dear, I cannot ask the grand duke to help you."

"But I can help him."

"I beg your pardon?"

"I know about your plans."

Tamara set her face in a mask. "I don't know what you are talking about, Kennet . . . I do think, though, that you better leave."

She stood up and crossed her arms under her breasts. Ash sat where he was and looked her in the eye. "I'm talking about a palace coup."

Tamara held her rigid pose. "You are frightening me, Kennet. What are you trying to do to me?"

Ash got to his feet. "I'm not trying to frighten you. I'm on your side."

"How is that . . . ?"

"I've come to take the Czar to England. King George has offered asylum."

"But . . . that's wonderful . . ."

"He won't go."

She sat down and folded her hands.

"Then I heard about Valery. And dammit, Tamara, I can tell you that too many already know about you."

She nodded. "That is the risk of asking people to help. They don't all say yes and they don't all keep quiet. But somebody has to do it. And Valery has the courage. The war is ruining Russia. The peasants are angry and the workers are impossible. Rasputin destroyed everyone's faith, and Nicholas still does nothing. Russia begs for a firm hand, like the old days."

"I see that Ivan the Terrible still has your vote. How did you get mixed up in this? Just for Valery?"

"I've told you before. Art demands order. For me to dance there must be a theater building, musicians, artists, training schools for the corps *and* audiences able to afford tickets. All of that demands order."

"Was a coup your idea or his?"

"I support him."

"Can you ever support yourself?" Dammit. He realized too late he wasn't talking about the coup.

"What is that supposed to mean?"

"You were already the greatest dancer in Russia. What did you have to fasten onto Valery for?"

"And leave you?"

"Yes."

"What could you do for me, Kennet?"

"Whatever I did I did for seven years. I thought I did it fairly well."

"You did. Yes . . . but it wasn't enough. *Stop* this. I won't talk about it. It's the past. What is happening now is more important. Russia. And Valery." She sat there, silent, angry, abstracted.

Ash got hold of himself. Something else she had said bothered him. He hadn't come to Russia to weaken the Allies. Just the opposite.

"What," he asked carefully, "does Valery propose to do about the war?"

"Win it."

"How?"

"He plans to start with the railroads. Our greatest strength is in our numbers. We can still field huge armies, but we can't move them or supply them. Surely you are aware of this."

"I am. I didn't know you were."

"Valery understands all this. He teaches me. He is a good man, Kennet."

"So how can I help him?"

Tamara sighed, walked to the windows and gazed at the palace lights that shone softly through the blowing snow. "My God, Kennet, you are complicating things."

"I knew that when I came here. But I think we need each other."

"Valery's worried about what to do with Nicky."

"Well, that works out fine. I'm here to take him away."

She turned to him again. "Kennet, the whole scheme is falling apart. Valery's supporters are cowards. I'm afraid it won't work."

"I heard that too . . . let me talk to him."

Tamara shook her head. "Oh, God . . . yes, I guess you must."

The butler knocked and announced a telephone call for Mademoiselle Tishkova. She was gone a long while. When she came back, she was smiling almost coquettishly. "That was Valery."

"What does he say?"

"Oh, I couldn't tell him tonight. The telephone is not safe . . . would you care to have dinner with me?"

"An understatement."

"Poor Valery. He is all the way out at Tsarskoye Selo and the Czar wants him to stay the night. Poor thing, stuck in that dreary household."

"What a shame."

"Don't you get the wrong idea."

"May I at least sit with you while you dress for dinner?"

Tamara smiled. "Of course—but no more talk of the coup. Wait for Valery."

It was an old habit of theirs. She dressed and did her hair behind a floral Chinese silk screen while he sat in a nearby armchair and talked with her. He told her a little about the trip from London. She had not traveled since the war. And he described Paris and London and Berlin as he had last seen them. She asked about fashions, and he told her what he had noticed and how women were working at all kinds of jobs. He told her about the new ballroom dances in Paris and London, the Nurse's Shuffle and the Saunter.

"I'll show you."

"No," she said firmly. "You stay right where you are . . . tell me about the dance." She meant the ballet. Ash said, "I saw Anna in New York. They loved her."

"Yes, she wrote me she saw you. Was she good?"

"Very."

"Good." Tamara liked Pavlova, they were friends. She was one of the few ballerinas Tamara had open, unreserved admiration for.

"And there's no more Ballets Russes in Paris, as you know. Nothing in London. Not a single ballet in London except for *divertissements* in the Christmas pantomimes."

"Stupid war. Well, for the dance, at least, it's a good time to be in Petrograd. It's a brilliant season."

"And Tishkova its star?"

"Of course." She snaked her hand over the top of the screen. Her arm was bare—creamy white and rippling with long, shapely muscle. "In fact I may dance my Jubilee . . . at last."

Ash laughed. It was traditional to celebrate a jubilee twenty years after a debut, a tradition Tamara had steadfastly ignored.

"What will you dance?"

"I haven't decided. Everyone's doing fantasies this season. Benefits for military hospitals and war bonds. Even lovely Kchessinska had a grand triumph last week—though I am told that the theater carpenters worked half the night to repair the stage."

Ash grinned at the screen. He personally thought Kchessinska a fine dancer and a good-looking woman besides, but saw little profit in convincing Tamara. Kchessinska too had a grand duke wrapped around her finger, but she had had a child by hers and Ash suspected that rankled, though Tamara, in her inimitable way, insisted that children should be kept in dark places to mature like wine.

She popped her head over the screen. Her hair was a wild tangle of black curls, her eyebrows high in inquiry. She had removed her dressing gown. Her shoulders were bare.

"Would you like champagne? It's next door."

Next door was her bedroom. The champagne stood in an ice bucket beside her vast canopied bed. Ash opened it, filled their glasses, carried them back to her dressing room and stepped behind the screen.

Her hands went to her breasts. "Don't look at me."

But Ash was already looking, gazing in open admiration. She was seated naked on an upholstered stool before a mirror. Full-bodied, toned like an athlete, she was at once hard and voluptuous, at once a finely sculpted machine and as sexual as a courtesan.

"Please don't look at me."

"Why not? You look so beautiful."

"My breasts are sagging."

"They're not. They're as lovely as ever."

"Liar."

"And if they ever did sag do you think I'd give a damn?"

"Liar . . . why do you say that? That you wouldn't care?"

"Because they're yours."

286

"Liar . . ." She kept her hands crossed over her breasts, but she watched his eyes flicker over the rest of her body. Slowly, she crossed her legs and arched her back. "Tell me about your women, since me."

"Don't twist me in circles."

"Why do you let me?" she asked.

"Your hands are different."

"My *hands?*" She thrust them under the light. "What do you—"

Ash knelt swiftly and kissed her breast.

". . . You tricked me."

Ash held the champagne glasses behind her back and nuzzled her with his lips. "Whatever you are, I love it. And I love you."

"Kennet. This is dangerous."

"Shhh."

Her hands closed behind his head. "Kennet?"

"What?"

"Kennet, you know me. I won't leave a grand duke for an American lieutenant commander. Valery's of the blood royal, Kennet, I won't give it up. I warn you . . ."

Ash drew her nipple between his lips and mumbled, "Commander."

"What? What did you say? Oh, don't stop . . ."

"Full commander. They promoted me. I could make commodore by fifty." He showed her the three broad stripes on his sleeve.

Tamara threw back her head and laughed. She looked at him and her eyes turned liquid soft. "Shall I congratulate you?" she whispered. "Just this once?"

36

Tamara let a cry escape when she opened to him. She drew him in and he kissed her lips, crushed her mouth with his and fought for more of her.

His eyes burned into hers. She felt him fighting to keep her, knew he was trying to force his taste and scent and touch into her memory. She felt herself drowning again, as she always had with him, as he drowned in her. She allowed it. Here the years between them didn't anger her, here he didn't mirror her age, here he was black glass, mysterious, promising. In their sex they were both without age, new, unhampered by time, at once precocious and knowing, and yet always astonished.

He filled her. With his eyes he begged, then demanded she be with him and share her spirit as she shared her body. And when she did, when she took his mouth as insistently as he took hers, begged back with her eyes, the hard lens of desperation melted from his look.

He exploded and set off a barrage in her which left her gasping, clinging and suddenly laughing as she hadn't laughed since she couldn't remember. He spoke gently and stayed inside her, kissing her face until he grew hard again and began to move. She pulled down his shoulders, clasped his legs, and felt the fire . . .

Now *she* was desperate, thrusting under him, lifting him with hard muscle, proud of the strength she had for him, demanding strength back. More. She had made him whole, told him what he was, so he was able to smile into her eyes and play, tease her the ways she had taught him . . . ways they had learned together . . .

"*No* . . ." She was too late. He retreated slowly, further and further. "No." Further until only a kiss of flesh seemed to remain to blind them, so small that it could break at the least unwary motion. But he was moving,

288

and he stroked her with his fingers, making her move too, making her shudder with joy.

She gasped, afraid that their flesh would part. Her body betrayed her, leaping for him. "No." The bond would break, they would part. "No." But though her body ached and heaved he kept them connected. And suddenly he had entered her again. Slid deep, but he was all gentle now, no longer desperate, easy and sure in these few minutes and hours, and filled her with a promise that he was hers to keep forever.

A gramophone on a marble pedestal near Tamara's bed provided Chopin between their lovemaking. They drank champagne and spooned gray caviar into each other's mouths while the music played. An old Russian woman brought the caviar, tsking angrily at Ash, refusing to acknowledge him even though they'd first met when she was Tamara's maid on the trip to New Hampshire.

"Don't worry, she's safe," Tamara said as she got up to change a record. She could feel his eyes track her.

"I love to watch you wind that thing," Ash said. Tamara gave him a wicked smile over her shoulder. Her breasts brushed the flared sound horn and her bottom wiggled as she turned the crank that wound the mechanism. She loved it when he admired her, but she said, "You, you just say those things. You don't mean them."

"Come back here."

He lifted the comforter. She covered her breasts with her hands again as she slid back beside him. "How is it you make me feel so naked?" It was a mystery. She actually felt herself blush.

In the night they woke up and made love sleepily. Then again with deep longing that erupted into a fierceness. Shuddering in each others arms, wide awake afterward, they whispered in the dark.

"Why wasn't it enough?"

"Love is more than sex and companionship and affection." For a long moment she was silent. Then she said, "More than seeing the world through double eyes."

"So why are you crying?"

"I am not crying."

"Something's making my chest wet."

She erupted into a half-giggle, half-sob and felt his chest, then traced her fingers to his lips. Brushed his cheeks. "The same reason you are, I suppose . . ."

"We were, as they say, made for each other, Tamara."

"But I'm old. My jumps are going."

"You said your jumps were going in 1908. Three years later, 1911 for Christ's sake, François Roland wrote that 'Tishkova employs an unfair advantage over ordinary ballerinas in that the rules of gravity do not apply to her.' "

"But they will go, someday too soon, and when they do so will my young lover."

"The rules of gravity may not apply to you," Ash said exasperatedly, "but the rules of time apply to me. I'm not the kid you met in Portsmouth. That was nearly twelve years ago. I'm older, changed. But still in love with you—I don't give a damn if you dance—"

"You don't." She was shocked, hurt.

"Not true. I do care. I admire your work. I'm overwhelmed by it. But I don't love you for your work."

"Why do you love me?"

"Why? Why is your hair jet? Why is your skin pearl white? Why are your eyes darker than black, your mouth—"

"My hair is jet because my mother was Italian. My skin white because my father was a Russian and like most Russians has Viking blood from some thousand-year-old rape. My eyes are dark because another ancient rape put Tartar blood in my veins as well. And my mouth . . . what did you say my mouth was?"

"I didn't get a chance, and I don't have the words. All I know is that I want it."

"I don't deserve you." She sighed.

"Probably not, but you've got me anyway so why—"

"What do you mean, probably not?" She climbed on top of him and grabbed his hands, and their talk dissolved into teasing and play and it was not until he was deep inside her again that she admitted to herself the fear that lay beneath all her decisions, the fear to take the final chance—risk everything without a man to support her—the fear that bastard Roland had intuited, in that same review, when she danced *Schéhérazade* with Vaslav Nijinski and Roland shrewdly guessed she could have done more. But Roland was the only critic who had. Not another soul knew that she could have danced Zobeide with even greater abandon than she had, but had been afraid. It wasn't really age. Everyone feared age. For all her brave talk of never marrying, it was fear one day of having no one but herself. A nightmare. Alone in the burning streets. Her audiences dead. Her lovers fleeing.

Sunlight was streaming into Tamara's bedroom. Ash's arms were filled with her warm sleepy flesh when the maid burst in. "Mademoiselle, mademoiselle!"

Ash couldn't catch all the Russian, but the way Tamara leaped out of bed told him that the Grand Duke Valery had returned from his business with the Czar.

37

Tamara pushed him toward a little dressing room down the hall. Her maid had hung up his scattered uniform as if she had planned for a quick escape. His boots were polished, his scabbard cleaned. Ash heard a commotion outside. He pulled on his trousers and glanced out the window.

A gigantic red sleigh, big as a house and drawn by eight Arabian bays, was swinging off the road from the bridge. Cossack outriders formed a protective cordon around it with long lances. The sleek horses were as fine a matched team as Ash had seen, their harness like the sleigh itself inlayed with gold. A footman in red livery leapt down to the snow, flung open the door and bowed.

The Grand Duke Valery stepped down and looked up at the mansion. He wore a long red Cossack coat and a high fur hat. Ash moved away from the window. Something in Valery's stance had told him that the grand duke didn't actually live here, merely had visiting privileges. It made Ash feel a little better that Tamara was at least still that independent. Not yet *totally* committed.

She hurried in, drawing an apricot robe over a silk nightgown. Her nipples stood darkly through the silk. "Give me a couple of hours to get used to the idea. Come back for lunch. We'll see what the three of us can work out . . . You better shave." She smiled.

"Quite an arrival down there."

"Valery's a damned fool riding around Petrograd like a target. I keep telling him he'll get killed by revolutionaries but he loves that sleigh . . . do I look like I had a good night's sleep?"

'You look like you had a good night."

292

She leaned against him, warm, pressed her forehead to his chest. "I did. My darling, thank you for coming to me."

"Thank you for having me."

The door knocker boomed through the house.

"Go on now," she said, closing her robe, covering her breasts. "Olga will show you the way."

The back door, again. He crushed her against him, then Olga, the old woman, led him down back stairs and through a maze of kitchen gardens and stable yards. Wet snow had started to fall. The air was chilly, damp seeped out of the ground. He startled a *moujik* shoveling horse manure. "Good morning!"

He boarded a tram at the Finland Station, got off at the Nevsky and walked up the boulevard, which was deserted so early in the morning except for servants and shopkeepers. A peasant woman was selling meat pies from a cart. God knew what was in them. He went into the Europa, shaved in François Roland's room, after which they walked to the fencing salle for another lesson. They had lunch. Ash was starving. By one o'clock he was back at Tamara's mansion. Trying to control a foolish grin that kept grabbing his face.

Valery's Cossacks stopped him at the door. Tamara's butler identified him. She and the grand duke were waiting in the solarium. Tamara had changed into black silk. As she stepped forward and let Ash bow over her hand, she allowed herself, and him, a secret smile for their night.

"Your Highness," Tamara said formally, "may I present Commander Ash?"

Ash bowed. Valery thrust out his big hand. "You ought to know from the start that I have agreed to talk because Mademoiselle Tishkova vouches for you. She has relayed everything you told her."

Not everything, thought Ash. But the grand duke seemed willing to let that other level of their entanglement hang unspoken between them. "Nonetheless," he continued, "I have questions."

"As I do, Your Highness." He had to establish a partnership to make this work, as he had with von Basel.

"Does the American government know that you've come to Russia to rescue Czar Nicholas for the English king?"

"My superiors hope that removing Czar Nicholas will make it possible for the United States to join the Allies' war against Germany."

"How is that?"

"Bluntly put, Your Highness, most Americans think of Czar Nicholas as a bloody tyrant."

"If they think Nicholas II is bloody, what, pray tell, did they think of Peter the Great? Did you inform King George of your government's interest?"

"No."

"You seem to serve two masters, Commander."

"No, Your Highness. I am an officer in the United States Navy. My mission to remove the Czar without knocking Russia out of the war *coincides* with King George's concern for his cousin—but now that the Czar refused to leave of his own accord, perhaps *your* goals coincide with ours."

"Perhaps. At the start, anyway . . . but tell me, Commander, why did you come to me? Why not the Vladimirs?"

"Idiots," Tamara murmured. The Vladimirs—the wife and sons of the Czar's uncle Vladimir—had figured prominently in the rumors Ash had heard about palace coups. Even Ambassador Hazzard had heard of them.

"For one thing, Your Highness, I heard too much loose talk about the Vladimirs."

"You heard of me too."

"More than I should have," Ash said pointedly. "But the main deficiency of the Vladimirs is they don't know what they're doing. Their plan to march on Tsarskoye Selo to seize the Czar is stupid—even if they could field the four regiments they claim."

"They *can't*," Valery said, showing emotion for the first time. "But why do you say the plan itself is bad?"

"They don't understand how to take control of Russia."

"And a United States navy officer does?"

"You don't have to *seize* the Czar, Your Highness. You merely have to isolate him."

Grand Duke Valery went to the windows and stared across the Neva at the Winter Palace. The snow had stopped. Sunlight flickered here and there, pale yellow on the ice.

"He's twenty miles from Petrograd," Ash prompted. "And it's winter. The roads—"

"Yes, Commander, you needn't draw the picture for me. I agree. Isolate the Czar. The Winter Palace there is where the power would be recognized. However"—he turned to Ash, his tiny blue eyes dark with worry—"easier said than done . . . my supporters are growing cautious."

"Cowards," Tamara murmured. She tossed her head, and her dark hair coiled around her neck.

"You are too harsh, my dear. The men of my class have been bred to inherit, not act. Nor were we trained to conspire. How can you expect them to act boldly?"

"You're too damned understanding," Tamara said. "What about *you?* They are deserting you—"

"Perhaps they are right."

"*Valery,* you can't give up now."

"I can help you," Ash said.

"Commander, you're not the first man to dream up blowing the rail line between Petrograd and Tsarskoe Selo. I presume you have a larger plan."

"I have some notions, and I think I can recruit some supporters you might not have thought of . . ."

The grand duke faced the window again, clenching and unclasping his hands behind his back. Tamara looked at Ash. Abruptly she came to a decision. "Valery, I'm going to the school to rehearse. Would you two drive me over, please?"

Valery's footmen sprang to the red sleigh's doors as they came out of the house. The Cossacks mounted, and a kitchen *moujik* ran up and poured fresh embers into the foot-warming brazier. The coachman bellowed. The footmen jumped onto their platform in the back and the sleigh slid into motion as eight horses dragged it off the road across a field toward the river embankment.

They sat shoulder to shoulder, the grand duke in the middle with Tamara's small hand curled in his huge fist. Surrounded in back and on the sides by the high seat, they were protected from the wind and the sight of the curious. Ahead was the circular bulk of the coachman and the heads of the straining horses. Overhead the sky.

The sleigh rode as heavy as a freight train, and Ash shivered as it crashed down landing stairs onto a path on the ice which was lined with pine trees stuck in the snow piles. Counting horses, the sleigh had to weigh six or eight tons. The coachman alone looked good for four hundred pounds, the grand duke another three, while beneath the ice the Neva ran swift and deep.

"The Czar has already isolated himself at Tsarskoye Selo." Ash broke the silence which had hung heavily while they waited for Tamara to dress. "He might as well be in England right now if it weren't for the railroad, and the telephone and telegraph. All we have to do is block the railroad tracks—north to cut him off from Petrograd and south to block him from contacting the Stavka at Mogilev. And cut the telephone and telegraph lines, of course. And they run right beside the tracks."

"I repeat," Valery said, speaking only after Tamara nudged him. "Do you think you're the first man who's thought of blowing that line? Even if you could find the men to do it, the First Railway Battalion would mobilize ten thousand troops in an hour. In two hours twenty thousand, *and* an armored train. In three they'd hang the survivors from the tele-graph poles."

The horses scrambled up the landing steps of the French Embankment —embassy row upstream from the palaces—and broke into a smart trot alongside the Field of Mars. Artillery men and horse soldiers drilling among the stacked firewood saluted as the red sleigh passed.

"I think Kennet has more to say," Tamara said. Her prompting kept them talking.

"I do," Ash said. "The First Railway Battalion's officers will think twice if they receive new orders from the Winter Palace, where you will be in attendence with key members of the Duma."

"You don't understand the timing," Valery said. "The Czar will march on the city the instant the line is repaired."

"I'll guarantee they won't repair it in three hours."

"How?"

"A little trick the Filipino Insurgents taught the U.S. Marines the hard way. There's more than one way to stop a railroad. Even the Czar's railroad."

When the sleigh turned left off Sadovaya Street onto the broad Nevsky Prospect, traffic police in high boots and white gloves halted trams and carriages to let the grand duke pass. Trotting up the boulevard they drew stares from the early afternoon shoppers, salutes from the guards officers and an occasional cheer for the grand duke, who leaned forward to show himself and nodded sternly left and right and raised his huge hand in a gesture that looked half salute and half wave.

"One must be visible," he told Ash. "One cannot rule an empire from one's country house."

"One is going to get a revolutionary's bomb tossed into one's lap one of these days," Tamara muttered. Ash, for his part, sat back, glad for the high seat. After a coup it wouldn't do for an American naval officer to have been seen too much in the company of the man who had plotted to become the new czar. A column of horse guards halted right in the middle of the boulevard, left-faced and saluted as the grand duke passed.

Ash glanced at Tamara, loving every minute of it even as she berated Valery for making himself a target. As indeed he was. Not everyone was saluting. A yellow tram had stopped to let them turn off the Nevsky into Catherine Square. It was packed with factory workers—on strike if they were off this early, Ash presumed—and each window contained a grim, angry face.

Valery sat back and took her hand. "We must be visible. Since the Czar-liberator Alexander was assassinated in his carriage, we Romanovs have become invisible, afraid of anarchists, afraid of revolutionaries. In a sense the assassin killed us all. What are the people supposed to believe in when they cannot ever see us?"

Tamara withdrew her hand. The sleigh had passed through Catherine Square, around the columned Alexander Theater and into Theater Street, the eight horses smartly navigating the tight turns. They stopped in front of the Imperial Theatrical School. Tamara stood up. "They can't see God either."

Valery gave her an indulgent smile as the footman helped her down. He called after her, "God doesn't have the responsibility for collecting taxes."

"Pick me up in two hours. We'll have *zakouski*—the three of us—and you'll tell me what you've decided."

Ash watched her disappear in the doors. He turned to see Valery's eyes on him. "Do you see that window?"

Ash looked where he was pointing. The ledge was twenty feet above the street. "Yes."

"Many years ago His Majesty was suddenly taken with a beautiful young girl, a dancer. The Czar was already married, and an uncommonly faithful man in the vows—he does truly love that woman—but he was enchanted, bewitched, as only Tamara can bewitch. He could not call on the girl himself, of course, so he sent me to fetch her to a little picnic. She sat on that ledge, and her hair was even longer then, black on her skin that was so white. She had her legs curled under her. She smiled down at me in my carriage. Romantic nonsense, some might say, but I fell in love with her at that moment. I was also obliged to tell her for whom I had come . . . You may think me an old fool to let her treat me the way she does. I certainly think that sometimes. My country is on the brink, but often when I sit with the men of the Duma, humoring liberals and Kadets and the Black Hundred reactionaries who want their serfs back, or with the generals at Mogilev and the munitions manufacturers and the railway managers, trying to get our house in order, her face forms in my mind and I hear her laughing and I see her dance . . . If you value your life, Commander Ash, you'll not see her again."

Ash thought of the first time he had seen her too, a beautiful woman in white, when he had known only girls, smiling up at him from the stern of a pretty sailboat. And he thought what a gentle soul lay inside this giant in a Cossack uniform.

The Cossacks had stayed on their horses, watching the street and the buildings, but Theater Street, insulated from the nearby Nevsky by the Alexander Theater and the twin classical buildings flanking it, was silent except for the horses' hard breathing. It was so quiet Ash could hear the riders' lances creaking in their black leather gloves.

"They'll skewer you like shish kebab on my command, but I'd prefer to do it with my own hands."

The sudden shift caught Ash by surprise. Was that all this talk was about? He met Valery's hard look with one of his own. "What's stopping you, other than the fact your country's falling apart and you with my help seem at the moment to be its only hope?"

A *kinjal*, the long Cossack dagger, hung from Valery's belt beside his *pallash*. His hand closed on the hilt.

"Go on, try it," Ash taunted him, feeling the years of frustration. "You think I enjoy watching you hold her hand in front of me?"

Two Cossacks edged into lance range. They did not know English, but they recognized a fighting stance, a potential threat to their master.

Valery sighed. "What's stopping me is that she would never talk to me again if I so much as bruised your pretty face."

Ash fought his anger. "Your Highness, I think we owe Russia a truce."

"What terms?"

"Neither of us touches her until you're the czar. Then she decides."

They shook hands, and Valery said, "You've made a good deal in the short term, but you will lose in the long term."

Ash shrugged. Anything not to watch him touch her. Now at least he could concentrate. Though Tamara, if he knew her, might have something to say about them divvying her up.

At five o'clock Ash met Count von Basel on the spit of Vassily Island. The German spy wore the shabby hat and overcoat of a stock exchange clerk again, and though he moved quickly down the steps, Ash noted, he took care to lean on his walking stick as though he really needed it.

"Not that way. The police around the palace would question a clerk with an American officer." They walked away from Palace Bridge into Vassily Island itself, toward the Bolshoy Prospect, the main thoroughfare of a middle and working class district.

"I'm in business. Right in the middle of a palace coup."

"The Grand Duke Valery's, might I ask? Don't be surprised. Considering your connection with Tishkova, which grand duke would you go to?"

"She's not involved."

"You made a good choice. Just the other day a police agent overheard the French ambassador suggest undiplomatically that Russia needs a Napoleon. Maybe you've found him. What do you want from me?"

What an unlikely alliance, Ash thought. Constrained to remove the Czar without knocking Russia out of the war, Ash felt like the middle horse inside the shafts of a troika. On one side a jealous grand duke galloped fitfully, and on his other a German spy who hated him.

"Before the grand duke can take the government, we have to block the rail lines in and out of Tsarskoye Selo, as well as telegraph and telephone. We have to draw troops hostile to the coup away from the Winter Palace, quietly. And we have to gag public figures who might denounce the coup."

"There won't be many of those," von Basel remarked drily. "Except of course for provacateurs taking advantage of temporary chaos. I will arrest them."

"Have you found Kirichenko?"

"Try the Moscow District. He's in there someplace."

"I'll need you to provoke an incident to draw off troops barracked near the Winter Palace that the grand duke can't persuade to his side."

"Whatever you ask," von Basel replied with a mocking smile. "As the Kaiser's servant, I am your servant."

Until later.

A Napoleon? Ash mused after he left von Basel. The Grand Duke Valery was no Bonaparte, but he just might be able to hold the whole mess together until something like one came along. Or at least until the U.S. got enough troops into France to make a difference. What, he wondered, did von Basel think of that? Or did he just do exactly what his beloved Kaiser asked and the hell with the consequences?

Kirichenko was his main problem, and best hope.

Valery had insisted on knowing exactly how Ash would blow the line. Ash had explained as best he could while the rode around the city waiting for Tamara.

"It's a trick the Filipino insurgents taught the U.S. marines. They blew a little hole in the main line from Manila to Cabanahuan. Just enough to knock out both tracks but too small to have been set by anybody other than hit-and-run amateurs. So the marines rode out on a couple of repair trains, one from each direction. Both hit mines. Now they had to clear *two* trains, repair three holes and search every inch of the line for more explosives. That's what we got for fighting in the other guy's backyard . . . It will slow them down considerably. The Czar is certainly not going to ride an armored train to Petrograd until they've checked the entire line. By that time you'll be greeting your fellow grand dukes and key members of the Duma in the Winter Palace. And I will take him to England."

"Who precisely will dynamite the lines?"

"I have contacts among revolutionary elements," Ash replied, which was stretching it. "People you will be able to deal with—and control— when you have restored order."

"There can't be so many that they would threaten me, I suppose."

"And a good government will defuse its enemies."

"And you think I will make a good government?"

"I doubt that you can make one worse than this one."

The grand duke nodded. No Napoleon, but a lot better than Nicholas II.

"But what about Nicholas? How exactly will you remove him to England?"

"The Czar, the Czarina and their children and servants—whoever wishes to accompany them—will be picked up by a British cruiser at Murmansk. They will arrive safe in Scotland a week after your government delivers them to Murmansk."

"Safe? Aboard a cruiser in the Norwegian Sea? I would remind you— and King George—that I have served my Czar, my cousin, like a brother for twenty years. I do not intend to take his throne to see him killed by German U-boats. His exile is vital to my rule, but not his murder."

299

"And I would remind you, Your Highness, that I have already given my word to the King of England to rescue his cousin."

"All very well, and I respect your word, but—"

"The Czar's safety has to be my responsibility," Ash said firmly.

"But how?"

"For reasons of safety, security, I won't share my plans with anyone not directly involved in the voyage . . . but I can assure you that His Majesty's cruiser will receive an untouchable escort."

And safety and security aside, Ash could not mention the Kaiser to the grand duke. He knew that Valery would cut off his own arm before he would shake hands with the likes of Kaiser Wilhelm.

38

"They've stolen my army."

The Imperial Guardsman keeping Kaiser Wilhelm company shook his head sympathetically, but the dullness that lurked like a sleepy animal in the man's vacant eyes provoked the Kaiser to emphasize the depth of his loss with the postscript, "And they didn't even have the decency to tell me themselves."

Down in the courtyard the major who had delivered Hindenburg and Ludendorff's curt message glanced up at the window as he climbed into his staff car. No salute. How quickly pawns ceased pretending respect. From this day on, it seemed, the Kaiser's two top generals were too busy to report daily in person. His Majesty was invited to call at general headquarters whenever he cared. But that meant living in Berlin in the awful Schloss Bellevue. Even Georgie was treated better.

He watched his reflection harden in the window as night crept from the forest up the palace walls and the servants scurried silently behind him lighting the lamps. He was getting thin in the face, but his sinking cheeks made him look strangely younger. His eyes, deepset, looked enormous and deep and liquid, almost like Nicky's, but not, thank God, with Nicky's rather vacuous stare. *His* glittered with intelligence, he assured himself.

The thought cheered him. He had been so depressed for so long, thanks to the war chipping away at his power and his crown, that he was surprised that at this moment, though he tried to mourn, he couldn't. Ludendorff and von Hindenburg had aroused something inside him. His upstart generals had thrown down the gauntlet. Well, by God he would pick it up. They had the army, but he was still Kaiser Wilhelm II, Emperor of Imperial Germany.

He had Victoria's blood in his veins and his tough old grandmother's spirits coursed beside the power that had been Frederick the Great's. He would put that upstart Colonel Ludendorff—colonel was his rank before the war—and doddering old von Hindenburg in their place. He had done it nearly thirty years ago to Bismarck, he would do it today.

. . . But how?

Inspiration struck. Yes. Like a great Krupp cannon—the war was his downfall but suddenly he knew how to win the war and take back his crown. He clenched his fist, pounded the window ledge. His crown and all the majesty, all the power. How? Simplicity itself.

He, Kaiser Wilhelm, would give Czar Nicholas asylum. *Not* Georgie.

He would parade the fallen Czar through Berlin. *His* prisoner of war. Leaderless Russia would collapse in days. Her armies would disintegrate He would command his eastern army to force a quick surrender, then order those million men and three thousand guns to wheel west and smash England and France before the United States could intervene.

His subjects would thank him for defeating the Allies by capturing the Czar. They would demand that Kaiser Wilhelm II take the helm of Germany once again. Germany would see him as the conquering general it had known before the war. He patted his left hand, securely perched on his sword hilt, and considered that if he took the initiative immediately upon winning the war, he could even abolish the Reichstag.

Poor simple Georgie, he thought, a smile appearing on his lips, and his reflection smiled back. "So kind and cousinly of him to try to save Nicky. I will save Nicky, whether he wants it or not. He will trust in cousin Willy . . ."

He gazed into the reflection of his own eyes and thought of all the times Georgie had outshot him . . . and outsailed him . . . and that damned Ash, too. Even Nicky had bagged more birds than he had on the Baltic marshes. Now he knew why. It took total concentration to marry a yacht to the wind, or hit every bird that flew over. Of course their concentration never wavered, he thought with amusement, because neither Georgie, nor Nicky, nor Ash had enough else on their minds to divert them . . .

"Guardsman." The Kaiser motioned him near and threw his arm around the man's shoulder. "Bring Count von Basel."

"Sedovina?" Tamara's eyebrows rose as if Ash had asked whether she wanted to assist her cook in the marketing.

"She's dancing Effie next Sunday. What do you think of her?"

"A talented girl, despite her unruly yellow hair and rather—how do you say it—gangling stance."

"I've heard her compared to you."

302

"Darling, that merely means she's caught their fancy for a season. She's actually quite good, but quite good doesn't mean she has the staying power. Ask me again in a few years."

"What do you know about her?"

"She runs with an unsavory crowd."

"That's what I really want to know. I don't care about her dancing."

"Darling, this is all making you very tense."

Ash looked at her smiling at him across a lunch table at Berrin's, a sweets shop on Morskava Street. They had walked here from the school after her morning rehearsal. The truce with Valery was working brilliantly; he was able to spend a good deal of time with Tamara between trying to put together the elements of the coup; it was like courting her, an old-fashioned life they had never had. But he was no closer to Kirichenko, the fighting squad leader, and von Basel, who ought to have been more help, had disappeared. Three notes at the wrecked German Embassy lay in the sconce hole, untouched.

"What crowd?" he pressed her.

"Revolutionaries. It's a miracle she hasn't been dismissed."

"Tamara, there was a time when you thought failure to say God Save the Czar aloud indicated revolutionary tendencies. What do you really mean?"

"I mean *revolutionary*, dammit, Kennet." Her small fist hit the table for emphasis, and their hot chocolate cups bounded in their saucers. "One more false step and the Imperial Theater will dismiss Sedovina. Her lover—"

"Lover? She's sixteen."

"*Lover,* and she's twenty. Dear heart, one learns early to conceal one's age. Anyway, her *lover* was exiled to Siberia for agitation. Shot trying to escape . . . What is your interest in her, may I ask?"

"What? Oh . . . her friends . . ."

A Russian armored car rumbled up to a trench a hundred and fifty yards from the German line firing its heavy machine guns. The infantrymen in the trench, which was a shallow morass of marshland, pleaded with their countrymen inside the slab-sided vehicle to take it elsewhere. A perfectly normal afternoon of exchanging sniper fire was turning to hell as evening lowered because the armored car was drawing terrible fire.

The Germans were trying to disable it by the unlikely method of shooting at the armored radiator grill and the laborious task of shooting the hard rubber tires to pieces. Soon it seemed as if all the enemy for two miles was flinging small arms fire at the car, which replied with murderously active machine guns and the sullen boom of a two-pounder. The Russians in the trenches hunkered down for the inevitable artillery barrage.

Count von Basel watched the iron beast with amusement. It was there at his orders, to provide distraction. A German shell suddenly screamed across no-man's-land and burst twenty yards from the armored car, throwing Russians in the air like toys. A second shell landed closer. Shrapnel rattled off its sides. The car lurched into motion. Armored cars and tanks were marvelous weapons, von Basel thought, movable fortresses, industrial cavalry. He had tried and failed to convince the Kaiser that such innovations could break the stalemate of machine guns and trenches, but the Kaiser had told him they were both too much of the old school to get involved with such modern contraptions. Look at the British tank failure. There was no arguing with him, but von Basel had secretly disagreed, thinking, what if . . .

Suddenly the car stopped moving. There was lull in the firing for a moment or two, and von Basel realized that its engine had stalled. Sure enough, a crewman popped out and ran around to the front to turn the starter crank. The Germans opened up and the Russians mechanic took hit after hit, doggedly cranking the engine. Von Basel did not wait to see what happened. He moved out of the Russian trench and started across no-man's-land, while every eye was on the stricken car and the artillery shells cratering around it.

Von Basel found the Kaiser, half-moved into the cold, drafty Schloss Bellevue, bellowing at his ragtag band of courtiers. Saddened by the sovereign's worn-out look, von Basel put on a bright face to try to cheer him up. But the Kaiser surprised him. No sooner had he dragged him off to a private room than he erupted excitedly into his plan for the Czar.

Von Basel was delighted. Blood always prevailed. The Emperor, battered by the war and his generals' treachery, was fighting back. Good. Could von Basel do it, the Kaiser asked. Could he somehow get the Czar out of Russia? Van Basel said he could.

The Kaiser wanted to award him the Iron Cross, First Class, on the spot, but von Basel respectfully refused. It was an honor to serve, not to mention, which he didn't, the answer to his prayers—*poor* Ash . . .

He made an obligatory report to Gruppe IIIb by telephone so they wouldn't detain him, then stopped to see his mother in the Berlin apartment she had moved to when the Russians overran their East Prussian estates at the beginning of the war. The land was German again, but little that was habitable remained.

She looked as beautiful as ever—a refined woman from an old Prussian family even older than the von Basel's. She had struggled all through his childhood to shield him from the simpleminded excesses of his father, a towering brute who wielded the saber like a battle axe and made them struggle for every quiet moment.

The conflict had flowered violently when von Basel was fifteen and the Kaiser had announced he would enjoy hunting stag on the von Basel estate. His mother was thrilled, his father resentful of the expense and disruption of installing indoor toilets and running water in the thousand-year-old castle, in addition to total redecoration.

His mother had prevailed, with the firm assistance of a Kaiserin court marshal who traveled far ahead of the entourage, making sure that host estates were in proper order. Exotic foodstuffs began arriving from Berlin weeks before the hunt, accompanied by enormous bills and soon by the Kaiser's own chefs and kitchen staff lent for a price by expensive Berlin hotels. Meantime, the peasantry had to be paid to paint and whitewash every farmhouse and hovel in the sight of the Kaiser's carriage ride from the distant railroad station, over a road which was ordered thoroughly repaired to provide a comfortable ride.

When at last the splendid Imperial Train steamed into East Prussia, the young von Basel was already dazzled by extravagances that delighted his mother and enraged his father, and ripe for the attentions of a charming member of the Kaiser's vast entourage, a colonel of the Imperial Body-guard who understood the boy's unrealized yearnings and ministered to them tenderly. And it was the very tenderness of a simple handshake good-bye which inflamed his father's suspicions.

When the last carriage disappeared, and quiet had descended on the estate like a blanket, Philip von Basel's father had dragged him, still in their dress uniforms, to the stable and beat him senseless with his fists. The boy came to, face down in the straw matting, vomiting. His father was sitting head in his hands, silent.

Philip dragged himself to the horse trough and plunged his head into the cold water until the dizziness passed. When he could stand he drew his saber. His father looked up.

The sharp rap, rap of steel against the trough was an unmistakable challenge. But in case the elder von Basel did not understand, young Philip added a remark about his father's sexual demands on his mother. His father came to his feet, promising worse punishment for the fifteen-year-old.

But von Basel had made his own promise—he would never let the stronger man inside his guard. If his father wished to punish him again, first he had to divest himself of the saber he had taught him to use. And that, the father discovered, was not easily done. He had honed the boy's remarkable speed from the day he had discovered it. What he had not realized was that his son's wrist had come into its own over the summer. Rage for ruining what he had shared with the colonel of the guard fueled the killing machine the boy had become, and the father had nurtured.

Philip laid both of his father's cheeks open to the bone, took an ear and extracted a tearful apology by threatening to slice off his nose. Hours later the humiliated count shot himself, guaranteeing that his son would come into his inheritance as soon as he reached his majority, and convincing the boy that the saber was a most satisfactory tool to redress wrong and restore order. The only thing that puzzled him at all about the affair was why his mother had grieved. . . .

She begged him now to stay a few days, but he was depressed by the way the food shortages affected even their class in Berlin—as opposed to Russia, where the only indication of shortage was higher prices that the rich could afford. Besides, he was anxious to get back across the lines. The Kaiser had asked what he would do about Ash. Von Basel smiled at the thought. He had told His Majesty about Ash's plan to support the Grand Duke Valery's palace coup.

"I think I will let Commander Ash do exactly what he intends to. I'll even help him. It would be more difficult to seize the Czar from his own Guard, or from a revolutionary government, than to take him away from a single American naval officer."

The Kaiser had clapped him on his back, then ordered a private car from his own Imperial Train attached to the express to occupied Riga so that Count von Basel might return to the front in a style befitting a German nobleman in service to his emperor.

Von Basel tried to luxuriate as the train thundered east, but he was too impatient to enjoy, too anxious to get back to Petrograd where he could keep an eye on how Ash was progressing.

39

Sedovina danced. A hush fell over the Maryinski Theater. Ash sat in the stalls, shoulder-to-shoulder with Russian army officers. When she finished her first solo the men surged, roaring, to their feet. Overhead applause thundered from the tiers of boxes and came down from the high gallery.

Ash had held her in his opera glasses. The great Karsavina performed the Sylphide, but Petrograd waited for Sedovina's solos and roared its approval again and again.

Sedovina danced with the icy precision the Russians demanded, the price of entry to their hearts. Without perfect form they would hiss her off the stage. To the precision she brought grace, also expected. Her style was youthful, an image as yet unformed, but her presence, in spite of her age, was irresistible.

And yet, thought Ash, an element was missing. Perhaps it was just her youth, perhaps she didn't have the drive to make it over the long pull, but she failed to display a distinct personality the way Karsavina did with her paradoxical double mask of prim sensuality or Tamara's exuberant sensuality. It was almost as if she was dancing with something else on her mind. Revolution? Or was that wishful thinking? He'd find out when the show was over.

The great blue curtain descended for the *entr'acte* and the officers broke into excited discussion about the new sensation as they headed for the stairs to the first box tier. Ash headed that way himself, hunting Sergei Gladishev. He squeezed past three ancient captains of the Jaegerski Life Guard, resplendent in their bemedaled dark green uniforms and arguing the merits of the performance. Choreography, they agreed, had fallen on hard times, but Sedovina . . . she was a *ballerina*. When would the Imperial Theaters award her a principal role worthy of her talents? But hadn't he heard? Sokolova, the great dancer of the eighties, was preparing her for *Giselle*.

In the first tier the ladies had thrown open their doors and were gathered in the anterooms at the rear of their boxes, smoking and talking with men visiting from the stalls. In the next tier pinkly shaven merchants were hurrying back to their boxes with chocolates for their wives, while down the stairs from the gallery streamed the "Gods," student dancers, laughing and chattering while the girls pretended not to ogle the officers in their bright uniforms.

Outside the Czar's box a royal guard performed its own sort of dance —a quick-time manual-of-arms executed with almost inhuman precision. Ash looked in the open door, but the Czar was not inside. Instead, a party of Roumanians, including a prince, whom Ash had heard was courting one of the Czar's daughters; despite the loss of his entire country to the Germans, and what the Czar insisted on calling "unrest" in *his* cities, the process of royal procreation still commanded obeisance.

Ash found Gladishev on the second tier drinking champagne with some grave-looking men he presumed were Duma members. To his relief, when Gladishev saw him hovering, the Kadet Party millionaire excused himself and motioned him to the champagne, where he bought Ash a glass. "I understand you've telephoned, Commander," he said.

"Five times this week. And I stopped twice at your mansion." He tilted his glass in silent toast and said, "This is the first time since I got to Petrograd that you haven't snubbed me. What's up?"

Gladishev had a big, round face and an almost perpetual grin, which was either good-humored or brusque depending on the squint of his eyes. They narrowed now and the grin turned hard, amused, but not mirthful. Ash was reminded of his father's friends in the coal and steel business— self-made and damned proud of it and straightforward. Gladishev said, "That's because I saw you on the Nevsky the other day with Tishkova." Ash had called the second time at Gladishev's mansion *with* Tamara. Apparently the ploy had worked.

"We're old friends."

"I admire her very much."

"So does the Grand Duke Valery."

"I always thought his tastes were much more advanced than the rest of his clan."

There was the opening Ash had been waiting for. So Gladishev had heard, or guessed, something about the grand ducal conspiracy to overthrow Czar Nicholas, and had surmised Ash was part of it. He said, "Mademoiselle Tishkova and I will lunch at Berrin's Wednesday afternoon. Three o'clock."

308

Ash returned to the stalls as the audience sorted itself out through the corridors and stairs. The lights dimmed, the blue and gold hall grew quiet and he heard one of the old Jaegerski Guards whisper happily, "And next month Tishkova's jubilee!" . . .

Provided, thought Ash, Petrograd wasn't in flames next month. He had seen his first street demonstration earlier in the week on the way to one of his fruitless calls at Sergei Gladishev's mansion. Factory workers marching up the center of Sedovaya Street had borne signs draped between long poles and chanted, *"Duma! Duma! Duma!"*—an angry demand to make the elected body more than a debating chamber. Let the Duma form a government that worked.

More of an immediate threat to Russian stability was another cry, a thin echo of single voices in the marching throng, *"Khleba . . ."* Bread. They were hungry. And Rasputin had prophesized again and again that hungry men would revolt.

The police made their stand where Ash had stopped at the intersection of Sedovaya and the Nevsky. The demonstrators advanced to within fifty feet of their black line, shouting and waving fists. The police stood their ground, and Ash thought them a disciplined force as they eyed their gray-coated officers for orders. Suddenly the police split apart on command, as if to let the demonstrators pass, but the gap was instantly filled as a mounted detachment wielding batons trotted into the space. An officer stepped in front of the line and bellowed at the demonstrators. There was a tense moment when neither side moved, then suddenly and, Ash thought, unexpectedly the demonstrators began backing away from the horses. The rear of their column melted into the side streets around the markets, but the leaders were left exposed in front and the police wasted no time pouncing on several dozen whom they clubbed into paddy wagons. In ten minutes the busy Nevsky was back to normal, but to Ash, who had been moved by the stolid courage on the faces in the front lines of the demonstration, it looked as if the police had won only the first of what promised to be many battles. . . .

A canal looped around the back of the Maryinski theater, iced and deep in snow. Carriages and motor cars lined up at the stage door. At intervals it opened on a cloaked figure that would scamper across the swept snow, revealing a glimpse of shiny hair or a pretty nose. A hand extended from the coach and the dancer slipped inside as it clattered away.

Other girls came out in groups, arm in arm, squealing at the cold, laughing excitedly, growing quiet when a group of young officers approached. Several cars were attended by drivers in the royal red livery. Ash wondered if one would take Sedovina. But after a while the last carriage pulled away, leaving only Ash and a few Russian officers. Had he missed her? Five minutes passed. No one came out. She could have been one of the cloaked figures hurrying into a car. Except he would have noticed her height . . .

One of the Russians knocked on the stage door. An old woman told him to go away. "Sedovina?" he asked; she nodded and he returned to his group. Ash looked over the competition—fresh-faced subalterns wearing the double-headed eagle and imperial red of the Cavalier Guard regiment. Aristocrats, newly commissioned. And younger than ever as the Russians accelerated their cadet classes to make up for the slaughter.

It was hardly a contest. He had waited outside a hundred stage doors for Tamara Tishkova, courting and recourting her over the years, and he knew the ropes. He let them go first.

She came out, wrapped in a wool cloak that completely hooded her head except for a gleam of golden hair and her nose with the little bump. The officers crowded up to her, shouldering each other aside to try to kiss her hand. Ash watched her eyes flicker over them. She seemed neither frightened by the onslaught, nor pleased. He was surprised to see a moment of disdain on her face. It passed, and she smiled noncommittally and turned away. Ash stood in her path.

"I saw Pavlova last November in New York City—I didn't know until tonight why she left Russia."

Big eyes met his—blue and young and startled, and still aglitter from the excitement of performing. Ash tried to hold them with a smile, but something was wrong. Either she didn't remember meeting him at the Exeters, or she hadn't liked what he had just said.

Sternly she replied, "Thank you for saying that. I know you mean it as a compliment, but artists are not competitors."

"Yours will be relieved to hear it," Ash said. "Do you recall, mademoiselle, we met in London?"

She looked at him. "Commander Ash. Poor Lady Exeter. What a strange death. I was so sad, she was awfully kind to me. I stayed at their home even after they left for Russia . . ."

"Would you have supper with me? . . . there's something I'd like to ask you."

"I don't, usually . . . I like to sort of think about things after a performance. What went right and wrong . . ." She glanced around. The Russian Guards officers were still waiting. Ash let his cloak fall away from his uniform. "Good *night*, gentlemen."

He received an obedient salute, some dejected good nights, and off they trooped.

"What did Pavlova dance?"

"*Giselle*. I heard tonight that Sokolova is preparing you for it. She coached Pavlova in the part too, didn't she?"

"How does an American know so much about the dance?"

"Tishkova is an old friend."

She looked disdainful again, the way she had reacted to the Guards officers, and Ash was puzzled by an undercurrent of anger. Perhaps Tamara had insulted the girl. She was capable of it, if she had been crossed. Sedovina said, "She and her entourage of grand dukes. They think the ballet is their toy."

"Shall we go?" Ash said. He had learned long ago to steer clear of the likes and dislikes that sprang up at the *barre* and flourished in the wings. "Will you join me for supper?"

"The ballet should be for everyone, not just the aristocracy. Tishkova encourages that exclusivity."

"Shall we go?"

"First tell me what it is you want to ask me."

"I want to meet a man named Kirichenko."

"Who?" she asked, but she looked briefly frightened.

"Kirichenko. He's a Social Revolutionary squad leader, allied with the Bolsheviks. Lenin knows him."

"We have nothing to talk about." She whirled away from the stage door and hurried toward the big square in front of the theater. Ash caught up. "Please. Have supper with me. We'll just talk—"

"I will scream for police if you don't go away."

"I'll swear to the police we were talking about *Giselle*—"

"I *will* scream." She looked around. A tram was coming.

Ash said, "Or should I tell the police we were talking about the Bolshevik sailor you met in Covent Garden?"

She grabbed his arm. Her eyes were now very large.

"I won't hurt you, I won't tell anyone but I must meet Kirichenko."

"Who else knows?"

"No one." Which wasn't entirely true, but the State Department operatives who tracked down the sailor were no threat to Sedovina. "I followed you from the Exeters. We're on the same side." Not really true again, but close enough. "I need your help."

"I don't know him."

"Think about it."

She looked around the square. The Maryinski stood alone, oddly Byzantine in its dome and facade. Theater Square was deserted now, except for old women sweeping the snow. Her gaze lingered on each.

"Let's walk."

Relieved, Ash let her steer him into one of the several streets that converged in the square. "This runs beside a canal," she said in a tight voice. "There's a bridge . . ."

It was suspended across the narrow canal by a pair of black chains anchored in the mouths of exquisitely sculpted black-and-gold lions.

Sedovina touched one of their heads. "My friends, when I first came to the Maryinski . . . this was the long way to my home but I preferred to see my friends . . ."

She looked down the canal, a graceful trough of snow that caught the light from the surrounding buildings and the regularly spaced street lamps. "I haven't come this way in a while."

"I'm lost," said Ash.

"At the next street you can see the Admiralty tower. Come, it's cold."

They walked quickly along the canal until it veered away and shortly came to a narrow boulevard, one of the principal streets that radiated from the Admiralty. The golden spire gleamed at the end of it, flood-lighted again now that no Zeppelins had bombed the capitol as once had been feared.

She began walking faster, and Ash had trouble keeping up with her on the slippery snow. The wind chewed at their backs, tossing their cloaks and cutting to the skin. Away from the canal the street lights were fewer, and they trudged for intervals in the dark.

When Ash did get a look at her face under one of the intermittent lights he was shocked to see a profound weariness. Or despair?

"What is it?"

"I am wondering what happens if the police break me."

"What?"

"I don't know that much, but it all matters . . . I should probably kill myself."

"What are you talking about? I'm not threatening Kirichenko. I just want to *meet* him. Why would I want to hurt Kirichenko?"

No answer. She had subsided into another of her long silences, one she had not broken by the time they reached St. Issac's Square. The domed cathedral loomed darkly on the far side, but the Astoria and the graceful Maryinski Palace spilled golden light onto the firewood piled in the square from nearly every window. Music from both drifted thinly on the wind.

Sedovina was walking with her head down and didn't see the sudden rush toward them from the shadows. An old woman darted out of a wood-pile and ran straight at them, clutching a stick of firewood. There was a shout as she scrambled past them, and a soldier came after her, raising his rifle like a club.

Ash acted without thinking, stepped inside the swing and doubled the soldier up with a fist to his middle. The soldier's gun clattered to the ice and he sprawled, moaning, as the old woman ran into an alley.

A second soldier came running down the narrow corridor between the piles, saw his companion on the ground and pointed his rifle at Ash. Sedovina whispered, "Give him money."

Ash let his cloak open, as he had done before. The soldier noted his dress uniform. Ash slowly reached into his pocket and extracted his billfold, pulled roubles from it and held them up. The soldier glanced once at his companion, who was starting to sit up, lowered his gun, took the money. Ash took Sedovina's arm and hurried toward the Astoria.

"You were kind," Sedovina said. "They would have beaten her. They don't realize that she's the widow and mother of ones like themselves."

"Thanks, but I didn't think . . ."

"Well, we're both lucky they weren't drunk. They's have shot us if they were."

Ash thought they were also lucky that she'd had the quick wit to suggest a bribe. He glanced at her. She seemed curiously unaffected by the incident, had already seemed to have put it from her mind. He reminded himself, as he often had to when he first got to know Tamara, that Russians were different, more emotional and more romantic than Europeans but at the same time so enormously fatalistic as to freeze all emotion with a cold dose of acceptance. She had meant it earlier when she said she would kill herself. No doubt about it.

He looked around the front of Astoria. It looked clear. Red Snow, by now, would have given up on the hotel. It was as good a place as any for late supper. He invited her in.

"No, I want to go home."

Ash signaled for a sleigh from the line at the curb. Sedovina settled back and watched the street. Carriages and sleighs were out in force on the Nevsky, and here and there a troika filled with gaily dressed men and women sped by. In London and Paris they would be rolling up the sidewalks at this hour, but Petrograd, like New York, was just getting started.

Sedovina had given the driver her address. A mile up the Nevsky he turned off and pulled up beside the mighty columns of the Alexander Theater. "I live down that lane."

The opening was too narrow for the sleigh, an almost invisible slit between two buildings. Inside, their footsteps echoed and Ash heard a crow call sleepily. He thought of New England. Tiny two and three story houses crowded close, like on a Portsmouth lane. The houses were wooden with pointed gables leaning toward each other. Sedovina headed toward an ally covered by a second-floor passage between two houses. There was a window in the passage and a lighted lamp in the window.

"My room," she said. "Isn't it wonderful the way it floats in the air?"

She passed under the room and worked a key into a wooden door that opened on a small, shabby parlor. The light from upstairs cast dark shadows on the floor wallpaper. She started to close the door.

"Kirichenko?" Ash asked.

Sedovina nodded. "Tomorrow at five. Can you meet me at the ballet school on Theater Street?"

Sedovina collapsed against her door, listening to his footsteps fade. She crossed her arms and pressed her hands to her breasts. She tried to make her mind go blank, to shed her panic. Who was he? Why had he followed her? What had she said? Would he come back with the Okhrana?

She had kept looking for detectives on the long walk from the theater, kept waiting for the sudden swoop of a police car; she could almost feel their rough hands clamping hold of her arms, dragging her inside.

Kirichenko. She calmed her mind with thoughts of him. Usually he frightened her—the few times they had met—but not now. She would tell him what Ash wanted. Let Kirichenko decide if Ash was dangerous. Kirichenko would know what to do with the American.

After turning out the light she opened the door, ran down the alley and roused a youth who slept in a flat off the courtyard. He came back with her, listened to her message and ran off, chewing one of the apples she kept by the door for delivery boys.

Calmed some by action, and reassuring herself that if Ash were dangerous Kirichenko would kill him, she got ready for bed. Her body ached from the fear and tension. She exercised to loosen the muscles, heated hot water to soak her new toe shoes. They were her one extravagance. She purchased them specially fitted instead of using the shoes supplied by the Imperial Theater and soaked to soften the hard glue and cardboard in the tip rather than protect her foot with too much padding.

She and her father were almost out of kerosene, which meant hours tomorrow morning on the *khvost* in hopes of buying more. How, she wondered, as she often did, did ordinary people survive? They were poor, but both had steady incomes and there were no children to feed . . .

She was still awake when Mikhailov came home, a little drunk but exhilarated by the night's playing. He knocked on her door and sat on the edge of her bed. "Where did you play?" she asked.

"The Paley ball. They came in raving about your Effie."

"I was terrible tonight."

"They didn't notice," Mikhailov smiled.

"They never do."

Her father worked the stiffness out of his big, blunt fingers. "You're too harsh, Vera."

She said nothing. The discipline she had embraced as a child, a student, and the discipline that made her a dancer had found new strength in the Revolution. She took comfort in the conviction that the cruel inequities of Russian life could only be relieved by total dedication on the part of those who could see the need to change. It *required* a cold eye.

314

Coryphée spilled down the stairs of the Imperial Theatrical School into the quiet trough of Theater Street. Laughing and calling, the young dancers dispersed toward the Nevsky in little groups, arms linked, heads bobbing for secrets. Cold snow fell hard, and a thin mist rose from the ground and haloed the street lights. By the time they reached the Alexander Theater Ash could barely see the girls.

Children burst next from the school, ducklings herding Sedovina in their midst, she like a swan bent over deep in conversation with a little ten-year-old. Ash hung back until she kissed the child and came toward him. She slipped her arm through his, affectionately, except that her body was stiff and the affection was quite obviously an act for anyone watching from the school. She steered him in the opposite direction of the Alexander Theater and the Nevsky. Her face was ghostly white, her mouth an anxious line.

Left at the end of Theater Street, across a tiny square, she stopped on a bridge that humped over the Fontanka River. "Listen to me. I am walking into the Moscow District. You are to follow twenty yards behind. If I stop, you stop. Do not approach me."

"Are you taking me to Kirichenko?"

"Comrade Kirichenko wants a good look at you first."

She continued across the bridge, her shoulder stiff. Ash waited twenty yards and went after her. Walking beside the river for a block, she turned left on Gorokhovaya Street, passed the building where Rasputin had lived. Within another block the factory neighborhood, which was wedged between the last vestiges of gentility east of the Fontanka and the railroad tracks of the Moscow line, had deteriorated from shabby to impoverished.

Sedovina hesitated. The narrow streets ahead teemed with factory workers and *moujiks*, street vendors and shoppers lugging pails for milk and kerosene. Long lines spilled from the shops and market stalls. A legless beggar slithered up and tugged at her skirt.

Sedovina recoiled, then caught herself and dropped a coin in his hand. She forged ahead. Ash followed, forcing himself not to look for whomever was watching him. The streets narrowed on the crowds. Lights were few. They *were* watching. He felt it. She saw a face in an alley.

Sedovina was easy to identify by her long blonde hair cascading from her hat, her height and the blur of milk-white skin when she turned her face to look back; but as the street narrowed again, squeezed into a *pereulki*, a lane deep in slush and half-frozen mud, Ash worried that his clothes stood out in the shabby crowds and might draw the attention of the police. His boat cloak covered his sword. His boots had gotten as muddy as everyone's, but the polished black visor and gold eagle on his service cap were beginning to make him feel as out of place as a Cossack at an anarchists' convention. Another face in the shopwindow . . . afraid?

He took it off, but a bare head stood out even more. No Russian would dare go hatless in the dangerous cold. In seconds it seeped through his thick hair and set a chill traveling down his spine. Ahead, Sedovina stopped, her way blocked by a wagon trundling out of a factory yard. The driver backed his horse to clear the turn. It would take a while. She bought an apple from an old woman in a tattered shawl. He had to blend in better, or they wouldn't approach.

Ash ducked into an alley where he had spotted an immensely tall, swarthy Tartar selling old clothes from a filthy sack, waved a couple of roubles at him and bought a used fur hat that had seen better days. As he crammed it on his head, he hoped it was not infested. A few kopecks paid for an old leather bag from a hawker of brooms and baskets. He stuffed his service cap into it and started after Sedovina as the wagon finally moved.

Down another lane past low glass-fronted factory buildings with arched roofs . . . through the dirty windows Ash could see men and women hunched over machinery. Sedovina stopped. A pair of drunken soldiers lurched at her from a doorway. She sidestepped them just as Ash moved to help. Before he reached her one of the gray-uniformed policemen patrolling the streets kicked the drunks away. Sedovina whirled and ran. The *gorodovois* ordered her to stop, but she disappeared in the crowds. The cop shrugged and kicked the drunks again. Ash circled around them, scanned the street quickly and saw no one who seemed to be watching. Sedovina?

He spotted the bright gold of her hair as she crossed a little square where half a dozen lanes joined. A wagon heaped with firewood and trailed by a mob of anxious shoppers blocked Ash's way. When it and the people had passed, Sedovina was gone.

He pushed into the square. Gone. He ran to each lane, looked down several alleys and ventured into courtyards surrounded by decrepit tenements. He had lost her. He went back to the square and looked there. A begger tugged his cuff . . . *"Khrista rady,"* a copper for Christ's sake. Ash gave him a few, looked further. The begger tugged his cuff again.

"*Nyet. Nyet.* You already got me—"

But the filthy hand which Ash had filled with kopecks now held a stubby revolver.

40

His long, ragged coat sleeve hid the weapon. Only Ash could see—though throngs of people were brushing past—and all he saw was the enormous circle of the muzzle. The beggar stood up. He had been perched on a box. He held Ash's cloak with his free hand and backed him into a doorway.

Ash heard two men clump down wooden stairs. They took him from either side, turned him around and marched him up three dark flights to a room with an oil lamp and a single window that overlooked the square. They gestured for him to lean against the wall, pulled off his cloak and patted him down for weapons. They left, but the beggar had followed them up the stairs, his gun still out.

Ash slowly lowered his hands and turned around. The beggar did not object until he tried to move away from the wall, then the gun shifted to him. Ash leaned back, waited. The square below the window seemed to be filling up with people. On the side of the square that Ash could see, a couple of men were stringing electric light bulbs between a pole and a tenement.

The two men came back, accompanying a third. Kirichenko? Definitely the boss. He planted himself in front of Ash, feet wide apart, looked him up and down.

Ash ran his own inspection. What he saw was a short, medium-built, clean-shaven Russian dressed like the others in a factory worker's short leather jacket and forage cap whose peak sloped close to his brow. Dark hair fluffed out from the back of his cap. He had a full mouth and long nose and kept his face turned slightly to the side, which gave him a wary look. His jacket hung open. Two guns were stuffed in his waistband.

"Who sent you?" His accent was heavy but he pronounced each word clearly as if he had learned English in high school.

"Are you Kirichenko?"

"Who sent you?" He was surprisingly young, but his darting eyes and tough expression made it easy to believe that he had survived underground since the war began and the police had decimated the revolutionary apparatus.

"I come for myself. But Lenin told me about you."

"Lenin?"

"In Zurich."

"Lenin is a coward. He is a bully. A backstabber. If he walked into this room this minute I would blow his head off."

"He expressed a good deal more admiration for you."

"Maudlin claptrap. You probably surprised him at a moment when he was feeling guilt for abandoning the Revolution . . . Have you any better reasons why I should trust you?"

"Your men missed my pistol. It's hidden in the small of my back."

"No, they didn't miss it, but we were curious how you would react."

"Did I pass the test?"

"No. The test hasn't started yet. In fact we haven't decided whether we'll even administer the test—what do you want with me?"

"I want you to blow up a railroad."

"Only a lunatic would come here and joke. What railroad? Why?"

"The Tsarskoye Selo line."

"Why?"

Ash looked at him. No complaints about the First Railway Battalion, no impossibles. Just *why*.

"You should be able to guess why."

"I have not survived three years of Okhrana pursuit guessing." He pulled a revolver from his waistband and pressed the muzzle to Ash's forehead. "Why?"

Ash knew he was dead unless Kirichenko thought he was of use. "It's necessary to isolate the Czar to bring off a palace coup—"

"*Whose* coup?"

"I didn't tell them your name and I won't tell you theirs."

"They perhaps didn't hold a gun to your head."

"They trust me."

"I trust this gun. Whose coup?"

"You'd never trust me if I told you."

"You expect me to blow up a railroad for someone I don't know?"

"I need to know more about you before I . . ."

One of the men looked out the window and spoke to Kirichenko. Kirichenko lowered his gun. "We'll talk about it and how I should help you, and particularly *why*, later. After your test. Take out your gun."

318

"Now?"

"In your hand, you damned fool, in case you need it. Come on."

One man stayed in the room and blew out the light. The other went upstairs. Kirichenko took Ash to a dark room on the first floor. The window was wide open. They crouched by the sill, a few feet above the hundreds of people who had crowded into the square. Suddenly the lights Ash had watched strung were turned on. The crowd surged around the bright circle cast on the muddy snow.

"What's going on?"

"Do you like the theater?"

"What are you talking about?"

Six men laid beams on the ground and covered them with heavy planks, taking care that they lay smoothly. A stage? The audience stamped their cold feet and murmured in anticipation.

Kirichenko made a gesture. Ash followed the direction. A man with a rifle stood on a roof across the square. Ash scanned the surrounding buildings. Three more rifles. Kirichenko held a pistol and slipped his other hand in his pocket. Ash held his gun at his side, hardly believing that he had been bamboozled into standing guard for Russian revolutionaries. His test.

"Theater?"

"We're the ushers. In case the *pharon* come. The cops, you call them."

They put a table on the wooden stage. For a moment it sat alone in the lights, then six men walked into the light carrying a coffin on their shoulders. They walked solemnly around the table, circled the edges of the light and finally laid the coffin on the table. A hush fell over the crowd. All attention was on the coffin. Suddenly, there was a loud bang, the sides fell open.

Rasputin lay dead. The crowd murmured. Rasputin sat up and made broad comic signs of blessing with his arms. The crowd laughed, and the man dressed and made up to look like Rasputin lay down again, dead as before. A play had begun.

A horn sounded a fanfare. Now actors representing Czar Nicholas II and Czarina Alexandra marched into the circle of light in tawdry regalia. The resemblance of the actors to the portraits all over Russia indeed seemed extraordinary. The Czar looked exactly like the Czar, from his pointed beard to his dreamy eyes, and the Czarina looked as imperious as she had the first time Ash had seen her in her mauve boudoir.

The horn blew again, and four young girls with the red sashes worn by grand duchesses skipped onto the stage followed by a boy in a uniform. The Czar's children. They filed part the coffin, and as each girl bent in prayer over the dead Rasputin, the monk's hand lifted her skirt and gave her bottom a pat. The crowd laughed. The boy pantomimed jealousy, putting his hands on his hips and pouting and the girls picked him up and carried him away as the audience laughed even louder. Again the crowd rippled with anticipation. Now only the Czar and Czarina and Rasputin were on the stage.

Ash noticed young men in leather jackets posted as lookouts at each lane. He glanced up at the riflemen on the roofs. This was one part of Petrograd where the Revolution seemed to be going along nicely, thank you. Ash looked at his own gun and hoped to hell the cops agreed—

The horn. The Czar raised his arms and yawned with elaborate gestures, laid down behind Rasputin, yawned again and shut his eyes. The Czarina stepped up to the table and put a hand on Rasputin's chest. She gazed out at the audience and chanted in Russian what sounded to Ash like a prayer.

The crowd began laughing again. A moldy carrot began to rise from between Rasputin's legs. When it was pointing skyward, the Czarina trailed her hand down his chest over his belly and clasped the carrot. The audience began shouting, encouraging her. It was the first joviality Ash had seen on ordinary people's faces since he had arrived in Russia.

The Czarina bantered back, asking what they wanted, and they shouted and catcalled, urging her on. The Czarina clasped the carrot in both hands and bent over it. The Czar commenced loud snoring, and she gave him a look of scorn, delighting the old women in the square. The Czarina raised her enormously painted eyebrows and her whole face seemed to ask the audience, What should I do? They answered by chanting encouragement and at last, with a gigantic shrug and another scornful glance at the snoring Czar, she bit down on the carrot.

Ash noticed that the older people laughed considerably more than the younger, many of whom looked away, embarrassed. But suddenly all laughter ceased in a single gasp, as Vera Sedovina burst into the lights. She wore white, a flowing white gown, a white peasant's headband around her golden hair and even a white mask that covered her eyes but not the little bump on her nose. She commenced a slow, stately arabesque, pirouetted and leaped into a deep and graceful bow. The musicians then began a haunting country melody on their guitars, and Vera Sedovina, ballerina in His Majesty's Imperial Theater, danced for the people . . .

A child watched near Ash from its father's shoulders, its face awestruck. The boards beneath Sedovina's slippers were like a polished stage, the string of naked light bulbs, stars. Even the shabby costumes on the Czar and Czarina seemed to glow. There was, though, nothing ethereal about Sedovina's performance. She knew her audience, danced as broadly as the actors had played, portraying peasant work with great swoops of her body —tilling soil, hammering machinery, carrying a divine figure in the flowing white robe, representing, *being* Russia herself. Now she glided up to the table where Rasputin lay in his coffin beside the snoring Czar and delivered a tremendous kick in the rump to the Czarina. The Czarina straightened up with a shriek, the carrot still in her teeth, reeled comically about the stage and fell backward over the Czar.

When the laughter subsided Sedovina reached for Rasputin. The audience gasped as the dead monk sprang to life and landed lightly beside her. Their *pas de deux* revealed that *he* was no renegade from the Imperial Theater, no *danseur noble*, yet a decent enough *porteur* and the audience shouted delight at Sedovina's leaps.

She dispensed with the earlier broad strokes, but again the point was clear—Russia and Rasputin were one. The evil monk in the eyes of the few was a fellow peasant to the many. Holding hands, they bowed to the audience, shared a chaste kiss and danced arm-in-arm as the guitars took up a peasant dance. Behind them the Czar crept off the table and pulled a long black gun from his scarlet tunic. The audience shouting warnings, but the Rasputin and Russia danced on. The Czar stalked, leering cruelly as a vaudeville villian.

Ash looked at Kirichenko, who ceased inspecting the conjunction of streets and alleys long enough to sneer. "A ham from the provinces."

"But a brave man."

"Valentinov would sell his own mother to play in Petrograd."

Valentinov, the actor playing the Czar, leveled his gun. Children screamed. The dancers, oblivious, broke into a lively mazurka. Valentinov flashed a final gap-toothed leer and pulled the trigger. At the loud bang of a blank cartridge Rasputin clutched his back and fell on the table. The Czar fired again.

Sedovina pirouetted a silent scream so real that the hairs rose on Ash's neck, staggered to the table and collapsed slowly across Rasputin until she and the dead monk lay still and silent like the arms of the Cross.

"Children," Kirichenko said. "Playing at revolution."

"Then what are you doing here?"

Kirichenko scanned the applauding audience. "Patience, Commander . . ."

Sedovina and her partner got up from the table and bowed to the square. Peasants, workmen, maimed veterans beat their ragged mittens together, and though it was obvious they were shouting for her, Sedovina made her *porteur* take every bow with her. Here and there parents bent down to explain to still bewildered children how the beautiful woman in white had come back to life.

The other players emerged from the alley that served as backstage. The audience greeted them with angry shouts and shaken fists and Ash was astonished by the gusts of raw hatred sweeping the square.

"They'll enjoy His Majesty's trial," Kirichenko remarked with satisfaction.

"What do you mean?"

"The Czar's trial, after the Revolution. His guilt must be exposed publicly before he dies."

"Why bother? Why not just send him into exile?"

Kirichenko looked at him sharply. "Your little friend Sedovina just brought the news back from *our* exiles. The Bolsheviks in Zurich, London and New York all agree. Imprisonment, trial, execution."

"Won't you have your hands full just holding the country together?" Ash was thinking that if the Grand Duke's coup failed and the Bolsheviks led a popular revolt instead he would somehow have to fight his way out with the Czar. It didn't seem very likely. "Won't you have more important problems, like fighting off the Germans?"

"We'll deal with the Germans when we have to," Kirichenko told him, his quick eyes sweeping the rooftops. "But the Czar is our real enemy. We can't let him form a government in exile and rally a counterrevolution. The party has decided and we Social Revolutionaries agree—the Czar stays in Russia, and dies in Russia."

"What about the trial?"

"His trial will be conducted publicly, immediately prior to his execution."

"Hardly seems worth the trouble—"

"Russia deserves a trial."

They were hardly allies, Ash realized. Kirichenko would tear Russia apart, pull out of the war and leave the U.S. holding the bag. His only hope was Grand Duke Valery supported by moderates like Gladishev. Lord Exeter had been right. Only a strong new leader could guarantee stability, a leader strong enough to squelch the fanatics like Kirichenko. But the question still was, could Kirichenko be used?

On stage the Czar and Czarina kept mugging for the wrought-up crowd. Finally, when it appeared that the more frenzied in the front rows would attack, the actress playing the Czarina lifted up her wig, revealing a rather ordinary-looking Russian woman with a long face and aristocratic nose similar to the Czarina's. Valentinov, the actor playing the Czar, waited until interest in her had passed before tugging off his beard, which he waved in the lights. He was a small, lithe, middle-aged actor—obviously the troupe's director and impresario, but when he stuck the Vandyke beard to his chin again, his resemblance to the Czar was uncanny. Ash thought he looked more like Nicholas than King George did.

Reluctantly Valentinov acknowledged the audience's shouts and brought Sedovina, still masked, forward for another bow. Her gaze traveled over the audience to the alleys. Suddenly she stiffened.

"*Pharons,*" Kirichenko snapped.

Shouts echoed from one of the alley's entering the square, and the crowd dimpled there as people tried to move away. A phalanx of Kirichenko's young men in leather jackets tried to form a defense line as the police stormed in swinging clubs.

Now they poured in a second alley, clubbing screaming people to the

322

snow. More police burst in a third alley, tall men in long coats, attacking in disciplined formation. The audience stampeded toward the stage.

The actors tried to run. Ash caught a glimpse of Sedovina, saw her golden hair, but lost her as the screaming mob swept her away. Valentinov herded the girls through a tenement door and then Ash lost sight of him too.

"Do something," Ash called to Kirichenko.

"Wait."

"For what?"

Quickly the square was divided. The police formed a battle line on one side, trampling on the injured, while forty or fifty young workers tried to hold them off until the audience could escape down the streets and alleys. A police officer shouted at them, and the workers responded with jeers and a barrage of snowballs. The catcalls, though, died on their lips when two dozen police reinforcements swarmed into the square.

"Come on." Kirichenko hurried out of the dark room. Ash followed, his gun at his side. Outside, the police were backing the workers toward the allies. A hard-packed snowball knocked an officer to the ground. On orders, they drew guns and started firing in the air.

Snowballs arced through the glare from the stage. Kirichenko trotted into the no-man's-land, his gun pressed out of view against his leg. Ash had only a moment to decide to join him or melt into the crowd, escape from the square. The police were forty feet away, firing in the air and advancing into the snowball barrage.

"You're in it now," Kirichenko muttered with a mirthless grin. "Get ready to run."

An officer blew a whistle and the police line tightened up in preparation to charge. Kirichenko walked calmly to the front of the worker line, where he reached into his leather jacket, pulled a snowball out of his pocket, lobbed it at the cop with the whistle.

The officer swatted it contemptuously with his club. Ash heard a loud *clang*. The club fell at the officer's feet and Kirichenko's "snowball" rolled among the police, freezing them, and then the white bomb exploded red.

41

The square echoed with blunt thunder. Before the smoke had cleared Kirichenko tossed a second bomb. Five police had fallen around the smoking crater. Four lay still. The fifth, the officer, clawed at a shattered leg. Kirichenko's second bomb landed beside him. He scooped it up, threw it back. It hit Kirichenko in the face, staggering him, and it dropped at Ash's feet.

"Six-second fuse," Kirichenko told him, reeling as he tried to orient himself. Ash started at it. It was slightly oval, the size of a baseball with a little nipple. Slush and blood smeared the white paint. He kicked it. The bomb rolled lazily toward the crater. Ash dove for cover, dragging Kirichenko down with him. Halfway to the crater the bomb blew up.

The police sent pistol fire from the alleys. A bullet went through Ash's fur hat. Another ripped Kirichenko's collar. A rifle sounded from the roof, driving the police back into the alley, from where they directed steady fire at the rooftops. Kirichenko got to his feet, extracted a third bomb from his pocket and threw it into the alley. A dud. The police answered with a burst of pistol fire. A bullet smashed one of the stage lights, extinguishing the whole string and plunging most of the square into darkness.

Ash followed Kirichenko into the night. . . .

"Why should I help replace the Czar with a grand duke? Another Czar?"

"Same reason you threw that bomb."

They sat in the back of a tearoom that sold vodka. The owner had come in moments after they arrived, took one look at Kirichenko and replaced the standard unlabeled bottle without a word. The first had tasted watered. This was like fire.

"You didn't need the bomb."

"And what would you have done?" Kirichenko said, seemingly unconcerned by their narrow escape or the dark swollen bruise on his face. He had led Ash down an alley, with a police searchlight flicking at their heels, into a tenement basement, through a long wet corridor and into an underground room that contained a printing press. A second tunnel had exited a hundred yards away in a well in a courtyard, where a lieutenant reported that the actors had made good their escape.

"I wouldn't have made the situation worse by throwing bombs. How many people were shot?—good God, Kirichenko, the only reason you stood guard was for the trouble. You knew the police would come."

Kirichenko shrugged. "So? Perhaps I informed them. Did you think of that, Commander?"

"That's why you'll help me help a grand duke replace the Czar."

"Why?"

"You and Lenin both—the worse the better."

Kirichenko poured more vodka. He tossed the glass back in a single gulp and looked at the drunks sleeping at the other tables. The room was thick with smoke from the few men sober enough to hold a cigarette. Two of Kirichenko's comrades sat at the door. Five more waited in the narrow street.

"The worse the better? Is that what you tell your grand duke? What Romanov would destroy to build?"

Ash said nothing. He was trying to play both ends against the middle. The only question was how far each side would go in its hopes of winning out in the end.

"You are betraying him. Or me. Or both of us."

"This isn't my fight," Ash said. "My government wants the Czar removed so the United States can enter the war against Germany. That's my *only* interest. As soon as the Czar falls, I'm going home." *But I'm also taking him with me, you son of a bitch . . .*

"Your grand duke will have the same fate as the Czar."

"That's between you and him. It's your country, although frankly the man I'm supporting seems decent enough, even for a grand duke. You ought to be able to work out something—"

"Don't be naive."

"Okay, okay, it's your country. You can be damned sure, though, the Germans aren't fighting among themselves."

"Do you think my comrades give a damn for fighting Germany?"

"The Germans will sell you down the river the first chance they get." Speaking of naive . . .

"We won't give them the chance—no, Commander, I'm not interested in your schemes. There are easier, better ways to use the worse to get the better than to risk my men blowing up the Czar's railroad for your convenience." He stood up, his men flanked the door.

"How much money would make it worth the risk?"

Kirichenko shrugged. "What good is money when I can't use it to buy what I need?" . . .

"You have a point . . . maybe I have an answer. . . ."

"Ash, I hope to God you know what you're doing."

"The revolutionaries want high explosives, Lord Exeter. Your factory has plenty of high explosives. We're going to trade dynamite for their support."

"A full lorry load to blow up two rail lines?"

"Could you lend a hand here, Your Lordship?"

The drive up the rutted roads beside the Neva had taken most of the day. Now, while Exeter's chauffeur waited in the limousine outside the factory gates, Ash and Exeter were loading wooden crates of high explosive into the back of a truck.

Independently they had both decided to dress in shooting tweeds, and it was apparent that while the enormous Englishman was powerful enough, he was hardly accustomed to ordinary manual labor. Nor did he seem, Ash thought, likely to develop a taste for it.

They packed the boxes in straw. The place was empty, though army guards were outside the fence because it was still on strike.

"I say, Ash, this is a lot more explosive than they need. I know this business. They could level the Winter Palace with this lorry."

"May I remind you, Your Lordship, that it was you who persuaded me to join up with the grand duke."

"And you were right to."

"Well, the grand duke needs the railroad blown up and the saboteur needs explosives."

"But I told you—"

"It's the only payment he'll accept."

"I really thought we were driving up here to get four crates. This is rather much. What else is he going to blow up?"

"I don't know. But he's not blowing up anything until after he does the railroad."

"How can you be sure?"

Ash told him.

"You're a treacherous bastard," Exeter said admiringly.

"I told you I'm learning. They intend to put the Czar on trial and execute him. If he and his group get control Russia's finished in the war.

And we'll be holding the bag. Besides, I've had enough of fanatics," he added, thinking of Exeter's wife dying in his arms.

He brought Kirichenko to an empty cow shed on an abandoned farm beside the Gulf of Finland and showed him the truck inside. Kirichenko opened the canvas. "Excellent."

"There are thirty-five crates," said Ash. "You can use four for the railroad. Leave the rest."

"Why?"

"If you remove five, the whole thing will detonate."

Kirichenko flushed. "You've sabotaged the truck?"

"I've marked these four crates which you can remove safely."

"You renege?"

"No. Ten days after you have blown the Tsarskoye Selo lines I'll show you how to disarm the detonator." . . . If Valery didn't have total control in ten days he never would, Ash had decided.

"I have men who can disarm it."

"They'll land in Zurich if they try. And you'll be out the whole truckload. You haven't seen this much dynamite in your whole life . . . just take your four crates and wait for the rest."

"You son of a bitch."

"I want my job done. Guaranteed."

Kirichenko jerked his head. The bodyguard grabbed Ash from both sides. "You'll tell me now, or I guarantee you'll die wishing you had."

"We're on the same side at the moment," Ash said. "We'll do a lot better being friends." He pointed up at the rafters. Lord Exeter and Chevalier Roland were perched there with a couple of Ash's double-barrel shotguns at full cock.

At Berrin's *confiserie,* tall elegant French waitresses served sponge cakes, ices and hot chocolate to well-dressed children in the company of grand-mothers and nannies.

"Will you look at them eat." Tamara shuddered.

Ash was watching the foyer in the mirrored wall, watching for Sergei Gladishev. "I already offered to take you to a bar."

"A bar? Then champagne. Moments later you're booking a room at the Europa—"

"Don't start."

She smiled at Ash and brushed the back of his hand with her fingernails. "Fun. Yes?"

"Yes." Fact was, Ash thought, they were having fun, despite the feeling she probably would never leave Valery for him, and despite Ash's promise to the grand duke which sat between them like a constant chaperon. Each was enjoying rediscovering the other, courting chastely. Enjoying it to a point. There were moments, like this afternoon, where the sexual tension flickered between them like heat lightning and Ash would not have been surprised if one of those children waving a metal spoon were suddenly singed.

"There's Gladishev."

Tamara checked her face in the mirror, touched a lock of hair and assumed her best professional smile. If the Moscow millionaire weren't eating out of her hand in half an hour, Ash thought, he'd be a man of strange tastes; the real problem, of course, would be to get Gladishev to eat from *Valery's* hand before the increasingly difficult grand duke bit his head off.

Gladishev, fortunately, looked anything but difficult. His round face grew radiant as he inhaled the aroma of chocolate and beamed at the gobbling children like a Santa Claus. He surrendered his cashmere coat and glided through the narrow aisle toward their table. He wore a gray suit, a red carnation in the button hole, a dark vest with a gold chain, spats and a cheerful polka dot silk tie. Greeting Ash civilly, he bowed over Tamara's hand when Ash introduced them, then sat down.

"I love this shop," Gladishev bubbled as he enveloped one of the tiny chairs. "But, mademoiselle, how do *you* eat here and keep your figure—"

"Glad you came," Ash interrupted. That was not a subject to endear him to Tamara.

"I have long admired Mademoiselle Tishkova on the stage. How could I resist coming?"

"There is an expression in Kennet's country," Tamara said. "Politics make strange bedfellows."

Gladishev got an interested gleam in his eye which Tamara, having gotten his full attention, coolly extinguished. "His Royal Highness, the Grand Duke Valery, and you, Monsieur Gladishev, have more in common than many bedfellows, however. In fact, I suspect, that were he to see you in an objective light, His Highness would admire you."

"On what basis, may I ask?" Gladishev replied, wary once he realized how swiftly she meant to get to the point of their meeting.

Tamara surprised Ash by rattling off three occasions on which Gladishev had triumphed in the Duma by a speech or adroit backroom manuevering. She had been surprising Ash a lot lately, since he had joined forces with her to encourage the grand duke. Over the years with Valery she had picked up a fair knowledge of the inner workings of Russian politics.

Gladishev looked impressed. "You are well-informed, Mademoiselle Tishkova. And you flatter me."

"With a purpose." Tamara smiled. "I am going to ask a favor."

Ash sat quietly. She was starting this meeting between Gladishev and the grand duke better than he could, employing a bold strategy of softening up Gladishev, whose temperament was an unknown factor, instead of concentrating on her own Valery.

Gladishev said, "If it is in my power, mademoiselle."

"I'm going to ask you to be accommodating."

"I think I've had some experience in the art of compromise—"

"But I am asking you to compromise your pride . . ."

"I'm not sure I understand."

"The grand duke is a very proud man. Very stubborn. He might seem narrow-minded, at first. He is also *blunt*, particularly with people not of his class—"

"I've had some experience with the nobility and aristocracy." Gladishev smiled.

"Well, you'll need it all this afternoon."

"Can you be more specific?"

Tamara gave him a look that said don't be coy. "I can think of only one subject we would have to discuss. *Oui?*"

Gladishev looked around as if belatedly concerned that the nearest nannies wiping chocolate off their charges' mouths might be Okhrana spies, and whispered back, *"Oui."*

Tamara sat back, her job done. "Kennet, I'm starving."

Ash waved for a waiter. For days they had prepared Valery for this vital meeting with Gladishev; in the next hour they would find out if they had succeeded in making an alliance between a rather hidebound royal and a liberal industrialist, or if the gap between old and new, autocracy and parliamentarianism was too wide to bridge.

Gap, hell, it was a chasm a century wide, with Gladishev embracing twentieth-century progress—with the glaring exception of labor unions—and the grand duke defending the eighteenth century—pre-Enlightenment eighteenth . . .

Suddenly the children scrambled from their tables and pressed to the glass as the Grand Duke Valery's great scarlet sleigh filled the shop window, and the Arabian bays and the Cossack escort's dark horses clattered to a halt on Morskaya Street. A footman entered the shop.

Ash paid, over Gladishev's protests. Outside the footman helped Tamara into the sled. Gladishev looked up from the sidewalk and eyed it dubiously.

"Get in," Ash said.

The millionaire politician glanced up and down the narrow curved street. "Ought I to be seen riding in the open like this, with . . . him?"

At that, the Grand Duke Valery poked his big, square head over the side. He was wearing a formidible bearskin *papaha* that made every hat on Morskaya Street seem somehow inadequate. His voice matched the annoyance on his face. "I've never skulked around Petrograd in my life and I won't start now. Get aboard or step aside."

Gladishev's big round face flushed angry red, but Ash already had his elbow, and the footmen helped lever his bulk onto the sleigh. Ash jumped on as it lumbered into motion. The vehicle was so large that all four could share the wide seat with the high back and wraparound sides. Tamara had arranged it so she and Ash had the opposite corners, which put Gladishev and the grand duke in the middle, side-by-side. Warm air wafted up from the brazier at their feet.

Gladishev, Ash noticed, relaxed a little when he saw that few could see them from the street. "Mademoiselle Tishkova said we should talk," Grand Duke Valery said bluntly. "What do you have to say?"

Gladishev looked at Tamara, who smiled back encouragement.

"Your Highness," he said, "the situation is desperate this winter. My warehouses are bulging with grain but I have no way to transport the grain to the cities because the Czar has let the railroads collapse. Starving people accuse my companies of holding back grain to raise the price . . . the Czar is responsible for this . . ." He glanced past Valery's stone-cold expression to Tamara, apparently gathering courage. "The Czar must pay, Your Highness. The war is an abomination. Russia and Germany have been too long related to destroy each other now."

Ash groaned inwardly. The notion of peace without victory was hardly the way to Valery's heart.

"How does a millionaire become a conspirator against his government?" the grand duke asked.

"We need change."

"But the kind of change the Duma discusses might well be more than a millionaire bargains for."

"Not if I'm in on it," Gladishev replied with a hard smile, moving happily into his own element. "There will be give and take, just as in business. All Russia will be better for it. You can't conduct modern business in a medieval state ruled by one man."

Valery looked at Gladishev. "I warn you, I have utterly no intentions of forming a parliamentary government."

"What about the Duma? Surely—"

"*If* I overthrow His Majesty the Czar and form a government, the Duma may sit and advise. *I* will act."

Ash glanced at Tamara. *If?* Was Valery merely cautious in front of Gladishev? But the expression on her face said she worried that the grand duke was cooling about his conspiracy. Typical. Ash had come to know him better in the course of preparing him to join with Gladishev and meeting with regiment commanders. Valery's response to adversity seemed to be to withdraw. And his blustering often masked retreat. No Bonaparte, the Grand Duke Valery . . .

The sleigh followed the gracefully curving Morskaya Street under a gigantic arch that connected the two wings of the General Staff Building and pulled up beside the huge Alexander Column in Palace Square at Valery's command. Ash looked at Tamara. This was the square, site of the Bloody Sunday massacre, that Valery's supporters would have to hold while he formed a government in the Winter Palace. The grand duke looked about somberly, taking in Gladishev last.

The millionaire spread his hands. "Many members of the Duma will agree wholeheartedly with Your Highness's position—"

"Good."

"Many others will not."

"And you?"

"Many highly respected *leaders* of the parties will not agree."

"And you?" Valery repeated. Tamara laid a calming hand on his sleeve.

"One man cannot rule a modern country."

"Then we have nothing more to talk about."

"Valery, wait—"

Gladishev raised a finger. *"Pardon,* mademoiselle. If I might." He turned to Valery. "However, I crave order. We are on the edge of revolution. *We* responsible people must act before the revolutionaries do. I crave order, Your Highness, it is mandatory—"

"Your order," Valery snapped. "Not mine."

Gladishev eyed the grand duke. "I won't let you off so easily. I am willing to compromise."

"What?"

"You have a responsibility to lead a coup, Your Highness."

"You dare to tell me my responsibility?"

"I dare to help."

Valery blinked, and Ash and Tamara began to hope again. They could see the grand duke responding to Gladishev's shrewd blandishments.

"Then help, support me, bring your Duma colleagues to the, Winter Palace. Instruct them to—"

"It's not that simple, Your Highness. There are pockets of democracy already in Russia and one is in the Duma. I cannot *instruct* fellow members to do anything. I can only try to persuade."

"Then persuade them."

"Give me some ammunition."

"What kind of ammunition?"

"Good ministers. The men you appoint will either save Russia, or lose her forever. We have no more time for fools."

"I will appoint good men."

Gladishev wet his lips and glanced at Tamara. "Your Highness, could you mention one or two names."

"Valery . . . go on, darling, you've made good decisions."

The grand duke was clearly not enjoying being put on the spot. Tamara closed her gloved hand on his arm again. "Tell him . . ."

Valery sat up straighter. "The Grand Duke Nicholas will take command of the army again. Brusilov second in command."

Gladishev nodded. "The troops seem to like the grand duke and Brusilov wins battles."

"Skobeleff will be foreign minister."

Skobeleff had been Ash's idea—the young career diplomat had been a vociferous supporter of the Allies before Rasputin exiled him—and Valery had bought the idea. "Excellent," Gladishev said. "But have you considered who will take the vital Interior post?"

"Rodzyanko." Valery named the current president of the Duma.

Gldishev laughed in genuine admiration. "You'll silence your worst critic by placing him in your own government. It's a wonderful idea if he accepts the post . . . have you thought of a ministry for Kerensky?"

"A *post* for Kerensky?"

"As leader of the Trudovik Labor Party, Kerensky is one of the most powerful members of the Duma, perhaps a bit radical—"

"A *bit* radical? The scaffold will be a perfect post for Kerensky."

Gladishev's good-humored mouth tightened. "Kerensky is a good man. Many people will rally to him. You can't go about hanging elected representatives as if the year were seventeen hundred and you were Peter the Great."

The grand duke said nothing.

Gladishev pressed on. "In order to manage a shift of power without undermining the stability of the government you are obliged to make your revolt as nonviolent as possible. You can't hang your opponents, you must follow the rule of law—"

"You sound like Commander Ash, here. All for stability. But stability and power go hand in hand. I will leave Kerensky be—if he stays out of trouble."

Gladishev looked out at the Winter Palace. Here and there the dark red paint was scaling away, revealing not stone but weathered plaster of paris crumbling from the damp. Valery waited, his silence daring Gladishev to find fault with his plans for Kerensky. He was feeling pleasantly in charge.

Dmitri Dan timed how long it took a shovelful of snow to fall from the top of the arch, which connected the two wings of the General Staff Building, to the square below. The assassin had perched himself among the galloping bronze horses of the triumphal chariot on top of the arch, nearly eighty feet above the ground. Grand Duke Valery's red sleigh was clearly visible in the lights that spilled from the thousands of windows in the walls around the square. In the sleigh sat four people, the grand duke, beside him a large man in a civilian coat, a woman Dmitri assumed was Tamara Tishkova and Commander Ash.

Dmitri had been stalking the American at the nearby Preobrajenski Barracks, where Red Snow observers had seen Ash several days running. He had already disguised himself as a *moujik,* a faceless peasant with a snow shovel and a lunchpail looped over the handle. But instead of a poor man's pound of moldy bread—a day's sustenance, if he were careful— Dmitri had stuffed his pail with rusty nails and fulminate of mercury, a highly unstable, powerful explosive ordinarily used to detonate dynamite because it went off on contact.

The Red Snow leader had been surprised to see the grand duke's sleigh trundle into Palace Square and stop in the middle beside the Alexander Column. Dmitri Dan had stared so hard that he almost gave himself away. *Moujiks* did not stare. *Moujiks* slumped in exhaustion or they worked. Dmitri had bent to his shovel. Ash and a Romanov together. Two birds with one stone.

But the Cossack outriders were the usual deterrent. A skilled horseman wielding a ten-foot lance tipped by a razor-sharp twenty-inch blade commanded a dangerously large area. Dmitri Dan was afraid of very little, but when one looked at the grand duke's escort with a practical eye one saw oneself slipping and sliding over acres of snow-and-ice-covered cobblestones chased by riders who had galloped bareback on the steppes before they had learned to walk.

Shooting several in an attempt to get close enough with the bomb was futile while the others were at large. As well as lances, each had a carbine slung over his shoulder. The grand duke turned out to be less vulnerable than he appeared, when one tried to kill him.

But then, when the sleigh hadn't moved after several minutes, it occurred to Dmitri that the normally cautious grand duke had made a bad mistake. It was getting dark, and if the Romanov kept to his usual habits, when he did move he would go directly to the Imperial Yacht Club for his evening cocktail. If he did there was only one logical route—back to Morskaya Street under the arch between the wings of the General Staff Building.

Dmitri had hurried into a service entrance of the General Staff Building, waved his shovel at the guards and shuffled to a back staircase, up which he raced to the roof. Seeing the sleigh still in place, he began shoveling snow over the edge, as other *moujiks* were doing on the palace and barracks roofs, timing the drop, calculating by how much to lead the sleigh when it moved in range of his bomb.

When Gladishev spoke again he had apparently decided to drop the subject of how the grand duke would handle Duma member and Labor Party leader Kerensky.

"If I were to support you I would need your word that autocracy would not last forever—a solemn promise that you will bring Russia's government more into line with modern practices—"

"I've made it clear to Commander Ash that my government will appear more benign than the present government so that his nation might be persuaded to enter the war. But I will tell you, Monsieur Duma Member, that my autocracy, as you call it, will last as long as Russia needs it."

"The people who support your coup will reserve the right to review that need—"

"*Russia* is my concern, and Russia has always fared best under a strong Czar. Peter, Catherine, the Alexanders Two and Three. Strong Czars made the power you see here." His big hand swept the circle of buildings that ringed Palace Square. The great semicircle of the General Staff Building—divided by the arch—the Imperial Archives and the barracks of the Preobrajenski Regiment loomed on the south and east sides. The gigantic yellow Admiralty blocked the west. North, the dark red Winter Palace hid all but a sliver of the snow-covered Neva, darkened to mauve as the sun settled earthward through a thickening scrim of cirrus cloud.

"Power forged by strong Czars, the power to build all this from nothing in a cold, stinking swamp—"

"Illusion, a hollow shell," Gladishev broke in.

"*Illusion?* A thousand rooms in that palace alone are packed with Russia's wealth and her prizes of war. We are not like ordinary nations that have to scramble around the world establishing distant, undefendable empires. We have multiplied our empire. In only a hundred years the Black Sea steppes, the Polish provinces, the Ukraine, the Crimea, Transcaucasia, Bessarabia, Finland, Amur . . . the list is endless."

"This is not true power," Gladishev insisted. "This is only, forgive me, the cream skimmed from an enormous vat of milk."

"Then where is the power?"

Gladishev pointed east. "Out there. The power in Russia is numbers. The peasants in their numbers have power. There are simply too many of them and not enough of us—forgive me if I include myself in your number, but in these terms I am hardly a peasant and I too have empires to defend. There are too many Russian peasants for one man to feed and clothe and control. All those victories? Too many borders to defend. We've won everything, you say, but we can't *hold* it, administer it without a modern government."

A lone figure trudged across the square. As was common in winter in many of the vast spaces of the flat and open city, the square was empty except for the man walking and the grand duke's sleigh, his restless horses and silent outriders still as ice sculpture. The only other motion in the square were plumes of snow falling from the triumphal arch where a *moujik* was shoveling snow from a level just under the bronze horses.

As the figure neared the furthest outrider, Ash felt a rush of excitement. He recognized Sirotkin—the captain of the Preobrajenski Life Guards— the one he'd been negotiating with for units of his regiment to hold the Palace Square. Sirotkin was wrapped in a dark cloak with no insignia. But what was he doing out here without a horse or carriage?

Sirotkin glanced inside the sleigh but didn't slow down as he kept going toward the arch that led to Morskaya Street. Only after he had passed close to the last Cossack and the rider had turned toward the sleigh did Ash realize that Sirotkin had handed something to the horseman, who brought it to a footman, who brought it to the grand duke. An envelope.

Valery tore it open. He glanced at Ash and for a moment his little blue eyes gleamed and a half-smile played beneath his mustache.

You cagey old bear, Ash thought. That's why we're freezing out here. The grand duke, always a little more complex than he appeared, had promised the Life Guard Captain Sirotkin Duma support and had used this debate—the ultimate result of which Ash still couldn't be sure of—to flaunt the Moscow millionaire Sergei Gladishev to Sirotkin. In spite of himself, Ash felt almost as proud of Valery as Tamara looked to be. He had to remind himself repeatedly that the grand duke was no fool.

Valery now pointed in the direction of the Preobrajenski Barracks, his expression speaking victory. "The autocrat is not alone, just because he doesn't have a so-called modern government. The Czar-autocrat's army protects his borders. The Life Guards protect the Czar. His Cossacks maintain order among the peasants. And the Czar's police control the cities—"

"Not anymore." Gladishev shook his head. "And we've lost at least two armies to the Germans. When will the third walk home? As for your Life Guards? Conscripts and officers dragged up from the lower ranks. The old aristocratic corps died in nineteen fourteen."

Valery nodded reluctant agreement, Gladishev pressed his point. "Even the Cossacks have fallen before the Germans."

"But a strong Czar can repair the damage," Valery protested. "A strong Czar not bothered by squabbling politicians."

"I would agree, *if* the destruction of Russian fighting forces were the real problem."

"What is, then?"

Gladishev glanced around the square. "Look at those windows."

Thousands upon thousands of windows were beginning to glow dim yellow as the dusk deepened, to shine in the endless sweep of the General Staff Building, the Archives and the Admiralty. "Behind each window a dozen clerks—little men in shabby coats who write reports all day long

335

about places they'll never see, people they'll never know, ships they'll never sail. Seventy thousand little men to administer our empire of one hundred and eighty million—our towns and villages, distant cities, railroads, post offices and schools, our armies and navies. They copy documents they don't understand and when they are deemed wise and trustworthy after many years service they are promoted to *stamp* the documents and affix seals."

"You agreed my selection of ministers was progressive," Valery said.

"It requires more than a few talented ministers. One-man rule has smothered the natural growth of *efficient* bureaucracy, which must be nurtured by good ministers *and* representatives elected by the very people who will be administered."

He pointed east again. "No one knows what's going on out there. What is Russia doing? What does Russia need? The first the Czar knew that Russia hadn't a modern navy was when the Japanese sent His Imperial Fleet to the bottom of the Tsushima Straits. The first the Czar knows that the peasants in some region are displeased is when they burn our estates. The first the Czar-autocrat knew his army had no rifles was when the Germans slaughtered us in Poland. The first the Czar knew our railroads were decrepit was when we tried to feed our soldiers and cities at the same time. You remember, Your Highness, before the war when a clerk lost a single salary voucher and schoolteachers in some eastern province nobody had ever heard of starved to death?"

Valery shouted angrily at the coachman and the sleigh lurched into motion, swung in a broad circle and headed back toward the arch in the General Staff Building. Ash elbowed Gladishev. Last chance. Gladishev didn't need much encouraging. He tapped the grand duke's sleeve, ignored Valery's glare and said, "Look at that window. It could be any of a hundred. If God came down to the province that civil servant administers and turned every man, woman and child to pillars of salt, the first the Czar's Imperial Bureaucracy would know would be when the price of salt fell in the neighboring provinces. *One man can't rule Russia.*"

Valery shook him off. "One man will try."

"He'll try alone. Stop the sleigh, damn you."

"Wait," Ash said.

Gladishev jumped down, caught his balance and walked off.

"Stop the sleigh," Tamara said. *"Stop it."*

Ash jumped after Gladishev. "Wait. Monsieur Gladishev . . ." He looked back. Tamara had persuaded Valery to stop just short of the General Building arch. He caught up with Gladishev. "Please, wait. His Highness is aware that I share your strongest reservations about autocracy. It's anathema to an American. But at the moment I feel it's *most* important to win this war and hold off the revolutionaries."

Gladishev was fuming. "Do you think I give a damn what an American thinks?"

"Maybe you'd like to start your own palace coup?"

"*Ach.*"

"He offers a chance for stability."

"What are you doing here, Ash?"

"I told you. My country wants a solid ally in Russia when we intervene in the war."

"And you think that terrapin brain is your man?"

Ash glanced at the sleigh. Tamara peeked over the side and shook her head. No luck with Valery either. "The war is killing Russia. Help me get the Czar out and America in and we'll end the damned thing in a year. The grand duke is man enough to be beholden to you. Make your peace now. Work out the details later."

"Details? He wants to be Czar of all the Russias, just like the one we've got."

In disgust, Ash looked skyward . . . and caught motion from the corner of his eye, focused on it and saw a figure lean out from the bronze horses on top of the arch. A man gripping one of the bronze hoofs and swinging something from his free hand, eighty feet above the sleigh where the grand duke sat arguing with Tamara—

"Oh, my God . . ."

42

Ash reached under his boat cloak. But the distance was too much for the short-barreled Luger.

"Gladishev, listen to me."

"No, enough, I'm going home."

Ash gripped the millionaire's arm and propelled him toward the nearest rider. "Gladishev, there is a man with a bomb on the arch. Tell this Cossack to shoot. Do it *now.*"

Gladishev wasted a vital moment looking up before he spoke Russian to the rider, who reacted with speed, flipping his slung rifle off his back, snicking open the bolt action and firing in a blur of fluid motion. The figure ducked, appeared ten feet to the side and threw his bomb. As it plummeted out of the dark sky, Ash got his Luger out and snapped two shots over the ears of the white Arabians . . .

"Valery you are being imposs—"

Three quick shots interrupted Tamara's outburst. The sleigh jerked forward, hurling her back against the seat. She heard a heavy boom, something rattled against the back of the sleigh. A horse screamed. She jumped up to look about. A Cossack was down and his screaming animal lay kicking on its side, disemboweled by shrapnel. The other horsemen were shooting up at the arch. She saw Ash running, so remarkably small and vulnerable on foot. Valery yanked her to the seat and threw his body over hers. More shots. The sleigh stopped inside the archway. The horse's screaming echoed on the walls, and the rage she felt for the kind of human being who could do that to a horse was directed at Gladishev . . . how could he believe that a Duma could stop the mindless violence in the Russian soul? Horseshoes rang on the cobblestones. From underneath Valery she caught a glimpse of the Cossacks blocking the ends of the archway. The shooting died down. A final sharp pistol crack and the horse stopped screaming.

Valery got up cautiously.

Ash dragged Gladishev into the passage and helped him up to the sleigh. He had a gun in his hand. His eyes met Tamara's.

"Are you all right?" she asked, choking off the word *darling*.

"Yes . . . you?" His eyes went to the mouth of the passage as the lieutenant of the guard clattered in; his men stayed in the square, aiming their rifles at the arch, trying to seek out the bombers.

"How is the rider?" Valery asked.

"The man is wounded, the horse dead, Your Highness."

The Cossack lieutenant, Valery and Ash quickly agreed to make a run for the Yacht Club across the Nevsky on the Morskaya while the outriders covered the top of the arch with their rifles. Several raced through the passage to take up position in front of the sleigh. The coachman called out and the Arabians burst from the passage. Tamara looked up, spine tingling in anticipation of the next attack.

They made it safely to the Nevsky, where they picked up a police escort. Gladishev gripped Valery's arm. "This *proves* things have gone too far, Your Highness. I will support you . . . for stability . . ."

Valery took his hand. "For Russia."

Tamara looked at Valery's determined face and believed that Czarism could still work, with a *real* Czar.

Ash decided not to spoil the new friendship by suggesting that the bomb was probably Red Snow's, and meant for him. Ironic, that an attempt on his life had apparently ended in making an alliance . . . never mind how temporary . . . between the two forces he so badly needed to bring off his mission . . .

Okhrana detectives slipped into Count von Basel's office in the Litovsky Prison to report Ash's movements. Some recited from memory, others read from their notebooks, but each of the Czar's policemen shed whatever swagger he affected on the streets of Petrograd when he addressed the cold-eyed security officer he knew only as Captain Moskolenko.

"Commander Ash was seen entering the home of the ballerina Tishkova. A short time later His Royal Highness the Grand Duke Valery arrived, having crossed the ice in his sleigh. In ten minutes, the Grand Duke Valery Romanov and Commander Ash came out together and rode across the river. They entered the Imperial Yacht Club at five o'clock and stayed for many hours." . . . "Heinrich Ballin, a waiter at the Imperial Yacht Club, was questioned. Ballin reported that Commander Ash and the Grand Duke Valery sat by a fire talking for hours and drinking little." . . . "It is reported by the assistant to the Imperial Yacht Club secretary that Commander Ash has been given a temporary membership in the club at the request of the Grand Duke Valery." . . . "Commander Ash was observed entering the British Embassy at noon. He reappeared half an hour later and lunched . . ."

Von Basel received their reports with brusque ill humor; the Kaiser's new plan to seize the Czar himself put the scheme to rescue Nicholas II in an entirely new light, and von Basel himself in a much more demanding role. Helping Ash at the Kaiser's request had been a sideshow, running concurrently with von Basel's military spying. Now it was center stage and the plot led not only to victory in war but ultimately to control of Germany. The Kaiser's plan rendered Kenneth Ash and Ash's progress vital. But Ash was annoyingly independent, close-mouthed and secretive, which put von Basel in the difficult position of having to keep track of what Ash was doing, partly to make sure he did not pull off any peculiar moves, and partly to keep him from blundering into trouble. This was, after all, and despite its many problems, still Russia, and Russia's rulers had never taken kindly to revolt, nor, if one looked at history, had they been all that susceptible to it.

When von Basel had pressed Ash for his plans—for details beyond the basic plan to dynamite the lines in and out to Tsarskoye Selo, seize the Winter Palace and have the Grand Duke Valery proclaim himself Czar in the presence of key Duma members, Ash had replied that he would tell von Basel when and where he needed police support and when to send the German U-boat escort to Murmansk. He had reminded von Basel that it was his show, not the Germans. Von Basel suspected that his sudden trip to Berlin had made Ash suspicious . . .

So it was a very anxious von Basel who received the detectives' reports in the guise of their own Captain Moskolenko.

"Commander Ash was seen entering the American Embassy. He left the premises some time later with the American ambassador's daughter, Catherine Hazzard, and took her by hired carriage to Berrin's in Morsakaya Street, where she ate sponge cake and ice cream and Commander Ash smoked cigarettes and drank coffee. His cup was obtained in the kitchen. The contents revealed no spirits added, but the ashtray contained many cigarette butts and it was the opinion of the observer that Commander Ash was anxious." . . . "Our man inside the American Embassy reports that shortly after Ash was there the British King's Messenger arrived with messages for Ambassador Hazzard and took messages for London in return. Ash had entered with a small despatch case which he was not in possession of when he left with the ambassador's daughter." ... "Commander Ash and Captain Putilov of the Ismailovsky Guard went ice yachting at the River Yacht Club on Krestovsky Island. Police Detective Borisov, who was captain of the Third District ice-yachting team before the war, commandeered a second yacht to follow Ash and Putilov. Commander Ash proved elusive and eventually drew the pursuing boat into a lead—"

"A lead?"

"A break in the pack ice, Captain Moskolenko, in this case a very narrow one between high walls of pack ice into which Police Detective Borisov crashed his commandeered yacht. The steward of the River Yacht Club expressed—"

"Dismissed."

". . . Captain Sirotkin of the Preobrajenski Guard, the Grand Duke Valery and Commander Ash went shooting on the estate of Baroness Balmont. No, Captain Moskolenko, the Italian was in Moscow." ... "Heinrich Ballin, employed as a waiter at the Imperial Yacht Club, reports that Ash and the Grand Duke Valery held a long discussion with Captain Putilov of the Ismailovsky Guard Regiment—"

"Bring this Heinrich Ballin." . . .

It always amazed von Basel how disheveled servants were in even the best establishments in Russia. The waiter stood forlornly in front of his desk, staring at the stone floor, expecting the worst. His clothes were dirty, his hair unkempt, his rheumy old eyes and dripping nose a clarion not to drink or eat from anything he had touched. And this was what the grand dukes of Russia allowed to serve them in their most exclusive club.

"How old are you?"

"Sixty-seven, Captain Moskolenko, and never have I been in trouble."

"Where were you born?"

"Riga."

"Your name and accent are German."

"I moved to Petrograd when I was two years old, Captain Moskolenko. For the past sixty-five years I have lived and worked in this city. And never have I been in trouble."

"For whom have you worked?"

Heinrich Ballin straightened up. "I have served in all the great homes of Petrograd. At all the balls and all the dinners."

Von Basel knew the German waiters of Petrograd—even one as awful as this one—were far superior to the Russian *moujiks*. It was not uncommon to see the same waiter at three different parties in a week, each night wearing the livery of the house that had temporarily hired him.

341

"But the war with Germany makes difficulties for you, doesn't it?"

"Yes, Captain. They don't always believe I am a loyal Russian."

"Well you've a chance to prove your loyalty," von Basel said with a chilly smile, and proceeded to extract from the frightened old man everything he had overheard between Ash, the grand duke, Captain Putilov, Captain Sirotkin of the Preobrajenski Guard and several other grand dukes with whom Valery was known to be close. It wasn't so much, but every bit helped in trying to keep even with what Ash was up to. He wanted no more surprises like the one in the Moscow District, where Ash, having gone into the slums with Vera Sedovina the ballerina, had disappeared from surveillance. The Okhrana detective assigned to him that afternoon had been set upon by hooligans who had taken his badge, gun and notebook and had broken his legs.

Shortly after that there had been a gun battle with revolutionaries, Kirichenko reportedly among them, but von Basel did not know whether Ash had made contact with the fighting squad leader. Ash had, however, hidden a truckload of dynamite outside the city, which the Okhrana explosive expert von Basel had sent to investigate reported was set to explode if disturbed. Von Basel had the truck under observation. Ash had asked him for help when he returned from Berlin, but merely the distraction of a police station near the Winter Palace on an as yet unspecified date, though Ash had suggested that von Basel prepare the German U-boat escort to be within a week's sailing of Murmansk.

Then more reports. A bombing . . . "Ash and Mademoiselle Tishkova were joined by Duma member Sergei Gladishev at three o'clock at Berrin's . . . the Grand Duke Valery's sleigh . . . an hour in Palace Square. A bomb from the General Staff Building—"

"What?"

"From the arch in the center, Captain Moskolenko. Only a Cossack hurt, by a miracle. The assassin escaped into one of the wings of the General Staff Building."

"Where were *you?*" von Basel snapped. What if Ash had been killed? The Kaiser's plan would die with the American. He needed Ash to do his dirty work, and take the blame.

"Across the square, observing, sir. As ordered."

Ash's luck had held again . . . *Gladishev.* Ash was getting close. The American and the grand duke were making the right contacts, building an alliance with the Duma, the Life Guards, the police through himself, and maybe Kirichenko. Soon, now . . . then suddenly a worrisome mystery. A very nervous detective who covered the railway stations reported. Von Basel could tell from his fear alone that it was bad news . . .

"Commander Ash was observed embarking from the Baltic Station. He previously purchased a train ticket for Reval. This information was sent by telegraph to Reval. When the train arrived, however, detectives waiting for Commander Ash apparently lost sight of him in the crowds of passengers—"

"For how long?"

"That was last night." The detective squirmed. "Unfortunately, Captain Moskolenko, sir, Commander Ash has not been resighted as yet."

"Get *out.*"

"The detectives in Reval are being severely reprimanded."

"Out." Von Basel was so angry he almost said *raus.*

Why did Ash go to Reval? *Apparently lost sight of him?* Ash allowed himself to be watched. Why did he suddenly change his mind in Reval? What was in Reval?

But before he had time to put more thought to the problem, an immediate and potentially deadly conundrum took its place. As a precaution, to protect the grand ducal conspiracy, von Basel had put surveillance on the growing number of conspirators themselves, among them Lord Exeter, the Grand Duke Valery, Tishkova, Captain Sirotkin and Captain Putilov. This last, the captain in the Ismailovsky Life Guard Regiment, was suddenly in serious trouble, trouble which threatened the entire conspiracy.

Another branch of the Okhrana which specialized in army loyalty had learned that Captain Putilov was persuading his officers to join in an as yet unnamed grand ducal palace coup. The Okhrana was debating whether to keep listening for more specific information concerning the identity of the grand duke in question or to arrest Captain Putilov and wring it out of him by interrogation. General Globatchev, chief of the Okhrana, was himself taking charge of the inquiry, which meant, von Basel feared, that Captain Putilov would be spilling his guts in damned short order, naming the Grand Duke Valery and Commander Kenneth Ash.

43

The ancient Baltic harbor of Reval, a town of narrow cobblestone streets and medieval houses, had been an important Russian port before the German navy sealed the Gulf of Finland. It was two hundred miles west of Petrograd, near the mouth of the gulf. The journey across Estonia had taken Ash thirteen hours crammed into a freezing train compartment with a half-dozen officers of the Czar's Motor Division who were trying to get back to the front's volatile northern sector. The German army, they told Ash, now threatened Riga itself, a city less than four hundred miles from the Russian capital.

On arrival Ash had shaken off von Basel's detectives and hid the rest of the night on a cot in the hall of a second-class hotel. In the morning he set out for the harbor, where he located the Royal Navy submarine base —and the depot ship *Dwina*, moored to a guarded, fenced pier.

A half-dozen smallish E-class British submarines nuzzled around the depot ship, which housed fuel, crew quarters, supplies and repair facilities. Thick coats of glistening ice softened the harsh, spiky lines of hulls and conning towers. The crews were making repairs in the sunshine—welding and beating steel with hammers. The clanging echoed to the foot of the pier, where the guards stopped Ash and made him wait until Rodney Skelton was located. He came jauntily into the guardhouse a half hour later.

"Yes, that's him, sergeant. He's harmless. How are you, Kenneth?"

"Hope I'm not interrupting anything," Ash said, indicating Skelton's greasy jumper and trousers.

"Just a major overhaul."

344

They walked out on the pier and Skelton proudly pointed out his boat. "Nasty little brute, isn't she?"

The submarine had a massive dent in its conning tower, as if something enormous and angry had punched it.

"What'd you do, surface under the *Dwina*?"

"Very amusing, Commander. I understand it's hell in Petrograd since the Czar banned the Tango."

"Rodney, what would you say if I told you you owed me your life for that time in India?"

To Ash's surprise, Skelton didn't bridle. To the contrary . . . he suddenly looked exhausted. "This bloody war . . . I feel different about a lot of things. Just between you and me, I guess the Indians would have slit our throats along with those poor horses . . . you were right." He looked up at Ash, openly for a second, before his feisty grin ended the confession. "Should I thank you?"

"No . . . but I do want a favor . . ."

Back in Petrograd, Ash telephoned Captain Putilov from the Baltic Railroad Station and walked across the Obvodney Canal to the Life Guard Ismailovsky barracks on Ismailovsky Prospect. Petrograd tram drivers had called a one-day strike, so the sidewalks were jammed with pedestrians.

Putilov was waiting, as planned, outside the barrack walls. Ash liked him. Putilov affected the lazy, bored air of a typical aristocrat officer, but it was a sham which the record and his character bore out. Wounded in Poland, and again the previous summer taking Stanislau during Brusilov's offensive, Putilov had refused medical retirement and, against his will, took his present post in Petrograd to recuperate sufficiently to be allowed back at the Front.

Unlike others Ash and the grand duke had tried to recruit, who were afraid to take the risk, Putilov's reservations derived from his oath of fealty to the Czar. He recognized the need to act to save Russia, but breaking his word was for him a deadly serious matter of honor.

Once he had finally come around, however, he had totally embraced the Grand Duke Valery's cause. Valery, who was unnervingly straightforward himself, had warned Putilov twice to be more discreet, and had finally confessed to Ash that he couldn't risk meeting Putilov anymore. Ash had agreed to make the next contact to assess what support they could expect from the units under Putilov's command.

It was dangerous. Putilov's natural honesty and ingrained bravery made him rather too careless a conspirator . . .

He waited now outside the main gates of the Ismailovsky barracks looking for all the world like a czar's officer preparing to review troops in full sight of the entire general staff.

He saluted Ash as Ash emerged from the crowds on the sidewalk, took Ash's hand, pumped his arm and started to proclaim in his fortunately, soft, aristocratic drawl that he had a half dozen subalterns eager to join their conspiracy. Ash steered him quickly into the crowds, scanning faces as he did. Almost immediately he was glad he had taken the precaution of putting on the fur hat and greatcoat he had worn in Reval to elude von Basel's men. The U.S. Navy service cap and boat cloak were too damned distinctive and were wrapped in his bag which he had sent back to the Astoria before leaving the Baltic Station. He suggested they walk.

"You're quiet this afternoon, Commander," Putilov remarked after they had gone several blocks.

"We're being followed. Don't—"

But the Russian aristocrat was already looking around like a tourist from Moscow. Among the throngs of pedestrians Ash had spotted the long raincoat and galoshes that usually marked the Okhrana detectives. What worried him was the man didn't seem to be making much of an effort to stay out of sight. He spotted a second and then a third, strolling purposefully after them. They looked less like they were following than pursuing. As if preparing to make an arrest.

Ash and Putilov were walking north, heading in the direction of the Astoria Hotel about a mile ahead. Ash looked for a place to hide. Immediately ahead was the Fontanka River. A block to the right, the Technological Institute.

"Closed today because of the strike," Putilov replied calmly when Ash suggested it. He was a compact man in his forties, with an open, innocent face; his wounds had left him pale, with a tremor in his cheek which his smile tended to obscure. "Are you sure we're being followed?"

"Damned sure," Ash said. "And they're closing up." He glanced over his shoulder. Half a block back the detectives were moving swiftly through the crowds, shoving people out of their way. Suddenly a long black automobile shot from behind a line of wagons, screeched in a tight turn over the tram tracks and slid against the curb beside Ash and Captain Putilov.

"Don't run," Ash said. "It'll only make them ask why."

"I won't," Putilov replied, squaring his shoulders.

But instead of police officers boiling out of the town car to arrest them, the window opened in the driver's compartment and Count Philip von Basel snapped, "Get in, they're on to you."

Ash yanked open the rear door, shoved a confused Putilov inside and jumped in after him. The car roared from the curb followed by the Okhrana men on foot, pushing people out of their way until one pulled a gun,

346

fired it in the air, which cleared a path as people dove for cover, then fired at the car.

Von Basel wrenched the large vehicle onto the narrow street beside the Fontanka, raced along it for several blocks, turned north, skidding and screeching the tires, shot over an Obvodny Canal bridge and started past the Baltic Station. The car hit an ice slick in the station square, slid out of control, spun in a full circle and slammed sideways into a tram-wire pole. The engine shuddered, coughed. Von Basel tried to coax it back to life as uniformed police officers came running from the station. It abruptly revved up again and he drove through them, past the station and deep into the Narva District.

"Who is this man?" Captain Putilov demanded.

"A friend, with police connections. It seems the Okhrana had a spy in your barracks."

The car went down lanes barely wider than it was, scattering peddlers and women lined up outside bakeries and kerosene shops. People fled, but none protested; they looked too beaten down to complain.

Von Basel turned abruptly into a noisome alley and got out. "Come quickly before the local police find it."

Ash led a bewildered Putilov after von Basel as the Kaiser's man hurried down the grimmest streets Ash had seen in Petrograd, or in any other city, for that matter. Drunks filled the gutters and vacant-eyed children huddled together for warmth. The sky appeared a dirty slit of gray between the leaning tenements.

"Where is he taking us?" Captain Putilov asked; he had the Russian gift for somehow not noticing misery, yet when a beggar raised an open hand with what appeared to be his last strength, Putilov, despite the fact that police were hunting him for the first time in his life, dropped a few kopecks into the shaking palm.

Von Basel stopped now in a doorway, motioned them both through, checked the street and bolted the door. He hurried down a half flight of stairs, and they emerged in a cavelike cellar with a heavy, vaulted ceiling blackened by smoke and mottled where pieces of plaster had broken off. Thin partitions formed cubbyholes with plank beds. There was one square window, high up in the wall, covered with ice.

"What is this?" asked Putilov.

"Home for the *boysaki*," von Basel told him. "The barefoot. Dock workers, when the port isn't iced in. The dregs."

"What—"

"This is for you," von Basel interrupted, handing Captain Putilov a sheet of paper he pulled from his coat. Puzzled, Ash watched an equally puzzled Putilov move closer to the smoking oil lamp. He read a few lines. "What is this about Grand Duke Dmitri Pav—"

Von Basel had followed. A dagger appeared in his left hand. He slid it quickly in and out of Putilov's back.

"*What?*" Ash couldn't believe his eyes as the Russian's knees folded and his body drifted quietly to the floor.

"Don't touch that paper."

The paper was clutched in Putilov's stiffening fingers. Ash reached for it. Von Basel whipped his sword out of his stick and touched the point to Ash's neck. "Don't," he repeated. "The Okhrana was going to pick him up. When they made him talk it would have ruined everything for us." Von Basel sheathed the thin sliver of whippy steel. "You must protect yourself. Go immediately to the Astoria. Go to the bar and have drinks with people. Stay in view. If the police question you, insist you walked from the Baltic Station to the Astoria and talked to no one. Get rid of that coat and hat, and stick by your story. They can't be sure what they saw in the crowds. If they're stubborn, go to your embassy."

"What's on that paper?"

"I had a forger construct a simple note from Captain Putilov to the Grand Duke Dmitri Pavlovitch informing His Royal Highness that he has changed his mind about supporting Grand Duke Dmitri's coup."

"*Whose* coup?"

"Some of the Grand Duke Dmitri Pavlovitch's cousins tried to convince him to lead a coup. They've gone so far as to approach regiment commanders, as you have. The grand duke, I understand, has refused to lay hands on the Czar—perhaps because he hasn't my help and yours," von Basel added with a thin smile, "to remove His Majesty—but the Okhrana is already onto the plot. You would do well to pray that this little charade convinces the investigators that Putilov was recruiting conspirators for Grand Duke Dmitri and not your Valery. Let the police presume he wasn't trusted."

"You didn't have to kill the man—"

"It was him or you, Ash. And I need you alive. They would have forced a confession, he'd have named you . . . as well as the Grand Duke Valery. *And* your friend Tishkova."

Ash stared at Putilov's body. He had no answer to that last.

Von Basel wiped his dagger on the dead captain's trousers and slipped it back into his coat. He tapped Ash's arm with his walking stick. "Get to the Astoria." When Ash didn't move quickly enough for him, he added, "Do you think the Okhrana would treat her any more kindly in their cells just because she happens to be a beautiful woman?"

Ash started for the stairs.

"By the way, Commander Ash . . ."

As Ash turned, von Basel thought how seriously Ash took death. It put the American at a disadvantage . . .

"What did you do in Reval?"

"The grand duke wanted me to meet a general from the Northern Sector. Reval was a convenient halfway point . . ."

What Ash had hoped would sound like a plausible reason, masking his real purpose in Reval, was to give von Basel considerable pause about Grand Duke Valery. At first von Basel puzzled over Ash's reply; the American had answered a little too quickly for a man as upset as he had appeared, and the stated reason for going to Reval had a somewhat glib ring . . . *but* if it were true, von Basel began to worry as he negotiated the dark streets of the Narva District, were it true that the Grand Duike Valery was including Russia's line commanders in his conspiracy, it pointed up a serious flaw in the Kaiser's scheme to win the war and take back control of Germany.

Grand Duke Valery would make a good Czar. Too good a Czar.

Von Basel had already hinted at the possibility in Berlin. Might the grand duke not rally Russia to a new war effort? The Kaiser had considered it unlikely that a usurper could replace a rightful heir without disrupting the already faltering nation. Perhaps, von Basel had agreed reluctantly . . . but at the moment Valery Romanov seemed to be conducting the grand ducal conspiracy in a step-by-step manner that was a little frightening in its purposefulness. Valery was becoming a threat . . .

Ash spent the evening in the Astoria Bar waiting to be arrested by the Okhrana. He ate dinner alone at a center table in the hotel dining room, then returned to the bar, where he bought champagne for any officer or foreign newspaperman who came along. At midnight he carried a half-empty champagne bottle through the lobby up to his suite to the horror of the hotel staff and the knowing smiles of the drunks.

Once upstairs he dropped the act, sent the floor porter for a brand of mineral water not at his desk and slipped out unnoticed to meet Vera Sedovina, who brought him circuitously to the fighting squad leader Kirchenko. Since the battle with the police, Kirichenko had moved operations to the northeast quadrant of the city and was holed up in the Vyborg District.

His men had chosen sites to blow the line on either side of Tsarskoye Selo; they had manufactured rail mines and had procured a pair of water-cooled machine guns to cover their retreat.

"The *pharon* are watching the dynamite truck," Ash warned him.

"I know. We've already got the four crates. How will you honor your promise?"

"I can get them away from the truck," Ash said.

"I repeat, if anything goes wrong, if you do not deliver on your promise, I will come after you, Commander Ash."

"Nothing will go wrong—"

"And if your government takes you away, I will take Tishkova as a substitute. I assume we understand each other."

44

"No Czar," said President Wilson. "And no Reds either. You *tell* him that, Mr. Banks."

"Mr. President, it seems clear from every report that Russia is about to blow up. Ash's plan might well save the Eastern Front—"

President Wilson cut Banks off with a slashing motion of his bony hand. "I want a *democratic* government in Russia. That is what you told me, Mr. Banks. An end to autocracy so that we might join *decent* Allies. The American people demand and deserve that."

"I said Ash would remove *this* autocrat, Mr. President, if I may be so bold to remind you. The present autocrat Czar Nicholas. But stability— Russia is days from an explosion, sir. Anarchy."

"No Czar."

Banks nodded unhappily, but Wilson was not through. "I cannot understand how an American naval officer could involve himself with one of those corrupt grand dukes. I've looked at Ash's records and am forced to conclude that fifteen years in Europe have somehow unsettled the man, diluted his sense of roots."

Banks jumped at the opportunity. "Perhaps Ash's experience with matters European suggests that the Grand Duke Valery's coup is the best course and in the United States' best interests."

"Violating every principle of free men? No, sir. Inform him. No Czar. No Reds. And when the war is ended, Poland and Finland are to be granted independence."

"Mr. President, you're giving Ash no leeway, no freedom of—"

"I will not compromise on principle. Tell Ash that this grand duke whoever he is must agree in advance to democratic ideals, principles and free elections or the United States will not recognize his government. And if he persists in his plot without such agreement, Commander Ash is to stop the coup."

"*Stop* it?"

"Mr. Banks, how can I ask young American boys to fight overseas for freedom without such a promise? How can I ask the American people to cease opposing intervention? They are still against me in this matter of going to war."

"If I may speak frankly, Mr. President?"

The President removed his eyeglasses, revealing what the glittering lenses had hidden, a stony, unbending gaze. "Of course you may speak frankly, Mr. Banks."

Harold Banks knew if he did so that his days in the backrooms of this administration were numbered. . . but someone had to speak the harsh realities that men of principle like Woodrow Wilson found so convenient to ignore.

"Mr. President, if you send American boys to France, and Russia pulls out of the war because she isn't ready for democracy, those boys will be annihilated."

Wilson returned his glasses to their perch on the bridge of his nose. "Mr. Banks, those who die for peace and democracy die the noblest deaths ever suffered. Remember that, as I do, and get on with it."

Harold Banks went to the Hay-Adams to get drunk.

He had cabled Andrew Hazzard using ciphers and code names they had established before the ex-Pinkerton left with Ash. And he had done his job right, giving Hazzard all the leather he would need to bring Ash under close rein. But he kept imagining what a mess Ash would find himself in having suddenly to stop the conspiracy he had started. His Russian partners were not likely to let him off the hook.

"You look like you lost your best friend, Mr. Banks."

Harold Banks looked up from his fourth bourbon into a pair of shrewd blue-gray eyes smiling under a ledge of brushy white brows. For a second Banks could not believe who had interrupted his morose thoughts. It was too bizarre, so macabre that it had to be a trick. But of course it wasn't. And he realized exactly how the man happened to be in Washington—for weeks President Wilson had been hauling state political leaders of both parties into the Oval Office, twisting arms to get support for intervention in the war.

"Charles Ash." The old man stuck out a large, gnarled hand. "We met at T.R.'s a few times."

Banks felt himself staring. Ash's father was a good three or four inches taller than his son, quite old, white-haired—must have been at least in his forties when he fathered Kenneth—yet the family resemblance was strong in the lean face and powerful nose, small ears and vaguely obstinate jaw. And it was obvious where Ash had picked up the habit of looking straight at you when he spoke.

"Of course, sir," Banks said. "How are you?"

"Fair to middling for an old guy. That's an empty-looking glass you have there."

"Thank you . . . What brings you to Washington?"

"Been in to see the President . . . he's trying harder than ever to shove us into that war."

"The President is also committed to a quick peace," Banks replied automatically.

"So he says." Charles Ash had a rather pronounced southern drawl that softened as he murmured, "Peace without victory? . . . it'll be the first time in the history of warfare . . . 'Course making history kind of excites this President, doesn't it?"

Ordinarily Banks would have greeted that observation with a noncommittal smile. One did not gossip disparagingly about the chief, regardless of one's disappointments. But Charles Ash wasn't the sort to pass around things said seriously over drinks, so Banks said, "President Wilson wants to leave his mark."

"I don't mind a feller wanting to leave a mark, but I do question one who's so darned interested in the *looks* of it . . . he doesn't want to leave a mark so much as the image of a mark."

That, Banks thought, was pretty much true. "May I ask what you told him?"

Ash's father fitted himself against the bar with the natural ease of a man who had hammered out a good many deals on polished mahogany. He nodded thanks to the bartender for refilling their glasses and said, "I told the President there'll be bills due on this war he's never maybe dreamed of. He said he didn't want to see killing any more than any decent man, and I said, no that wasn't the bills due I was talking about. Though I'll tell you, Mr. Banks, I fought in the War of the Rebellion and I've noticed since then that men who haven't gone to war are just a little more anxious to fight one than men who've already had the opportunity." He grinned suddenly and Banks couldn't help smiling back at the charm the old man employed to distill West Virginia's diverse populace into a solid bloc of deliverable votes.

"No, I said, I'm talking about the effect of going to war. Mobilizing America will change this old republic forever. Big government snooping into people's business, standardization of industry—it's all happened in England and France since the war, and it'll happen to us. To fight a big

353

war means big organization, and big organization can mean the death of a democracy. No room to argue, no questions. Do what you're told—"

"But it's going to be worse for democracy if Germany wins."

"Yup . . . but don't forget, if we win the war we're going to win Europe, want it or not. We're going to have to call a lot of shots, help feed and rebuild. The whole damned world will be our responsibility. And I'm not sure that collecting empires will be so good for our republic."

"What did President Wilson say?" Banks asked after the old man had gone silent.

"He said something like that the dictates of humanity demand that an association of nations forge a permanent peace. Sometimes I think President Wilson writes his answers down ahead of a meeting . . . Say!"—he brightened suddenly and turned to Banks—"I got a card from my boy. Did I tell you he's in Petrograd?"

Clinging to the snow in a thin wood a quarter mile from the Tsarskoye Selo line, Ash was with the SR fighting squad leader Kirichenko hiding from a mounted detachment of the First Railway Battalion that trotted slowly by, patrolling the tracks. The rails rode an embankment several feet higher than the snow-covered flatlands between Petrograd and the Czar's village, silhouetting horse soldiers like paper cutouts in a shadow box.

Kirichenko confirmed the time of their passage on a tin pocket watch. "Snow," he said, "is our friend and our enemy. When it falls it covers our mines. When it stops falling, we leave tracks."

Ash had already seen his men retreat from the embankment when the patrol was due, sweeping out their footprints with birch branches. He looked at the sky, lowering for night. "Snow in the morning?"

Tomorrow the Grand Duke Valery was to seize the Winter Palace. Kirichenko's lieutenants had a second group of saboteurs working ten miles south of Tsarskoye Selo, mining tracks and telegraph wires just as they were doing here. "Do you think it will snow?" Ash repeated. Not that they could postpone for the weather. Czar Nicholas was leaving in two days for Mogilev.

Kirichenko shrugged, but one of his constant bodyguards who understood a little English and was apparently a countryman nodded. "Yes, snow."

At the *Stavka*, the Czar would be inviolable. It was now or never.

"Make it a blizzard," Kirichenko said grimly.

The bodyguard looked north in the direction of the Gulf of Finland, from where the heaviest snow came. "Maybe."

"It will still be fairly dark at nine when you set the charges," Ash pointed out. Slightly longer days hinted at spring, which was due by the calendar

354

in little more than a month, though unheralded by either rising temperatures or lessening snow. The sun came up at nine lately on the rare days it was seen at all and hung in the afternoon sky until nearly four, a slight improvement in light unattended by warmth or the promise of warmth. All Ash could see from their hiding place in the wood was snow, ice and more snow broken only by the stubby telegraph poles, their almost invisible strands of black wire and a fence beside the rails.

Kirichenko shook his head. "But I can't arm the mines until daybreak. We don't want an early train setting off mines before your grand duke is sufficiently awake to receive his friends in the Winter Palace."

"He's not quite as dull as you think, Kirichenko."

Kirichenko smiled, obviously not convinced.

He was wrong, thought Ash. Only this afternoon Valery had warned him that they ought to guard Petrograd's main telegraph offices in case revolutionaries considered taking advantage of temporary chaos to send their own messages across Russia and Europe.

"How will you know if my explosions are successful tomorrow morning?" Kirichenko asked when Ash prepared to return to the city.

"I'll know the minute you've cut the line," Ash told him, though he would not know at the moment Valery headed for the palace whether the secondary explosions had the hoped-for effect of holding off the Czar's regiments long enough for Valery to seize control.

Aivazovsky's *The Ninth Wave,* a gigantic seascape portraying the most convincing shipwreck Ash had ever seen in a painting, loomed ominously over the smoking room in the palatial Imperial Yacht Club where several hours later Ash met to confirm final details with the Grand Duke Valery and the captains of the Guards' regiments they had rallied to the support of Valery's palace coup; all the painting showed of the sinking vessel were its mastheads disappearing into a riled sea and a single boat of survivors about to capsize on a broken spar.

Ash and the grand duke sat in armchairs beneath the painting. Facing them was a third chair, and in the center, a low table with vodka and caviar on a gold tray. It was as close, Ash thought, as he at least would ever come to holding court, and it was a heady few hours. In the next room a covey of grand dukes, not in the plot, glared over the tops of their cards as their rounds of quinze went on and on. Through another door Ash could glimpse Ambassadors Buchanan and Paléologue hunched together like a pair of owls, pretending interest in their own talk while, it was obvious from their expressions, they would cheerfully have sold their own children to Afghan slavers to hear what passed between Ash and Valery and the men who one by one joined them in the smoking room, shared a vodka and left.

In fact, had they been able, they would have heard little more than a series of toasts. *"Boje Tsaria Khranee,"* Captain Sirotkin said to Valery as he raised his glass, and Valery repeated, "God save the Czar." In Sirotkin's case it meant his Preobrajenski units were ready to seize Palace Square and storm the main gates if the light palace guard proved troublesome.

An artillery officer, Kustodiev, came next. *"Boje Tsaria Khranee."* He had charge of the main guns in the Peter and Paul, which commanded the palace across the river, and had pledged to keep them silent in the event that the Czar got a message past the blown lines to fire on the Winter Palace.

"Boje Tsaria Khranee!" Sergei Gladishev said, his face wreathed in nervous smiles. Forty men of the Duma, mostly Kadets, had agreed to follow him into the palace provided the square was in Valery's control. Another twenty reactionaries had given Valery himself their pledge.

Captain Sokolov of the Semonovsky Regiment, whose men would surround several police stations after von Basel had maneuvered most of the detectives away from the area; half a dozen grand dukes who had promised to stand by Valery when he announced his new government; the Guard Cossacks lieutenant who would protect the main telegraph offices . . . all filed casually into the club, had their drink with Valery and wandered back into the night. The only ones missing were von Basel, who would be right at home here if Germany and Russia weren't at war, and Kirichenko, whose appearance might raise a few grand ducal eyebrows even if they didn't realize his line of work.

Ash kept deliberately moving his glass out of reach; nervous and keyed up, he had to stop himself from tossing back the vodka out of need for something to do with his hands. One of the grand dukes who had promised to stand beside Valery when he announced the coup jarred Ash by replying to Valery's *"Boje Tsaria Khranee"* with *"Bye Jidoff."*

Beat the Jews, the traditional Russian reply to the old drinking salute, God Save the Czar. People said it automatically, but in "Beat the Jews" festered the canker of middle-European anti-Semitism, a virulent bigotry that made a lie of Europe's grandeur and history and culture. If this ancient civilization were so grand, so rich and refined, why did otherwise normal people sink to the level of hating the Jews?

Ash's father had fought in the Civil War against slavery. And Ash's mentor, Admiral Mahon, had reduced anti-Semitism to its ultimate Christian absurdity—"That Jesus Christ was a Jew covers the issue of His race for me." So how had Kenneth Ash ended up on the edge of it, politely lifting his glass as Valery and his troglodyte cousins traded *"Bye Jidoffs"* the night before they seized the throne of Imperial Russia?

Relieved when the last conspirator had paid his respects and Valery glanced at him to say they had stayed long enough, Ash reminded himself that removing the Czar to end the war was *still* the most important thing . . . Still, it was strange how he could never escape from the shadow smiles of diplomatic compromise . . .

At that moment one of the old waiters came in with a message. A gentleman in the foyer insisted on speaking to Ash. Von Basel, was Ash's first thought. A hitch in his arrangements to neutralize police stations near the palace? A problem arresting the Duma member they had considered too likely to support Nicholas II? Or not von Basel at all but a real Okhrana detective announcing that the Czar's secret police had broken their plot?

"I'll meet you at Tamara's, Your Highness," he said to Valery and walked casually from the smoking room. As soon as he was out of sight of the curious ambassadors and the grand ducal quinze players he nearly ran through the club's ballrooms and reception, slowing only when he arrived at the foyer, where he found not von Basel but Andrew Hazzard, the American ambassador's nephew. They shook hands and Ash said, "What's up?"

Hazzard glanced around the foyer. He still had not adopted the Russian custom of removing his coat instantly upon entering a building and stood sweltering in it now while the hall porters watched disapprovingly.

"We have to talk—private."

"Can it wait? I'm kind of busy—"

"That's what we have to talk about."

Ash got suddenly alert. Andrew looked both nervous and a little smug, as if he had some advantage over Ash. Ash drew him into a corner, away from the staff.

"What's wrong, Andrew?"

"I have a message for you from Mr. Banks," Andrew whispered.

Ash's heart skipped. "I don't understand."

"Harold Banks, Commander. He says you got to stop what you're doing."

45

Ash left the Imperial Yacht Club in a daze, vaguely aware of collecting his cloak and hat and escorting the smirking Andrew into the street. They walked beside the Moika. The triple-globed street lights sparkled on light snow . . . it looked as though Kirichenko's bodyguard had been right about the weather.

Andrew was barely concealing his pleasure. "Before we left London, Admiral Innes asked me to sort of take charge of you, if necessary . . . Mr. Banks cabled today. Both ways, I might add, across Europe and Siberia, to be sure he got through—"

"Take charge?"

"Well, how the hell could he control you six thousand miles from Washington if you got out of hand doing whatever you're doing . . .?"

"He sent me here to do a job. I don't know who the hell you are to—"

"I happen to be Harold Banks's deputy, Commander. You have to do exactly what I tell you, and I'm telling you what *he* wants. Stop the whole business unless the big man agrees to a democracy. In *advance,* he said."

"How did you get this message?"

"We set up a secret code."

"Have you said anything to Ambassador Hazzard?"

"I didn't tell anybody."

"Good, please don't. If Banks had wanted you to he would have said so."

"Commander, I don't think you have much respect for me. Well, you better believe Mr. Banks does. And he represents the President. I'm not the dummy you take me for. Mr. Banks and Admiral Innes told me in

358

London that I should remind you about the difference between an order and a command."

"Innes?" Ash looked at Andrew, wanting to knock the half-smirk off his face. Until Andrew had mentioned Innes, Ash could tell himself Harold Banks had stepped out of line . . . Ambassador Page was his real boss— except no, he wasn't. His *real boss* was the United States Navy in the person of Admiral Innes . . .

"He said you'd know the difference," Andrew repeated, "and he said to tell you this is a command."

"I absolutely refuse," Valery was saying before Ash could get the new terms out of his mouth.

"*Kennet,*" Tamara put in, "you are out of your mind?"

"Well, damn it, my government tells me that it will be impossible for the United States to recognize a new government that isn't at least pledged to a democratic government. What the hell more can I say . . . ?"

Valery and Tamara were sitting side by side in Tamara's solarium; snow hissed against the windows, yet between gusts of the hard, frozen pellets the lights of the Winter Palace could be seen across the Neva.

The grand duke stretched to his full height and glared down at Ash. "Do you really think that I would sacrifice my family's three-hundred-year dynasty as the Czars of all the Russias for recognition by *America?*" He pointed across the river. "Catherine the Great sat six thousand nobles for dinner in that palace when you people were still living in log huts."

Tamara stood beside him and took his enormous arm in her tiny hands. "Kennet, what can you be thinking, you must be mistaken . . ."

What Ash was thinking was that all his compromises and small evasions were coming home to roost. Banks had knocked the props out from under him, and as he fell everything he'd done looked to be crashing down . . . "Both ends against the middle" had been a plausible-sounding phrase to mask the implausibility of joining the radical Kirichenko with the reactionary Grand Duke Valery in an effort which Ash alone, it seemed now, thought would serve democracy, his country . . . but it *would,* damn it, if only temporarily . . .

"Kennet Karlovich?"

Ash looked at Valery. The grand duke had never addressed him by his patronymic before. Only as "Commander."

"You people of the west do not understand us. You think Russians are barbarians. Incapable of your high accomplishments in government and economics. We are not as highly developed in some skills as you, but we are not barbarians. We are, actually, rather simple people, with deep faith and much bravery."

"That's absolutely true—"

"Kennet Karlovich, I ask you, could England and France have stood this long were it not for Russian bravery?"

"No, Germany would have taken Paris long ago."

"And pushed the British Expeditionary Army into the sea . . . Kennet Karlovich, this is my promise to you—Russia will fight until Germany surrenders."

Tamara said quietly, "*My* life has been possible under Czarism. Perhaps a czar can't solve all of Russia's problems, but a good man like Valery will do better than a quarrelsome Duma. Kennet, you yourself *know* democracy won't work now in Russia. If a weak government, which a democracy would be, replaces the Czar, who will control the revolutionaries? Anarchists?"

"Maybe a democracy would defuse the revolutionaries." He didn't believe it himself. Not an imposed democracy in a place like Russia. Not yet . . .

"The bomb throwers?" Valery asked. "The assassins? No, Kennet. The Social Revolutionaries and the Bolsheviks would slice through a democratic parliament like my *pallash* through flesh. They already are organized. The labor unions would seize the railroads and the cities. Soviets, workers' councils, would strangle your democracy."

"I thought you don't care about American recognition."

"I care about yours."

"As I do," Tamara said.

"Also," the grand duke added shrewdly, "I would imagine your new orders go beyond *threatening* to withhold support.

Ash looked away.

"I thought so . . . Kennet, I don't want to fight you, but I will."

"*Why?*" Tamara asked.

"He's been ordered to stop us. Can't you see it in his face?"

Tamara looked at Ash. "No. No, Kennet, you wouldn't . . . Valery, would you leave us a moment?"

The grand duke walked out of the solarium. Ash stared at the Winter Palace. For a while he and Tamara just stood there in silence. Then he said to her, "Look . . ."

Valery's Cossacks were spreading out in front of the house. Ash nodded at the side window. The lancers were surrounding the house. "He doesn't trust me, it seems."

"Should he?" she asked coldly.

Ash walked to the side window and stretched to see toward the back of the house. The flaw in the Cossacks' cordon was the kitchen yard . . . the riders who guarded the back door, which led into the maze of kitchen gardens from a number of mansions, would be forced to dismount in the confined space. From there it was less than ten minutes on foot to the Finland Station, where he could stop the grand duke with a single telephone call.

"*Should* he?"

Admiral Innes's order, actually a command, had activated a sense of the whole of Ash's eighteen-year naval career. The Academy had trained man o' war's men by enlarging their capacity for judgment *and* obedience. To obey and decide were an officer's skills. But to insure that under fire an officer would act instantly, not wasting time weighing alternatives, well, certain mottos were issued as ironclad articles of faith—

"Should Valery trust you?" Tamara demanded again. "Kennet, don't go against us. Please. What do you care what happens in Russia? It is Valery who will fight the war. You will get what you want. Tell me we can trust you."

Be fearless in the face of duty . . . Seared in the mind of an eighteen-year-old midshipman was an image of standing firm while enemy shell splinters screeched across the bridge. But who was the enemy? They didn't teach that one, not under circumstances like these.

Trust yourself . . . he *knew* the grand duke was the best hope of saving Russia's army . . . Admiral Innes and Harold Banks were six thousand miles across the world in Washington, D.C. But *Trust the Navy* and *Bye Jidoff* kept ringing in his head . . .

"Then do this for me. *Please*, Kennet."

And Andrew had given him a final warning from Admiral Innes—Ash would never get a ship if he disobeyed his new orders.

"So you can be the empress?" A cheap shot, he knew as he said it, confirmed when she reached up and deliberately slapped his face.

"I don't want to be anything over your dead body . . . don't you understand? Valery will kill you if you try to stop him. It is in his grasp. He will shoot you down like one of your pheasants."

"I can take care of myself," and immediately winced at the sound of the empty boast.

"Do you think I would choose the *victor?*" She sounded insulted.

Ash turned back to the windows and again inspected Valery's grim picket line. "This isn't about us," he said quietly. "We're just pieces in a—"

"But you *know* what is right. You've made this happen. Valery couldn't have done it alone. Why did you help?"

"I thought it was the best chance to get rid of the Czar and end the war."

"And now? Because some fool thousands of miles away thinks Russia should bow to an upstart who . . . who doesn't *know* . . . Kennet, Valery will kill you tonight. And then he'll proceed with the plan. And if something goes wrong along the way you won't be there to help him. Or me . . ."

Or her ... Ash had a sudden vision of a dark car at the door of her house, plainclothes Okhrana detectives emerging to arrest her ...

"Get Valery."

She slipped her arms under his, squeezed him tight and ran from the room. Ash turned the other way and headed for the back door.

Off their horses, and without their lances, whips and carbines, the tall, blue-eyed Cossacks looked somewhat more like ordinary men. Ash knocked down the first at the kitchen door with a right uppercut. The second Cossack went for his *kinjal.* Ash feinted a jab as the dagger flashed out of the sheath and hooked him with a left. By the time the yelling started he was three houses away, bleakly confident that no one in the pursuit had quite the experience he did in exiting ladies' lodgings by the back door.

It was three in the morning, but thirty women had already lined up outside a shuttered bakery. Others hurried toward the line, yawning and rubbing sleep from their pinched faces. In the Finland Station Square thousands of soldiers milled about in the cold. Ash asked an officer what was going on; it looked like an insurrection.

It was not. Two regiments of Caucasian Rifles were stranded on their way to the front. "No locomotives," the officer explained. "The boilers burst from the cold when they ran out of fuel."

In the dark window of every shop was the same sign. *Nyet.* No bread, no oil, no kerosene, no potatoes, no carrots, and of course no meat. Ash took a last look at the crowds in the square, turned his back on the mobbed station and started walking toward the Alexander Bridge. He spotted a *rissak* whose driver was afraid to enter the square and hired the fast sleigh. As it headed toward the Neva a cry drifted from somewhere on the snow. *Khleeeee-ba.* Bread.

St. Issac's Square lay smooth under new snow. Ash stared a moment, wondering what was different outside the hotel. It took a moment, and then he realized ... the firewood was gone. Inside, the Astoria felt very chilly. ...

Andrew Hazzard grinned when he saw Ash walk into the bar.

"Took you long enough. I been waiting two hours. Bartender, a drink here for the officer and gentleman who obeys orders."

Ash was freezing. He tossed back the vodka, searched his mind for one single thing that made sense ... "I need your help, Andrew."

"What?"

"I'll explain in the sleigh."

Outside, the *rissak* he had hired at the Finland Station was waiting. It was colder. The snow was turning thin and icy.

"Where are we going?" Andrew asked as they headed for the embankment.

"Tell me something," Ash said, ignoring the question, "what were you supposed to do if I didn't obey Mr. Banks's orders?"

"Oh, don't worry. We had you there. Another hour and I'd blow the whistle on you *and* your big shot Russian. Christ, Ash, how the hell did you get mixed up in such a mess?"

It was Andrew's first intelligent question.

"Say, where are we going? It's cold as hell . . . you need my help stopping them?"

"Andrew, what was Ambassador Hazzard supposed to do if I got arrested?"

Andrew tried to shield his face from the snow. "They had some kind of paper showing you were on leave. You know, doing all this on your own . . . Hey, how we going to stop them?"

"You got your gun?"

"Sure." He laughed. "I figured you might pull something."

"Give it to me."

"Why?"

"Because I have mine, too, and Andrew, it's about two inches from your gut."

Ash marched Andrew past the Cossacks into Tamara's solarium, explained who he was to a relieved-looking Valery and concluded, "Lock him in the cellar."

"May I ask why you changed your mind, Kennet Karlovich?"

"Just don't be surprised if I apply for a commission in the Imperial Navy."

"Traitor," Andrew shouted at him.

"Andrew," Ash replied gently, "you just don't know what's going on here. It's not your fault . . ."

Tamara waited silently until Valery left the room with Andrew and the Cossack guard. "I hope you didn't come back for me," she said with the suggestion of a smile that said she hoped he had.

"I came back for a lot of reasons," Ash said. "But you're the only one I'm sure of."

Andrew Hazzard knew he'd made a mess of things again, but who the hell could be expected to figure a fellow *American* to pull a gun on a guy in the middle of Russia? No wonder Mr. Banks had hired him to keep an eye on the louse. Ash was trouble, all right . . .

They had locked him in the coachman's room, half-underground in the mansion's cellar. A fire in the grate flickered on a low, vaulted ceiling. There were hooks in the stone walls for cloaks and hats, and in a couple of huge wooden chairs by the fire draped with furs were two enormous coachmen drinking vodka nonstop.

The bigger one, wearing red, was probably the grand duke's driver; he'd clumped in a little while ago with one of those metal foot-warming braziers the Russians used in their sleds and plunked it down on the hearth; later some peasant would fill it with embers when the grand duke's sled was ready to go.

The other driver was probably Tishkova's. He seemed to live here, being the one who went back and forth to a cabinet for fresh bottles. After the Cossacks who'd tied him to the chair in the corner had left, the coachmen draped a heavy fur coat over him so he wouldn't be cold so far from the fire. Nice of 'em . . . gave him a chance to try and untie the knots.

He'd be ready to make a run for it when they passed out from the vodka. He knew he didn't understand everything going on, but he had a powerful feeling that Lady Luck and Mr. Banks had got together to put Andy Hazzard right smack in the middle of something really important. Finally . . .

Strike-breaking for Pinkerton had gone nowhere—no money, no future, not as exciting as the life of a Pinkerton op was supposed to be. Nor was getting shot in the leg his idea of a success. Selling railroad wheels to Russia was turning out to be a frustrating job too—big deals cooked up at all-night dinner parties, on his tab, always seemed to peter out by the end of the week. Diplomacy looked like an interesting line of work, but he was too old at twenty-eight to start at the bottom like the young Eastern snobs from Harvard and Yale who were courting Catherine. A better way to get into diplomacy was to start at the top like Catherine's father, but you had to be a success at something else first so you'd have the strings to pull. Nobody worried too much about experience. A first secretary in the Petrograd embassy had come straight from the warden's office of the Nevada State Penitentiary. But he'd had the strings. Andrew had the feeling that when he got himself untied and the coachmen passed out he was going to perform a service for Mr. Banks that would earn Andy Hazzard some strings of his own.

Problem was they weren't passing out. The night was wearing on, and they were tearing the seal off bottle after bottle but nothing happened. Andrew lost count how many times they had brought the bottle to him and held it cheerfully to his lips while he sucked the fiery vodka, clapped him on the back and returned to their chairs by the fire. He dozed off in his dark corner. When he woke up the Russians were *still* at it, chuckling at their jokes and swigging in front of the fire with their feet propped up on the sled brazier. Under the fur he pawed at the ropes until they ambled over with another coachman's highball.

Finally, as gray light appeared in the barred window high in the wall, the grand duke's coachman stood up, belched mightily, buttoned his red coat, jammed a tall hat on his head and rumbled out into the dawn. A while later Andrew heard the sound of a team being hitched to the grand duke's big red sleigh.

Tishkova's coachman, meantime, finished the bottle and ten minutes later stretched out on a bunk in a corner opposite Andrew, where he broke into thunderous snores. Through the barred window Andrew caught a glimpse of sun reflecting off the tip of a gold spire. He tugged at his ropes. He had one hand already free under the fur and—

The thick wooden door creaked open, slowly.

Andrew froze, half closed his eyes and pretended to sleep while he watched. A *moujik* crept in. His sheepskin, which Andrew could smell twenty-five feet across the cellar room, hung open, revealing in the fire-light a blood-red peasant blouse underneath. Andrew figured he had come for the sled's foot-warming brazier. But he looked around instead, checked that the coachman was asleep, missed Andrew in the dark corner and motioned to someone else behind the door.

The second guy was no peasant. He wore a long gray wasp-waisted coat, a snap-brim hat and carried a walking stick. He went straight to the brazier on the hearth, opened the top and snapped his fingers. The *moujik* produced a bundle of greasy red cylinders.

Andrew's eyes opened wide. He'd been a Pinkerton long enough to know dynamite when he saw it. A dozen sticks, wired up to a detonator and set to go, enough to blow this house into the next block. They put it in the brazier. He was still trying to figure that out when he noticed the bundle had an odd fuse, very stiff. The guy in gray had to bend it with both hands to coil it. He scooped up a shovelful of red-hot coals from the fire. A fearful shout stuck in Andrew's throat when a second later the man dropped the burning coals on the dynamite. Andrew ducked instinctively, as if that would have helped—nothing happened. The guy poured some more coals in and closed the brazier while Andrew, scared, tired and still a little drunk on the coachmen's vodka, tried to figure out why they hadn't all been blown to kingdom come . . .

Fire alone wouldn't detonate dynamite right off, but the fuse would as soon as it hit the detonator. The blasting cap. Lead! That's why the fuse was stiff. Wrapped in lead, which made a crude time bomb.

When the hot coals melted the lead wrapping the fuse would ignite, detonate the blasting cap and—it might blow any second . . . He looked up at the vaulted ceiling, imagined the entire mansion tumbling on top of him, squeezed his eyes tight shut and screamed, too panicked to notice that the *moujik* had started to carry the foot-warming brazier from the room.

"Help! *Help* . . ."

Count von Basel, halfway out the door and watching for the Cossack guards, whirled at Andrew's cry. The sleeping coachman stopped snoring and got to his feet. The *"moujik,"* one of von Basel's German agents dressed for his part in von Basel's scheme, put down the brazier, which he was about to carry out to the grand duke's sleigh, and hit the coachman with the shovel. The big Russian sagged back on his bunk, and the *"moujik"* again snatched up the brazier and headed outside.

But the coachman hadn't shouted *help* in English.

In the moment it took von Basel to locate the figure huddled beneath the furs in the darkest corner of the room, he flicked the sheath off his sword cane, set to thrust.

46

Ash watched the sun light the golden tip of the Admiralty spire as Tamara Tishkova picked up the telephone in her solarium and asked the operator to connect her with the Alexander Palace at Tsarskoye Selo. So much for Kirichenko's bodyguard's snow; the damned stuff had stopped before dawn, and it was anybody's guess whether the First Railway Battalion patrols had uncovered the track mines.

When the palace operator answered, Tamara identified herself as Madame Egersky—one of the longest-lived of the legion of mistresses entertained by Count Vladimir Fredericks—and asked to speak with the ancient chief minister of the Imperial Court. Count Fredericks was the same old man whose name Ash had used to bluff his way into the Alexander Palace with his gift for the Czarina. He saw no reason not to use him again, since at the Czar's New Year's reception he had observed a pair of red-cloaked equerries ease the old nobleman gently into a chair when he dozed off in the middle of a conversation with the Italian ambassador.

The Grand Duke Valery betrayed some anxiety by repeating aloud what they all already knew: "The poor old man's so dotty it will take them a quarter hour just to find him."

Ash nodded. Fifteen minutes was plenty of time for the line to go dead. If Kirichenko hadn't blown the telegraph poles by then it would be because he was already hanging from one. Ash was nervous too, but it made him silent. He leaned close to Tamara and listened to the telephone popping and hissing. Her perfume was heady. What a time for such a reaction. She wore a quilted silk robe, black, black slippers, and her hair coiled around her neck. Before the telephone call she had been sipping dark French coffee from a Limoges cup. Now she stared through the solarium's windows at the frozen Neva and the dull red Winter Palace, its north face in cold shadow. She felt him watching her, met his gaze with large eyes. Two hours from now it would all be over, one way or the other.

The palace operator came on the line again. "We apologize, madame, for the delay in locating His Excellency Count Fredericks."

"*Merci.*"

Outside her mansion Valery's red sleigh faced the river. The eight white Arabians were groomed as if for a dress parade; a triple guard of Cossacks waited on their mounts; two more sleighs carried armed men from Valery's own household. They had a Maxim "Sokolov" machine gun under canvas in the back seat of the rearmost sleigh. As Ash watched, and Tamara waited on the line, a *moujik* in a dirty sheepskin and bright red blouse appeared from behind the house and hoisted a brazier of fresh coals into Valery's sleigh.

Tamara started. "They found him," she whispered. "He's coming. Kennet, what happened to the line? It still *works.*"

Valery's lips tightened. The key men of the Duma who had pledged to support him were breakfasting at this unlikely hour at the Astoria and the Europa, less than five minutes from the Winter Palace, waiting to install him on the throne of Imperial Russia. He looked at Ash. Why wasn't the line blown?

"*Bonjour,* Your Excellency," Tamara said in a choked voice, her eyes wild with panic as she turned to Ash. "What should I do?"

Ash thought of Andrew tied up in the cellar, living proof that he had virtually committed treason in a cause that had just collapsed. Kirichenko? Had the revolutionary double-crossed him? Or were the horsemen of the First Railway Battalion at this moment trampling his men into the snow?

"*Je suis . . . allo? allo?* . . . It's *broken,*" she said.

Ash grabbed it, hit the plunger one, two, three times, then cradled the telephone and looked at the grand duke, and then at Tamara. "The railroad line is blown. Your Highness . . . good luck."

Grand Duke Valery took a deep breath. The color returned to his face. He put his hand on Tamara's shoulder and she touched his fingers with hers. He kissed her black hair, put on his fur hat and took Ash's hand. When their eyes met he impulsively clasped Ash's hand in both of his.

"I wish you could ride with me."

"So do I." They had already decided there was no place for the U.S. Navy in Grand Duke Valery's sleigh this morning.

"I have one more favor to ask you, Kennet Karlovich. If something happens . . . take care of her—"

"Nothing's going to happen," Tamara interrupted with annoyance. "And please remember that I can take care of myself."

Valery bowed over Tamara's hand and walked out to his sleigh. He stood up and waved once as it started moving, trailed by the horseguard and the two sleighs that were flanked by more Cossacks. Standing beside Tamara in the window, Ash wondered how they would appear from across the river on the Palace embankment. The convoy grouping was unusual. Yet the Cossacks always carried their rifles slung over their backs, and lances. And grand dukes often traveled with bodyguards. The Maxim gun was under wraps . . . and the Winter Palace was empty except for servants and a small guard . . .

The sleigh plunged down the bank and onto the Neva and headed southwest, diagonally across the river on a course that would take it straight to the landing on the quay in front of the Winter Palace. The sun had risen high enough now so that its rays splashed the ice a pale yellow. The Arabians broke into a fast trot, pulling ahead of the sleds of armed men. The Cossacks, red figures on dark animals, stayed close—

Fire spouted under the sleigh, mushroomed until the horses seemed to be crossing burning ice. Thunder sounded across the river. The blast lifted sleigh and horses above an enormous black hole in the ice. The animals kept running, galloping on flame.

But where the ice had been was only the Neva, dark and swift, and into it vanished the grand duke, his sleigh and his horses.

BOOK

IV

The Czar

47

The silver button on François Roland's foil swam in front of Ash's eyes. He blinked, and it seemed to shatter.

"Get your guard up."

"I can't . . . I think—"

Roland slipped his foil under the stump of his left arm, caught Ash with his right hand and helped him off the strip. "Too much too soon, my friend. What do you expect, swimming in the Neva?"

Fencers crowded around as Roland eased Ash, dizzy and nauseous, to the floor of the *salle d'armes.* The Frenchman banished them with an annoyed look.

It was two weeks since the Grand Duke Valery had been killed. Ash himself had nearly died when he had fallen among the floes in a futile attempt to save him from the river and the swift current had slammed his head into the ice. He had been delirious when he woke up in a hospital. As he slowly recovered his memory, he tried to figure out who had bombed Valery's sleigh, and why. The timing and the sword cut that had killed Andrew Hazzard pointed to von Basel, but the German's motivation was less clear—von Basel was, after all, his strange partner, at least in the scheme to remove Czar Nicholas—which opened the possibility that Kirichenko had betrayed them in the best, or worst, revolutionary tradition. Or did von Basel have some other irons heating?

Then two days ago Roland had burst into his hospital room with the news Ash had most worried about, and he suddenly stopped caring about von Basel, Kirichenko, Czar Nicholas or even the war. Okhrana detectives had just arrested Tamara Tishkova for plotting to overthrow the Czar. It was a secret arrest; the censors allowed nothing in the papers, though this, like most Russian secrets, had not escaped the French ambassador. Ash knew it meant Tamara was held beyond the law. They could do anything to her . . .

He brushed Roland's hand away and tried to sit. "Gotta get limbered up . . . François, help me. I *have* to."

Roland sighed and pulled Ash slowly to his feet. "You've had a severe concussion. You are not fully recovered. You are lucky you're not dead."

Ash picked up his foil. "I'm just *stiff*, dammit. Come on, *en garde.*"

Roland looked hard at him. "Am I to assume that you intend to rescue mademoiselle by fighting your way into the Peter-Paul Fortress with a sword?"

"I have to do something, what else *can* I do?"

Ash had gone everywhere, begged help from everyone he knew who had influence. No one could help. He had found Sergei Gladishev, a trembling wreck at the Duma, waiting at any moment for his own arrest. Tamara's old friend, the director of the Imperial Theaters, was devastated but helpless. Her friend the police chief of the Fourth District blustered, then admitted he could do nothing. And Ambassador Hazzard's counselor had already warned the ambassador that the United States had neither business nor interest in the legal difficulties of Russian citizens.

When he went to Lord Exeter the Englishman had said, "I'm very sorry, Ash, but I'm afraid the real issue is . . . what are you going to do about the Czar?"

"I just got out of the hospital, Tamara—"

"I'd get cracking, my friend. You must put personal considerations aside. There isn't time to spare. The railroads have collapsed. The food is gone. The police expect bread riots within days. What they've been told of the grand ducal conspiracy has frightened the Czar and Czarina. He's gone back to the Stavka, she's consulting mystics."

Ash had stared at the Englishman without seeing him, his mind on Tamara.

"*Mystics*, Ash. And he's left her in charge of Petrograd while he's gone back to the army. Meanwhile no one's found this Red Snow assassin, Dmitri Dan. Can you imagine the chaos if the Czar were murdered now? You've got to get him out. Quickly."

"Yes, I know . . ."

"And there's something else you ought to know. Kirichenko got impatient. His men tried to defuse my lorry. What the hell did you do to it?"

"Just attached a detonator to the springs. Take off too much weight and—"

"Well, they did. Kirichenko had already lost men blowing the Tsarskoye Selo lines. He of course blames you for everything. I'd say you've made a rather dangerous enemy . . . whose stock can only rise as the Czar's sinks."

Ash thought, hoped that Exeter was exaggerating the situation to jolt his

374

mind off Tamara, but when he telephoned the Alexander Palace to plead for her, he discovered that Exeter wasn't far off the mark. He first ran smack into the same impenetrable wall of the Court that he had had to vault to present King George's offer of asylum. He got no further than a remote-sounding Colonel Riazhin. "Russia's peasants have an old saying, Commander. 'Father Czar would save us from this unhappiness, if he only knew.' "

"*Tell* him."

"It would be the end of my career to even mention Tishkova's name in the Czarina's palace."

"The woman's life is at stake. God knows what they're doing to her."

"As for the Czar," the colonel went on coldly, "His Imperial Majesty has more on his mind at the Stavka than interceding on behalf of a woman accused of turning the Grand Duke Valery against him."

"That's malicious rumor—"

"Perhaps, but I can tell you another rumor . . . if His Imperial Majesty's government were not reluctant to trouble a potential ally in his war against Germany, there is a certain American naval officer whom the Okhrana would have hanging by his thumbs in the Peter-Paul beside the great Tishkova."

This was not news. The Okhrana had apparently satisfied itself with several interrogations in the hospital. But the cruelty about Tamara was unforgiveable, and Ash let the pretense of courtesy drop from his voice.

"May I ask how His Majesty could leave when Petrograd is about to explode?"

To his surprise Colonel Riazhin answered him seriously, which Ash took as an indication of how frightened the Court must be. "Minister Protopopov promises quiet in Petrograd. Hooligans who won't work and exaggerate bread shortages are not such a threat that the Czar of all the Russias can't lead his armies in the field. And I am told," the colonel continued in confidential tones, "that a lady-in-waiting to Her Majesty returned from a week in the city and saw no serious disturbance. Nothing the police can't put down."

What makes you think my spies in the Russian Court are all men? the Kaiser had boasted. Why not a lady-in-waiting? . . .

"*En garde*, then," Roland said. "If you insist."

But Ash lowered his foil and walked off the strip.

"Where are you going?"

"Von Basel."

"Are you insane?"

No, thought Ash, but I'd deal with the devil to save her. He left a note in the sconce hole at the German Embassy, and the Kaiser's spy agreed to a meeting in front of the Stock Exchange on the spit of Vasily Island. Ash waited an hour. Von Basel did not show. He went back to the wrecked embassy. No message. But on his desk at the Astoria was a typed note.

"You're still being followed by Okhrana detectives investigating the explosion. Try Grisha's on the Bolshoi Prospect. Alone."

Ash took it as a warning he was coming unhinged by worry over Tamara. He went out, spotted the detectives, lost them on the Nevsky and took several trams to Vasily Island. Grisha's was a middle-class restaurant. He sat for an hour, drinking glasses of tea. There was not much left on the menu. Von Basel sat down and ordered herring, which he ignored. Ash marveled at the attention he paid to details. He leaned on the walking stick as if he needed it, and buttered a piece of bread in the careful, reverent Russian manner by which bread was buttered in middle-class restaurants. When the full slice was thickly and smoothly covered from crust to crust, he brought his cold eyes to bear on Ash's anxious face. "I've made arrangements for a special train on the Murman line."

"Why did you bomb the grand duke's sleigh?"

"I did not. And why would you think I did?"

"All I can figure is you thought he'd make too good a Czar."

"And defeat Germany?" von Basel smiled. "Not very likely."

"Then Kirichenko?"

Von Basel shrugged. "It makes no difference now. But *our* problem remains unsolved. Do you have a plan to get the Czar to the cruiser at Murmansk?"

"Not until I get Tishkova out of the Peter-Paul."

"Tishkova?" Von Basel sat up, suddenly alert now. Ash cursed himself. He had assumed that with his police contacts at the Litovsky Prison von Basel knew Tamara had been arrested. He *hadn't*. And the interest in his eyes made Ash wish he could erase his slip.

"Can you help me get her out?"

"No. It's beyond my power."

"Can you see her for me?"

"And have Tishkova start screaming that's Count von Basel, the German spy?"

Ash slumped back. Von Basel was right.

"Your first and overriding objective . . . which we share . . . is to remove the Czar from Russia. But I wouldn't worry so. If the revolution is as imminent as my sources indicate, Mademoiselle Tishkova will be free quite soon . . ."

Clinging to those words like a drowning man Ash followed von Basel out to the street, where the German spy added with a quick smile ". . . provided, of course, that the revolutionaries don't hold her monarchistic tendencies against the lady . . . Tell me when you're ready for the

376

U-boats, and of course please do ask for any help you need with the Czar. I've made some contacts for you in the railroads. I can probably arrange a special on the Murman line, even if the Czar is no longer able by the time you get to him . . . I emphasize that time is running out, Ash. It is fifteen hundred miles to Murmansk. Once the Revolution is underway, there will be many people trying to stop you."

Are you one of them? Ash suddenly found himself wondering. Von Basel barely concealed his pleasure in Ash's misery about Tamara. A highly tenuous, makeshift at best, link, this thing of getting the Czar out of Russia . . . for two men who otherwise were enemies. Had it broken, without a found declaration or acknowledgement? Were they now, as they parted in front of Grisha's restaurant, backing away from each other, each at least privately acknowledging to himself that the other was, after all, an enemy?

What was all that talk about Murmansk? The Murman run certainly seemed to be importantly on von Basel's mind . . . "Keep in touch," von Basel said, and limped toward the tram stop.

"Soon," Ash said, and his telephone conversation with Colonel Riazhin came to mind—the babbling of that frightened courtier reminded him of the sorry crowd in the Kaiser's Court . . . strong evidence that Kaiser Wilhelm was on the losing end of a power struggle with General Ludendorff and the German army.

Volatile fellow, the Kaiser, Lord Exeter had warned . . . Could it be that the Kaiser might have broken the link among a pride of royals, had maybe changed his mind about rescuing his cousin the Czar? If so, wouldn't the German U-boat escort suddenly become a killer and torpedo the cruiser? . . . Possible . . . but not likely . . . the Kaiser had enough troubles with Ludendorff, why get involved in a dangerous plot to kill his own cousin? Even the Czar had said that Ludendorff had all but taken over the real power in the German Empire. Trouble enough for the Kaiser, more than enough to keep his mind on that overriding problem, any threat to him . . .

Ash stopped walking abruptly and two old women lugging an oilcan bumped into him. His logic about the Kaiser began to weaken . . . had von Basel killed the Grand Duke Valery not only because he feared Valery would be too good a Czar, and so make Russia a stronger enemy, but more, because it would be more difficult to seize the Czar when Valery was firmly in control of the situation? Had the Kaiser decided to use the Czar as a pawn in his own power struggle with Ludendorff and the army? That, dammit, made sense, too much sense for Ash's comfort . . . explained why von Basel was his enemy even in the plot, and why the link among the royals had likely been broken. Kidnap the Czar . . . though the Kaiser, of course, would call Nicholas a prisoner of war—an enemy captive to refloat the Kaiser's sinking fortunes. Power-lust was thicker than blood . . . It made sense, too much sense . . . well, at least Ash could be glad he'd cinched backup arrangements for a sub with Rodney Skelton at Reval. Von Basel probably had his suspicions about that. Had to. But one thing was damn sure—there was no way von Basel could persuade Ash to let him help transport the Czar, much less get within a hundred miles of the Czar . . . In refusing to help with Tamara, the *way* he had refused, von Basel had betrayed his hand, made too clear that they were enemies again, in *everything* . . .

She was cold for the first time she could remember since the Yusupovs had plucked her from her father's circus. She thought longingly of her solarium—so warm that tropical plants Valery brought her from the Crimea stretched to the sunny windows even as the snow scurried past, and big enough to dance in if she liked. Strange how a whole house in a memory became a single cherished room, a whole life a single moment—Valery marching a giant clerodendrum into her house, bellowing at his Cossacks to shield it from the snow. All dead, now. His entire guard had perished with him as the weakened ice gave way. Only Kennet and her coachman, who had run to their aid, had survived.

Her cell was tiny, silent and cold despite the stoves she had seen buried in the passage wall. Part of her mind, which thankfully had detached as if to protect her sanity, suspected that soon something would happen to make her afraid. So far, confinement itself was the horror—the inactivity, the cold. The jailers, rough and coarse, she barely noticed; but when the commandant had come personally to greet her in her cell, she had granted him a hint of civility in her response, acutely aware that with Valery dead this man had power over her.

The warder had ordered the guards to remove the chains from her wrists. She caught herself debating whether a smile might suffice to free her legs.

Vera Sedovina was standing on the *khvost* when the Czar's police found her. This particular shadow was attached to a bakery just around the corner from the Alexander Theater. The line of shivering women seemed ten thousand miles from the columned portico where lavish court carriages lined up each night to whisk the rich from their entertainment to their dinners in the expensive restaurants that somehow still had food.

On the way home from rehearsal she had seen an enormous *khvost* stretching from the Railway Ticket Bureau up Mikhail Street all the way to the Nevsky. Her father had told her that people who could were leaving Petrograd, fleeing south to the Crimea or north to Finland over to Sweden, and even on the luxurious Trans-Siberian Express to Vladivostok and America across the Pacific Ocean. Those who couldn't get out were burning rowboats and cemetery crosses for firewood.

She was talking with two women—a housewife with a cruel cough and cook for a middle-class family. Were it not for the bitter cold and the need to rest her legs after a full day's rehearsal, she would almost enjoy the *khvost*. They were wonderful places to talk. There was nothing else to do, so people ignored social barriers that before the war would have prevented the work-worn housewife from speaking to a cook, and the cook, who fancied herself superior because her employer was richer, from talking to the housewife.

The newspapers had been proved liars too often to believe, so it was on the *khvost* that the people of Petrograd learned something of the truth about the war, the shortages, the treason in high places, and as the *khvosty* lengthened the police withdrew, knowing the anger they would provoke. And so people spoke more freely than usual. The *khvosty* was also a perfect place for a revolutionary to spread the word.

The explosions two weeks ago were still high on the list of favored rumors this snowy afternoon, second only to the story that six trains of grain and cooking oil had been diverted from Petrograd on Sunday and sold to the Austrians. Sedovina dutifully repeated the diverted food story, as her comrades were doing on every *khvost* they stood at, then listened politely to yet another retelling of the explosions.

The cook claimed her master had seen it with his own eyes from his desk in the Stock Exchange on the spit of Vasily Island, which had a clear view up the Neva. A sleigh had fallen into the river. Sometimes the story said two. This man had seen three. They were said to belong to a grand duke. Scarlet, it was said . . . and Sedovina wondered was it coincidence that last week haughty Tishkova was seen weeping in the theater?

Sedovina had looked from the Palace Embankment the day after, but if there had been a hole in the ice the deep cold had frozen the river again. Now a piano teacher she knew slightly from their neighborhood interrupted the housewife.

"Not one explosion, three." She held up her mitten as if to show three fingers. "Three," she repeated.

"On the river?"

"No, silly, the train to Tsarskoye Selo."

"Three explosions on a train? Was it the engine?"

"No," Sedovina said. She had heard this rumor several times. "They say the tracks were blown up. And then when trains came to repair it they were blown up too."

"Who did it?"

"Revolutionaries."

"German spies," the cook said, and the housewife and the piano teacher nodded grave agreement, which provoked a conversation about *izmena* —treason—and traitors. The housewife looked around carefully and said, "The German woman," and the others nodded, knowing they meant the German-born Czarina Alexandra.

Sedovina had heard that the police had swept through the factory districts after the explosion, breaking down doors in the Vyborg District, Narva, Vasily Island, Alexander Nevsky and particularly the Moscow District, where she had performed with Valentinov's revolutionary troupe. Hundreds were arrested. She hadn't seen Valentinov since the night Kirichenko had rescued them—partly from fear, largely from the intense preparation she was putting into her *Giselle*.

"They say she would betray her own husband the Czar."

"Perhaps the Czar agrees with her," Sedovina said softly.

The others looked at each other, suddenly alarmed, and she knew she had gone too far. Confused, frightened, cold and hungry, ordinary people like these could only accept so much uncertainty. The housewife and the piano teacher and the cook might question the competency of the Czar's government, but they weren't ready to turn against him, yet. She smoothed it over by saying, "They say he loves her deeply, it's hard for a man to resist a woman he loves," and the cook and the housewife and the piano teacher smiled tentatively and switched to how poorly the city government was removing the snow this winter; it lay in drifts in some places, and the cook had heard that in the outlying districts the government was paying ordinary people who had never held a shovel in their lives a few kopecks to clear it, such were the shortages of manpower.

It was then that two police officers in black uniform led by an officer in gray stepped out of the swirling snow and took hold of her from either side.

"Vera Vadimovich Sedovina?"

"Yes," she said, hearing her voice tremble and sensing the other women back away.

"I place you under arrest for crimes against the Czar."

An old lawyer with a white beard came to Vera's cell. He looked appalled by the wet stone walls, as if he had never seen a prison before. Vadim Mikhailov had somehow persuaded him to help. He had vague connections at court that garnered him a small amount of respect from the prison guards, but they still wouldn't allow him in the cell with her alone.

Speaking slowly, with a shaky voice, he explained what he knew about her situation. "A conspiracy to overthrow the Czar has been detected. The police have arrested hundreds of suspected revolutionaries. Among them, the members of a theatrical group that had been performing seditious plays in clandestine theaters. Under questioning a member of the troup, a child—"

"A *child?*"

"They interrogated the child," the lawyer continued, "and the child revealed your name. I certainly don't believe that you would be involved with such people, and neither does my friend Vadim Mikhailov, but the police were obliged to act."

"What's going to happen to me?"

He couldn't face her. Her stomach clutched, her mind raced so that she couldn't think. The lawyer tried to make her sit down on the filthy cot. "Can you help me?" she asked.

"The offense is considered very serious, but I will do what I can."

"In other words, you can't help me."

"Do you suppose that the Imperial Theater might help you?" he asked, and she was certain then that she was lost . . . he must know that not only wouldn't the Imperial Theater help, but at the slightest hint of political scandal she would be dismissed.

"No, I suppose they won't." He answered his own question. "I will do my best . . . Mikhailov sent you this warm cloak." He draped it over her shoulders, after the guard inspected it for contraband.

Sedovina twisted it around her trembling hands. Had her boyfriend Anton been so frightened when they arrested him? She glanced at the guard leaning against the cell door. He stared back with a lewd smile. How long would her modest fame protect her from people like him?

The lawyer started to go, and suddenly she thought of a last desperate straw . . . "Tell Vadim—" The guard was listening.

"Yes, my dear," prompted the lawyer, grateful to perform any small service.

"Tell my father to speak to his friend from America."

The commandant of the prison in the Moscow District looked surprised to see him. "What are you doing here, Moskolenko?"

Von Basel indicated his short, round assistant. "I've brought Lieutenant Orlov to interrogate a prisoner. Have you a room we can use?"

The commandant barely concealed his distaste for Orlov.

"Which prisoner?"

"Vera Vadimovich Sedovina."

"The dancer?"

"Yes."

"Sorry, you missed her."

"I thought the charges were too serious for bond."

"No bond, Moskolenko. Not likely. They've moved her to the Peter-

Paul." And then because he didn't like Moskolenko either, the commandant added what von Basel already knew, "You'll have a hard time prying her out of the Peter-Paul. They do their own interrogating."

Von Basel brooded in the car on the way home to the Litovsky Prison. In one real sense he regretted having to separate from Ash because to abandon Ash he would also have to abandon "Captain Moskolenko," and with it all the information that "Moskolenko" was able to gather for Germany. But it looked as if Ash may already have abandoned him.

Reval was the question. The more he thought about why Ash had gone to the Baltic port, the more likely it seemed Ash had gone to the British Royal Navy submarine base. What else could possibly have drawn Ash? The Russian Baltic Fleet—bottled up for years? The merchant port—blockaded by the German High Seas Fleet? Ash claimed he had met with a Russian general from Riga . . . but what Russian general would travel to Reval when he could make Ash come to Riga?

A British submarine? A submarine, instead of a cruiser with German escorts to take off the Czar. It would be a long, dangerous voyage to England. But if Ash no longer trusted him, might Ash not risk it? If that was Ash's plan, then von Basel would have to kidnap the Czar himself, not wait for Ash to do the job for him. Yes . . . it would mean the end of Captain Moskolenko, and worth that *only* if he had no other choice. He had to find out without question what Ash had done in Reval. He couldn't risk his whole carefully built cover on the basis of speculation . . . no matter how plausible it might be. Too much was at stake.

"I retained a very famous lawyer," Vadim Mikhailov assured Ash.

"What's he done for you?"

"He used his influence to see Vera."

Better than I've done for Tamara, Ash thought.

"Also, he learned what the charges are."

"What are they?"

The old tappeur looked on the verge of tears. "They are charging Vera with acting in seditious plays."

"Why did you let her?"

"How could I stop her?"

"You're her father—"

"Ever since her mother died I've tried to protect her, but she's always been so . . . angry. You must help me, Commander Ash. Please . . ."

"I wish I could, but how?"

"She asked for you," Mikhailov said quietly.

Ash walked to his window and looked down at St. Isaac's Square; a sledge was pulling away from the Maryinski Palace heaped high with furniture.

He glanced at François Roland, who met his look, thinking what Ash was thinking.

"My own very dear friend Tamara Tishkova has been imprisoned three days. I've tried everything just to see her. They won't let me."

"Tishkova? A performer so famous and once the Czar's friend?"

"Even a fling with the Czar doesn't seem to make a woman immune from the Okhrana," Ash said bitterly. "You're lucky, Vadim, at least they admit they're holding Vera. She'll have some legal protection." Even this old gossip hadn't heard . . . they could do anything to Tamara.

Vadim sat on the edge of a love seat wringing his hands. A tear drifted down his cheek, dried in the wrinkles.

"Where are they holding her?" Ash asked.

"They moved her to the Peter-Paul."

Ash looked at Roland again. God, if he could somehow get permission to see Sedovina then he might see—but that was impossible. He'd been locked in the Peter-Paul himself. Each cell was isolated, each prisoner chained alone, buried inside an impregnable prison hidden in an equally impregnable fortress.

"The lawyer couldn't do a thing," Vadim admitted. He clenched both fists and got to his feet. Grief and fear had made him look even thinner. He turned to Ash, his eyes intense. "Do you still want to see the Czarina?"

"I beg your pardon?"

"Do you still have business with the Czar?"

"What are you saying?" Damned right he had business with the Czar. Pressing business, if it weren't already too late. Ambassador Hazzard had related news from America—President Wilson was making some headway in his efforts to convince Congress to declare war on Germany. Popular resistance was still fierce and would remain fierce, in the opinion of Harold Banks—who had sent a cryptic message congratulating Ash, as if Ash had bombed the grand duke's sleigh, for God's sake—until the Czar-autocrat was removed. But Germany had resumed unrestricted submarine warfare.

U-boat attacks on American ships might provoke American sentiment toward intervention which lent a new, and dangerous, wrinkle to the Russian situation; if the Czar hung on so long as to set off a cataclysmic revolt, American soldiers might land in France to find their most important ally collapsed. So Ash's "business with the Czar," the need to remove the autocrat, was doubly pressing—triply, considering the havoc if Dmitri Dan and his Red Snow nihilists managed to assassinate the Czar.

"Yes, Vadim, I believe I still have business with the Czar—what are you getting at?"

"If you help my daughter, I will bring you to the Czarina."

François Roland saw that Ash was about to explode and intervened.

"Monsieur Mikhailov, if you could take Commander Ash to the Empress, then you yourself could ask Her Majesty to help your daughter."

"And while you're at it, see what you can do for Tamara Tishkova."

"I can send you to her, but that's all."

Ash went to the window. Roland took the old man's arm. "It would be best if you left now, monsieur."

"You don't understand—"

"I do understand," Roland told him, steering him toward the door. "Your daughter is a lovely child and a beautiful dancer and I'm sure *you* can understand that Commander Ash is as upset as you are. *Bonjour, monsieur.*"

Vadim Mikhailov clamped one of his big hands on Roland's wrist and tore loose. "I didn't say *I* have influence with Her Majesty. I said I could get Commander Ash to her. Commander, I can get you a private audience with Her Majesty."

Ash turned from the window. He was nauseous and another headache had started. He felt perspiration suddenly cool on his temples. "How come you never offered this to me before? You know I was trying to get an audience."

"I couldn't before. But now I have an old friend who suddenly has access to Her Majesty's chambers—"

"Suddenly, Vadim? Just like that?"

"Yes."

"Vadim, I wish I could help you but I can't. Don't claim you can help me unless—"

"It's *true.* My friend has become her friend, I mean since Rasputin."

"What?"

"He . . ." Vadim hesitated. "Her Majesty grieves . . . my friend . . ." He trailed off as if reluctant to tell or as if he didn't believe it himself.

"Can't your friend speak for Vera? A word from Her Majesty and Vera would be released."

"I begged him. He can't. His position is not that secure . . . But he could bring you with him."

"Why would he?"

"You'd see why if you talked to him."

"Who is he?"

Vadim crossed his long arms. "I won't tell you until you help Vera."

Ash and Roland shared a skeptical glance. Was he lying or just exaggerating? Would the Czarina see him, again, even if the old man were telling the truth? Roland shrugged. Ash wondered if they'd overlooked some better way? But the fact was that when the tappeur had telephoned a half hour ago from the lobby, Ash and Roland had just come to the grim conclusion that Ash was stymied on both fronts—he had no plan to present King George's offer again; and even worse, no way to help Tamara . . . In the end, Tamara tipped it. Ash was desperate. Vera Sedovina was held in the Peter-Paul. So was Tamara. If their cells were at opposite ends of the prison, separated by a hundred walls, he would still be closer to Tamara than sitting in his suite in the Astoria Hotel.

The Okhrana captain inquired about Ash's condition when Ash telephoned. Ash said he was much better.

"And your memory?"

"Clear . . . I wonder if I might ask a difficult favor."

"Commander, I can tell you right now that if this favor concerns a certain woman—whom I shall not name—I can do nothing more for you than repeat my earlier advice that you disassociate yourself from her completely."

Ash tried to stay calm; he could hear in the police captain's voice that the Czar's government was terrified that news of the grand ducal conspiracy might reach the Russian people.

"I understand what you're saying. I'm not referring to that woman. But this is very delicate, nonetheless. Very delicate."

"Let me judge that, Commander."

"The daughter of a friend, a young girl, has been arrested. Her father is beside himself. I would like to see her."

"Who is the girl?"

"Unfortunately, Captain, it is a political matter about which she was arrested."

Ash waited. The police officer was silent. "And she's being held in the Peter-Paul Fortress."

"That is very difficult—"

"I wondered if you could direct me to the proper authorities who might get me permission to see her."

"Her name?"

"Sedovina."

"*Another* dancer?"

"Purely coincidental, sir."

Silence. Then: "It would be extremely difficult . . ." Again silence. Then: "Perhaps you might tell me something . . . ?"

"If I can."

"When we spoke last your injuries had affected your memory . . ."

"I'm almost fully recovered."

"Good. We now have evidence that the third sleigh in the Grand Duke Valery's entourage carried a machine gun. Do you know anything about it?"

"Of course."

"Of course?"

"It was a Maxim 'Sokolov' seven-six-two millimeter, 1910 model."

"Do you happen to remember why it was aboard the sleigh?"

"Well, it's my understanding that His Royal Highness had requisitioned several machine guns to test at his estate. He had been informed that the manufacturer had been skimping on certain specifications . . . the feed blocks were jamming . . . in fact, now that we speak"—Ash embroidered the lie—"it was my impression that His Highness was preparing charges against certain officials in the Ministry of Interior."

"Interior? Surely you mean the army—"

"No. His Highness indicated the culprits were in the Ministry of Interior." *Figure out who, you son of a bitch.*

When Ash finally hung up the telephone, Vadim's eyes were on him. "Yes?"

"Yes, Vadim. A visit." Ash stood up. The blood rushed from his head. He steadied himself on the chair.

"A visit?"

"I think I have permission to see Vera." And maybe, God willing, the girl might know something about Tamara.

"How will you get her out?"

"Out?"

"Out," Vadim Mikhailov shouted. "Free. You must *free* her."

"Vadim, I'm just—"

"I won't help you get to the Czarina through my friend until you free Vera from the Peter-Paul . . . *and* take her to America." . . .

"Out?" Roland echoed, when the old man had gone. "Is he crazy?"

Ash shook his head as he watched the tall, thin old man scurry down the hall. "He's crazy terrified. Just like me."

"There wasn't enough time to make her talk," Lieutenant Orlov was saying. "These revolutionaries take time and patience, Captain Moskolenko. Particularly the women. But the commandant wouldn't let me have her long enough—I think he has his own ideas—all I could do was soften her up a little."

Orlov's pudgy face wrinkled up with sincerity. "I know I would do much better in my own work space, Captain Moskolenko. Can't we bring her here to the Litovsky?"

Von Basel slowly nodded. He had begun thinking along slightly similar lines. Why not kidnap the women? Let Captain Moskolenko maintain the

386

deception at least for a while longer . . . and give him a considerable hold over Ash by having Tamara Tishkova.

He really needed Ash . . . the Czar was impregnable at both the Stavka and the Alexander Palace, where Tsarskoye Selo's mansions screened an armed camp; only aboard the Imperial Train was the Czar even slightly vulnerable to a seizure, but von Basel couldn't wait for the Imperial Train to move at the Czar's pleasure. Nor did he have to with Ash doing what he told him.

Kidnap the women from the Peter-Paul. Hold Ash's beloved Tishkova hostage. For ransom. A trade. Czar Nicholas II for Tamara Tishkova.

Ash would persuade the Czar to leave for England, then Ash would hand the Czar to von Basel, and von Basel would take the Czar to Germany. Orlov could have Sedovina, and thus occupied the Okhrana lieutenant would hardly challenge von Basel's claim that Tishkova had somehow escaped, disappeared . . . Two hours later von Basel had every forger loyal to him preparing papers to show the Peter-Paul prison commandant, while von Basel himself paid a call on the man to determine the proper bribe.

48

The commandant of the prison in the Peter and Paul Fortress was an immense, jowly man, a muscular blond who had gone to fat. He looked like he enjoyed his work. He addressed Ash through the Okhrana captain, who had agreed to the visit.

"He says, 'We don't often get them so attractive.' Then he asks, 'Who is she to you?' "

"A friend," Ash said.

The captain translated. The commandant laughed as he looped a ring of keys over his arm. He said something, and Ash told the captain, "I would just as soon not speak to him anymore."

The commandant continued to talk, however, and the colonel translated. "He says that no one has ever escaped from this prison. He hopes you will describe its innovative design to jailers in America."

Ash looked at the commandant and wondered if the man knew Ash himself had been a prisoner here this same winter. "Tell him we don't have political prisons in America—no, wait, don't. I don't want to offend him. Just tell him I'm ready to see her."

But the commandant knew some English, and answered Ash himself in a thick accent. "You will when you need them."

Whistling cheerfully, the commandant led Ash from his office in a low building that housed barracks and offices out to the snowy yards of the sprawling fortress. The gold spire and the onion dome atop the Cathedral of St. Peter and St. Paul flashed red in the afternoon sunset. The fortress walls hid the river and the city so that the yards and drilling fields could have been anywhere in Russia, thousands of miles off in the country, a bucolic impression enhanced by the lines of horse sleds delivering fire-wood.

The commandant turned into an alley between two long structures, one of stone, the other the more common Petrograd stucco painted yellow. He entered a heavy door at the end and gave a shout in Russian so that as Ash entered the small, dark room the guards turned and faced the stone wall, just as they had the night Ash had been arrested.

He followed the commandant into a second room, bare except for a wooden table and hooks on the wall—the search room where they had taken his clothing—then up a flight of stone steps through a guarded iron door and into the long corridor lined with pairs of wooden doors. It was colder than Ash remembered.

The commandant gestured to raise his hands. Ash did, and the Russian searched him thoroughly. He took his sword and leaned it in a corner, patted down his arms and legs and felt for a shoulder holster and belly gun. Then the neck, the back. His grin froze when he hit the hard lump of the chamois holster.

He snapped his fingers. A guard came instantly, pointed a pistol at Ash. The commandant gestured him to open his tunic. Ash undid the buttons and raised it. The commandant reached behind him and removed the contents of the holster.

Ash held his breath. The commandant closed his huge hand and ordered the guard away. When they were alone again in the corridor of wooden doors with iron mesh peepholes the commandant opened his hand. His grin had returned, wary, speculative, interested.

The gold clinked dully as he opened the leather sack. British sovereigns. Twenty pounds each. Fifty of them. Ten thousand roubles? Twenty thousand on the black market? He stared at the gold, hungering to take it, and finally shrugged with an almost sheepish expression.

Only in fantasy had Ash imagined he could buy a prisoner out of the Czar's chief political prison. But could he buy a moment alone with Tishkova? He said her name.

"Tishkova?" A complex expression replaced the sheepish disappointment on the commandant's face. She was here, all right, but the commandant was wondering how Ash knew. Ash had asked Vadim for the Russian word for "visit." He tried it now, massacring the pronunciation, tried it again.

The commandant's eyes widened some. Twenty thousand roubles for a *visit?*

Ash indicated the money was his for just that.

The jailor weighed the coins in his hand, then poured them back into the pouch and jammed the pouch in his pocket. He led Ash to a door, pushed a key in the slot, threw it open. Ash stepped in, the door clanged behind him. The cell was like the one he'd been in. There was a high barred window and, turning from it, a frightened Sedovina. Hope flared in her eyes; Ash put down his disappointment and tried to smile. Maybe the commandant would take him to Tamara afterward . . . maybe . . .

She stayed by the window, cut near the vaulted ceiling. She had been holding the bars and staring out at the red sky. They had put her in a shapeless muslin dress and felt slippers, but at least her long golden hair still looked attractive. The cell was chilly. She had chains on her wrists and on her ankles. Chains, for God's sake.

Ash looked at her and imagined Tamara. "How are you?" His voice was, unaccountably, a whisper.

Sedovina said, "No one can hear you. They put felt in the walls so we can't talk to each other between cells. I was so frightened, you were the only person I could think of . . ."

The electric light switched on from somewhere in the prison, and Ash could see her a bit more clearly than by the fading daylight from the window. He was shocked.

"My God . . . what happened to your face?"

"They hit me."

He felt sick. An ugly welt cut across her cheek from her lip to her ear.

"Who did that?"

"They asked me questions." She faced him, but still held the bars with one hand, her body extended as if she were dancing. "When I had nothing to tell them they hit me and they told me it was to remember . . . that they would come again for me."

Ash crossed the few steps of the cell and took her face gently in his hands and turned her cheek to the light. "What did they ask you?" he said, feeling ridiculously helpless, his eyes riveted to her cheek while his mind traced the welt on Tamara's face.

"They told me tomorrow." She started to cry. "They said they're coming back tomorrow, at sunset. They said to watch the sun and when it was gone they would come and get me—"

"They are just trying to frighten you . . . but don't do anything foolish . . . Valentinov has been arrested with all of his actors." The police, her father's lawyer had discovered, had made a clean sweep of the revolutionary troup—Czar, Czarina, Rasputin and the five children. "You can't protect them, Vera. They've all been caught. Just answer their questions." But what are they asking *you*, Tamara?

Sedovina pulled away. "They didn't ask about Valentinov . . ."

"Kirichenko? Don't worry about him. Nobody's caught him yet. You don't know a thing that would hurt him. Just answer their questions."

"They asked about you."

"*Me?*" That was crazy. He'd been flat on his back in the hospital ten days. He'd been there for the plucking anytime they'd wanted. The grand

390

duke was dead, his conspiracy died with him. What could they ask her they couldn't have asked him? There were limits to how far they'd go to avoid annoying even a potential ally . . .

"What did they ask?"

"They said they wanted to know what you did in Reval . . ."

Von Basel.

Her blue eyes filled with tears again. "I didn't even know you had gone to Reval. How could I? I told them. They said I was lying."

"Is that why you asked Vadim to come to me?"

"No, I didn't know. It was at the first prison. I just thought you could help somehow . . . I didn't know anyone else. Then they asked me about you . . . I don't really understand."

Ash put his arms around her. She had nothing under the thin muslin, and she felt soft and surprisingly slim for such a powerful dancer. Fright shook her body. "What can I tell him when they question me tomorrow?"

Ash took a deep breath. Von Basel had access to the prison, access to the prisoners . . . "Tell them I went to Reval to meet a Russian general from the Northern Sector." Swiftly he sketched in details to make it seem plausible. "I did it for the Grand Duke Valery. He was asking for the general's support." Sedovina looked puzzled. "It was an attempted coup, a palace coup, Vera. The duke was going to make himself Czar."

"What general?"

Brusilov, Ash started to answer, then thought twice. Brusilov was too good a general to put in jeopardy with an Okhrana investigation. If Ash had to condemn an innocent man to protect Sedovina and his real reason for going to Reval, at least let it be a nonentity whose absence from the battlefield might even reduce casualties.

"Were you part of the coup?"

Ash took another breath. This attempt to save her more agony was getting out of hand, but he saw a chance to help Tamara. "Some might think so . . . they're confused . . . arrested Tishkova instead, and she had nothing to do with it."

"They arrested Tishkova?" She seemed incredulous that such a symbol of the establishment could have been scooped up in the same net as she.

"She's in the Peter-Paul too. Have you seen her?"

"There's a woman in the next cell, I think. They keep us alone, I've only seen guards and the commandant. But when they opened the food slots I heard a woman crying."

Ash looked at the wall. A foot of plaster, stone and felt . . . he touched the wall. "Are you sure?"

"No. And there are many cells, Commander. And many prisoners." She put a hand on his arm. The chains dragged on his sleeve, but his own misery seemed to calm her. Finally Ash pulled himself together to ask, "Who questioned you about me?"

"The guards who held me called him Orlov . . . Lieutenant Orlov."

The name meant nothing to Ash. Just a name von Basel could have used . . .

"An Okhrana lieutenant?"

"I believe so."

Ash stared at the wall. "Was he Russian?"

"Of course."

"What did he look like?"

"Short and fat and he had no hair on his head."

Not von Basel . . . but who else cared why he went to Reval? "Who was with him?"

"Guards."

"What did *they* look like?"

"Just guards."

"Was there one about my height, very thin and a bony face?"

"No."

Could von Basel have an assistant? Or was all this unrelated to the German spy? "Do you have any idea why this Lieutenant Orlov would have thought I might have told you about Reval?"

"I wondered, then I recalled . . . twice you took me home. And you met me at the school. Someone saw us once and told Vadim, and Vadim boasted that you were courting me."

"Me? What would Mikhailov brag about me for? I'm an untitled and very unrich American naval officer. Your father's social sensibilities—"

"You're American," she said. "Vadim is afraid of the Revolution. He's begun to think that American is a very good thing to be."

Was Orlov simply unrelated to von Basel? "Did the commandant come with Orlov?"

"Just to my cell, he didn't come outside."

"Outside? What do you mean outside?"

"They took me to another building."

"Where?"

"I'm not sure . . . in the fortress. They seemed rushed, in a hurry to bring me back here."

"Did you go outside the same way you were first brought in?"

"I think so, it was dark the first time but we walked between those two buildings before we crossed a yard."

Her hand suddenly went to her face, her eyes grew large. "My God, Tishkova . . ."

"What?"

"He was frightening me and I started to cry and he said I'd have company tomorrow and they'd make us dance . . . that's what he meant . . ."

Ash sagged to the bunk. Orlov was von Basel's man, all right. The German couldn't risk Tamara exposing his true identity, so he'd sent

392

Orlov to question Vera first and then Tamara. He couldn't explain himself questioning Vera and then someone else—Tamara. Orlov would do both jobs . . .

And then a terrible realization . . . Tamara didn't know the real reason he had gone to Reval either. He had to give her more than the lie he'd given Sedovina. He'd put the girl in real danger, even though he'd tried to protect her. Besides his mission was still paramount . . . except when it came to Tamara, who was more important than anything . . .

The door burst open. The commandant motioned him out. When Ash hesitated the man stepped in, grabbed his arm and pulled him into the corridor while two guards slammed the cell door shut. Sedovina was left there, watching in her chains.

"Tishkova?" Ash said to the commandant.

The man let go Ash's arm, hitched up his pants so Ash could hear the gold coin clink, and grinned. *"Nyet."*

Ash slammed him aside and threw himself at the door beside Sedovina's. "Tamara." He called out the name as loudly as he could, clawing open the peephole. "Tell them I went—"

Two guards hit him from behind, wrestled him to the floor and carried him out of the prison, the face of a stranger locked in his memory—young and frightened, with bruises to imagine a hundredfold on Tamara's face.

He left notes for von Basel in their drop in the wrecked German Embassy and slipped into the shambles several times in the night and hourly the next morning.

Von Basel made no reply. The sun faded as the day wore on, and by early afternoon the snow had begun falling. Laden clouds promised another Gulf blizzard. As for Lieutenant Orlov's taunt about sunset, today its moment could only be guessed at by Sedovina and Tamara as they watched the sky from their barred windows.

49

The widowed peasant woman's son had come home from the war with one leg and a rusty German pistol. God provided, in His fashion; the boy guarded her sledloads of green birch logs from the thieves and deserters roaming the countryside. Green or dry, the fortress bought firewood and paid cash. They paid no more than before the war when everything else had cost a quarter of what it did now, but at least they paid. Her son said she was a fool, that she could get three times as much from the palaces across the river, but she had never crossed the Neva and did not intend to start now, not a widow with a crippled son.

He sat grumbling, driving the horse. She stood on one of the wooden wings that stuck out a yard each side to stop the sled turning over and worried how few potatoes were left in the root cellar under her log hut. Ten *versts* from the fortress, still on a sparsely traveled lane, a strange vehicle bore down on them. It looked like a motorcar, but the front wheels were attached to skis and it had no wheels at all in back, instead a wide, ribbed belt spun underneath and made the motorcar go by clawing the snow like the hundred feet of a caterpillar.

Her son cursed and forced the pony to the side while she shouted at him to look out for the ditch. Imagine her and him with his one leg trying to free the sled. The caterpillar belt stopped turning and the vehicle skidded to a halt, blocking the road.

Three men got out. Her son reached for his rusty pistol, but she stopped him. These were not the type to rob wood. The eldest was lean as a stork, gray-skinned and bony and even older than she was. He wore a long tailored coat, what country people called a *diplomat*, though this one was frayed. The young ones wore the cloaks of aristocrat soldiers. One had an officer's mustache, the other had lost an arm. God provided—if her son had lost only an arm instead of a leg he would have gone to the city and left her alone.

The old stork addressed her in labored Russian heavy with German and French accents and words she didn't know. He reached into his *diplomat* and pulled from the coat pocket thick wads of roubles. She had never seen so much money in her life but she could count and it looked like enough to buy a horse and a cow and roubles left over for potatoes to last until summer. The old stork said she could have the money if the gentleman with the mustache could ride into the Peter-Paul Fortress under her heap of wood.

She asked how he would get out again. She said when she took manure from the fortress stables in her empty sled the guards stuck bayonets into it as she left.

How he would get out was not her concern, the old stork answered sharply. All he wanted was to get in. Her son shrugged. A crazy man with money was no concern of theirs. They drove the sled into a copse, out of sight of the road, and hid the wood they removed to make room for the man. The snowcar followed; her son was bewitched by it . . . he said it made a railroad track out of the snow. She told him to shut his mouth; the aristocrats were speaking. Her son knew some French words but he shook his head. They were speaking English.

"This is less a plan than a hope," Roland chided as Ash prepared to climb into the sled.

"It's also my only hope."

"I wish you would reconsider, let me come in with you—"

"I need you outside. I want that snowcar warmed up and raring to go in case I come out with a posse after me."

" 'Posse'? What is 'posse'?"

"*Gendarmerie*, is what it is. The sheriff and a whole bunch of deputies." Ash lay down in the sled, and Roland motioned the peasants to cover him with the logs. "Like the cops?" Roland asked, and Ash said, "Yes, except on horses."

Roland touched his shoulder. *"Bonne chance, ami."*

When they had buried the one with the mustache to the satisfaction of his companions, the old stork and the one-armed aristocrat did a strange thing. The stork held the money in both hands for her to see. The one-armed man pulled a silvery blade from his walking stick and sliced the roubles in half. His blade cut the thick wad like butter. He gave her one half and kept the other. The stork said she could have it when their friend got out safely.

She protested how could she be blamed if he didn't get out of the fortress, they were taking advantage of a widow, but the old stork fixed her with his beady stare and she knew in her heart that he knew that she had had every intention of telling the guards and demanding a reward . . . because the money for a horse and milk cow was not enough. Before she could buy them she had to pay the *koulak* to whom she owed her debts, and then the tax collector who would demand his share for the horse and cow.

Ash ducked down as a squad of conscripts, fresh from the farm by the look of them, marched past the woodpile where he had crouched for the hour he'd been watching the prison entrance. The drill sergeant bellowed, and the unit right-flanked away from the firewood, except for one gawky kid who turned left, straight toward Ash.

The fortress, which housed some twenty-five thousand troops within its walls, was busy as a city this evening; in spite of the steadily thickening snow the lamplit yards between the low barracks and storehouses echoed tramping feet and the rattle of rifle bolts. When the sled had first left him in the woodpile, which covered nearly a quarter acre, Ash had worried that the soldiers would still be drilling when von Basel's man came for Tamara and Sedovina. After a while he began to wonder if he'd somehow missed them.

The boy kept coming. Ash edged deeper into shadow. It was dark now, later than Lieutenant Orlov's sunset taunt, but the soldiers continued to drill by the light spilling from the windows.

The exasperated drill sergeant ran after the kid, leaped in the air and slammed both boots into the small of his back. The kid crashed face-first into the logs. Ash heard him grunt, then saw him jump up, bleeding from the nose, and hurry back to his laughing comrades, where he executed the next turn correctly while Ash finally let his breath out.

A cannon boomed six o'clock. The soldiers fell out, and minutes later the yards were deserted except for some black-robed priests walking slowly toward the cathedral. Ash stood up and walked boldly toward the passage that led to the prison. Two men in civilian clothes were approaching the passage from the direction of the main Neva Gates. Ash veered close enough to get a look at them, then headed for the cathedral. Neither was von Basel, but one looked fairly short and squat. Sidelong, he watched them turn into the passage beside the prison.

He went up the cathedral steps now, and when he looked back again he could barely see the two-story yellow building through the snow. He went inside and knelt by a tomb near the door. The priests had gathered before a huge altar at the far end; there were no pews but many tombs.

Ash timed the progress of the two men in his mind, following them into the prison while his eyes played over the surprising sight of Roman letters. He was praying at Peter the Great's tomb, the Czar who had built the city, this fortress and cathedral and the prison . . . visualizing now . . . up the passage, in the main door, the foyer and the search room, then presenting some passes of some sort and waiting, perhaps, while the guards went up the stone steps, through a door down to the end of the first corridor, turn right and to the end of the second corridor, halfway down the third to Sedovina's door. Key in the lock, throw the door back, take the frightened girl with Tamara nearby. Key in the lock, throw the door back, take Tamara. Throw blankets over their shoulders, walk them out the door, down the corridor, left turn, down the corridor, left turn down the corridor, through the door, down the steps and hand them to the two men, who take them from either side, through the search room and the foyer and into the snow. Ash got up and hurried out of the cathedral, loosening his saber.

The yard was still deserted, the snow thick. No one came from the passage. Ash looked both ways. No one. He ran to find their tracks before fresh snow covered them—and just then they stepped out of the passage. They had taken the extra minutes to remove the ankle chains.

Tamara. She was holding herself erect, stiff, as if angry. Ash prayed that angry meant she wasn't hurt. The short one was holding Sedovina's arm, the other Tamara's. Ash drew closer. The short one was speaking to Sedovina in Russian, his voice insinuating, threatening. He became silent when he saw Ash approaching, confirming that this removal was clandestine and that at best the prison commandant had been paid off to look the other way.

Sedovina looked terrified. Ten feet from them now, and Tamara saw Ash. Her face lit up for a moment, then went blank. She drew back, momentarily distracting the man holding her. Ash took the opportunity, pulled his saber like a boarding cutlass and smashed the man with the hilt. For once it worked like they'd promised at the Academy. Surprise and slippery footing helped. The man went down hard as Ash whipped the point to the throat of the second man.

"Translate," Ash told Tamara. "Tell him I'll kill him if he doesn't hand over his papers." He pulled his Luger and held it under his cloak. Orlov's eyes went from Ash's blade to the gun and back to the blade pricking his throat.

"I speak English. You can't use my papers, they know me at the gate—"

"Take us with you."

"They won't let me."

Ash slid the saber back into his scabbard and aimed the gun at Orlov's eyes. "Try."

Orlov's companion stirred on the ground. Ash yanked the man to his feet, snapped his arm into a hammerlock, held the pistol on Orlov again. "We're walking across the yard to those woodpiles. Tamara, stay close.

Hold Sedovina." He looked both ways. A group of officers was approaching but they were distant, barely distinguishable in the swirling snow.

"Go on." He jerked the man he was holding and shoved the pistol in Orlov's back. They crossed the yard, passed dangerously close to some of the lamps, finally made the woodpiles. Ash looked back. Had they been spotted from any of the windows? He waited for an alarm.

Ash let go the hammerlock and hit the Russian in the back of his neck. Orlov started to move again. Ash covered him, ordered him to kneel. He looked down at Orlov. "I know you hit Sedovina, I can imagine what you planned for both of them tonight—"

"Nothing, just to frighten them—"

"Where were you taking them?"

Orlov hesitated, then: "The same as yesterday. A barracks room. I was only going to question—"

"Shut up and listen to me . . . I'll kill you the first hint I get that we can't escape from here. You're taking us out of here . . . your life is in your own hands. Now get up and get us out."

Orlov did and turned toward the Peter Gates.

"No." Ash stopped him. "The river gates. Take us to the river, damn you."

Count von Basel found the lingering aroma of his police chauffeur who'd gone to relieve himself sufficient to impel him to pull down his window, ignoring the cold snow the wind was blowing up the river. He was parked on the ice a hundred yards from the fortress, which was a dark, barely visible presence, looming in the night. A faint light marked the river gates, where Orlov would soon emerge, if there was still a God in heaven, with Vera Sedovina and Ash's Tamara Tishkova.

Von Basel and the commandant had reached a fair bargain after von Basel provided a blizzard of official memoranda to make the commandant appear properly innocent. And Lieutenant Orlov, completely unaware of what was going on, his primitive mind slathering over the young ballerina, was armed with the finest papers signed by the most important officials money could buy. There were moments, von Basel thought with a smile, when one could really learn to love Russia.

The needle tip of a saber touched his throat. Carefully, slowly, he looked to see, framed in the car window, hat and cloak covered with snow, Chevalier François Roland. For a moment the silence was so complete he thought he could hear the river rushing under the thick ice.

"Step out of your car, Count von Basel."

In all these years in Russia von Basel had never been caught by surprise.

And now, by of all people . . . it was almost worse than if Ash had done it himself.

"You goddamned French queer."

Roland's eyebrows drooped. "If that is a proposition, my dear, I must confess I never couple with leprous Arabs, syphilitic dogs or German counts. Put your hands where I can see them, and get out."

Von Basel saw the returning driver moving up in a crouch behind Roland. The man straightened up, raised his pistol like a club. Perhaps instinct warned Roland, von Basel thought, perhaps the abrupt cessation of snow on his back when the police chauffeur blocked the wind with his body . . . whatever, once warned, the Frenchman was impressive in his speed and accuracy. He whirled, slashed—and not, von Basel noted as he made his way across the seat and out the opposite door, not just anywhere. Right to the throat, so that the man died instantly. Von Basel rested a gun on the roof of the car and aimed at Roland. Roland allowed himself a smile. "Put it away . . . you can't use a noisy gun any more than I can. If you could you wouldn't be lurking out here." He walked around the car. Von Basel pulled his sword out of his walking stick and opened the hilt bars.

Roland shook his head. "Surely your psychotic tendencies do not include the suicidal. Keep in mind that my training was somewhat more rigorous than yours, which I gather consisted of butchering impetuous, untutored university students."

Von Basel ignored the taunt. "I'm a duelist—" he raised his saber— "you're only a fencer."

"I think I saw enough killing at Verdun to last me a lifetime, but I can and I will kill you if you don't surrender that weapon—"

"I also have a second advantage," von Basel said, no smile on his face. "Two arms." He pulled out a long dagger, rapped it twice against his saber. *"En garde."*

"Drop back," Ash said. "Let them out first." Ahead, officers leaving for the night on passes were converging on the brightly lighted river gate from various paths. They stopped under a tree, one of many lining the path which contributed at this point to the feeling of an urban park.

"Vera, take his other arm, and Tamara you take mine. Hold her, Orlov. She's supposed to be your prisoner. Show your chains, Vera." Her wrists were still shackled, Tamara's weren't. As they neared the gate Ash held Tamara's arm conspicuously and nudged Orlov with the gun through his cloak.

The gate was a pass through the wall, about fifty feet long with a vaulted ceiling. Iron grills barred it inside and out, and soldiers guarded the grills, which were kept closed until they opened them to allow someone through. Ash reflected that while they were crossing the fifty feet between the two grills the guards had time to change their minds.

Orlov slapped his papers in the guard's hand and answered insolently in Russian when the soldier asked him something. Ash looked at Tamara, who nodded it was all right. The guard opened the gate grill and they passed through, Orlov starting to hang back.

"Keep moving."

They reached the second, outer, grill, and Ash again watched Tamara's reaction as Orlov spoke to the head of the guard. The conversation was longer this time, but at last the grill swung open. Ash nudged Orlov. He pushed Sedovina through and Ash followed with Tamara. Shouts echoed through the stone pass. The guards looked toward them.

Ash saw a commotion at the first grill, saw the man he had left at the woodpile shouting and pointing. Sedovina called out a warning. Orlov had pulled a gun from his coat.

"Raise your hands, Commander."

50

Ash shot through his cloak and caught Orlov's gun as the Russian detective fell. The startled guards had no idea where the shot had come from. Their officer, however, quickly took a revolver from his flap holster. Ash knocked him down with Orlov's gun, but the officer kicked Ash's feet from under him. Ash was put on his back with a bone-jarring crash.

The guards lunged at him. Tamara scooped up the revolver the officer had dropped and shot the nearest guard. Ash got to his feet, ordered the other guard to put his hands on the wall. Tamara waved her gun and translated. The guard did as he was told, and the officer buried his face in the snow.

"Run," Ash said, pushing Tamara toward the river. She caught Sedovina's shackled wrist, and they ran together across the stone terrace, down the landing stairs. Backing after them, Ash fired shots down the vaulted gateway, scattering soldiers now running through it. He made for the landing and caught up on the ice. Sedovina had fallen and Tamara was pulling her to her feet.

Ash scanned the dark. "Where's Roland?"

Muzzle flashes showed beneath the black cliff of the fortress. The crack of pistols was joined by the deeper sound of rifles. The cutting wind carried snow so thick that the lights of the Winter Palace had vanished only half a mile across the river. Ash took Tamara's hand, she held Sedovina, they ran onto the river.

"Roland . . ."

The muzzle flashes homed in on his voice. They went quickly to the ice, crawled from the gunfire. Ash spotted the dark shape of a car, got up, stumbled over a snow-covered body. Roland? He turned him over. A stranger, his throat slashed. And it wasn't the snowcar. He heard another motor, and the snowcar now loomed out of the dark, Roland at the wheel. Rifle fire again, bullets snapping past their heads, caroming off the car.

Roland turned it clumsily. Ash pushed Tamara and Sedovina in the back, jumped in beside Roland as the rifle fire concentrated once again. Roland reached for the gear stick, groaned, slumped against the steering wheel. His face was a white blur in the dark. He managed to get out . . . "Von Basel . . . *poniard* . . ."

Ash pulled Roland from the wheel. The weapon was stuck in his chest . . . von Basel had stabbed Roland with a heavy dagger while Roland had tried to fend off von Basel's saber with his single arm . . . God, how in hell had Roland cranked the car? How long could he last?

The fortress searchlights flung white beams into the night. Ash eased his friend into the passenger seat, climbed over him, found the clutch and gear stick and skidded into a tight turn—a circle of light came swiftly over the ice and caught the car.

"*Down,*" Ash instructed. "Heads down."

But Tamara had already stretched over the front seat and was cradling Roland in her arms while bullets slashed the canvas top and ricocheted off the metal.

"He beat me . . ." Roland whispered.

"He had a *poniard,* friend, not exactly an even-up fight . . ." Ash found second gear.

The Frenchman tugged his sleeve. "He's better than we thought . . ."

Ash felt the caterpillar track bite deep, but the searchlight blinded him and he skidded back toward the fortress.

"Kennet—"

He veered too late, a second light caught the car—a pair of hugely wide-set eyes. Ash tried to steer away. Cat's eyes, gauging when to pounce. Ash slewed a hundred and eighty degrees, put the lights behind the car, headed for darkness. "Got to find a hospital—"

Roland was silent. A machine gun opened up with a grinding noise that overwhelmed the rifles and the laboring engine. Bullets chewed up the ice, seeking the car in bursts; Ash turned hard left, hard right, repeated the maneuver, zigzagging to confuse the gunner, but the man was too skillful and the heavy slugs continued to crack past their heads, ricochet off the car. The left ski shattered. The car lurched, and sagged to the ice.

A third searchlight closed in. Ash risked a glance back. The fortress looked on fire with white lights and the flickers of rifle shots and the steady red tracing of a machine gun high up on top of the bastion, its bullets sticking the snow.

But the snowcar was pulling out of range; the damaged ski held and the blowing snow had begun to curtain them from the guns and lights.

Sedovina shook Ash's shoulder. "The tram. The tram on the ice. It's downstream, you can't drive over it."

Ash nodded, started to put the crippled car into a gentle turn upstream with the blazing fortress on his left when he heard a dull boom and the ice exploded next to the car. Artillery. A two-inch gun. Chunks of ice blasted by the shell shook the car and tore off its canvas roof. Ice splinters tore at Ash's face. Another sullen boom and the shell exploded on the ice thirty feet away. Bracketed. Lights were converging again. The next shot would surely be a direct hit.

"*Out.*" Ash stopped the engine, the snowcar skidded to a halt. He ran around the car and grabbed at Roland. A third explosion simultaneous with the boom of the cannon hit in front of the car, rocking it and hurling Ash against Tamara.

"Leave him—"

"I can't—"

"He's *dead,* Kennet. Please . . ."

The cannon boomed again, the shell splitting the air with its terrible keening sound. Tamara tugged Ash from the car, and he reluctantly went with her. They found Sedovina and ran together downstream as more searchlights found the car. Ash looked back. Roland's arm was stretched toward the lights, his head was thrown back against the seat . . . almost, it occurred bizarrely to Ash, as if he were acknowledging applause from the fortress.

The car exploded under a direct hit, and as they ran into the night and the swirling snow, and the noise of the rifle and machine-gun fire died away, they heard a new sound—hoofbeats—the rumble of Cossack lancers coming after them . . .

They ran from the lancers, from the searchlights, from the glare of the burning car. The ice was rough, and the new coating of snow made it difficult to see the variations in it. Sedovina stumbled, she had lost one of the felt slippers. Ash managed to retrace their steps, found the slipper and brought it to her. Tamara knelt and put it on. The girl seemed in shock.

"I can't keep up . . . go ahead and—"

Tamara and Ash took Sedovina's hands in case she got any more crazy ideas about stopping. Suddenly ahead was another searchlight. Ash was about to dive into the snow when he saw it was moving rapidly. Tamara saw it too and guessed what it was. "The *tram.* Come on . . ."

Behind them horses sounded closer; the riders were calling to each other, their voices moving apart as they spread across the ice. Ash spotted the slight ridge of the tramline and then the headlight illuminating the power wire overhead and the line of poles that held it, and finally the gleam of the steel rails.

Behind the headlight shone the windows of a two-car tram. People were wiping at the iced glass, peering out at the flashes of gunfire and the burning car. Tamara went onto the track and proceeded to hail the speeding tram like a taxi.

Sedovina scrambled after her. The tram screeched, locked wheels scattered sparks. Ash pulled Tamara over the embankment as the tram slid past and banged to a halt. Now the faces switched to the other side and stared down at the three people struggling to stand up in the snow. A few jumped down to help. Ash didn't know which way to go . . . the Cossacks would reach the line in seconds. Downstream was the icy empty waste of the river . . . and the embankments were too far to run to . . .

But Sedovina suddenly came to life, took control. She went aboard the tram and raged at the occupants in Russian. Some backed away from her. Others glanced in the direction of the Cossacks. Some started shouting at the driver, who crossed his arms and shook his head.

"What'd she say?"

"She's asking, *telling* them to help us," Tamara said.

"Come," Sedovina called out. "Hurry."

Ash looked at Tamara. They could hear the Cossacks. "We'll be trapped," she told Ash.

A group of men who had been shaking their fists at the driver surged into the aisle, ran to the front and pushed him away from the controls. Moments later the tram jerked forward.

"Come," Sedovina repeated. *"Hurry . . ."*

Ash looked at Tamara. They ran for the rear step as the car picked up speed, swung aboard the hot stuffy car to the cheers of the passengers. They increased speed, but suddenly the lancers galloped into the light that spilled from the windows, came alongside and kept pace while their officer shouted for the men driving the tram to stop.

Ahead, Ash saw the light pick up the distant Palace Embankment through the blowing snow. The officer drew his heavy saber and slashed at the window in the driver's compartment. The passengers driving the tram ducked from the shower of broken glass, and one grabbed the stick used to raise the electric contact, leaned half out the broken window and swung back at the startled officer, who pulled his horse up and gave a command.

The Cossacks whipped their rifles off their backs.

"Get *down*," Ash called out.

But instead of doing what Ash told them, the passengers climbed to their feet and stood in the windows.

"Tell them to get down, they'll be killed—"

"They won't get down," Sedovina said. "Not again."

The officer slashed and shouted again. Tamara pulled at Ash's arm. "He's telling them to shoot."

The passengers stood firm. A few horsemen halfheartedly raised their guns, but none fired even as the tram picked up speed and the track began rising to the Palace Embankment. The officer continued to shout and be ignored as one by one the lancers stopped their horses. Ash watched until they were lost in the dark. The last he saw of them was the officer turning his horse and riding slowly back to the fortress.

The passengers broke into a cheer, and as the tram slowed and they prepared to run before the police came, two workmen hurriedly opened a sack of tools and chiseled the manacles off Sedovina's wrists. One, a worn-looking man in his forties, knelt, whispered something to Tamara, kissed her hand and hurried back to the tram . . . .

They crossed the Nevsky and hurried by back streets the short distance to the troika-stand behind the Kazan Cathedral.

When the racing sleigh had finally left the city behind and was breaking into the woods of Krestovsky Island, Ash, who was sitting between Tamara and Sedovina with an arm around each, saw that Tamara had tears in her eyes. "Is it something the man from the tram said to you?"

She shook her head. "I was thinking of Roland . . ."

Sedovina, huddled against Ash, said, "He told Tishkova that when he was a young man, before he had a family to feed, he had waited two nights in the snow to buy a ticket in the highest seat of the gallery to see Tishkova dance. He said it was the most magnificent moment of his life and in twenty years he'd never forgotten."

Vadim Mikhailov sat alone in a crowd of drunken Russians singing to gypsy guitars. Wondering if any were police spies, Ash hurried through the revelers and sank down on the cushions beside the old piano player. "They're okay, at the River Yacht Club."

"Thank God."

"Have you found a place to hide? They can't stay there."

"Can I see her?"

"What about your friend, Vadim . . . you promised—"

"He's coming any minute, he will come and help you, and hide the ladies."

Ash wasn't sure whether he believed Mikhailov. He was exhausted, and heartsick over François Roland. The gypsy songs were a grating din and there seemed more cigarette smoke than air . . . He'd willingly risked his whole mission to save Tamara, but really never thought Roland would be the price . . . "Dammit, where the hell is your friend?"

Vadim Mikhailov fidgeted, poured tea from a nearby samovar and looked anxiously at the door each time the candles blew. Suddenly he turned to Ash. "You said yesterday that Tishkova had an affair with the Czar."

"Years ago," Ash said bleakly. "What's that got to do with—?"

"It troubles you—"

"Dammit, Vadim, it's none of your business."

"Well, it's not true. They were friends, briefly when she was a girl and more recently again. He was taken with her—so beautiful, such a splendid dancer, but I believe no affair. I know people who were commanded to perform in the *Firebird* at the Alexander Palace—"

"The ballet?" Ash asked, aware how good it felt to believe she hadn't slept with Nicholas.

Mikhailov, relieved to have been able to distract Ash, nodded, vigorously. "Right after it was performed in Paris the Czar invited Tishkova to dance *Firebird* for the Court at the Alexander Palace. A great honor. The sets and costumes were shipped from the Paris production—the Czarina canceled it."

"Why?"

"Jealous, perhaps . . . or perhaps she just did not like Stravinsky . . . anyway, as a result the sets and costumes lie in the cellars of the Alexander Palace, and the great *Firebird* has never been danced in Russia."

Ash looked at the door. "*Where* is your friend, they're not that safe at the club" . . . Nor, judging by the mood of that crowd on the tram, Ash thought, did the Czar have much more time.

Tamara refused to stop moving. If she did she would think, and if she thought, she would remember . . . the running and shooting, the explosions, and Roland dying in her arms, and the thunder of the Cossacks. And if she let herself remember that she would be as frightened as Sedovina.

Kennet had done well indeed . . . a warm room, a huge bath, clothing, boots, even a wig to cover her all too famous jet black hair. She bathed quickly, though she ached so from tension in every muscle she felt it would take a year to rid her body of the strain and the stench of the prison. She vacated the tub for Sedovina and left her to soak while she made up, arranged the auburn wig and chose her clothing.

She got Sedovina out of the bath, got her dried off and into one of her dresses, which was a bit short in the hem and full in the bosom. She sat her in front of a mirror and began pinning up her beautiful golden hair, envying its thickness.

"I couldn't believe such things would happen in Russia . . . the guards were despicable, look at your face. No wonder people are angry—"

"The guards are brutalized by the established order," Sedovina murmured. "That's how the Czar rules."

"They're brutes," Tamara said, stuffing the girl's hair under one of her sable hats.

"No . . . the guards are Russian too. The Czar has ruled by making us hate each other. Peasants, Cossacks, artists, soldiers—*we* are Russia. We don't have to fight each other—"

"Good," said Tamara, "at least you seem to be snapping out of it." She looked closely at Sedovina. God she was beautiful, bump on the nose and all. What did Kennet think of her?

"I was terribly afraid," Sedovina said, on the edge of tears. "I wanted to be brave but the noise—"

"You were very brave when you had to be, when it counted. You saved us on the tram . . . Well, we have to cover that mark on your face."

Wielding her softest powder brushes, Tamara worked pale rouge over the welt. Sedovina winced. Tamara made her laugh by saying, "Haven't you heard it hurts to be beautiful?"

When she was done she draped one of her coats over the girl's shoulders. Sedovina said it was too fine, her father had left her own coat.

Tamara insisted. "The police aren't so likely to be hunting escaped prisoners in sable."

"There!"

An old man shuffled in. He seemed ancient, haggard-looking, thinner, if that were possible, than even Mikhailov. He had the aloof stare of an aristocrat.

"My friend," Vadim said proudly. "His Royal Highness Prince Kurakin."

Ash was not impressed. Russia was littered with impoverished nobles, and this one's cape looked a hundred years old. "How is he going to get me to the Czarina?"

"Prince Kurakin is a necromancer. He holds seances. He has raised the ghost of Rasputin—"

"Mikhailov, I warn you—"

"Yes, yes, it's true. He has raised the ghost. Protopopov himself attends his seances—asking the ghost for advice."

Ash groaned. Why had he even for a second believed Vadim—

"He is summoned by the Empress. He's been to Tsarskoye Selo every night this week. He'll bring you with him, now."

Ash held back and considered . . . Lord Exeter had claimed that the Czarina was consulting mystics. He looked at the prince. "Sounds like a faker who got lucky. Why would he help me?"

"Faker or not, I won't judge, but Prince Kurakin has concluded that the Czar must leave. Someone, Rasputin when he was alive, or the Czarina herself told him you had come to rescue the Czar." Ash looked at Vadim. He had never told the tappeur his intentions. "How come he's friends with a piano player?" To hell with being diplomatic at this point.

"His Highness is poor, very poor. He permits me to buy him drinks . . . Whatever you think, at least pretend to take him seriously."

Ash glanced again at Prince Kurakin. For a moment the moving shadows of the gypsy candlelight made him look like the villain in a William Gillette melodrama. "All right, let's hear what he's selling."

Ash caught the prince's eye and indicated with a nod that he should join them. Kurakin looked away and stared at the gypsy dancers. Mikhailov said, "He is a nobleman, Commander. We must go to him." Ash bit his tongue and they did. Prince Kurakin invited them to sit. He spoke in a quavering voice with a funereal tone that struck Ash as intended to promise intimacy with the supernatural. But instead of the hocus-pocus Ash feared, he got to the point matter-of-factly.

"Rasputin has repeatedly warned me that revolution is imminent. Last night he informed me that His Imperial Majesty the Czar is the cause of the people's anger. He told me to tell the ministers to form a new government."

Ash refrained from remarking that Rasputin seemed to have assumed the attitude of an anxious nobleman.

"Mikhailov tells me I can help you . . . Your Highness."

Kurakin raised a spidery hand. His eyes were bright, no doubt with a mystic light. It wasn't hard to imagine him holding a seance in thrall. But again he spoke like a nobleman who had suddenly come to realize that the mob was about to pull Petrograd down around his ears.

"The Czar must be removed. But not harmed. Rasputin was adamant. Their Royal Imperial Majesties must not be harmed."

"They won't be—if you bring me to the Czarina tonight."

Prince Kurakin hesitated, finally said, "I will try. She is Empress of all the Russias. I am but one poor lowly prince who happens to be able to communicate with her friend, the peasant Rasputin—"

Mikhailov broke in. "If I may, Your Highness, relate to Commander Ash how Protopopov has taken advantage"—the prince gave a slight nod, Mikhailov became more indignant with each word—"His Highness admitted Protopopov to his seance. Now the minister runs to the Czarina with each of Rasputin's utterances—reports them himself as if *he* and not Prince Kurakin were the one who had the vision." The piano player glanced around and lowered his voice conspiratorially. "Do you know it is said that two days ago while reporting to Her Majesty the minister suddenly threw himself on his knees and said, 'I see the Savior standing behind you, Your Majesty.' The man has no shame."

Wondering if his last hope of reaching the Czar lay with two deluded old men, Ash said, "Your Highness, may I ask your interest in this? What do you want from me?"

"I am a Russian," Prince Kurakin said. "I see visions of the future, and that future is red with blood . . . still, I have hope Rasputin might be our savior. By removing the Czar, as Rasputin directs, maybe we can stave off the slaughter."

Ash nodded. Whether Kurakin meant that, or was merely competing with Interior Minister Protopopov for the favors of an apparently highly suggestible Czarina didn't matter a hell of a lot if he could help him get the Czar off his throne and thereby keep Russia stable enough to go on fighting Germany . . . and make Russia a palatable ally for the U.S. Strange how it all came back to Rasputin . . . almost as though it had been preordained or something . . . dammit, Ash thought, I'm thinking like a Russian . . .

The police stopped their troikas at the palace bridge. Ash and the prince were in the lead, on their way to the Tsarskoye Selo Railroad Station. He tried to signal Tamara, Sedovina and Mikhailov in the second troika but it was too late. Mikhailov was taking them to the prince's apartment near the Moscow Railroad Station—as unexpected and therefore safe a hiding place as they could find in the city. Ash hadn't expected a roadblock at the palace bridge so many hours after their escape.

The women were dressed like a pair of wealthy Petrograd matrons out for a big night, their faces almost hidden in fur . . . Still, if the police launched a full search . . . but it turned out the police had their hands full diverting traffic from the palace area because thousands of demonstrators were marching down the Nevsky. The windblown snow carried thunder —*Khleba. Khleba. Khleba . . . .*

They could still hear the chanting at the station. Prince Kurakin was recognized and ushered aboard a waiting train with elaborate courtesy. "Bread," he intoned as they settled into an otherwise empty parlor car. "That ought to keep Minister Protopopov busy until we've seen Her Majesty . . ." He then became silent and remained that way for the thirty-minute ride through the night. There was no sign in the dark, or on the smooth Tsarskoye Selo roadbed, of Kirichenko's explosions. Where, Ash wondered, had the fighting squad leader gone to? Probably to the middle of Petrograd, tonight . . .

Kurakin was equally silent in the court carriage that took them past the aristocracy's mansions and the Catherine Palace, but he suddenly rapped his stick on the roof of the carriage. It stopped, bowing footmen opened the door and Kurakin climbed out in the snow. The lights of the Alexander Palace were still far ahead, but Kurakin's attention was drawn to a cluster of flaming torches some distance off the drive. Wrapping his black cape around his shoulders, he motioned Ash to join him.

"Where are you going?"

"Rasputin's tomb."

Through the snow Ash could just make out a small structure, and as they drew nearer he saw it was a chapel, still under construction. Prince Kurakin followed a path of wooden planks. "He won't be here long," he said in his most dirgelike tones.

A carriage was parked outside. Ash waited for an explanation.

"Rasputin predicted that his ashes would be cast to the wind—his body returned to God."

Footmen attended the carriage. An equerry who looked like he hadn't been outside in years shivered in patent leather shoes and the red cape embroidered with the double-headed Imperial Eagle of his office at the entrance to the chapel. He bowed to Prince Kurakin, who said, "Inform the Empress that her friend appeared at my seance tonight."

The equerry took this information as routine and retreated into the chapel. Kurakin turned to a skeptical Ash. "I don't make things up."

"Of course . . . Your Highness."

Kurakin glowered and drew his threadbare cape closer around his scrawny throat. The equerry returned. "Her Imperial Majesty requests that you pray with her." He led them into the chapel, which smelled of freshly sawn wood and hot wax. There, praying before a candlelit icon on a flower-spread altar, knelt Czarina Alexandra.

Her head was bowed and her eyes were closed and she made no sign as the equerry cleared flowers on either side of her to make space for Ash and Prince Kurakin. Ash knelt and watched sidelong. She wore a sable coat, the hood thrown back, and a lace shawl over her auburn hair. She looked remarkably well, Ash thought, far better than the rumors had led him to expect, her face smooth, her expression calm, almost placid; erase, as did the flickering candles, the hollows of pain and suffering normally under her eyes, and a girl of exquisite beauty shone through. Between Her Majesty, Kchessinska and Tamara Tishkova, Ash had to admit, the Czar, whatever his shortcomings, certainly had picked beautiful women.

She opened her eyes, looked past Prince Kurakin to Ash. Her eyes became wide, and for a second Ash expected her to scream as she'd done when she'd seen him in the Czar's billard room. "You again push yourself into my life, Commander."

Ash said nothing, tried to meet her steady gaze while hoping for the prince to interrupt. The prince kept silent. Ash waited . . . "When I was informed that you had accompanied Prince Kurakin, I wondered whether you would have the nerve to desecrate this holy place. What sort of monster are you?"

Ash knew this was his last chance to convince the royal family to leave. The Romanovs were finished and Russia was finished with them, but a disintegrated Russian army was too high a price to maintain this one family in splendid isolation twenty miles from the capital, even one extra day.

"Begging your pardon, ma'am, but you're acting like a damned fool,"

410

Ash heard himself say, and rushed on before he lost his nerve. "If you want to save Russia, not to mention the lives of your children, and if you want to win over Germany, you'll accept King George's generous offer right now. For God's sake, they'll burn the city down and then come out here and burn your palace down around you."

"*Get out . . .*"

Ash thought of Tamara, hunted like a felon in her own city, and of François Roland, dead on the Neva, and of the Grand Duke Valery, under the ice, Lady Exeter in a marshy grave . . . "You stupid, selfish bitch." He stood up, stalked to the door.

"*Wait.*" Her voice was like a whipcrack.

"What for?"

"*Wait . . .*" And then, quietly she added a distinctly nonimperial "please."

Ash stopped at the door. "Does it occur to you that's just about your last imperial command?"

She got up from her knees and beckoned him. There were, he saw as he came closer, tears in her dark, violet-blue eyes.

"Don't leave me," she said in what could only be described as a frightened voice.

The Empress was a woman, after all. He'd hardly considered her human . . . She reached for his hand, spoke to Ash as if they were alone and Prince Kurakin had disappeared to join Rasputin's ghost.

"I came here tonight because my children are sick, they have measles. Whenever they were sick Father Gregory comforted them. My son, my little boy, suffers from a blood disorder which causes him the most excruciating pain, pain such as neither you nor I have ever known. Before he faints from it, while he can still cry, he says the only words a little boy can say. He says, 'Mummy, it hurts. Please make it stop' . . . Do you have any children, Commander Ash?"

Ash shook his head.

"Even if you did, you couldn't understand, because a child doesn't turn in its last resort to its father, it turns to its mother. Did you not turn to your mother when you were a child?"

"I was very young when my mother died . . . I suppose I did, though . . ."

"My baby begged me to stop the pain, screamed for it to stop but I could do nothing but sit beside him until he fainted, wait through the night to see if he died. Then Father Gregory came. Because of Rasputin my son lives, and because of Rasputin, when my baby screamed to please make it stop, mummy, I could make it stop . . . until they murdered him . . . My own family killed my only friend. Now, alone, I must support my husband. The Czar needs me. I am his and our love is the only sun in his life . . ." (Ash noted the word "sun," coming in the con-

411

text of her talk of her *son* . . .) "But with Rasputin gone, I have little to offer him but love . . . Father Gregory had the power to divine the loyal from the disloyal around us, to help me choose who should serve my husband. Without Rasputin, we are lost."

Well, thought Ash, here we go. He glanced at Prince Kurakin, who obviously was overwhelmed by his Czarina's presence. Ash stood up, gave a meaningful look at the old prince.

It seemed to work. Clutching at his cape, screwing up his courage, he said in a quavering, sepulchral voice, "Rasputin knows, Your Majesty. Rasputin said you should leave this place of turmoil . . ."

The Empress smiled faintly at Kurakin. "You are his messenger." She turned to Ash. "And you are his instrument."

"Can the children travel?" Ash asked her.

"Yes."

"Then we must go, before it is too late."

"Just for a while . . . to England, just for a while . . ."

"Of course, until matters settle down." Their voices echoed in the chamber, though both had begun to whisper. Kurakin seemed to realize his work was done and, bowing, backed out the door. Ash said, "How soon can the Czar return here?"

"He's on his way."

"His Majesty has left Mogilev?" Ash asked with sudden alarm.

"Sometime after midnight. What is wrong, Commander?"

Von Basel was what was wrong. The Czar's person was inviolable at the Stavka, just as it was in Tsarskoye Selo, protected by an enormous Imperial Guard, Convoy Guard and bodyguard, but not aboard the Imperial Train. In spite of the Convoy Guard and the railway battalions the route between Mogilev and Petrograd passed through enormous empty stretches of Russian countryside—thirty and forty miles between towns. And what was more predictable than the route of a train confined to its lonely rails?

412

51

"**A** German spy will try to kidnap your husband from the Imperial Train, Your Majesty."

Her forehead wrinkled as if she were reassessing her opinion of an officer who would have dared to make an absurd statement.

"It's true . . . he has already infiltrated sections of the Okhrana. He had an office in the Litovsky Prison, and a Russian assistant named Lieutenant Orlov—that's all I know, but it's the absolute truth. You must believe—"

"Help me walk," the Czarina snapped, and limped on Ash's arm from Rasputin's chapel. The carriage took them quickly across the Imperial Park. In moments she had the head of the Ohkrana on the telephone, and an answer minutes later. "He used the name Captain Moskolenko. He has disappeared. The Okhrana assures me they will have him soon, *and* that he presents no threat to my husband."

The same Okhrana, Ash thought, that von Basel had infiltrated; the same Okhrana that, the French ambassador had informed François Roland, routinely forged letters of respectful appreciation to the Czarina purportedly from loyal subjects. Ash said, "May I have your *laissez-passer,* Your Majesty? I need to meet your husband's train."

She wrote it out in a swift, broad hand and said she would telegraph the Czar that Ash was coming.

"Ma'am, I suggest you not—"

"Don't worry, Commander, we telegraph in code." When Ash still looked dubious, she added, "We give people our own names . . . including you. Nimrod—the hunter—we called you when we discussed your visits."

Ash took the document, and asked for an airplane.

The airfield was north of Petrograd. By the Czarina's order a special train returned Ash to the city and a police convoy escorted him through the night. But though the lights of the airplane hangars were on and a pilot stood beside a warmed up British B.E. 2C, the snow was hopeless.

The sky was lightening in the east, but dawn promised nothing except more snow. Ash watched the sky; the B.E. 2C was as stable a plane as there was, but he also knew that a thousand feet off the ground the pilot wouldn't be able to distinguish up from down.

The police drove him back to the city to put him aboard the morning express at the Warsaw Station. But what greeted them in Petrograd was ten thousand men and women marching up the Liteiny Prospect under the red flag, ignoring both the snow and the police. They seemed in a gay mood, bantering with the soldiers and Cossacks who hemmed them in on both sides.

The trams had stopped running, his grim-faced police escort informed him, and a strike had immobilized taxis and horses, carriages and sleighs. A machine gun suddenly started firing on the marchers from a rooftop. The crowd ran, screaming and shouting, but to Ash's amazement the soldiers and the Cossacks directed a withering fire at the roof. Seconds later a police officer tumbled dead onto the street.

Ash thanked his police escort, jumped from the car and headed for the Warsaw Station. The Nevsky Prospect writhed black in the gray morning light as thousands of workers marched down the broad boulevard shoulder to shoulder and from sidewalk to sidewalk. They were pouring off the Liteiny Prospect, coming from the Alexander Bridge, which meant they had probably marched on the center of the city from the Vyborg Factory District across the Neva, beyond Tamara's mansion. There seemed to be more women than men.

Khleba. Khleba. Khleba.

The railroad terminal was mobbed. Ticket lines spilled into Ismailovsky Prospect. Ash pushed through them, found the stationmaster's officer and presented his pass. An empty private compartment was found on a train heading south. Lunch was promised aboard, despite whatever rumors the "honorable commander" might have heard to the contrary. There were no difficulties on the trains outside the corrupt and pestilent city of Petrograd, he was promised.

A special train? Unfortunately, impossible. Not only were there no extra crews, thanks to the strike, but no train, literally, no locomotive. He hoped the commander would understand.

But when the stationmaster had gone his young assistant refused a tip and looked Ash in the eye. "I'd be careful who I showed that particular

414

travel pass to, Commander. If the wrong person sees it you're carrying your own death warrent."

Ash showed his pass to the chief conductor, requested a map of the railroads between Petrograd and Mogilev. "This and everything else I say to you is to be kept in the strictest confidence. You're to keep me informed of the whereabouts of the Imperial Train."

"The Imperial Train has left the main line, Commander."

"What?"

"His Majesty often shunts to secondary lines so as not to interfere with military trains."

Secondary lines passed through even more isolated countryside, desolate and remote. Ash had the conductor point out likely routes on the map.

"At each station," Ash told him, "you're to confirm by telegraph the exact location of the Imperial Train."

The conductor said he of course would . . . Ash stared gloomily at the birch trees—ghostly white shadows on the snow. It wasn't hard to imagine von Basel in a similar conversation with a railroad official, in spite of the Okhrana's claims, and von Basel was miles ahead of him. Ash poured over his map, shaking off sleep, and tried to figure out where the German would strike.

The express was making speed at last, after a slow start, highballing, Ash presumed, between supply trains fore and aft. They roared through local stations and ignored express stops, halting only for coal and water and to disgorge bewildered passengers. Ash dozed between stops, where he checked the telegraph. Then at noon, at Dno—crossroads between the Petrograd-Mogilev line and the west-east track between Pskov and Bologoye—word came over the wire that the Imperial Train had reached Smolensk.

The Czar was shunting onto the Moscow-Petrograd line. Ash saw by the map that the northbound Imperial Train and his southbound Mogilev express would steam past each other on separate lines fifty miles apart.

Ash got off at Dno, telegraphed his intention to the Czarina and boarded a train heading east so as to intercept the Czar at Bologoye. But a hundred miles down the line—just sixty from Bologoye—his new train stopped outside the town of Dolmatova. A palpable shiver passed through the first class carriages; rebellious troops were reported blocking the tracks.

The conductor decided to hold his train until troops arrived from Dno. When none came and dusk began to fall he decided to go back to Dno. Ash climbed down. The train backed away. Its headlight receded to a pinprick, and then he was alone on the rails, in the snow, where flat, frozen marshes met a line of hills. He began walking toward the hills and came soon on the lights of Dolmatova. The town looked peaceful enough except for a big bonfire near the station. Some soldiers were drinking and singing around the fire and watched Ash curiously; deserters, it seemed, but not

bothering anybody and certainly not blocking the tracks, though the telegraph had somehow been cut.

Ash showed the stationmaster the Czarina's pass and asked for a train
to Bologoye, thinking that if he were von Basel he would telegraph reports
and then cut the lines to confuse the railroad situation and perhaps force
the Czar's train to change routes. Which direction? West, toward the front,
closer to German territory . . .

The stationmaster scared up an ancient yard engine with driver and
fireman and Ash resumed steaming toward Bologoye. Thirty miles short
of the junction town they were shunted, permanently, onto a siding to let
pass an endless stream of battered food and munitions trains struggling
west to the front beyond Pskov. The engine crew began loudly debating
what they should do.

Ash borrowed cleats and a key and scrambled up a telegraph pole. He
was just tying into the line when a snort from the yard engine told him
the crew had reached a consensus. The engine backed off the siding onto
the main line and disappeared back in the direction from which they had
come.

The snow quickly swallowed its headlight. Ash discovered the telegraph
was still dead. He slid down the pole and tried to read his map by the light
of windblown matches. The terrain was hilly, the roads grim, but by
angling north overland he might intercept the Czar thirty miles up the
main line from Bologoye. The alternative was to flag down an eastbound
train that might never come.

Six o'clock. Ash's last report on the Czar's train had indicated a speed
to bring it to Bologoye by nine and Likhoslavl by ten. Likhoslavl was
twenty miles overland.

He dog-trotted up the tracks, looking for the lights of a village, spotted
a handful of crude huts that serviced the siding. There were no cars and
no trucks, but a peasant came by on a sledge pulled by a half-starved horse,
and when Ash waved roubles at him he drove Ash the few miles to a
village, where there were lights in the windows but again no sign of a car
on the frozen, rutted street. "Likhoslavl?" Ash asked, pointing at his map.

The peasant gestured at the snow and the condition of his horse and the
sledge bumped away, leaving Ash alone once again, standing between two
long rows of whitewashed houses built of squared logs. Snow lay thick
everywhere. Smoke trickled from the chimneys, and smelled like they
were burning dung. Ash decided if he'd come to the end of the road, this
was an appropriate place . . . and aroma . . . for it.

None of the cottages even remotely resembled a tavern or any sort of
public building; he was going to have to knock at one of the windows in
which candlelight flickered dimly. Which window? He doubted anyone in
the whole village knew a single word of English; the closest he'd ever

416

come to such a place was bear hunting one winter years before the war with Skobeleff . . . which at least gave him an idea . . .

He already had a map and the name of the town he wanted to go to—Likhoslavl. What he needed was a fast ride overland through snow that was beginning to look very much like another blizzard. So instead of knocking at any window Ash started down the street peering behind stable gates at the people's sleds. There were a few light ones and a half-covered one in front of the largest cottage. But even the smallest hovel had a *rozvalny,* and it was those crude sledges made of two long runners connected by a frame of rope and lath that Ash inspected closely. Commonly used in the country to haul hay and firewood, the *rozvalny* had neither back nor seat and the driver knelt on his load. But at the twelfth house Ash found one with a sturdy board seat big enough for two drivers. He knocked at the window. It was a bear finder's sled, designed to run all night deep into the forest to remote caves where the hunters took wealthy sportsmen. Their fee, Ash recalled, was calculated by the weight of the bear.

An old man in a high wool hat opened the door; beside him stood a hefty son. Ash greeted them in Russian, said, "Likhoslavl" several times and held up the map and a wad of roubles. They motioned him inside, and it wasn't until they had taken him through a cold dark passage into a room with an enormous brick-and-plaster stove that Ash realized how terribly cold he was. An entire family was grouped around the stove drinking tea, and staring at him. In the light of the candles around the icon Ash showed the old man the map and the money. He took the money and spoke to his son, who put on a sheepskin he'd been drying by the stove and went out to hitch a team. A woman poured Ash a glass of tea and indicated the communal sugar bowl from which Ash gratefully took a lump of sugar, put it between his teeth the way Tamara had once laughingly taught him and drank while the family, including children tucked into shelves above the warm stove, watched closely. Thanking them, Ash pulled his watch and showed it to the old man, pointing to nine.

Father and son sat on the front plank. Ash lay full length on a bed of straw in the sling between the runners and covered his face with his cloak. Two ponies proceeded to pull the sledge into the forest. The runners hissed, the fresh snow muffled the horses' hooves, the drivers murmured to each other, sharing a bottle and occasionally talking to the horses. Ash dozed, abruptly awakened sensing danger. The *rozvalny* was crossing open ground and the snow was drifting. He could hear the worry in the drivers' voices as they searched for *veshky,* bushes that had been planted in the snow as roadmarks . . . then the track returned to forest and they were again sheltered from the wind.

Ash dozed off, awakened again and pulled the cloak off his face. The boy was cracking the whip while his father unlimbered a shotgun. Ash looked over the side. Wolves were pacing them through the trees, flitting black on white between the thin, straight birches. The old man jerked the trigger. The gun misfired. He jammed in another shell; a second hollow click and the wolves came closer. Ash worked his Luger out from under him and fired twice. When he could see again the wolves had vanished, except for a mournful howl that followed them for miles. The snow stopped and gradually a mantle of stars spread through the feathery tops of the birch trees.

The lights of Likhoslavl were few and dull by comparison to the long, orderly string of lighted train windows pulling swiftly from the station.

"Faster," Ash called to the drivers. "Faster, dammit."

They understood his tone of voice, whipped up the horses and the *rozvalny* careened down a hill into the little town. But they were too late. The locomotive was pounding a steady beat. The train was up to twenty and pulling steadily into the night.

Ash wanted to kill somebody.

"Sir, sir . . ." The boy was pointing. A second train appeared from behind the station.

"Da," Ash yelled. "Go." He remembered that the conductor had told him a special always preceded the Imperial Train. "Faster . . ."

The *rozvalny* hit the first street of the town, went through startled spectators who had gathered to salute the Czar as he passed through their station; the majestic beat-beat of the steam engine was accelerating, and when they swung around the last building the train was already moving at a fast clip. Ash leaped from the *rozvalny* and ran, clawing the Czarina's pass from his tunic. He caught up to the last car, waved the paper at a soldier who guarded the doorway with a rifle and managed to swing aboard.

He was instantly surrounded. Two men held bayonets to his chest while an officer took over. When he'd read the pass he told Ash welcome aboard. At least, Ash decided, von Basel would find a direct assault similarly impossible without an invitation. Direct, yes. Indirect . . . ? "What's the news from Petrograd?"

"Not good, sir. Not good at all."

Ash nodded, asked them to take him to the Czar.

The city burned.

Prince Kurakin's shabby apartment was on a barely reputable block near the Moscow Railroad Station at the upper end of the Nevsky; the drawing room was entirely black, the site of Kurakin's seances, though through the day that Tamara Tishkova and Vera Sedovina hid there, whatever spiritual mood the gloomy rooms evoked was thoroughly dispelled by the chanting demonstrators below in the street, the sudden bursts of gunfire, the screams and then the songs resuming—songs of triumph.

Sedovina wanted to go into the street and join the parades, but Tamara had persuaded her to stay. When the fires broke out after dark it was Tamara who left first. Sedovina could go into the streets if she insisted . . . but Tamara was too concerned about the safety of her house to sit still anymore. Besides, it was becoming clearer hour by hour that the police had more to contend with than arresting ballerinas. She tried not to think about the corollary—that they might also be too busy to protect ballerinas, or their beloved homes . . .

Tamara threw one of the prince's black cloaks over her own sable, which Kennet had left at the River Yacht Club, and walked out, clutching the gun she had picked up outside the fortress and which she'd used to shoot the guard who had hit Kennet. It was a mile along the Liteiny Prospect. The mob had broken into the Liteiny Arsenal, so now they were armed. She made it to the Alexander Bridge, across the Neva to her home. From her solarium, she watched the fires turn the night sky red . . . her fire dream at last. *Kennet, where in God's name are you . . . ?*

The Law Courts burned. So did the arsenal on the Liteiny and the Litovsky Prison, which she prayed von Basel was still in. Dotted across the darker districts of the city where the poor lived were red balls of flame, each marking one of the Czar's police stations.

But as the fires spread Tamara realized that the mob was indeed breaking into homes as well. She could actually see the people surging along the embankments, because now the flames reflecting on the snow made whole sections of Petrograd as bright as day . . . Earlier Prince Kurakin had reported after one of his timid excursions out to the Nevsky that something that called itself the Petrograd Soviet was meeting alongside the Duma in the Turide Palace. Sedovina had been delighted at the news . . . Fascinated and shocked by the sheer numbers of people parading through the city and crossing the river on the ice when the police blocked the bridges, Tamara watched for hours. Until she saw a mob crossing the ice merge with another surging off the Alexander Bridge, overrunning the police and heading straight for the necklace of mansions on the embankment—of which Tishkova's was the jewel.

She rang again for her maid.

"Bring me red ink and a large sheet of paper. *Quickly.*"

Vera Sedovina had run into the street from the prince's home when she saw a crowd of workers carrying the red flag up the Liteiny join hands with a unit of a Guards regiment marching down the Nevsky. Not a shot was fired by the soldiers, not a stone thrown by the people. Soldier and worker, conscript and peasant walked together through her city. The police had vanished. There was no one to arrest her. No prisons to hold her. She thought of Anton, dead in Siberia two years too soon to see his dreams happen. She joined the march, linked arms with an old man on one side who told her he'd been in jail since the 1905 rebellion, and with a woman who said she had been a servant and was going to go back to her village where she believed her family would at last have a piece of land. They sang the *Marseillaise* and the *Internationale* and surged down the Nevsky.

The Admiralty, though, was still in Czarist hands. Revolutionary soldiers laid siege to it with rifles and machine guns. Just then Vera saw a palace burning on the Moika, and she suddenly was afraid for the beautiful Maryinski Theater. She ran when the march ended at the besieged Admiralty, ran past Kennet Ash's hotel and St. Issac's, straining to see smoke and flame from the direction of the theater . . .

Theater Square was deserted except for an empty tram stalled at a broken wire. The theater was intact. She went to the stage door and knocked. The old woman who guarded it opened and let her in. She heard loud voices from the stage and slipped into the wings.

Valentinov was declaiming from center stage, gesturing wildly as he bellowed Chekhov at an empty auditorium. His wife sat in the front row while their children gaped at the glorious gold-and-blue proscenium.

Sedovina walked on stage.

Valentinov gave a glad shout. "We're free, they burned the prison to the ground."

He tried to throw his arms around her. Sedovina backed away. Valentinov gestured at the theater. "Now this is for everyone, now people like me can perform here—"

Sedovina slapped his face. Valentinov had no business here. He was a terrible actor.

When the drunken soldiers who had been exchanging rifle and machine-gun fire outside the embassy wheeled three cannon up to the corner of the Liteiny Prospect Ambassador Hazzard ordered the American flag hung out and illuminated. Earlier, when the firing had died down a bit, he had gone for a walk with Catherine to see what was going on. Before rifle fire had chased them in again he had decided that students seemed to be egging the soldiers on . . .

He was standing now with his daughter by the windows of his office

420

when, amazingly, Ambassador Page managed to get through on the telephone from London.

"What's happening?"

"There's an insurrection in the city," Hazzard told the ambassador. "Revolutionists have taken over the streets, I've been told they're bringing prisoners to the Duma and the Duma has arrested the Czar's ministers."

"Where's the Czar?"

"The last I heard he was at army headquarters."

"And where's Commander Ash?"

Hazzard glanced at his daughter. "I've no idea," he said coldly. He didn't know the whole story, but goddammit, his nephew Andrew had died in Ash's girlfriend's cellar . . .

"Will you find out, please?"

"I'll *try,* Mr. Ambassador."

There was a long pause. Ambassador Hazzard thought the line had been cut. Then Page asked, "Do you have any idea what's likely to happen to Russia?"

Hazzard sighed. Page was a wily old gent who could be a useful friend if he thought well of a man. He wanted to answer properly, but had no idea what to say.

Catherine leaned over his desk and wrote a note in her clear, square hand. She had overheard Page's question. Hazzard read the note, nodded gratefully at her and said, "In my opinion, Mr. Ambassador, what will happen here all depends on the Czar."

"Marvelous," Page said. "Please do find Ash," and to himself Page said, Maybe Ash knows what's going on.

A general wearing the staff pin N-2, one of several officers clustered about maps spread on the long dining table while stewards watched from the galley, was explaining that Ash could not possibly see the Czar before morning. He was interrupted when Czar Nicholas himself appeared, looking for Ash. He wore a plain tunic with colonel's shoulder straps and A-3, in gold, for Alexander III, his dead father and commanding officer.

The generals snapped to attention. The Czar appeared to be the calmest man on the train.

"Good evening, Kenneth," he said as the general propelled Ash forward like a prize of war.

The Czar insisted on holding doors as he led Ash onto the platform between the dining car and his carriage, through a vestibule and into a wood-paneled study. In the absence of noise, drafts or vibration it was hard to remember that the Imperial Train was hurtling through a bitter cold night at fifty miles per hour.

The Czar's study was furnished with a map table, some comfortable-looking leather armchairs and a desk. Photographs on the walls showed him at the helm of a racing yacht, on a bicycle, on horseback and posed in front of Balmachan House in the Scottish Highlands with a Westley Richards draped over his arm, a Russian fur hat on his head and wearing a Savile Row shooting jacket especially tailored with long deep pleats for easy movement and big pockets for extra shells.

He went to the table and stared down at the map.

"Our destinies seem connected, Commander . . . the Czarina telegraphed about this German spy and added a strong suggestion I listen to you . . . you've come with another offer from King George?"

"The same offer, Your Majesty."

The Czar shrugged. "We won't concern ourselves over a single German . . . what does he want?"

"He wants to kidnap you and take you to Kaiser Wilhelm as a prisoner of war."

"Willy . . . ?" He shook his head. "I always thought my end would be sudden. A bomb, like my grandfather the Czar-Liberator. I thought I would die in blood. Instead I'm dying of slow disease, like my father, but mine is not of the body. It is of my people. Insurrection, Commander. Spread by the vermin of deceit, treachery, cowardice." He glanced vaguely at the maps again, and when he raised his hand to rub his eyes Ash saw a man deeply tired, weary unto death . . .

The map depicted the railroad triangle Ash had traveled trying to intercept the Imperial Train ahead of von Basel—Petrograd and Tsarskoye Selo in the north, Pskov and the Front west, and the Moscow-Petrograd line on which the Imperial Train was currently steaming in the east.

"I'm chased by rumors," the Czar said abruptly. With a red pencil he circled the town of Tosno near Tsarskoye Selo, and Bologoye to the rear, and Pskov in the west. "Rumors that some monstrosity calling itself a Provisional Government will stop my train at one of these towns."

"Where are we now, Your Majesty?"

The Czar gave another shrug. "About ten miles south of Malaya Vishera —it looks bad but there is still hope. The Czarina has telegraphed that the situation is improved in Petrograd, and the troubles do appear to be confined to Petrograd." He crossed himself.

"That's excellent news, Your Majesty."

"I have loyal troops headed there at this very moment."

The train jolted and slowed rapidly. There was a knock at the door, and when the Czar gave permission to enter, a general walked in and saluted. "We're coming into Malaya Vishera, Your Majesty."

"We were closer than I thought. Is the station signaling a telegram?"

"No, Your Majesty."

"Then why have we stopped?"

"The special has stopped, Your Majesty."

"Why?"

"The special has received a report that rebel battalions have blocked the tracks with machine guns, Your Majesty."

52

Von Basel, Ash thought as the Czar's staff circled the map-strewn dining table and debated what to do. The rebel units were supposedly at Lyuban, the next station up the line, but to Ash a report of machine guns on the tracks, which no one had actually seen, sounded like Dolmatova all over again—a minor disturbance cooked up by von Basel's German agents to provoke an exaggerated response from the jittery train crews and the panicked imperial entourage. A trick to steer the Czar nearer the Front. And it seemed to be working.

None of the Czar's staff had the stomach to run a machine gun gauntlet, even with the special train leading them; some wanted to retreat all the way back to Mogilev, though the majority pressed to reroute the Imperial Train west to Pskov. Pskov, they argued, was nearer to loyal troops at the front. Ash knew he was powerless to interrupt, and it was obvious that Czar Nicholas, facing the disintegration of his entire empire, had now forgotten entirely about von Basel. The state of his armies concerned him far more, as he'd said, than a single German spy, yet each time the Czar said, "I must learn where my armies stand," his generals shuffled their feet and gazed intently at the steam dancing outside the double windows of the stalled train. Aides ran in and out of the dining carriage with telegraph messages.

The Czar stared at his maps while his staff went on debating.

"What is the news of Petrograd?" he asked.

"Apparently an isolated situation, Your Majesty."

"Moscow?"

"Reports are inconclusive—"

"Is there any news of the army?"

424

"No, Your Majesty."

"And these insurrectionists?" he asked, pointing at the railroad map.

"Apparently they hold Lyuban and perhaps Tosno, Your Majesty."

"Are we sure?" He raised his eyes to his staff, all of whom began talking at once. Beneath the hubbub Ash heard Nicholas murmur, "I want to go home."

"Your Majesty," Ash ventured. *Home* was just where Ash wanted him —away from von Basel and close to the Gulf of Finland.

Czar Nicholas turned to Ash, who had remained just behind him since the staff had filled the carriage. "Yes, Commander, what do you think of all this?"

The generals and noblemen turned to him, worried what the stranger would say. Ash decided to grandstand, give them their money's worth . . . "Tsarskoye Selo will remain center court, Your Majesty, for as long as you play there."

The Czar nodded. "Yes."

"But your armies, sir," a general said. "You must know more about your armies."

"Yes . . ."

"Might it not be better to first join your family, Your Majesty?" Ash needed to try to keep him from the generals long enough to consider the danger of being separated from the Czarina and the difficulty of escaping to England if they weren't together.

"Yes, I suppose," Nicholas said, but it was clear he wasn't yet ready to surrender, not yet prepared fully to acknowledge the danger.

"Your armies," the general repeated. "You must contact your armies, Your Majesty. What are a few traitors in Petrograd compared to the fifteen million Russian soldiers under Your Majesty's command?"

"Yes, of course."

And another general put, "We must communicate with loyal units, Your Majesty."

"*Yes*, of course," and then he asked, peering at the map, "Where is the nearest Hughes terminal?" He was referring, Ash knew, to the American-designed Hughes keyboard telegraph printer which the Russian army used for internal communication.

"Pskov, Your Majesty," his entourage said almost together—and Ash knew von Basel had won.

The Czar touched the map. "To Pskov then, before this matter is ended."

The Imperial Train backed into the Bologoye Station at nine in the morning and sat there half the day, bombarded by rumors that the Duma was preparing a plan for a constitutional monarchy. But in the afternoon no delegates had arrived from the Duma and the blue-and-silver train steamed west.

In the last carriage, an additional barracks coupled on for extra guards, a young officer of His Imperial Majesty's Own Convoy struggled to take off his boots in the cramped cubby where he slept. He felt older than God. Not a single man of his cadet classes who had gone into the line regiments was still alive. He was wondering if the dead were the lucky ones now, gone in a burst of glory for Czar and Russia while a few like him waited to be overwhelmed by a new world of strangers' making. The steward knocked at the door and brought in tea.

"Put it there."

The steward closed the door and leaned against it; there was hardly room for two in the compartment. The officer looked up, gasped. *"Dmitri?* What are you—" He leaped up, even before he completed the thought . . . *Dmitri Dan* . . . his fellow officer had disappeared weeks ago. An assassin, they said. And apparently they were right. Dmitri had a knife . . .

When it was done and he had shoved his old friend's body out the window, Dmitri Dan put on the Convoy officer's uniform over the servant's costume he'd worn to board the Imperial Train, cleaned his dagger and lay down to wait. He was calm. His mind was empty of all but the thought that he, and the Revolution, were only two carriages behind the Czar's private quarters.

Ash sought out some Convoy officers and got himself invited to share tea. They were jumpy, knowing that there was little they could do if the tracks were mined or the rebels managed to obtain artillery. They were essentially bodyguards, not a military tactical unit, and to guard the Czar they had to assume that the rest of the world was still in order, which, it became apparent when the train reached Dno, it was not.

The rumors resumed flying that Duma delegates were coming by train from Petrograd. As the Czar had not invited Ash back to his own car again Ash was as in the dark as the rest of the entourage. The Convoy officers admitted they were watching for a German spy, but none of them seemed to take von Basel's threat very seriously, not compared to the fate of the Imperial Russian Empire. Ash, however, was not surprised when the train headed west again and the new rumor promised that the Czar would meet the Duma delegates at Pskov.

He got his cloak and went forward. Armed soldiers stopped him at the barracks car behind the locomotive. Ash claimed he wanted a breath of

426

air and persuaded them to let him stand in an open vestibule. Outside, alone in the biting cold, he climbed onto the roof.

The train was doing close to forty, and the wind was fierce. Sheltering himself behind a ventilator, Ash watched the flat, empty white landscape for signs of von Basel.

The endless open fence flowed beside the rails beneath an equally endless row of telegraph poles. Snow-covered fields disappeared toward an horizon of trees. The vast sky was clear and starry except for a dense cloud line in the north that marked another Gulf of Finland blizzard over Petrograd, a hundred and fifty miles away. Some five miles ahead of the locomotive's smoke spume he could see the red lights on the back of the special that preceded the Imperial Train.

The lights of a town shone ahead. Porkov. The special passed through the lights and stopped, followed by the Imperial Train, which slackened its pace and glided to a stop in the station. A trainman jumped down and questioned the officials lined up in dress uniforms on the platform, as similar ones had manned every platform the train had passed through today. Petrograd might be burning but here in the countryside the passage of the Imperial Train was still an occasion for respectful salute.

The trainman got aboard and they started rolling, which meant, Ash presumed, no new telegraph messages from Petrograd. Ahead lay fifteen miles of desolate field, marsh, birch forest and the occasional dark village. Ash glanced back. The town officers and railroad officials were still at attention. The graceful onion domes of their church floated in starlight above the station.

The next town on the map was Podsyevi and beyond it, thirty empty miles to Pskov. It was in that last long stretch that Ash expected von Basel to strike. The trains would be alone for nearly an hour, more than enough time to stop them with a barricade and a few machine guns, plus maybe some armored cars. It was so simple—stop the train, a show of force, remove the Czar and drive away. But a hundred and fifty miles overland was still a long run.

Ash scanned the sky. He thought he heard music, pressed his ear to the roof and heard it louder and remembered the officers in the lounge car had a gramophone. Then another sound intruded on the rumble of the wheels and the rushing wind and the beat of the locomotive, a steady hum from behind that grew swiftly to a drone. An airplane swooped over the train and flitted through the upper glow of the locomotive headlight like some great bat. In the instant Ash saw it flash ahead of the train he thought it looked like a two-seat British-built DeHavilland bomber.

Von Basel's men had probably commandeered the airplane from the Russian Imperial Air Service, and Ash hurriedly repainted the picture in his mind of how the German would seize the Czar—a fire on the tracks, or the special would be mined, anything to stop the Czar's train midway between Podsyevi and Pskov. Then a half-dozen armored cars on either side, courtesy of turncoat army units recruited by von Basel's German agents, headlights and machine guns and artillery pointed at the Imperial Train . . . the Czar hustled to the airplane waiting on the frozen snow, strapped into the rear-gunner's seat. In two hours Nicholas II would be in German territory. And twelve hours later von Basel would present his prisoner of war to the Kaiser . . .

The lights of Podsyevi appeared dead ahead. The special slowed and passed through the town, by which time Ash could see the silhouettes of the onion domes. Most of the town lights seemed to be on the railroad platform. Four officials waited, coming to attention as the Czar's train neared. They had a telegraph. What did they think when they heard the news from Petrograd—the elderly stationmaster bent from the long years of his life for the Czar, the freight manager who had watched his rolling stock disintegrate before his eyes, the telegrapher whose key must have clattered relentlessly all day, the wounded war veteran leaning hard on his cane? What did they think . . . if they dared think at all?

53

C ount von Basel had positioned himself some distance from the civilians, as befitted a veteran in the service of the Czar, and none had presumed to question his presence on the platform. A gleaming black locomotive glided past, and von Basel raised his hand to his service cap in reverent salute. He was close enough to the blue-and-silver train carriages to touch the double-headed Imperial Eagles on their sides.

A trainman leaped down while it was still rolling, shouting—were there telegrams? The telegrapher stepped forward, holding his salute, and pressed sheaves of paper into his glove. The trainman disappeared inside as the train ground to a stop.

Von Basel followed the telegrams' passage. They appeared next in the hand of a Guard subaltern who had walked them through two carriages and turned them over to a captain in the dining car in front of the Czar's own carriage. A group of generals pored through them.

Next the Czar himself appeared from his carriage, third from the end of the train, just ahead of his servants' lodgings and the Guards' car at the end. He looked, von Basel thought, worried but calm. The Czar took the telegrams and leaned over his maps.

Von Basel knew the contents of every one of those telegrams, except, of course, the private wires from the Czarina, who'd been bombarding the Czar with unfathomable references to Nimrod, the hunter; he'd had an agent on top of a telegraph pole tap into the line a mile from here since dark. Conditions had gotten so bad in Petrograd that he no longer had to plug his own electric forgeries into the line; his last false message had been eighteen hours ago, warning the Czar of nonexistent rebel troops at Tosno and blocked tracks at Malaya Vishera.

The Imperial Train had turned back, just hours from the Czar's Palace, and since then the Russian populace and the madmen of the Duma, already fighting among themselves, had kept the Czar on the run. But once the train had left Bologoye its route was absolutely predictable. Pskov. The Czar was escaping to his army. Too late, Your Majesty, too late . . . Von Basel slipped into the shadows, and when the train whistle blew, he was already crouched in the snow on the dark side of the train.

Ash had seen too much indecision bordering on paralysis aboard the Imperial Train to attempt to convince either the Czar or his Guard that a German agent was going to stop the train fifteen miles down the line. Simpler to stop it first, explain later. As the train started from the station he ran forward over the rooftops. He'd show the locomotive engineer his snub-nosed Luger and let him draw his own conclusions.

From the vantage point of the stalled engine, Ash would be in a much more practical position to convince the Convoy Guard to wait for reinforcements to clear the line. Preparing to jump the slot between two cars, he glanced back at the station to make sure he wasn't seen . . . they'd shoot him down if they saw a shadow heading for the locomotive. No guards. The three railroad officials were still saluting like statues, but the old soldier had gone. He faced the wind, jumped the first slot and ran forward.

He was creeping silently over the final car just before the tender—it was a Guard's barracks car—when he glanced back . . . something nagged. He noted that Podsyevi station appeared as a single bright light. As in the previous town, and the towns before, the silhouettes of the onion-dome church steeples were the last shapes seen from the desolate plain, standing as patient a watch as the last men loyal to the Czar had stood on each railroad platform . . . Why had the soldier left, where had he gone . . . ?

Von Basel.

No armored cars. No machine guns.

Ash ran for the back of the train, cursing his stupidity, fighting the wind at his back that filled his boat cloak like a sail.

Of course . . . von Basel intended to kidnap the Czar alone, force him to leap from the moving train, take his chances on the snow, then aboard the two-seater bomber, with a knife in the ribs for the pilot.

Ash jumped the gap between two cars and raced toward the rear of the train, crossing the two cars of officer accommodations, the roof of the lounge car. He was starting across the dining car when he hit a patch of cooking grease beside the galley smoke vent and lost his footing.

The wind ballooned his cloak. One moment he was falling, trying to tuck his shoulder into a controlled roll, the next the cloak lifted him off the roof and suspended him, flailing in the air. He saw the snow rushing beside the train, felt himself plunging toward it.

Abruptly the wind let him go and he crashed hard on the roof. Spreading his arms and legs, he scrambled on the tin surface until he stopped moving. Then, back on his feet, he ran again and leaped the space from the dining car to the Czar's car. He was about to drop to the front vestibule when he saw that the last two cars that carried the Czar's personal servants and the additional rear guard were separated from the rest of the train. Already a hundred feet back, they were disappearing into the dark.

Von Basel . . . he'd disconnected them and gone into the rear vestibule. Ash crossed the Czar's car, treading lightly as possible, and lowered himself to the vestibule. The door was slightly ajar. He opened it, slipped in and let it shut. He drew the Luger from the small of his back and moved silently across the vestibule. He opened the inner door. The car was swaying, having lost the stabilizing tail of rear cars.

He reviewed the layout of the Czar's car. It had a huge bedroom and bath and two sitting rooms, one in mauve and gray, which must have been the Czarina's before the war, and the Czar's at the front, his study.

Gun now in hand, Ash stepped into the rear room, found it empty, moved into the bedroom. A servant was sprawled on the bed, unconscious and bleeding from a bruise on his temple.

Ash opened the last door.

Von Basel rushed him. The German had been waiting at the forward vestibule door at the front end of the Czar's study. He had his sword cane in one hand, a gold pocketwatch in the other. He needed to time the ten minutes until the train reached the airplane. The Czar had not returned from the dining car, where he customarily conferred with his generals and aides when telegrams arrived.

Von Basel had shed the bemedaled Russian army greatcoat he had worn on the station platform and now wore a black leather flying jacket and service hat. In a single, smooth motion he clicked the watch stem and went at Ash, raising the cane in a tight arc that twisted into a long thrust. He covered half the study's twenty-foot length before Ash got his cloak off his arm and let him have a look at his gun. Von Basel appeared to stop short, but stole four more feet doing it. He came to rest, lightly balanced, countering the sway of the train, two yards from Ash.

Ash gestured with the Luger.

"I wasn't aware we had agreed to new weapons for our long-deferred duel," von Basel said, trying to give the impression that he'd given more ground than he had.

"Some other time. Drop that damned cane."

Von Basel lifted his hands, the watch dangling in his left, the cane in his right.

"Drop it."

Von Basel's gray eyes seemed to glint at his watch. The cane dropped from his other hand. For an instant everything was in motion—the cane, the watch, his eyes, both hands. He caught the cane, it flashed like a dark snake and bit the small bones in the back of Ash's hand.

Before Ash had made a sound or his Luger had thudded to the carpet, von Basel drew steel from a hardwood scabbard. Roland had warned him about the man, that he was better than they'd thought. He'd obviously meant the German's speed.

Ash wanted to go for the gun but von Basel was too close. He feinted a lunge at the floor. Von Basel replied with a wide slash an inch over the gun butt, but at least Ash was able to use the time to draw his dress sword.

"Much better," von Basel said. He pocketed his watch, gripped the cane in his left hand and brought his sword to his nose, point vertical in salute, then whipped the blade down and advanced.

Ash knew he needed more room. He backed through the door into the big bedroom, which was nearly thirty feet long. Russian trains were wide, and the room approximated a fencing strip with the exception of the bed intruding into the middle and the ceiling, which would have the good effect of limiting the high slashes Ash expected from von Basel. The servant was still unconscious on the bed; it appeared that von Basel had clipped him with the cane, which he held in his left hand in case Ash tried to in-fight. Was there also a dagger in his jacket, like the *poniard* he'd put in Roland's chest?

Von Basel followed his leading blade, steady, the point tracking Ash like a finger. The blade, Ash thought, looked lighter than his, consequently more flexible. It was sharp the length of the leading edge and half the back. A slash in either direction was lethal, as was the point. An ingeniously designed set of prongs had folded out of the hilt, forming a protective bell for von Basel's hand, which was already protected by a heavy leather glove.

Ash's eyes fixed on the razor edges of the long, whippy blade. This man had beaten François Roland, Ash's own master. *Poniard* or no damn *poniard*, von Basel had had to breach Roland's guard to get in close enough to use it. The razor edges nearly mesmerized him; he was a fencer, not a duelist, and not even a professional fencer, just a very good sportsman. And this man in black, lean and flexible as his blade, his face a white slash, was the most dangerous swordsman in Europe.

Ash was afraid. I'd be crazy not to be, he thought.

Von Basel advanced. Ash retreated. He had ten feet to his back, then the bed to climb over or squeeze past, two yards more a narrow door, fifteen feet of the Czarina's sitting room, the tiny vestibule—and then nothing but tracks roaring under the train at forty miles per hour.

Von Basel seemed to read his thoughts . . . "The Czar's servant was waiting to help him dress for dinner, which means he'll come in alone. So you see, merely *occupying* me will not serve your purpose. If you warn the Czar you must warn him *before* he enters this carriage. But for that you'll need to get me first . . . which is to say, a clever defense will not suffice. Though I suppose you could simply turn tail and throw yourself off the back. The snow will break your fall."

Ash said nothing. What was there to say? Somehow he had to keep von Basel, as they said, at bay, and himself alive.

"You've got ten minutes," von Basel said. "Then I shall be obliged to end this. After all, I've promised to take His Majesty flying . . . In fact, I believe I'd prefer you further back until His Majesty arrives." He kicked Ash's gun under a leather armchair, and advanced. Ash watched him come, fascinated by the eerie stillness of the point of his sword. It floated as if it had a life and powerful will of its own.

All right, Ash lectured himself, a little less respect and more action. This man intends to kill you . . . He proceeded to test von Basel's grip with a pair of hard beats. Von Basel replied with a pair of his own. The car rang with the sound of steel on steel. Ash tried a thrust. Von Basel parried, thrust and lunged. Surprise momentarily showed on his face. Ash's speed had saved him when clearly von Basel had thought it would not. A pleased smile replaced the surprise. Ash had escaped the thrust, but he'd also, in so doing, retreated.

His morale lifted some by his escape, it crashed when he realized von Basel was past the bedroom door. The German lunged again. Ash went back as he parried, but von Basel's lunge had been a feint that bought him space to kick the door shut behind him so that now when the Czar entered his carriage he'd see nothing wrong in his study.

Von Basel, Ash realized, had manipulated him like a damn novice. He sensed the bed behind him. Von Basel thrust again. Ash riposted, and von Basel retreated to the door until his left heel was touching it. Ash pressed his attack. Von Basel drew back even closer to the door until it appeared he had no more room to retreat.

Worried about a trick to entice him dangerously close, Ash attacked cautiously, still feeling him out, testing what the German could do. Thrusting, parrying—striking at von Basel and shielding himself from von Basel's thrusts—Ash hunted for a weakness. He discovered a frightening strength.

Von Basel's sense of distance was so acute that it allowed him to parry late—wait until Ash's point was an inch from its target—then reposte with remarkable speed at the moment Ash was too extended, too stretched into his thrust to counter-parry effectively.

It was with a late parry-riposte that von Basel drew first blood.

It flew scarlet from Ash's right sleeve, and his forearm felt as if it had been pierced by a hypodermic needle. Von Basel jump-lunged. Shock and anger goaded Ash to swift recovery, parry and counter-thrust. Von Basel parried late again and repeated the riposte. Again it caught Ash off balance and too far extended to parry, and Ash did something that wasn't in the rules—neither was von Basel—and whipped his boat cloak around von Basel's saber with his left hand. He pressed his sudden advantage, and von Basel let him close enough to lash his head with the hardwood scabbard. Ash fell back on the bed, seeing stars and the point of von Basel's saber corkscrewing toward his eye. He tried to roll out of the way, got tangled in his cloak and collided with the unconscious servant. Von Basel thrust again. Ash flipped backward, kicked blindly at the blade, drove over the servant and hit the floor.

Von Basel was winning, and he knew it. Ash squeezed his tunic sleeve to soak up the blood so that it would not drain into his hand and ruin his grip. He was ten feet further from warning the Czar than he had been before the exchange. But *was* the son of a bitch really that good? Was he perfect? Ash had to find a flaw. Maybe von Basel was overconfident. Well, Ash thought, he had every reason to be at this point. But did his famous refusal to have his face scarred derive from fear? The man's gray eyes showed nothing. Maybe his broad style, the wide slashes, indicated too much saber training and not enough in the exacting foil. Clutching at straws, Commander. *He's better than we thought*, Roland had said, and he'd been right.

Never mind now. The options were gone. Ash attacked.

Von Basel was rather impressed. He admired Ash's timing, his speed, his point control and his sense of distance. The precision of his hand was superior—almost up to Chevalier Roland—what one might expect of an Italian professional of the sort von Basel had secretly trained with when his mother had bundled him off to the Jewish doctors in Vienna when his father killed himself. Ash also possessed a considerable ability to recover from disaster—a flexibility that came, he knew, from the power to relax. The American had control of himself and his skills. He also detected in Ash a gift for combat—the ability to restart after each phase. Then why, he asked himself as Ash came gliding around the bed and opened a new attack with a hard beat, couldn't the American launch a convincing attack? He shrugged him off with a spanking parry. Ash's brilliant defense seemed all he had. He couldn't attack. And in the long run a brilliant defense was a map to the cemetery . . .

Here he came now, dead-steady point, marvelous control, a lightning thrust. Short. Another. Short again. Von Basel parried and countered. Ash parried masterfully, thrust. Short. Had he lost his sense of distance? Von Basel thrust. Ash parried at the last instant and reposted. Short again.

Von Basel established a series of parries while he retreated into his mind to puzzle it out. Ash had begun to imitate von Basel's late parries—the mark of a great fighter was the ability to learn in action—and he cut it very fine, showing his distance was perfect. But his ripostes still fell short. What was wrong with the man? He had never really believed Ash was a coward, but he was fighting like a man afraid. Of what? It was a question von Basel had to answer before he risked his final, killing attack.

He couldn't wait much longer, though. The Czar would walk in at any moment—a fact that von Basel realized was affecting his own concentration, since he had to keep himself ready to throw the Czar off his feet while he finished Ash. And the airplane was waiting several miles up the line. Five minutes. No more.

Von Basel attacked, spanked Ash's blade aside and jump-lunged, slashing wildly to unnerve the American . . .

The blades clashed, kissed, sparked in the dim electric light, seemed to whip around each other in impossible embrace. Ash felt his grip tightening, which made his wrist rigid and reduced his point control. *Relax*, Roland demanded. Relax. In Paris he had put Ash in the on-guard position and left him there for five minutes while he strutted about his *salle d'armes* instructing his other students. If Ash's grip had tightened when Roland came back he was told, "You'll never be a fencer," and banished for the rest of the day. *Relax*.

Steel rang on steel.

Von Basel bore in on him with frightening skill and intensity, and Ash steadily retreated, trying to recover the strength he'd lost in his own futile offensive and waiting for von Basel to make an unlikely mistake. He looked for openings in the wide slashes, watched von Basel's face for a sign of fear of being cut, and for overconfidence. That last seemed the best bet, he thought uneasily.

Chimes began to play the Brahms Lullaby.

Von Basel extracted his watch from his pocket with the hand holding his scabbard. The watch was playing the melody. Von Basel showed it to Ash and put it back in his pocket again. It happened so quickly Ash hadn't been able to react. Von Basel said, "Your time is up, Commander. You've done quite well, for a sportsman . . ."

And von Basel attacked. He had his man now, knew what ailed Ash. It was Chevalier Roland. Ash thought von Basel had beaten his master. So how could he be expected to beat von Basel?

What neither Roland nor Ash understood was that dueling was more than skill. Roland, for all his reputation, had turned out to be a gentle soul, a brilliant technician but even in a death fight more interested in technique than killing . . . His death had killed Ash's belief in his own strengths. His thrusts and lunges, perhaps always his weakest skills in any case, fell far short because he no longer *believed* he could launch a successful attack. And now it was too late, because now von Basel knew everything he needed to know to kill him.

Von Basel also had the ability to adjust to an opponent and a situation. When Ash's parries and the relatively confining walls and ceilings of the Imperial Train proved too much for his broad saber cuts he began to thrust as if his saber were a foil.

Surprised, Ash retreated rapidly while he adjusted. And when Ash had adjusted, at the cost of being driven back around the bed and halfway to the door of the rear compartment, von Basel feinted with the sword and smashed his face with the cane.

Ash fought back any sound to give away his pain, and in spite of himself, it occurred to von Basel that if he had ever felt the need for a friend beside his sovereign, the Kaiser, it might have been a man like this—and then he cauterized the thought. The brain tended to play tricks in combat.

Ash launched an angry attack energized by pain. Von Basel tried to capitalize on the American's show of temper, but it served to drive Ash, not unsettle him . . . anger helping to make up for low confidence. Von Basel realized that Ash might, after all, succeed in making a forceful attack. He retreated, looking to regain initiative.

Ash broke his defense, slashed at his scabbard, sliced it in half. By the time von Basel realized it was only a feint, Ash's saber whipped up from the downstroke. The razor edge jumped at his cheek. With an astonishing twist of his entire body, von Basel wrenched his face out of the path of Ash's blade, which left him far off-center—his body in one plane, his weapon in another. He threw himself backward onto the bed, collecting space and time to regain his equilibrium. He landed hard on the servant he had earlier knocked unconscious, who groaned and rolled over as von Basel levered himself off him and landed on his feet on the opposite side of the bed in the *en garde* position.

Ash felt the fight go out of him. Von Basel had made a shambles of his best attack. The servant groaned and tried to move again, and in doing so revealed a long knife that had been lying under him. While Ash was still trying to figure where it had come from, von Basel, closer, grabbed it up and started toward Ash with a blade in either hand.

Ash ended his silence. "I'm flattered. You needed two for Roland, too."

"Don't flatter yourself. Roland slipped on the ice. He was not properly balanced with one arm—"

Smug bastard—Ash hurtled at von Basel, onto the bed, across it, slashing down at von Basel like a horseguard. Von Basel allowed him close, then thrust the servant's dagger. Ash was ready . . . a darting thrust, and his saber skewered von Basel's left wrist, slid between the bones, in and out like ice.

The ice left a trail of fire. Von Basel dropped the dagger. Ash slashed at his face. Von Basel parried, his own blood spraying in droplets from

Ash's blade. Ash went at him, drove ahead, *around* . . . and suddenly von Basel realized that Ash was done fighting, was forcing his way past him to get to his gun in the study and warn the Czar . . .

Exhilarated that he had finally bloodied von Basel, sinking his point exactly where he'd aimed it, Ash now slashed and thrust, tried a couple more late parries. He had maneuvered von Basel half out of his way and was preparing to break for the door to the Czar's study when the German caught on to his intent.

"*Nein.* Fight. For this." He snapped his left arm and the blood flew. "*Fight.*"

And von Basel exploded into a new attack, driving a startled Ash against the wall and leaping back to his old position between Ash and the door to the Czar's study. Slowly, he drove Ash backward with cold skill, to the bed, around it, and past. His thrusts were long and rapid, his parries like Roland's spinning steel shield, the shield Roland would raise when he wanted to remind Ash who was master and who was student.

Ash tried to break up the attack. He riposted with a stop-thrust and paid for it. Von Basel let loose a slash that tore through Ash's cloak and stung his shoulder. Warm blood spread onto his chest. Von Basel kept attacking.

Ash retreated, hoping von Basel would exhaust himself. It was clear now to Ash that he intended to drive him through the rear sitting room and out the vestibule and off the back of the speeding train. Ash retreated because the alternative would be to be slashed again, run through.

Von Basel was fighting at his peak. Ash knew he had lost the earlier initiative. He backed through the door into the sitting room and retreated suddenly as he slammed the door on von Basel's sword. Von Basel was ready for that, moving forward and kicking the door open so it threw Ash backward.

The rear door opened out against a hydraulic spring. Von Basel worked Ash through it with thrusts like jets of flame. The spring kept Ash from slamming the door on his blade. Von Basel held it open with his boot and came through. Trapped in the narrow vestibule, Ash backed through the last doorway.

Cold air blasted into the vestibule. Ash tried, and failed, to hold his position. Von Basel's thrusts were too accurate to parry with his back pinned to the door. Ash retreated to a last stand on the open platform. The wind tore at his cloak; the rear trucks thundered on the beaten-up roadbed.

Von Basel seemed to get tangled up in the door. Ash thought he saw his chance. He leaped up the ladder on the back of the car and climbed for the roof, to run forward and warn the Czar.

Von Basel slashed up at his leg, his saber slicing through Ash's cloak, his heavy boot and wool trousers. Ash felt a narrow tug of pain on the back of his calf, inches above his Achilles tendon. Von Basel slashed again, lower, hunting the tendon.

Afraid of a crippling cut, Ash dropped down to the platform with a last-ditch off-balance parry. He was wide open when von Basel riposted, and took the thrust in his upper arm.

His fingers opened convulsively. His saber began to slip from his glove. Ash clamped his left hand over his right, held his fingers on the hilt and just managed to parry von Basel's next slash while he maneuvered for a little more room on the platform. He was running out of room . . . von Basel had driven him the length of the Czar's car from the study in front, through the big bedroom, through the rear sitting room, through the vestibule and now outside on the open rear platform. Ash tried to hold one side while von Basel thrust and slashed to drive him the remaining six feet to the back and over the edge to the tracks racing away below . . . .

Czar Nicholas pushed open the door, and peered outside, into the dark where the servants' car had been. He called, squinting to adjust his eyes to the change of light. Von Basel shot out his left hand, grabbed hold of the Czar's tunic and yanked him out onto the platform while he tried to spank the blade from Ash's stiff fingers.

Ash held on, parried von Basel and pushed the Czar back to the door. He lunged at von Basel. The German's stop-thrust slid the length of Ash's blade. They slammed hilt-to-hilt, and a scream whirled them both around with the same thought—while fighting for him had they somehow run the Czar through?

The Czar's back was to the door, but the scream had turned his head too.

Twice the duelists had fallen on him and the second time Dmitri Dan surfaced to consciousness. The last he remembered, he had been waiting in the Czar's bedroom, where Bloody Nicholas was sure to come along to dress for dinner. Then he heard a loud noise and the car began swaying as if it were the last car. He started back to investigate when a man with a cane suddenly appeared from the sitting room behind the bedroom.

Dmitri had quickly bowed, playing his servant role, and the cane, preceded by a heavy *swish,* had crashed into his head. It knocked him onto the bed, half-conscious. He had pulled his knife from inside his tunic and was preparing to counterattack when some movement must have alerted the man with the cane. The second blow blanketed him in darkness . . .

His head was splitting. He felt something warm on his face, touched it, spread it to his lips. Salty, blood. His own? He opened his eyes. Someone had shaken him.

It was Czar Nicholas. Incredible.

The Czar was already turning away from the bed, hurrying toward the back sitting room that led to the rear of the train. Dmitri felt for his knife. It was gone. It had been under him, he remembered. The Czar disappeared through the door to the sitting room. Dmitri groped for the knife. He was too weak to strangle the Czar. The knife wasn't on the bed. He stood up slowly, reeling a bit. The blade shone in the lamplight, on the rug at his feet, with drops of someone's blood already on it.

Dmitri reached for it. His own blood rushed to his head and he fell. He managed to grab hold of the knife, willed himself to stand up and head for the rear door, after the Czar.

Nicholas had already crossed the rear sitting room and was pushing through the vestibule door at the back, calling for his servants. Dmitri lunged after him, gaining strength with each step, eyes fixed on the Czar's back. From the vestibule door he could see the Czar leaning out the last door, peering into the night, where the last two carriages of the train had been.

Beyond the Czar, outside on the rear platform, Dmitri saw the man who had hit him with his cane, and he saw Kenneth Ash. They were fighting with sabers, and the sight clearly had all the Czar's attention. Running into the vestibule, Dmitri Dan felt a scream . . . an explosion of triumph well out of his chest—a scream, by his lights, for every Russian ever starved and tortured, a scream for his brother and their comrades, especially a scream for the last Romanov—he lifted his knife high and plunged it toward Czar Nicholas's back, just as the tyrant was turning his head to look at death.

54

"**N**ein" and "*no*" came simultaneously from von Basel and Ash. The object of both their affections was about to be dispatched and both their missions violently aborted. They disengaged their sabers and almost as one thrust at Dmitri. The Czar was bracketed by their blades. Ash tore the assassin's knife arm, von Basel pierced his left shoulder. Dmitri Dan crashed into the Czar and slid down his back to the platform, where twice wounded he grabbed his fallen knife with his left hand and made to slash up at the Czar.

Ash kicked the knife out of his hand, stepped on it. Von Basel reached inside his jacket with his left hand and Ash realized it wasn't von Basel's knife on the bed . . . it was this knife, the assassin's knife . . . But now the German's *poniard* had already emerged.

Ash threw what he really knew best—a left hook, his best punch at the Academy. Von Basel tumbled sideways, hit the low railing at the edge of the platform and fell over it. Ash saw him roll down the embankment, flailing at the snow. But before the train had sped too far into the night Ash caught a glimpse of the airplane, a black silhouette, like a crow sunning itself in starlight. His vision was blurred by increasing distance, but he could swear he saw von Basel staggering toward it . . .

"The German spy?" Czar Nicholas asked with rather impressive calm.

"Yes."

"And this one?" The Czar looked down at Dmitri Dan at their feet. Ash kicked the knife from his fingers.

"Russian." Ash heard his voice moving into the distance . . . still pursuing von Basel . . . ?

"You've been hurt," the Czar said.

440

"I'm all right, Your Majesty," Ash replied, and collapsed on top of Dmitri Dan.

He awakened with a yell, which the Czar cut short by clamping a hand that smelled of expensive soap over Ash's mouth. A second man, a doctor by his plain frock coat, was dribbling iodine into the puncture in his upper arm, and with the pain came memories of the same hideous burning.

The Czar ordered silence with a finger over his lips. Ash gritted his teeth and tried to look around. Daylight was evident behind drawn shades. The train had stopped moving. He was propped up on a heap of blankets and pillows in the bast white bathtub in . . . my God . . . in the *bathroom* of the Czar's personal car. The doctor untied a bandage around his forearm, revealing a long wide slash already liberally oranged with iodine and crusting on the edges. Ash vaguely remembered his wounds being dressed the night before, recalled the crash of railcars coupling—the guard and servant cars von Basel had detached. Then a second crashing as the train pulled into a station. Pskov?

The Czar tightened his grip on Ash and the doctor poured iodine the length of his forearm; the pain arched his back, tears popped out of his eyes.

Ash hung on the thought that somewhere, if he had survived the fall in the snow, von Basel might be going through the same thing. The doctor rebandaged his forearm while Ash tentatively flexed his fingers. Not so bad. The doctor nodded to the Czar, who removed his hand from over Ash's mouth, but instead of explaining why they were hiding he said, "Kenneth, if you would turn over there seems to be another wound on your leg." His calf, Ash recalled—von Basel had tried to cripple him. He noticed a small window up high and open a crack, and he recalled hearing a steady parade of footsteps outside the train on the station platform and low-voiced, somehow urgent conversations.

Another dose of liquid fire and the doctor was through. He washed his hands in the sink, cautiously opened the door and disappeared through it. Ash noticed his sword and clothing hung on the back of the backroom door. The Czar lowered the toilet lid and sat down. Good lord, Ash thought, the Czar of all the Russias sitting in a bathroom talking to him. What would history say . . . the irreverent thought was quickly dispatched by the Czar's remarkably sad tone of voice, as though it were almost too much for him to speak.

"No one knows about the German but you and me. Only the officers' doctor and the officers who removed the assassin secretly to the Pskov hospital know about the assassin. I told them that you received your wounds defending me from him."

"But why?"

"I've not been able to contact the Czarina. I want nothing to prevent you from going to Tsarskoye Selo to tell her what has happened here . . . When we arrived in Pskov last night Petrograd was in flames. Police stations were destroyed, my ministers arrested, regiments ordered to put down the insurrection had gone over to the insurrectionists. I dined with my generals aboard the train and telegraphed others. It was the opinion of my generals that I must grant a full constitution—grant full power of government to the Duma—otherwise Russia would plunge into anarchy and my armies collapse."

Good, Ash thought. The American people would accept a *constitutional* monarchy as an ally against the Kaiser's Germany. The Czar stared at the tiles above Ash's head. What about Tamara, Ash wondered . . . he wouldn't put it past her to pull some lunatic attempt to defend her precious house . . . he had to get back to Petrograd, *then* to the Czarina at Tsarskoye Selo . . .

"But this morning," the Czar went on, "I learned that the political situation was far worse. Particularly inside the Duma itself, which is divided. There are two factions . . . the majority have formed a Provisional Government to lead Russia in these difficult times, but they are opposed by the Social Revolutionary Party and the members of workers' committees—the soviets, that are opposed to my having *any* part in the government. So the ministers of the Duma are helpless, the workers' soviets already control Petrograd and the railroads and the telegraph." He nodded at the little window. "And so our visit to Pskov . . . while my wife is alone at Tsarskoye Selo."

They've isolated him, thought Ash, just like Valery and I tried to do.

"A strong government must be formed to resist these soviets, restore order and continue the fight against Germany. It is imperative that you carry this message to the Alexander Palace. Tell the Czarina to stand fast, tell her it is God's will that I defend my throne—"

"May I ask you how, Your Majesty?"

"How? I will command our loyal troops to march on Petrograd. I have fifteen million men under arms, they can't *all* be disloyal—"

"Sir, what can the Czarina do when I tell her this?"

"Provide an example, encourage the garrison—"

"Has the Tsarskoye Selo garrison remained loyal?"

The Czar hesitated . . . "I don't know . . . we are cut off here on the train . . ."

"Sir, I know this sounds presumptuous of me, but I ask you to reconsider what you are saying. If the soviets threaten the very existence of the provisional government, aren't they likely to resist you as well? Even you . . ." And added to himself, Especially you . . .

"I will crush them with Cossacks, Brusilov's soldiers, cavalry."

442

Ash realized there was nothing more to be gained in debating the Czar. His father used to say there was a time to tell the truth and a time to tell a man what he has to hear.

"Of course you have loyal regiments, Your Majesty . . ."

"Then you will make your way through the lines to Tsarskoye Selo, to my wife . . . we must not give in to fear."

But he hardly sounded convinced by his own words. Lenin had cautioned Ash in Zurich not to misunderstand Russian patriotism, nor underestimate it. He looked the Czar in the eye. "But what will happen to Russia, sir, if your capital is destroyed . . . ?" For a moment Ash thought the Czar might hit him . . . after all, here he was, a distinctly nonloyal upstart American not very subtly suggesting to the Czar of all the Russias that he end three hundred years of Romanov succession and a thousand years of Russian monarchy for the good of his nation.

The Czar's fists clenched. He looked away. He was still wearing his gray Cossack uniform. Ash decided to press one last time, *this* time to say to Nicholas what he knew was the truth but could not say to himself. "I believe there's a saying, Your Majesty . . . that there are many tests of a soldier's courage . . ."

It had happened. The Czar, with Ash's prodding, had made a soldier's decision. Late that night Ash watched the Imperial Train steam south toward Mogilev, where the Czar had received permission—God, Ash thought, what *that* must have done to him . . . receive *permission*—from the Provisional Government to say good-bye to his army. He hoped to rendezvous with his mother there to explain to the Dowager Empress why he had abdicated, as he had put it, "my father's throne."

He had asked Ash to report to the Czarina, to tell her he was safe, that he would be with her soon.

"May I tell Her Majesty that you will go to England?"

The Czar had only shrugged. His thoughts of the future were his own. He had precious little else left.

At the Pskov station a machine gun covered the empty platform as the Czar's train steamed into the dark. When the train lights had disappeared Ash closed his boat cloak, straightened his service cap and walked slowly to the ticket office.

A ragtag gang of soldiers stopped him; their battle-scarred sergeant wore the gray face of the trenches and an officer's coat with its epaulets ripped off. He read Ash's pass and sent a man running. Ash was trying to explain that he was an American citizen when the runner returned with the Social Revolutionary fighting squad leader Kirichenko.

443

Kirichenko returned the sergeant's respectful salute. He looked the same as Ash had last seen him preparing to blow the Tsarskoye Selo line. He had the same leather jacket, open as usual as if he didn't feel cold, a peaked forage cap over his eyes and a pair of guns in his waistband. His heavy lips and long nose seemed more prominent in a face drawn with fatigue. Somewhere, he had picked up an incongruous-looking pair of spats. He regarded Ash with little interest, as if meeting him were a minor event in an otherwise important day.

"What are you doing in Pskov, Commander Ash?"

"On my way to Petrograd."

"But why are you here?"

"I'm passing through on American government business; that safe-conduct pass was issued by the Provisional Government—"

"Ah? The *Provisional* Government." Kirichenko held the pass to the light and carefully read the signature, then tore the paper into small pieces which drifted to the railroad platform. "You need passes from the Railroad Workers' Soviet, and, of course, the Petrograd Soviet . . . But there's no need, in your case. I'm sending you to Petrograd anyhow. Your train will leave in the morning. And your room will be waiting for you in the Peter-Paul."

"You're arresting me?"

"Certainly."

"On what charge?"

Kirichenko lifted the peak of his hat enough for Ash to get a good look at his eyes. "Suspicion of counter-revolutionary activities. Your monarchist associations are well known. And there's also the matter of the death of several of our comrades murdered in an explosion you arranged—"

"You have no authority to arrest me—"

"I have the authority of the Railroad Workers' Soviet throughout Russia. And the authority of the Petrograd Soviet in Petrograd." He nodded at the sergeant and two soldiers grabbed Ash's arms; he stifled a yell when one inadvertently squeezed the puncture in his upper right. Kirichenko noticed, but a second group of soldiers came running out on the platform, carrying a stretcher and shouting, "*Tovarisch* Kirichenko."

They had found Dmitri Dan. The Red Snow leader was wrapped in hospital sheets and heavy blankets. He looked weak, but when he recognized Ash he managed to lift his head as surprise turned to rage. He then started shouting at Kirichenko, introducing himself, it seemed. Ash recognized a few of the words he kept repeating: *Krasnyi*, which meant both red and beautiful; *sneg*, one of many Russian words for snow; *vozhd*, leader; and again and again, *tovarisch*, comrade.

Kirichenko listened until he was done, then pulled one of the pistols from his waistband and shot Dmitri Dan through the head. The bullet passed through Dmitri's skull and through the stretcher and ricocheted on the cement platform; the report echoed in the train shed. The soldiers holding his stretcher gaped white-faced at what they were carrying. The ones holding Ash let go, stunned.

Kirichenko addressed them briefly. They looked at each other, looked at Kirichenko still holding his gun, and tentatively saluted. Kirichenko returned their salute and turned to Ash. "He said you prevented him from killing the Czar."

Ash looked at his gun. "Am I next?"

"Oh, no. The soviets are grateful. The Czar must stand trial, be made an example of. There will be no summary execution for the Czar."

"Why did you shoot him?"

"We have no place in the Social Revolutionary-Bolshevik Revolution for fanatics." Kirichenko slipped his pistol back into his waistband, and with a look at the soldiers added, "Or for dissenters."

Ash knew then, here in Pskov, that even the Czar's abdication wouldn't change Russia's course. Hours old, the Revolution was hurtling toward chaos, and the soviets intended to use the Czar to justify it, to provide it with legitimacy. That above all must be avoided if the U.S. were to get involved, and if Russia were to continue as an ally against the Germans. More than ever it was necessary for Ash to get the Czar *and* his family to England.

BOOK

V

The Death of Kings

55

A sh was among the first new prisoners in the Peter-Paul Fortress. Many more joined him in the next few days—bloodied ex-ministers, actually grateful the Red Guards had saved them from the mob; frightened aristocrats, their clothing ripped and smeared, or wearing hastily put on and transparent disguises; Life Guard officers, scabbards empty, insignia cut away; and even bewildered citizens who were once functionaries in the Czar's bureaucracy. They were all herded into large communal cells.

Ash tried to get disinfectant and bandages to patch up the new arrivals, pumping them, as he did, for the latest information. Two governments, it seemed, were running Russia—the Provisional Government, which represented the establishment, minus the Czar, who was rumored to be under arrest; and the soviets, who represented the workers. The Provisionals spoke for the nation, the soviets controlled the major cities and communication between them, and it was the soviets, Ash heard over and over, who demanded that the Czar be arrested and tried. A single name emerged from the chaos and seemed to promise stability: the Duma member Sergei Gladishev had so strongly defended—Alexander Kerensky. Appointed Minister of Justice by the Provisional Government, Kerensky was taking charge, bridging the gap between the old establishment and the soviets. Kerensky promised to keep fighting Germany.

But a crippling debate raged over the Czar. Ash got hold of an English-language newspaper a new prisoner had held to a wound in his chest and read around the blood. It was filled with lurid accounts of supposed eyewitness reports of sex between Czarina Alexandra and Rasputin, as well as stories about religious desecration and the Czarina's connections with German spies.

Summing up the debate were two opposing columns under a single heading: WHAT TO DO WITH THE CZAR?

A minister of the Provisional Government suggested that after a "suitable investigation of alleged wrongdoing" the Czar should either retire or be exiled. How convenient. The catch, of course, was the "suitable investigation." The second article was by a radical member of the Petrograd Soviet and he echoed Kirichenko. Bloody Nicholas must pay. He added that a former Czar abroad in exile would become a rallying figure for counter-revolutionaries. The Provisional Government hadn't the courage or the power to let him go, and the revolutionaries considered him as too dangerous to let go, too important a villain not to punish.

The Czar was the focus. The whole country could blow up on account of him. Ash had to get him out . . .

Four days later they brought in Lord Exeter. Ash watched the Englishman fight hard for his dignity. He had been struck repeatedly about the face; he was bloody and bruised, his eyes were closed and blood dripped from his nose. A revolutionary guard pushed him into the cell with his rifle butt, which caught him hard in the kidney. He staggered, grunting with pain. Ash caught his arm and guided him into a distant corner where he'd been trying to help new arrivals. When Exeter's lungs finally stopped wheezing Ash asked him, "How'd they get you?"

"Had my name on a list . . ."

"Can your embassy help? Mine doesn't even know I'm here."

"They'll try to get me deported."

"We've got to get the Czar out before he sets off total civil war—"

"The soviets are dead set against him leaving."

"I know. We need to make it seem that the King has withdrawn the offer of sanctuary, make the soviets think the Czar couldn't go if he wanted to. And then we must secretly get him out."

"You seem to forget you're in prison, Ash."

"Get word to Gladishev to get me out of here. He's Kerensky's friend."

"Kerensky's hanging on by his fingernails."

They were eating a vile thin soup when the guards came for both of them and locked them in a small cell. After a few hours they appeared again, with an attaché from the British Embassy. "Deported," Exeter said. "I'll give your *regards* to our friends in England."

Ash pretended to ignore him. The guards left and came back once more after Ash had been expecting to be shot. They took Ash down to the courtyard. Ambassador Hazzard was waiting in a hired car.

"Don't thank me, Commander. Thank the U.S.A. The Petrograd Soviet wanted to throw away the key but the Provisionals, who're running the rest of the country said it was more important to be friends with the United States. You've certainly made some bad enemies, Ash."

"Do you think we'll declare war on Germany soon?"

"President Wilson is addressing a joint session of Congress on April second. We're getting closer. If this whole damn country doesn't blow up first."

"Mr. Ambassador, I'm going to need passports to get out of Russia . . . ten of them."

"*Ten?* What the hell for?"

Ash took Ambassador Hazzard's arm. The movement caused a dull twinge in his own arm in both the places von Basel had scored.

"Please cable Ambassador Page, sir. In code, and don't use my name. Ambassador Page will know what you mean."

"I'll bet he will . . . Ash, what the hell are you up to?"

"See what Ambassador Page says, Your Excellency—"

"Lay off the 'excellency' stuff, Ash. You're not talking to one of your European bluebloods . . . Ten?"

Ten, thought Ash. The Czar, Czarina, four grand duchesses, the boy, Sedovina, as he had promised Vadim and who could be very useful if he could persuade her to leave . . . that was eight. He was nine. And Tamara was ten.

"Well, one thing's for sure," Hazzard broke the silence as the car drove onto the Palace Bridge. "If and when we get into this war, we're going to end it damned soon."

"Not without Russia," Ash said.

"Of course not without Russia. God . . . what a mess if they pulled out. Shall I drop you at your hotel, Ash?"

"The Winter Palace."

Ash was taken through halls and chambers so huge and extravagant as to reduce the palaces of Europe and England to pallid imitations of royal display. Their classic proportions were perfect decisions of height and breadth, embellished with rococo ornamentation, gilded and fantastic.

"There are a thousand rooms like this one," Sergei Gladishev said, greeting him. He was standing over a billiard table in a room with lapis walls. "What is it you want, Commander?"

While Ash explained, Gladishev puttered about the table with his cue, missing shots and flicking the balls with the back of his hand.

"Everything is set," Ash said when he had concluded telling the Duma member what he had told Exeter. "I've got a route out. The Czar will go. King George's offer still holds, regardless of what you might hear. I'm ready to go."

"Except that the Petrograd Soviet won't let him leave the Alexander Palace. Kerensky himself is interrogating the family—"

"What *for?* The Provisional Government doesn't want to put him on trial, does it?"

"No. I believe Kerensky is hoping to persuade the soviets that the Czar should not stand trial. Let him go into exile."

"They won't," Ash said. "The Bolsheviks won't let him go."

Gladishev shrugged. "The situation is volatile. Give Kerensky time, we'll help you if it becomes necessary, but attempting to get the Czar out of Russia at this moment would be dangerous for us all . . . wait."

"There isn't time, you're not going to make the Bolsheviks change their minds. And meanwhile things are getting worse, more dangerous—"

"Wait."

For your own funeral, Ash thought.

General Ludendorff had requisitioned an hourglass. His aide-de-camp delegated a secretary to fill out the forms, and in due course an hourglass appeared on the desk of the quartermaster general. He took to turning it regularly, often before the hour was up. The sand fascinated him. His grains of sand, his casualties on the East and West, had kept mounting through the cold winter, and with spring approaching might accelerate.

There were boys in the line now, children stunted by nearly three years of short rations. And there were old men, hungry too, and cautious. Ludendorff laid the hourglass on its side; the sand settled into two imprisoned heaps, one larger than the other. He stared at it a while, then turned the large heap eastward. Russia. The small pile of grains on the other side, Germany.

His aide-de-camp knocked, sparing him from his increasingly morbid imagination. "You asked to see me, General?"

"What's happening in Russia?"

"There are now virtually two governments, sir. The Provisionals say they speak for the state; the Provisionals pledge to pursue the war. The soviets—workers' councils—control the cities and the railroads; the soviets would sue for peace."

"Which would you bet on?"

"I don't bet, General, but if some rival faction were to seize *our* railroads, I'd make every effort to dislodge *them.*"

"Can the Provisional Government dislodge them?"

"It might. An appeal to patriotism over politics. They say the Russian soldier believes in God, the Czar and Russia. And he's still got God and Russia."

"That's what bothers me," Ludendorff said. "There are too many, and they are too brave. We've got to undermine them . . . what do you think of this von Basel situation?"

His aide-de-camp hesitated. It was not an idle change of subject.

Ludendorff said, "All right, this is how I see von Basel. Number one, he has decided the Kaiser is hopeless. Hence the renewed reports to Gruppe IIIb . . . Number two, whatever his demented condition, he is a German patriot. Number three, though he was forced to go underground when the Czar abdicated, he is still a potent force inside Russia. Do you agree?"

"Yes, General. His reports indicate he is still working for Germany under difficult conditions."

"And Count von Basel's advice?"

"Divide Russia by creating conflict between the soviets and the Provisionals."

"My feelings exactly," Ludendorff replied. "I think it's time to gather up those scum in Zurich and swing the balance of power."

"The Bolsheviks, sir?"

"Yes. Bolsheviks, SRs, Red Snow, Mensheviks, every damned one you can find. Offer them passage to Russia." He upended the hourglass and the large heap began trickling into the smaller. "Be sure not to let them off the train in Germany even to stretch their legs. They'll infect our people . . . and order von Basel to give them all the help he can."

An ecstatic Lenin received the news while he was writing a letter about the revolutionary role of the soviets, about which he knew little. News from Russia was still sketchy, but one thing was sure. The soviets could appropriate the Revolution if they were armed. And the Bolsheviks could appropriate the soviets.

Red flags flew from the Admiralty and the Peter-Paul. Anarchists dressed in black roamed the streets of Petrograd carrying machine guns. Ash tried to call Tamara from the Winter Palace, but the telephones were out. On her embankment across the river he could make out black holes where houses had recently stood. He couldn't see hers. There were no cars for hire. He caught a tram part way and ran on foot the rest of the distance to her mansion. But as he neared the embankment, he slowed . . . Up close the burned-out hulks looked as if they had been shelled. Here a wall stood free, there a chimney, and beside it a garden filled with bits of furniture, too big for the looters to carry or damaged beyond saving. He rounded a final bend—and there was Tamara's, still standing, with its windows dark.

A sign on the door told why:

PROPERTY OF THE PETROGRAD SOVIET
TRESPASSERS WILL BE SHOT

Ash pushed open the gate, walked up the unshoveled front walk and banged the door knocker. Maybe the bastards knew where she'd gone . . . been taken . . . But no one came to the door. He thought he heard movement inside, knocked again. A curtain slid from a side window, a face peered out. The door opened wide.

"Kennet."

As she threw her arms around him, Ash caught a glimpse of her black boots, black fur, black hat, cheeks pale and hair so very beautiful. "Inside, quickly."

It was bitter cold in the house. Ash embraced her. "God, I thought they'd done something to you—"

"Not yet," she said with a steely note in her voice Ash had heard only in her rehearsals. "Are you all right? You disappeared."

"What's that sign about?"

A quick smile. "I wrote it myself. No one's bothered me. They took Kchessinska's house. A mob of Bolsheviks are living in it. Others they burned."

"You can't stay here."

"I don't intend to. I'm going to Paris."

"Paris? How?"

She looked away. "I've made arrangements."

"Tamara. You can't go across town without a pass from the revolutionaries."

"I've got one."

"You?"

"Now, listen. There's someone I want you to meet and I would appreciate it if you would behave yourself."

"Who?"

She hurried without a word toward the solarium. Ash followed. All the plants were dead. Across the river many of the buildings flew red flags.

A Russian Guards officer stood warming his hands before a small fire made from a smashed-up chair. He too wore a coat and hat against the cold; he had a big red cockade on his hat, and on his shoulder where the Czar's insignia had adorned his epaulets was a red ribbon.

"A friend, my dear?" He smiled at Tamara and turned to Ash. "We worried when we heard your knock."

"This is Prince André. He has a travel pass to the Crimea. He is taking me to Paris."

"I am honored to perform that service."

"This is my friend Commander Ash."

"Honored, Commander."

"Would you excuse us?" Ash said.

454

"I beg your pardon?"

"Tamara," he said quietly. "Get him out of here or—"

"André, Kennet and I must discuss something of a private nature."

Prince André stood up, smiling. "I'll be right outside. Don't forget, we're leaving very soon."

Tamara closed the door and turned to Ash. "Kennet . . . understand . . . you know damned well what the revolutionaries will do to me when they find out I'm here. They've burned all my neighbors' houses already. Sedovina warned me to get out. I'm a monarchist, I was the Grand Duke Valery Romanov's mistress. *You* have your American diplomatic passport. How am I supposed to get out of the country with the Czar abdicated and these damned Provisionals and soviets and God knows what taking over—?"

"Not this way, Tamara. Who is that idiot—"

"He's a liberal, the revolutionaries need him."

"For the moment. And what does he need you for?"

"He's a gentleman, he'll respect my grief for Valery."

"Like hell he will. Tamara, you're fooling yourself. This is no good—"

"Can you do better, Kennet?"

Ash hesitated. "Yes . . . but it's going to be a little while, a week or—"

"A week or? Kennet, don't you see what's going on here? I'll be back in prison in a week. Or worse . . . André's got a pass. For two. He said my jewels will help as bribes. And I don't have to wait while some damned soviet decides to arrest me because of Valery." She looked at Ash at last, and her defiance softened. "What can I do, Kennet?"

Ash understood . . . The Czar's police had locked her up like an animal. Now the revolutionaries wanted to do it again. He opened his arms to her. She came into them, then pulled back and looked up at him. "Oh God, Kennet, I'm a coward, it seems. I'm frightened. Sedovina . . . I think she's tried to defend me, but she's just one girl . . ."

She pressed against him. She whispered against his chest. "Sedovina is organizing benefit performances for the troops."

"Oh?"

"Many artists are contributing, they're afraid not to."

"Is she dancing?"

"She says she wants to, but she's busy presenting the events . . . Kennet? Perhaps *I* could dance."

"A benefit?"

"For myself. For a pass. Would you come and see me dance for a pass?"

Ash smiled. "Sure would. You wouldn't even need to bribe me with jewels."

Tamara shuddered. "God, dancing for a mob of revolutionaries."

"They're just men, Tamara. You've never had much trouble handling the breed before."

She moved close to him again. ". . . But most have never even seen ballet."

"Neither has anyone else who hasn't seen you dance." She squeezed his hand and started pacing around the solarium. The dead plants rustled like snakes when she brushed their brown leaves. "I keep thinking about that man on the tram who saw me dance . . ."

"Why not dance at the Maryinski?"

"I was thinking the same thing. If I do this I'm not going to do it halfway . . . Good God, Kennet, two thousand revolutionaries?"

"Make it your Jubilee."

"Kennet—"

"I'm serious. Go out in style."

Tamara stared out the window. Across the Neva a silken red flag flew over the Winter Palace; it stood straight out, blown by a hard spring gale off the Gulf. Snow swirls raced up the frozen river. She had no choice. She was going, whether she wanted to or not; but *how* she went was still her choice. Wasn't that what Kennet was saying, asking her to be what he admired, be what she *was* . . .

"I wonder what I would dance? . . . *Swan Lake,* I suppose. I've rehearsed it already. It's pretty and it's simple enough to understand . . . what do you think?"

He was looking at her strangely. "What about *Firebird?*"

56

Increasingly anxious to rid the Provisional Government of the Czar's divisive presence yet at the same time not up to challenging the soviets who were hell-bent to put the Czar on trial—a forum from which they could attack the aristocratic and bourgeois elements of the Provisional Government as well as the Czar himself—Sergei Gladishev and Justice Minister Kerensky allowed Ash to persuade them to take what seemed a good way out of their dilemna. Kerensky ordered the captain of the guard holding the Czar to help Ash hide Nicholas and his family in the stage sets of the *Firebird* ballet, which had been stored for some time now in shipping crates at the Alexander Palace.

After that, Ash would be on his own. The crated sets would be sent to the Maryinski Theater, where Tamara Tishkova would perform *Firebird* to honor the Revolution. From the theater it was up to Ash to smuggle the family, disguised and carrying American and British passports, to the Finland Station, then by train across the Finnish-Swedish border.

Ash persuaded Rodney Skelton, with an indirect nudge from King George, to station his Royal Navy submarine at the edge of the ice at the west end of the Gulf of Finland as an emergency alternate escape route, should something go wrong on the train.

But it was the first twenty miles of the escape that was certain to be most difficult. The Tsarskoye Selo village soviet, the Railroad Workers' Soviet and the Petrograd Soviet had an iron grip on the route between the Alexander Palace and the Maryinski Theater. And the revolutionary guards that served them were more than likely to inspect any crates that passed through their territory . . .

Vera Sedovina was Ash's only friendly contact among the soviets—

Kirichenko had been less than pleased when the Provisional Government had released Ash from the Peter-Paul—Sedovina's bravery, her courier missions for the Bolsheviks and her dancing in the slums were widely known, as were her efforts since the Revolution to bring dance, music and theater to "the masses."

Ash found her in a bitter-cold rehearsal hall near the Maryinski, overseeing acts to be presented to revolutionary soldiers. Valentinov, the provincial actor whom Ash had seen play the Czar when Sedovina danced in the Moscow District, was badgering her for a role.

"It is *ballet*," she told him firmly.

Valentinov gave an enormous shrug. "You are a hard young woman, Vera." At the door he slipped his Czarlike beard around his chin and called out, "I, Nicholas the Deposed, *command* that Valentinov play Petrograd. What do you say to *that*, Vera Sedovina?"

"I say *out*."

"Is he that bad?" Ash said after the man had gone.

"He would take advantage," she said bluntly. "It's wrong."

Ash looked at her. Her blonde hair was crushed into a tight bun. She wore wire-frame reading glasses and a heavy wool sweater over her rehearsal clothes. Dancers were working out at the barre, their breath steaming in the frigid air. Vera sat at a desk covered with neatly stacked papers. And Ash thought she did not look very happy.

"You seem upset. What's wrong?"

"I'm just tired, there's so much to do, so much confusion . . ."

"I'd have thought you'd be happier, I mean with the Revolution here—"

"Yes, of course . . ." Except she didn't sound very convincing.

"Vera . . . would you have lunch with me? I need to talk to you about something."

She started to refuse, changed her mind, gave some instructions to a few people and got her coat. They walked along the Ekaterine Canal. "First of all," Ash said, "you convinced Tamara. She'll dance the *Firebird* at the Maryinski for whatever audience you invite."

"Tishkova?" Her eyes lighted with pleasure.

"She'll want a travel pass. She wants to go to Paris . . ."

"Yes, I guess I can understand that. Things must seem strange now to a woman of her position . . . well, if she dances I think the soviets will give her permission . . . Why *Firebird*?"

At that moment a huge limousine roared by, diverting her from waiting for his answer. Armed soldiers lay on the running boards and poked guns and red flags from the windows. They saw Sedovina and gave out admiring catcalls. Sedovina moved closer to Ash. He slipped her hand through his arm.

"They're patrolling for counter-revolutionaries—"

458

"They're joyriding," Ash said. "When they run out of gas they'll steal another car. Except they'll call it appropriating. It's getting out of hand, Vera. The whole city's going to blow up again."

Sedovina's voice sounded very tired. "Those men in the car are still the poor, the Provisionals are still the rich . . ."

"Whatever, but you've got a civil war coming if you keep thinking that way. Is this the Russia you imagined?" He looked at her and saw tears in her eyes. Her guard had come down. For a moment the frightened young girl had reappeared. "Your father asked me to take you to America—"

"*No*, damn it. This is my country. We just somehow have to move ahead—"

"Russia's not likely to be moving any place as long as the soviets try to destroy the Provisional Government."

"But I'm a Bolshevik, Commander . . . the soviets *should* destroy the Provisional Government—"

"I saw Kirichenko murder a man in cold blood because he happened to belong to another political party."

"The fanatic Dmitri Dan? I heard."

"Doesn't that bother you?"

"Yes . . . of course . . . but as the peasants say, when you chop wood, chips fly—"

"Well, those chips are going to catch fire, Vera. How much more chaos can Russia stand? Do you want a civil war? My father fought in one. A million men died. And we were a very small country at the time. At least the Provisional Government stands between you and anarchy. Sure . . . let the Bolsheviks take over in time, but let it happen slowly, Vera. Let the soviets take power peacefully; if they really represent the people, let them do it without fighting."

Sedovina shook her head. "I'm confused, I don't like what I see. I know it's wrong to feel this way, but it's almost as if we've discovered a new oppression, our own stupidity—I don't want to talk about it anymore . . . Why did Tishkova choose *Firebird*, of all things? You never answered me."

"Because I asked her to."

"You? Why?"

He took a deep breath. "Do you know the story about how Tishkova was suppose to dance *Firebird* for the Czar?"

"I've heard it from my father . . ."

"The sets and costumes were shipped direct from Paris to the Alexander Palace."

"But why—"

He would have to trust her. "Vera, the Czar is what the soviets and the Provisional Government are going to fight over. And in the process wreck the whole country. The Czar is the real issue . . . You can help me get him out of the country and save it . . . Removing him will be like dousing a fire, it will give Russia some time to get on its feet—"

"Help you? How could I do that?"

"The soviets won't let him go. You can help me smuggle him out of the Alexander Palace."

"With the sets for *Firebird?*"

"Yes . . . exactly."

"Have you told Tishkova?"

"She's going to have enough, dancing her Jubilee for two thousand revolutionaries without worrying about a Czar hidden in the cellar . . ."

"You really trust me, don't you?"

"Vera, there are three people in Russia I would trust. You, Tamara Tishkova and myself."

Tears filled her eyes again. "I guess that's why I'm crying," she murmured. "My list is no bigger. Everyone seems to have lost their way . . ."

57

The cavernous stage was bare from wing to wing, empty from the proscenium arch to the back wall. Tamara looked more sad than angry, but her eyes flashed as she paced a tight circle. "I am performing in thirty-six hours and still there is no set? No scenery. No drops. No scrim." She clutched up a fistful of her thick practice sweater. "And *this* is not a costume, for the information of gentlemen who keep promising miracles."

Her friend, the former director of the defunct Imperial Theaters, glanced imploringly at Ash, who had his own considerable reasons to be concerned about the delayed sets. Ash said, "I'm sure everything will arrive in time for the carpenters to fly the sets tonight."

"*You're* sure."

"Sedovina persuaded Kirichenko to issue new passes for her crew. She'll get through to the palace this time, I'm sure."

Tamara ran both hands through her thick black hair. "Why did I let you talk me into *Firebird?* I could have done *Swan Lake.* Every theater in the city has sets for *Swan Lake.* Damn it, why didn't you let me go to Paris with Prince what's-his-name?"

Ash massaged her shoulders. "You're tense. You've rehearsed yourself to death. Everyone thinks you're wonderful—"

"Absolutely," said the director.

"*Tense?* How would you feel if they sent you to sea without a ship?"

Which was just about how Ash did feel. Yesterday and the day before the soviets had turned the Maryinski's haulers back from Tsarskoye Selo in spite of Vera Sedovina's reputation and credentials. The reasons were less political than bureaucratic . . . with responsibility so divided among Petrograd city soviets, railroad soviets and Tsarskoye Selo soviets, chaos reigned. There always seemed to be one more official demanding a pass than Sedovina had passes.

"Tonight," Ash promised.

"Where are *you* going?"

"The embassy," Ash lied.

"You can't leave me today."

"Tamara, I do work for the United States government and its ambassador has told me to show up . . . good luck at rehearsal."

"You are an out and out bastard."

Ash reached for her and she dodged; she relented on his third try and let him hold her. "It's all going to be over soon."

"Try to get back early. I'm going to be a wreck tonight. Seriously, Kennet, I'm going to need you very badly."

He saw no way to tell her he was heading out to the Alexander Palace; Tamara was getting her pass by dancing, which was a far surer way of getting out alive than knowing about his scheme to rescue the Czar. . . .

Tamara was not the only one with nerves on edge. Sergei Gladishev greeted Ash with a strident warning. "Last time, Commander. If you don't get them out today it's over. Two times I have driven you to the Alexander Palace pretending to interrogate the Czar for Justice Minister Kerensky. My colleagues wonder how many more times I can ask why he appointed bad ministers. Two times we put the Czar and his family in packing crates, and two times no theater crew collects the crates."

"Last chance," Ash agreed. "Tomorrow's the performance."

They were, as usual, stopped by two roadblocks on the way to Tsarskoye Selo, and on one occasion Gladishev's bodyguards exchanged fire with gunmen hidden in the trees.

Slovenly guards admitted them to the palace grounds. The captain of the Provisional Government's guard, a taciturn front-line officer, conducted them to the cellar; only he and a few loyal officers and ladies of the household were aware of the plan.

The family was waiting. It was nearly a month to the day that the Czar had abdicated his throne and the right of his son to inherit; time and events had affected him and the Czarina differently. The Czar looked like an old man; deeply scored wrinkles had added twenty years to his face, yet he was calm and if Ash had to guess at his emotions he would have thought sorrow was the dominant one. Czarina Alexandra, on the other hand, had blossomed. Indeed she looked quite beautiful, in charge of the situation. She greeted Ash cordially when he bowed over her hand . . . a considerable change from previous encounters. Perhaps it was that the

462

ghost of Rasputin's injunction for the Czar to resign had been carried out, and her husband and family were about to fulfill her mentor's prescribed destiny.

"Better luck this time, Commander?" She was almost cheerful.

"To be sure, Ma'am. An audience of two thousand revolutionaries must lend weight to the idea that the show must go on."

Her children were strangers to Ash. Four girls aged sixteen through twenty. Olga the eldest, quite pretty and rather serious looking. Tatiana, as regal a beauty as her mother; Marie, a pretty girl about Catherine Hazzard's age; and Anastasia, a happy-looking child. The Czarevitch, or ex-Czarevitch, Ash reminded himself, stuck close to Czar Nicholas as if most sensitive to his father's grief. He shook hands with Ash gravely, as did his father. Both greeted Sergei Gladishev as "Mr. Duma Member."

The captain of the Provisional Government's guard reappeared shortly. "It looks like they're getting through. The Tsarskoye Selo Soviet has allowed them to enter the Imperial Park. They're less than a mile from the gates."

The Czarina hugged each of her children, and kissed the Czar.

The flats, backdrops and scrims had been broken down in Paris seven years earlier to fit railroad cars. There were a dozen crates eight feet high and eight to fifteen feet long in addition to costume trucks and prop boxes. All but the boy and the Czarina entered them singly. Alexandra feared the boy would hurt if he were alone; and she was unable to stand for a long time on account of her sciatica, so in the center of a huge prop box they had constructed a bed of blankets on which she would lie down holding the boy.

There was no one to say good-bye. Closest friends had already been sent away from the palace. Those few who remained were upstairs in the royal apartments maintaining the charade and fiction that the family were in their rooms.

Ash and the captain of the guard nailed each crate shut. Ash saved the Czarina's for last. She thanked him when he wished her luck. He was pounding in the last nails when the cellar's huge outer doors banged open and a gang of roustabouts trooped down the ramp, Sedovina in the lead.

As a leader of the newly organized Theater Workers' Soviet, she had put together a crew from various theaters, men not known to each other, and who therefore took little notice of Ash, who like them was dressed in sheepskin, forage cap and *volanka*, oiled felt knee-high peasant boots. He joined the crew hoisting the crates onto dollies and wheeling them out the cellar and up the ramp to freight sledges waiting on the frozen snow. Nor did they notice when one of the haulers—the actor Valentinov—stayed behind in the cellar, until the captain of the guard escorted the actor upstairs to the royal apartments . . .

Outside the Alexander Palace, Provisional troops stood around a fire roasting one of the tame deer shot in the park. When the sledges were loaded, the horses started for the gates that led to the Imperial Park, and the theater crew hopped on wherever they could find space. The Provisional troops waved them through the great grill gate. The troops of the Tsarskoye Selo Soviet promptly stopped them on the other side.

Ash sat on the prop box housing the Czarina and Alexis and tried to look as unconcerned as the theater workmen. Red Guards swaggered around the sledges while Vera Sedovina presented papers to their officer.

Sedovina was having a hard time keeping her temper. "We passed this way an hour ago," she reminded the officer.

"Quite right, comrade, but now you have cargo."

"Which you and I discussed an hour ago, comrade, when I showed you these permits and informed you that you yourself will be a guest at the people's ballet tomorrow night, provided these sets and costumes arrive there on time."

"I would be derelict in my duties to the Tsarskoye Selo Soviet if I did not inspect the contents—"

"*I* would be derelict in my duties to the comrades of the Petrograd Theaters' Soviet not to inform *you* that two thousand Russian soldiers, Red Guards, sailors of Red Kronstadt, SRs, Bolsheviks and the workers' soviets are invited to the Maryinski Theater to see a performance by Comrade Tishkova using these sets."

"I am responsible—"

"Then get *on* with it." She pointed to a crate. "Open that one."

"Why that one?"

"Because, comrade, that is the only crate I did not have time to inspect myself." She nodded and her crew levered it open with crowbars.

"Careful," Sedovina shouted as a soldier reached inside. "Do it yourself, comrade," she told the officer. "That is part of a scrim, very fragile." He poked around, then noticed another crate on another sledge while the workman nailed the first crate shut again.

"Comrade, please," Sedovina asked with a smile. "We're really late."

He glanced at the papers. "This is signed by Comrade Kirichenko?"

"Comrade Kirichenko told me that he is very curious to see why the great Tishkova was the Czar's favorite. You understand?"

"Proceed."

Flying red flags, a small black locomotive wheezed onto the Tsarskoye Selo freight siding with a boxcar. Sedovina's crew slid open the doors and started hoisting the crates up from the sledges. A delegation of the Railroad Workers' Soviet bustled officiously among the horses, crates and sledges, shouting, waving papers and generally getting in the way. The Maryinski roustabouts indicated Sedovina was boss. The ballerina reached for her own papers but the chief of the railroad workers' delegation recognized her, tugged off his leather cap and tried to kiss her hand. "Little Mother," he called her, an almost mystical phrase of peasant respect. He told her he had seen her dance in the Moscow District with Valentinov, and that she had given him courage so that instead of running from the police he had fought back. He then ordered his delegation to help load the crates.

The ground was slippery under the boxcar door and a man fell in the mud and ice as he helped lift a crate; it teetered precariously. Ash went to help, but at that moment the half dozen men decided as one that it was going to fall and scattered. The crate crashed a full five feet to the ground.

Ash heard a loud cry from inside as he sprinted toward the falling crate, which was almost obscured by the sound of splintering wood; he was wondering whether the others had heard the cry when the narrow side of the long crate fell off, and the Czar's boot slid half out of the box onto the ice.

Ash snatched up the fallen side and tried to cover the opening to give the Czar time to pull back his foot. But Nicholas was dazed and the boot stayed there for what seemed like years.

Sedovina pushed through the gaping workmen, berated Ash in angry Russian and made a show of peering inside the broken crate, blocking the opening with her body as she did so. She pushed the boot into the dark interior by bending the dazed Czar's knee. Nicholas came to his senses with a shaky smile and whispered, "Thank you," and in spite of herself Sedovina found herself smiling back.

Ash stood by with the broken side and slapped it on as Sedovina emerged backward from the crate and warned that if even a single prop were lost a ballet could be ruined. A workman promptly nailed the piece Ash was holding and secured the damaged crate with ropes.

They rode in the boxcar with the crates. Ash again stationed himself on the box holding the Czarina and her son as the locomotive moved slowly toward Petrograd. The man on the next box tried to make conversation and when that failed, passed a bottle. Ash drank as little as possible without raising suspicions so that he was still reasonably sober when the train reached the city.

Things, it seemed, were finally looking up, Ash thought as he backed onto the platform holding a corner of the Czarina's prop box and muttered as much to Sedovina as she brushed close by.

Then he saw Kirichenko.

The SR fighting squad leader and representative of the combined railroad soviets was striding down the freight platform trailed by bodyguards. Ash ducked his head and tried to turn his back; the prop box was enormously heavy and he could not let go his corner without provoking dismayed shouts from the men holding the other three.

Sedovina froze. She could bully and cajole the workmen; she could receive homage from those who considered her a young female revolutionary hero. Not with Kirichenko. She looked at Ash for help. Kirichenko was only twenty feet away. Ash had to keep carrying the prop box.

"He likes you," Ash muttered. "Use it."

Sedovina couldn't believe it . . . Kirichenko?

Ash shuffled past with the box, trying to keep his head down. "Imagine you're Tamara, do *something* to distract him . . ."

"*Tovarisch* Kirichenko," she called gaily. He looked surprised. No wonder . . . not a word of scandal had ever been connected to his name, not a hint of a mistress. Kirichenko personified the dour, puritanical side of the Revolution. His eye went to the box that Ash and others were struggling with—the box that secreted the Czarina and the Czarevitch—and Vera Sedovina moved quickly into territory she had up to now only seen from a distance . . . she slipped her arm through Kirichenko's, smiled and sickened herself by saying, "We never would have made it with these sets without your name on the passes."

Kirichenko looked at her as if she were out of her mind. She waved her hand at the other crates, and turned him away from Ash. "There's confusion among even the soviets," she said. "Your name cut through it. The people's ballet will be danced at the Maryinski, thanks to you, *Tovarisch* Kirichenko." She even squeezed his arm. Kirichenko scarcely reacted. Sedovina was reminded of a caged wolf. Fighting squad leader Kirichenko was sweet on no one, clearly not very susceptible to her reluctant wiles. Still, the distraction had apparently worked; Ash had disappeared in the direction of the trucks carrying the crates across Petrograd to the theater. She let go of Kirichenko's arm. "I hope you enjoy the ballet," she said, more coolly.

"I'll be there, I've never seen you dance indoors."

So he was human. "I'm only dancing the princess. *Firebird* will be Tishkova's night."

Was that a flicker of humor animating Kirichenko's sharp features? He had been looking around the train platform, at the broken crate wrapped in ropes. Now he turned back to Sedovina, who pushed a wisp of blonde hair back under her hat.

"I'm sure it will be interesting to experience the pleasures of the Czars —but I for one am grateful for the opportunity to see you dance without having to watch that ham Valentinov. There were nights I thought of

466

turning him into the Okhrana as a public service . . ." He took a final look around and nodded to his bodyguards. "Well done, Comrade Sedovina. And good luck tomorrow night."

There remained getting the Czar and his family out of the scenery crates without being noticed by the theater carpenters, who urged on by a near-frantic stage manager were eager to fly the flats. Ash went ahead of the trucks to the theater, changed into his uniform in Tamara's dressing room and sat in the front row of the darkened house until Tamara and her Prince Ivan rehearsing their *pas de deux* took a break.

She came out of the lights with a towel around her neck and smiled down at him. "Thank you for coming so soon."

"I had to lock the ambassador in the closet . . . You look marvelous."

"Getting there . . . I'm told the sets are on the way."

"Sedovina thinks it would be a nice gesture to address the stage carpenters before they start. They'll be working all night."

"You tell Sedovina I grew up in the circus and I've never slighted a single member of any company in my life—even *before* I had to call them comrade."

"She's young—"

"And then tell her that when I was her age in the Czar's Imperial Theater, dancers who cut rehearsal the day before a performance ended up dancing in Turkestan."

The Maryinski's acoustics were near-perfect, carrying Tamara's and Ash's words to the top of the gallery, where Count von Basel sat listening in the dark. As soon as the posters announcing the great Tishkova's Jubilee were pasted up beside the strident revolutionary broadsides that covered every blank wall in the city von Basel suspected that at the Maryinski he would likely find Ash, and what Ash was up to.

He was considering going into Tishkova's dressing room, laying his saber across her face and asking her, but the tone of the conversation rising to the dark gallery suggested that Tishkova was not involved in whatever Ash's plans were. The subject was her performance, and what Ash was saying was what anyone would say to encourage someone he cared very much about . . .

But why had Ash stayed in Petrograd? A week ago the United States had formally declared war on Germany, as was expected once the Czar was overthrown. He had to smile about that. Yes, the Czar had abdicated and the United States could now feel easier about being Russia's ally . . . but

467

what kind of an ally? Russia was being divided by the soviets and the Provisionals. The Bolsheviks wanted to put the Czar on trial, the opposition didn't. The Czar was *still* the trouble, and as long as he was in Russia the country would be torn apart. Some ally . . . Still, he wondered why Ash hadn't been immediately recalled for sea duty? The United States was badly unprepared for war. It would take a year to mobilize a major army in France. Wouldn't they call home every experienced officer?

It was a puzzle that worried von Basel, a concern more important even than his fury at Ash for frustrating his attempt to capture the Czar for Kaiser Wilhelm, almost as important as the debt of honor Ash owed for hitting him with his fist to end their duel—

Ash and Tishkova had stopped talking. Von Basel leaned over the gallery balustrade and looked down. The entire theater was dark except for low lights on the stage. Tishkova was sprawled face down on a blanket. Ash had climbed on the stage and was kneeling beside her, massaging her shoulders.

Von Basel's bony head made him look like a wary hawk. Ash's government, he decided, hadn't recalled him because Ash was still involved in some intrigue in Russia . . . which could only mean trouble for his Kaiser and Germany.

He tried to flex the fingers of his left hand as he gazed down at the figures on the stage. Ash had severed tendons with his lucky thrust. Two of his fingers had curled up almost like the Kaiser's . . . Still enemies, Ash and himself. More than ever.

Thirty years earlier, deep in the cellars of the Maryinski, a pack rat of a stage manager had stored the gas lights when the theater was electrified. There was no reason for anyone to enter the storeroom, and so it was there among discarded foot and border lights, coils of copper tubing, an old gas valve switchboard table and ancient limelights that Ash had hidden Czar Nicholas and his family.

They were chilled from the long ride in the crates, and because the theater backed directly onto a canal the walls were wet, the room cold. The Czar insisted he had not been hurt when his crate fell off the train, except for some stiffness in his back. They huddled in blankets. Ash spirited a hot samovar out of the stagehands' workshop. They made and drank tea while Ash displayed the clothing he and Sedovina had assembled to go with their various passports.

"Nuns?" the Czar said with a smile for his three eldest daughters.

"A good way to hide a pretty face. Olga, Tatiana and Marie have British passports listing them as nursing sisters with the Anglo-Russian hospital."

"And my wife's pretty face?"

468

"Gray hair, for Her Majesty. Alexis and Anastasia will be your grandchildren."

"And who am I?"

"An American secretary of the Young Men's Christian Association. The YMCA. You've been visiting the *Mayak,* the Lighthouse brother organization here in Russia. Her Majesty's passport is British, to explain her accent. Yours is flatter and can pass for American."

The Czar took him aside afterward.

"We are grateful, of course, Commander, but are you still convinced we can—?"

"Can I guarantee to get you aboard a train and across the Swedish border? No, though I'll promise you a damned good try . . . Can you guarantee your family's lives in Russia?"

"Not without the Provisional Government's protection."

"Well, I wouldn't bet on them too long . . . tomorrow night every revolutionary leader worth his salt is going to be sitting upstairs watching Tishkova dance."

"She *is* distracting." The Czar smiled.

"She is more than distracting to me," Ash told him, a chill in his voice.

"I did not mean disrespect, Commander, merely admiration . . ."

Ash broke the brief silence that followed. "I'm afraid you're also going to have to say good-bye to your beard."

The next afternoon, while Tamara Tishova and her friend, the former director of the Imperial Theater, drove their company through dress rehearsal, two corporals of the Automobile Unit of the Engineer Corps concocted what they decided was a brilliant idea as they roared up and down the Nevsky Prospect in a commandeered armored car.

The great Bolshevik leader Nikolai Lenin was due to arrive from Zurich late that night. Why not go out to Tsarskoye Selo, arrest the Czar in the name of all the soviets and to hell with the Provisionals, and then present their prisoner to Lenin when he got off the train at the Finland Station? A magnificent welcome-home gift.

They were sharing a bottle, and the one who had had the least cautioned that the Provisional Government troops might resist a single armored car. So they drove out to the Smolney Institute, rounded up three more cars with like-minded crews and headed out to Tsarskoye Selo in convoy. One car crashed on the way, but the rest made it in an hour, a remarkable time considering the ice and frozen ruts.

Smashing through the front gates, scattering the sentries, they skidded to a noisy halt at the main entrance, leveled their cannon and machine guns and announced from their steel turrets that they had come to arrest the Czar in the name of the Petrograd Soviet. A hard-bitten Provisional captain came down the stairs and threatened to arrest them.

It was the first resistance they had met, and while they could have shot him, he was no imperial dandy but a soldier more like themselves. In that moment of reflection some began to wonder whether the Provisionals might be readying an artillery piece. Someone offered a compromise . . . "Let us see the Czar so that we can tell the soviet the prisoner is in your custody."

The captain did not like that idea at all, but there were three cars and among them two cannon and at least six heavy machine guns. "You may come in . . . the prisoner Nicholas Romanov will be brought to you."

"We want to see the royal apartments."

"The children are ill—"

"We want to see the heir."

"You can't," the captain said. He had regained some control of the situation and led them into the palace and lined them up at one end of the central reception hall. He then went up to the royal apartments, after mustering a ragtag Provisional guard to keep an eye on the armored car soldiers.

The actor Valentinov had never entered a stage tentatively, and he did not propose to do so now. The captain of the Provisional Guard had tried to soothe him by promising his guard would stand between him and the soviet soldiers who demanded to see the Czar, but that, he was certain, wasn't necessary . . . he was, after all, wearing the Czar's own clothes, and the soldiers had seen only pictures of Nicholas II. Now here he was in person, dazzling in scarlet and dripping gold braid, medals and a silken sash. He even had a sword, which the captain took away, explaining that as a prisoner he would not logically be allowed to keep it. And the captain reminded him again that the servants weren't to be trusted, since many had been enlisted as spies for the soviets.

"Act like a prisoner," the captain had told him. "Not Caesar."

Valentinov had promised but when he entered the reception hall and saw the soldiers waiting, he lost control. Instead of parading back and forth at a distance to make clear that he was in custody, he marched straight at the soldiers and offered to shake their hands.

Astounded, several did. Others just gaped in disbelief. Finally the captain of the guard clamped Valentinov's arm in a grip of iron and marched him away.

"How did I do?" Valentinov asked on the stairs.

"They will tell their grandsons that they shook the hand of Bloody Nicholas, Czar of all the Russias."

470

"Thank you, sir."

The captain eyed him. "Valentinov, have you no idea of the danger you will be in if the real Czar is caught?"

"No more than you."

"I am a soldier. And when he's gone the Provisional Government will thank me. The soviets will kill you if they learn what you're doing today . . ."

"For three years before you were a comrade, Comrade Captain, my acting troupe played under the noses of the Okhrana."

"But now you have your revolution. Why risk—"

"I agree with Comrade Sedovina. Now that we have our revolution, we have to risk our necks to save it."

"Well, with luck you'll be back in Petrograd tomorrow."

With luck, or a miracle? Valentinov wondered. Impersonating the Czar was going to be the performance of his life.

58

Tamara Tishkova watched strangers invade the Maryinski. Gone were the colorful uniforms of the Life Guards. Gone too old friends gathering for Society's entertainment. No laughter trilling from the first ring as the ladies of Petrograd inspected the officers parading in the stalls.

Ordinarily, with the dance settled in her mind, she would be relaxing these few minutes between dress and performance, staring into space, jumping up to prowl her dressing room, adjusting to the elaborate head-dress, but tonight she was irresistibly drawn to the stage manager's peep-hole at the side of the curtain to watch the people trooping into her theater.

The soldiers wore frontline khaki, the revolutionaries shabby suits if they were moderates or black leather jackets if they were radicals like Kirichenko, who was taking a seat of honor in the Imperial Box—*the Czar's own box*—flanking an anxious Justice Minister Kerensky with an equally nervous-looking Duma member, Sergei Gladishev.

The soldiers and revolutionaries made an oddly quiet audience as they gaped at the dancing figures painted on the great domed ceiling, the gold decorations, the crystal chandeliers and the plush blue seats. Many seemed awed by the splendor, but as many looked angry.

Tamara turned away from the peephole. Backstage was chaos as she had rarely seen. Monsters, demons and goblins huddled in the wings; the dancers were terrified of crashing into each other, almost unable to see out of the grotesque masks which had arrived only the previous night from the Alexander Palace. Because Igor Stravinsky's music was so unusual they were afraid they might not hear their entrances. And if the late sets and costumes, the at least partially hostile audience, the panicked stagehands and murky cues were not enough to unsettle the company, everyone, including the golden princesses perched on the stairs of Kostchei's enchanted castle, knew that Pavlova herself had turned down the part of the Firebird in Paris on the grounds that the music was incomprehensible.

Tamara looked out the peephole again, and suddenly knew she had been fooling herself this whole season. She was too old. A young girl like Sedovina could charm men like those in the audience. Not Tishkova. Not any more. She hadn't worked enough this year. Hadn't rehearsed. Hadn't practiced beyond her normal daily workout. Valery's coup had taken so much. And then Kennet had come . . . yes, she knew the tricks of experience that allowed a dancer to accomplish movement with less effort, but they were limited by aging bone, sinew and muscle. How could she ever drag herself out there and—

"Five minutes."

She brushed past the stage manager and ran to her dressing room. Of course it was filled with mirrors. She closed her eyes and felt her way to an easy chair, sank into it and listened to the blood rushing through her brain.

Someone started knocking on her door.

"Go *away*."

"Five minutes, mademoiselle."

"I'm not a horse you drive from the stable, go away."

Silence.

She felt with closed eyes for the ivory elephant her father had given her when the Yusupovs took her from the circus. When she had it firmly in both hands she slowly gathered her strength to open her eyes . . . The mirror. Tamara looked back in wonder. The Firebird was a most beautiful costume—a crown of gold and bright feathers, a scarlet bodice shimmering with sequins, gold dust sparkling on her bare shoulders. Slowly she stood up. The sparest *tunique*. She leaned to the mirror. Not a hair was out of place. Not a line showed through her makeup. She turned. Her legs, at least, were still Tishkova.

Tamara touched her lips to the little ivory elephant and put him down. She had, after all, rehearsed for two solid weeks with the constant help of her oldest friends in the theater. She was as ready as she would ever be. She gave the Firebird a rueful smile. What was a dancer without a mirror to remind her who she was and what she could do? What indeed . . .

Hurrying out to the stage, she ran into her partner, a boy with just the air of simplicity to play the Prince Ivan she was supposed to enchant. He looked terrified. Tamara kissed him, and reminded him that Diaghilev's original presentation of *Firebird* in Paris had also gone on with only one rehearsal. And when he still looked doubtful Tamara added that today's dress rehearsal had convinced her that she was extremely fortunate to be paired with him. He melted.

She commenced a brisk walk around the stage, stretching her arms and legs. Under ordinary circumstances the stage manager would have ordered her shot for such behavior only moments before curtain, but this was no ordinary night. Ordinarily the Grand Duke Valery would be sitting in the Czar's box, his enormous hands pounding out adoration she could distinguish from all the rest of Petrograd's applause.

Her purpose now was to calm the company as well as herself. She paused often as she circled the stage to smile and nod at the monsters, goblins and demons. She curtsied to the terrified princesses on the castle and coaxed them to curtsy back. She hugged Vera Sedovina, the first princess, and told her her Russian dance had been spectacular in dress rehearsal. Sedovina was either frozen with nerves or possessed of a remarkable *sang froid* as she straightened one of her feathers and told Tamara she was beautiful.

"Two minutes," said the stage manager, nodding approval as Tamara returned to the peephole by his desk and again looked out at the audience.

Kennet was taking his seat in a box with the American ambassador and his pretty little daughter. They were among the few nonrevolutionaries in the theater, but the Americans were heroes to many since they had recognized the new government so quickly. Looking at Kennet, Tamara recalled her shock an hour ago in her dressing room when he had told her that he had been suddenly recalled to London. His train would leave tonight. His last sight of her would be on the stage. He had held her and told her he loved her. They promised to meet in Paris. She recalled her thought that these were frightening times to be making promises . . .

Abrupt movement now drew her eye to the Czar's box in the center of the first ring. Kirichenko, ignoring Gladishev's attempt to make conversation, was leaning forward to see across into Kennet's box.

Kennet looked at his watch.

The musicians began tuning again. Tamara took a final look at the expectant throng and retreated to the wing as the houselights dimmed.

The music began with cellos and bass throbbing in the lowest registers, like an insistent, quick-timed *Dies Irae.* Sullen horns mounted the strings, threatening. To Tamara it was ancient Russia, vibrating with medieval, pre-Peter-the-Great eastern rhythms one either felt in one's bones or didn't feel at all. Russian music for a Russian fairy tale. An enchanted half-woman, half-bird—a Firebird—tried to free a handsome prince and a beautiful princess from a terrible ogre. But first she had to free herself.

The curtain rose on a dense forest and Tamara felt her audience shimmer with recognition. Had they not fought the worst battle of the war in the gloomy Pripet marshes? Hidden from the police in evil slums? She started counting. The tempo increased. Flight. An amber spot circled the

474

stage, heralded the Firebird, and Tamara swept into the light on a chain of swift leaps and poses. She heard a single gasp from the audience, seized it, wove their wonder into the music and took wing . . .

She moved, Ash thought, like a light in a mirror, crossing the stage with enormous *grand jetés*. She returned, weaving *tours en l'air* among the jumps. A ricochet, leaping, turning, back and forth in constant motion, flaming through the dark forest as beautiful as a bird, as free.

The lights flashed on her scarlet costume, her crown of gold, but Tamara's dark eyes shone even brighter. Ash decided that Stravinsky might have written it with her in mind. Ash expected her to continue the showy jumps through her long solo, but she suddenly shifted to the great strength that distinguished her from nearly every other dancer alive. The Firebird was beautiful and the Firebird was free, but the Firebird was also a woman, and to Tamara Tishkova, dance and sex were inseparable.

Her timing was perfect. Ash could feel the audience release into fantasy . . .

Some deep instinct had said *now*. She danced as if each man of the two thousand were finally coming home after three years of war. She danced to welcome, imagining a room full of children and grandparents. She danced to entice, imagining their room when the others had gone to sleep. She danced until they were utterly silent, until they knew she had given all she had to give.

And when she cast off every restraint she had ever clung to, she exploded again into the exuberant apparition she had first introduced. *Grand jetés*—a sudden focus stage center where she whipped through *fouetté* turns—and more *grand jetés* into which she wove her airborne turns. And then she tripled them, astonishing even herself—three full turns in the air before touching the stage to rise again.

Tishkova reminded revolutionaries they were Russians. They came roaring to their feet.

The music kept going. She could not stop for applause. Stravinsky had written no pauses in his score for the conductor to stop and let her take a bow. The soldiers clapped and stamped their feet even as the orchestra kept hurtling her through her solo. Prince Ivan was waiting to come on knowing full well that they would probably tear him limb from limb. She was very happy, but couldn't figure out what to do as she launched into the high-speed spin that would climax the solo when Ivan would seize her. Finally the conductor realized her predicament and the music stopped, quieting for a moment the screaming audience.

Tamara opened her climactic spin into a deep curtsy. Again she felt the applause thunder out of the house. She took bow after bow, exhilarated and proud, and finally raised her head to blow Kennet a kiss.

He was gone.

Old Vadim Mikhailov, Sedovina's father, was in Kennet's seat next to the

American ambassador's daughter, as if, she realized through her disappointment, the old tappeur had filled the seat to make it look as if Kennet hadn't left. . . .

Kirichenko was leaning forward again, as he clapped, obviously trying to see into the shadows of Kennet's box, and Tamara now felt a sudden chill . . . Kennet was up to something . . . and Kirichenko suspected . . . The conductor's baton rose tentatively and the soldiers settled into their seats as the orchestra found a place to resume the music.

Kirichenko half stood now, craning his head. Tamara counted into the music, rose *en pointe* and played the rest of her solo toward the Imperial Box, where she had directed many a performance over the years with, she was pleased to see, similar results as Kirichenko slowly resumed his seat.

Perhaps, she thought, her performance was bringing time for Kennet . . . in whatever he was up to . . . as it was buying her passage to Paris. Where, if they were lucky, they would meet again one day . . .

59

A brass band started playing as they entered the Finland Station and the Czar stiffened automatically to attention before he remembered the music was no longer for him. He shared a wan smile with his son and took the boy's hand. Half-bald and beardless, having shaved his widow's peak as well as his Vandyke, his face lined by his ordeal and wearing an inexpensive suit Ash had filched from the United States Embassy, the man whose portrait had hung in every public room in the Russian Empire was virtually unrecognizable.

Nicholas II looked instead exactly like what his passport suggested, a tired, old underpaid American YMCA official heading home in second class, accompanied by his gray-headed wife—a woman who walked with a limp but had, if one bothered to look, remarkably serene and beautiful eyes—and their two grandchildren, who seemed subdued and no doubt a little frightened by the huge, enthusiastic crowds gathering in and around the station to greet another exile—this one coming home and not in disguise.

Outside, searchlights from the Peter-Paul Fortress split the sky above the station square where the crowd waved red and gold banners. An armored car was parked outside the Czar's reception-room entrance, defying the Provisional Government's futile ban on such vehicles in the city streets. As Ash had helped the Czar and his family off the tram they had taken from the Maryinkski Theater, he had seen a couple of hundred Bolsheviks march into the square in smart formation from their headquarters in Kchessinska's appropriated house.

Draped in the nuns' habits of the Anglo-Russian field hospital nursing order, the Czar's daughters led the way across the station. Many in the

477

throng bowed and pushed other people out of their way. As Sedovina had predicted, the field nurses were about the only unassailable heroes left in the war. Even the Red Guards at the train platform gates treated them with respect, glancing at the papers and waving them through. Ash went next. An unshaven English-speaking functionary in a dirty uniform read his diplomatic passport and told him to board the train. He then thrust out his hand, demanding the Czar's papers.

Nicholas looked momentarily confused. The Czarina pressed forward and spoke for them in imperious tones that she was either unable to curb or oblivious to. "We are returning home to America," she announced sternly. "If you will kindly expedite our passage."

Ironically, her tone had the desired effect. The functionary waved them toward the train and even inclined his head in the semblance of a respectful bow. But there was a second blockade at the platform just on the other side of the gate. Red Guards had set up an impromptu customs inspection and were searching luggage. They had already let the grand duchesses in their habits pass, and the Czar's daughters were walking out on the platform toward the waiting train. A line of Russian sailors were standing at attention on the next platform, an honor guard awaiting the next arrivals. Ash caught a glimpse of a locomotive headlight far off in the yards, heading for the station.

The Red Guards pointed at his valise. Ash showed them his diplomatic papers, which made his valise inviolate. They told him to put it on their table and called someone over who could speak English.

"You travel light, Commander."

"This is a diplomatic pouch, you can't open it." But a brief exchange convinced him he had no choice if he wanted to get on the train. The Czar, the Czarina and the boy and Anastasia were still stuck behind him. He opened the case. They pawed through his clothing, pulled out a heavy wooden box and opened it.

"What is this?"

"A sextant."

"For what?"

"For determining a ship's location by the stars or the sun."

"But you are traveling by train."

If I'm lucky, thought Ash. If not, it will be damned hard finding Rodney Skelton's submarine without a sextant. "It's a gift for my commanding officer."

The Russian turned it over in his hands, noting the mirrors and lenses. "But this is made in Leipzig, in Germany . . ."

"I *bought* it on the Nevsky. Yesterday. The receipt is there."

"It is German-made. A store here selling German products?"

Ash put his hand on the box. "Russia and the United States are allies now, *Tovarisch*. We've recognized the new government. The Czar has

478

abdicated. I'd like my sextant back . . . who knows, maybe it will help my commanding officer sink a German submarine."

The Russian grinned, nodded and passed him through. And then he turned to the Czar.

Ash made a show of rearranging his bag so he could stay near, and was relieved to see that they ignored Nicholas and the children. But their attention fixed on the Czarina, who went pale when they ordered her to open her valise.

Ash's heart sank. The expression on her face told him she had disobeyed his order not to smuggle her jewels. The Red Guards ordered her to open the bag. She had packed a second traveling suit, several pairs of sensible looking low-heel shoes and a collection of modest embroidered linen underwear.

The Czar's face reddened as they went through his wife's clothing. Was there, Ash wondered, a bulge in the bag's lining, or had he heard a dull clink as the Red Guard pushed a garment aside, disturbing a necklace sown inside a hem?

Ash repeated rearranging the contents of his bag. Their train was less than a hundred feet away, but to him it might as well have been on the other side of Europe. The Red Guard probed deeper. He tapped the bottom of the Czarina's valise. It sounded hollow . . .

The floor trembled as the arriving train trundled into the station and came to rest beside Ash's. The naval guard sprang to attention, and a moment later a mob ran past the gates, past both guard points and raced cheering onto the platform.

"Lenin . . . Lenin . . ."

Hundreds surged onto the platform as the cry rose through the Finland Station and echoed back from the square beyond. Ash, the Red Guards, the Czar and Czarina and the two children were buffeted from both sides. The crowd started pouring back, bearing the stocky, bald figure of Lenin on their shoulders and calling for him to speak. The naval guard saluted and a travel-weary, happy-looking and somewhat surprised Nikolai Lenin saluted back.

Someone jumped up and pressed a bouquet of red roses into his hands. The crowd kept chanting for a speech.

"May I go now?" the Czarina took the opportunity to ask.

The Red Guards, held by Lenin's first words, waved her along . . . "Yes, yes, tell the world what is happening here . . ."

The Czar helped her close the bag. As they started toward the train, he asked, "Who is that?"

"A Bolshevik named Lenin," said Ash. "One of their leaders."

The Czar stopped, in spite of his wife's imploring, and stared across the empty track at the gesticulating figure delivering a speech from the shoulders of his comrades. Did Lenin notice his stare? When the mob interrupted him with applause, Lenin looked back across them in the direction of the Czar some forty feet away—at Ash, and puzzled recognition showed on Lenin's face.

The Czar shook his head. "He just told them there will be worldwide revolution. Isn't Russia enough for him?"

"Be grateful he came when he did," Ash said, taking his arm. "He just saved our lives. Please come along, before they change their minds." And before, he added to himself, Lenin gets curious about where he saw me first and what I'm doing now.

The Czarina took the Czar's other arm and said under her breath to Ash, "I am sorry, Commander, about the jewels . . . I just couldn't bear to leave them. One must keep something . . ."

Lenin now did remember the worried-looking officer urging the old man toward the train on the next platform, but he couldn't fit Ash's face to his boat cloak and naval service cap. Nor could he recall where they had met, though it had been recently, and the man had not been in uniform . . . Well, events were swift and wonderful. He had wondered if the Provisional Government would put him into the Peter-Paul. Instead a naval honor guard from Red Kronstadt was drawn up on the train platform as if for a Czar; people stuffed his hands with flowers, lifted him on their shoulders like a conquering hero and demanded a speech. Over their heads he saw a cadre of Bolshevik men and women march into the station in strict formation. Discipline. Perhaps Russia was ready for a *real* revolution . . .

The cheers sounded a little subdued. Locked in a struggle with the Provisional Government, not many among the soviets had thought about the Revolution going *beyond* Russia's borders. Looking at their faces, trying to gauge their response better to estimate the struggle ahead, Lenin noted the old man with the naval officer he was certain he knew.

The old man was staring at him. The officer held one of his arms and a gray-headed woman the other, apparently urging him to board their train. And suddenly Lenin remembered another train, another station . . . Zurich . . . a United States Navy officer . . . *Ash* was his name . . . off to Russia to rescue the Czar . . . too late . . . But why was this American officer still in Petrograd? Was it his imagination that the man seemed worried, anxious? He didn't think so . . . The welcome dinned around him, distracting . . . And then Lenin thought he saw why the officer had seemed anxious. A woman, hooded by a fur cape, her face hidden behind a dark veil, slipped through the mob and ran toward Ash. Everything about her seemed delicate and precise, from the small valise she carried in her black glove to her shapely high-heeled boots. When she threw back the veil and drew the officer's head down to kiss his mouth, Ash's face transformed. Worry and anxiety seemed to melt into astonishment, which in turn became intense pleasure. Nikolai Lenin turned away, uneasy at having looked on so intimate a moment in another man's life.

"It is *my* pass. I can travel anywhere I want. And I *want* to travel with you."

"But I'm—Tamara, I can't let you." They weren't even on the train yet. The whole scheme could blow up any second.

"I suddenly knew I would never see you again if I didn't go with you—"

"Tamara, believe me, it's impossible, too dangerous."

"That's what I mean . . . Kennet, I don't know what you're doing, but I must stay with you . . ." She touched a black glove to his mouth. "I'm coming with you. The subject is *closed.*"

And now she saw Vera Sedovina hurrying toward them. "Why is she here? Is there something I should know about Vera?"

Ash glanced at the train. The Czar and Czarina were boarding. Lenin was disappearing on his supporters' shoulders toward the station. Red Guards were everywhere. Maybe there was a chance to protect Tamara. He glanced at Sedovina, who was wearing a cloth coat and a babushka that hid her hair and much of her face.

Tamara reached into her handbag. "I think I will kill her," she said, pulling the revolver she had taken from the guard at the Peter-Paul.

"Put that away, for God's sake, you'll get us all arrested—"

"Is Vera traveling with you?"

"Only to the Swedish border, she's got some comrades in the train crew . . . Tamara, meet me in Paris, go out alone, it's much safer—"

"Believe me, Kennet, one of us won't live if we go alone. I know, I can feel it." She took his arm and steered him toward the train. Sedovina caught up, passed them and whispered, "Kirichenko's spy at the Alexander Palace spotted Valentinov. Hide in the luggage store-room at the far end of the platform. Comrades will take you to the baggage car. Go with him, Tamara, if Kirichenko sees you . . ."

It was a dimly lit room lined with trunks in storage racks bisected by a tall heap of packages wrapped in brown paper and string. Ash checked the other side, but Sedovina's friends had not come yet.

"Kennet?" Tamara was calling from the door.

"They're not here, yet—"

"Kennet . . ."

Ash rounded the heap in the middle of the room, and stopped dead.

Tamara was pressed against the door, the point of Count von Basel's saber at her throat.

60

"First, the gun you carry in the small of your back, Commander
. . . Now, yours, mademoiselle, from your purse . . . Now, mademoiselle,
you will bolt the door . . . Thank you, and now you will come here—oh,
I've cut you, I am very sorry. Perhaps you should move with the blade, as
if it were your partner—"

Ash lunged for him, stopped abruptly when von Basel moved his saber's
needle point from her throat, slid it under her veil and laid the razor edge
alongside her cheek.

"Commander, you've already struck me with your hand as though I
were a peasant . . . and crippled me." He held up his left hand. Two fingers
were curled like barbed wire. "Draw your sword."

"Half the Red Guard is out there—" Ash began.

"It will give me pleasure as a German soldier to inform them that you
are attempting to take the Czar. His trial by the Bolsheviks will tear Russia
apart, which is good for Germany. But I am going to finish you first,
Commander. Once and for all. *En garde*—stay there, mademoiselle. Tell
her, Ash, if she moves I'll slice off her lips."

Ash pulled his saber and told Tamara he could and would do it. Von
Basel backed her into a corner, one eye on Ash. Through the veil Ash saw
a dark trickle on Tamara's neck where von Basel's saber point had broken
her skin.

Ash shook the cloak off his sword arm, feinted with a pair of hard beats
and thrust at von Basel's face.

Von Basel parried. "It seems love makes you aggressive, Commander."

God, Ash hated his posturing, goddamn Teutonic smugness . . . Ash tried
a high slash, again at the face, repeated two more, and thrust. Von Basel

483

easily stopped all three slashes and nearly got Ash's hand late-parrying the thrust. But now a slightly wary look moved into his eyes . . . he was too experienced a fighter not to know that Ash was up to something . . .

Ash had learned two important lessons in their first encounter. The fact they weren't wearing fencing masks had held him back. He was unaccustomed to such vivid eye tactic and it had intimidated him, no question. More important, he had concluded that von Basel's chief concern was protecting his face, his chief desire to mutilate before he killed.

Ash now slashed repeatedly at his face, high, broad swings, risking each time he raised his saber that von Basel would breech his guard and thrust into his exposed belly. They fought as if they had picked up exactly where they had left off on the Czar's train. Neither was wasting time feeling the other out. A month was a long time to consider the other's strengths and weaknesses.

Suddenly von Basel went on the attack. Ash retreated, concentrating on breaking it up by frustrating the German, relying on his own speed and eye to parry and occasionally unsettle von Basel by imitating one of his own late parries. The inevitable price was a touch. But even as the pain lanced through his forearm, Ash knew von Basel was a captive of his own deep-grained cruelty. He always went for the extremities, it was predictable . . .

Von Basel's saber leaped again like a snake. Just missing Ash's forehead, it knocked his hat off, slicing the visor and reminding him that knowing von Basel's weakness and exploiting it were two different matters.

"Get *back*," Ash called out as from the corner of his eye he saw Tamara break for the door. She froze at the urgency in his voice, and he was grateful that for once she did as she was told.

Ash broke up von Basel's next attack with a stop-thrust and another slash at his face. The German retreated, winding up as he gathered for his next attack. Ash tried to use his point control and sense of distance to slash closer and closer to von Basel's face without sacrificing his own.

"That's a dangerous game, Ash. No one has ever marked me. Not even your precious Roland."

Ash cocked his arm to raise his saber up high. Von Basel's blade leaped to protect his face and counter-thrust—but Ash dropped his arm and jump-lunged a long, low thrust into von Basel's belly . . .

"*Nein*," von Basel said. His voice was a deathly whisper. His gray eyes opened very wide. He stared, first into Ash's eyes, then down at the hilt pressed to his belly. His own saber fell from his fingers. He pushed at Ash's hand, trying to push the steel out of his body. Ash backed away. His blade seemed to slide forever.

Von Basel fought to keep his feet but his knees collapsed underneath him. He looked up at Ash, eyes clouding. "You did not mark my face . . ."

"No . . . but Roland would have, which is why you murdered him with your *poniard*."

Tamara was twisting handkerchiefs around his cut forearm when the knock came at the door. Outside a pair of frightened-looking railroad workers had a baggage cart ready with a narrow slot between trunks and mailbags for Ash and Tamara. Tamara translated, "Sedovina has everyone aboard."

Inside the slot, which the railroad workers covered with more bags, Ash felt his knees begin to go. The iron-wheeled cart ground along the platform to the train. He heard the locomotive blow its whistle. Bells answered.

"Are you all right?" Tamara whispered.

"I felt him die through my blade."

She pressed against him, "Oh God, this can't be happening. We weren't supposed to end our lives like this."

"It's been happening since 1914," Ash managed to get out as the cart bumped aboard the train and the train started moving.

Von Basel was not dead yet. The floor shook as the Finland train rumbled out of the station, shaking him back to consciousness. He felt no pain, only a massive numbness from his waist down. He found his sword, found the walking stick, sheathed the blade. When he tried to crawl to the door he felt an unknown, profound weariness. He forced himself to keep going, reached the door, somehow got it open and crawled onto the platform. Overhead was the train shed roof; in the distance, the station.

Halfway there, he looked back. The lights showed a long, dark trail of blood, as if some ghastly, wounded insect had slithered up from the rails. Von Basel gathered himself, planted the walking stick on the platform, pulled himself erect.

Leaning heavily on the stick, he made himself walk to the station. It took tremendous concentration to move his legs. Each step demanded purpose. The few people left in the station stared at him.

Then the Red Guards came . . .

Moments later the SR fighting squad leader Kirichenko was leaning over his stretcher. "Who are you?"

Von Basel found he had trouble talking.

Kirichenko leaned close, put his ear to von Basel's mouth.

"The train . . ." von Basel got out. "He's on the train."

"Who?"

And von Basel suddenly knew his last words on earth.
"The Czar."

Ash and Tamara had just located the Czar's family crammed into a steamy compartment two cars ahead of the baggage car when Sedovina ran down the corridor from the front of the train. "My comrade in the crew says the soviet has signaled the train to stop at the next station."

"Kirichenko?"

"Probably. They'll search the train."

Ash went into the Czar's compartment. The family looked at him with a mix of gratitude and misery. "They're stopping the train, I'm afraid we have to jump off."

"Now?" the Czar asked.

"Now," the Czarina said. "Children!"

The grand duchesses pulled their valises down from the luggage racks.

"But you can't jump," the Czar protested. "The girls can, but not you and Alexis—"

"I can jump if Commander Ash says I must. It's Alexis I'm worried about."

"I can jump," the boy insisted.

"I'll go off with him," Ash said.

"No. You'll hurt him if you fall on him. Better a scrape we can control. The snow will cushion our fall."

Ash lead them to the vestibule at the back of the car. Sedovina guarded the front. The moon on the snow showed a steep embankment ending in forest. It could not have been worse, even though the broken-down engine was doing less than thirty miles per hour.

Suddenly the trees stopped at an open field. Ash heaved the bags. The Czar went first, followed by his daughters. The Czarina saw them slide across the snow, across a frozen crust.

Tamara took the boy's hand. "He will jump with me," and to the boy said, "I was in the circus, no one can jump like me. We're going to jump and run. Can you do it?"

Alexis murmured he didn't know as he eyed the ground racing away beneath him. "Jump," Ash told the Czarina.

And she did, over the side onto the snow.

"Hold tight," he told the boy. "Ready—go."

Ash watched them, black figures against the white snow. They hit the crust running hard to keep their balance, down the embankment and onto the field, still running, nearly a hundred feet before Tamara broke through the crust and fell hard. The boy sprawled a moment later.

Ash signaled Sedovina and jumped. He slid down the steep bank and crashed through the crust, tucking his shoulder and rolling to his feet only to fall over his sword. Sedovina skidded on top of him. The train rumbled past, trailing silence.

For a moment she was soft in his arms, and he asked her why she had come.

"You are more convincing, Commander, than you apparently know. You, and they, are not out yet. I want to see that you are."

He let it go at that . . .

They found Tamara, rubbing her ankle and watching anxiously as Alexis's sisters grouped around him. Tatiana held snow to his face.

"A nosebleed," Tamara whispered, and when Sedovina looked puzzled because no one in all Russia but the immediate family knew, she added, "He's a bleeder." Valery had told her, and even he didn't know all the details.

It was, Ash thought, one of the ruling family's worst mistakes to keep it secret and short-circuit its subjects' sympathy. "We can't stay here," he told them. "Everyone, let's go, find the bags and let's move—"

"Where?"

"Down to the Gulf, onto the ice, break our trail and find a place to hide."

"Then what?" asked Olga. She was the oldest, twenty.

"Help your mother," Ash told her. "We'll take the boy. Alexis, on my back." . . . And then what, he thought, was a damned good question.

Alexis, obviously an experienced patient, threw his head back and pinched his nostrils. "What if I faint?" he asked.

"I'll be right next to you," Tamara said. "I'll hold your nose if you faint. It's not far."

She looked at Ash and together they surveyed the long moonlit slope. Half a mile to the treeline and another mile through the trees. And below the trees, the barren ice of the Gulf of Finland.

Aggravated by the fall from the train, the Czarina's sciatica made each step agony. They stopped in the trees, and Ash hacked off some pine boughs that he and the Czar bound with strips of clothing into a crude litter. They laid Alexandra on it, let her examine the boy, whose bleeding had not stopped, and then started down again through the soft, deep snow of the forest. The girls, the Czar and Sedovina spelled each other, dragging the litter in pairs. Ash carried Alexis while Tamara pressed snow to his nostrils. "What circus?" he asked suddenly. His voice was weak, as if he were growing sleepy. Tamara thought he had fainted.

"My father's. I was younger than you are now," she told him.

"Your *father's*. You're lucky . . . Father Gregory told me about two humped horses."

"Oh, we had lots of them," Tamara said, replacing the snow as she struggled to keep up with Ash.

Suddenly the boy said, "I hear a wolf."

"Just saying good night to us," Ash said, wishing it were a wolf, instead of a train whistle. The first search party.

The forest stopped at a frozen marsh—one of the northern extremities of the Neva delta. Ash had them cross in single file in case a spring flood had weakened the ice. When they reached the Gulf of Finland it was three o'clock and the moon was inclining toward the west. Surface thaws and freezes and an afternoon rain several days ago followed by two days of hard freeze had left the ice flat and smooth. A hard wind blew from the north. The trees had blocked it, but here in the open it stung badly.

"Bring me Alexis," the Czarina called from the litter. Ash sank to the ice beside her and caught his breath while she examined the boy and the Czar and their daughters crowded around. Tamara and Sedovina watched the slope for moving lights.

"The bleeding is better," the Czarina said, "but we can't go on dragging him around. He must lie still."

Ash pointed up the slope. A train moved slowly along the line, probing the snow with searchlights. "They'll find our tracks at first light. We have to move."

The Czar looked at his wife. "Then we must surrender. I will not kill my son for my freedom."

"Nor will I," the Czarina said. "How long could we hide anyway?"

"Do you know this area, Your Majesty?"

"We have sailed the Gulf every summer of our marriage."

Ash opened his valise, removed the sextant from its wooden bow and found the Gulf of Finland charts he had hidden under the navigational instrument. The charts did not cover this far east . . . he'd had no intention of being here, but he had a land map that showed the coast of the Petrograd Bay where they were at the head of the Gulf. The wind nearly tore the map from his hands. "Exactly where are we?"

The Czar turned a slow circle, examining landmarks and skyline. Ash held the map to the moonlight and the Czar pointed. "Here. There are dachas, all along the shore." Ash looked at the slope. Forest and field alternated. The occasional light showed in the clearings. Ash turned his back on the slope and faced the endless expanse of flat ice.

The Gulf of Finland extended three hundred miles west to the Baltic

Sea. Ash imagined he could see the entire distance, the moon and stars were so bright, the ice so empty. Somewhere out there was Rodney Skelton's submarine . . .

"Your Majesty, how far do you think the Gulf is frozen?"

The Czar looked up from where he had crouched beside Alexis and the Czarina. "Ice? Middle of April? Still some two hundred miles."

Ash held up the map to him. "Isn't the Balmont dacha near here?"

"A few miles north," the Czar told him, tracing the coastline with his finger. "If you are referring to the Baroness's shooting marsh."

"That's the one. Let's go—"

Tamara broke in. "Kennet, just because you went shooting there doesn't mean she'll hide us."

"There are," the Czar added, "closer places to hide. Estates all along the shore, though of course they will search them."

"We're not hiding," Ash said. "Wait until you see her neighbor's iceboat."

"Iceboat?"

It had snowed one afternoon, too heavily to shoot or sail, so they had piled into troikas and visited the next estate, which was owned by a tall, elderly Finnish nobleman who had two passions in life—his neighbor the Baroness, and sailing.

"A monster, Your Majesty. Six hundred square feet of canvas."

"Have you ever sailed an iceboat, Commander?"

"Not one that big."

"But you do know it's not like sailing on water."

"Hardly . . ."

It was slow going into the relentless north wind. The footing was treacherous, the litter heavy with the Czarina and Alexis. They hugged the shore, to avoid being silhouetted against the moonlit ice. Another train probed the night on the slope, and above the tracks along a road truck lights scoured the snow.

They had gone two miles when Ash spotted a break in the shoreline, the channel the Baroness Balmont had dug through her marsh into the Gulf. It was another mile to her lover's estate.

Kirichenko cruised the rail line in the cab of a locomotive festooned with searchlights and hauling a dozen flatcars. Red Guards jumped off every few hundred yards to patrol on foot. Telegraphers were perched each mile on telegraph poles. And half a mile up the slope motor and cavalry squadrons were searching house to house.

"Comrade Kirichenko." The engineer pointed ahead and quickly eased off his quadrant and throttle. A telegrapher was scrambling down a pole, gesturing for the train to stop.

"A trail in the snow, Comrade Kirichenko. Down to the ice."

61

Smooth ice stretched like a tongue into the dark mouth of the boat-house, which looked like a big barn with the front wall gone. Behind it, a quarter mile up the slope, the main estate mansion loomed darkly. Smoke plumed white in the moonlight from the servants' cottages that circled it, but the boathouse and the lower fields were uninhabited.

The slim frame of the boat—a cross with steel runners on either arm and a rudder in the back—was painted white. The enamel gleamed ghostly in the moonlight that bounded up from the ice. Ash kicked the runners to unstick them and pushed her outside with the help of the Czar's daughters.

Thirty-five feet long and twenty wide, the iceboat was light and glided easily; the two parts of the frame—the long, narrow hull and the thin runner arm that crossed it—were virtually the entire boat. Hull and cross-piece were braced with wire cable, but neither cables nor the small flat cockpit in back added any significant weight.

"We need the mast," Ash said. "Stays, mainsail, jib, lines and running gear."

The Czar spoke and his daughters hurried into the boathouse, and reappeared almost immediately dragging the mast. Nicholas and Alexandra exchanged a quick glance, and the Czar said to Ash, "We did not raise helpless young ladies."

The mast was a brute, pear-shaped to reduce wind resistance but much heavier than a yacht mast so as to stand the extraordinary strains of an iceboat. It took Ash, the Czar, the four grand duchesses and Tamara and Sedovina to step it up into its hole, where the hull and runner arm inter-sected, after Ash had run the sail halyards through the top. He fastened stays fore and aft and rigging on either side and tightened them with turnbuckles.

The rig was modern, a triangular Bermuda sail. The much smaller jib had its own boom and was rigged to be self-tending, which Ash knew would be a blessing on a crowded cockpit, as would the roller reefing.

"There's not enough room for all of us," the Czar said. The boat looked designed for a crew of five . . . they were ten. Ash extended the cockpit with the spare jib, stretching the canvas between the iceboat's frame and the wire cables that braced the arms of the cross. The Czar rigged safety lines to hold onto. Ice axes, chisels, files to sharpen the runners, spare runners and heel spikes were already aboard in the lockers built into the long, narrow hull. The Czar lashed their valises to the deck in front of the mast, checking clearance for the jib boom. The deposed sovereign would be a help.

Anastasia laughed. "We'll look like gypsies, papa—"

"I see lights at the main house," Tamara called out.

It looked like two trucks or cars. Ash heard doors slamming, shouts. More lights flared in the cottage and the mansion.

"Tamara, get them on board. Leave room aft for the Czar and me—"
"Aft?"

"The *back*. By the tiller." Ash and Nicholas fitted the boom to the mast and started attaching the sail while the grand duchesses helped their mother stretch out on the canvas cockpit with Alexis in her arms, still holding a compress to his nose.

"They're lighting torches," Sedovina called. "They're coming down."

Ash's fingers were numbing from cold as he forced the last of the mainsail's parrel balls into their groove in the mast. He glanced up the slope. Soldiers were racing down with flaming torches.

"Hoist the main, I'll rig the jib." Ash didn't have time to feel awkward ordering a recent Czar as though he were a midshipman.

The Czar and his daughters heaved the iceboat around until it was facing dead into the north wind, raised the big sail which glowed in the moonlight and crackled like rifle shots. Ash finished clipping on the jib, hauled it up and tied off its sheet. He'd try to figure how to set it once they got moving.

"All aboard, tend the main."

"Perhaps I should take the tiller, I know the coast," the Czar said.

"Beg your pardon, sir, but we've got one skipper and I'm afraid I'm it. Tamara . . ."

She came running around the boathouse . . . "Soldiers."

"Get on. Sedovina, sit by the Czar. Do what he tells you. Ready on that sheet, sir. Let's kick her around." He grabbed the tiller and swung his leg over the side, dug his heel spike into the ice. The Czar, Tamara and

Sedovina did the same, but the boat wouldn't budge. The runners had frozen to the ice while they were sitting.

Two soldiers waving torches and rifles careened off the slope.

"Push," Ash ordered.

The soldiers sprawled on the ice. A third planted himself in the snow, started firing a pistol. Sedovina and Tamara jumped off, ran to the right runner and pushed hard against the arm. The runner broke loose and the boat lurched to right angles with the wind, which filled the mainsail.

"Get aboard." Ash hauled in the tiller, and the iceboat started to move. Sedovina sprawled onto the cockpit and reached for Tamara. The iceboat picked up speed. Rifle shouts sounded behind them. Tamara slipped from Sedovina's hand. Ash lunged for her, missed. She grabbed the lifeline, and the boat pulled her off her feet at the same time she tried to get her legs onto the cockpit. Still holding the tiller, Ash tried again, caught her other hand, pushed the tiller to head the boat into the wind to slow it, and managed to drag her aboard.

Now a truck had made it down from the main house, crashing onto the ice and skidding after the iceboat. It caught them in its lights, and the men in it started firing.

"Down," Ash ordered. "Haul in, sir."

The Czar pulled the sheet, the sail tightened. The boat picked up speed . . . but the truck still gained.

"Sedovina, pull that line, *pull* it!"

It was the jib sheet and the effect of her action was immediate. The iceboat seemed to leap forward, the truck fell back. Bullets still spewed in their wake, but moments later they were alone on the Gulf of Finland, heading across a moonlit, ice-covered wasteland at sixty miles per hour.

Half an hour later Ash and the Czar were still experimenting with the sails when the Kronstadt Fortress came into view. Some twelve hundred pounds of passenger weight slowed the boat markedly whenever the wind dropped, which it did with disturbing frequency since they were still in the narrow head of the Gulf. They were down to fifteen or twenty miles per hour, and Ash was looking anxiously for the point where the Gulf broadened to its true hundred-mile width when the searchlights of the island fortress's gunbattery split the night.

Kronstadt was Petrograd's main sea defense, and the huge beams were capable of sweeping the ice for miles. Twice they caught the boat, but the operators apparently couldn't distinguish the white sail from the surrounding ice. The third time they focused better and the gun battery opened up with a flash.

Roaring like a freight train, a shell passed overhead and a moment later detonated a mile away.

"Twelve-inch gun?" Ash asked the Czar incredulously.

"Of course," and Ash thought he looked proud of it in the glare of the searchlight. A second shell rumbled through the sky, so close they all ducked. It exploded a quarter mile away, and Ash could feel the heat on his face. A third shell landed just ahead of the boat, blowing a huge hole in the ice. The water was black, and Ash decided the gunners were trying a new strategy—drowning them would be just as effective as a direct hit.

He swung around the hole and headed straight for the battery, five or six miles to the south. Dead ahead the cannon flashed.

"Where are you going?"

"I'm betting he's got that gun depressed as far as she'll go."

He steered into the glare of the light for a mile, saw the cannon flash. "Easy with the main, she doesn't like going downwind . . . all right, back on reach, we're heading west again." Two shells rumbled high overhead . . . apparently the frustrated gunners had stopped firing—

And slowly they passed out of the searchlight's range. Another hour, with the wind freshening, they moved out of the narrow Petrograd Bay into the main Gulf. The boat built to speed, and the rigging began a metallic whine.

Kirichenko pursued Ash by a train manned by soviets—a special train that highballed west paralleling the coast on track cleared straight to Helsinki. Coal and water were waiting along the way, and telegraphers listened at open keys for news of Ash's iceboat. At Vyborg Kirichenko learned that Ash had somehow managed to escape the guns of Kronstadt. At the next coaling stop he telegraphed the bad news to naval soviet in Helsinki.

Dawn lighted the tips of the high-pressure ridges a translucent red. Here at sea, fifty miles from the nearest coast, the ice had been forced up in wild, angular eruptions thirty feet high. The wind was blowing a near gale, and the boat was carving a beautiful mist of shaved ice. Ash was getting tired. As he tried to gybe between two of the pressure ridges, trading the wind from one side to the other, he misjudged the tiller. The sails smacked over, and the force spun the boat in a complete circle.

Tamara, Sedovina and two of the girls were thrown to the ice as the boat crashed into the nearest pressure ridge. The Czar had gone to his wife the instant he felt the boat gather the speed that led to the spin, holding her and Alexis.

494

"We'll have to lash them down," Ash told him. The women got back to the boat as Ash inspected the runners for damage. They had survived, and when the Czar had tied his wife and son in place Ash got underway again, veering north toward the Finnish coast to escape the pressure ridges.

He shot the sun when it rose higher, and checked the chart. "That smoke's Helsinki. We've got a ways to go."

The smudge on the horizon grew darker as they neared, developed a hard core. It puzzled Ash . . . it looked like a steamer but there were surely no steamers out here on the ice. But by the time he made out what looked like a domed cathedral in the city and a lighthouse, he realized that it definitely was a ship, and that it was moving.

An icebreaker, pouring black coal smoke from a huge stack and blasting a narrow channel from the port to a pressure-ridged icepack several miles off shore.

"Why is he doing that?" the Czar asked. "The ships can't get out yet."

"I'm afraid he's after us. Hang on everybody, we're gybing about . . ."

But as he looked back, Ash saw horsemen galloping onto the ice from a promontory east of the Helsinki Peninsula. The wind was gusting this close to the shore, and he knew he couldn't outrace the cavalry back to the clear ice. He had to pass the icebreaker before she cut the ice all the way to the ridged pack.

He played the sails for speed, steering a weaving course around rough ice and angling for the best wind. A mile from the laboring icebreaker he began to hope he would make it. "Get your heads down, they probably have something to shoot . . ."

They did . . . a slow-firing one-inch cannon, nearly useless as the vessel plunged up and down while it charged the ice, backed off and charged again. They were nearly in front of the icebreaker. It had backed into the path it had opened and was charging forward again, bellowing smoke. It hit the ice and was again thrown back, but the heavy bow had done its work. A crack twenty feet wide zigzagged from the icebreaker the two hundred yards to the pack ice.

Ash ordered the Czar to haul in the main and Sedovina to tighten the jib as he steered a little closer to the wind for speed, which also put him on a collision course with the iceboat which was pushing triumphantly into the open water it had prised through the ice. Ash veered away at the last moment and shot at the black water. The grand duchesses, in front, screamed. The icebreaker went airborne, skimmed the water, and crashed onto the ice on the other side.

Kirichenko ordered three boxcars filled with cavalry when he had his special train shunted onto the coastal line that served small towns west of

Helsinki. A few of the Finns were reluctant to bow to his every wish, and one in particular demanded, "Just who is aboard that ice yacht?"

Kirichenko put a gun in his face. "None of your business." And it damned well wasn't, Kirichenko thought. All Russia did not have to know that an American named Ash was trying to escape with its Czar. The last reports still had him heading west along the Finnish coast. Exactly how Ash had managed up to now Kirichenko didn't know . . . but one thing was certain—he was running out of ice.

Ash shot the sun from the moving boat, calculated their position. "Steer southwest, sir."

"I think I see open water—"

"It's just a lead, I'll tell you when to stop."

Fifteen minutes later he shot the sun again. As he did he felt the iceboat move strangely, rise and fall like a ship. He looked at the others. They had felt it too. They were near the open sea, and ground swells were rocking the ice as if it were a great white rubber sheet.

Tamara said, "How far are we from land?"

Ash was taking a bearing with his hand-held compass on the point of a peninsula. "About five miles . . . All right, sir, turn her into the wind."

The Czar brought her around, and the iceboat stopped, facing the north wind—and the Finnish coast. It was nearly noon. The high sun had melted the surface, making a skim of slush and water.

Ash took an ice axe from the locker and started chopping. The Czar followed his lead. The ice was over a foot thick. "I hear horses," Alexis said. Ash looked at him. He had been so quiet in his mother's arms. Now he raised his head, moving tentatively, not wanting to start his nose bleeding again. "I *hear* them."

"I don't," Anastasia said.

Ash scanned the coast with the binoculars he'd found in the locker. A tight pack of black dots was moving toward them. He dropped to his knees and hacked at the ice.

"What is it?" the Czar asked.

"Cavalry. Alexis is right."

Seawater welled up in the hole. Ash widened the edges, submerging his hand in the bitter-cold water. He ran to his valise, pulled out the wooden sextant box and smashed it to pieces with the ice axe. A pair of hand grenades rolled out of their hiding place: signals for Skelton's submarine.

"Make way." They stepped back from the hole. Ash released the safety pin, dropped a grenade in the hole and ran. Nothing. And then seawater fountained out of the hole, and the ice shook with a dull, muffled bang. No answer to the relentless drumming of the oncoming horses.

496

He looked at the coast. They were closer, distinguishable through the glasses as men on horseback flying red flags on their lances. He waited two minutes, counted forty, fifty riders in the glasses, and dropped his second grenade. Again the water geysered. Nothing more. Where the hell was he?

The Czar and Czarina looked forlornly at the advancing cavalry. Their children moved instinctively closer.

"Get your things off the boat," Ash said.

"Is there really any point?" the Czar was saying, and Ash knew he had no good answer.

Rodney Skelton's submarine crashed out of the ice a hundred feet away.

It still had the big dent in the conning tower. What wasn't dented was rusted and it was still absurdly small, but Ash thought it was beautiful.

Hatches popped open, and Skelton himself was first out.

"You can't bring that, friend," he said, pointing at the iceboat. He cut the forced levity when he saw the cavalry, and started issuing orders. Seamen laid a plank gangway from the sub to the ice and stood by on their end to help all aboard while a gun crew unlimbered a heavy machine gun.

Ash guided Tamara and the Czar's family onto the gangway.

"Take it sort of easy with that gun," Ash called out. "They're still allies, more or less . . ."

"Always the diplomat, Ash. But I don't think they see it your way at the moment;—all right, men, at least give them something over their heads to think about."

The gun cut loose with a clatter as Skelton turned to salute the Czar and Czarina coming aboard. His sailors helped them through the gun hatch. Tamara stepped aboard, then paused in the hatch, for a last look east toward Russia . . .

The gun fired again. The horsemen spread out, still charging.

"Come on Ash, we don't have all day—now where the hell is *she* going?" Sedovina was walking across the ice toward the cavalry.

Ash ran after her, caught her arm. "What are you doing?"

"I'm going home, Kennet. I have to. You were right in what you have done. I am glad I could help. But I belong—"

"Kirichenko will kill you. Is your life worth a revolution that's going to hell?"

She removed Ash's hand from her arm, touched his glove to her cheek, and suddenly kissed his mouth. "It's just starting. I have to believe that . . ."

62

The American Embassy reception for General Blackjack Pershing and the one-millionth United States Army soldier to land in France, by coincidence the son of a prominent midwestern senator, was typical of the afternoon parties taking over Paris during the summer of 1918. It was only July, but the pattern was set; an energetic cosmopolitan crowd was too happy feasting on itself to mind the heat.

U.S. Staff officers outnumbered their British and French colleagues. American businessmen ran a close second. Most of the women were French, which never hurt a party, though there was the usual contingent of wealthy American ladies who had come to Paris to nurse at the more fashionable hospitals or raise hell in what the enormous American Expeditionary Force was making the hottest city in the world. Painters, scientists and aerial aces wandered in and out, and a wall of war correspondents blocked the bar talking about their novels. Sprinkled about the guests like diamonds on a veil were Russian emigres whose dazzling manners and easy laughter camouflaged from all but each other who they might have been before the Revolution, and whether they felt sadly uprooted or merely transported to a smaller Petrograd-on-the-Seine. Ash arrived late and got onto the tail end of the reception line. He thought General Pershing looked like William S. Hart would have looked if he had spent his life chasing Pancho Villa around Mexico instead of making movies. Resolute looking with a hard broad mouth, military mustache, squint lines around the eyes and a long, solid nose, he had the sort of caved-in cheeks that came from a lifetime spent out of doors. Lafayette, we are here. Indeed.

"Sailing that transport desk late again, Commander?"

"I had to convince a French harbor master that we like our gunners and their artillery to arrive at the front together. Good to see you, sir. Congratulations on your million troops, sir."

"Are they ever going to give you a ship, Commander?"

"Same old story, sir. They're convinced I talk better than I sail because I supposedly know the Europeans, so I'm stuck coordinating transport . . . Now they're promising a ship at Christmas—"

"The war's going to be over by Christmas."

For the first time since 1914 that seemed true. The Russian Provisional Government had held out until November, when the Bolsheviks finally gained enough control of the soviets to take power, and it wasn't until March that Russia made a separate peace with Germany. By then American soldiers were pouring into France.

The music stopped, and the American ambassador climbed the podium. "Ladies and gentlemen. *Monsieurs, mesdames.* May I have your attention, please. News has come over the Reuters wire . . ."

The party went silent.

"From Russia we have word that the Czar, the Czarina and all their children have been murdered by Bolsheviks in the city of Yekaterinburg in the Ural Mountains."

Kaiser Wilhelm received the news in his bathrobe. Though it was late afternoon there were many days since Count von Basel's death in Russia that he did not really care to put on a full dress uniform and make grand entrances into empty rooms. With that noble German's death, von Basel, had died his last dreams of somehow stopping General Ludendorff and probably winning the war.

Ludendorff had won Germany, but Georgie's American allies were almost surely going to win the war. And now Alix and Nicky, murdered by revolutionaries. How could the world have gone so wrong?

He prowled his empty rooms until he found a gold-framed photograph of Nicholas and Alexandra at their wedding. God Himself could not have made a more royal union. "I tried to save you," the Kaiser told their picture. "We tried . . . if only you had listened, Nicky . . . I told you something like this would happen."

General Pershing looked stunned when the ambassador had finished. "Why in hell did they have to kill the whole family?"

"Russia's a grim place, sir. And getting grimmer."

"You knew the Czar, didn't you, Ash."

"Yes, sir, I did . . ."

Lord Exeter came toward him as soon as Ash was alone. There still seemed to be an empty space at his arm where the lean figure of Lady Exeter had maintained escort.

"Tragic news about the Czar."

"Tragic," Ash agreed, "though I doubt they'll find any bodies."

Exeter glanced around before adding, "Not unless they kill those poor actors . . . Have you read the latest news of the charade?"

Ash nodded. "I read the interviews, and that article by the boy's tutor. I'm glad they finally got around to ending it before somebody realized it was a phony."

"Well, it's over, and the water is good and muddy—by the way, the King asked me to remind you he's looking forward to shooting whenever you can get to England. And I promised to give you this."

It was a thick, heavy brown envelope.

Ash went out on a terrace for privacy. An American battalion was marching down the boulevard like occupation troops. In the envelope were two small boxes, one long and one square, a packet of newspaper clippings and a letter written on stationery that smelled of Penhaligon's lily of the valley.

Ash looked at the clippings first. They were articles about the Czar in captivity, and being moved from Tsarskoye Selo to the Siberian town of Tobolsk and finally to Yekaterinburg. Witnesses who had met the Czar before the Revolution reported on brief meetings overseen by his jailers. There were even photographs.

A haggard-looking Valentinov sitting on a tree stump. Ash had to smile to himself. The symbolism was so heavy that Valentinov must have come up with the pose himself and directed the Bolshevik photographer. Other photographs showed Valentinov's "family" in costume portraying the imprisoned Romanovs gardening or sitting together under the watchful eye of revolutionary guards.

Kirichenko had made the best of a bad deal, and afterward Ash had expected him to rise high in the new government, but just two weeks ago he had been shot in a purge of some fifteen hundred leftist Social Revolutionaries who were too radical even for the Bolsheviks. A mistake, Ash thought . . . he would have been an asset, he was flexible . . .

Vera Sedovina, as it turned out, had actually arrived in England ahead of the submarine, dispatched by Kirichenko with a deal for King George. If the King would keep the Czar forever under wraps, hide him and never allow Nicholas to reveal that he had escaped, Kirichenko promised that Russia's revolutionaries would not hunt the Czar to his death.

"He can live in fear, and be murdered. Or he can live peacefully in seclusion." What the soviets, the Social Revolutionaries and the Bolsheviks asked in return was that they be allowed to keep the Czar in legend. That he and his family be forever acknowledged as dead at the hands of the

Russian people. A dead Czar Nicholas could never lead a counter-revolution . . . And a troop of terrified actors, including their "Czar" Valentinov, was not likely to reveal their role in the deal.

King George had ordered all aboard Rodney Skelton's submarine taken secretly to Balmoral Castle in Scotland when it arrived at Scapa Floe. He had urged the Czar to accept the offer. George V had no desire for Britain to be a staging place for a counter-revolution; nor did he want the Czar murdered on British territory, for there was no doubt that the revolutionaries could carry out their threat, even if it took years. Nicholas, also encouraged by his wife, had agreed . . .

Ash next took up the letter, which was from the Czarina. It was, of course, unsigned, but she had written Ash several times, and by now he knew her quick style and recognized her brisk dashes and ellipses.

"My dear Commander,

We have settled in comfortably in a cottage and even have a vegetable garden in—though that is hardly a guarantee in the brief Highland summer—next year perhaps Poland or Finland—or perhaps stay here if the natives don't notice. The girls are adjusting, though I know that T. more than the others chafes to enter society, which sort, of course, we can't fathom . . . A. is extremely well and it is beginning to look as if the doctor's predictions that he might have a normal life if he survives to adulthood might come true . . . He's taller, filling out and talks about going home some day. I tried to tell him he can't and suddenly realized he meant it—in some manner he might . . .

My husband is—I hesitate to say happy—perhaps peaceful is more correct. I astonish myself how happy I am here—my grandmother's simplicity seems to flow in my veins, more than I ever imagined. But of course it is easier for me than my husband. I started out as only a little princess while he was—well you know what he was—and I know what he hoped to be . . .

We have always thought ourselves to be the most fortunate people because of what we are to each other. The worst moments were those apart when he had to be at the Sta—there, I've almost used a forbidden word. You must burn this—but my husband and I still have each other and our children. It is they, of course, who have lost the most—we have already had our life. But they, being young, can best adjust. And will have to . . . Forgive this chattiness, but we did share a long, long ride, didn't we, during which we almost settled some of our earlier arguments . . . The small package is from my husband. He is aware that recent events diminish the cachet of an ennobling honor, but he wants you to know it comes from his heart. From mine too."

Ash opened the box and gave a silent whistle of amazement. It was the star of the Imperial Order of St. Andrew.

"As the collar and badge are rather a cumbersome affair," the Czarina wrote, "we sent them to your shooting friend who will hold them for you."

Cumbersome? If he remembered correctly the collar was made of seventeen gold medallions studded with diamonds.

". . . The longer box I'm sure you recognize. It was a lovely gift, but I shan't be wearing that sort of thing. Perhaps your lady . . ."

Tamara Tishkova was surrounded by an admiring covey of U.S. Air Service aces when she noticed Ash alone on the terrace. Detaching herself from the fighter pilots with a smile that left each man convinced life back in the States would never seem the same, she started toward Ash only to be intercepted by Ambassador Walter Hines Page. The trip from London had obviously exhausted the poor man, but nothing, not even the sickness which would surely kill him within the year, could conceal Page's delight with events.

His manners were a blend of graciousness and informality which lent certain Americans she had met an easy elegance she once associated only with fellow artists. Kennet would grow older this way . . .

Page kissed her hand and said how much he had enjoyed meeting her at Balmoral Castle. He nodded toward Ash, alone on the terrace. "He used to call himself a glorified mailman when he was my courier. Now he says he's a glorified traffic cop, directing troop transport. I hope he isn't too miserable. He once said he wanted to grab history, make it instead of observe it . . ." Page looked around the reception, grinned at the sight of General Pershing marching out with his staff, heading back to the front. "Well, I'd say he's done all right—excuse me, he seems headed this way and I don't think that gleam in his eye is for an old man." . . .

Ash turned her toward a mirror and draped the pendant over her head by the chain. She reached back and touched his hand as the pearl-crusted, double-headed eagle settled between her breasts.

"From an old friend, to me, to you."

"It's beautiful. My God, I could open a dancing school with this."

"Maybe you won't have to," said Ash. "I got one too."

He showed her the eight-pointed star on his chest.

502

"Kennet."

"Haven't you ever seen a Russian nobleman?"

"Good lord, Kennet. The Order of St. Andrew is the highest honor in Russia."

"Was . . . but I have a feeling it could still come in handy." He glanced around the still-crowded reception. "I love you, I have always loved you and you know it. I also think you are the most beautiful woman in the world. Hell, I know it. Tell me, if you won't have a lowly American sailor, how about a Russian nobleman?"

Tamara, forever the performer even in love, raised an eyebrow, touched the star of St. Andrew, and raised her dark eyes to Ash. "But of course, Your Excellency."